Bloom books

Dear reader,

In this book, the curtain gets pulled back.

You will get a peek into Slade's past, and finally discover the real reason behind his nickname. (And it's not really because he ripped people's heads off on the battlefield, although, you can't really put it past him.)

I loved being able to show more parts of his background and reveal some of his secrets, and I hope you like learning more about him too.

For Auren, *Glow* is all about facing truths, forging new paths, and standing on her own two feet. But of course, the road will be rocky.

Bright side?

Auren can handle it.

GLOW

RAVEN KENNEDY

Bloom books

Copyright © 2022, 2024 by Raven Kennedy
Cover and internal design © 2024 by Sourcebooks
Cover design by Audrey Troutman of A.T. Cover Designs
Cover images © Peonies May/Shutterstock
Internal design by Imagine Ink Designs
Map by Fictive Designs
Illustrated quote by Alicia McFadzean
Editing by Polished Perfection

Sourcebooks, Bloom Books, and the colophon are
registered trademarks of Sourcebooks.

The characters and events portrayed in this book are fictitious or
are used fictitiously. Any similarity to real persons, living or dead,
is purely coincidental and not intended by the author.

All brand names and product names used in this book are trademarks,
registered trademarks, or trade names of their respective holders.
Sourcebooks is not associated with any product or vendor in this book.

Published by Bloom Books, an imprint of Sourcebooks
P.O. Box 4410, Naperville, Illinois 60567-4410
(630) 961-3900
sourcebooks.com

Originally self-published in 2022 by Raven Kennedy.

Cataloging-in-Publication data is on file with the Library of Congress.

Printed and bound in the United States of America.
PAH 10 9 8 7 6 5 4 3 2 1

About The Book

THE MYTH OF
KING MIDAS REIMAGINED.

This compelling and dark adult fantasy series is as addictive as it is unexpected. With romance, fae, and intrigue, the gilded world of Orea will grip you from the very first page. Be immersed in this journey of greed, love, and finding inner strength.

Please Note: This series will contain explicit content and dark elements that may be triggering to some. It will include explicit romance, mature language, violence, nonconsensual sex, emotional manipulation and abuse, sex trafficking and on-page sexual assault, and other dark and potentially triggering content. It is not intended for anyone under 18 years of age. This is book four in a series.

To those who stand on their own two feet
despite their stumbles.

CHAPTER 1

QUEEN KAILA

The air is full of screams.

The entire front of Ranhold Castle is an ocean shore of people washed up on the courtyard. They ebb and flow, frothy cries making waves as they undulate in a shallow mob.

Behind me, Ranhold guards are trying to push out the subjects through the gate, with frenzied command that barely cuts through the chaos. Half the people are trying to come back in to see what's going on, the other half fleeing for their lives.

Manu and my guards got us outside, but only just. My heartbeat is a hammer, and the breath that I'm sucking in is just as rushed as the adrenaline pumping through my veins. It's the sort of harried vulnerability that makes me feel no better than a cornered animal. One who's frozen in snow, unable to move. And yet, what's really keeping me still are the sounds coming from the castle. Sloshing. Dripping. Clanging. Smashing. *More screaming.*

Another sharp slap of shrieks erupts when liquid gold suddenly bursts through the front doors. Everyone flinches back, gasping bodies caught in the swell of panic, shoving into the mass behind them as they try to get further away.

Manu and Keon stand in front of me, facing Ranhold Castle, and they both push me back protectively while our guards surround us. Not all of my guards made it out, yet I haven't wanted to look around to see just how many I lost.

The gold spews from the doorway and curls around the castle walls, gushing down the front steps. Like outstretched hands, it nearly grabs hold of a man, but he gets yanked out of the way by some guards at the very last second.

The liquid metal slams down from its unsuccessful reach like a petulant child smashing fists in a fit against the ground and sending splatters flying. Mottled gashes of gold streak across the snow-covered steps, marring the stone. More of it drips like blood from the window sills, staining the glass and peeking past the frames.

We're surrounded by the castle's lantern-lit outer walls, and even though it's supposed to make us feel protected, it's only keeping everyone trapped out here together. I'm about to suggest to my brother that we get away in case the gold keeps pouring out and we become trapped with the crowd, but another loud crash happens somewhere inside, cutting me off.

My eyes wildly veer between my brother's and Keon's forms, wondering what else inside has been destroyed, who else has been killed. But then, as if that last noise was a signal for the end, the gold that's gripping the front walls suddenly stops glinting, stops rippling.

It hardens in place as the castle goes suddenly quiet.

The screaming of the crowd cuts off too, everyone waiting with bated breath to see if it's actually over. I'm not sure how long we all stand there, watching and listening, but the splotches of gold along the grayed, frozen stone are no longer moving, and despite the torches casting off firelight, everything seems darker. Colder.

The movement and sounds may have ceased, yet those things instead spring to life inside of me. My body begins to tremble, my mind a funnel of noisy thoughts swirling around.

What in the Divine just happened?

My shoes are soaked through as I stand here in the snow, my skin pebbled from the awful frigid night air. I wasn't meant to be outside in this dress. I should be in the ballroom right now. I should be celebrating my engagement announcement and making plans for my control to now spread to Sixth Kingdom.

At the very least, I should be warmer.

When I look down, I see blotches of gold splashed onto my deep blue dress in a motley of gleaming spots. I don't dare run my finger over it. Not after what I saw in that ballroom.

"Has it stopped?" I ask.

The question is overly simplified for what just happened in there. Has it stopped—*it*. The berserk gold that just rose up with furious motive. I already know my mind is going to be stuck with the memory of tonight for a long time, that I'm going to replay it over and over again.

I won't be able to erase the way the gold moved with violent precision. How it dripped down the walls. How it pooled on the ground. How it splashed, and stabbed, and *consumed*.

"Has it stopped?" I ask again, my voice shriller than I've ever heard it.

I've never been so close to mortal danger before, and my body knows it. Which is why my pulse is still racing, why the tempo of it is pounding in my ears.

Why I can't stop shaking.

"I think so," Manu finally answers as he turns around.

His husband still watches the castle, as if he doesn't trust taking his eyes off it. As if he expects the violence of the liquid metal to lash back to life.

"Damned Divine," I hear him say beneath his breath.

Perhaps his murmured curse has pulled the stopper from the bottled-up crowd, because a flurry of voices starts to pour through the courtyard. Automatically, my power sweeps out, pulling their words to me. My magic sweeps down, catching what they're saying and stringing them up in my mind.

"What's happened?"

"This is King Midas's gold-touch."

"Where's King Midas? Where's King Rot?"

"Our prince is dead."

"Did Midas do this on purpose?"

"But what happened?"

The words flow from their mouths to my ears, where they gather like threads in a web for me to spin. Yet soon, I don't even need my power to hear them, because the crowd begins to shout, demanding answers in frenzied cries loud enough for all.

"Shit," Manu hisses, turning toward me. "Maybe you should—"

Someone suddenly shouts, "I know what happened!"

All eyes slam onto the woman, who staggers to the front. She points a shaky finger toward the doors, gold bleeding from their depths like a gaping wound.

"This wasn't King Midas's doing!" she spits out, a long curtain of black hair hanging down her back, her dress looking like part of it melted off. "It was his gold-touched pet! She stole his magic!"

I rear back in surprise, her words tangling up in my head.

"Who is that?" Manu murmurs.

A man from the crowd shoves forward. "What are you talking about, woman?"

She straightens up, sweeping a proud look over the crowd. "I am one of King Midas's royal saddles, and I can tell you all right now that this was all because of Auren. She did this! The gilded whore stole his magic when he gold-touched her, and she figured out she could use it for herself. She lied to him, and now she's attacked him. I saw it with my own eyes when I was running out!"

Shock cuts like an oar through a surf.

"What the fuck?" Manu hisses beneath his breath as he turns to me.

When the woman places a hand on her stomach, it occurs to me who exactly this is.

Mist. The saddle Midas impregnated.

As her words sink in, I start to shake my head in denial at first, and yet, it *must* be true, because what I saw in that room... It was like the gold wasn't in Midas's control at all, like someone else was doing it...

How did I not discover this secret sooner?

5

"Look!" someone shouts. "Timberwings! Someone's fleeing on timberwings!"

"It's her! The gilded murderer!"

My head angles in the direction of the man who spoke, my gaze following where he's pointing. I only get a split second before the view is swallowed by the darkness of night, a flash of feathers and talons disappearing into the clouds.

Was that King Rot with Lady Auren?

"I told you!" Mist cries out. "She's a deceiver. A cheat. She seduced Midas and took his power, and now she's going to do the same to King Rot!"

A crescendo of voices surges, and within moments, the rumor is caught up in a current too forceful to stop.

How in the Divine-damned could I have missed something like this? How could I not have known?

"You're trembling," my brother says, yanking me out of my flooding thoughts. His gaze casts over my shoulder. "Your queen is cold. Find something for her."

There's shuffling behind me and then the weight of a cloak being draped over my shoulders. "Here you are, Queen Kaila."

My fingers grip the front of the cloak, pulling it tight around my chest, though it does nothing to ward off the chill, because it's seeped all the way through to my bones. I need to be back in Third, walking along the beach at the height of day in order to feel any sort of warmth again after being stuck here for so long.

However, I can't go home yet. Not when everything I've worked so hard for is falling through my fingers. I can feel the eyes of the crowd glancing at me, waiting to see what I'll do.

"Manu, have someone confirm that Ravinger just fled with Lady Auren."

My brother nods at my command before moving out of my line of sight, where I hear him issuing orders to someone. I glance around the courtyard, noting that only Ranhold's guards are gathered outside. Not a single guard of Midas's. Not a bit of gold-plated armor in sight.

"Keon," I call, and he immediately turns to me. "Have some of Ranhold's guards go inside and confirm that the danger has passed. See if they can find Midas and if he needs help."

He moves away with a nod, pointing at a couple of Fifth's guards standing around a splatter of gold on the snow, kicking at the solidifying puddle warily.

As I continue to stare at the castle, the wind picks up, glazed slush starting to spit from the sky, as if it wasn't miserable enough out here already.

Three of the Ranhold soldiers break away, walking forward with grim faces as they head for the broken doorway. The first one holds out his hands to the others, then kneels at the first splash of the spilled gold that lies motionless on the steps.

He presses his finger against it, and when it does nothing, he stands again, nodding to the others. Together, they walk up to the doorway, boots clicking over the solidified gold before they disappear inside.

We wait.

The crowd still gathered in the courtyard has grown quiet again, the anxiousness of the wait seeming to clog up their throats.

Despite my own warring thoughts, I walk to the front of the

castle, stopping to face everyone as I put on a calm yet strong demeanor. Their prince is dead, Rot has fled, and Midas isn't here, so I'm the one they need to look to, and it's important that I cultivate that. Right now, I need to be seen.

"Do not fear," I announce. "The danger is over, and I will find out if what has been claimed is true."

The people murmur, my powers gathering the whispered relief, the admiration, the respect they have for me.

"Well done, sister," Manu says beneath his breath.

When one of the guards reappears, I nod to Keon to go collect his report. My brother-in-law steps over, expression stoic before dismissing the man, but my eyes scan the crowd, magic picking up their mumblings.

I break off my magic when Keon comes over.

"Well?" Manu asks nervously.

"All the gold seems to have stopped its movement and is solidified," he says quietly, keeping his voice down.

"And Midas?" I press.

His brown eyes center on me. "They believe he's dead."

I suck in a shocked breath. It stays stuck to my throat, just as the words themselves weave in my head, wrapping around my skull in trapping strands.

Dead.

My lips press together, and I feel my eyes chiseling into the face of the castle. All my hard work...all this time I've spent on my machinations, and now this.

King Midas does *nothing* for me if he's dead.

I came here to negotiate deals, to exert my own wants through an impressionable prince and a rich king. Things

8

changed, but they were for the better. I had a *plan*. I was going to be the first monarch in history to join two kingdoms together through marriage, while having a hand in a third.

Because power is everything, and though I may not have a physical magic like gold-touch or rot, I have words, and a queen can do a lot with a web full of people's secrets.

I have been working endlessly since I took my throne to ensure that my people see me as just as much of a power threat as any other monarch. That would've been solidified even further with these alliances. Now, all of that is crumbling.

All because of Lady Auren. *Lady*. As if a saddle pet warrants the term.

Anger and fear clash inside my head, though I don't let it show. Not when so many people are watching. As a woman in power, you can never let people see your true emotional reactions because they would only use them against you.

"I want to see."

Before either of them can stop me, I stride toward the castle, toes frozen as more snow saturates my silk slippers.

"Sister," Manu calls, but I don't stop. I hear rushing footsteps as he and Keon catch up with me just before I make it to the steps.

"At least let me go first," Keon says as he abruptly cuts in front so he can walk up before me.

"Be careful," Manu cautions.

With a brisk nod, Keon heads up the steps, and as soon as he does, I follow behind him. "Kaila," Manu hisses beside me. "Just because it's stable right now doesn't mean it's going to stay like that. We don't know how volatile it is."

"It's solidified," I say, shoes rasping against the slick gold just before we make it to the top step. The doors are hanging from their hinges like teeth knocked loose and crooked.

"It was solidified *before*, *too*," he retorts. "And look what happened with that."

"Looking to see what happened is exactly my intention."

I hear him sigh as I walk through the doorway, but my footsteps slow as soon as I'm inside. The flames from the wall sconces are flickering erratically, as if they too are jumpy, still recovering from the assault.

The entry hall echoes with our footsteps as Manu and I follow a few paces behind Keon until we reach the ballroom. All three of us stop in our tracks when we make it through the doorway.

I blink at the darkness that's settled over the room. At the darkness and at the gold inside that glints in shadowed warning. Before, flames from the chandeliers and sconces lit up the entire space, making it rival the daylight. But now, everything's been cast in shadow. The only light comes from the iron furnaces still burning in the corners, their presence only now visible because the ballroom is empty. This room doesn't even look remotely the same. It's as if the entire space was made with wax, and someone held a burning candle to it.

The walls look half melted off, gold frozen in its drip. The ceiling, too, has strings of it cast down like icicles, ends pointed down at us with sharp purpose. The plated pillars are bare of their gilt, every bit of golden adornment melted away.

The floor is a rippled mess, clumpy in some areas, raised with motionless shapes that make me cringe. A visible hand reaching up, frozen in place. A gilt lump of a body curled beside the raised platform. A frozen wave caught below the mezzanine, as if the balcony melted clear off and splashed to the floor below where I can see someone's leg sticking out.

"Gods..."

Manu's whispered declaration spurs me back into motion. My footsteps take me across the ballroom, gaze cautious, skipping from one spot of gold to the next. Yet as I get further in, a horrible groan comes from the walls. The floor. The ceiling. Like an old home settling with cracks and creaks, only this is far worse. It's eerie. Like the gold is a ghost, bemoaning our presence, threatening to haunt.

I go still, pulse spiking even more than before. Beside me, Manu grips my arm. "Kaila, we should get out of here."

The groan tapers off like a sigh, the room falling silent and still once more.

Shrugging off my brother's touch, I continue in my search. "I want to see."

Keon points forward and says, "There."

As soon as I lay eyes on what he's pointed out, my feet take me forward, all the way to the far end. To the bulbous spot now marring the space of the wall.

"Great Divine..."

It's him.

His crown is missing from his head. Perhaps melted into the gold that now encases him. He looks like he's being melted into the wall itself, like it was trying to suck him into its depths and swallow him whole. His agonized face is on display. Wide eyes held with shock and fear.

King Midas is now nothing but a corpse encased in a gold tomb.

The gold groans again, as if staking its claim.

"No…"

We whirl around at the woman's voice to find Mist stumbling forward, looking at Midas with horror. "My King…" She falls to her knees, clutching her belly, the tinged, demolished room carrying the echo of her cries. "She did this. She did this to him."

"But *how*?" Keon murmurs as we watch her sob. "How is that possible?"

I think back to each interaction, to everything I've been told. I stare at Midas's face as I think. As I hear. Flicking past strands of old webs that I've collected, words swaying back and forth in my mind.

Monarchs are secretive about their magic. It's strategic. Knowing when to show your hand and knowing when to conceal it. In some cases, it's best to make people underestimate you. In others, monarchs are known to show enough power to make everyone either revere you or fear you. Sometimes both.

Midas gilded the dining table—it was the first time I saw it with my own eyes. He also gold-touched this entire ballroom for tonight's celebration. Two perfect spectacles.

Yet, tonight, his gold behaved as if he wasn't in control of it at all. Because he wasn't.

The gold-touch power was real, there's no doubt about that. And he's never gold-touched another living person, other than Auren.

This must be why.

I thought her greatest secret was that she was sleeping with an enemy army commander. I thought the gold-touched favored was just that—a favorite royal saddle for him to ride.

I was wrong on both counts.

I *detest* being wrong.

Midas made her into something ostentatious, a gaudy prize to flaunt. Men always have their fixations, especially when it comes to women. Their enthusiasm for their obsessions always straddles the line between infatuation and hate. One simple move, and the master will turn on their pretty pet.

But perhaps in this case...the pet was the one to turn on her master.

The fear in my mind digs down into my belly. If she can truly thieve powers, then what if she tried to steal mine? What if she *succeeded*?

My teeth click and grind. Instead of falling into panic, I need to figure out how I can weave things to my own advantage. Because if Lady Auren tried to steal what is mine, I will *ruin* her.

Seeing the hardened metal is what solidifies my own spinning thoughts. Midas is encased in gold like he's been cast in a mold, ready to be plucked out and sharpened by a blacksmith.

I thought he was useless to me dead, but perhaps not. Perhaps all I have to do is use what he's been forged into.

A weapon.

"When he gold-touched her, some of his power must've transferred to her," I say quietly. "He wouldn't have wanted anyone to ever know that."

Midas was secretive about *everything*, but this? This is an entirely different layer of dangerous secrets. Is that why he kept

13

her around? Because he trained her to take on the powers of others to use to his advantage?

"This isn't good," Keon says.

"Kaila," my brother begins. "What if it wasn't a fluke? What if that's *her* magic? Being able to take on the magic of others if they use it on her? Did you…?"

"I did," I say with a sharp nod, fresh anger budding through me.

"What if she steals *your* power?"

I don't like hearing my own worry spoken aloud. My knees lock together, tongue pressing against clenched teeth. My gaze on Midas shifts to my blotted reflection shining from his gilded chest.

This wasn't how tonight was supposed to go. I wasn't supposed to be in danger of someone taking my power and using it against me.

"How are we going to use this?" Manu says, because like me, he's grown up learning how to always spin every instance to our own political advantage. Tonight is no different.

I glance around the ballroom, but we're still alone other than a blubbering Mist, who's sobbing into her hands. "We tell people the truth," I say. "That Midas's favored turned on him. That she had an affair with King Rot to make him jealous. That she was jealous of my engagement with Midas."

"Make sure everyone knows she's the villain."

I nod. "All of Orea will hate her."

"But what about Sixth Kingdom?" Manu asks. "Now, there obviously won't be a marriage."

"But we publicly announced our engagement," I reply. "It will be difficult, but if I play it right, I can still push for control."

"The people there are still rioting," Keon says. "Plus, they *murdered* their old queen. What makes you think they'll accept you with Midas dead and no marriage ceremony?"

I shoot him a smile. "Because I'm not the Cold Queen. I'm the warm, charismatic, beautiful Kaila Ioana. I'll make them love me as my own people in Third love me."

"We know how beloved Kaila is to our people. She can sell it," my brother says with a definitive nod.

"We will have to move fast," Keon says. "As soon as we can, we will need to visit Sixth, do some sort of ceremony to honor Midas's life, make you the grieving betrothed for them to sympathize over."

If there's one thing I know how to do, it's to make a kingdom love me.

"I can do that."

More sharp, gasping wails behind us make me want to grit my teeth, and I spare Mist another look.

She will still have to be dealt with.

If I'm going to try and take Sixth, I certainly cannot have her bastard heir being born from her womb. But that will be a problem for another day.

"There will be a lot happening now," I go on quietly. "Once the other monarchs find out about Lady Auren's ability to steal power, they'll want to get involved. Plus, there's the issue of Fifth."

"I actually have an idea about that," Manu says, and my attention immediately sharpens.

My brother isn't my advisor for nothing. He has a brilliant mind, knows how to play a room, knows how to read people, and above all, he will always be loyal to me.

"Since our focus now needs to be on how to secure Sixth, as well as how to take care of Lady Auren, the last thing we want is to lose all the work we've done to create a foothold here in Fifth. So, I propose that we immediately put in the search for the closest kin of Fulke, because now that the prince is dead, Ranhold needs an heir. We will track down whichever ones have power, and sift through the best candidates. Then *we* will choose which heir gets the throne. *We* will determine who takes power. And in exchange for our support...they will support us, and us alone."

I smile. "You are perfect, brother."

He gives me a matching grin.

"And if anyone tries to oppose us in claiming Sixth or with having our hand in naming a Fifth heir?" Keon questions worriedly.

My smile grows sharp, twisted with ruthlessness. "Any voice that speaks up against me, won't have a voice to use after that."

And if Lady Auren thinks she can take what I've worked for, she's going to realize soon that she's not the only one who knows how to steal what she wants.

I may not have gold-touch, and I may not have rot, but words are the most powerful weapon of all, and I will wield them.

CHAPTER 2

SLADE

There's a *tempest dredging the* sky, while I hold a lifeless body in my arms.

The impending storm is coming in with bared, frozen teeth to scrape the air with malice, its sharp frigidity beating at my face as it roars.

In my head, I'm counting the seconds. It took sixty for my timberwing to get to me, called from the whistle bursting between clenched teeth. Another forty to get on Argo's back, for Lu to strap me in as I held Auren in my arms.

Another sixty seconds has taken us here, into the clutches of the clouds that are closing in. The night's weather has decided to turn on me, the signs of an impending storm clogging the horizon like tufts of cotton in a drain.

Ice scrapes against my cheeks like jagged fingernails as my timberwing rushes on. I hold Auren closer, keeping my cloak over her, angling her face against my chest as my arms tuck her tightly to my body.

She's too cold, too exposed, too *still*.

Her heart doesn't beat, her chest doesn't rise, her skin has gone sallow. All because of me. Because of what I did.

With a quick glance over my shoulder, I see Ranhold Castle below, lit up with torches. The face of it has now been marred with a splash of angry, solidified gold, erupting through the mouth of the doors and staining the gray stonework like insipid gilt magma that went inert before it could do any further damage.

It looks like the gold was trying to eat its way through the whole damn castle. To inhale it from an unforgiving mouth and devour it with wrath. Like a dam giving way, this is what happens when power is suppressed for too long, left to collect, to rise, to beat against its containment until the cracks form and it can finally *break free*.

I turn back around and hold Auren a little bit tighter.

I've got to get away from the castle—from the gold—but *how much further* is the question. Because every second I wait puts her in even more danger.

There's a double-edged sword, and Auren's life is balancing at the tip of it.

I have to get her as far away as I can, but I can't risk leaving her in this rotted stasis for too long. Without knowing how far her power can reach, it's a guessing game as to how far we need to go.

All I want to do is get the rot out of her. Her body can't take more depletion. I need to have her on land too, settled and secure, because when I remove my power, there's a chance she can still call on hers, and I can't have that happen in the air.

Her aura is nothing but a pale wisp, like dying mist in the light. If I wait too long, my power that's infested her will do more damage than I can reverse, and I can't let that happen either. I can't let *either* of those things happen. So this will be down to the very last second.

Time and distance are my enemy *and* my ally.

With anxious worry, my heels come up to nudge my timberwing. He lets out a call, either to show his displeasure or to signal to the rest of the flock. I know the others are following.

"Faster, Argo," I urge the feathered beast, though my voice gets ripped away like hands snatching stolen trinkets.

Although the wind beats at us, Argo pushes on in a burst of speed, and I keep the reins loose to give him his head as his giant wings stretch out and cut through the night sky, lit up only by a veiled moon. I get jerked back, and if it weren't for the leather strap from the saddle hooked to the buckled belt around my waist, there's a good chance I would've fallen right off.

Wouldn't be the first time.

Yet right now, I'm not riding for sport or for scouting. This is life and death.

Her life.

We fly as fast as possible away from Ranhold, and Fifth Kingdom's skies seem to punish us for it. Perhaps the deceased King Fulke and Prince Niven want someone to blame for their demise.

Some of Auren's hair slips out from beneath the hood of my cloak, its golden strands whipping around in the wind. With one hand, I pull the cloak tighter around her ear, trying to keep the cold from touching her even though I know she can't feel it.

Thirty more seconds have passed.

Dread is stacking up in my gut like the heavy bricks of an insurmountable wall. It feels as if I'm counting the increments of Auren's soul slipping away bit by bit.

I've seen what happens when I wait too long to reverse the rot, and I know just how damaging it is. I know how much danger I put her in.

Guilt ravages me for what I've done, for the magic holding her hostage, but my resolve to keep her safe hardens. I spare another glance behind me, but Ranhold is now out of view, the clouds blocking the kingdom completely.

From the corner of my eye, I see a dark shadow cut through the clouds, and I'm not at all surprised at the timberwing and rider that swoops in. The beast's size somehow makes even Osrik look small in comparison. He watches me wordlessly, hands tight on the reins, and I give a nod.

I hope I've gone far enough, because I don't dare wait a second longer. With a tug on the reins, I make Argo dive. My timberwing lets out a call, and I curl over Auren, bracing for our descent.

When Osrik sees I'm making to land, he lets out a sharp whistle and follows suit. In the distance, I can hear the call of more timberwings answering back.

Where I go, my Wrath follows.

20

My eyes burn with the force of the wind that rushes up at me as we continue to drop, cutting through heavy clouds saturated with the impending storm.

The lines of power along my jaw writhe and snap as I monitor the link of my magic now swirling inside of Auren. Rot. Corrosion. *Death*. It doesn't belong anywhere near her, and yet, *I* put it there.

I fucking hate it.

My knees lock in as I lean forward and grip the hold of my timberwing's strap. "Come on..." I murmur.

Maybe Argo can feel my rushing panic, because he somehow manages to dive even faster. Water freezes at the corners of my squinting eyes, and my heart pounds against my chest loud enough to compete with the rushing wind.

"Almost," I say against her hair. "Just hold on a few seconds more."

Finally, we cut through the last of the mist and clouds, only to be greeted by the frozen ground below, brandishing the world like a sheet of gray. When it looks like we're going to crash right into it, Argo lifts up at the last moment and swoops in a circle right alongside Osrik's timberwing before both land on their taloned feet, kicking up a spray of snow like the sea crashing into the hull of a ship.

My frozen fingers are already unhooking the buckle holding me in place. I slip down, taking the impact of the jump with my knees so as not to jar Auren too much. Before I can take a single step forward, Os is there, ripping off his cloak and laying it on the ground just as I see more timberwings landing like shadowed spectators.

"Stay back," I call over my shoulder.

I lay Auren down on the cloak, the faintest traces of rotten lines stretching up the veins in her neck. Her hair is spilled in a halo around her, somehow gleaming even in the darkness. She looks so small with my cloak tucked around her, so lifeless.

I kneel over her, immediately focusing as I snap my eyes closed. My magic is there, clinging to her prone form like a poison. Unnatural decay is slogging through her veins and withering the heart in her chest. It's slinking up her deteriorating throat, barred by her unmoving lips.

Tension rolls through me. Instinctually, I want to yank the magic out of her as quickly as possible, but I've found pulling it out too fast is like ripping a blade from a wound. I don't want to do any more damage than I've already done.

Carefully, I call the power back inch by inch so as not to shock her system. Behind me, I can hear the murmured words of the rest of my Wrath, uncertain footsteps shifting in the snow, timberwings chuffing at one another, and thunder from the clouds we just departed signaling a cold front blowing in.

I shove all of that away and keep my awareness on the magic coursing through her. Like the roots of a weed, I drag it out as gently as I can manage. Fingers dig through soil, removing the rotten stasis I buried her in, letting her body reacclimate. I'm meticulous, lifting each bit of corrupted patches like drying clay, ridding it piece by cracked piece.

Despite the biting air, sweat beads at my temples. My teeth clench as I pull the power back to me, back to the recesses carved from my veins to simmer in my own spoils. I get it all out of her, until there's just one single fragment left. One seed left buried in the center of her chest.

Yet when I call to it, try to unearth it from her depths, I find resistance. Instead of withdrawing like the rest, this piece sinks in its thorns as if it's trying to stay.

As if it's trying to *keep* her in its clutches.

My brow furrows and my hands shake, while the rotted roots on my skin stretch down the length of my arms. It slinks past my palms and cloys beneath my fingertips, the dark lines rubbing me raw from the inside out, threatening to pierce through my very skin.

A war of confusion and fear jumps in my jaw.

Never has my rot been so reluctant. Never has it been so persistent in *staying*. I haven't struggled with controlling it like this for years, not since I was a boy. I had to learn very early on how to handle the malodorous magic before it destroyed everything, including myself.

So what the fuck is happening?

Frantically, I check over the rest of her, but there's no other blight in her, not a single other part besmirched. The rest of the rot is gone, leaving her as she was before, so why won't this last piece leave?

"Let go." My tongue is heavy with the taste of unrelenting toxins. "Let go of her."

It writhes in reply, like brambles twisting around her chest, like it wants to root inside of her. Panic slices through me like the sharpest blade.

"Get the fuck out of her!"

Magic and might unleash from me, stronger than the

torrent of the storm trying to rend from the sky. With a crack that splits the air and clangs my teeth, I give one massive *tug*.

The force of my violent pull sends me flying back, while Auren's entire spine bows up from the ground like an arcing wave.

"Rip!"

I lie stunned and out of breath, eyes locked on the shadowed outline of clouds covering the night sky above me. Snow flies up from the impact of Lu's knees as she hits the ground next to me, eyes wide with worry. "Are you okay?"

"What the fuck just happened?" Osrik demands.

I hear Judd let out a whistle... "Your roots..."

My eyes drop, gaze falling to where the veins in my hands are writhing and snapping angrily. I can feel everyone's gaze lift to my neck and face, but I don't need them to say anything, because I can *feel* the lined roots beneath my skin. Fucking everywhere. As if I haven't used my power in months, as if it's pent up inside of me to an unstable magnitude.

But it doesn't matter, because I just ripped that last bit of rot out of her, so everything will be okay.

Lu tries to help me sit up, but I push her fretting hands away, a pained groan escaping me. I quickly lean over Auren again, but the moment I see her face, I realize that she's still not awake.

She's still not moving.

My panic stems and swells.

Rot bleeds into the ground, shooting into the depths of the earth just as thoroughly and as violently as my stomach falls straight through into my feet.

What did I do?

Fingers dig into the snow, rotted mulch spreading from my touch, corrupting the ground with putrid lines. I don't just feel it spreading into the snow—I feel it wrapping around my heart, squeezing, crumbling, making it wither right here in my chest.

My eyes slam shut, and my roots stab up against the skin of my neck. They wrap around my veins like furious snakes, constricting and biting, making me hurt all over, but it doesn't matter.

Because I killed her. I fucking *killed* her—

Her lips suddenly part. The movement makes my eyes snap open just as a shuddering breath lurches out of her. Wisps of black expel from her mouth, the poisoned air evaporating between us.

Relief pounds through my temples. "Auren?"

But her eyes don't open, and dread pulls at my chest.

I close my eyes to focus on the inside of her again, and immediately, the blood drains from my face. Because that piece—that single scrap of rot that I should've just ripped out of her when I got knocked on my ass—is still there.

It's still. Fucking. There.

Stunned, I mentally try to grip around it again and yank, again and again, but it won't budge. It won't leave.

She breathes, another exhale of murky black misting past her lips.

My heart pounds like fists against my ribs, ready to punch through and fight. And still, no matter how much I call to my power, that piece in her chest won't come out. It's sunken in, like a stain of ink in gold fabric that I can't get out.

Yet her chest is rising and falling. Her heart has begun to beat. She's *alive*.

I can't get that fucking last drop of rot out of her, but she's alive, and that's what matters.

"Wake up, Auren."

Seconds go by. Five, ten, twenty. I count them all.

"Is she okay?"

My back tenses at the rough question spoken from Digby, his voice hostage to both injury and disuse. I don't answer him, and I don't know if anyone else attempts to. I keep watching her. Willing her to open her eyes.

"Come on, Goldfinch…" I murmur, urgency notched around my neck like a noose.

There's the sound of shuffling footsteps, then Digby is pushing his way forward to kneel next to me. "Is she okay?" he demands again.

When I still don't answer, his hand grabs the front of my shirt, and he tugs me to face him with surprising strength, considering the bruised state of him. "What did you do?" he snarls through swollen lips split with blood and frost.

Osrik is there in an instant, lifting Digby and pulling him away. "*What did you do?*" Digby's shout is mangled, hoarse with accusation, but it melds with the voice of my own inner terror. The two of them exchange some heated words, but fear is too busy slamming in my ears for me to hear what they say.

What did I do?

The panic and fear that's been latched to me since the moment I used my power on her comes flaring up in the form of a tremor through my hands.

"Why isn't she waking up?" Lu asks beside me, but I don't know. I don't fucking *know*, so I can't say a damn thing.

I clasp her cold cheeks in my hands, hissing at the pain throbbing in my fingers. Even now, it's as if my power wants to split from my skin and go back to her.

Her aura is dull. Just wisps of dreary gold barely skimming against her silhouette. It should be gleaming brightly despite the night, yet it's nothing like the flare of potent power and life that usually shines from her.

I waited too long.

I should've rotted her sooner, before she'd nearly drained herself. I should've landed faster, ripped my magic out of her earlier.

"Don't do this," I grit out. To her, to the gods.

Not now.

Not after everything. Not when I just fucking got her.

"I need you to wake up," I order, but really, it's a plea pulled from the pit of my soul. What if she *never* wakes up? What if that clinging seed of rot has taken root inside of her and won't let her go?

The whole reason I used my magic on her was to stop her from draining herself to death. But I made it fucking worse. I made it worse, and now my own power is lashing out against me like a thousand serpents ready to bite, while she's been tainted with my magic.

My head drops, forehead pressing against hers, my hands still on her cold cheeks. "Don't do this," I plead, eyes shut tight. "You're stronger than this, Goldfinch. You are. So. Wake. *Up*."

She doesn't.

"Fuck!" Jerking upright, my fist pummels the snow beside me, the meat of my hand splitting open from the sharp ice packed into the ground. "*Fuck, fuck, fuck!*"

I can hear Digby fighting like hell against the others, cursing me, threats and profanity slung against my back like a whip. Beating me with the realization—

"I did this." Three words cut from the keenest guilt.

Lu's lips press together at my declaration. "So *undo* it."

"I fucking tried!" I snap, frustration bringing my hand up to drive through my hair. "I *am* trying."

I can't think straight. My pulse is pounding at my temples, the ground is shaking beneath my feet, something is roaring in my ears. My magic wails inside of me, bleeding into my irises, making me see lines that are not there. I'm pouring rot out now, too much, too fast, making it melt down into the ground, weakening the earth, spoiling its surface.

I hear shouts, or maybe that's the wind or the power bucking in my bones.

"Rip, your power..."

My entire body is shaking, every inch of my skin being prodded and stretched, wanting to lash out, and my rot starts to flood the ground, reaching, hissing, wanting to spread and *explode*...

BAM!

I go flying back at the force of a fist to my face, falling back into the snow for the second time in the course of a minute, once again stunned.

"Get your shit together," my brother fumes over me,

kneeling even as he lifts me back up from where he sucker punched me. My furious eyes latch onto his face. "You're leaking rot all over the Divine-damned place. Suck it up *right now*. You don't have the luxury of losing control."

I blink, Ryatt's snapped words somehow grounding me to the present. A glance down shows that the snow at our feet is browned and sickly, veins like poisonous threads come to spread their toxins. It stretches out in a perfect circle, spoiling the ground and sucking up the moisture from the snow, collapsing it in rubbled ruin.

I take a breath and fist my hands, managing to pull it back before my power can spread any further, managing to pull it back in and in and *in...*

"You got it?" Ryatt demands.

"I got it," I snarl at him.

"Good." He lets me go, and I equal parts want to slam my own fist into his face and thank him for snapping me out of the power pull.

Turning away, I find all of my Wrath and Digby huddling around Auren. Judd casts me a wary look. "She's breathing, that's a good sign," he says, as if that will settle me.

"But she's not waking up."

"Did you get all of it?" Lu asks, hands dancing around Auren's sleeves, not quite touching her, just in case.

"Something is wrong. I couldn't get the last piece out."

Lu's eyes go wide, and I hear someone else suck in a breath.

"Maybe I waited too long."

"What does that mean?" Digby asks.

29

I shake my head at my own loss.

"Well, we need a plan," Lu says, standing up and dusting herself off before she casts a look at the sky. "This storm is coming, and coming in fast. What do you wanna do?"

Taking a moment, I roll back my shoulders, subduing the tyrannical pull of magic as I flex and clench my fingers, forcing the roots to cease their incessant coiling. As soon as I get a handle on them, I push my way past everyone and then carefully gather Auren into my arms, tucking her against my chest, hating how lifeless she still feels.

I start to walk away, but Digby hobbles in front of me, expression murderous. "I told you *to fix her*."

"She just needs to rest," I reply, but even I can hear the uncertainty in my tone. "I need to get her out of the elements."

Mutinous hate is there on his face, but before he can say anything else, I turn to Osrik. "You all fly back to the army. I want our soldiers moved out of Ranhold tonight. I don't trust Queen Kaila. Get them back to Fourth as quickly as they can march." My mouth sets into a grim line. "We'll need them."

Osrik nods, but Judd asks, "What about you?"

I cast a glower at the sky. "I'm going to fly like hell ahead of this storm and get Auren somewhere safe."

"You can't go alone," Lu argues. "And you can't fly all the way to Fourth with her unconscious. It's too far. What if she wakes up and gilds you to death?"

Argo tucks in his bark-colored wings and kneels as I approach him, his talons sunk into the deep snow. "I'm not going to Fourth," I call over my shoulder.

"Where are you taking her, then?" Digby demands.

But it's Ryatt who answers as I grab hold of the saddle strap and hoist myself and Auren onto Argo's back. I lock eyes with my brother's angry gaze just as he answers for me.

"He's taking her to Deadwell."

CHAPTER 3

SLADE
Age 8

S lade!"

My shouted name is louder than the birds' song, startling a few into taking flight.

I turn to look at the estate through the branches of the tree, and when I bend one back, one of the buds under my hand puffs out a cloud of blue. Ahead, the black stone building is stained with lines of white from all the times it's rained, the top of it flat except for the square chimneys standing up like stacks of blocks.

My eyes drop down to the sloped grass where she's walking up the hill toward me. I huff out a sigh and let go of the branch, more carefully this time so that I don't get hit in the face with another puff from the tree buds. They smell good at least, but they're awfully messy.

I turn back to the pin bird sitting on my finger. She's just a nestling, tufts of down covering her spindly body, but her eyes are open and she coos low in her throat. "It's alright. You'll grow your real feathers soon," I tell her. In a few weeks, she'll have a plume of them at her tail for her to show off, each one as thin as a pin, the ends as sharp as them too. "Then you'll be able to fly off with the rest of them."

My name is shouted again, so I gently place the bird back in its nest before I swing my leg over the branch and start to climb my way down.

When my bare feet land in the grass, I look up at my mother standing over me with her hands on her hips. Her black hair is in a long, loose plait, and she's wearing the same red-colored clothing as me, except she's in a dress. "And what do you think you were doing up in that tree?"

I shrug. "Nothing."

"Mm-hmm," she says as she wipes off some of the blue powder that landed on my shoulder. "I suppose you weren't climbing up there and playing with the birds again."

My face is in a frown when I turn it back up to her. "I wasn't playing. That's baby stuff. I was monitoring."

My mother's lips twitch. "Of course," she says, green eyes flicking down. "And your shoes?"

Another shrug. "It's harder to climb with them. I didn't put them on because I didn't want to fall."

She shakes her head, but all sternness has left her expression as she kneels down in front of me. "Well, I certainly can't have you falling. And how are the birds this morning?"

"They're good," I assure her, feeling excited again now that I can tell she's not angry. "There's a little nestling, but I think its mom left already, so I'm gonna help teach it to fly."

34

The shape of my mother's green eyes crinkles as she smiles. "If anyone can do it, you can. You've always had a way with them."

Her hand lifts and she combs her fingers over my hair, but I jerk my head away and press down on it. "I combed it earlier."

She laughs and then fixes my upturned collar. "Come on. It's time to eat."

When she reaches for my hand, I tug it away. "I can't hold hands anymore. I'm eight," I tell her.

"Oh, right. Of course," she says, though the side of her mouth has lifted up into a smirk. "I guess I just miss holding my son's hand."

I don't want her to feel bad. It's not that I don't want to hold her hand, it's just little kid stuff. "You could hold Ryatt's," I tell her. "He's only three, so that's alright."

She gently pats my cheek. "That's a very good idea."

Together, we walk away from the copse of trees, passing by the birdbaths and the line of point-shaped shrubs. I look at the estate at the bottom of the slope, but I don't want to go inside. I'd much rather stay out here with the grass and the birds.

There's nothing wrong with the house, really. We've got forty-three rooms, a load of fancy things, and a bunch of servants too. None of the other families in the city have a house as big as ours with as many horses as we do.

But I hate it. I'd rather live in the smaller houses on the city streets. Because then I wouldn't live here. With him.

We're almost to the back door past the gardens when a figure appears in the doorway, and I immediately jerk to a stop, my mother stopping next to me. My father stands there, red shirt buttoned all the way to his neck, not a crease out of place. His bald head cuts into a thick brown beard, and his mouth is already pinched with irritation. It usually is whenever I'm around.

His black eyes skip from her to me, and I stop myself from swallowing. He'd see me do it, and I'm supposed to always be something called stoic. I think it means not to feel.

My mother reaches down and takes hold of my hand, and I don't yank away this time. My sweaty palm is held tightly in hers as she takes me the last few steps until we stand in front of him.

"I didn't know you were coming home tonight, Stanton."

"I was able to cut things short with the king," he replies.

His attention drops down to my bare feet, and it makes me want to scrunch up my toes and try to bury them in the grass. My heartbeat turns quick when he gives them a withering look before snapping his eyes back to my mother.

"I see that you've been shirking your motherly duties while I've been away, Elore."

My head instantly drops, eyes finding my dirt-smeared feet while shame falls on my shoulders. If I knew my father was coming home, I never would've come outside without shoes. I never would've even come outside at all. This past week that he's been gone has been the best time I've had in a long time. My mother has let me come outside every single day, and I even got to skip my weapons and history lesson yesterday. The last thing I want is for my father to be mad at her.

"He was just having a run in the gardens," she tells him, her voice calm and nice. She always sounds like that, even when Ryatt is throwing a fit, and he throws fits a lot. "Fresh air is good for a growing boy."

"His studies are good for him," my father snaps. "Now take him inside and get him cleaned up. We have guests, and I've already ordered dinner to be brought in within the next twenty minutes."

After he turns on his heel and walks away, my mother hurries me inside. She goes with me to my room where she helps me get ready. I don't complain once, even when she runs a wet comb through my hair. By the time I'm dressed in fresh clothes and she's collected Ryatt from the nursery, our twenty minutes are almost up.

Inside the dining room, Father sits at the head of the table, and there are three other people sitting to his left. One of them is my Uncle Iberik. His land shares a border with ours, and he's older than my father. The two of them do business together a lot, though I'm not sure exactly what kind. I know my father owns ships at the harbor, and I hear them talking about blacksmiths a lot, but other than that, I don't know. Yet unlike my father, Iberik lives alone and never had any heirs.

The other two people sitting at the table aren't familiar. It's a male and female, both of them with the shiniest hair I've ever seen. The female has red hair and eyes that look like bricks, nearly the same color as the empty fireplace at the left of the room. The male has a brown beard like my father but with slightly bucked teeth. Both of them have piercings *through the pointed tips of their ears, jewelry dripping down them like teardrops and chains.*

My mother sits to the right of my father, while I help Ryatt into his chair before I take my place between them. There's a set of red flowers in a centerpiece in front of us, but it partially blocks the people, so I'm glad one of the servants put it there. It makes me feel a little more hidden.

The talking at the table doesn't stop as we sit, and I'm glad about that too, because the last time Uncle Iberik was here for dinner, all he did was talk about how I should already be going out on hunting trips by myself and that it didn't do well to raise a soft son.

Uncle Iberik eyes me and my brother with his usual scowl. I want to scowl right back, but there's a prickling sensation between my shoulder blades that distracts me before I can get in trouble for being disrespectful.

As soon as we're settled, a servant comes over and sets plates in front of us, and I see Ryatt scrunching his face. I reach over and put his napkin on his lap so I can catch his eye. When he sees the look on my face, he quickly loses his scowl and picks up his fork. He's a picky eater, and when Father is gone, Mother lets us choose what to eat. But he can't be picky now.

Ryatt takes his first bite of boiled spinach and doesn't make a word of argument, and I let out a little sigh of relief before I pick up my own fork. I was so worried about my brother getting into trouble that I didn't pay any attention to what anyone was saying until my mother goes stiff beside me.

"I understand, of course," the unfamiliar male says, fork

and knife held in either hand as he speaks and eats at the same time. "It's a valid argument."

"Of course it is, Tobir," Uncle Iberik says to the male. "It's what the loyalists maintained for decades and why, ultimately, we won the war. I for one am glad that we put a stop to Oreans coming and going into Annwyn and for the old king's campaign to destroy the bridge. It needed to be done."

I can't help but glance over at my mother to see how she's reacting to this conversation. Her eyes are on her plate, the grip on her fork tight.

I've had history lessons about the war and the breaking of the bridge, but those are mostly boring, and my tutor always talks about how bad Oreans were. He talks about how they were using up all of Annwyn's resources and starting fights, and how they wanted to take land here for themselves so they could have long life.

I much prefer it when my mother talks about Orea. She is Orean, after all. She was one of the last to come through on the bridge. Sometimes, when she's putting Ryatt and me to bed, we can get her to tell us stories about it. She always looks different when she's talking about her world. Softer and sadder.

I know she misses it.

"To be sure," the red-haired female says. "And the Oreans that are still here are very lucky in my opinion. They were waived from the law and are allowed to stay and given long life in the process. Not to mention the fact that some Oreans have magic because they bred with us for hundreds of years. They should be thankful."

"Quite right, Netala," Tobir says next to her before

shoving a thick piece of meat into his mouth, his fork clanging against his tooth.

Netala tilts her head, mean eyes cutting across the table, and I see how her gaze lingers on my mother's blunt, rounded ears. Ryatt inherited that from her. I used to be so glad that mine were pointed like my father's. It was just one less thing for him to pick on.

"You have magic," Netala says.

I see my mother glance at my father. He doesn't usually like for her to talk about her magic. I don't know why. Her magic is the best.

"She does," my father answers, adjusting in his chair. "My Elore is remarkable."

"What is it she can do?" Tobir asks, watching her curiously.

My father looks over. "Show them, Elore."

Beneath the table, I see my mother's knees lock together. "I'm not sure if I have the calling for that right now…"

The look on my father's face makes her words dry up like dew in the desert. She casts her gaze back to Tobir, and my brother and I watch in awe as her eyelids flutter closed. When she opens them again, the green of her eyes is gone, and in its place, pale irises churn with some type of ancient scrawl, the letters so tiny they're impossible to read.

Across the table, Netala gasps. "Her eyes…"

"Elore is a diviner," my father says smugly. "She divines words from the gods and goddesses."

Netala's and Tobir's eyes widen in surprise. I personally have only seen Mother do this a couple dozen times over the years, but I know my father makes her use it when we aren't around.

I watch her face, watch the way the scrawl spins in her eyes, the way the rest of her face has gone calm and relaxed. Ryatt is watching just as closely as I am, and excitement leaps in my belly. I love watching her do her magic, but I know it tires her out. Soon, the words stop spinning, and her strange gaze sharpens on Tobir. I hear the fae male suck in a breath.

"The red-cloaked bearer shall give you two truths and a lie. You will believe the wrong one." Her voice is deeper, not her normal speaking voice, and just like the other times I've heard her make her foretellings, goose bumps go up and down my arms.

Then, Mother blinks quickly, and the strange words disappear from her eyes, the green in her irises fading back into view.

Tobir's brown brows are knotted deep into his skin. He stares at her for a second, like the words are replaying in his head. "What is that supposed to mean?" he demands.

"Elore's foretellings are not always clear to us at the time of speech," my father says.

"So this is why you took an Orean for yourself, Stanton," Netala says. "Was she able to predict the outcome of the war?"

Father shakes his head. "Elore's magic only works on people, not worldly events. Some foretellings can be as inconsequential as buying a bushel of spoiled apples, and some…more significant."

"Ooh, I am curious what she predicted about you," she says to my father, her eyes lighting up with curiosity.

41

Beside me, my mother goes stiff.

Anger slides over my father's features like slime under a slug, but he wipes it away quickly. "She has not made one for me as of yet," he says lightly, but I'm not tricked by it. He might try to sound calm, but there's something sharp underneath that makes me squirm.

Netala nods, taking another bite of her meal. As she swallows, her eyes lift. "It is a very impressive power, Elore. Your ancestors must have bred with very powerful fae. Tell me, you were one of the last Oreans to come into Annwyn, is that right?"

My mother tips her head. "Yes, that's right."

"Part of the agreement for my support in the war was that I was able to bring in a last batch of Oreans," my father explains. "They make up all of my groundskeepers and servants. Very efficient. They get long life, and I get a long-lasting staff."

I try not to scrunch my nose up. I hate it when he talks about my mother and the others like this. I scratch the back of my forearm, trying my best not to let my anger show up on my face.

My mother's lips go thin, so I reach over and place my hand on her leg under the table and pat her like she does for me sometimes when my father is making me upset. She glances over at me, and her face softens for a second.

"Stanton, your sons are the spitting image of Elore," Netala says, and even though she's smiling, she doesn't look nice.

I don't like that everyone keeps talking about my mother instead of to her, either. It's nothing new, though. Most fae that my father has over are rude to my mother. It's not her fault that my father saw her in Orea and brought her here. It's not her fault that she's Orean, and I don't see why it matters anyway. Just like I don't know why it matters that Ryatt and I are only half fae. She just proved that she's powerful in her own right. Her magic is better than most of the fae in the city, so they shouldn't be mean to her.

I shove a bite of meat into my mouth, chewing through my anger, but I immediately grimace just like Ryatt does when he eats something he hates. The food tastes off, like it's been left too long. I try some of the boiled apples instead, but it's overly sweet and mealy, like it's started to go bad. Yuck.

"They do," my father says. "But it is not a bad thing. Elore is very beautiful—and her magic is impressive. It's why I chose her."

My mother twitches. The back of my arm itches again.

"I hope they don't take after her completely," Uncle Iberik says with a laugh, hand swirling his cup of wine.

Tobir keeps chewing away. "Mmm, yes. I've seen plenty of fae and Orean pairings where the child doesn't develop magic. Dreadful."

"My sons will both have magic," Father says, voice like a whip to punish anyone who should say otherwise.

"Of course they will." Netala smiles. "I'm sure they're more fae than Orean, at any rate. Elore herself has been fae-blessed as a diviner. And you—you're The Breaker. The most powerful fae in the kingdom, aside from the king."

I look over at Ryatt as he squirms in his seat, and I want to do the same.

The Breaker. That's what everyone calls my father, and for good reason. Because his magic does just that—it breaks.

I've seen him break rocks, break fingers, break a lame horse's neck. I've seen him break a roof, making the whole thing cave in.

His magic is scary.

Before he retired, he used to help break whole cities for the king. It's why he got this estate. It's why we have forty-three rooms and Orean servants. It's why he was allowed to go for one last trip to Orea to bring people back with him just before both he and the king broke the bridge and ended the tie between our worlds. It's why he was permitted to choose my Orean mother.

But just because she lives here and has two half fae sons and amazing magic doesn't mean that the rest of the fae will ever look at her as an equal.

The three of us continue to eat dinner while everyone else talks, even though every bite of food I take tastes gross. I eat it anyway, because no one else is saying anything, and I don't want my father to notice me not eating.

Finally, the servants come in to clear the tables, and I set my fork down, feeling queasy but glad to be done with it. All of the servants are Orean, just like my mother. I think she feels guilty sometimes that they're serving her.

One of them, a man named Jak, comes to collect my mother's plate, and she turns her head up to smile warmly at him, and he gives her a smile right back. All the servants love my mother. I don't know if it's just because she's Orean like them or if it's because she's so kind, but when my father isn't home, it feels more like they're family than our servants.

Luckily, the adults decide to go into the parlor for pipes and drinks, so my father excuses my mother to take us to bed. Even though we're free from being around his guests, I'm still feeling mad and gloomy. My mother's brows are pulled down, and Ryatt is scowling.

But when my mother brings us into our bedroom, we get ready for bed, and then she sits down in the chair set between our beds and tells us a story about Orea. About a place split up between seven kingdoms. About a land where people didn't even have power until fae came. And it doesn't matter that Orea doesn't have magic of its own, because hearing her talk about it makes the whole place seem magical anyway.

When my eyes get tired, I shift on my pillow and yawn. "If the bridge of Lemuria weren't broken, I'd take you back to Orea, Mother."

I'm too sleepy to open my eyes, but I think she sounds both happy and sad when she replies, "I know you would, Slade. I know."

CHAPTER 4

SLADE

I've raced against a storm before.

Many times, in fact.

Most of the storms have caught up to me in the past. Drenched me in a pouring shock of tepid water that smeared my mood and cut through my clothes with benign heat. Or pelted me with icy sleet so sharp it cut through my skin.

But to have to race against it now feels like a betrayal of the gods and goddesses. That they could be so fucking cruel as to add this to an already dismal fucking situation.

So I refuse to let the storm win this time. I refuse to let it catch up to Auren.

Argo is the fastest timberwing in Fourth Kingdom. Probably the fastest beast of his kind, and his stamina and skill alone give us a fighting chance. I demand every burst of speed he can give me, drive him harder than I ever have before, and he allows me my demands.

We race the tempest who's clotting the clouds as she wails and beats at our backs, throwing a fit to catch up to us. But Argo isn't going to let the bitch win, and neither will I. I won't allow another storm to touch Auren. She has been flooded and wrung out, left to take the barrage without shelter. But so long as I'm here, *I* will be her shelter.

We fly, like lightning shot across the skies, arcing over the ground.

Against my chest, buried beneath two cloaks, Auren breathes. Breathes, but doesn't wake, doesn't stir.

Wretched hours pass as we fly. Every single second of them, the cold batters us, the very air sodden with overflowing dampness gathered from the pursuing storm. My face has long since gone numb, my ass soaked through on the saddle, my fingers unable to feel the clutch of the leather reins. If my eyes could still water, each drop would be nothing but frost against my skin.

Miserable cold and suffocating dark is all I know, but I trust Argo to guide us where we need to go. I keep Auren so far buried beneath layers that I can't see a single inch of her, but I feel the hot press of her breaths against my neck, and that is all that keeps my protective fae nature in check. Keeps me from rotting the clouds and raining down the poison from my rage. I count her breaths like my own heartbeat, using it as the tempo to quell my seething power.

Time and distance drag on.

Then, out of nowhere, a sudden gust of wind knocks into us from the left, and Argo balks out a furious cry as his entire body is slammed from the force. The slippery saddle shifts from the jarring movement, sending both me and Auren tipping.

I lurch forward, hands scrabbling to tighten my grip on the reins, but my numb hands miss the grip. My heart leaps into my throat as we go sliding over.

Digging in my knees, I throw my weight to the side at the same time that Argo banks, shoving out his full wingspan to catch my knee. He straightens us with furious attention, another roar of indignation crawling up his throat as I slump over the saddle, breath heaving from the close call.

All that holds us to this saddle is a single leather strap buckled around us both. If Argo hadn't caught himself...

As if the shoving wind was a personal affront to him, Argo turns feral.

He continues to roar at the sky with a renewed vigor to his flight, like it's now his personal mission to battle the wind, refusing his own tiredness and beating it back with sheer fury.

It takes an hour for my hands to stop shaking, for my heartbeat to go back to normal, to not hold the reins to the point of pain. The crash of adrenaline seeps out of me like blood from a wound.

I need to get Auren somewhere safe, somewhere warm, and Deadwell is the closest option I have. Yet the dark landscape mocks me, like instead of moving mile after mile, the snowy world of Fifth beneath us isn't passing by at all. Instead, we're glued to its ether, the shadows mocking us as endless distance stretches, threatening to never give way.

But Argo's sheer will and pissed off determination is unmatched.

Our race brings us closer to the dawning morning, though

I thought it would never come. It brings the hint of an angry, curdled sky. I blink against the brightening horizon, and I don't know whether to be relieved or filled with dread at the coming of the sun.

Yet even when the first spikes of daylight cast through the corrugated clouds, Auren doesn't stir. I make sure the cloaks are still wrapped around her, every inch of skin covered. I don't know if she even *could* produce gold right now in her current state if something were to touch her bare skin, but it worries me. She can't afford to use any magic, and if it starts spilling from her uncontrollably, even Argo won't be able to keep flying.

Beneath my thighs, Argo's chest heaves. His breath is ragged, muscles shaking from the strain. In the gray light, I can see patches of feathers have been ripped out of his tree-bark wings from the violent gusts that have assaulted him. Stalactites of frost hang from his foamy muzzle like extra fangs, but he doesn't stop roaring, doesn't stop racing.

"Keep going," I urge him, though whether my voice reaches him over the wind, I don't know.

Guilt churns in me as he dives for another pocket of air to help carry him. Even with the burst of furor, he's tiring. I'm pushing him too hard, too fast, too long, but there's no other alternative.

Dawn finally wins over the last of the night. It shines like a beacon, lighting the way for the storm raging. I look behind us, eyeing the clouds that seem to be galloping forward, ready to crush us beneath frozen hooves.

In my arms, Auren shivers, making me grit my frozen teeth and gnash the ice caught between. Thunder rumbles with a grunting nicker and threatening huff, yet Argo rages back at it in a guttural roar that's hoarse with fatigue.

A thousand scenarios play in my head. That we aren't going to make it. That Argo will have to land. That Auren will be even more exposed. That the storm will overcome us.

But somehow, the familiar silhouette of cracked mountains comes into view.

Deadwell.

We made it.

Hope leaps in my chest at the sight of it.

From the ground, all you see is rotted snow and cracked peaks. From the air, all you see is a shadowed, frozen valley caught between the mountains like a row of crooked teeth. It's inhospitable. Ugly. Empty.

But that's only if you don't know where to look.

Out of habit, I cut a whistle through my teeth to signal Argo, though the beast doesn't need the heads-up even if he can hear me. His eyes are sharp, his sense of direction far better than mine. After all, he's been flying me here for years. He could probably make the trip with his eyes closed.

My chest expands as we get closer, and I cup Auren's cloaked head against my chest. "Almost there. We're almost there," I murmur.

Leaning into Argo's turn, I keep Auren and myself braced as he swoops down toward the craggy tops of the mountains. The tips are shaped like a serrated knife, with cracked crevices that make a jagged sightline and dangerous rockfall. The largest mountain in the middle tilts slightly, like the wind has shoved at it so much for so long that it's finally beginning to bend to its will.

Mountains should know better than to bow to the wind.

But the ridge isn't the only eyesore here. It's the stretch of my magic that truly taints the land.

What once was an empty and bleak breadth on the border of Fifth, is now a crisscross of rot-infected ground. Fetid roots reach all the way from Fourth's border, delving through the snow to curl around the base of the mountains here like insipid crawling vines.

My magic responds to the massive amounts of power that I've already leached into this land, my skin snapping with its presence like it's welcoming me. I can feel it soaked into the snow-packed soil, can feel the call of it thrumming like bloodlust in my veins. But my power has to wait.

Although the mountains below are cracked and crooked, and though the massive roots of rot have made this land ugly and spoiled, it's still the best damn sight to see. I brace myself as we drop down below the clouds at a breakneck speed, my stomach nearly coming up my damn throat as Argo dives.

For years, this small strip of land has eluded my control. But now, I finally lay claim to it. With the deal I made with Midas, we are officially out of Fifth Kingdom and in my own territory.

Argo swings wide, heading directly for the tallest mountain, right where the rotted lines of rubbled rocks make up the base.

It's the combination of all of it, really. The leaning mountains. The dumps of snow and piles of rock. The festering rot. It all distracts, it all hides.

Anyone who might pass by this part of the world would have no reason to linger and no desire to. Argo bypasses the cracked fang-tipped peak, heading for the smallest mountain. It has a side like a mantel, and the rocky shelf overhangs far enough to offer shelter to the hidden village below. This nearly invisible lip in the leaning mountain looks inconspicuous but it calls to me as much as my rot does.

You'd only see the small town if you purposely came poking around or knew where to go. The buildings are all made of the same gritty rock, blending against the mountainside effortlessly, hidden beneath the snowy shelf.

It's here, shrouded in the forbidden cold, that my greatest secret hides.

Drollard Village.

Just then, the chasing storm lashes out, punishing us for reaching our destination. The clouds slash open and frozen rain pours, soaking through my clothes immediately.

Argo heads straight down to the village, rain streaming off his outstretched wings and freezing against his feathers. He only circles once before his exhausted body slams into the ground so hard my teeth clack. He sways where he stands but manages to stay upright, his talons digging into the snow for purchase as frozen froth batters from his mouth.

"Good beast," I praise him. He turns his head to blink at me, and though he looks exhausted, the gleam in his hawklike eye is also smug. "Yeah, you earned every fucking jerky strip you want."

I look around, squinting through the downpour, but all is quiet in the early morning pause. Twenty feet away, rows of rocky houses are lined, lazy smoke rising from chimneys beneath the lip of the mountain, ice gathered on top of the overhang like sheets of shingles.

My frozen hand reaches down for the buckle on the saddle, but it's a struggle to unstrap myself. My fingers are too numb to get them to work right, and now with the sleet lashing down, it's slippery. But I can't risk letting go of Auren with my other hand because I need to keep her dry and secure.

A noise of frustration tears from my lips like a growl. "Come the fuck on."

"Sire?"

My head snaps up at the voice, and I zero in on one of the villagers walking up from the small pavilion that's stuffed between the cracked cave of the mountainside. He hurries over, hood pulled up to try and fend off the deluge that's just started to pour, his bulbous nose showing beneath. "Let me."

With deft fingers, he quickly undoes the strap, and I jump down with Auren.

"Thank you, Theo," I say. He's not as wary of me as some of the others, but he still won't quite look me in the eye.

"Should I alert the watch?"

I shake my head. "No need. Just see that Argo's taken care of in the Perch. Tell Selby to give him whatever he wants and as much of it, including extra blankets in his roost. He's more than earned it."

Theo tips his head, already walking over to grab Argo's strap. To his credit, he only slightly balks at the timberwing's appearance before leading him to the Perch where he can be cared for.

As soon as they walk away, I hurry off with Auren, my booted feet stepping onto the white stone path that blends into the slushing snow. My rot doesn't spread into the village itself, instead kept strategically around the border like a barbed rampart to keep our enemies out. And although it doesn't spread here, this place is still steeped in dreariness.

By all accounts, Drollard Village doesn't exist. Maybe that's why it's always felt so dismal. By keeping it secret, I've somehow made it feel even more devoid.

This place is by no means picturesque. It's harsh and cold and gaunt, with lonely homes cut into the hollowed mountainside, cast in perpetual shadow. The people who live here don't have the conveniences of being in a city where travel and trade are abundant. Instead, they toil to live off this bleak land, while supplemented with the supplies I can bring them. Even so, not one of them will ever leave.

They can't.

Aside from the village watch, everyone is asleep at this dawning hour, windows shuttered in anticipation of the storm. I quickly pass by the slanted walls of the slate-faced houses, each wooden door not even a stone's throw apart from one another. Yet the sizes of the homes themselves are deceiving since their depth is made up within the recesses of the mountain. Prickled lace vines stretch up from craggy splits in the rock floor and spider web around the doors and windows, their white-skinned berries still hanging in clumps from their stems.

The stone beneath my feet is slick with the new rain, so I take measured steps. I don't want to slip with Auren in my arms, but I still try to go as fast as I can, boots digging into every step.

There are a few hardy evergreen trees clinging to life along the path, their frosted limbs carrying the weight of the endless cold and giving me some reprieve from the rain as I tuck Auren closer against my chest.

When I get to the bend in the path, I follow the curve of the mountain where the homes end, leaving the rock face bare save for the snow frozen against it. Above, the mountainside curls like a riptide, creating a giant, protective awning. A sheet of frozen rain drips down from it like a thin waterfall, and I hesitate, trying to think of a better way to get Auren through without soaking her completely.

"Here, let me."

My arms automatically tighten around Auren, and I whip around at the sound of my brother's voice. "What are you doing here?"

Ryatt stalks through the rain and, without a word, removes his cloak and flings it over both our heads to block the downpour. I have a feeling he does it more for Auren's sake than mine. We duck beneath the sheet of rainwater as quickly as we can, and once we pass beneath the rock shelf, we're blessedly out of the storm and into the mountain's cave.

"Thanks," I mutter.

Ryatt lowers his arms and brings the cloak down again but doesn't bother to put it back on.

Now encased in the shadows of the cave, it would be completely pitch-black if it weren't for the soft blue glow that comes from the fluorescent veins that run through the belly of the mountain. These cerulean streaks branch off in every direction, running through the walls, floor, and ceiling, while colorless beetles cling to their surface to nibble on their sediment. Stalactites reach down from the ceiling, pointing at us in accusation.

"So? You going to tell me what you're doing here?" I ask as we walk, my voice echoing bleakly.

"Did you really think I wasn't going to come?" Ryatt's hands clench around his cloak in bitter twists. "I wanted to come here the moment Midas issued his threats, and you know it, so you can just save your fucking commands," he snaps, jaw locked tight.

I feel my own teeth grind in response. I probably have no right to be frustrated with him, because I understand his anger, and yet, I am. As he often is with me.

"Fine," I relent. I'm too cold and exhausted to argue. "We'll talk more tomorrow. But I need to get her warm and dry."

He glances at Auren from the corner of his eyes. "Fucking storm had to hit tonight of all nights."

My brother and I walk in tense silence through the cave. Without even trying, our strides match, our shoulders at the same height, our clothes nearly identical. When my fae nature isn't out, we could pass for twins, a fact that I've used to my advantage many, many times.

Despite the fact that we always effortlessly fall into stride with one another, we always seem to step on each other's toes.

I would die for Ryatt, and he's given up a lot to be at my side, but most days, we'd gladly pummel each other.

Tonight is no different.

We eat up the rest of the distance, and then, we're here, at our house in the cave, descended in blue shadows with stalagmites like standing guards.

The Grotto.

"Home sweet home," Ryatt mutters.

Something sours in my stomach. "Yeah. Home sweet home."

CHAPTER 5

SLADE
Age 8

S lade!"

I look down at Ryatt, his chubby legs scrabbling as he tries and fails to climb up the tree after me. I knew he was going to try to follow me up here. But every time he sees that he can't, he starts whining like a baby, scaring all the birds away until I come down.

"Slade!"

Knowing I can't keep ignoring him, I roll up the sleeves of my shirt and scratch at my arms. "I'll be back," I tell the little nestling.

It chirps at me.

When I hear Ryatt scrabbling again below, I lean over my branch, moving aside some of the brown, dead leaves. "You can't come up here. You're too little."

His face rumples with anger as he stares up at me. "Am not."

"You are," I tell him. *"Besides, you're not allowed to climb trees yet."*

He drops his feet to the ground again, just so he can stomp one of them in a fit. His socks are rolled down unevenly, both of them covered in grass stains. Mother always clucks her tongue when we come in with our white socks streaked with grass, but tells us that it's the same color as our eyes, so at least it matches.

I swipe some sweat off my forehead and sigh, abandoning my tree branch so I can jump down next to him. "Happy?"

He nods. "I'm hungry."

"You're always hungry." But now that he's mentioned it, I'm hungry too. "Come on. I bet Cook will give us something."

"It's hot," Ryatt whines.

"It's summer, stupid," I tell him with a snicker.

He shoots me an angry look. "I'm gonna tell."

"No, you're not." I grin over at him, because Ryatt and I never tattle on each other. It's our rule.

He shrugs.

The two of us head toward the estate. Now that I'm not under the shade of the tree anymore, I realize just how hot it really is. No wonder Ryatt's face is all ruddy and his black hair is sticking up with sweat. I probably look the same.

I got done with my lessons earlier, and the nursemaid let Ryatt come outside for fresh air, so we've been out here for a while. I don't know how long. I get distracted when I check on the bird nests.

"Let's go to the pond!" Ryatt says out of the blue, just as we're almost to the shrubs.

I shoot him a look. "You just said you're starving."

"Pond!"

"Fine," I relent with a groan. "But just for a little. Then we're going in to eat."

Ryatt nods and starts racing down the hill. I run after him, pretending like he's faster, and he laughs with a screech. We run around to the side of the estate, making it about halfway before Ryatt's legs get tired and he has to stop.

"I'm thirsty," he whines.

"I'll dunk your head in the pond then."

He scowls at me, but I laugh and nudge him right in the ribs where I know he's ticklish. He tries to fight it for a second, but he loses in a fit of squirmy giggles.

Past the house are the stables, and just on the other side of that is the pond. We pass by the paddock where a couple of Father's horses are standing around, grazing on the grass.

I think nothing of it at first.

Thwack.

It sounds like our stablemaster whenever he uses the riding crop on one of the horses. I hear the slap on the hindquarters, the swift whack of correction.

Thwack.

Ryatt doesn't notice a thing either.

But I stop for some reason, my hand shooting out to my brother's arm so I can stop him too. "Hold on."

"Why?" he whines.

I scratch my arm. "Just stay here for a sec."

He frowns, and I know he's going to argue, but luckily, one of the horses comes over to the fence just then and distracts him. He climbs up on the fence and starts to pet it, and I immediately hurry forward. But when I pass the stable, there's no one inside.

Thwack.

I whip my head to the right, my feet carrying me forward. And then they jolt to a stop.

It's not the stablemaster. It's not a crop. It's not a horse.

It's my father, standing over my mother, the two of them against the outside wall of the stable. I can't figure out what I'm seeing right away, so I just stand there and watch.

But then my father's hand comes down, and he slaps my mother so hard that she falls down onto the ground. His mouth is moving, hissing out angry words, but I can't hear them.

Shock freezes me in place.

There's a loud sound in my ears. Or maybe the sound is in my blood, because I can hear it and feel it at the same time. My back itches. My arms feel like ants are crawling all over them. My veins feel cold. Even my head feels weird.

For a second, I'm just standing there like a statue, feeling and hearing. My blood, my skin, it's so loud I think I might pass out.

But then my father raises his hand again. My mother ducks her head. And I get so mad that it mixes with the noise and all of it just...bursts.

Before my father can bring his hand down again, I'm screaming at him. "Stop!"

I move faster than I can think, and then I'm shoving him with all my might. There's a look of shock on his face as I push him, but I look at him with hate. So maybe hate is stronger than shock, and that's why I'm able to make his body slam into the stable wall.

But...I didn't think hate was strong enough to bring down a wall.

The wooden stable was built solid and strong, but somehow, the wall collapses as soon as he hits it.

The wall falls in, making my father fall with it, and I watch as the wood disintegrates, tiny splinters puffing up into the air like dust as he goes crashing to the ground in a heap. The noise in me is now the noise of part of the roof caving in, and the rest of the wall going with it, burying my father beneath the boards.

"Slade!" my mother calls, scrabbling backwards with fright.

I start to go to her, but my father's fist punches through the scraps, and he snaps his fingers, making his power lash out, breaking the wood on top of him with a crack. It falls away from him as he gets to his feet, and the look on his face makes all the blood drain from mine.

"How dare you!"

He's furious. Black eyes stuck in a netting of bloodshot veins that make him look even angrier. I know he's going to strike me next, but I don't care. I don't care, so long as he doesn't hit her again.

He steps toward me, and I brace myself, feeling like all the coldness in my veins drops right down through my feet, and my father lurches to a stop. He pauses, staring at the ground around me. "What the—"

I follow his gaze. The grass around my feet isn't green anymore. It's the pale, dead color of wheat. There are patches of dirt where I can see weird looking lines drawn through it, and those same black lines have spread up what's left of the crooked stable like ugly roots. The wood itself looks like it's been in hard weather for years and that a single exhale will knock the rest of it down.

"Slade..."

At my mother's voice, I look over at where she's still crouched on the ground, but the lines didn't touch her. She's on the only spot of ground where the grass is still alive and green. Her gaze isn't on my face as she watches me with wide eyes. She's studying my neck, my arms, my back.

Right then, it sinks in that I hurt. All over.

My father spins toward her, but I jump in front of her. I'm breathing way too fast and feeling way too short, but I'm not going to move. I'm not going to let him hit her again.

"No," I tell him, and my voice is the last thing that's loud, because everything I was hearing inside of me has gone quiet, and I'm suddenly really tired.

Behind me, I feel my mother grab my leg and try to push me away, but I ignore it. Father has taken the cane to me before, and I was fine. I can handle it again because I'm not a baby. I want to tell Mother this, but then Father strides to me and grips me by the shoulders, his eyes wide.

At first I think it's a trick, but when the shock doesn't leave his eyes, when his hand doesn't come up to strike me, I finally look down to see what he's looking at. To see what my mother was looking at before.

My arms are bleeding, which is probably why they hurt so bad. But it's not the blood that makes my eyes go as big as saucers. No, it's the black things sticking out of them, sharp little points that have driven through my skin like they pierced straight through me.

At first, I think maybe some of the splinters from the stable broke off and stabbed into me. But the longer I look, I see that's not the case. The things are identical on both of my arms, and they didn't stab into me. They came out of me.

I'm frozen in shock as my father reaches forward and presses against one of the black things. Both of us hiss in pain. I look up and notice that his thumb is now bloody, as if the black spike was so sharp that it cut him.

All the previous rage from his face is replaced with a strange grin as he looks at the blood for another second before he moves his attention to me. "My son."

He quickly grips me by the shoulders again and makes me bend, and then I feel another jolt of pain when he presses a spot on my back, making my spine arch as I jerk upright again. "Ow!"

My father laughs as he releases me. "Look at you!" he says, his grin wider than I've ever seen it before. "Only eight years old, and look at this!"

"What is it?" I ask worriedly, staring at the bloody drips coming from the sharp black bumps. There are black veins stretching from the base of them, going down my arms like Ryatt took a quill to my skin and drew all over. I try to rub it off, but it won't go away.

"You transformed," Father says excitedly. "Your power came in."

I feel myself go cold all over. "What?"

He grins and then yanks up my arm to show me. "See! You've already manifested."

My eyes track from the veins in my arm to the veins in the ground that trail up the rotted outer boards of the stable wall. They're the same.

"I knew my son would be powerful."

I don't feel powerful. I feel tired and everything hurts, and I'm so angry and so scared...

When I start to cry, I know it's a mistake, but I can't help it.

The pride instantly leaves his face, and he looks at me with disgust. "Stop that. I will not have a blabbering baby for a son," he says coldly before his black eyes track to my mother. "Get him cleaned up and then send him to the gardens. I want to start testing what he can do," he tells her, and then he adds, "and you, stay in your room. I don't want to see you for the rest of the night."

My mother's grip on my leg tightens.

He turns and stalks away, and so many tears fall down my cheeks that I can't even keep track of them all, but I'm glad he's not here to count them. I try to stop, I really do, but everything hurts and I don't understand, and my mother...

Just then, her face appears as she kneels in front of me, her eyes red-rimmed to match the mark on her cheek, the split in her lip.

"Am I...a Breaker?" I ask, and it makes me cry a little harder, because I don't want to be anything like my father. But I somehow broke the stable wall, and I broke the ground, and these spikes broke through my skin...and I feel like a monster.

She shakes her head, gently tipping my chin up. "No, Slade. Not you. You don't break things. You protect them."

But when I look around the yard, this doesn't look like protecting. This looks like ruin. My father ruins things too. Just looking at my mother's face reminds me of that.

Even though my arm hurts a lot to move it, I lift my hand and softly touch her cheek. "Are you alright?"

Now she's the one whose face crumples as tears start to run down her cheeks. Dropping my hand, I reach forward and carefully take hers and squeeze, trying to ignore all those black lines spreading to my fingertips.

"Don't cry, Mother. I'll protect you."

This doesn't make her feel better, because she just cries harder. My eyes drop, and I wish I was older, wish I could do something. Looking down, I see the grass stains on the hem of her white dress, from when Father hit her and she fell to the ground.

"Slade?"

We both turn to see Ryatt behind me, frowning and holding a bunch of strawberries in his shirt. He must've wandered off to the garden for a snack. I forgot he was out here. I'm so glad he didn't see.

"Look, Ryatt," I say, keeping his attention on me. His mouth drops open, and he whips a finger in my direction, making his strawberry hoard fall to the ground. "What's that?"

"I got my magic," I say, trying to sound happy, sniffing so that I can make myself stop crying.

Excitement flashes over his red-stained cheeks. "Can I touch it?"

"Sure."

He hurries forward, his red-stained finger smoothing over one of the black spikes. "Does it hurt?"

I shrug. "A little."

He grins, turning to our mother, but whatever he was going to say to her gets tossed away, and he frowns. "Mother?"

She has a pasted-on smile, and she's already wiped off her cheeks, but she still looks all wrong. "Ryatt, those strawberries look very good."

He's not deterred. "You're crying?"

"I'm alright, darling. Just took a tumble. See?" she says, motioning toward the bottom of her dress.

He nods and then slips his red sticky hand into her other hand. "That's okay, I fell too," he says, pointing to his soiled socks. "And know what?" he asks.

"What?"

"The grass stains match your eyes too."

I don't think I ever saw a smile that looked so sad.

CHAPTER 6

SLADE

Aside from the stalagmites that reach up from the ground in the cave, there are also bold stalactites hanging from the ceiling too. They perfectly taper around the front door of the Grotto like an archway, the craggy pillars hanging down in sharp peaks. They're wrapped in thin coils of fluorescence, casting blue shadows upon our faces as we pass beneath them.

I have warring emotions when it comes to being here. On one hand, it's a comfort. On the other, it feels like a punishment. It might be strange for some that we have a house inside a cave, but it's private and hidden, and despite the bleak gray walls, I have found some comfort here.

Ryatt steps in front of me and shoves the front door open, its hinges squeaking from the perpetual damp in the air. I rush through the dark house, not needing the light, knowing where everything is by memory.

I quickly make it to the front room, scant shadows making up the shapes of furniture that I know by heart. I feel my boots hit the white fur rug that sits in the center of the room, just beneath a circle table that has rings stained on the wood from all the glasses of alcohol my Wrath and I have set on it, condensation be damned.

I stop when my shins hit the cushioned sofa, and by the time I set Auren down on it and start to pull off her wet shoes, Ryatt is already behind me, getting to work on lighting a fire.

Using the cushions, I carefully prop Auren up so that she's not lying directly on her back. Because her back…

I can't bear to think about it.

About what he did to her.

Rage surges inside of me, and I wish I was in Ranhold, that I could turn back time and bring Midas to life again so I could kill him myself. I'd do it slowly. Cutting off limb after limb. Rotting him one vein at a time. Crushing his heart in my fist.

Making him suffer.

The strike of a flint draws sparks at my back, and I calm my anger to focus on my task. I need to get her warm and dry, or the rot inside of her won't matter, because she'll die of hypothermia instead.

I strip the wet layers of cloaks off of Auren. I toss them both to the floor, clumps of ice breaking as they land, water puddling beneath them. I'm thankful to find that her dress beneath is damp but not soaked-through, only small pebbles of snow stuck to the hem. I quickly yank the blankets off the back of the sofa and pile them on top of her, tucking them in tight around her body.

A soft orange glow begins to light up the house, and I waste no time pulling the sofa forward, its legs screeching in protest as I drag it across the floor and settle it right in front of the fireplace. I can hear Ryatt moving around the room, lighting sconces as he goes, trying to ward off the chill.

I hold my hand in front of her parted lips, feeling Auren's breath come out slow and steady.

"Auren?"

I'm not expecting a response, but I'm filled with disappointment nonetheless. The only way I can swallow the dread is to keep moving, keep doing, so I remove her sodden leggings. Then I check her fingers and toes, cupping them in my gloved hands to blow warm exhales on them. I don't care if her power did kick in now that it's morning. I need to warm her up. When I'm satisfied with their temperature, I cover them in the blankets once again and then gently wipe the frost from her hair.

"Why isn't she waking up?"

I hadn't heard Ryatt walk up behind me, but my shoulders tense at his question. I glance at her face, while something cold writhes in the pit of my stomach. "I don't know."

Both of us watch her, chest rising and falling, the crackle of flames crowning her skin with an orangish hue.

"Auren."

My call brings absolutely zero movement from her.

I hear Ryatt step away, and then a clanging in the kitchen draws my gaze. I peer past the archway where he's now standing in front of the iron oven, just barely visible from this vantage point. Its front grate is already closed and glowing with fire as he works over a pot that's sitting on top of it. Outside, the storm is growing wilder, the hollows of the cave echoing with the wind's cries.

Turning back to Auren, I tap into my power again, but just like before, I see that last grain of rot inside of her, and it won't budge. I can't even get a grip on it anymore. It's embedded into her like a seedling taken root. Yet her essence is as pure as before, the inner workings of her body just as it should be. Aside from that single fragment, she feels the same.

So why isn't she waking up?

My brows draw together, eyes watching her serene face while worries assault me left and right. The faint, rotted veins that had crept up her neck are gone, her skin back to her usual color. She simply looks like she's in a deep slumber.

"Auren, you need to wake up."

Of course she doesn't listen. She never listens to me. Always argues, always has a simmering fire just beneath the surface, which I fucking love.

"Wake up and argue with me, Goldfinch."

I watch her placid face for another moment before I turn and slump to the floor beside her. Balancing my back against the sofa, I draw up my knees so I can brace my elbows on them. I scrub my hands down my face, feeling exhaustion tugging at my limbs like knotted strings.

Reaching down, I tug off my wet boots, tossing them onto the hearth before yanking my gloves off and holding my palms up to the flames. I don't feel their warmth.

I think I'm too frozen through with fear.

I'm still staring into the flames, still not feeling a thing,

72

when the front door suddenly bangs open. I'm on my feet in a second, ready for some unknown attack, but when I see two sopping wet figures hurry inside and slam the door shut behind them, I pause.

I look at Lu and Digby incredulously. "What are you two doing here?"

Lu tosses back the hood of her cloak, breathing hard as she holds Digby up, the guard's arm slung around her shoulder while rain and ice sluice off them. "He insisted on staying with Gildy Locks. Pitched a fit back there until I agreed to follow you and take him along."

I cast the surly man a look, but he just scowls at me, making a puddle on the floor. Despite his glare, he looks like he's about a second from tipping over. "I stay with her."

"Fine," I say with a sigh.

Digby blinks, like he's surprised I relented so easily, but I want what's best for her, and I know Auren would prefer for him to be nearby anyway.

With Lu's help, he hobbles over to come look down at Auren, a frown forming between his brows as he takes her in. "She never woke up?"

"No."

Clearly, Digby's temper hasn't been cooled off by the winter storm, because his eyes blaze just as angry as before. "This never should've happened," he growls. "You're supposed to be something to her? You supposedly care?"

My hands curl into fists. "Of course I fucking care."

"Well, why'd you let this happen then?" he challenges, but it's nothing that I'm not already repeating to myself.

"You're supposed to be the most powerful king in the world, right? So *do* something."

If only I fucking could.

"She just needs to rest," I say again, all the anger bled out of my tone.

He stands there, dripping and seething, his cheeks wind-chapped and nose red from the cold.

"Come on. You saw her, and Slade's right. She needs to rest." Lu starts to pull him away. He only resists for a second, looking down at Auren one more time. Then he turns, letting her lead him toward the corridor that goes to the back of the house where it branches off into several bedrooms. "Let's go raid Osrik's room. I'm sure we can find something for you to wear."

When their footsteps fade, I watch Auren again, but she only lies there, still as a corpse. The one thing that keeps the wild fear from exploding out of me is the fact that I can see her golden aura hovering around her silhouette. It's still weak. Lackluster. But it's there, so I hold onto that scrap like a single thread holding up a boulder.

She just needs to rest.

It's a mantra playing in my head.

She used too much power. It drained her, almost to the point of death. Yet what concerns me even more is that she used an entirely different facet of her power that she's never even tapped into before. Who knows what kind of toll that took on her?

"Here."

I look to my right as Ryatt walks up, holding out a

74

steaming mug. Taking it, I peer inside to find some watery broth with a few bits of onion and celery roots tossed in. "It's all I could scrounge up this quickly," he says with a shrug. "We'll need to go to the Cellar tomorrow."

I toss the drink back, not tasting it save for the heat that burns my tongue and swims into my hollow stomach.

Ryatt drinks his own much slower, and I can feel his dark green eyes watching me. "What?" I ask.

"This hasn't ever happened before."

I look down at Auren's face. "No. It hasn't."

"Not to sound like a jackass, since I'm sure you've already done this, but you can't just...get the rest of the rot out of her?"

"Unfortunately, you do sound like a jackass, because *I fucking tried*."

"What's different?"

Setting the empty cup on the wooden mantel, I brace a hand against the dark wood, head hanging as I look at the flames. "I don't know. Maybe I was too forceful when I used my power on her in the first place. Or maybe I left it too long inside of her."

"Is it...I mean, have you ever left rot inside someone before?"

I shoot him a look. "Obviously I have. When I wanted to *kill* them."

He waves me off. "I mean someone you weren't trying to kill?"

"No," I spit out, grip squeezing the mantel hard enough to make the wood creak in protest. "My rot follows my direction. It's never fucking done this."

I don't understand it. Even now, I can sense that it's there, but I can't grip it. I can't call it back to me. It's not answering to me.

"Will she wake up?"

Rage has me spinning with a snarl on my face. "Of course she's going to wake up!" I shout, the skin along my arms bulging, spikes threatening to break out. "Fuck you for even asking that."

"Well, fuck *you* too. It's a valid question."

My hand curls and I'm about ready to slam a fist into his face when Lu comes back in. "Already not playing nice, boys?" She's changed out of her wet clothes and is wearing massive fur slippers bigger than bear paws. They're her favorite fucking thing whenever she's here, even though they look ridiculous on her. Digby is nowhere in sight.

"He's resting. He tries to pretend otherwise, but he's in pretty bad shape. Gave him Osrik's bed," she says without me having to ask. She comes to stand next to us with her hands on her hips. "So? What's the problem?"

"I'm just trying to have a fucking conversation," Ryatt grumbles.

"About Gildy?" Lu guesses, then snorts and strides over to Auren. "How about you don't poke the rotten beast?"

My brother rolls his eyes.

"What are you doing?" I ask when she strips off Auren's blankets.

She shows me a bundle of clothes in her hand. "Is it safe to touch her?"

I hesitate. "I'm not sure. It's technically daylight, so her gold-touch shouldn't be dormant anymore, but..." My words trail off.

"But she just snapped like a rabid animal and turned the castle into a giant mouth of gold that swallowed everything up during the night even when she shouldn't be able to?" Lu quips.

"She didn't gild any of the blankets or the sofa."

"Too bad. I hate that green color," she says, gaze drawing over the cushions before she passes over a pair of thick fur-lined leggings and socks. "These are for her."

"Thanks."

She turns to Ryatt and slaps him on the arm. "Come on, let's go make ourselves useful by lighting the fires in the bedrooms and getting more wood. I don't think this storm is going to break for a while."

The two of them disappear down the hall, voices muffled. Slipping on my gloves again just in case, I carefully pick up Auren's feet one at a time, feeding the soft leggings onto her legs. I move her gently, especially when I need to maneuver her to pull them the rest of the way up. When I'm done, I carefully prop her up on her side again so that all her weight isn't resting on her back.

Then I put the socks on her feet before covering her up with the blankets once more. One delicate hand is hanging off the sofa, and that's when I spot the tattered remains of her cut ribbon still tied to her wrist.

Emotion, hot and heady, suffocates my skull, my sorrow pressurized and congested.

With the barest of touches, I pick up her hand, my fingers

skimming over the cut end. It lies unmoving and leaden, a severed, silken corpse.

Use your ribbons.

I can't.

Oh, she didn't tell you? She lost that privilege.

A tic in my jaw pulses, rot pushing at my neck like punishing whips.

Gently, I untie the ribbon and slip it into my pocket—the only part of me that stayed dry. Then I tuck her hand back beneath the blanket before I slump down to the floor again. I don't know how much time has passed when Lu comes back into the room. She smells of firewood and smoke and looks tired, but that doesn't stop her from sitting down on the floor next to me.

If she asks me why I can't fix Auren, I might just snap.

Instead, she's quiet. We both just stare at the flames, listening to them crackle as the storm wails outside.

When she does talk, I almost flinch, so lost in my thoughts that I forgot she was here. "Do you remember when I first joined your army?"

I go still, glancing at her from the corner of my eye, studying the ridge of her contemplative brow. She never talks about this, never talks about herself back then. We've always respected her silence on the matter, because we sure as shit have things in our past we don't like to speak on either. The few times one of us has brought it up, she's shut it down, so I'm shocked that she's bringing it up now.

Feeling like I'm treading on ice that can split at any moment, I carefully nod. "I do."

With wrists balanced on her knees, she shakes her head. "I was a hissing cat who couldn't go through a single conversation without picking a fight."

My lips tilt up when I remember that scrappy, vicious girl who used to spew some of the meanest, crudest shit I'd ever heard, and she was only fourteen. "I was surprised you never sprouted claws."

She snorts and flicks at the wooden piercing in her lip, the firelight making the set-in ruby gemstone glint. "I walked right up to you, looked you dead in the eye, and told you that your captain was a bony-assed whiner who couldn't dodge a wad of spit, and that you needed soldiers with better judgment."

The memory makes a chuckle slip out of me. "All while he had you by the collar until you kicked him in the knees."

"Bastard shouldn't have wrongfully accused me of trying to steal shit."

"You're right. Which is why I gave you a uniform and told you to get your ass to the barracks."

Her lips tilt up. "You said if I was going to try and replace one of your captains, I needed to at least learn how to swing a sword."

"And look at you now," I reply. "Captain of the right flank."

Lu rubs a hand over her shorn hair, finger lingering over the shape of the blade cut into the side. "Let's be honest. You saw a half-starved and feral girl on the streets that day and felt sorry for her." Her tone is nostalgia topped in something bittersweet.

"On the contrary," I tell her honestly. "I saw a wicked

sidekick and a person unafraid of a fight, who could be a great leader if only she was given the chance to learn."

Lu turns to me, and for the first time in years, it's almost like I'm looking at that fourteen-year-old girl again. Served a shitty platter of an undeserving family, caught in the prongs of their shortcomings. She was fucked up, tossed out, forced to fend for herself. Her combative attitude wasn't a character flaw. It was her fortitude. "I hated you that day, you know. For drafting me into your army and making me into one of your fucked up soldiers. I didn't want to answer to you. Didn't want to answer to anybody."

"Oh, I know. You cursed me out on more than one occasion for it. I think you were on latrine duty for a solid nine months."

"It was twelve," she counters, almost proudly. "And I secretly hated you more because I was so damn thankful." Brows lifting at her candor, I watch as she shakes her head and lets out a sigh. "Let's face it. If you hadn't scraped me off that street and given me a sword, I would've died, Rip."

I shake my head. "I don't believe that for a second. You were strong, even then."

Her brown eyes are cast down, staring at the charred wood burning on the grate. "I don't mean die physically, but mentally. Emotionally. Spiritually." She presses a hand to her chest, thumping it twice. "You can't contemplate or settle or thrive when you're living like that. I was dead and running, just trying to keep up with survival. Just making it one day. People don't get that, you know? If they've never lived like that. It's *one day*. A whole slew of one-day-at-a-times, just getting through, squeezing by. Always running, never expecting anything else. Never having anyone or anything but that running and fighting and dying through it."

"You're not that girl anymore. That's not your life."

"You're right," she replies. "Just like Osrik isn't the mercenary, and Judd isn't the thief. Because you picked us to fight at your side and showed us that it wasn't just one day. It wasn't just running and dying." Her gaze meets my own head-on. "I'm the woman I am today because you tossed my ass in your army and let me make myself into a captain."

Unexpected emotion tightens in my chest. "You earned it every step of the way, Talula Gallerin."

Her nose wrinkles up, and she leans over to punch me in the arm, but it's not anywhere near her real strength. "Don't call me that."

I smirk and rub my arm. "Still vicious."

"Always," she laughs, and then she tips her head toward Auren. "She's gonna wake up, you know."

I swallow hard, all the light amusement draining back out of me. "You sound sure."

"That's because I am," she says before she unfolds herself and gets to her feet. "You took my belligerence and tossed a uniform in my face. You met Osrik's kill drive and decided to give him your sword. You saw every jail cell that couldn't hold Judd and, instead of tossing him in another one, let him keep the keys. This time, you found your goldfinch and watched her leave her cage. She'll open her eyes, just like you got the rest of us to do."

"This is a little more literal. I fucking rotted her."

Lu just shrugs. "We've all got a little rotten in us, and I wouldn't change that for anything. It's how we've survived."

CHAPTER 7

SLADE
Age 8

I'm so tired. My body hurts all over, but it's the worst on my arms and back where the spikes come out. Even now, they're poking from under the skin, making it stretch and turning my skin gray.

"Again!"

My father's command makes me flinch, but I raise the sword in my hand, even though it's heavy and my whole arm shakes as I try to keep it up.

My sparring teacher is a fae named Cado, who's bald like my father but with dark brown skin and no beard, and when he wants, he can bring blades from his fingertips. It's never a good day when he brings those out.

I used to train with Cado three days a week for only an hour, but ever since my power came out a few weeks ago, Father has been making me do this every day for hours. He *says that I have to get stronger physically so that I can learn how to wield my new magic. All my other lessons are on hold for now. But so far, I haven't been able to bring my spikes or my power out on command.*

I try. I really do. I'm tired of being out in this field day after day, while the sun burns and my sweat drips and my father makes me train with a real sword instead of the wooden practice ones. I hate it. But he says that pushing myself is the only way to make the magic come.

I barely get my sword up in time for Cado to slam his own blade into mine. I'm supposed to be practicing blocks, but he hits me so hard that the metal clang goes all the way up my arms and makes my teeth feel funny.

Staggering back, my feet dig into the crunchy grass as I sway.

"That wasn't a block," my father barks.

Glancing over, I see him standing several feet away with Uncle Iberik right next to him. I hate that they're both watching me, calling out every single little thing I do wrong.

"I'm tired," I pant. I have to wipe the sweat from my forehead because it's dripping in my eyes and making them sting.

"You're still weak," he counters, his arms crossed in front of him, red shirt matching my own. It reminds me of blood. The same color of the split lip I got yesterday when I missed my block and Cado rammed the hilt of his sword into my mouth. The same shade that drips down my arms every time the spikes poke through.

84

"You need to push yourself, Slade. Push physically and call to your magic."

Clamping my teeth together, I turn back around, barely ducking in time when I see Cado already whirling. I try to swing my sword, but I can't get it up in time for the second advance. Cado pulls back at the last second so that it's his arm that slams into my side, instead of his blade, but it still hurts.

I go sprawling, face mashed against the ground. I'm breathing so hard that the blades of dry grass move back and forth. The taste of copper in my mouth lets me know that my lip probably broke open again.

"Get up," my father orders.

I try, but my whole body is shaky, and I dropped my sword, too. I'm not sure where it landed.

"Get up."

"Stanton."

I sit up at the sound of my mother's voice. She walks over, stopping next to him, her face pinched. I hate seeing her worrying about me, so I try again to get to my feet. It's hard, and I'm a little dizzy, but I manage. I still can't find my sword, though.

"He needs a break," I hear her say.

Uncle Iberik shakes his head. "Ach, he's fine."

My mother's black hair rustles a little in the breeze I can't feel. I wish I could, because I feel like I'm a loaf of bread baking in Cook's oven. "You've been out here for hours, and he's tired."

My father doesn't even spare me a glance, but I see

his eyes darken on her, and I start to sweat for an entirely different reason than the heat.

"He's a fae," Uncle Iberik tosses back. "We aren't built like you Oreans. We're stronger."

I wonder if anyone else sees the way my mother's hands fist at her sides.

"Yes, well, he's half Orean. And he's also only eight years old. Even fae boys can't be expected to be out under the hot sun, practicing sword fighting for hours on end. He needs a break or he could become overheated and be too sick to practice again tomorrow. Most fae don't even get their power until they're fifteen. You're pushing him too hard." She says this all with a firm voice, her eyes focused on my father.

But I know what will happen. Later, when no one is around, my father will be mean to her. Maybe hurt her. I don't want that.

For the past few weeks, I've been sticking to her side like glue. If my father comes around, I distract him from her. He's been so excited about my power manifesting itself this early that it's been easy so far. I don't want his attention to go back to her.

I dreamt about that sound of him hitting her, woke up to my mattress shredded from the spikes on my back poking out, the sheets ripped from the ones on my arms. The lines in my skin spread to my bed, rotting the wood until it collapsed. Because that's what it is—rot. I might not be a Breaker, but I still destroy.

"I'm okay," I say, but my throat is scratchy, and it would be so nice to dunk my head in the pond right about now. I'd

also like to throw this stupid sword right into the middle of it so that I won't have to practice again.

Cado keeps silent as his eyes dart between all the adults, though it's not with concern. He'd gladly train me into the ground if that's what my father wanted.

"See?" my father says, arm gesturing to me. "The boy's fine."

"Stanton—"

"Get back inside, Elore," he snaps. My mother looks just as angry as he does, but it just doesn't fit on her face the way it does my father. She's always smiling with me and Ryatt. Laughing with the Orean servants, kind and calm to the horses. She wears a different face with my father. It's either shy or angry or scared or sad. They don't fit. They don't belong.

I want her to always wear the face that she wears for us.

"I'll go inside with my son," she says stubbornly.

My heartbeat goes crazy as I look between them.

Uncle Iberik gapes at her. "How dare you show such disrespect to your lord and husband! He's a fae. He brought you to our world, let you live here, gave you long life and children and the ability to live in our world."

My mother doesn't even pay attention to him, but my father does. His temper always gets worse when Uncle Iberik is here. He doesn't want any of us talking back or behaving poorly, especially when other people are around.

The anger in my father's face makes me feel a surge of emotion. When he takes a step closer to her, the grass suddenly turns brown at my feet. Black lines flood down my arms. Spikes pierce through my skin, each one a different length.

My father's head whips toward me as the rot spreads through the grass. Instead of being excited like the first time, his lips press together in a hard line. "Your power comes out now?" he growls. "You should've been able to bring it forward during training. This is proof that you're not trying hard enough."

"I promise I am," I tell him. I try to reach down to my leg and wipe off the blood dribbling from the jagged gashes in my arms, but all I manage to do is tear a rip in my pants from one of the spikes.

"You need to learn," he tells me, walking forward. His eyes skim over the way some of my spikes are longer than others, the messiness of my sliced skin. "You can't be controlled by your magic or fall to foolish emotions," he spits out. "You're my son, and you will learn to make me proud."

Or else.

That's the unspoken threat.

My head falls. "Yes, Father."

His chin jerks up. "Get him inside."

My mother wastes no time in hurrying forward. Her soft hand takes hold of my upper arm not riddled with spikes, and we start the long walk back to the estate.

We're quiet all the way there, but my head is loud with my father's words.

You will learn to make me proud.

Because I don't make him proud. I just disappoint him, again and again, and he's going to hate me forever.

My eyes burn, but I keep sniffing, trying not to cry. I've been doing it way too much lately. But I just keep hearing my father's words in my head. I've always wanted him to stop being disappointed in me, and I thought once I started to show signs of magic, he would. But that's not true at all.

Once I get back to my room, I'm quiet as I bathe and then quiet still after I dress for bed. My mother comes back in with food and some supplies to clean my sore, torn skin, and I don't say anything through that either, even though the stuff she pours on it stings. At least the spikes went away again, so I don't have to sleep with them.

When the last of the blood has been wiped away, my mother places her hands on my cheeks, forcing me to look at her.

"I want you to listen to me, Slade, and I want you to remember this, alright?"

My head nods slowly.

Her eyes are fierce and full of love. "You are my son, and you already make me proud. Every day."

It feels like I'm going to bawl like a baby, but I swallow hard.

"But I'm weak. My magic only comes out when I'm feeling emotions, and Father says that's wrong."

"You are not weak," she says firmly. When I start to argue, she goes on. "You don't have to be cruel to be strong. You don't have to be mean to seem brave. You don't have to look down on others in order to stand tall. Having emotions does not mean you're weak. It means you're smart enough to let yourself feel."

When my stinging eyes get too much to sniff away, her

*thumbs wipe along my cheeks. "I don't want to be like him,"
I whisper, and even though we're shut away in my room, I
still look to the door, afraid that he somehow will have heard
me. "I don't want to break or rot or hurt things. I want to be
good."*

*My mother's face turns sad. "You are good, Slade. Every
single day, I am proud of you. And it's not because of these
spikes on your arms or the magic in your veins. It's not for the
blood you are born from or the status you will one day have."
She drops a hand and places it on my chest, right over my
racing heart. "I am proud of you for this. Not for what you
can do, but for who I know you will be."*

"Who will I be?"

*She leans forward and kisses my forehead, combing
my damp hair away from my face. "You will be completely
yourself. And you will be proud."*

CHAPTER 8

SLADE

I'm not sure how or when I fell asleep. All I know is, the front door bangs open again and my head jerks up, my neck cricking instantly from where it was lying back on the sofa. Ryatt apparently fell asleep here too, though I have no idea when he came back. He lurches up from the chair he was slouched in just as I jump to my feet, pulse hammering from the rude awakening.

Wind howls through the cave, and I realize it's gone dark again, either because I slept longer than I realized or the storm has completely overrun the sun. I pause when I see a mop of yellow hair. "Judd?"

"Miss me?" He shakes his head like a wet dog, sending water droplets flying around in the entryway.

I let out a sigh and drag a hand down my face. "Does no one actually listen to my orders?"

Ryatt gives me a scowl and then stalks into the kitchen.

"Not when your orders are stupid," Judd answers jovially.

I need to punch something. I really do.

But then he moves aside just as a slight man clad in a long coat with red bands stitched around his biceps walks in and closes the door behind him.

Hojat.

Relief floods into me, and my eyes widen, flashing back to Judd. "You went all the way to the army to get Hojat and bring him here?"

"Yep."

Surprise, gratitude, irritation that I didn't think of it—all of those things knock around inside my skull.

"You're welcome," Judd says, flashing me a smile as he pulls off a satchel from his shoulder and sets it on the ground.

"Thank you." Having Hojat here to check over Auren is already loosening some of the panic fisted around my gut.

Both of them come into the living room, and then Judd helps our army mender out of his soaking wet cloak, while Hojat checks his own bag that's slung around his shoulder. I can hear vials tinkling together as he rummages around. "Good, everything in this stayed dry."

"Your other bag wasn't so fortunate, I'm afraid," Judd tells him, motioning toward the satchel that's now not much more than a puddle by the front door.

"That's alright, Captain Judd," Hojat says as he shakes off some of the water from his brown hair.

A tired Lu appears from down the corridor and takes in the scene. "Took you long enough," she says through a yawn.

"You know I hate flying," Judd replies as he strips off his

cloak and hangs it on the peg, beside the fire where the rest of our cloaks are already hanging. "Plus, we went right through the damn storm. That rain turned to sleet, and that sleet turned to hail. Ever been pummeled by hail while you're trying to stay on a frozen saddle with a mender who hates heights?" he asks as he yanks off his boots.

"Not recently, no."

He gives another hair shake. "Well, it's hard."

Hojat frowns. "It was my first time on a timberwing, Captain Judd," he says, shuddering slightly as he too takes off his wet boots. "And your flying...it is not the best."

Lu snorts. Ryatt walks back in with a pair of steaming tin cups. He hands them to Judd and Hojat, who take them gratefully, gulping the broth down.

My patience has gone paper thin, this banter tearing right through it. "Does anyone want to explain why you're not all back with the army like I told you to be?"

The four of them look at me like I'm a kid throwing a tantrum. They give me this look *a lot*.

"Calm down," Judd says as he comes over to clap a cold hand on my back. "Os is with the army, and they've already moved out on his command. He's got everything in order. Besides, Lu and I agreed that you'd need Hojat. For Digby and for..." He trails off, glancing down at where Auren is still lying on the sofa. "She still hasn't woken up?"

I give a terse shake of my head.

"Excuse me, Captain Lu," Hojat murmurs before scuttling around her to stand in front of Auren. He looks down at her, the left side of his burned face creased with concern. "Captain Judd said we cannot touch her skin during daylight, yes?"

"Correct," I tell him. Aside from my Wrath, Hojat is someone I trust implicitly. He knows quite a lot of secrets, and now that he's here, I'm so fucking relieved, because he can help Auren where I'm failing. "But she never gold-touched the cushions or Lu's leggings. I don't know if that's a good or a bad thing. She could just be too drained."

Hojat hums thoughtfully. "Well, it's night now. May I?"

With a nod, I move away so he can begin to carefully look her over. He starts by feeling the temperature on her forehead, holding his fingers in front of her lips to count her breaths, checking her extremities, and then pressing his ear against her heartbeat.

"Well?"

"All appears as if she is simply resting. Perhaps the power drain, as you said. I seem to remember a few times that you passed out from too much power use, Majesty," he says with a reassuring smile.

"I left a piece of my rot in her," I blurt. "I can't get it out."

Creased brown eyes blink at me. "Does it seem to be doing any damage?"

I check her again just in case, and then I shake my head. "None that I can sense. It simply won't come out."

He makes another humming noise. "You will keep an eye on it, yes?"

"Yes."

With a nod, he glances at Judd before looking at me again. "Captain Judd said she may have wounds on her back."

My shoulders stiffen.

Judd holds up his hands. "I know I told him a lot, but he has to know in order to help her."

I shake my head, because I'm not angry with him for telling Hojat these things. I would have too. I'm mad that I didn't do more than simply prop her up on her side. "I couldn't..." I clear my throat, trying to sound a hell of a lot stronger than I feel. "I haven't checked it."

Because I'm a coward.

Because I couldn't bear to.

Hojat doesn't chastise me, even though I deserve it. Instead, he tips his head toward Auren. "Best if I do. Lean her forward so I may check her and treat as need be."

With a nod, I walk around to the other side of the sofa. Gently, I take hold of Auren's shoulders and roll her until she's lying on her stomach. As soon as I have her positioned, Hojat has already gone through the bag slung across his chest and dug out a pair of scissors. He wastes no time carefully snipping down her dress until he can fold it away.

The moment her back is bared, a jagged inhale cuts through my lips and slices down my throat. I hear my Wrath take in a collective gasp, all of them stepping in closer to see. Yet I don't step closer. Instead, I'm rooted to the spot.

Her back is in ruins.

The satiny gold ribbons that used to sprout along her spine like feathers of a wing have been utterly destroyed. Those twenty-four delicate strips, draped down like the train on a gown, moving alongside her as an extension of herself, they've all been torn from her, barely an inch or two of length left on her bloodied back.

Auren's ribbons were beautiful. Unique. Fae. They were as bright and alive as her. Now, they've been cut away like the branch of a tree, hacked off and shredded, left in splintered ruin.

Use your ribbons.

I can't.

My eyes blur as I stare at each chopped stub, at the dried blood caked to the ends and smeared along the skin in spatters of gold. Her ribbon ends are frayed and bent, her skin bruised up and down her spine from the trauma.

Even now, some of the shorn ends weep with golden drops of blood, and I curse myself again for jostling her too much, for not seeing to this immediately. For being a coward.

"*Fuck…*" I hear Judd say.

"That fucking monster," Lu spits, turning away.

My throat is too clogged to say anything at all.

"Okay." Hojat straightens, the only one in the room who isn't grim-faced or full of horror and pity. He doesn't make a single mention of the way they bleed gold or the fact that she has them at all. Instead, he's fallen into his mender role effortlessly, methodically, and without hesitation.

"Commander Ryatt?" he says, turning to my brother. He's one of the only ones aside from my Wrath who knows I even have a brother and that he takes the lead from me when I'm being a king instead of a soldier. "I will need you to boil some clean water." He turns to Lu next. "I'll need a big shirt for her that ties or buttons all the way up. Preferably Captain Osrik's size." Both Lu and Ryatt immediately disperse, heading in separate directions.

"You two," Hojat says, motioning toward Judd and me, "she needs a bed where I have more room to work and she can be more comfortable."

"I already started a fire in your room," Ryatt calls to me from the kitchen.

With a nod, I carefully gather Auren in my arms. Judd walks ahead of me down the corridor, and we pass by the flickering firelight from the sconces hanging along the walls. He opens the last door at the very end of the hallway and then hurries over to the bed, yanking the furs and blankets down. The room is warm, the fireplace crackling and casting off both heat and a comforting orange glow, though it can't stave off the musty smell from disuse. It's been a while since I last stayed here.

Judd wastes no time as he starts to light the lantern on the bedside table before pulling open the thick brown curtains. We wouldn't have bothered to put windows in the Grotto at all since we have no true view of the outside, but we did so that it seems less claustrophobic, and because the glowing fluorescent rock in the cave casts off a comforting blue that almost resembles stars.

"On her stomach, please, Sire," Hojat tells me, striding into the room.

I set her down as gently as I can, making sure her head is turned and that she doesn't look too uncomfortable.

When I have her settled, Hojat practically shoves me away, setting his bag down at the bottom of the bed as he begins to rifle through it and pull things out.

When Judd and I just stand there, he casts a look over his shoulder. "No time to waste. Captain Judd, you'll need to get out of those wet clothes, and I'm afraid I'll need to borrow some as well until my own dry out."

"I'm on it." Judd turns and leaves, and then Hojat is eyeing me, a line forming between his brown brows. "Sire, you didn't change out of your clothes from the storm?"

I glance down at myself, wondering how he could tell, but my black leathers have wrinkled and stiffened, white frost lines stained into the material. "No."

"Best get changed."

I hesitate for a moment, watching him with Auren. "Hojat, anything to do with her—"

He holds up a hand, stopping me. "You saved my life, Sire. The least I can do is save your secrets. Anything that happens with you or the others will always be protected by me."

I already know this. Hojat has long since earned my trust. Yet when it comes to Auren, I need to appease myself, because my fae nature is wound up tight. I'm struggling with having anyone near her while she's in this vulnerable state. I catch a growl in the back of my throat, find myself jerking toward her, as if I'm going to block everyone away.

I have to tell myself that this is *Hojat*. I trust him with my life *and* with hers. So although the protectiveness punching through my pulse makes it incredibly difficult, I somehow force myself to nod and turn away from her.

Heading for the door on the right, I enter through my washroom that has an adjoining closet, finding the sconces already lit with low-burning oil. If I thought my bedroom was musty, my closet is even worse, despite the sprigs of pine someone left hanging on the clothing racks to ward off the closed-up scent. I quickly strip, dumping the stiff clothes in a pile.

When I'm yanking on a fresh pair of pants, I catch a glimpse of myself in the mirror. The veins of rotten power beneath my skin have multiplied and stretched from my chest to my abdomen. They've crept down my arms and up my back, squirming with aggravation along my jaw. They're only this widespread and this unsettled when I've repressed my rot for too long. But this time, it has nothing to do with magic I've held back and everything to do with the female lying prone on my bed. My magic is reacting to her, my fae nature pumping power through my veins like a heart pumping adrenaline.

As if it knows the direction of my thoughts, the roots on my hands prickle and shift until I clamp them down into my fists. With gritted teeth, I finish getting dressed, covering up as much of them as I can.

By the time I've washed up and come back out into the bedroom, Hojat has also changed his clothes and is hard at work. He's finishing up cleaning away the blood on Auren's ribbons, his touch careful and perfunctory, the steaming bowl of water filled with some sort of mashed leaves that make the whole room smell of herbs.

Judd comes in carrying a clean bowl and another set of rags, and he sets both on the bedside table.

"Thank you, Captain Judd," Hojat murmurs as he continues to concentrate on Auren. Both Judd and I watch as he puts some sort of salve along the ruined edges, and then he gently begins to lay strips of cloth along her back to cover the short ends. He's not at all bothered or hesitant at her differences, not at all fazed by the fabric-like strips that he's now treating. Hojat has seen many things during his time with me.

When he's finished, he washes his hands in the clean bowl and turns to me. "Everything is cleaned. I will need to keep an eye on them to make sure they don't get infected. She should rest on her stomach or side as much as she can." He begins to collect his things, rolling up bits of dried herbs and stoppering vials as he puts everything back into his satchel.

"Should I do anything?" I ask, hating how helpless I feel. I'm not used to sitting back and doing nothing.

"Let her rest. Magic depletion can be very hard on the body, as you well know." He sifts through his bag once more, pulling out a dried peony and stuffing it under her pillow before he gathers up his bag and both bowls. "I'll go see Master Digby now and begin to treat him if I have your leave?"

"Yes, thank you, Hojat."

He gives a slight bow. "It is always my pleasure to help you, Sire."

When he leaves, I blow out a breath, hands shoving into my pockets. "Thank you, too," I say to Judd where he's leaning against the wall next to the fire. "For bringing Hojat. I should've thought of that."

"You were a bit preoccupied," he says before giving a jaw-cracking yawn.

"Go to sleep, Judd. You look like shit."

He chuckles, rubbing a hand down his tanned face before scratching at his chin. "You really know how to build a man up. But you're right. I'm the handsome one in the group, so it's important I get my beauty sleep. Holler if you need anything, we're all right down the hall."

"I will."

With a nod, Judd walks out, shutting the door behind him, and despite dozing off earlier, I still feel wiped out. I bank the fire and grab the chair next to the small table, dragging it forward as close to the bed as I can get. I settle down into it, resting my head in my hand while I study her. With her head tilted toward me, my gaze skims over the relaxed planes of her face, the curves of her cheeks, the plush form of her lips. Her skin glows beneath the firelight, and I can't help but reach over to tuck back a piece of her hair.

"Rest, Goldfinch," I murmur. "Rest, and then wake up for me."

I fall asleep sitting right there next to her, listening to the tune of her even breaths threading in and out. It's the only reassurance I have. Because even now, while her aura still wisps faintly around her and her eyes stay firmly shut, I can sense the seed of rot that's settled into the soil of her chest and taken root.

And still, it does not answer to me.

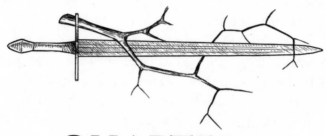

CHAPTER 9

OSRIK

The moment I landed back in Ranhold, I got the army moving.

It was a disorganized, rushed shitstorm, but there was no time to waste. Hopefully, the soldiers are restless and rested, because we have to get the fuck out of Fifth Kingdom.

On my horse, I gallop up and down the lines as the rest of the soldiers finish packing up. There are shouts and clangs, things being tossed unceremoniously in carts and barrels, tents being rolled up, and horses being saddled.

Within ten minutes, I had the front of the army moving. Another ten, and the middle was underway. Now, I'm getting the soldiers at the back in motion. Of course, a prick of a winter storm starts boasting its grit right as the last of us get going, blowing snow on top of us like it's trying to prove it's stronger.

Fuck that.

The army might be slightly unprepared in our hasty withdrawal, but they're strong. Lu, Judd, Ryatt, Rip and I have all made sure of it.

Taking my horse around the ranks, I encourage them to go faster as they hastily get moving, while also making sure all the stragglers are accounted for. "Alright, Keg?" I holler.

The man dumps a pile of snow on top of the cooking fire, extinguishing it in a mess of steam and smoke before tossing a pot into the back of his cook's cart. "Alright, Captain," he calls back. "But this really cuts into my meal prep time for breakfast."

"I'm sure your breakfast will be fine."

He places his hand over his chest. "Aww, are you saying I'm the best, most capable cook in the army, Captain?"

I roll my eyes. "Keep an eye on things back here, will you? Whistle if you need me."

"Will do."

For the next hour, I tromp my horse up and down the lines, shouting encouragement and orders, getting everyone going quicker as we start to march away from Fifth. Normally, I'd wait for the storm to pass, but I don't trust Queen Kaila, and considering what happened in that ballroom tonight, we can't afford to sit around while they decide if they want to risk attacking us or not.

Rip wants the army back in Fourth, so I'll get it back to Fourth.

But the sky is a dick. Slapping our faces with frigid air, spewing out streams of wet sleet. It's turned the ground into a sloppy fucking nightmare, and the dripping wind just keeps groaning and crying like a little bitch.

I hate this Divine-damned kingdom.

I think that's the consensus of every single soldier as we march all night, so at least the shitty elements are making us even more motivated to get the fuck out of here.

By the time I call for the army to stop, dawn is about to crest and the storm is still jacking off, dumping its endless load on us.

Fucking prick.

The mountain pass where I have us stop gives us some protection at least. Everyone pitches their tents, flint sparked to start hasty fires so we don't all freeze to death. The mountainside blocks most of the wind, and if we angle the tents right, we keep most of the snow from tearing right through them.

Much to my horse's irritation, I don't stop checking the perimeter until I get a full headcount from all of the lieutenants and the first watch patrol has been put into effect. Only once most of the army are bundled up inside their tents or hovering around fires do I finally stop my vigil, bringing my horse to where the others are being sheltered.

As soon as I dismount, a soldier named Himinn rushes over. "I put up your tent, Captain," he calls over the wind, snow battering his chapped face.

"I keep saying that you don't have to do that shit for me," I tell him.

The boy is barely ranked, only joined the army this past summer, and he's been grateful for me accepting his application ever since. Caught him spit-shining my shoes once when I didn't remember to put them away.

He shrugs with a smile, showing off his chipped front tooth, and then immediately takes the reins. "I'll put your horse with the others, take good care of him."

"Himinn," I start to say, but I'm cut off when a sharp whistle sounds.

The soldier takes the opportunity to slink away with my mount, while I turn around and find Keg strolling up, twigs tied into his long, twisted hair.

"Remember when you told me to whistle if I needed you?"

"Yeah?"

"Well, that was a shit suggestion, Captain, because no one could hear a damn whistle in this storm."

My eyes scan the surroundings, but tents and people are so jam-packed in the narrow mountain pass that if there is a problem, I can't see it. "What's the issue?"

"You'd better come see for yourself."

Great.

I follow his zigzagging path as we trundle through the thick snow in the camp. We stop at his cooking fire, where a line of soldiers are serving themselves from a massive pot hanging on iron spokes over the flames.

"Did you drag me over here just to make sure I eat?" I ask.

Keg snorts. "No, but I am going to make sure you get a bowl, you know that."

To demonstrate, he shoves past the line and scoops the thick stew into two tin bowls and hands them both to me.

I cock a brow. "Two?"

"You'll see," he says cryptically before he waves me forward.

With a sigh, I follow him, but the boiling hot broth keeps spilling on my damn fingers, burning right through my gloves and making me hiss. "Did you have to fill these so fucking full?" I grumble.

"You should practice your lightness of foot," he calls back cheerfully. "That stew's the best dinner in the camp. Those other army cooks are jealous as hell, as usual."

With a laugh that comes out as a grunt, I keep walking until he stops in front of a tent. He holds the flap open expectantly, and I cock my head, stopping just in front of it. "If this is your way of propositioning me, you're shit at it."

Keg lets his head fall back as he laughs loudly. "Captain, you wound me. I'm romantic as fuck. If I was propositioning you, I'd knock your Divine-damned socks off."

"Just so you know, my socks smell like shit."

He jerks his head at the tent. "Get in there, you're causing a draft, and the stew's gonna get cold."

Rolling my eyes, I duck inside. As soon as I'm in, he lets the flap fall closed with a "have fun" tossed with the wind as he walks away.

Frowning, I straighten up, and then my eyes adjust to the darker lighting and the warmer air, and my gaze immediately zeroes in on the woman wearing some fancy ass dress that has no business being worn out here in these conditions. The little coat she has on isn't doing shit either.

The blonde stands up to face me, crossing her arms in front of her indignantly. "And just who are you?" she demands.

I blink at her, then at the *second* woman who's lying on the pallet next to her, white as a sheet as she sleeps.

"I'm captain of the whole damn army right now. Who the fuck are *you*?" I counter, though she looks familiar.

Her lush lips press together in a thin line. "I'm Rissa. When I was leaving Ranhold, I ran into someone named Lu. She told me if I went to the army, you would take me with you out of Fifth Kingdom. She said Auren had talked to you all about it—that I could come with you."

My thoughts snap back to that night when Auren told us about Rissa. About how the bitch was basically blackmailing her. I suggested we kill her.

I suggest killing a lot.

"Yeah, she did. Gildy is way too fucking nice," I grumble under my breath.

"Excuse me?" she says in her uppity voice.

"You heard me," I retort, looking at her with disgust. "You threatened her, made her give you shit in return for your silence, and still, all she wanted to do was help you. I said we should just kill you. Because if there's one thing I hate, it's disloyalty."

A flash of outrage flares through her blue eyes. "*Disloyalty?*" She eats up the space between us, shocking the hell out of me when she pokes a manicured finger into my chest. "You listen here, you savage hairy giant. I'm a sex worker and a woman. You think I have the privilege of living my life on some moral high ground?" she spits out. "Well, let me tell you, *I don't*. Saddles give the world the pleasure it wants, and what do we get in return? We're controlled and judged, and that's just best-case scenario. So you can hate me all you want, want to kill me even, but I do what I have to in order to survive in this world, and if that means I use information to my advantage, then I'm going to do it."

She's breathing hard, chest rising and falling, pink dots cropped up on her cheeks, and for some reason, my wall of irritation suddenly cracks, and out leaks the realization that she's really fucking beautiful.

Damn the Divine.

How did I go from the killing suggestion to *this*?

Her speech was emboldened enough that I know she meant every word. A part of me even respects her for it. I know what it's like to have to do whatever you need to in order to survive the world. For so much of my life, it was kill or be killed, and I chose to be alive.

I guess she did too.

But survival is also about choosing your loyalties wisely. When it comes to those *I'm* loyal to, I'm a fierce fucker.

My tongue flicks over the twisted wood piercing in my bottom lip. "Auren is loyal to you, but you're not loyal to her. Simple as that. I don't let disloyal people march with my army."

The blonde stiffens. "Fine." She turns around and starts shoving things into a bag, half her body lit up with the pile of simmering coals set in the center of the tent. "We'll leave. I hope you sleep better at night knowing that you tossed out two helpless women into the Barrens and saved your precious conscience by upholding your high and mighty *loyalty*."

My head tips back as a long-suffering sigh comes out of

me. "Quit with the martyr shit," I snap. "That's not going to work on me. You can stay because we told Auren you could, and I always keep my word."

Rissa stops what she's doing, the skin at her eyes tightening, while I continue to stand here like an idiot, still holding two steaming bowls of stew. I shove one toward her. "Here."

She hesitates for a moment, but I guess her hunger is stronger than her dislike for me, because she stands up and quickly takes it. When my eyes wander down to the way her lips close over the tin bowl, to the way she starts sipping it politely down, all sorts of dirty images pop up through the cracks of my thoughts.

Not good.

Shifting my focus, I down my own stew in a mess of slurps and chews and one hearty burp at the end. After I wipe the dripping broth from my beard with the back of my arm, I look up to find her watching me with her nose wrinkled in repulsion. "Are you not house-trained?" she sneers.

I grin back, all teeth. "You're gonna learn real quick that those dainty sips aren't gonna do shit when you're starved and freezing. There's no kings and nobles for you to sit around and impress. Just me."

"As if I would ever strive to impress you," she shoots back after taking another delicate drink. "You wouldn't even be on the bottom of my list when I mark a room. I only ever go for the rich and cleanly."

This time, I'm the one who eats up the space between us, my long strides taking me right in front of her. The way her pretty neck bends to look up at me is oddly attractive. Never thought I'd think someone's fucking neck was a turn-on.

I've been in Fifth Kingdom too damn long. Blue balls from the weather must be real.

"Good news for both of us, Yellow Bell."

She frowns. "Yellow Bell?"

I shrug. "It's fitting. Flower's yellow like your hair, and it tricks some people, because it might be pretty on the outside, but it's pure poison."

Her eyes go dark. "My hair is *blonde*, not yellow, you incompetent brute."

I grin. "So you don't deny the poison part? Interesting."

She shoves the bowl back at me. "You can go now."

"Since I'm the captain of the army, I'll be giving the orders around here."

"Great," she mutters under her breath before she turns her back on me to sit down next to the sleeping woman.

I have to say, not many men would dare to turn their backs on me, so the fact that this woman is doing it without a care in the world makes me hard.

Yep. Definitely been in Fifth Kingdom too damn long.

"What's with the broad?"

"Her name is Polly," she bites out as she picks up a cloth and dabs the woman's brow.

"She sick?"

"What do you care?"

I shrug. "Guess I don't. But if she's gonna be using up army resources with one of the menders, I need to know."

She shoots me a look that's colder than the storm outside.

"She's not contagious, and I don't need anything from you or this army."

"Other than our shelter, food, protection..."

I can practically hear her grind her teeth. I don't know why riling her up makes me so fucking excited, but it does. She's got spirit, and I didn't know I liked that in a woman until right now.

Standing again, she turns to me with something fierce blazing in the depths of her blue eyes. With her gaze locked obstinately on mine, she starts to strip off her coat and then toes off her boots. But when she starts to pull at the sleeves of her dress and tug them down her shoulders, I startle. "What the fuck are you doing?"

"What?" she says with careless indifference. "This is what you want, right? You want me to pay for your *services*, Captain? I'm just a disloyal saddle, so I'd better compensate you for your generosity."

I stand here like a fucking idiot as she tugs the sleeves the rest of the way off, revealing a set of perfect tits inside a dainty corset that's squeezing them for dear life, making her curves swell with plumpness that begs to be let out and handled.

I go rock fucking hard. So hard, in fact, that all the blood I need for my damn brain to work has rushed in the wrong direction, so it takes several seconds for me to realize what she's said.

As soon as I do, I get really fucking pissed.

"Pull your clothes back on," I snap.

"Why?" she lobs. "This is what men want in exchange for anything. I'm just doing what I do."

When she continues to stand there like an indignant tempest, I toss the bowls down and then stomp over to her. But when I move to jerk off my coat, she flinches.

She fucking *flinches*.

Like I was going to hit her or some shit.

And that just pisses me off even *more*, because flinching is a learned response, and now I know that she's been hit before. Probably by some of those saddle-toying fucks who like to mistreat women. Maybe even by Midas himself.

Glowering, I go more slowly as I take off my coat and drape it over her. She stares at me without moving, not even breathing.

"I'm an asshole, but I would never take advantage of a woman," I say gruffly.

Despite doing her best to shock me, it looks like I've shocked her now. She blinks like she doesn't understand that I'm putting clothes *on* her instead of taking them off.

Graceful fingers come up to clutch the coat.

"You're...giving me your coat?" she asks, and her voice is in a completely different tone now. Quieter. Confused. A hint of vulnerability behind that thorny exterior.

"I am," I say with a nod, and I can't help but let my eyes drop down to her lips. Fucking pretty. "I'll make sure you both have some extra clothes. You can't be tramping along Fifth Kingdom in a fucking gown and corset."

Rissa eyes me dubiously. "You're going to give me all of that?"

"I just said I was, didn't I?"

"And...you don't want me to fuck you?" she asks bluntly, as if she can't quite believe it.

113

A grumbled chuckle comes out of me. "I didn't say that. I said I won't take advantage of you," I reply, making the frown between her brows deepen. I give in to temptation for a second and lean in closer, and just like I suspected, she smells faintly of flowers. "When we fuck, it'll happen because you want it to happen."

There's a spark of heat in her eyes right before she puts it out, and that petulant, pouting look comes back over her face. "What makes you think I'd ever want to?"

I give her a crooked smile before I turn and scoop up the bowls. "Because, Yellow Bell, you might be poisonous, but you're not immune. There's something here."

"Yeah, loathing."

With a grin tucked behind my beard, I head for the tent's opening, stopping to look over my shoulder at her one more time as I push back the flap. "What's the fun in it if you don't loathe each other just a little bit?"

I walk out, leaving her sputtering, but I didn't miss the blush that covered her cheeks.

The long journey back to Fourth Kingdom just got *a lot* more enticing.

CHAPTER 10

SLADE

It's been four days.

Four days, and Auren still hasn't stirred. She lies on my bed silently, only moving when Hojat changes her dressing and adjusts her sleeping position so she doesn't get sore. And despite the fact that the sun has risen and set multiple times, not a single thread has been gilded by her touch. Not the fabric of the pillow beneath her cheek, not the new gloves or leggings on her body. Not an inch of power has come out of her, and I don't know what to think.

The storm has raged and raged, as if trying to seek revenge for the fact that we avoided its wrath and beat it here. To get back at us, the tempest has now decided not to leave.

My attention jerks to the door when Ryatt strides inside without warning, a pissed-off look on his face, green eyes flashing as they level me with a glare.

"Ever heard of knocking?" I say, though there's no energy behind my words.

He stops in front of my chair, toeing past the half dozen books discarded on the floor beside me, forgotten and shoved aside since my mind won't allow me to actually read anything. I can't—not when Auren still lies here unmoving.

"You need to get out of this room."

I snort. "You're giving me commands now, brother?"

"No, *brother.* I wouldn't dare to order the great King Rot around," he bites back. "But you aren't eating, you're barely sleeping, and you smell like shit."

I roll my eyes, ready to shove him out of my room. My mood plummets more each day when Auren doesn't wake up. I haven't left her side a single second, concern and fear risen up to my ears so it's all I can feel and hear and think of. "Get out, Ryatt."

He lets out a disappointed sigh. "You need to get a grip."

My eyes flash up to his face. "*Get a grip?*" I snap, on my feet in an instant, my face in his. "You think that I don't have a white-knuckled grip on myself every second of the day? I don't have the luxury of never *not* having a grip on myself." My entire body is tense, my tone gnarled. "Since the moment I had to use my magic against her, I've been *this* fucking close to snapping. Do you get that? I have to hold the reins around my power constantly, can't give it a single fucking inch. So no, I don't need to get a grip. Because I haven't been able to loosen it since I got here and realized she's not waking up."

Ryatt takes in my fuming expression, but we've gone head-to-head many times, and while most people would back down in the face of my anger, he's not one of them. "This is exactly why you need to get out of this room."

I shake my head, spikes trying to shove through the sleeves of my shirt. Even now, I can feel the smallest ones punching through the curve above my eyebrows.

"Look at you," he says with a note of disgust. "Let me see how bad it is."

Scoffing, I turn away, stopping in front of the fireplace. "Who sent you in here? Lu? Tell her she doesn't need to worry about me."

"No one sent me, but we're all sick of your shit," Ryatt replies. "Now let me see."

"Fuck off."

"You think I want to babysit you? I've got better shit to do. So roll up your Divine-damned sleeves and let me see. I'm not leaving until you do."

Fuming, I spin around and shove up both sleeves, just to get him to go away. As soon as my arms are revealed, Ryatt's lips press into a thin line. "Fuck."

I shove my sleeves back down. "It's fine."

"It's not fine," he retorts. "You need to go expel some power before it eats you alive."

"What about the scouts?"

"Don't try to change the subject. I'm handling Midas's scouts, don't worry. Now you go handle *your* shit."

"I'm not leaving her alone."

Ryatt strides over to the chair I was sitting in and plops his ass down while I stare at him incredulously. He even goes so far as to brace an ankle on his knee and grab one of *my* books from the floor to start reading.

"What the fuck are you doing?"

He shrugs a shoulder. "I'm staying with the golden girl so she won't be alone. Now go away and rot some shit before you explode and destroy all of Deadwell."

My fists ball together, the roots along my fingers writhing and snapping against my skin, trying to pierce through me like thorns. "I can't." Watching her, staying by her side, it's the only thing that's keeping me from losing my shit entirely. Because she's still not awake. She's still not okay.

Ryatt looks up at me, and for the first time since he strode in here, his expression sobers. "The sooner you take care of your magic, the sooner you can get back here by her side," he tells me, his tone no longer biting. "So go. I'll stay right here with her. I promise."

I start to shake my head, but he cuts me off. "Slade. You're about a second away from snapping. Sitting here watching her isn't going to help, because even when she does wake up, you'll have to leave immediately to take care of your magic. So go do it now before you fucking implode."

I agonize in indecision, but now that Ryatt has very unapologetically pointed out how strained I am, I can no longer ignore it. My power is writhing beneath my skin, prickling over my back and chest, snapping at my arms, and making my fingers throb as it pushes against the underside of my fingernails.

"Fine," I finally relent, realizing I can't even let out a full breath. "I'll be back as soon as I can."

"Take your time. Make sure you expel enough so that I don't have to shove you right back out into the storm again two hours later."

"How cold is it?"

"Been dumping snow for four days with no end in sight and a wind chill that can chap your ass cheeks in a second."

I groan. "Fucking perfect." Heading into my closet, I grab the first coat and gloves I see, yanking them on before I pull on my boots. "Watch her," I tell Ryatt. "And have someone signal me if she so much as twitches."

He gives me a mock-bow without actually getting up from the chair. "Yes, Sire."

"Shut up."

With his chuckle sounding at my back, I stomp out of the bedroom for the first time in three days, just to find both Lu and Judd leaning against the walls in the corridor. I stop short for a second when I see them, but then roll my eyes and keep walking. "What was the order going to be?"

Lu follows behind me with light steps. "It was going to be Judd next if Ryatt couldn't convince you with his brotherly love," she tells me with a smartass smirk. "Judd can usually cheer you up enough to get you to stop being a prick and listen. But if that didn't work either, I was going to go in last and just issue some good old-fashioned threats."

Despite my bleak mood, I feel my lips twitching. "What kind of threats?"

"As if I'd spoil the surprise. I might need them down the road."

I stop at the front door, turning back to look at the two of them where they're still perched in the corridor. "Fancy a fly?"

"What, in that storm?" She lifts her foot, shaking her fluffy slipper. "These would get ruined."

"Of course. Judd?"

He grimaces before hitching a thumb over his shoulder. "I've got some firewood I need to re-stack."

"Such loyalty," I say dryly.

Lu gives a wave before turning to walk into the living room. "Have a nice rot trip," she calls.

A snort escapes me before I yank open the door and walk out, letting it shut behind me. My eyes quickly adjust to the darkness of the cave, the air so frigid that even the blue fluorescence seems to shudder.

The closer I walk to the mouth, the louder the storm becomes. I stop just inside, watching as it rages in front of me in a swirl of white and wind. At my feet, snow has blown in and piled up past my knees like frozen rubble warning me of the battle outside. It's late afternoon, but you wouldn't know it with how thickly the clouds are covering the sunlight.

"Of course I'd have to do it in this weather," I grumble to myself before I snap up the hood on my coat and bury my hands in my pockets as I step outside.

Immediately, the wind shoves into me, and I tuck my head down, barreling through it, turning right to head up the curve of the mountain rather than left to go back toward the village center.

The flakes come down in constant streams, but luckily, someone has been keeping up on the pathway, scraping away the snow before it can build up too high. I keep my head down against the gale, my hood threatening to rip off every step of the way, all while I curse my magic's temper tantrum.

The way to the Perch is all uphill, which isn't ideal when

it snows, which it does quite often. It takes me longer than usual to get there, but I finally reach the entrance of a smaller, jagged-mouthed cave. It looks like an open maw with fangs ready to clamp down as you enter, but the real biting beasts are the ones inside.

As soon as I breach the entrance, the weight of the wind is gone, but the weight of my power pushing against my skin seems to have doubled. I kick my boots against the stone before stepping onto the tufts of straw laid down on the ground. My shoes crunch over it, and I look around the domed cave, so high up that it's a struggle to see the beasts who perch at the very top.

Rivulets of blue fluorescence glow deep and steady, while a dozen timberwings sleep in wooden roosts built like enclosed balconies along the walls of the cave, their heads tucked beneath bark-colored wings.

I walk across the cave, a few of the beasts chuffing at me with irritation as I pass them by. Argo likes to roost at a perch thirty feet up, and I stop just below, arms crossed in front of my chest, waiting for him to stir, but he doesn't. "I know that you know I'm in here," I call up to him. "We have to go for a ride."

He doesn't move.

Rot starts to seep from my feet, making a patch darken the straw. "*Argo.*"

If anything, he buries his head further beneath his wing.

"Look, you've been sleeping for days now. You've had more than enough treats and rest."

He finally deigns to pop out his muzzle, iridescent eyes

glancing down at me before he lets out a little clicking chirp through his razor-sharp teeth. "Yes, yes, you'll get more treats after this flight. Now come on before I rot the whole damn Perch."

Argo gets up with all the lazed enthusiasm of a cat who was interrupted during sunbathing. Finally, he leaps down, landing nimbly before he shakes out his wings with a giant stretch.

"Enjoy your nap?" I drawl.

He licks his chops in response.

With a snort, I walk over to where the saddles and reins are kept at the right hand side of the cave and get to work buckling him. When I'm done, I swing my leg over and strap myself in. I barely have the thing tightened in place before Argo takes off through the opening at a breakneck run. The minute we have the sky above us, he lets out his wings and launches into the air.

I grapple with the strap, holding on before my ass slips right off the back, while Argo streamlines straight up through the storm. My hood flies off and the snow pummels my face, the temperature so cold that it feels like all the warmth has leached from my skin and frozen through my clothes. All I can do is hold on, my eyes closed, teeth gritted as I'm soaked through and left freezing while the wind howls its complaints against me.

When we finally break through the clouds and Argo straightens out, I'm able to catch my breath enough to give him a glare at the back of his feathered head. "Proud of yourself, are you?"

He harrumphs in response, but I know there's a damn gleam in his eye.

Now that the worst of the storm is below us, I pull the reins, directing him where to go, but my rot stabs against my fingers and hands, making me seethe at the pain and nearly lose my grip.

Argo shoots across the sky while I pant in shitty, ineffective inhales. It feels like the roots are wrapping around my chest like a boa constrictor, not letting me take in a full breath. The lines are cutting through my neck, clamping down on my jaw and snapping down my collarbone.

With sweat beading at my brow, I tap Argo with my heel and direct him to land. I don't want to go too far, but I also can't be too close when I let my magic out. I need to be far enough away from the village and to also get this over with as quickly as possible so I can get back to Auren.

Argo lands in the middle of nowhere, the snowstorm just as harrowing. I jump off his back and give his hindquarters a tap. Knowing exactly what to do, he launches back into the sky, circling beneath the clouds.

I look around the sparse white landscape, but visibility is down to maybe thirty or so feet. Rolling my shoulders back, I quickly take off my gloves, shoving them in my pocket, and then I shake out my arms and close my eyes, focusing on my power. It's pent-up and overwrought, pushing against me with irritation.

Forcing myself to breathe in and out, I make sure I'm centered enough to grapple control over the monumental force pumping through my veins.

Then, I let it out.

Rot ruptures out of me like a spewing volcano.

My knees hit the ground as violent torrents shoot through the snow like demonic roots come to poison the earth. And that's exactly what it does.

Power flows from me in waves, and I feel every inch of it as it pours from where I'd kept it dammed up.

Now unleashed, it rumbles from my feet and spreads from my hands, delving into every inch of ground it can get to, rotting, decaying.

Destroying.

In a matter of seconds, there is no untouched snowy ground. Streams of toxins have spanned out in all directions, while I stand in the center of the wicked timepiece, counting down the seconds until the power stops pushing, stops punishing.

My body shakes from the amount of magic expelling from my body, and when it finally ceases its endless torment and I feel like I can breathe again, I close it down. Like a fist around a straw, I strangle the flow until the rot drips out its last drop.

Exhaustion drapes over my limbs and scours down my back, leaving me raw and heavy. I blink blearily around me as the roots in the ground settle and stiffen, their movements finally going still.

With shaky hands, I try to curl my fingers, noting the roots of power on my skin have receded and I no longer feel them crawling up my neck or down my back. A hefty price, considering the fetid and impure land I'm standing on that's now dead and desecrated with an awful stench.

After taking in several labored breaths, I have enough strength to lift my head and let out a sharp whistle. Argo comes down within seconds, feathers frozen, maw covered in patches of snow. He kneels down more than usual so I can heave my body on top of his back. Once I'm buckled, he takes off, not once chattering at me for my slumped over position. He's carried me in far worse postures.

It's dusk now, and I look down at the land as he lifts us into the air, seeing the stretch of rotted lines polluting the ground like venom spread through the earth. He carries us up above the clouds, cutting off my view, and even though I'm tired, the relief of expelling all that pent-up power is immense. I can finally take in a full breath now, and all my rot has retracted back to the thin, painless lines that I can feel around my chest.

I barely feel the wind or the snow as Argo flies us back to the village, but by the time he lands and steps back into the Perch, I'm frozen through. When I slip off the saddle and land at his side, I give him a scratch on his muzzle, and he nudges my arm for another. "Good beast," I murmur.

Although I no longer feel like a dam about to burst, shoving out that much power at one time is debilitating. I do my best not to look as drained as I feel while I start to unsaddle Argo. Just as I'm doing the first buckle, the caretaker, Selby, hurries over, though I hadn't even noticed him in here. "I've got it, Sire. Just brought in a fresh feast for them as well. He'll be eating good tonight."

With a grateful nod, I start to walk out, but his voice stops me. "Did Captain Lu or Captain Judd find you, then?"

Slowly, I turn back around. "Find me?"

A confused look crosses his face. "Oh, beg your pardon, Sire. They saddled a couple of timberwings just a minute or so ago. I thought they'd gone to meet up with you."

Dread fills my stomach, and I don't even answer him before I turn and sprint from the cave. They wouldn't have gone out in this storm to look for me unless something was wrong. My steps slip and slide as I rush downhill, but I don't stop until I make it to the Grotto, with fear and worry biting at my heels.

Hojat nearly barrels into me as soon as I step inside, his brown eyes wide, scarred face gone pale. "Thank Divine you're back."

A shot of adrenaline surges through me, spikes ready to burst through my back. "What's wrong?"

"It's Lady Auren."

Panic drives through the center of my heart.

I knew I shouldn't have fucking left.

"Is she awake?" I demand, already stalking down the hallway.

"Not her," he calls after me, making me stop in my tracks to pin him with a fierce gaze. "It's her gold."

CHAPTER 11

QUEEN KAILA

At the very heart of Ranhold City, there's a gleaming white building with a portico two stories high. The pillars are the width of a tree, solid and presumptuous, though the building itself isn't as impressive looking. It's here that the funeral processions take place for every monarch of Fifth Kingdom who has ever died, which is why I find myself standing with my brother on the second level, overlooking the gathering below.

From my spot on the pillared balcony, I have a spectacular view of the city itself, plus the castle's turrets just beyond the wall. On the ground level, Fifth Kingdom's advisors are carrying out the passing rites for the deceased Prince Niven.

Citizens from all throughout the city have gathered in droves to spectate, though most of them can't see a thing since they're too far away. Still, they've come, their figures buried beneath mounds of purple tapestries with Fifth's sigil of jagged icicles embroidered on them, erected like awnings up and down the streets. I don't believe they even realize the symbolism of the royal crests casting them in shadows.

Beside me, I feel my brother, Manu, shiver. "Why in the Divine do the people of Fifth Kingdom have to hold their passing rites *outside*?" he whispers between the teeth he has clenched to keep from chattering.

"I do believe that we are simply less acclimated to the weather here."

He glances at me from the corner of his eye. "And yet here you sit, not shivering in the least."

On the contrary, my skin is raised with chills even beneath the thick layers of my gown and cloak, but I would never shiver in public. Even something so small as that innocent gesture could be taken as a sign of weakness when it comes to a widowed queen.

Looking to my left, I catch the eye of a few Fifth nobles, one of whom keeps pretending to dab her eyes with her handkerchief anytime she hears the rite bell toll from below. There are six rows of benches, all of them full, where the nobles are sitting straight-backed as they try to catch a glimpse of the proceedings in the promenade where Prince Niven's body is set upon a sarcophagus.

But in the front row with us, sitting a few paces down, is Hagan Fulke. Only twenty years old, with a pudgy face and washed-out blond hair, the man keeps yanking on the front of his high-necked collar, obviously unused to wearing such formal garments. Though he might not look like much, he's the first kin of the late king, and heir to the throne.

Well, he is *now*.

We had to get rid of his father first—the king's cousin once removed—but that wasn't much of a hardship. Based on Manu's reports, he was a stodgy, set-in-his-ways old man. Not a good candidate for us.

His son, on the other hand, is impressionable. Shy. Without much money or many prospects, he was ready to sink to his knees and do whatever we suggested if we backed him in order to become king. He's the perfect heir to mold and to guide into acting in both Fifth's *and* Third's best interests, and he has enough magic to justify wearing a crown.

His magic of impenetrable skin will do him well, because arguably, he looks easy to get rid of, so his magic will probably save his life a time or two once he's king.

Hagan's pale face turns a little green, and loath as I am to do it, I follow his gaze back to Prince Niven. The sight of the dead prince makes my stomach churn in disgust. It's been five days since he dropped in a heap in his own ballroom, choking on poison. The body didn't look good then, and it looks even worse now.

"If you put my body up for display like this after I've died, I will come back and haunt you," I murmur beneath my breath.

Manu continues to look ahead as if I hadn't said a thing, keeping the same politely piteous look that's on both of our serene faces. "Dear sister, you should know I would never let you look so garish. I would display you dressed up and dazzling with beauty so that you could gain even more admirers and love in your death."

The corner of my mouth threatens to curl up, because I know he means every word. "That's why I trust you most in this world."

We're the only ones on the portico who don't have some purple patched on us. Instead, the two of us, as well as Keon, are all wearing the traditional Third Kingdom's cream and blue formal attire. My black hair is lifted up in silver coils, while my brother's hangs down his back like a sleek midnight river, just as thick and shiny as my own.

"Poor Prince Niven," I say, loud enough for the people behind us to hear. Several of them nod their heads, murmuring it themselves.

It's amazing how the very same people who whispered and snickered about the spoiled boy prince now pretend to grieve for him. Then again, death always manages to create misplaced adoration and loyalty. But murder? That brings an entirely different level of fanaticism.

There are two things that I've learned firsthand while being here in Fifth. One, it's always cold. And two, the people of Ranhold love nothing more than to warm themselves by spreading the flames of gossip. It's a good way to keep spirits heated.

As the queen of whispers, it couldn't be more convenient.

The rumors of that fateful night have run rampant throughout the kingdom. That the gilded pet cheated her way through Midas's heart and stole his power. That when he announced his engagement to me, she went crazy in a fit of rage, using his magic against him before she tricked King Rot into helping her flee.

Unfortunately for poor Niven, his death has been overshadowed by better, far juicier news. Like the fact that the king of Sixth Kingdom is dead, his corpse gilded and stuck against the wall in the ballroom in Ranhold Castle.

I have to admit, it's all quite scandalous.

Then, of course, there is the gossip about Hagan Fulke. The obscure relative who never thought he'd ever sit on a throne. He went from a nobleman bachelor, who nobody was interested in, to a man about to be crowned king. He still has stars in his eyes about it, doesn't even seem to bat an eye over his father's death or the prince's.

Not when he gets to be the new king because of me.

But they aren't the only ones the people are talking about. My name has its fair share of churning in the rumor mill too.

To them, I'm the heartsick queen who lost her betrothed and is now going to step up and help piece together a riot-torn Highbell, bringing stability back to Sixth Kingdom.

This wildfire gossip has burned through the city. I wouldn't doubt that thousands of messenger hawks have spread from here to all over Orea by now. Manu and I have confirmed the narrative, and now, once these passing rites are finished, I can continue to herd the fires in the direction I want them to burn. So long as they keep seeing me in a favorable light, I can get what I want in Sixth Kingdom and solidify my alliance here.

A singing voice drones out across the promenade, hitting my ears in an unwelcome wave. Keon shifts his legs, no doubt hating the fact that we have to sit here just as much as Manu and I.

Finally, the last bell is rung, and Fifth's advisors shroud the prince's body in the same purple tapestry hung up along the streets. They carry him away in a chorus of that awful singing until finally the rites are over, the prince's body taken in to be properly buried in his tomb right beside his father.

The people on the streets don't disperse yet. They want to watch this macabre parade since most of them probably never get to see their own royals, let alone ones from neighboring kingdoms. They watch as I'm led down from the portico and across the plaza. They call my name as I pass by the empty sarcophagus on my way to my carriage, its blue flags the only disruption in the endless array of Fifth's purple.

Manu and Keon follow me inside, and the way is painstakingly slow and bumpy as we travel back to the castle. I keep the tranquil expression on my face as I turn toward the window, hand lifted in a wave to the people we pass who shout my name. They all want a glimpse of me. Most of them talk about my late husband, who died most suddenly, which is amusing since I haven't thought of him since the moment I watched his body drift out to sea.

That's the way I prefer it.

Finally, once we enter the castle's walls, I let the placid expression fall from my face, dropping the curtain of the carriage window before I sit back against the seat with a sigh. "What a horrible way to pay homage. I don't know what the people of Fifth were thinking, creating something as dull and grotesque as that. Their traditions are far inferior to ours."

"Most boring thing I've ever had to sit through in my life," Manu says, kicking his feet out as far as he can stretch in the cramped carriage space. "Can you imagine dying a horrific and very public death, just for the kingdom to stuff you up on a corpse stage for everyone to see your decaying body? All while everyone is trying to get a look at your carcass, bored out of their minds while they listen to a bunch of old men ring bells and sing wordlessly for three hours straight." He shudders. "Their singing voices were the real tragedy here."

Keon gives him a sidelong glance, but I let out a throaty laugh.

"So, sister," he says, turning his attention to me. "Gather anything interesting?"

He's talking about my power, of course. He knows very well that any time I'm in a public setting, or even a private one, I'm always using my magic. I let it delve out, like a bee seeking pollen. Voices constantly buzz in my head, and I gather the ones I want, collecting them to use whenever I please.

"It's nothing we didn't already know," I admit. "Niven was only well loved because he was a born-prince and still young. But now, that's all changed. They act as if he was their beloved child prince, and they've readily accepted that Lady Auren must've tricked Ravinger into killing him, or she poisoned him herself."

"Good," Keon says, his rumbling voice always held at an octave lower than my brother's. "Although I suspect now we'll never know whether he was poisoned or rotted. The state of his body..."

I can't help but wrinkle my nose, once again remembering

the grotesque veins that ran through his skin, the bulging eyes, the frothing mouth...

"Yes, his corpse was not a pretty picture," Manu says as he fiddles with the silvery buttons down his vest. The cream fabric is fabulously embroidered with subtle waves, the only pop of color coming from the cerulean blue cravat tufted at his neck.

If only I'd been able to get Midas's secret notebook. We searched everywhere in his rooms for it, had my own personal decipherer on standby, but we never found it. It's probably tucked away beneath his shirt, now gilded with the rest of him.

Useless.

For a moment, we ride in silence, but even when no one is actively talking, I'm always listening to the whispers that my power has wrapped up tight in my mind.

"You've prepped Hagan?" I ask Manu.

"Of course. We've been over the coronation many times. He knows what to do."

"Perfect."

Everything is falling into place.

All our plans are going to go off without a hitch. We feed the information, I monitor the rumors, we've handpicked the heir, and soon, Fifth Kingdom will be settled, and I can focus on Sixth. It's been running rampant without a monarch to rule it. The city of Highbell has been ransacked, the nobles have all fled. I need to get there soon, before people with magic try to claim the throne for themselves. I'm surprised they haven't already.

When the carriage comes to a stop, I fix my skirts just

before the footman holds the door open for us to descend. As soon as I stand in front of the castle, my eyes rove over the front where the splashes of solidified gold still mar it. The carpenters had to work night and day to fit a new set of doors to the entrance and drag away the incredibly heavy old ones by hacking them up into pieces. The new set looks light and out of place amongst the old gray stonework, even more so with the gold that's clawed its way out, its tendrils hooked onto the castle's walls and front steps.

Once inside, I go up to my room to change, my maids quickly outfitting me in a silk dress that cuts into a low square at my chest, beaded with crystals along the sleeves. When I'm ready for the formal dinner, I meet Manu and Keon in the hall, both of them already changed into new clothing as well.

"You ready?" Manu says quietly beside me.

"Yes."

I stride forward, shoulders back, a pleasant smile in place. I pass by the purple flags hanging from the rafters, the ten-pointed star sparkling on the ceiling of the entryway. When I reach the dining room, I'm greeted with the scent of sweet food and the sound of nasally voices.

When the three of us come in, the conversations go quiet, and everyone inside bows at the waist as I pass. As I am now the highest ranking person in Ranhold until Hagan is crowned, I take my place at the head of the table, with Manu and Keon sitting beside me on my left and Hagan at my right.

For the next hour, I nod encouragingly at the king-to-be, listen as the advisors recount today's passing rites they performed for the prince, and hear endless stories about Niven when he was a toddler throwing fits in the stables. I subject myself to every conversation, drink their syrupy wine, and eat their too-sweet food, all with pleasantries on my tongue or a smile on my face.

Finally, when the plates are being cleared, I stand.

One by one, the advisors around take notice until the room once more falls silent. Even the servants clearing the tables have gone still, pausing their ministrations. With my hands clasped in front of me, I look down the length of the table at each man's face. There isn't a single woman on Fifth's advising panel.

"I would like to take a moment to express my gratitude for being able to be present for the late prince's passing rites. I believe his spirit has been rightfully honored by you all."

Their heads bow in agreement, pride puffing up their pompous chests.

"Now that he has been so respectfully laid to rest, we can crown the new heir tomorrow, Hagan Fulke," I say, gesturing my hand toward him, watching as his cheeks go blotchy. "I know you will bring stability back to Fifth Kingdom, and you will always have an ally in Third so long as I rule."

A quiet applause spreads over the table, people giving me accolades, already buttering up Hagan. "Right in this room where the prince sat, King Midas gold-touched this very table." I let my fingers scrape across the glass top, remembering how the gold had spread over it like liquid until it gleamed and went solid. But this gold, just like every other bit in the castle, peeled away that day, melting into the ballroom to wick vengeance against the walls.

I lift my eyes, my expression gone sad. "Two monarchs were brutally murdered," I go on, enjoying the way some of them flinch at the harshness of my words. "Both of them killed by someone they believed they could trust. The beloved prince as well as King Midas, who was betrayed by his own favored. Because of that night, I lost my betrothed."

I let my lip wobble. Let my eyes shine. I have every single person's undivided attention, the room so quiet you could hear a pin drop.

"Now more than ever, it's important that we unite together. That we support Hagan's rise, and that the rest of Orea stands against the golden traitor." I see Hagan nod emphatically, trying to seem kingly, though it's far too strained to look natural. "Lady Auren has fled the kingdom and is trying to trick King Rot just as she tricked King Midas. Which is why I'm going to call for a royal Conflux."

Shock ripples through the room at my declaration.

I brace my hands against the table, looking at every single one of them. "It's time Lady Auren answers for her crimes."

CHAPTER 12

SLADE

ometimes, when adrenaline slams through your body, you move without thought. It's a force that takes over, and there isn't a chance to do anything else *but* act.

So I have no idea if I say anything at all to Hojat when he tells me that Auren's gold is awake. I don't even remember running down the hallway to my room.

But my body jolts as soon as I pass through the doorway, coming face-to-face with what's inside.

No longer are the blankets black and the furs brown. In fact, I can't see them at all. The bed is now covered in a pool of lustrous liquid gold, and Auren's inert body is in the center of it, floating on top like a lily pad on a pond. Her power weeps out of her skin in little rivulets of slow draining water, beading against her skin and covering her in golden dewdrops. It's sweating from her every pore, soaking into her borrowed leggings and shirt, collecting on the bed like a puddle.

Ryatt is off to the side, holding his hands up the moment he hears the growl tear from my throat. "*What happened?*" I demand.

"No idea. I was just watching over her like you said, and all of a sudden, she started leaking gold all over the place, and I still couldn't get her to wake up."

I'm at her side in a second, eyes skating over her figure.

"Auren." My call to her whips through me, but she doesn't wake. "Auren, can you hear me?" Gold continues to drip from her, just as calm as her expression.

The bed is losing the battle to its slow but constant rise, as the metallic liquid begins to spill over and drip onto the floor. It doesn't gild anything, just puddles there like water from a leaky roof. My hands hover over her as I call her name again and again.

"You cannot touch her, Sire," Hojat says from the doorway, not daring to come in any further. It seems even my unflappable army mender knows to fear her magic.

"Fuck."

The fact that I can't touch her makes frustration needle through me.

Turning, I rush to the door, and Hojat jumps out of the way as I dart down the hall. I hit the first bedroom next to mine—Ryatt's—stripping his bed of every blanket before I come running back to Auren's side.

"What are you doing?" Ryatt asks.

"I have to get her out—get her away from here in case she starts gilding the whole fucking village," I tell him as I dump the blankets onto the floor before draping the two thickest ones over my arms. Even with my gloves on, this is risky, but the gold doesn't seem to be doing anything other than staying in its collected pond. It's not turning anything solid, it's not gilding the fabric on the bed. Instead, it's just pooling out of her and keeping her buoyed.

But at any moment, that could change. It could start moving, rushing, *attacking*.

"Ryatt," I bark out, and in an instant, he's at my side.

"Got it," he says with a grim nod, and as if he's read my mind, he grabs a blanket and lets it drape along his arms the same as me. "Ready?" he asks.

As soon as I give him a nod, he goes to Auren's side.

"Even with your gloves and sleeves, you need to be careful," I caution. "I don't know if the gold is going to do anything."

With complete confidence, he carefully rolls her body, keeping the blanket as a layer between them. As soon as he moves her, the pooling liquid begins to cascade down the side of the bed.

"Watch it!" Digby calls from the doorway, rushing over with another blanket to toss over the liquid spilling on the ground.

Ryatt doesn't get deterred, even when the viscid substance splatters on his boots. He's able to turn her enough so that her body is out of the deepest parts of the pooled gold, and as soon as he does, I swoop in. Using the covering of the layered blankets, I gather Auren into my arms, though some of the gold seems like it tries to stick to her inert body like honey on a stick, not wanting to part with her.

"Sire—" Hojat's worried voice cuts off when Digby starts to drape another blanket over Auren for good measure, until all that's visible is her face, beaded in gold perspiration.

Wasting no time for the gold to react to me taking her, I rush out of the bedroom and down the hall, while Digby limps as he tries to keep up with me. "Where are you going to go?"

"As far away as I can." When I make it to the front door, Hojat is already there, yanking it open for me.

"What do you want us to do?" Ryatt calls behind me.

"Keep an eye on that gold. If it starts to spread, get the fuck out of the Grotto and evacuate the villagers," I call back. "It won't be safe if she can't pull it back."

"It won't be safe for you either," he says back, but I don't have time to reply. I rush out of the house, and I hear the door closing behind me.

Hurrying, I race out into the storm, debating for a split second which direction to go, before I turn to the right. This time though, I don't go to the Perch. With gold already starting to soak into the blankets, I can't risk bringing her on top of Argo. Not only could her gold suddenly lash out at him, but the worst place to be when it happens is up in the sky where a fall could kill us all.

"Auren, wake up," I tell her.

Dusk is clutching the sky as securely as I'm clutching her. I'm trying my best to keep her tucked securely against my chest, taking the brunt of the wind and the snow as I carry her. A new line of gilded perspiration smears her brows, and panic crawls up my throat. "Listen to my voice. You have to listen to me and wake up."

Perhaps it's the howling wind, but I swear, I hear a moan.

"Auren?"

This time, I know I'm not hearing things, because I *feel* the moan vibrate from her chest. It sounds pained and exhausted, and her brow puckers in the tiniest of grimaces.

My heart leaps into my throat and grips my airway, making it hard to breathe. Not once has she made a sound or an expression since she collapsed.

I sprint up the incline of the mountain, bypassing the timberwing's roost. I pass a cluster of craggy trees where the stone path stops, and with it, the shoveled maintenance. With labored steps, my legs slog through three feet of snow as I head along the incline of the mountain's base.

"Keep trying to wake up, Auren."

Every foot of distance I put between us and the village could be a matter of life and death. I have no idea what will happen if her gold fully awakens, but I have a feeling that this steady drip is just the beginning.

My chest heaves with the effort of trying to run through deep-set snow, and several times, it almost tips me over. It's by sheer determination that I keep hold of her as I climb. Every second that passes, the blankets grow more weighed down, and I feel the syrupy heft of more and more gold soaking through the fabric, and it's *heavy*.

The whistling wind freezes my ears, and the punishing snow makes it nearly impossible to see, but I finally get to the bend of the path just as her gold starts to drip onto the ground, no longer contained by the layers.

Rivulets burst free of the blankets, landing in splashes on the snow, and with it, Auren starts to tremble. Her pained moans are now constant along with the shivers racking her body, but I have a feeling it's not due to the cold.

When I adjust my grip on her, my gloved hands come away sticky. The gold is no longer simply wicking away like oil, but soaking into the fabric, gilding every fiber as it continues to pour from her skin. I don't know how far off nightfall is, but the sky is darkening, though not fast enough.

"Fuck."

When I reach the crevice cracked through the side of the mountain, I practically dive for it. Once we're hidden in its fluorescent depths and out of the storm, I kneel to the rocky ground and set Auren down.

With gold-smeared gloves, I peel back the layers of the blankets, and as soon as I do, her body quakes. Thick, syrupy gold comes pouring out, gathering against the ground of the cave. This is no longer a slow, steady drip. It's pouring from her in streams, snapping and groping around the room like it's searching for someone to maim.

It soaks into the knees of my pants where I kneel, while some of it starts to creep toward the cave's entrance. I reach up to try and hold her steady as her body thrashes, while fear pummels against my chest and rings in my ears. If she doesn't wake up, if the night doesn't stop her and her gold reaches the village…

My glove sticks against her cheek when I cradle her face. "Wake up, Goldfinch. You *have* to wake up!"

Her power is splashing, her aura gone erratic, and panic surges through me so thoroughly that I might be quaking too. "I'm not going to rot you again, do you hear me? I can't fucking do it. *So wake up!*"

Her lips part, and then she lets out a scream that echoes through the hollows. The gold seems to snap in answer as it clambers up the walls, masking the dim fluorescence as it covers the veins of blue etched into the rock.

Yet the force of her scream and the floodgate of her power makes her aura suddenly flare to life, the brightest it's been in days. I have to squint against the sight, but then it flickers back to near-nothing, and my heart halts in my chest, barricading any breath that might've passed through my lips.

Her gold thrashes, rushing back toward her, like it's going to encase her whole so that nothing else can get to her. "Auren!" I call as I start shaking her by the shoulders. "*Wake. Up!*"

And then, so suddenly that it makes me rear back, her eyes snap open.

My voice is nothing but shock caught in the net of an exhale. "*Auren.*"

I see her pupils dilate. See the golden depths of her irises shimmer. All around her, the gold goes still. It stops dripping. Stops flooding. Perhaps night has fallen, and now the gold is watching me as closely as she is.

My pulse pounds in my head, but I don't dare move. A deeper intuition is keeping me rooted to the spot. "Goldfinch?" I ask.

But I already know. I can see it in the depths of her eyes.

It's not fully Auren looking back at me.

All I have time to do is suck in a breath. Because in the next second, she attacks.

CHAPTER 13

SLADE

Huge tendrils of liquid gold lash out, wrapping around me like ropes and then tossing me away. They send me crashing against the jagged wall of the cave so hard that I see stars. I land on my side, the breath knocked out of me for a moment, and it's only because of the endless hours of training I've had that I leap right back up to my feet.

Déjà vu rushes over me, because twenty feet away, Auren stands with a wave risen behind her like a gilded crest. Her chest heaves with rapid breaths, her dripping hands curling into fists at her side while her eyes glow with narrowed attention.

"Auren."

I try to take a tentative step forward, but a snarl rips from her throat. My eyes rake over every inch of her, assessing. When I take a step, she thrusts out her hand, sending a rope of gluey gold shooting out at me like a whip. But it doesn't make contact. Instead, it was merely a warning.

My lips tip up into a smirk, while her eyes taper in suspicion.

Oh, Goldfinch, I see you.

"So, you've finally woken up," I say casually, barely glancing at the whip of gold hovering mid-air, like it's ready to strike at any moment. "Not a morning person?"

Another snarl comes gnashing through her teeth.

"I didn't think so. That's alright, Ryatt's worse. Although," I muse, glancing toward the cave's darkening entrance, "it's nighttime now, anyway."

With slow, measured steps, I shift to the left, starting to circle around her. I keep the same amount of distance between us as before, but this makes her shift with me, makes her become acclimated to movement. She's not dripping new gold anymore, but everything she has is coalesced around her, gathered with perfect synchronicity.

Her gold mirrors her motions, stretching up behind her, its surface rippling like an ocean's wave. But my attention is on her and her aura flickering around her silhouette.

"You've been asleep for days, did you know that?" I ask, keeping my tone conversational. "Lying on a bed, not waking, not eating. In fact, I'd be willing to bet that you're probably feeling a bit weak."

As soon as I say the word *weak*, her anger bursts through her gold, which she sends hurtling toward me. But this time, I'm ready for it, and I dodge the viscid whip before it can make a hit. Behind me, it slaps against the rock, a splatter left behind from the blow.

I tsk. "That wasn't very nice."

Her face pulls together in a furious sneer.

"Oh, I see," I say casually as I take off my stained coat, letting it drop to the floor, before slowly rolling back the sleeves on my arms. "You don't want to be nice. You want to *fight.*"

My body shifts with a thought, black spikes punching through my forearms and curving down the length of my spine. They line my brows, and I touch my tongue to the fangs now dropped from my jaw. She watches my transformation with rapt attention, like a beast trying to size up another predator in her midst. With my ears now pointed and the slash of gray scales against the bones of my cheeks, the smile I flash her is pure fae.

Her chest heaves, and her body is so tense, like she's a string pulled too tight. She's not going to listen to soothing words to get her to come back to herself. No, what she needs is to *snap.*

Which is why I lift a hand, gesturing for her to come near. "You want to fight, so fight *me.*"

That's all the invitation she needs.

Auren sweeps her arms out to her sides, and the wave of gold behind her splits. Then she claps her hands together, the gold moving to mirror her movements, but I drop to my knees and roll before it can smash into me. The focus of her fight is good. She's not depleting herself like she did back at Ranhold Castle, and her aura is holding steady, although, she's also not wholly herself.

But I know a thing or two about dual natures.

"Is that all you got?" I taunt as I leap back up.

She whirls around to face me, eyes blazing. The gold moves with her, blowing her hair back, tightening in a cocked wave to hold itself in a predatory stance beside her. With a curl of her fist, she sends it shooting toward me, trying to squish me to a pulp. I leap away, but not without it splattering all over me from the force of its crash. I see her eyes glow, her jaw tighten, and I smirk in return.

She starts sending the waves at me again and again and again. Yet not only am I fast, but I *know* her. I can read her every move before she makes it, giving me time to anticipate exactly what she's going to do and dodge the gold before it can slam into me.

Each time she tries to pin me down, I slip away out of her gold's grasp, chuckling as I circle her. The gold keeps up with me, sloshing against the ground, arcing and twisting with my movements. Her irritation is clear on the pull of her brows, on the way her eyes barely blink. But she is so attuned, so fucking gorgeous like this, wielding her power so effortlessly.

When I dodge another splash slamming toward me, I wipe away the spray that landed on my cheek with a grin. "You've got to be quicker than that if you want to land a hit," I taunt.

She screams in frustration and abandons her tactic. This time, she breaks apart her gleaming wave into a hundred different twisting ropes and sends them lashing out at me like a wall of whips. When I duck, she manages to move one strip down in time to slam into my stomach, smashing me against the rocks.

I grunt upon impact, my eyes flashing up to see her

reaction. Satisfaction edges her mouth, but when she sees me get back to my feet with a smirk, it slips right back off.

"That was better, Goldfinch. But why don't you drop the gold and hit me like you mean it?" I croon.

She blinks, taken aback, but then her lips press together in anger. With a snap of her fingers, the gold immediately loses its shape and drops to the floor in a splash, soaking through the soles of my boots. Instantly, the gold hardens, and even though it's only about an inch thick around my feet, it's enough to pin me in place.

Clever girl.

Now that I'm stuck, she comes walking over, hips swaying in satisfaction. When she stops in front of me, there's a gleam in her eye. Anyone else standing here would probably be pissing their pants. At the very least, trying to yank out of their boots and run. But me? I'm just turned on. And I stay right where I am.

"You're gorgeous when you're unhinged," I tell her.

Then, I slam my lips against hers.

Her mouth is warm and supple, droplets of gold dotted along the seam, and I can't help but let my tongue dart out to get a taste. I have barely a second of feeling her against me before she's shoving me back, the solidified gold turned back to liquid. I fumble backwards from the force of her push, feeling it splash around my shins.

She pants, looking even angrier than before, her golden eyes alight as she brings her fingers up to her lips. For a moment, she just glares at me, fuming, the gold rippling at our feet.

Come on, Goldfinch.

I keep my body loose but poised, readying for another hit from her. When she drops her hand, my eyes dart down to the gold, expecting it to come up for an attack.

Which is why I'm completely caught off guard when *she* launches at me instead. I go tense, just as her body slams against mine, forcing me to take a step back to keep myself upright.

It takes me exactly a heartbeat to realize that this is an entirely different sort of attack. She's not trying to hit me anymore. She's trying to *devour* me.

My lips part against the assault of her mouth on mine, and my hands come down to grip her thighs that wrap around my waist so I can hoist her up higher. This time, instead of pushing me away, she's got her hands in my hair, yanking me closer, demanding more. When my tongue slips against hers, she moans, this time not in pain or aggravation, but pure, hedonic thrill.

Fucking sexy.

When she nips my bottom lip hard enough to split it, I pull away, locking eyes with her challenging gaze. She tries to dive right back in to continue with our kiss, but I lift a hand up and thread it through her hair, yanking it firmly to hold her in place, but not enough to hurt. She growls in response, making me smirk.

"Come out to play, Goldfinch, and I'll kiss you all you like."

Her eyes flash with warning, and a moment later, she's on her feet and I'm pinned against the cave wall by her gold. It's not liquid enough to seep into my clothes, but it's firm enough to hold me in place. She stands in front of me with a look of pure victory on her face. I'm like an insect caught in the strands of a spider web.

"Very good," I praise.

She smirks in satisfaction, trailing a hand down my neck, streaks of gold smearing against me wherever she touches—like she's marking me, which my fae nature really fucking likes.

After she trails along the stubbed spikes above my eyebrows, she leans in and skims her mouth against my neck. I have to bite back a groan.

"Come out, Goldfinch."

A delicate, warm hand comes up to my cheek, and she turns my head to look at her.

"Come back, baby," I say softly before I reach out and cup her jaw, letting my thumb drag across her cheek. "Come back to me."

Something flickers in her eyes. Like flecks of shimmering light. Then, she blinks, and her expression suddenly morphs.

Sheer and complete relief pummels into me like a fist to my chest. "There you are."

Her breath catches. Her lips part, and I watch her eyes focus on me before she whispers, "*Slade.*"

"I'm here. You're here."

She gives herself time for one breath, and then she fuses her mouth against mine. Her hold on the magic seems to disintegrate in a blink, and it goes splashing to the ground, splattering us both.

But she doesn't even seem aware of it. She's too busy

trying to climb up my body, like she can't bear to have any distance between us. I let the spikes on my arms sink beneath my skin, but everything else in me comes flaring up. All the worry and dread is shed into the pooling gold at our feet as carnal heat takes their place.

Because she's awake. She's alive. She's warm and writhing and pressed against me.

Thank fuck.

Her lips yank away, just long enough for her to gulp in a breath. "I need..."

"What do you need, Auren?" I ask, letting my fang scratch against the pulse of her throat. Her hands cling to my neck, legs wrapped around me while I hold her ass, hands splayed and squeezing.

"You, please. I need it. I need it *now*."

Her hands drop to the strings of my pants, already loosening the ties. So different from our first time together when she was shy and unsure. But all thought leaves my head when her hand darts inside and she grips my length.

"*Fuck.*"

She strokes me up and down, frantic and fast, like she's desperate for me, desperate for escape. "I need you to make me feel."

Her touch makes my balls tighten, and all I can think of is sinking into her and giving her exactly what she needs.

I put her down on her feet, making gold splash up around us.

"What are you doing?" she growls out in protest.

I grip her jaw, tilting her head up to look at me. Without saying a word of warning, I reach with my other hand and shove her leggings past her feet, her borrowed shirt barely covering her from my gaze.

She gasps, but when I cup her pussy, the sound turns into a moan. "Please..."

"You're begging, baby."

"I know!" she shouts out, head lolling back when I swipe my thumb over her clit.

I lean forward and lick a line up the curve of her neck, making her shudder. "I like it."

Hands at her ass, I pull her up again, and the feel of her bare heat against my length makes me grit my teeth in pleasure.

"Rub yourself over me," I command. "Get that slick pussy all over my cock."

Wetness drips from her as she does exactly as I say, her hips rocking over me and coating me in her juices. "That's it," I purr. "Just like that..."

"Slade..."

The pitch of her voice seems to shoot directly to my cock, and I can't wait a second more to sink into her waiting heat. I shift my hips and she reaches down between us, lining me up with her entrance.

I hold still, staring into her eyes while she trembles over me.

"Hurry," she pleads.

I punch my hips forward and thrust into her, sinking all the way to the hilt.

Auren's body latches onto me inside and out, hands digging into my neck, her inner walls clamped down tight.

Squeezing her ass, I lift her up and then bring her back down with a forceful grind, tearing a cry of bliss from her throat.

"Is this what you needed, Auren?" I say as I lift her before bringing her back down once again. My arms flex with every move, my spikes wanting to punch right back through my skin.

"Harder."

Her breathless appeal tips over my restraint, and there's nothing I want more than to oblige. I start slamming her down onto my cock so hard that her entire body tightens up, letting me have her completely at my mercy.

"Harder," she cries, just as her head falls to my shoulder. Her blunt teeth bite into my skin and make my cock swell impossibly larger.

I go harder, faster, driving into her with carnal fervency.

"Harder," she says again. And again. And again.

And *again*.

I jerk my head back, seeing sweat slick her face, her lips parted in quickened pants.

But I also see an edge of something else in the depths of her wild eyes. Something that makes me pause.

"No! Keep going," she says, fingernails clawing at my neck and yanking my hair. "Go harder. So hard it hurts. I need to hurt."

My hips stop punching up, my hands pausing on their lift. I raise a hand and fist her hair, tugging her face to the side. She hisses out a breath that turns into a groan.

"You need this?" I say, pinning my hips against hers,

keeping my fingers threaded through her hair so she will look me in the eye. "Need to be punished?"

Her throat bobs, and I see a flicker of something in her gilded depths. "Yes..."

I thrust into her in a slow drag that makes her eyes roll back.

"Well, guess what?" I say, bringing her lips close enough to mine that I can sip in her exhales. "You don't deserve punishment, Auren."

She goes stiff in my arms, eyes widening.

"I see you." I start fucking into her slow and steady, just as I slowly release her hair and instead bring my hand between us to stroke her clit. "You need an escape? You need me to make you feel good? I can fucking do that."

I punctuate my words with my fingers rubbing against her, making her shake, her teeth biting down on her glistening lip.

"Listen to me," I command, making her watery eyes latch onto mine. "You don't deserve punishment for *anything*. You deserve *reward*." A sob churns out of her, and I don't need her to say a thing, because I see it all there in her eyes. "I will drive myself so far into you all you'll feel is pleasure for how fucking glorious you are as you burn for me. But there will be no punishment."

A golden tear drops from her lid and falls on my chest, soaking into the fabric of my shirt.

Before she can let out a protest, I sit us down on the ground. I lie beneath her, my cock notched so deep inside her that she lets out a whimper. But from this angle, she can be in charge. "I'm going to thumb your clit and make you scream, proving to you that you're a goddess who takes her pleasure because *that* is what you deserve," I growl out. "Now ride me."

Her palms press against my chest, and with an angry glare, she starts lifting her body and then slamming back down on me hard and fast, her pace relentless, her expression determined. But all the while, I just stroke her clit with slow, smooth movements, circling her nerves and waiting.

Waiting.

Another frustrated tear slips down her cheek, and she looks down at me with anger burnishing her cheeks. "Fuck me," she says.

"I will," I tell her. "As soon as it's about your pleasure and not your punishment."

She slaps her hands down on my chest hard. "I need to be punished!" she snarls, chest heaving, aura flaring.

"Why."

It's not a question, it's a demand.

Her expression falters. "Because I...I..."

I sit up fast enough that she sucks in a shocked breath, my cock angling deep. "I'll tell you what you did. You finally broke free and you *conquered*."

She stares at me like I'm her lifeline. Like I'm her only hope of not being torn to shreds. But I will always ground her. I will always remind her of who she is.

Because I see her. I always fucking have.

I wrap my hand around her throat, my other hand still stroking her clit, slipping through the wet desire she's gushing. I make my grip *just* tight enough to cause the slightest restraint to her breaths. The moment I do, her chest heaves faster, more moisture slicking from her pussy, pupils blowing wide. "The only thing I would ever punish you for is the way you tried to give up on me."

Her pulse slams against her veins, and she lets out a small, shaky noise. I tighten my grip and thrust my hips up into her, making her shudder and moan.

"You'll never give up like that again, will you, baby? You'll never let your power overwhelm you." I thrust again, hips snapping up and making her gasp out my name. "You're going to remember who you are and how fucking powerful you are, and you will not—ever—fucking—give—in— again." Every word is a thrust, every letter a faster stroke over her clit.

"Say it," I demand, my growl vibrating against her ear. I want to consume her. Bury myself so far into her that she will feel me forever, sear my words into her thoughts.

"I won't ever give in again," she cries. "Slade, *please*."

Bliss to my ears.

My fingers rub over her clit, my speed a blur. My hips punch up again and again, making her mouth drop open in a scream that echoes through the cave.

"Come, baby. Take your pleasure on my cock and fucking *flood* me with it."

Her orgasm seems to implode.

I feel her body clamp down on my cock, and my thrusts stutter. She calls out my name, shaking all over, her pussy surging with wet heat that sends me right over the edge with her. "*Good fucking girl.*"

I come so hard I'm surprised I don't black out, spilling hot jets of cum deep inside of her, marking her as mine. But I don't take my hand off her clit until I wrench the very last wave of pleasure from her singing body, not until she slumps against my chest, shaking from the aftershocks.

Only then do I move my hand and start to stroke her arm instead. Slowly, gently, fingertips grazing up and down. We stay sitting there for several long moments, and I don't rush her. I don't push. My cock has no complaints, and neither do I. I wish we could stay in this cave, I wish I could keep her safe in my lap. But despite my wishes, reality comes trickling in.

Her pliant warmth turns stiff, her mind racing fast enough that I can hear it whirring. I watch as her head lifts from my shoulder, eyes flicking around, taking in the dark cave, seeing the swill of gold still puddled on the floor just a foot away.

"Slade..." she says, but this time, it isn't with the plea of pleasure. It's a call of *fear*.

"You're okay, Auren," I say, but she's already scrambling off me, yanking up her discarded leggings from the floor.

I get to my feet and pull up my pants, tying up the laces as I watch her circling around, her eyes wild as she takes in the cave, her fingers spearing into her hair as she shakes her head. I don't know if it's the shock of taking in this unfamiliar place, but the pain in her eyes as reality comes crashing down around her makes me want to roar, want to *protect*.

She stumbles on her feet, eyes wide, hand snapping up to grab her throat, right over the subtle slice of a scar. She's staring at the gold on the floor like it's utter demise looking back at her. When the gold starts to move, starts to come closer to her, she flinches back with a cry. "*No, no, no, no, no!*"

"Auren."

Panic has set in, her head shaking nonstop. For the first time since she woke, worry creeps up the back of my neck. Before, when she was attacking me, I had complete confidence that she would snap out of that state and come back to me, had complete confidence that she was in control of her magic.

But now...

Her breathing starts to go quick and hollow, like no matter how much she inhales, she can't get enough air.

"Auren, look at me."

She spins in place, looking around wildly. "I don't... Where am I? I can't let the gold go. I need it away from me! I need it to *stop*!"

I stride forward, but the sound of my boots splashing through the melted gold makes her flinch. "It's okay," I start to tell her, but she isn't hearing me.

"What did I *do*, Slade?" Her arm grazes the cave wall, making the gold splatter there stick like syrup against her sleeve. She wrenches back from it, cowering with a full-body tremble. "Oh goddess," she breathes, a hand clamping over her mouth in horror. "What did I do?" The question is a shaken whisper. A cornered recognition with its hindlegs backed against a wall.

Sidestepping, I slip in front of her, gripping her by the arms. "Look at me." She tries to jerk away, but I keep my grip firm. "Auren, *look* at me."

Her gaze snaps to mine, her pupils blown with fear, the pulse in her neck racing. "What did I do..."

"Breathe with me."

I take in a deep breath, pursing my lips slightly to blow it back out. I do this again and again until she starts to mimic me. At first, her breaths are still too quick, her eyes too wild, but slowly, her breathing calms down enough that she's no longer hyperventilating.

As her panic ebbs, her gold no longer dollops with movement. I can tell the moment she severs her hold over it, because it no longer seems alive. Instead, it's just liquid left to dry on the floor.

"That's good," I soothe, running my hands up and down her arms. "You're doing so good. Keep breathing."

She lets out a shuddering breath, watery eyes lifting to mine like she's seeing me for the first time. "Slade."

"I'm here, baby."

My chest has gone tight. I'm so overjoyed that she's awake, that she's herself, but I don't want her to feel fear, to feel despair.

Her gaze drifts to the gold splatters along the cave walls, to the pool of it solidifying on the floor. "Great Divine."

I watch it—the memories—as they seem to fall into place one after the other. There's a whole host of expressions that cross her face, but all I can do is brace myself, waiting for the onslaught. Of blame. Of hate. Of guilt.

I think that's what will cut me deepest. Not her blaming me or even hating me for rotting her—I deserve that.

But the guilt? Her feeling guilt over killing Midas, now *that* will kill me.

I don't know how many seconds pass as her mind recalls

what transpired, but finally, her eyes hook back onto mine, and my heart nearly drops down through my feet at the tears gathered in them.

"How?" she whispers. "I felt my power leave me when the sun set. That shouldn't have been possible, but I—" Her words choke off. "There was something inside of me that just snapped open."

"And it was fucking *glorious*."

She flinches. "How can you say that?" she asks, her voice cracking. "I became a *monster*."

But I shake my head, brush my thumbs over her wet cheeks. "No, baby. Not a monster. A *fae*."

CHAPTER 14

AUREN

F *ae.*

The moment he says the word, I know it's true. I know that's what this beast inside my chest is, the one that even now, lies in wait, talons gripping the rungs of my ribs.

I look around the shadowed space of the strange cave, and that grip tightens. Gold is splashed everywhere in messy blotches, most of it congealed in puddles around the ground. When I look at it, all I can think of is how the fae in me took over. How it tore through me, hooking onto the reins of control, yanking them right out of my hands.

And with it...

Great Divine, the *noises.*

Every glint of gold in the cave is a glint in the castle as it shuddered and spread. Every reflection gleaming back at me is me seeing this wild version of myself tearing through people, killing them with merciless sweeps.

There were so many sounds of splashing and crashing, but mostly, what rings in my ears are the screams.

There has only been one other time when my gold acted like that. One other, and I swore to myself it would never happen again.

But it did.

When I back up a step, my heel soaks into the gluey liquid, and I jerk away from it with a flinch. It tries to creep up my leg, tries to come alive again and react to my emotions and movements, but I kick it away. Fisted hands shaking, I slam up my walls, cutting off the gold. Cutting off the fae beast. Shutting it all away so that those things can't overtake me again.

I won't let it.

A shudder goes through me, and I feel incredibly heavy all of a sudden, as if those walls I just erected inside my chest are weighing me down, pressing against my bones and cementing through my feet.

"Auren?"

Turning, I look at him with all that cumbersome weight straining my gaze. "Where are my gloves?" I ask. "I need to cover my hands."

He hesitates and then slips off his own gloves, striding over to hand them to me. I can't help but grimace when I see how stained they are or when I hear the squelching sound beneath his boots when he steps in one of the hardening puddles.

"Thank you," I murmur.

I can't quite look at him. I'm too embarrassed by the way I jumped him, for how I admitted that I wanted to be punished for the things that I did. I basically just used him so I didn't have to think, so I could feel pain for the pain I subjected on others.

"Auren," he says firmly, and despite how heavy my eyes are, they rise up. "Nothing about what we just did is anything shameful. You don't need to feel embarrassed."

I scoff, shaking my head as I pull on his gloves, feeling slightly better at having my hands covered.

"It's true," he says firmly, his eyes pulling me in. "You're *fae,* just like me, which means we're going to have wild, raving urges. Like fighting and fucking. Those two go hand in hand."

My cheeks heat at his bluntness, and then I go hot all over when he carefully slips a hand to the back of my neck. His hair is disheveled from my fingers spearing through it, some of the strands stained with streaks of gold, even more of it dragged down his cheeks and gleaming on his lips. Something in me wants to purr at seeing all my marks on him like that.

"It's completely natural," he goes on, his voice rumbling through me with decadent heat. "And I, for one, fucking love it when I see more of your fae nature coming out."

I let out a shaky smile. "I must not be *that* fae, considering these," I say, tapping against the rounded tips of my ears.

"I have them too," Slade points out, and as if to prove his point, his body shifts. His spikes absorb back beneath his skin, stealing away the wisps of his aura and the shine of scales along his cheek. When his eyes are green once more and his ears no longer pointed, he taps against them. "Though, mine are rounded in this form because I'm only half fae."

"You are?" I ask in surprise. "Maybe I'm only half fae too. I don't remember my parents well enough to know."

"Could be."

I'm relieved that we're off the other subject, but now that reality is settling in, there are about a hundred *other* subjects cropping up in my mind. Subjects I don't want to think about yet. I wrap my arms around myself, suddenly feeling incredibly tired.

The second he notices me shiver, Slade takes me by the hand. "Let's get you back to the Grotto where you can rest."

I don't even have the energy to ask what the Grotto is. I simply let him scoop me up in some gold-stained blankets that he insists on wrapping me in. Once he's satisfied that I'm bundled up, he carries me out of the cave, where we're blasted with a snowstorm.

My spirit sinks a little at the cold, shriveling away from the drab, frigid sky. Without the shelter of the cave, the howling wind that I'd underestimated whips through us so hard that I'm surprised Slade doesn't get knocked over.

Night seems to have fallen, and it's spun with flakes of snow that whip around us. This is no soft and silent snowfall by any means. Fortunately, he has me so bundled up that only part of my face is out in the open. Even still, I feel frozen through within a minute of being outside.

Yet even in these less than ideal conditions, I find myself being lulled into an almost-sleep. With Slade's arms around me and the steady gait of his walk, I burrow closer to him, a sigh passing through my lips as I close my eyes and turn off all my thoughts, turn off all my memories.

Because I don't want to think of those. I don't want to face them.

Not yet.

For now, I just want to feel his arms around me and ignore everything else.

I must doze off more than I really intended to though, because I'm roused again by the sound of voices. Instantly, I can tell that I'm no longer outside in the cold, because there's a warmth that surrounds me, and the sound of the wind is gone.

"...let her sleep. It's late." That's Slade's voice. I realize even though we're now inside and he isn't carrying me through a blizzard, he's still holding me. Like he doesn't want to let me go.

My heart breaks a little at that.

I hear someone else scoff. "I don't care if it's late, she needs to eat. She's been sleeping for four days. She's done. Gildy Locks, you're done. Wake up!"

My eyelids flutter open when I recognize Lu's voice, and I blink up at a smooth wooden ceiling before my gaze shifts to Slade's face. He sighs when he sees I'm awake.

"Did that work?" Lu asks a second before her face appears above me.

"Of course it worked, it's not like you were quiet about it," he replies.

She grins when I glance up at her. "There you are. Stop being lazy."

Slade makes a noise of warning, but I feel my lips tugging up into a smile.

"I'm in a house with five damn men, and they're driving me nuts," she tells me. "I need someone to commiserate with."

"Gildy should commiserate with *me*," I hear Judd cut in from somewhere across the room. "You've been mean."

Lu spins around. "Beating your ass at cards every night doesn't make me mean. It makes me superior."

"Yeah, but stealing the wine *does* make you mean."

She sniffs. "I don't know what you're talking about."

With Slade's help, I sit up, but he keeps me tucked against his lap on the oversized chair.

I look around curiously, taking in the unfamiliar space. It's dark, save for a brick fireplace with a raised hearth that's putting off a glow from the healthy fire. Not counting the exposed chimney, the rest of the walls in here are paneled wood, their color rich and polished. Aside from the forest green chair we're currently sitting in, there's a matching sofa to our right and another chair across from us. In the center of them all sits a wooden table with a thick white fur rug beneath it.

All in all, the space feels cozy. There are little touches too, like the coats hanging on hooks on a stand near the fireplace, the five pairs of boots lined up beside the hearth. There's a savory scent coming from the open doorway that leads to a kitchen, and when I crane my head around, I can see what looks to be the front entryway door. This place has a homey sense, and I automatically relax when I note that it's only Judd and Lu in the room with Slade and me.

When I turn my head back to Lu, my eye catches on the single window across from me. Frowning, I cock my head as I peer out. At first, I think the haze of blue must be the stars—though I've never seen them look like that. But the longer I study it, I realize that's not right. I can see close shadows nearby, like maybe there's a house with that strange lighting next door, but that doesn't quite match up with what I'm seeing either.

"Where are we?" My voice comes out slightly cracked. Beside me, Slade keeps one hand loosely at my hip, his thumb slowly stroking over the fabric of my clothes as my side rests against his chest.

"Welcome to the Grotto," Judd says with a wave of his arm from his spot on the sofa to my right. Lu walks back to the sofa next to him, curling her feet beneath her, though I don't know how she manages to do that considering she's wearing gigantic slippers on her feet.

"What's the Grotto?"

Lu and Judd look to Slade, as if they don't know how to answer. I thought this would be an easy question, but considering the hesitation that's settled in the room, I guess I was wrong. The first drip of anxiety filters into my stomach, which is the last thing I want. Turning my head, I look up at Slade.

I finally get a chance to get a really good look at him, and what I see makes even more of those worried droplets fall down. He has circles under his eyes, and his five o'clock shadow has turned into the start of a thick beard. There's tension held at his brow that he can't hide from me, and he's still wearing his wrinkled, gold-splotched clothes.

His eyes soften as he watches me. "The Grotto is our home in Drollard Village."

"Okay...and where's Drollard Village? Are we still in Fifth Kingdom?"

Judd grins and chucks his hands behind his head as he stretches his legs out in front of him. "That's an interesting question. See, because it *was* Fifth Kingdom, but now it's not.

And technically, Drollard Village doesn't exist. Neither do the people who live here."

My mind swims. "Um. What?"

Slade shoots him an impatient look before turning his attention back onto me. "We'll explain all of that later. How are you feeling?"

That's not what I want to talk about. Not at all.

Ignoring his question, I shove the blankets that are still wrapped around me. Now that I'm awake, it's sweltering under all these layers. When Slade loosens his hold enough for me to do that, I take the opportunity to stand. My bare feet sink into the soft fur rug as I pad across the room to the window. I look out, squinting at the swirl of glowing blue. "What is that? It's almost like we're—"

"In a house built inside a cave? Yep, we are," Lu tells me.

"And it glows," Judd pipes in.

My brows lift up in surprise. "Wow. It's pretty."

"Auren?" Slade calls my name tentatively, but it makes the skin around my eyes go tight.

Instead of answering him, I look back to Judd. He seems like a safe bet. "What kinds of card games have you been playing?"

I can tell that he sees right through me, especially when his eyes dart over to Slade for a split second before he answers me. Still, he plays along. "Oh, you don't want to know, Gildy. Lu cheats."

"I do not!" she says with outrage. "It's not my fault you can't hold your wine while we're playing, and you make awful bets."

He rolls his eyes. "See? Mean."

A little laugh escapes me, but that quickly gets washed away when I hear, "Auren."

I paste on a smile and turn to face Slade, but my stomach churns when he slowly stands up. "Yes?"

"I asked how you're feeling," he says carefully, his eyes the color of summer grasslands.

I can feel Judd and Lu staring at me, and my face goes hot. "I'm fine."

Seconds go by. Time's pendulum swings like a spectator, eyes ticking from Slade to me as we watch each other.

He wants to talk. I can see the agonized words held back in his mouth. I can see the emotions he's ready to face. But when I snapped back into consciousness in that other cave, those very emotions were too consuming. The memories too raw. I didn't shove up walls only for my gold and my fae nature. I barricaded everything else too.

"I'm not ready."

My lips are protective over that truth, pursing together defensively as soon as I've said it. I'm not ready. I can't go there. Because if I go there, then I'll have to think and process and feel. I don't want to feel yet. The clock can count down all it wants, but I'm still not going to give in.

It's apparent that Slade doesn't want to give in either, but I get saved from whatever response he was going to say when a man walks in through the front door. A man who looks just like Slade.

Fake Rip.

CHAPTER 15

AUREN

It's only the second time I've seen him without the concealing armor and helmet he always wore when he pretended to be Rip. It's a bit jarring. He looks so much like Slade that I can't help but stare, trying to pick out the small discrepancies.

He comes in carrying a wooden crate that looks to be overflowing with sacks, bottles, and root vegetables poking out of the top. He stops just inside the room, taking in the silence before his eyes land on me. "Good to see you without the puddle underneath you."

I blink.

Did he just say I peed myself?

I look around to see if Judd is smirking. He seems like he'd laugh if I'd peed myself. Only, there's no smile to be found. Hopefully that's a good sign.

"Excuse me?" I ask.

"Your gold," he says slowly. "When you started to come to, it was leaking out of you all over the place."

Oh.

An awkwardness descends, because I have to go from possibly peeing myself to realizing that he's talking about my power so openly. The fact that he just casually mentioned seeing gold stream out of me is more than a little disconcerting, and I can't quite wrap my head around this new version of normalcy. It's become second nature for me to hide my power, to hide from touch, so this feels almost...wrong.

"Sorry about that," I say awkwardly. Then I squirm on my feet. "Umm, since we're on the topic, where's the washroom?"

He frowns. "We were on that topic?"

I feel heat flood my cheeks. "Oh. Nope. No, we weren't," I blurt before I look over to Lu, hoping she'll take pity on me. "Washroom?"

"Come on, Gildy," she says, unfolding herself to lead me out of the room. Her slippers really are very large and furry. I'm surprised she's still so light of foot with those on.

I follow her as she takes me to a door down the hall. "This is my room, the washroom is right through there, and grab some clean clothes from my closet too—I set a pile aside for you."

With a nod of thanks, I quickly go inside, do my business, and wash up as best I can. Then I take off my ruined, gold-splotched clothes, feeling like they dried with paint splattered all over them. Though as soon as I drag the shirt off my back, I freeze at a sharp stab of pain that shoots down my spine.

I stop.

Suck in a breath.

And I slam walls up so fast that I make my own mind spin. I'm not going there. I'm *not*.

With determination as strong as steel, I carefully pick up an oversized shirt and slip it on and then drag on a new pair of leggings. All while I breathe through braced lungs, fortifying my mental walls.

With one last breath, I force myself to unclench my teeth, to relax my arms at my sides. When I've secured myself, I head out, going back into the main living room. As soon as I do, everyone's murmured voices go quiet as they all turn to me.

"Better?" Lu asks from her spot on the sofa next to Judd.

"Much," I reply, hovering in the doorway. Everyone in the room is stilted in silence, and I don't miss the way they keep shooting questioning looks at Slade.

"Okay..." his brother drawls out, shifting on his feet before he glances at the others. "Well. Like I was saying, I went to the Cellar for supplies because I know none of you had dinner. But it's not my turn to cook, so one of you assholes can do it this time."

Judd gets up from the sofa to take over the duty, but I rush forward, beating him to it. "I'll do it!"

Everyone looks at me, but I pretend not to see as I head for the open doorway.

"I didn't mean you," Fake Rip says.

"I'm hungry, and I want to help," I call over my shoulder.

"Auren..." Slade begins, but I sidestep him before he can reach for me.

As soon as I pass into the kitchen, I hear quiet murmurings behind me, but I ignore them and instead look around the space. It's just as homey as the living room, except instead of wood paneling, smooth white walls make up three sides, and then the fourth is made up of the same brick as the fireplace. It's here at the brick wall that an iron stove sits, its grate glowing slightly from embers within and a stovetop just above it. There's a round black table with curved benches tucked beneath it off to the right, and the rest of the walls have hanging shelves along their length stuffed full of cookware, with wooden countertops just below.

After a few more seconds, I hear footsteps, and I turn as Slade's brother comes inside. He heads for a small door just past the dining table, which I'm guessing is the pantry, where he sets down the crate. I hear him rummaging around before he reappears a few seconds later.

We stand facing each other awkwardly before he says, "I guess I never got the chance to properly introduce myself. I'm Ryatt. Nice to formally meet you." He reaches up to scratch the back of his head full of black hair. It's the same as Slade's.

"You two really do look alike," I blurt out.

He snorts. "Yeah, I've heard that a time or two."

I think there might be an edge of bitterness to his reply, but I don't know him well enough to be certain.

"I'll just get to work on making dinner," I say before I move toward the pantry. It's bigger than I thought, with cabinets against the bottom and shelves lining above them. There are all kinds of ingredients stuffed in bottles and sacks, and what looks to be strips of jerky hanging on a drying rack.

I circle the room, trying to come up with an idea for something I could make. But then I remember that I don't actually know how to make anything.

"Dammit," I murmur under my breath. I was in such a hurry to escape conversation that I didn't really think about the follow-through. But how hard could it be?

Squinting at the labels on the different containers, I finally find rice and dried peas, along with some eggs. That's a good meal, right?

Right.

I grab the ingredients and head out, but when I eye a bottle of wine on the cabinet just in front of the door, I swipe that too.

I'm going to need it.

Once I come back into the kitchen, Ryatt is gone, and I let out a breath of relief that I can just have a moment alone. A moment where I don't have to pretend, don't have to talk.

Placing everything on the counter, I eye the spices on the shelves above, but none of them are labeled, and I don't recognize a single one.

"Want some help?"

I flinch at Judd's voice, pasting a smile back on my face before I turn around. "No, thank you. I've got it."

His hazel eyes watch me for a moment before he nods and ducks back out of the room. More murmurings erupt in the living room, and I can hear Slade's rumbling tone cutting through right before Lu's softer voice says, "Just give her some time."

Yes. Time. That's exactly what I need. The more time I can have, the better.

I spend the next hour running around the kitchen, trying to make something edible.

It's not going well.

Bright side though, the wine is fantastic. Not only does it taste great, but it's taking off the edge. And when I'm nothing but edges and sharp points, where one stray thought is all it would take to make me ram against one and burst, I could use a little dulling.

By the time I plop bowls down onto the table, the kitchen is filled with steam and smoke, and I'm a little drunk.

It's lovely.

"Dinner's ready!" I shout.

Everyone comes in. Quickly. As if they were all standing just outside the doorway. Everyone takes a seat except for Slade, who pulls out one of the benches for two and waits for me to sit.

Giving him a smile, I take a seat, and then he lowers himself next to me. Our thighs touch, which seems like such a silly thing to focus on, considering we've done much more intimate things than touch thighs, but my stomach flutters anyway.

"So," Judd says, rubbing his hands together in front of him. "What's on the menu?"

I reach over and pluck up the lid to the serving bowl with a smile. "Rice!"

All four sets of eyes stare down at the contents. After a moment of silence, Lu says, "Why is it green?"

"Oh, that's the peas. They sort of melted."

Stirring it with a spoon, it slops together, stickier than honey. I start scooping it up and serving a spoonful on everyone's plates, but when I try to give Ryatt a third heaping, he holds up a hand. "That's good."

With a nod, I uncover the half a dozen eggs next, but there's a bit of a smell.

Judd wrinkles his nose. "What kind of spices did you put in that?"

"I have no idea," I answer honestly before I spoon some onto his plate.

After I've served everybody, including myself, I lift my fork but notice no one else has. As soon as they see me looking around expectantly, Slade clears his throat pointedly. Everyone picks up their forks very quickly after that. Then, with Slade being the first, they each scoop up some rice and take a bite.

Smiling, I follow suit.

Regret. Instant, immediate, firm—*nope, mushy*—mushy regret.

"Oh goddess," I say around a huge bite of the sticky slush, because it's bad. Really bad.

It doesn't really resemble rice. It's more like overcooked porridge. The spices I put in it are at war with each other, and somehow, there are parts that are absolutely boiling hot, and others that are stone cold, with little stiff grains that seem like they weren't boiled at all. Somehow, I manage to swallow down the bite.

Honestly, the green color was the least of our worries.

Embarrassment floods my cheeks as the others all make faces. "It's bad," I say.

"It's *really*—" Ryatt jolts mid-sentence, and he scowls across the table at Slade. "Good," he finishes before looking at me. "It's really good."

"Really?"

Judd and Lu nod their heads in unison, but I notice they're still chewing.

Beside me, Slade swallows. It's a testament to how sticky the slop really is, because I can hear the struggle of his throat to get it down.

"Try the eggs?" I say helpfully.

"Mm-hmm," he replies, and everyone watches him scoop up a giant spoonful and stuff it into his mouth, their eyes widening slightly like he's doing some amazing feat.

I let out a sigh and set my fork down. "Okay, you can all stop pretending for my sake."

"Thank fuck," Judd says, just as he spits out his bite into the cloth napkin at his place setting. "My tongue is so confused right now."

Lu smirks. "I've heard women give you that very same critique."

Judd tosses his napkin at her, but she somehow bats it away with her fork before it can land on her.

I clear my throat. "I should probably confess that I don't actually know how to cook…"

Ryatt snorts. "You think?"

"Right. Who wants wine?"

Everyone speaks up immediately, and I rush up to go

grab the wine bottle from the kitchen counter when I feel my back twinge painfully.

I freeze.

My breath hitches.

And agony, glowing and hot, pours down my thoughts and scalds its way down my back.

This hurts me a lot more than it hurts you.

You caused this.

You did this to yourself.

I can't I can't I can't

Goddess, please...

My eyes squeeze shut as I force myself to breathe through the pain. I won't think of it. I won't. I slam up another wall. Barricading it high, blocking every bit of misery notched in my back.

"Auren?" Slade asks quietly.

I snap my eyes open, realizing that I've halted with only one leg slung over the bench, so I paste that awful smile back on my face. "Stubbed my toe," I lie before I swing my other leg over—carefully this time—and move to the counter.

With my back toward the table, I let out a shaky breath, thankful that no one can see my face. The pain twinges and prods, like it's trying to fish through the very depths of me, but that's exactly the last place I want to feel.

I give myself one more strained breath before I turn back around, bottle in hand. Somehow, Lu has already brought cups to the table, setting the last two down in front of her and Judd as I unstop the cork and start to pour. It's not nearly enough for all of us, especially since I helped myself earlier, but it's something.

Yet even with the distraction of the food, my careful mood is threatening to tip. I'm up on the point of a blade, trying not to fall and cut myself open, but I know I can't keep upright forever, no matter how stiffly I sit at this table.

Beside me, Slade is tense too, and the others are watching me, though they try not to be obvious about it. I grab my cup, holding it tightly, staring at the deep red color.

"Auren."

"Not tonight," I say without looking at him as I take a drink.

I'm not ready. I need more time. Not tonight.

I hold those words against my chest like a beggar's coins, clutching at them because I know they'll offer me the tiniest reprieve for a little while, until I'm empty-handed once again. "Tonight, I just want this."

When I glance back up at the now quiet table, no one is pretending not to look at me, and I hold my breath with anxiousness until Judd jumps up. "Well, alright then," he says with a nod. "We're going to need more wine."

He lopes over to the pantry and comes out carrying two more bottles along with some bread and jam he found. "Something a bit more edible," he says with a wink as he sets everything down.

I let out a shaky laugh, relaxing when they all start to drink and talk and eat, relaxing even more when I join in.

And for a while, that's all there is. That's all that matters. I clutch my words and stay balanced on the blade, and for now, it works. For now, I don't have to reflect or process or talk. I don't have to face anything real.

For now.

CHAPTER 16

AUREN

I *don't* wake up *so much as a hammer* slams against my skull so hard that it knocks me into consciousness against my will.

My breasts are smashed against the mattress from lying on my stomach, and I feel tickling fur on my cheek. Cracking open an eye isn't as painful as I anticipated though, because the room is blessedly dark. I suppose there are some perks to having a house inside of a cave.

I roll over, but the tug against my back makes a grimace pull at my lips and a pained groan slip free. That small noise in this quiet room seems to be amplified, and when I look up, my heart sinks.

Slade is sitting in a chair beside the bed, watching me.

There's a book on his lap, its pages fanned out like he wasn't really reading at all. His legs are spread before him, one elbow bent and leaning against the armrest, finger and thumb cocked against his jaw.

I sit up the rest of the way, forcing the grimace off of my face, though I immediately notice that nothing is gilded. Not the blankets, not the pillow, not my clothes. *Is it still night?*

"How long was I asleep?"

"I'm not certain," he tells me. "But you needed the rest to sleep off the wine. Plus, your body is still recovering from the power drain, among other things."

I let out a noncommittal noise because the "power drain" and "other things" are firmly in the *I'm not talking about this yet* territory.

"I was hoping you could show me the cave today," I tell him as I get to my feet and look around the room. The only light is coming from the low-burning fire and glowing blue just outside the window. "Are there any shoes I can borrow? Do you think Lu has anything?"

When he doesn't answer, I risk a glance at him, just to find that he's still watching me steadily, the greens of his eyes pitched in something heady and attentive. The silence of his study makes my skin crawl. Because somehow, despite not knowing him for long, he has always been able to sift beneath my surface and find truths I thought were long-buried.

"...Is that a no on the shoes?"

He carefully tosses the book on the floor and gets to his feet, and I find myself backing up a step. It's a knee-jerk reaction, because I don't want him to get closer. I don't want him to start to dig in my depths.

The second he sees me back up, he jerks to a stop and something unsettled flashes through his expression before he shutters it.

I hate that I'm standing here, putting distance between us. But distance is the footpath of avoidance, and it's the track I have to cling to for my own sanity.

Because if he gets close, he'll see the truth. He'll see how the ground at my feet is riddled with potholes and bumps. He'll see the stark fear in my trembling lip and the guilt in my eyes as I try to keep backing away. He'll see the reality of the destruction that surrounds me, while I desperately try not to trip. Distance is all I have between me and having to come to terms with the carnage that's piling up to my knees.

But leave it to Slade, because I swear, he can see this too.

"We need to talk."

Just four words from his lips, and heat presses against the backs of my eyes and makes my nose burn. Shoving them back, I shake my head at him, try to straighten my shoulders. But I can't. I can't, because it hurts, because—

"No."

The word wrenches out of a cinched throat, lashed from a whipping tongue.

His lips press together in a thin line, and I see the first peeks of his roots moving beneath the collar of his shirt.

"I want to go see the cave," I say, my voice stronger this time.

But what is the value of strength when it's just a facade?

After a long moment that stretches between us, Slade tips his head. "Alright, Goldfinch. I'll show you the cave."

Relief pilfers through the stack of my anxiety, stowing some of it away for later.

"I have some boots for you in my closet, so we'll need to go into my room first."

I look around in surprise. "This isn't your room?"

He shakes his head. "Your gold has taken up residence there for the time being, so we're staying in here."

My gold—what? But then the other part of his answer snags my attention. *We're staying in here. We.*

"You slept in here with me?"

To say I'm taken aback is putting it mildly. The idea that he would stay with me makes me feel oddly vulnerable.

He cocks his head. "Where else would I be if not with you?"

My breath catches, heart twisting.

"But the daytime…"

"I was up before dawn," he assures me, the shadows cast in the room making the sharp angles of his bearded jaw more pronounced. "Does that make you uncomfortable?"

I look down, eyes skating over the rough threads of the thick socks I have on my feet. They're not gilded either, and something uneasy tempers in my chest.

"No. Yes. I don't know."

My ears perk with the sound of him taking a single step forward. My body wants to sway toward him, to move with the force of his approach, because his nearness has *always* been a force of its own. One that's always held power over me.

I feel the heat of his body in front of me, the shadows cast from his body mingling with mine. "I claimed you that night in Ranhold," he tells me, his tone so full of unfaltering fire that it draws my gaze back up. Heat flushes my face, as if he really were ablaze, his words igniting the packed-down snow of my spirit. "And then you claimed me right back, in the middle of a ballroom for everyone to hear. Or don't you remember?"

Flashes.

A crowd of faces.

Lines of armored guards.

Cruel, angry eyes beneath a golden crown.

The heat of a body at my back.

And then my own clear, unshakable voice. *He's mine.*

It wasn't just a claiming, it was a *challenge*. As if I was ready to destroy anyone who tried to refute it or take him away from me.

Do I remember? Of course I do. I remember every single encounter with him. I walked off a pirate ship and fell at his feet in the snow, and ever since then, it's like I've just kept on falling.

"I want to go see the cave."

"You want to keep avoiding everything," he counters.

A barbed laugh scrapes past my lips. "And if I do? That's my prerogative. I have been controlled and owned for over twenty years of my life," I say, eyes flashing. "So if I want to avoid something and see a damned cave, then that's what I'm going to do."

The muscle in his jaw jumps, but he doesn't argue, doesn't try to talk me into anything else, and I'm grateful for that, because my head is pounding and my back is twinging, and I just need to get out.

Turning around, I head for the door, but right as I reach for the knob, I jerk to a stop, snatching my palm away in hesitation.

There's a moment's pause, but then Slade says, "It's nighttime."

Because he knows without me saying anything. He somehow understood my sudden spike of anxiety that I was going to gild the whole damn door.

I hesitate. "So, I only slept a few hours, or…?" My question is pregnant with pause, with another question that I'm not voicing yet.

"No, you slept the day away."

My eyes flick down to my black and brown clothes, and then I give a jerky nod.

Swallowing hard, I turn the knob and walk out in the hallway. It's just as dark as the bedroom was, the wood paneled walls broken up by sconces. They're made up of rough, clear crystals that seem like they were plucked from a mine and hung here, their basins full of oil to feed the flickering flames.

My shadow casts along the walls as I walk, but Slade's voice stops me. "You'll need those shoes, Auren."

Stopping, I turn around to see him heading in the opposite direction. He disappears into the last doorway in the hall, returning several seconds later with a pair of boots and a leather coat.

When he reaches me, I expect him to hand them both over. He doesn't.

My eyes go wide as he drops to one knee in front of me. I watch as he picks up my left foot and slips on the boot, lacing it up one row at a time. Each deft movement of his fingers has me entranced, and my heart beats so hard in my chest that I worry he'll feel the pulse all the way down my leg.

Setting my foot down, he picks up the other to do the same thing, his hand gripping my calf with steady surety. Heat bursts from the spot of his touch, and my skin tingles despite the layer of clothing between us.

Finished, he stands up, so close now that I can see every fleck in his eyes, from the dappling of a summer's lush green pasture to the onyx shadows lurking just behind it.

Without saying a word, he moves around me and, with excruciating gentleness, helps me into the coat. It's entirely too big, but it hangs loosely around my shoulders, the fabric warm without the oppressive weight.

I feel his breath against the side of my neck, his hands gently skimming the collar to make sure my skin is protected from the cold. He moves reverently, and it's these moments of surprising intimacy that burn into my heart.

I've always been treated *like* treasure, but with Slade, I'm simply treasured.

I bury my nose deeper into the coat so I can breathe in his scent that's covering it. The smell of damp earth and sunned bark, of the sweetness of chocolate charred by bitter richness.

Almost reluctantly, his hands drop away, and I feel more than hear him take a step back. "Ready?"

With a silent nod, I follow as he leads the way to the front door. The living room is empty, so we don't pass by anyone else, and then Slade pulls open the door, stepping aside for me to go first.

I look up as I take my first step out, mouth dropping open at the giant stalactites hanging from the ceiling. The cave itself is massive, so much bigger than I could've envisioned, with so many pockets and crevices and cracks that it would take years to map it all. But what's most enchanting of all are the veins of blue that run throughout the rock, like frozen waves of a glowing sea.

I pass beneath an archway of stalactites, their points wet with gathered water, the slick ground reflecting the cerulean fluorescence. It's almost hard to blink in a place like this, because I don't want to miss anything. My head swivels and my body turns, and I keep myself as quiet as I can, because the cave seems so ancient and apart—a hallowed wonder in the middle of a village that shouldn't exist.

"It's beautiful," I whisper.

Soundlessly, Slade comes up to stand beside me, though I don't move my craned neck. "What the Grotto lacks in daylight, it makes up for tenfold with this."

Nodding in agreement, I let my lungs wash through the air that somehow feels both fresh and timeworn. "It's peaceful."

I'm not sure how long Slade walks around with me, but I eat up every moment of it. Everything—from the darkness of the cave to the veins running through it, from the mysteriousness of the endless crevices to the stark reveal of each hanging point—reminds me of him. There is a depth here that feels fathomless and untouchable, and all I want to do is stay here beneath its shadowed glow.

But then Slade steps beneath one of the brightest fluorescent fissures in the cave, the underbelly of the mountain glowing so brilliantly that it lights up his face, illuminating his eyes.

"We need to talk, Goldfinch."

My chest instantly goes tight. "No."

I start to turn away, but he reaches out and grabs my hand, stopping me. "We have to speak about this."

I jerk my palm away. "I want to go back inside."

He shakes his head in frustration. "You want to cook dinner, you want to see the cave, you want to go back inside... you can't keep running from this, Auren."

"I'm not running."

"You are, and you're stronger than this," he says firmly, the dark green of his eyes hidden beneath the illuminating blue.

"Oh, so you think I'm being weak, now?"

He runs a hand down his face. "No, that's not what I'm saying, but I—"

"I'm not talking about it yet."

His jaw muscle jumps. "Yes. We are."

My anger is so thick I can taste it burning on the back of my tongue. "Go ahead and talk then, but I'm going inside." I turn on my heel and start to walk away, tossing my next words over my shoulder. "You can think I'm a coward all you want, but I'm not going to stand here and talk about how thoroughly I fucked up."

I can't.

Not yet.

Already my body is shaking, but not from anger—from fear. Fear to face what I did, fear over how spectacularly I lost control. It's like getting black-out drunk and having no recollection of what you did except for jumpy fragments that pop up unwanted, none of the memories good.

"You didn't fuck up," Slade calls behind me. "I did."

I whirl around, stopping just beneath the tail-end of the mountain's blue vein. "If you're going to try to make some male chauvinistic claim that everything I did was really somehow *your* doing, then you can save it, because that was all me. I don't care if you're trying to say that to be noble or because you think it will help assuage my guilt, but—"

He gives me a tortured look and bites out, "I fucking *rotted you*, okay?"

His words don't just cut me off—they splice right down my middle, making me sway. My mouth opens and closes as I try to come to terms with what he just said.

"What?"

He stalks forward, booted steps echoing on the rock, while cold air presses up against my back like a frigid bystander. When he's right in front of me again, one side of his face is lit up with blue, the other cast into shadows.

"I rotted you," he repeats, but hearing it again doesn't help. "What do you remember?"

My brows pull together and I shake my head, glancing away, eyes locked on the rifts in the cave. "I..."

What *do* I remember? It's hard to tell since I've been actively trying not to.

I remember I snapped. I remember that this depth of pure, unmitigated *power* suddenly coursed through me. I remember killing. It was so easy—I think that's what gets me the most. That, and this sense that I wasn't wholly *me*. There was a beast inside me, famished and furious, ready to devour the world.

But before I could go on that rampage, someone stepped in front of me.

I see it now, flashes of fragments, like torn bits of paper held briefly under the candlelight. The way he begged me to let the power go, the chokehold that terror had on me.

I couldn't do it. I couldn't, because without the beast to control the magic, I was incapable. I didn't know how to stop it. All I could do was hold onto the reins, hoping Slade could get out before it snapped. But of course, he didn't. Of course he refused to leave me.

The ashen kiss he placed against my gilded lips was all I felt before an invasive breeze slipped down my throat. And then a whisper, echoing in my ear, *Forgive me.*

My eyes flick back to Slade, and he must sense that I'm remembering, because he nods.

"You rotted me?"

Images spring up in my head, none of them pleasant. Rotten corpses of soldiers left at Sixth Kingdom's border, their bodies puffed up and reeking in the snow. Then, Midas's guards barring me from getting out of the room, Slade coming in and rotting them where they stood until their faces went sunken and hearts decayed. And another, of him walking toward Ranhold, leaving roots of rot in every step's wake, poisoning the snowy ground.

Was I like one of those sunken-in corpses? Lips peeling back, organs decayed into husks? I look down at my skin, as if I'm going to see evidence, but everything looks normal.

"The rot wasn't visible like that," he tells me, once again so in tune with my train of thought that he seems to always anticipate what I'm thinking.

His expression turns agonized. "You were...dying." The

words choke out, his shoulders bent with blame. "I didn't fucking know what to do, but I couldn't just stand there and let you drain yourself. So I used my power against you."

I let his words settle in, slowly shaking my head. "No. You used your power *on* me, not against me. Because you're right, I was dying."

He flinches—so subtly that I barely catch it. "I... You're not angry?"

A frown plants itself between my brows. "Why would I be angry?"

Now he looks positively bewildered. "I fucking *rotted* you, Auren. Stole into your body and shut it down, putting you in a stasis of spoiled decay."

My nose wrinkles. "Well, I could do without the visual of *stasis of spoiled decay*," I mutter.

"I risked your life," he goes on, and I realize these are the words that have been running through his head since the moment he used his magic on me, that he's been tormenting himself with self-proclaimed blame. "I used my power against you, and then I kept you like that when I took you and got you as far away from your gold as I could, risking your life *again* with every minute that I waited." He pulls at his hair in frustration, glancing around the darkness like he's looking into the crevices of his own guilt. "What if I'd waited too long? What if I hadn't been able to reverse it?"

"You've been hating yourself this whole time." It's not a question—I can see the truth plainly, can hear it in the way he's talking. Gently, I take his hand in mine, squeezing his fingers. "You saved me," I say quietly, and he looks at me like he's desperate to see me, like he can't bear to look away or else be swallowed by those shadows of fault.

He slumps slightly, head tilted up at the ceiling as he lets out a breath. "There's something else."

My stomach tightens. "What is it?"

He tips his head back down to look at me. "When I reversed the effects of the rot and removed my power from your body...a piece of it stayed behind."

A piece of it stayed behind.

My eyes widen, and my stomach gives an involuntary roll. "What do you mean it stayed?" I press a hand against my chest like I'm trying to feel it. "Are you sure?"

He gives a terse nod. "Positive. Even now, I can sense it, but it's rooted into you. No matter how many times I've tried, it won't come out."

Uneasiness shuffles down my spine, and I swallow hard. "Should I be worried?"

"No," he says with such decisive confidence that I'm not sure if it's actually true or if he's just willing it to be so. "I've checked you countless times, sometimes for hours on end, but the rot isn't doing anything harmful. It's just... there."

"Has this ever happened before?"

"Never."

I'm still pressing a hand to my sternum, so I let my hand drop. "You'll keep checking?" I ask, unable to keep the worry from my tone. "You'll tell me if anything changes?"

"I promise."

I nod slowly, trying to acclimate to this new fact, though

I have a feeling I won't be able to for a while. "I want to go inside now."

Slade looks like he wants to say something else, but he stops himself. "Okay, Goldfinch."

On near silent steps, I follow him back through the cave to the Grotto, passing by its stone walls, all the more appreciative of its shadowed haven. Of all its secret splits and nooks, because I feel like I have just as many crannies hidden in myself.

But even a haven stops being a refuge at some point.

So when we walk back inside and the door closes behind me, I shouldn't be surprised at the sudden chill that spreads over my skin. It's a warning that the first knot in the string I've been trying to ignore has been pulled out, and now, everything in me feels looser. Unsteady.

And I have a feeling that no matter how much I try to bunch it back up, all of me is going to come unbound anyway.

CHAPTER 17

AUREN

That chilled premonition doesn't take long to come into effect.

I barely have time to slip off the boots next to the fireplace when I hear someone come up behind me, and I automatically tense.

"Lady Auren."

I spin around, surprise making my eyebrows jump. "*Hojat?*"

The army mender is wearing borrowed clothes that are a bit too big on him, his brown hair longer than the last time I saw him. The dragged-down scarring of his eye seems more pronounced from the lighting of the fire, his skin mottled with red and white.

"It's good to see you awake," the mender says, wearing a soft, crooked smile. "How are you feeling?"

The answer is automatic. "I'm fine."

Hojat tuts as he comes over to me, giving Slade a nod in passing. "Come into the bedroom, please, so I can look you over."

Every muscle from my toes to my neck goes tense.

"No, thank you, really."

His burned mouth creases into a frown. "My lady, I understand it is sensitive, but this is for your health, and I must—"

"I said I'm *fine*." My hands go to the coat I'm wearing, pulling it tighter around me like a wraparound shield. Even to me, the *I'm fine* sounds like a collection of lies. A platitude of denial made up of heated stalling and forced ignoring.

Hojat's eyes flick over to Slade, and they seem to communicate something silently between them. A thick hesitation fills up the room, pushing up against me like a turbulent wave come to knock me under.

"It's imperative, Lady Auren," Hojat says carefully, and I hate the pity I see in his eyes, because it certainly doesn't bode well for me. "You do not want infection to set in." His accent pulls at his *t*'s like his tongue wants to drag them under, but the only thing dragging me under is this descending panic.

I can't have him look at me.

I just *can't*.

Because if he does, then I won't be able to keep ignoring...*that*.

As if it knows my conscious thoughts are skating around it, my back suddenly twinges with a sharp, prodding pain. I suck in a breath, my very inhale braced against the barbs in my chest.

"Auren, Hojat will be gentle," Slade tells me, but he doesn't get it. There is nothing *gentle* about this. What he's asking me to face is rough hate and slashed violence. What he's asking me for is to take on a soul-deep trauma that I want to keep ignoring.

He wants to yank out the stopper holding in my anguish while I'm still desperately trying to keep my fingers pressed to the cork.

I've just been told I have rot inside me, but maybe it's not his fault at all. Maybe it's *mine*. Maybe the things that have happened to me, the things I've done, are the reason that the rot stayed rooted inside of me.

"I don't care if he's gentle," I say, turning around to shove my feet back into the boots. I don't even bother to do up the laces, because I just need to get *away*. Out there, in the depths of the cave, where its secrets stay hidden and depths stay untouched. "I'm going back out."

"Auren—"

"He's not looking me over, and I'm going back out to the *fucking* cave!" I shout, chest heaving, my cheeks flared with angry, defensive heat—heat that I cling to, because I can't bear to plummet into the ice-cold reality of loss.

Why can't they just let it be? Why are they being so horrible and pushy? I just need to stay in that cave. Because I can't, I *can't*—

"My lady."

It's barely above a whisper.

But that hoarse, quiet voice makes everything in me suddenly grind to a jarring, weighty halt.

Slowly, I turn around, and my entire world tunnels down to the person standing slouched in the doorway.

"*Digby*."

He doesn't move. Doesn't speak.

For a second, we simply look at each other.

He's been a tight coil in my chest, a leak in my heart that's been stoppered along with the rest. I can't even fathom that he's here. In the crevices of my mind's cavern, he was there, buried in the shadows dark enough that I wouldn't have to face the grief of loss. But he's *here*. Somehow, he's gone ahead and stepped out of the corners and come out safe and sound.

The wet blur that fills my eyes distorts him, so I blink furiously, forcing myself not to cry, because I need to see him properly, need to assure myself that he's okay.

But he's not.

He might be safe and sound and *here*, but he's not unscathed.

His face is made up of mangled blotches. All different colored bruises, their shades marking the severity of the swelling beneath. His brown eyes have a haunted look in them that they didn't before, his gray beard and hair so disheveled that it doesn't even resemble my tidy, stoic guard. I don't miss the way he's leaning against the arched doorway, the arm wrapped tentatively around his waist, the padding of wraps beneath his shirt.

"You're here," I say, my voice sounding like I'm standing on quaking ground. "I thought I...in that room. You were there, and I just... I mean, I was so afraid that I... *Did* I...?" The choppy question stands on tenterhooks, balancing on the edge I'm too afraid to peer over.

Did I hurt him?

Did I hurt anyone else I care about?

The coil condenses and tightens in my chest, reeling around my ribs, keeping it too taut for a single breath.

Digby frowns at my question like he's not sure what I mean, but it's Slade who answers. "No, Auren. You didn't hurt him or any of us."

A whoosh of relief passes over me, but I don't miss the way he said that I didn't hurt any of *us*. He didn't say I didn't hurt *anyone,* because that would be a lie.

"My lady," Digby says, making my eyes hook back to him instantly. "Let the mender care for your wounds."

I go rigid, my head shaking.

When he hobbles a step forward, his face contorts into a grimace. Hojat starts to rush over to go help him. "You should really be in bed, Sir Digby…"

My stubborn guard holds up his hand to ward him off, and with painstaking steps, he limps all the way over to me. When he stops in front of me, when we're eye to eye, he just stands here, watching me.

No words. No argument or reasoning. He doesn't need them. There's so much more right there in his watery gaze.

Simply looking back at him makes my heart squeeze into itself, makes my ears scream with memory.

Miss Auren.

I'm going to save you.

Hold her.

You brought this on yourself, Auren.

Then, the screams.

It's all there. In the deepest, sharpest crevices. In the most frightening, sunken-in abyss. The sound of a sword swinging through the air. The explosion of pain. A spinning room. Rough, strong arms holding me down. Blots in my vision. Howls torn through my throat. That whistling blade, coming down again and again and *again*.

And this man standing in front of me, he's watching it replay right along with me. That haunted shadow in his eyes is cast from the very same shadows, because he was there. He saw every second of it. The two of us were the only ones who were in that room, and the truth is, I'm not sure if either of us will ever truly be able to get out of it.

That's the thing with trauma to the body—it shows up instantly. In breaks and bruises, in burns and in blood. But the trauma on the *inside*, that's harder to see. It creeps around your mind, poisons you with disquiet. It can hit you out of nowhere, debilitating and ruinous. There are no marks visible for those. None, save the shadows in your eyes.

Finally, within the recesses of those shared shadows, Digby speaks. "You've got to have it looked at, my lady."

No one, save him, would've been able to do this. To break down this one wall I have constructed around such a painful piece. It must've been keeping my spine upright, because as soon as it comes tumbling down, so do my shoulders. I ache as the bricks of refusal rain down at my feet, showing me exactly the sort of rubbled ruin I truly am. And to think, this is only a single wall.

When I say nothing, Digby gives me a firm look. "It's got to be done."

With the debris useless and scattered, I have nothing to hold up my resolve. Not with the recognition of his gaze. So I swallow hard and say, "Okay."

Because I can't say no to him. I can't look him in the eye and say *I'm fine*. I could with the others, but not him, not when we were both in that room.

Digby steps aside, deferring to Hojat. "This way, my lady," the mender tells me.

My numbness comes off in layers as I walk down the hallway. It feels like dead skin peeling away, left in a scattered trail behind me.

By the time I reach the borrowed bedroom I woke up in, I'm already raw. When Hojat covers me with a sheet so I can slip off my shirt, my body starts to tremble. When he has me lie face-down on the bed, my skin breaks out into a cold sweat.

Slade stays at my side, his hand gripping mine, and I squeeze and squeeze, because his touch is the only thing that's steady against my convulsing rupture, but I also can't bear for him to see. "Don't look at them," I say quietly, my voice a plea.

I don't know if he already saw, but I can't stand him looking at it now. Can't stand for him to see what's no longer there. At the wounds left behind.

His jaw muscle strains, but he gives a nod, his eyes never leaving mine, never straying down my spine.

I turn my head on the pillow, and there's Digby, standing guard at the door like he's done my whole life. Face grim, mouth quiet.

One of these males watches over me, the other sees right through me, no matter where I tell him to look.

"Alright, Lady Auren, I'm starting now," Hojat says quietly.

I brace myself, but I could never really be ready. The pain is hot and angry, almost bitter at how I've tried to ignore it, ready to lash out in punishment.

The first pass of Hojat's gentle hands as he starts to clean the wounds makes my spine bow up in shocking pain, and I suck in a noisy breath.

Every single swipe of his rag, every trickle of water and the herbal smell that fills my nose, I feel it all with stark alertness. But I feel the phantom pains of what happened in that room, too. The lightning bolts of agony that cut through those pieces of me, leaving me to bleed out onto the floor in golden tatters.

It's the smell of herbs tainted with the memory of metallic blood.

It's the dipping of his water mixture wrung out in the bowl that's morphed into the sound of blood dripping into a puddle.

It's the swipe of his motions merged with the swipe of the sword.

It's Digby watching me now, just as he was then.

But it's the window that really does me in. The dark glass may as well be a mirror for how well it reflects. And with my face turned toward it, there's no hiding away from the sight of my exposed back.

It looks so *empty*. Devoid. When I see it like this, the true reality of my loss slams into me full-force in a way it hasn't before. Because I wouldn't let myself think of it. But now, I can't ignore it. Because there it is, like scalloped edges jutting from my back that I can no longer cling to.

They're gone.

I don't have their comforting hug around my middle or their graceful twirls along the floor. I don't have the satiny brushes against my skin or the steadying weight at my back. They've been taken away, hacked away like a length of hair, leaving me to ache with the loss. All that's left are two rows of jagged, throbbing stubs that bleed and fray in the wake of what they once were.

And it's right here, right in this moment, that the pent-up sob finally tears past my lips. My stopper is yanked out, and there are no denials, no *I'm fines*. There isn't a cave in the world that's deep enough for me to hide away from this.

Because I've passed the point of no return now, and it's not just that there's no going back—it's that my back doesn't even *exist* anymore.

Eruptive emotion pushes out of me, so loud I feel it must burst from the house and echo through the cave. As if it cries with me.

And everything, *everything*, comes spilling out. Like a broken bottle, its contents leaked past the cracks.

Truth be told, I don't know if I'll ever feel full again.

I sob and I grieve, and it's not subtle or quiet, but a violent wracking of mourning that digs itself out of me and lands in a messy, hurtful heap. But all the while, Slade squeezes my hand and Digby stands watch.

I may be empty, but I am not alone.

And that, at least, is something.

CHAPTER 18

AUREN

When you hit rock bottom, you feel it.

You break down, walls crumbling until you're free-falling. The feelings that you tried to run from suddenly rush up around you in an unstoppable force, the gravity of your thoughts now nothing but a punishing plunge.

When you slam into the bottom, that landing jolts you all the way to your very soul. You hit hard, and it cracks the very foundation of the world. The ground fragments beneath you, lines stretching far and wide.

And then you're left, a pile of rubble.

But I realize something as I lie here, surrounded by the destruction of my plummet. These cracks that have spread out from my caustic landing, they're not evidence of my ruination.

They're paths.

Each jagged line leads from me and then diverts away, showing me all the different ways I could go from here.

I lie on the bed with Hojat's hands tending to my hacked back, with tears streaking down my face, where even breathing hurts. But I'm also in my mind, staring at the fissures around me, seeing where each one leads. Because now that I'm forced to feel what I didn't want to, I have a decision to make.

I can choose to stay stagnant here, at the bottom of the cliff, broken and unmoving. I can rage, I can wallow, I can blame, I can hide. I can let the severed parts of me sever all the rest.

Or I can get up, dust myself off, and look back up. I can find a path that ensures I'll never fall again, ensures that I don't lose any more parts of myself. All I have to do is turn and follow my feet, one step at a time.

So that's what I'll do.

I let myself cry until all my tears dry up. It's not ragged or turbulent anymore. Instead, it's quiet. Slow. The kind of tears your expression lets fall without fanfare. There is no choked breathing or scrunched up nose. No pulled lips or furrowed brow. This is the suffering of the silent. A hurt so deep it doesn't show itself on a face. The tears fall down my wooden expression, leaking from slowly blinking eyes while I stare at my reflection through the window. While I grieve for twenty-four strands of me that have been plucked away like petals from a flower.

When Hojat finishes, he's treated the wounds, my nose long since acclimated to the scent of the sharp herbs. I don't know if he did something to help dull the pain or if I've simply gone numb, but I barely feel a thing now.

He's also given me a new oversized shirt that he has me

wear backwards, so all the buttons are down my spine, making it easier to tend to my wounds.

"Alright, Lady Auren," he says quietly. "It's all done now."

It's all done now, I tell myself. So I wipe away the last of my tears and take a deep breath.

"Thank you, Hojat." My voice comes out as a mere rasp, but the mender hears, because he gives a gentle pat on my shoulder.

"I'll need to check it each day for a while until the healing process speeds up."

I nod, feeling wrung out, lethargy tugging at my bones.

"Sir Digby?" Hojat says. "How about I take a look at you next?"

When Digby doesn't reply, I turn my head to face him. He's still standing sentry in the doorway, and I don't think his gaze has left me for even a second. I notice how heavily he's leaning against the wall, how his arm is tucked in tight against his ribs and how one leg seems to be giving him trouble. He won't go without prompting, just like he never once ducked out early on a shift to guard me.

I give him a nod. "Your turn, Dig."

He hesitates for a moment before his eyes pass over me and land on Slade. I'm not sure what the two men communicate, but Digby glances back at me with a tilt of his head, and then he and Hojat walk out, closing the door behind them.

As soon as they're gone, I start to sit up, and Slade is instantly there to help me. Despite how much I've been sleeping, my body feels exhausted again, but my mind is too wired to sleep.

I hold the borrowed shirt against my chest, the back still undone. "Can I clean up a little?"

"Of course." Slade helps me to my feet and leads me to an attached washroom. It's small but clean, with a round tub, a washbasin, toilet, and a wooden vanity.

"I could fill the bath for you, but we'd have to keep the water quite low so we don't get your bandages wet."

"No, that's alright. I'll just clean up as best I can for now and do that tomorrow before he wants to change the bandages."

With a nod, Slade walks over to the vanity and pulls out a small stool. I take the hint and pad over to it, gingerly taking a seat. I watch as he moves around the room methodically, quietly, and I wonder what he's thinking. But I've never been able to read his thoughts as well as he's been able to read mine.

He grabs a glass vial from the vanity before going to the washbasin. The bowl set into it is a deep blue, the wood around it the same color as the floor. He pours some of the mixture into the bowl and then reaches up, pumping out water from a silver spigot on the wall. Water splashes into the basin, filling it with small bubbles, and he grabs a washing cloth from a hanging rack before dunking it in.

I watch as he wrings it out, his forearms visible from the rolled up sleeves of his shirt. The twisting movement of his hands fascinates me, especially in the low lantern light. From this angle, I'm able to study the profile of his face, and something in me aches just to look at him.

When he turns and walks over to me, I hold out my hand for the cloth, but he says, "May I?"

Taken aback, I hesitate. Washing someone, tending to

them in this way, it's intimate—intimate in a completely different way than sex. I clutch the shirt against my chest, my mind trying to come up with what I want, and he doesn't rush me. He just waits, and I know that if I say no, he'll pass me the cloth and that will be the end of it.

But I don't want him to pass the cloth.

Swallowing hard, I stand up and reach back, undoing the top two buttons at my shoulders. Since the shirt is so large, I'm able to peel the sleeves off one at a time, letting it fall to the ground. Even with the strips of bandages wrapped around me, I still feel exposed. I twitch, arms ready to come up to cover myself, but Slade is always a step ahead.

His calloused hand comes down to circle my wrist, and he gently encourages me to sit. As soon as I do, he starts to drag the cloth over the skin of my arm with the gentlest touch. I suck in a breath, jolting a little at how cold it is.

Slade chuckles. "Sorry, I should've warned you."

Yet every stroke he makes against my skin doesn't stay cold for long. How could it when he's touching me?

He works quietly and thoroughly, my arm being swept with soap and water, while his free hand threads his fingers between mine, gently bending my wrist backwards and forwards. He bends my fingers next, releasing the tension in each one, before he starts to slowly stroke up my other arm.

By the time he's finished with that, my entire body has gone supple and soft. He moves his attention to my shoulders, massaging into the tense muscles, careful not to get close to my spine, meticulous in his gentleness so he doesn't hurt me.

It doesn't turn sexual, even though my nipples harden into

points and my breath catches a few times. Slade just continues to take care of me, easing the stress and the tension from my body one muscle at a time.

When I help him peel off my leggings next, he kneels at my feet, that slow drag of the cloth making me just as languid as before. But when he digs his fingers into the arches of my feet, my eyes nearly roll into the back of my head.

His quiet care has calmed the thrumming of my mind, helping me to see everything so much more clearly, while he's won over my body so thoroughly.

But then, he always does.

When the cloth comes up to wipe at my forehead and cheeks, I blink up at him. Our eyes lock, and he brushes a thumb along my chin. He drops the cloth into the bowl and then, still watching me, he reaches into his pocket and holds out his hand.

There, sitting in his palm, is a frayed piece of my ribbon. The same one Midas had tied around my wrist.

My eyes fill as I reach out and tentatively take it. The moment I feel the satiny fabric, a sob passes my lips, tears spilling over my cheeks.

A twinge pulses at a single spot beside my spine, as if my body knows where this ribbon was. As if it wants it back.

For a long time, I just sit here. Slightly bowed over, staring at the dulled gold of the unmoving ribbon, thumbing over the tattered end still stained with blood.

Then, I raise my head, look at Slade where he's leaning against the wall.

"I don't want to be weak anymore."

My confession stands on a tension line between where I

am and where I want to go. It's a precarious balance, but I curl my toes and stand up straight, hearing Slade's words whisper back to me.

Don't fall.

Fly.

We've been transported back into that moment in the library again. Except now, parts of me are missing. Taken away. The wounds on my back twinge, but it only serves to make me feel more resolute. I twist the ribbon in my hand.

"I don't want to be weak ever again."

He absorbs my determined declaration with quiet study. I see his dusky green eyes flicker just beside my face, as if he's looking at my aura. His is stowed away, the black vapors that hug his form hidden right alongside his spikes and scales.

"I want to master my own strength—physically *and* magically," I tell him, my words sounding out of breath with the exertion of what lies ahead. And even though it no longer feels, no longer moves or lives, the ribbon still offers me its fortitude.

I wait, my breathing erratic, the feel of my heartbeat thumping hard against my bones. I'm not exactly sure what I'm waiting for him to say. Maybe that I don't have to worry. That I have him and the others in my corner now.

But none of that changes my determination.

I need to be strong for *myself.* Because I will never forget that feeling of being held against a wall while I was mutilated. I will never forget that feeling of utter helplessness.

Perhaps things are born from trauma. An anger. A clarity.

A beast.

It scares me. Terrifies the hell out of me—of what I did that night. Because I don't know my own power. But that's been the problem all along, hasn't it?

Maybe none of us truly know our own strength. Not until the world has hacked away at us. But the point is, we aren't strong *because* of our trauma. We were always strong to begin with. We just needed to figure it out for ourselves.

Which is why I meet Slade's eye, and I don't waver when I say, "I want to be so strong that I never have to fear anyone else in this world. That if I need to, I can make them all fear *me*. And I want you to teach me."

Silence reigns like a rigid monarch.

For a moment, I wonder if I've crossed a line. If I've shocked him. Worry makes me want to gnaw on my bottom lip.

But then, Slade *grins*.

I can see it right there on his face—the pride. The *excitement*. It's wholly fae too, something almost animalistic about it. As if his own vengeful beast is ready to rise up and roar alongside mine. It's contagious, and maybe a little unhinged, and I feel my own lips tipping up too.

He comes over, reaches up to grab hold of my chin, and then he leans down until his lips are skimming against mine so that I can *feel* his words when he murmurs. "Oh, Goldfinch. I'd thought you'd never ask."

CHAPTER 19

RISSA

The first time I traveled across Fifth Kingdom with the army, I was a captive.

The royal saddles were kept together like pigs in a pen, guarded day and night. Our tent was bursting with all of us in it, which isn't a good mix at the best of times but certainly not when everyone is cold, stressed, and scared.

I thought one of the saddles was going to yank someone's hair out or slap a few cheeks by the time we finally reached Ranhold. I had to constantly intervene between them, trying to manage short tempers and help to resolve issues so no one clawed anyone's eyes out.

This time, the traveling experience is different. I'm not a captive, but a grudging guest instead, and I'm not sharing a tent with a dozen saddles—only Polly. But I'm still managing bouts of short tempers, and if anyone's eyes are going to be clawed out, it will be mine.

It's been weeks since we left Ranhold, and it's so difficult to keep up with such a punishing pace. Even though Polly and I ride in a carriage all day, I'm exhausted by the time we make camp every night.

Though my exhaustion isn't just due to the travel.

I glance over at where Polly is sitting hunched on her pallet bed, shivering over the coals where they burn in a cauldron in the middle of our tent. I give it ten minutes, and then she'll be snapping at me that she's having hot flashes again, and she'll start pouring out sweat, demanding ice packs.

All this time, and she's still going through withdrawals.

The first few days, she was in a rage. Screaming at me for taking her away from Ranhold, crying about the news of Midas being dead, threatening to leave and walk back on her own. It was only because her bursts of energy were very short-lived that I was always able to drag her back to the tent before she could get too far.

She hates me.

I hate that she hates me.

Yet I still take care of her, because she is the closest friend I've ever had. Or at least, perhaps the longest one.

Polly and I received our contracts to become King Midas's royal saddles together. We started at the same time, probably accepted because we look so similar. Very quickly, we decided to become allies to help solidify our place in Highbell Castle. We made ourselves desirable as a pair, superior over the rest of the saddles in Midas's stock. We played to each other's strengths, we gossiped, we had each other's backs. Our friendship was strong while we were in Highbell.

Until we weren't.

It seems like as soon as we left, things began to change.

Maybe it changed that night on the Red Raids' ship. Maybe *I* changed that night on the Red Raids' ship.

The thing about being a saddle is that it was a profession I chose. I chose to go into sex work because I was beautiful but had no highborn family or money to protect me. I'd already been accosted by men, so why not turn around something that made me feel powerless and use it to be powerful instead? By making it my career, I put sex under *my* control.

And I was good at it.

Becoming a royal saddle is what so many workers in the brothels dream of. The contracts always pay very well, the clients are rich and powerful, and many saddles in that position can simply retire when the contract ends, sent away with a pouch of coin and that's that.

The problem is, somewhere along the way, I didn't want to do it anymore.

The seduction, the flirting, the makeup and hair and tight dresses. I got tired of having to smile and bat my eyes, to suck cock and spread my legs when I wasn't in the mood.

I wanted something different. So I started to save up the money I made when nobles and visitors stopped by the castle. I started to work even harder to please, to be the favorite, so I could fill my hidden purse instead of spend it on frivolities.

When we left Highbell, I thought Ranhold would be a new start.

But then, the Red Raids happened.

Captain Fane happened.

Auren happened.

Every night, while I tend to Polly's feverish fits, my mind replays the events from the moment we left Highbell all the way to the ballroom when I grabbed Polly and started to flee. I nearly didn't make it out. We were stopped in the entry hall by some of the guards, but a woman with smooth umber skin wearing army leathers and the shapes of daggers shaved into her scalp spotted me, told me that Auren had mentioned me and that I needed to go to Fourth's army. Then she somehow distracted the guards, and Polly and I were able to slip away.

It feels as if I owe Auren, when my last assurance was that she owed me. But now, I'm not sure if she'll help me again. Or if she even can. Because apparently, she stole Midas's magic in front of *everyone* and killed him right there in that ballroom that I fled.

Men. Why is it that my life's events always seem to revolve around the deaths of men? First was the death of my father, whose loss left me nothing but debts and vulnerability. Now Midas, marking the time for me to flee.

But I can say with complete certainty that the death of Captain Fane showed a distinct point in my life. Because that moment on the Red Raids' ship, that's when I realized I was finished with that life.

I've been assaulted before, hurt before. As a saddle, these things happen, though it's no excuse. I've had to come up with ways to manage reactions over the years, to steer men to behave in ways I *could* manage. I couldn't do that with Captain Fane.

That's when I decided I was well and truly *done*.

Done being a saddle. Done managing men. Done trying

to walk this fine line of powerless and powerful when it comes to sex.

Does he haunt my dreams? No. Apart from the nights I've tended to Polly, I don't think of him at all, nor any of the other violent encounters I've had. Because I refuse to give them any more of me than they've already taken or that I've already given.

They had my body, but so what? Hundreds of others can claim the same. However, they will not have my mind. I won't give it to them.

Including Captain Fane, whose gilded dick is probably buried beneath a hundred feet of snow somewhere in the Barrens.

I have to admit, that does make me smirk.

"I'm hot!"

Right on time, Polly shoves herself away from the coals and starts fanning her face. My eyes are burning with exhaustion as I get up from my pallet to drag myself toward the tent's flap.

I don't bother to go outside, not with my stockinged feet padding across the rolled-out fur laid on the ground. Instead, I simply grab the bucket and rag and scoop up some snow from just outside. There's never a shortage of snow on the ground, though I do notice every night someone has come to shovel the space in front of the tent's entrance.

I don't have to wonder who.

There's only one man in this army who's big enough to fit the shadowed silhouette I see when he does the chore. The captain drags the tool beneath huge piles of snow and then packs it in against the sides of the tent to help insulate and stabilize it.

He does it each night. Just as he delivers our food and makes sure we have plenty of coals to burn. And never, not once, has he propositioned me. He hasn't asked for a single thing in return.

I'm not quite sure what to make of that.

I close the tent flap again and walk back over to Polly, tying the ends of the rag as I go. Kneeling down in front of her, I gently press it to her flushed forehead.

She groans, clutching her stomach and licking her lips. "You're killing me," she says with accusation.

I pause in my ministrations. Truth be told, Polly hasn't said much at all. Not since those first few days when she screamed and raged at me. Other than exclaiming how terrible she feels, she's quiet. Something between us has strained and shattered, but I know that once her body recovers, once it stops needing and craving the dew, she will feel better. She'll be back to her old self. *We* can be back to our old friendship.

Though, I have no idea why this process is taking so long. I hadn't expected for her to be this sick for this long. She vomits nearly every time I try to feed her, only keeping down the smallest bits of bread and water, along with the herbs that the army mender has brought. She's lost weight, her pallor is gray and pale, and there are deep circles under her eyes that seem to deepen every day, even though she spends nearly all of her time in fitful sleep.

I so badly want her to get better, for her to see that I took her away from Ranhold to *help* her. This strain between us is just the drug talking. Once she's back to normal, she will realize that I'm doing all of this to save her.

"You're making snow drip down my dress," she hisses.

"Sorry." I gently start to stroke the snow over the back of her neck, but she jerks away, so I set it down again. Reaching for the little pot I've been given that hangs over the coals, I tip it over into the small tin cup. "How about you try sitting up again to sip some broth?"

"Don't want it," she says, eyes closed, teeth nibbling incessantly at her bottom lip. She does that a lot now, like a nervous tic from the dew that she craves. She's doing it so often that she's peeled off the skin, leaving her mouth swollen and raw. It's the same with her cuticles. The army mender brought a cream for me to apply onto those areas, but unless she's asleep, she won't let me put it on her.

"Come on, just a bit—"

Polly turns her face away again and lies back on her pallet. "Go away."

A pang of hurt pierces me, but I shove past it. This isn't her fault.

"Alright, I'm going to empty the chamber pot. I won't be gone too long."

She doesn't reply, but when she starts to shiver again, I gently pull up a fur to cover her, just as her eyes fall shut. I tuck in my overly large shirt that I've been given, step into my boots, and then slip on the captain's coat and some gloves before grabbing the chamber pot and heading outside.

Almost as soon as I've stepped out of the tent, a giant mountain is looming over me so close that I nearly barrel into it.

"Watch it!" I bite out as I try to steady the pot so it doesn't splash all over me. I only have one other set of clothes, and I like wearing this shirt. I refuse to ask if it's his. I already know.

When the liquid is safe from spilling, I look up, shooting a glare at the intruder. "What do you want?"

Captain Osrik arches a thick, bushy brown brow at me. Honestly, there's not a single part of him that doesn't need trimming. His beard is so long I could braid it, his hair is always windblown around his shoulders, and from what I can see at his wrists beneath his sleeves, he's hairy there as well. I just *know* that he's one of those men with chest hair. The male saddles always had to use sugar wax to remove theirs. I would pay good money for someone to strap down the captain and yank on his skin, strip by painful strip.

"You're staring again, Yellow Bell."

My gaze cuts away from his hands, flying up to his face. Flustered, I shift on my feet. "I'm not staring, I'm simply amazed at just how much of a hairy giant you really are," I say, curling my lip up with distaste.

"If you're interested in seeing my body hair, all you have to do is ask."

Why I suddenly picture his groin hair is beyond me. I don't want to think of that. I'm not interested in anything to do with his groin. Not at all.

I roll my eyes and start to shove away from him, though the annoying oaf just follows me. "What do you want?"

"I brought you some more food," he says as he tries to pass me over something wrapped in a bit of cloth.

"You already left the soup earlier, and my hands are a bit full at the moment."

"What's that?"

I feel a slight blush of embarrassment climb up my neck. "What do you think it is? It's our..." I trail off, not wanting to say it out loud.

The boor actually *leans over* and looks inside of it, much to my horror. "Oh, why didn't you just say so?" He looks behind him. "Himinn," he barks out, and somehow, a reedy soldier appears from nowhere.

"Yes, Captain?"

Captain Osrik yanks the chamber pot out of my hands before I can stop him, and shoves it at the younger man. "Take this and go clean it out. Then return it to Lady Rissa's tent."

The soldier actually lights up, as if this is an honor. "Right away, Captain!"

As soon as he bounds off, I cut a look at the captain. "Don't *do* that! Now some strange soldier is dealing with our...void."

He laughs and then tries handing me the food again. "Piss and shit aren't anything to be ashamed of, and trust me, Himinn is going to be excited about that job for the rest of the night. Now take the food, woman."

"My name is *Rissa*," I say tartly, but then I rip off my gloves, stuffing them into my pocket, and take the food, because I haven't eaten yet tonight and I'm starving. When I peel back the small bit of cloth, I find a pocket of bread with meat stuffed inside.

"Come on, Rissa," he says, gesturing ahead. "Come sit by the fire, eat your sandwich and drink some wine."

I shake my head. "I'll eat in my tent. I need to keep an eye on Polly."

"Isn't she sleeping?"

I hesitate for a moment too long, because he smirks. "Thought so. Come get some fresh air and sit with me, woman. You can listen to Polly pitch a fit when you get back."

For the most part, I've kept away from the captain, ignoring him at all costs, but somehow, it seems like he's always nearby. I find him riding his horse outside of our carriage, getting battered by wind and snow, yet never seeming to mind it. I see him at the cook's fire or talking with soldiers or walking around camp every time I venture outside. I see him tending to our needs, but never barging in. And even though I try to avoid him, I still...watch.

I'm not even sure why. It's silly, really. He's a crass, boorish, uncivilized giant. Definitely not my type. For one, he's a man, and I've sworn off men for the time being. Maybe even forever. I haven't found a single one who's ever been worth much of anything.

So I've no idea why I find myself following him to the fire. Perhaps I really do need a break from the stagnant air of animosity brewing in the tent.

When the captain leads me to the tent set up just in front of mine, I stop and stare. "You...why is your tent so close to mine?"

He ducks inside it for a moment, pulling out a fur, and then grabs two buckets. He overturns them both and sets them in front of the small fire he has going, placing the fur on one. "Here, sit."

I blame it on the fire that I obey. It has nothing to do with the way my stomach tightens at his gruff order. Nothing to do with the way his leathers hug his tree-trunk thighs.

Nothing at all.

Yet as soon as I do sit, I nearly slump against the warmth of the flames, a sigh escaping me. I start nibbling at the sandwich, and while it's cold and the crust too tough, it tastes so good that I could eat a whole plate of them right now.

I'm finished and licking my fingers before I even realize what I'm doing. Of course, *he* realizes. Nothing seems to get past him. "Good to see you eating for real, Yellow Bell."

"When are you going to stop using that ridiculous nickname?"

He hands me a waterskin. "Oh, you're stuck with it."

With a huff, I tip the skin back and take a big gulp, only to sputter and cough, nearly dropping it. "What...is...that?"

"Mulled wine," he says with a shrug. "It'll put some warmth in your bones."

"I thought it was water."

"This is better." He takes it from me so he can have a swig, and I have no idea why watching him drink after me makes me squirm, but it does. So does the way his tongue moves the wooden piercing through his bottom lip.

"So," he begins, letting his legs stretch in front of him so his boots are nearly inside the fire. I'm glad that for once, it's not snowing tonight. The moment we're out of Fifth Kingdom, I'm never going back to the cold. "How's your friend doing?"

"She's fine," I say automatically, just as I've said to him the three other times he's asked. Although, I suspect he's the reason the mender keeps visiting every couple of days, so my answer probably doesn't mean much. "She will be," I amend.

The captain nods. "I've seen plenty of soldiers come down off things. It's not easy to be a nursemaid through that."

"She's my friend."

"Is she?"

I stiffen. "What's that supposed to mean?"

He lifts a bulky shoulder, and I try not to stare when he

crosses his arms in front of him, making his muscles bulge. I shouldn't have let him give me his coat. Then his physique wouldn't be so visible. "Just a question."

"Is this about that *disloyal* talk about Auren?" I ask defensively. "Want to judge me some more?"

His eyebrows lift. "Retract your poison, Yellow Bell, I'm not judging shit. Just seems to me that this friend of yours isn't being very friendly to you."

"How do you know?"

He gives me a dry look. "Tent walls are thin."

Embarrassment heats my face. "She's just not feeling well."

"Mm-hmm."

I start to get to my feet. "If you're just going to be an ass—"

He taps his foot against my shin, making me pause. "Sit down, Rissa."

My butt hits the bucket. Hearing the gravelly tone of his voice say my name sends an odd thrill down my spine.

What the hell is wrong with me? I absolutely refuse to be attracted to this man. I *refuse*. I have been with countless beautiful men—men that looked like sculptures, they were so pretty. Men that...bathed regularly. So why, every time I leave my tent, are my eyes looking around for *him*?

It doesn't make any sense.

He's infuriating, and coarse, and I shouldn't think of him at all. Yet, I do. That first night, he said a little loathing makes it better, and I haven't been able to stop thinking about it ever since.

I can't deny that there is *something* in the air that charges between us like lightning caught in the belly of a cloud. And I'm…curious. Curious about what would happen if we did clash together.

Maybe it could be a perfect, raging storm.

With all of this anger and worry churning around inside of me, the thought that I could take it out on him sounds sublime. That we could come together in a violent flare where I didn't hold back. Where I wouldn't have to be the perfect, most beautiful seductress. But that I could take instead of give, make him work to give *me* pleasure. He's the only man I think could handle the real me like that, and *that's* why I can't stop thinking about him. He's not a client.

"What's your plan?" he asks, yanking me out of my wanton thoughts. "When we get to Fourth Kingdom."

"To go away," I say quickly, because I need to keep that goal in mind. I can't let him or anyone else deter me from my plans. "I'm going to get the gold Auren promised me, and then I'll leave for the first ship I can afford, to the farthest city I can go. Maybe to the deserts of Second Kingdom, since it's about as opposite of Fifth Kingdom as I can get."

He nods. "What will you do then?"

"I'll do whatever I like. I'll do nothing at all."

"You don't want to be a saddle anymore?"

My eyes tighten. "No."

There's a lull between us for a second where all I hear is the spitting fire and the gulp of wine as he takes another drink. "You could stay."

I frown over at him. "What?"

"In Fourth Kingdom. You could stay."

"Why would I stay there?"

"It only snows near the border at the mountains, so you wouldn't have that in the capital. Plus, I'll be there. So will Gildy."

"And you think those are incentives?" I ask sharply.

He only shrugs. "Could be. If you let them be."

I open my mouth to make some rude retort, but for some reason, I stop and shake my head. "You pointed out yourself that I've blackmailed and used Auren. Why would you even suggest I stay?"

"Seems to me you got one woman who you're bending over backwards for who wants nothing to do with you...and another woman who's done nothing but try to be there for you, who you're happy to step on. Just thought you could consider another way."

Anger is my natural, knee-jerk response, but this time, it simmers beneath a surface of sadness. This sad feeling is like a slap to the face, startling me so much that I'm horrified when I feel my eyes burning, and not from exhaustion, but from *emotion*.

I try to tamp it down, try to swallow it away, because I detest crying.

"Hey."

Turning my face, I refuse to look at him, hating how vulnerable I suddenly feel. But of course, the barbarian can't let it lie. I feel him vividly as he stands before me, and then his finger and thumb are gripping my chin, turning my face up to look at him. He's got a deep frown, muddy brown eyes caught in a perpetual glower. "What's wrong?"

"Nothing."

"Bullshit. What's wrong?"

I should jerk my head out of his hold. I should stand up and shove him away. But instead, I find myself leaning into his touch, find a tear tracking down my cheek that he thumbs away. The touch leaves behind a streak of tingles, as if I'm some innocent maiden. Ridiculous.

"It won't matter if I leave," I say, my voice sounding far too fragile for my liking. What is it about this man that leaves me so upside-down?

Somehow, his glowering eyes soften. I didn't even know he was capable of such a look, or why he's giving it to *me*.

"It would matter to me, Yellow Bell."

I swallow hard. "Why?"

Why would you care? Why do I keep watching you? Why are you trying to help me? Why does my heart quicken every time you're near?

"I like your peppery attitude," he says with a smirk. "I've always enjoyed a little bite."

The vision of him biting *me*, peppering nibbles along my flesh, suddenly flashes through my mind in a far too realistic vision.

"I have a plan, and you're not in it," I say as I finally gain the strength to pull away and get to my feet. Of course, he doesn't back away, doesn't give me space. Now, with both of us standing, he's so close that his body brushes against mine, my head tilting back because of how ridiculously tall he is. Despite the thick coat I have on me, I can feel the heat burning from him to me.

"Change your plan," he murmurs, eyes dropping down to my lips.

My breath catches, but I shove it away and pull up a sneer. "Men just want to conquer. I'm not playing hard to get so that you work extra hard. I don't want you, Captain."

Instead of getting pissed off, he gives me a crooked smile that nearly curls my toes. "You don't want me?"

I sniff and lift my chin. "That's right."

"So then...you *don't* sit awake in your pallet at night, thinking about arguing with me just enough to get our blood heated, and then wrapping those long legs of yours around my hips and fucking me till you see stars?"

My pulse quickens. Everything he said becomes vivid pictures in my head, making my core throb.

I can't deny it. I can't, because I'm breathing way too hard and I know I'm blushing, and I realize that all of a sudden, I don't *want* to deny it.

How the hell did I crumble so quickly?

Then, I do the stupidest thing I have ever done.

I lean up and *kiss* him.

I dive into his mouth like it's holding the nectar of the Divine. He's so shocked at first that he does nothing, but then his huge hands come to my waist, making it feel smaller than it is. His hairy beard scratches my cheeks, but instead of it being irritating or gross, it scrapes my fevered skin in this primal way that somehow makes me like it even more. I nip his piercing, lick his tongue, kiss him in a way I haven't ever kissed anyone before.

Because this *isn't* for my job. This *isn't* for coin. I'm not trying to seduce or put on a show. I'm just kissing him because I wanted to know...wanted to see.

I yank away, panting, eyes wide, wondering how the hell I could be so stupid. "That was a mistake," I sputter out.

He laughs. Doesn't let go of my waist. Keeps holding me there in a far softer touch than I ever would've expected from him. It makes me wonder what kind of lover he really is. If he's the rough or the gentle.

"That was a damn good mistake. We should do it again sometime."

Pulling away, I start to stumble over the bucket in my haste, but he easily catches my arm before I can fall.

"Leaving the fire so soon?" he calls, his rough voice somehow teasing.

"I'm hot enough."

He laughs. I blush harder.

As I scurry away through the snow, inwardly kicking myself, he says, "When you're ready for another mistake, you know where my tent is. Right next to yours."

Stupid lout of a man.

Stupid *me*.

When I rush back to my tent, when I topple onto my own pallet and press my hands to my cheeks, my lips are still tingling. My heart still racing. My core still throbbing.

That was a stupid, horrible, ridiculous mistake.

And yet, all I can think is, *we should do it again sometime.*

CHAPTER 20

AUREN

T he Grotto's cave holds *more* secret crevices than I first realized.

Because here we are, inside of one, in what Judd fondly calls *the Teeth*. Judd and I squeezed through a serrated fissure from the main cave's walls, and after a short, albeit very claustrophobic passage, it opened up into a new room—the place where the Wrath come to train.

It's not overly large, but it has plenty of space, and the veins of fluorescence that run through the walls and ceiling are so abundant in here that the entire area glows. The ground has been covered with thick layers of half-frozen hay that crunches beneath my shoes, and there are three wooden chests stacked off to the side that Judd told me hold practice weapons.

I'm not allowed to use those yet.

When we first got here, he'd grinned, turning in a circle with his arms up, his normally yellow hair turned luminous blue, right along with his tanned skin and the army leathers hugging his lean body. "Welcome to the Teeth—the mouth of the mountain where you're going to get chewed up and spat out."

He sounded excited about it.

On the ceiling above, the stalactites hang in a perfect row—just like razor-sharp teeth ready to do exactly as he claimed.

I was hoping he was exaggerating.

He wasn't.

I really *do* feel like I'm getting chewed up in here, though it's not his fault.

For the first half hour, he simply showed me some stances. Explaining how to hold my weight, how to secure my posture, how to stand, and why.

Simple stuff.

Easy, basic, bare bones knowledge so that I can learn from the ground up.

I first noticed there was a problem when he kept pointing out that I was tilting one way or the other and having to correct my stance. I dismissed it in the beginning. I thought I was still a bit weak and out of shape for all the days spent in bed. I just needed to warm up.

But now, as I pitch to the left again and *again*, reality lands hard and heavy, like bricks sinking into my gut. I stare at Judd, eyes gone wide, and it feels like my internal temperature plummets, ice filling my tightening veins.

"Gildy?"

His lips move, but I can't focus enough on his words. Couldn't hear them anyway with how loudly my heart is pounding.

Judd takes a step forward, blond brows pulling in.

"Water," I croak out before I totter toward the crates. I pick up one of the skins he brought, lifting the nozzle to my lips and taking a hefty drink as if the ice-cold liquid will help to wash away my realization.

It doesn't.

I swallow it down, feeling it land in my stomach like I've plunged into a lake and too much of it rushed into my mouth.

Judd comes up and takes a sip from his own. "I know this stuff seems rudimentary, but it really is important. Strong, stable footing is the foundation for everything else."

I glance at him from the corner of my eyes. Does he think all of my struggling and stumbling is due to distraction because I don't think this is important?

"I trust you," I tell him honestly. "I know everything you and the others will teach me is what I need to know."

He nods, but then cocks his head as if he's reconsidering. "Except maybe Ryatt. He might teach you something just to fuck with you."

I catch my lips curving. "Good to know."

"So, why do you want to do this?"

"Train?" I ask with a frown.

"Yep. Rip told me that you wanted to train, but I want you to tell me why."

Why.

The *why* has been driving me since the moment I woke. Before that, even. Maybe the *why* first started solidifying when I met Judd and the others, when I was in that fighting circle with them and realized the possibility of being capable of *more*.

My eyes flick up to his, meeting his gaze steadily. "My

whole life, I have been a thing for other people. A thing for them to have, a thing for them to use." Stark honesty makes my tone flatter, without any divot or protrusion to hide the plain truth. "But I'm not a thing."

His normally amused expression has gone sober. "No, you're not."

"The next time someone wants to try and use me, control me, I want to be ready. I want to crush those who would keep me under their thumb."

His hazel eyes glitter with something like pride. "That sounds good to me, Gildy."

It sounds good to me too.

He takes another polite sip of his water, since I know he's only drinking because I am. It's not like he's expending a lot of energy when I haven't even gotten past stances.

"Shall we get back to it?"

I nod and set down the water, slipping my hand into my pocket as I follow him back to the middle of the space again. For a moment, I let my fingers brush against the rolled up satin length that's tucked away before I drag my hand back out again.

"Alright, basic defensive stance. Left foot forward. Push that shoulder back a bit. I want that elbow down in front protecting your midsection."

I try to follow his every direction for the different stances he barks out, and for a while, I do okay, as if our talk and my determination alone helped steady me. But when it's time to start moving my body quicker, I falter again.

Embarrassed heat flushes my neck, but I continue to pretend that nothing is amiss.

"Left foot forward, right foot back," Judd instructs as he circles around me, studying my form. "Good. Now twist—like someone is coming at your back."

I try. Really, I do.

As soon as I start to spin around, my weight topples, my spine jerking while my feet attempt to correct my movement and keep me upright.

"I'm sorry," I blurt out with frustration. "Let me try again."

Judd doesn't hesitate, nor does he laugh at me. "Your posture is still wrong," he tells me, coming up to tap my right shoulder. "Straighten out here, and get that heel down."

I slam my heel into the ground, making sticks of hay split beneath my foot. I shove my shoulders back for the umpteenth time, silently screaming at my body.

"Relax your hands," Judd says when he notices they've curled into fists.

Reluctantly, I release my fingers, shaking out my hands slightly.

Judd cocks his head. "Are you up to this? If your wounds—"

"Nothing is bleeding anymore, and Hojat wrapped me up and said I could do this," I cut in. "I'm just getting used to these boots. I think they're too big."

I'm not sure if he knows I'm feeding him bullshit, but he nods. "Alright, get those feet planted. Good. This time, I want you to move left, raising that arm up in a defensive block. Ready? Three, two, move."

It doesn't matter how much I try to keep my feet planted. As soon as I try to do even the simplest maneuver of control, I realize I don't have any. Just like all the times before, I lose my balance, one of my feet picking up before I can stop it, making me waver.

Judd frowns and looks down at my feet. "Do you want to try it without the boots?"

Frustration bubbles and boils inside of me, the heat of it splashing against my eyes.

"No. Let me try again."

He hesitates. "Is something wrong?"

"Not at all," I say with false brightness. "I'm probably just your worst student because I've never been trained before."

"You were bad in the fight circle, but you weren't *this* bad."

I cut him a sharp look. "Thanks a lot."

"You know what I mean," he says with a wave of his hand. "Do you want to stop for the night?"

"Just keep telling me the moves."

Stubbornness rides me, taking me by the reins. It steers my movements, propelling me to try again and again, but even dogged determination doesn't help. Doesn't make me balance any better.

My wavering just gets worse, and no amount of trying to hide it or making up stupid lies can excuse it away.

I'm failing.

Day one, and I'm already *failing*.

And yet, I have to do this. I *have* to learn how to be strong. But I can't even fucking *turn* without teetering and—

Caught up in my growing frustration, I try to pivot too quickly. I'm topsy-turvy, like a spinning top that can't stay on its point, and this time, my feet can't catch me.

I crash to the ground on my side, landing hard, the ice-cold hay splintering through my coat and needling my skin. Needling my confidence until it deflates.

I shove up onto my hands and knees, but then I just stay there. Eyes slightly blurred, staring at the broken and dirty hay, the scent of it thick in my nose, the fluorescence dousing it all in blue.

"Fuck." My whisper is sharp and galled, mind furious with the incapabilities of my body.

"It's fine, Gildy. We all fall," Judd says, and somehow, his amicable optimism just makes it worse.

"It's not alright," I snap. "I can't be *ready* if I can't even do a *fucking stance*."

"Auren."

My head snaps up at Slade's voice, and I see him standing just at the entrance of the fissure. Shame crawls up my limbs, and my heart drops at the sight of him. Looking away, I push up to my feet, but even doing that makes me stumble slightly to the right. I'm disoriented. Off-balance. Feeling weak and wobbly like a newborn foal.

I hate it.

Slade's footsteps crunch over the hay as he comes near until he's standing right in front of me. "I thought you were going to take it easy until Hojat gave you the go-ahead for more?" he asks, question posed to Judd.

"We are…" Judd's words trip to a stop.

"He's not having me do anything difficult," I admit, my jaw tight with frustration. "I just can't do it."

The admittance falls from my lips with disgust. I tear a hand through my hair, fingers getting tangled in the gold strands that fell out of my braid. "This is my first session, and I'm already failing. How pathetic is that?"

"It's not pathetic."

I let out an ugly laugh, yanked from the center of my chest. "I can't even *stand*," I spit out, but my tone isn't directed at him or Judd, it's directed at *me*. "Because I keep losing my balance. Because I let him…I let him…"

My words choke off. Strangled, like a fist around my throat.

I let him.

For ten Divine-damned years, *I let him.*

Let him silence me. Let him lead me. Let him fool me. Let him cage me. Let him hurt me.

I let him drug me and hold me against that cold wall, let him take *another* part of me that I'll never get back.

Understanding dawns in Slade's eyes like mist on a shadowed field. "Your ribbons."

The two of them trade a look, and I know what's on their expressions, because it's on mine too. The recognition of exactly what I lost.

I never noticed before how much my body relied on my ribbons. I have to learn all over again without the comfort of their presence.

But it's not just that.

The weight of them is gone, yes, but they were more than just satiny strips that hung from my back. I miss the way they trailed behind me. I miss being able to lift them to help me comb my hair or wrap around my waist like a layer of armor. I miss the way they snaked around Slade's leg.

They caught me. Defended me. They were my instincts.

My unconscious impulse and sentiment. They made me more. And without them. I'm less. Less steady, less sure, less free.

You never notice what's keeping you balanced until you realize you're not standing straight anymore.

I took my ribbons for granted. For years, I hated them, hid them, tried to pretend that they weren't a part of me. It wasn't until I was with Fourth's army that I even let them truly breathe—let *myself* breathe. It was just one inhale, but it led to a cacophony of gulping air.

I wonder if this is what it feels like for a bird whose wings have been clipped.

I didn't comprehend until they were gone just how important they were to me. They were an extension of myself, they were my heart on my sleeve. And now, they've been torn away. I'm already trying to cope through my loss, but I *never* anticipated this other aspect to it.

It's not just my balance that I lost.

"I let him make me into this, and I didn't even realize it until it was too late," I say as fury fills my eyes, red-hot heat raining down my cheek like acid. The ribbon in my pocket feels like it's taken on the weight of a brick. "How am I supposed to train to become strong if I can't even stand?"

Slade's fists tighten at his sides, as if he's envisioning wringing Midas's throat. "You've had your ribbons for a decade, Auren. It makes sense that you need to adjust to being without them."

I glare at him. "Don't."

"Don't what?"

"Don't placate me. Don't stand there all confident and encouraging."

"Would you rather I be doubtful and disparaging?"

Anger rises like a tide, but I push past it and start to walk away. I only make it a couple of steps before Judd appears in front of me. "You think you're quitting, Gildy?"

"I'm not quitting," I hiss through my teeth. "I'm just taking a break before I try to punch your kingly army commander."

He snorts. "As much as I'd like to see that, Hojat gave me strict orders that you're not to be hitting anything yet, so we'll save that for another day. In the meantime, you told me you wanted to train, so I'm training you. I'm afraid you're stuck in the Teeth until I say so."

"You *just* asked me if I wanted to stop."

"Yeah, and you said no."

A frustrated sigh clatters past my lips. "I can't even turn around without losing my balance, Judd. How are you going to train me?"

He sweeps an assessing gaze over me. "Well, if you'd have just told me what was going on, I would've been able to account for it and rethink my strategy," he says. "Now that I know you're having to adjust to the loss of your ribbons, we'll start out our training a different way."

"You think that will help?" I ask dubiously.

"Gildy, don't wound my pride," he tells me, placing a hand over his heart. "I'm an excellent trainer."

"Who told you that?"

He frowns. "I'm sure someone's said it."

I find myself letting out a bemused laugh. With just a few words, my anger has been replaced with frustration.

"Why didn't you just say so?" Judd asks me, not with judgment, but curiosity.

My shoulder lifts. "You're not supposed to admit weakness, right? Even I know that."

"That's not a weakness, Gildy," he says with a shake of his head. "And don't lie to your trainer. When I ask you what's wrong, I expect you to tell me the truth."

I glance over my shoulder, expecting Slade to still be standing there, but he's now next to the wooden crates off to the side, hip perched against one as he watches us. Just having him in here observing is making my chest tight with tension. He was so proud when I told him I wanted to train. The last thing I wanted was for him to see me flounder.

"Alright, sit your ass down."

My head snaps back to Judd. "What?"

"You heard me," he says before plopping down on the ground in front of me.

I follow suit, instantly adjusting when I feel sharp sticks of hay stab through my pants.

"We're going to start over with some stretching. You're going to go slow, and you're going to tell me when certain movements hurt or if you start to feel off-center. Then we're going to try some positions from here."

"Sitting down?"

"Yep. You're going to have to re-learn to balance and move without the help of your ribbons. So for now, I'm keeping you planted on your ass so you can stop psyching yourself out and falling over. Besides, Rip will get all pissy if you're covered in bruises. Now shut up, stop thinking that you're failing, and let's figure this shit out one step at a time."

My lips pull up. Just like that, I feel the last of the clogged up tension roll off my shoulders. "Are you *sure* people say you're a good trainer?"

He shrugs. "I'm paraphrasing."

Laughing, I shake my head. "Alright. Let's figure this shit out."

Judd flashes me a grin. "Thatta girl."

CHAPTER 21

AUREN

There's a glint of a golden blade. A blade I gilded with my own hands. Everything else has gone drab in gray and white—even King Fulke, who pins me against his chest with that very
blade and slices into my neck.

I scream and struggle, but the sharp sting of the edge just sinks in more, slicing through me and making blood drip down to my chest. Yet when the king leans in against my ear, it's not Fulke's voice at all. It's not his pudgy body at my back.

It's a clean-shaven face and gilded sleeves and carob-pod eyes. It's deceit and abuse and golden reins clutched in his hands. Reins that he's tied around my wrist, holding me still. Keeping me where he wants me.

"If I can't have her, no one can. Isn't that right, Precious?" His voice is vile, pressed against my ear with an offensive purr, trying to wind around me just as much as his words always did.

We're in Ranhold again now, with so much gold in the room it's blinding. As if it's glaring at me—glaring at *him*. We're right here, stuck in the middle of the ballroom, reliving it all.

Slade is in front of me with his Wrath, while *my* wrath burns deep in my gut. Churning like magma ready to spew.

"Auren, use your ribbons."

"Oh, she didn't tell you? She lost that privilege."

The dagger changes now, and I'm no longer pinned against Midas's back, but pinned against a wall. It's not gilded reins tied around my wrist, it's my ribbon.

And then there's a sound that the sword makes as it comes swinging down. It's not a slice in the air, it's not a whispered whistle. It *shatters*. Like a body being flung out a window, or a fist slamming into a mirror.

Or the shattering of a soul.

With it, comes the pain.

Pain and pain and pain again. Pain as I fracture into a million pieces. Pieces that look like strips of satin falling frayed and bloody to the floor.

"This hurts me a lot more than it hurts you."

I can't hear my screams. Can't hear myself wail or beg or grieve. It's just an endless cracking of crystalline glass.

And then, it's suddenly over. Jarring in the ringing silence, caught with daggers and ribbons and splintered shards beneath my feet.

Broken. I feel so *broken*.

"You did this to yourself."

I just stare at the shards of mirror, seeing my face in a thousand different pieces. Seeing my ribbons in a thousand more.

Seeing him.

Hearing him.

Over and over again.

"Don't disobey me anymore, Precious."

"If I can't have her, no one can."

"This hurts me a lot more than it hurts you."

"You did this to yourself."

My reflection in these mirrors shows every range of emotion looking back at me. Judgment, disappointment, pity, anger, numbness, anguish. My broken faces surround me as I drop to the floor and start digging through the shards with frantic desperation.

I snatch up the ribbons, but the mirrors make it confusing, and just when I try to grab hold of the satin strips, my hands hit the glass instead. I slice open my palms, my fingers, my knees.

Still, I dig through it desperately, tears and blood dripping down simultaneously, while the cut-away ribbons evade me at every turn. But I can't give up.

I need them back.

I need them back I need them back I need them back

My grip comes away bloody, mangled, not a single scrap of ribbon safe in my hold. Then, I start to sink. Tied at the ankles and dragged under, so the glass starts cutting into my stomach, my arms, my chest.

No matter how hard I try to dig my way back up, I get pulled further down, dragged by a million shards of myself that broke, tangled in the lengths of ribbons I'll never get back.

And a single gilded dagger, sharper than all the rest, digging right into my throat.

"You did this to yourself."

My eyes burst open, lids rimmed with the dampness of tears. My hand is already at my throat, frantic movements checking for blood that isn't there. I take several gasping breaths, sitting up in the otherwise empty bed. I'm shaking all over, covered in sweat, and I fling the covers off the bed, because it feels like the walls are closing in on me.

I pace around the room.

Back and forth, socks gathering static with every quick tread. My back feels battered and aching, as if the dream implanted it with phantom pain. With another particularly nasty twinge, I grab the lantern from the bedside table and pass through the bathroom before heading into the closet. I hang the lantern on the doorknob and then lift my shirt, standing there in front of the floor-length mirror.

When another stitch of pain jumps at my lower back, I turn around and carefully lift the wrapping Hojat keeps bound around my back.

My breath has gone rickety, nearly creaking from my throat in derelict protest. And when I look over my shoulder at my reflection, gaze zeroed in on the spot that's hurting me, this time I *do* make a noise that scrapes past my lips.

The pair of my ribbons at the very bottom of my back are hanging on by a thread. Like skin that's started to peel, left attached to harden and shrivel. My fingers barely skim over them, but even that faintest touch has them both falling off.

Just like that.

Like browned leaves on a stem, dead and brittle they fall. Swaying to the floor in near weightlessness until they land on the rug, two sorry pieces of shrunken and emaciated ribbons that have lost their gleam.

My eyes burn as I look down at them, and they fill when I press my fingers to the indents in my back. Nothing there but a pair of thin scratches on either side of my spine.

As if my ribbons were never there at all.

The sob that comes out of me is cut off as I slap a hand to my mouth. Muffled more when I lean against the closet wall, shoving my face against the spare coat hanging up.

My ribbons are going to flake off like that, one by one, until my back is bare and there's nothing left.

I think a part of me believed that they were going to heal. Grow back. But all hope of that has flaked off, left to wither and wilt with the pieces at my feet.

So that's it. That's it now.

They're gone, and I'm not going to get them back, and I just have to deal with that.

I breathe against the coat, trying to exhale out this chiseled-in mourning, though it's carved too deep for me to get rid of. So when I've steadied myself again, I swipe away the tears that have leaked down my cheeks, and then methodically replace my bandages and pull down my shirt.

I pick up the dried, disintegrating ends. Hold them carefully in my palm. My mourning melds with my anger, stoked fresh with prodding and sparks.

With a shored-up sigh, I grab the lantern and leave the closet, going back into the bedroom where I place the ends and the lantern onto the bedside table. There's no chance of getting back to sleep now.

Passing the banked fire, I leave the bedroom and walk down

the dark hallway, my feet going faster, like they want to break out into a run. When I get to the living room, the flames in the fireplace are burning a bit more brightly, and one look at the clock on the mantel tells me that it's early evening, though the house is quiet.

Movement from the kitchen catches my eye, and my gaze settles on the lone figure sitting at the table with a cup clutched in his hands and a bottle in front of him. I pause for a brief moment before I drift over, taking a seat directly across from him.

Digby lifts his gaze, settling his steady bark-colored eyes on me. For a moment, we just look at one another. Without bars between us. Without a king who had no business wearing a crown. Without rules or expectations. We look at each other as two people who have a culmination of shock still working through their systems.

I don't know what Digby can see in my eyes, but I know what I see in his. I see countless hours of torture. Of imprisonment. Punishment. I see racking guilt and bone-deep injury and stark regret. I think that's what pains me the most. That I can see, despite everything that's happened to him, that he's suffering right here, for *me*. For what I endured and what he was forced to watch.

"It was always you with the power."

I smile shakily at his words. "I imagine it was a big shock when you saw me in Ranhold. Probably seemed foolish to you once you knew what I could do and how much I let him walk all over me for so many years. You must think I'm very stupid and weak."

He shakes his head fiercely. "Even the most powerful people can be made to feel powerless. Finding your strength even when you believe you have none is what makes you a true force. Nobody made you into what you are, my lady. You were *always* strong. You just had to prove it to yourself."

I swallow hard, still brushing off that awful dream, still feeling those ends fall off my back like petals flaking off a flower. "I wish I hadn't waited so damn long."

"And I wish I'd never let the bastard hurt you in the first place. I should've been there for you. Should've shielded you from what happened."

With my shaky hand, I reach across the table and grip his fingers still tucked loosely around the cup. "It's not your fault, Dig." My words are a hoarse whisper with nothing but crystal-clear truth.

And his face just…buckles.

Haunting exhaustion and crippling wounds are like a hand curling around the parchment of his expressions, crumpling them in one grappled fist.

And then, my stoic, steady, inscrutable guard *cries*.

Right here at the table, pain etches out of him in unwanted waves. His other hand covers his face, as if he wants to try and smother the grief. His fingers are bruised, his pinky stained permanently black and held at an awkward angle, lost against its battle with frostbite, just as he's lost the battle with his unflappable disposition.

His outward display shocks me, making tears spring up to my own eyes because seeing someone so indomitable suddenly break down is a shock all on its own. Makes all my own emotions so much sharper.

When he drops his hand, Digby's face is puffy and mottled,

his lips cracked and his body more slumped than I've ever seen him.

"I'm sorry," he utters on a single shaken breath trying to be stable. "I'm sorry."

"Look at me, Digby," I say, and his wet eyes lift. "It was *not* your fault. Not any of it."

"I was supposed to protect you."

My fingers squeeze his. "You did," I tell him. "You always did."

He takes in another breath, an inhale raked over rubble. He wipes at his eyes. "I'm proud of you. For what you did."

He means it, too.

I pull my hand back. "You were a Highbell guard for a long time."

Digby waves dismissively. "I could've retired years ago," he tells me, making my brows shoot up in surprise. "Stayed for you."

Shock pools at my chest, lapping in warm waves against my heart. "You did?"

He nods, running a hand through his thick gray beard. "You needed someone watching your back. Didn't trust anyone else to do it." His mouth twists in disgust. "I should've just let you out of that fucking cage. Thought about it. Many times. But I should've fucking done it."

"If you'd done that, you would've been tortured and killed. Head on a spike that I would've been forced to gild."

"Or I would've gotten you out," he says stubbornly. "Gotten you free. That's what matters."

The fact that he'd even considered it speaks volumes.

He lifts his cup, takes a long draw from it and then says, "Midas wanted to take you along with him on his own caravan to Fifth Kingdom, you know."

My brow furrows. "Really?"

Digby nods slowly, eyes down in his cup. "I was the one who suggested it would be smarter to send you separately, in case anything happened to the royal envoy. Convinced him that he needed to assess things at Ranhold before he should send for you. To make sure you would be secure there. I gave him a vow that I would protect your travel to Fifth. That you would be safe with the other saddles."

His face is troubled again, forehead wrinkled in thought, while I just slump against my seat, taking it in.

"But really, I knew after what happened with King Fulke, you just needed time apart from the bastard. He always kept you so fucking tight in his fist." His own hand curls together as if he's imagining Midas's grip around me now. "But I almost got you kidnapped by fucking snow pirates."

My mind whirls with this information. I had no idea that Digby's guilt ran this deep.

"If it weren't for you, I might never have gotten out of that cage. That trip was the catalyst to it all," I tell him. "And you're right, I did need time apart. That was my first taste of freedom in a long time, and if it hadn't happened, I wouldn't have met Rip that night. I wouldn't have started to question...*everything*." I shake my head, my chest feeling tight. "You can't keep blaming yourself, Digby. Because all the horrible things that happened to me, they led me here."

Digby watches me steadily, and I let him see the truth in my face. Let him see that I mean exactly what I've said.

"And I'm glad I'm here, Dig," I add on a murmur. "Despite it all, I'm glad I'm here with you."

I see him swallow hard, his eyes gone glassy just before he sniffs it away. The two of us, we understand the progression, witnessed the journey from there to here over all these years. So I take a deep breath, and then I shrug off my clinging ache. Because we aren't there anymore. We're here.

And I want to make the most of it.

I take the bottle, pouring more wine into his cup. "So, what do you say we finally play that drinking game?"

He blinks at me, letting out a husk of a laugh as he drags his cup toward him. "Alright, Lady Auren. You can have your drinking game."

My lips curve up, and I hold up the bottle in a toast. "No longer live the king."

His mouth curves in a rare smile that I'm not sure I've ever seen. "No longer live the fucking king. And may you kick anyone's ass who ever tries to hurt you again."

I think it's the perfect way to start our game.

I clink the bottle against his cup. "My thoughts exactly."

CHAPTER 22

QUEEN MALINA

The man sitting across from me is polished and poised, as if he'd grown up in royal court all his life. In actuality, he's been a rootless nomad. He's traveled all over Orea doing odd jobs, helping the poor, chasing away thieves and raiders.

Why he decided to come to this frozen edge of the world, I don't know. But he showed up to visit Highbell, and when I saw him appear at court the first time, our eyes locked. He's been here ever since, though I still can't quite fathom it. He seems to have just dropped from the sky.

"You are very beautiful."

My lips curl up at the compliment. "I know."

I'm certain that my reply catches him off guard, because his brown eyes widen a fraction before he gives off a small laugh.

But it's true. I do know I'm beautiful. Any beautiful

person who says otherwise is lying. Sometimes, it's to fish for compliments. But mostly, it's because they have been taught by society—men, in particular—that we have to downplay our beauty, to only let them determine it. To seem humble. But I don't have to be humble.

I'm a princess.

Of course, being a princess has its downsides too. Right now, for instance. Instead of being able to have this conversation privately, there's an audience. Three of my ladies-in-waiting are embroidering by the window. Though even I can tell they're more interested in eavesdropping than making their stitches. I should walk over to the fireplace that's tucked into the corner of the tea room and toss their hoops into the flames, letting them balk. Yet my mother taught me to never let my temper burn hot. Rashness, fiery tantrums, outbursts, those are never well thought out.

Punishment is best served cold.

"You told me you've frequented theaters during your travels throughout the other kingdoms," I reply, eyes flicking back to him. "I'm sure you've met many beautiful women."

He tips his head as if in thought, lets a hand run down the gold thread along his collar. "None like you."

I know this too. There isn't a single family line whose heirs are born with snowy white hair—that's a Colier trait. I have had sonnets sung to me, artists who have painted my likeness as a white rose growing out of the Highbell snow. I have been praised since I was a little girl for my unique beauty.

I have also had many offers for my hand in marriage, but this time, it's different.

258

This time, the man sitting across from me has charmed my father. And there are only two things that my father can be charmed by: power and wealth.

Tyndall Midas just happens to have both.

Leaning forward, I reach to pick up the teapot from the table in front of us and pour out more tea before I take a sip. It's still warm, despite the fact that we've been sitting here talking for the past hour.

"So, is that something you like to do here? Go to the theater in the city?" Tyndall asks.

After taking another sip, I place the cup back down on the glass table. I can see both of our legs beneath, mine shrouded by the skirts of my white dress, and his encased in brown trousers, the buckles on his boots solid gold.

"I do not enjoy the theater perhaps as well as I should," I admit.

He tilts his head slightly, making the flames from the fireplace cast his golden hair in an orangish shadow. "And why is that? I thought most young women loved watching plays."

"But that's just it, isn't it?" I reply, stroking a hand against the hair that's swept over my shoulder. "They're playing. I get enough of people pretending on a stage while I'm at court."

"I suppose I won't ask you to attend one with me, then." A wide, bright smile comes over Tyndall's face. I have to admit, the sight makes my stomach flutter. I am not one to be so casually charmed. Another aftereffect from court adulation. Yet this is different. I don't dislike his attentions. For one, he's not from this kingdom, and therefore, he's something new.

For another, when he looks at me, it feels like he's actually interested in me.

Unlike the other possible suitors, he doesn't constantly meet with my father. Instead, he puts all of his attention on me.

"On the contrary," I tell him. "I have a feeling I wouldn't be nearly as annoyed as I usually am when I go with my ladies."

When he smiles again, I find my own lips curling up too. The motion makes my cheeks hurt. I don't smile very often. I'm not one to give fake grins or to simper. I only smile when the person or the moment truly warrants it.

Is this what it feels like to fall in love?

The smiling, the stomach tightening? I have no one to ask. Not with my mother dead and buried, certainly not with my father, who only ever speaks to me either from across a formal dining table or during a court function. I'd rather scoop out my own teeth with a serrated spoon than ask my simpering ladies.

I suppose the theater will be good for something after all. The romances played out on that stage are the only examples I can go by.

"You'd make a very fine leading man," I tell him, eyes sweeping over his figure.

"Well, from what you've explained, there will be plenty of opportunity at court for me to try my hand at a good pretend."

I let out a small laugh. "I look forward to watching your performance. Actually, you will be performing from what I understand?"

"Indeed," he says. "If all goes well, I will present myself to your court with a formal show of magic."

"I must admit, I'm especially excited to see it. From what my father has said, your magic is fascinating."

"I'll gild something just for you," he says with a wink.

My heart skips a beat. "I'd like that very much."

His smile softens, but when I reach out to grab my teacup again, he captures my hand instead. A gasp sucks through my lips at such a bold move, and my eyes dart to the right again to see if my ladies noticed, but thankfully, they're actually keeping their heads down on their needlework for once.

"Your hand is quite cold," he says quietly as his thumb skates over my skin.

"They're always like that." I'm embarrassed at how shaken my voice sounds. "Everything about this kingdom is cold. Its princess included."

He hums beneath his breath, eyes locked on my pale skin, while I take the moment to be able to study his face. He's handsome, there's no doubt about that. With his clean-shaved face and arched brows and so much charm packed into a single expression. It's no wonder my breath catches again when he lifts his eyes to mine.

For a moment, I get lost in the depths of his eyes, and I wonder if he gets lost in mine. I've heard some men say that the pale blue of my eyes is unnerving. Yet when he looks at me like this...I don't think he's unnerved.

No, he looks at me like he's thinking about doing things far too inappropriate during high tea.

"May I ask you a question, Princess?" he purrs, making a shiver travel down my back.

"Yes."

"If I asked for your hand in marriage, would you want to accept?"

My eyes go wide. Of course, I know that he and my father have been in discussion about it. Yet that's something that the men always decide—especially when it comes to royals, and even more so when it has to do with a powerless princess.

"You're asking my opinion?" The idea is ludicrous. None of the other would-be suitors have ever asked me whether or not I wanted to marry any of them. The fact that he is asking is a bit mind-boggling.

"I am," he says.

"My father's opinion is the one that matters." There's a hint of bitterness crawling over my words like biting ants. "You have an incredible power and wealth that could restore Sixth Kingdom's glory and stability."

"Yes," he says slowly. "But I am not asking about your father or your kingdom. I'm asking about you."

Startled, I blink at him, my straight spine hitting the back of my chair.

"If you don't want this, tell me at once," he says, eyes looking between mine, his hand still holding my own with a steady warmth that's so foreign. "I would never wish to move forward with something that you didn't wish for. Would it make you happy, Princess?"

Sincerity drips off his tone like honey from a spoon. Slow and sweet, making me want to lean forward and lap it up.

This must be what it's like. This must be what all those silly romance plays are about.

"I would be happy," I finally answer quietly, though that

word...I'm not sure I truly know what being happy means. I haven't been happy since before my mother died years ago. But I would like to be happy again.

I would like to have a husband who I actually liked. Who actually liked me. I would like to have control over my life and not always be thrust away by my father, forever punished for being born a girl without any magic. If it weren't for my white Colier hair, I suspect he may have tried to denounce me as his heir years ago.

I don't even realize that a tear has dripped down my cheek until Tyndall lets go of my hand to reach up to brush it away.

Not once has a man ever touched my cheek. My own father never even placed a kiss there when I was young. So perhaps that's why it feels like such an intimate thing. Perhaps I am so starved for and startled by touch, that it's the reason I freeze beneath it.

"None of that," he says quietly, and I don't know whether I want to cry or smile, but he's somehow gotten me to do both in the same hour, when I've gone without either for so long.

I marvel at the feel of his hand cupping my cheek. Marvel at how, for the first time in my life, I actually want.

Yet the moment is broken with the sharp hit that comes from the clearing of a throat. Suddenly remembering we're not alone, I jerk away from him, gaze darting over to my ladies. They're all looking at me now, disapproval pulling at their brows. Yet their chastisement doesn't quite ring true. Not with the glint of excitement in their eyes now that they have a piece of gossip to later spread throughout the castle.

How I loathe them.

Clearing my throat, I take a moment to gather my composure as I run my hands down my skirt. Yet it's not the fabric that I feel, it's his touch, the way his fingers curled around my palm. The warmth that seeped in from his skin to mine. The trace of the tear he swiped away with his fingertip.

"Princess—" Tyndall begins, but that gets cut short too.

The door to the tea room opens, and my main guard walks in with a bow. "Pardon, Your Highness, but your father has requested to see the gentleman."

I try not to let the disappointment show as we get to our feet. "Of course," I say as we head for the door. "I'll join you."

Yet the guard shakes his head. "King Colier was specific. He wants to meet with only the gentleman."

My spine stiffens, anger pressing my lips together tightly. Tyndall sweeps a light yet comforting brush against my back as he passes. "It's alright, Princess. I will speak to your father, and then we can see about getting out to that theater, yes?"

I give a stilted nod. "I'd like that."

He lowers himself into an elegant bow and then turns and leaves the room. The guard removes himself once more, while I return to the table and sip on tea that's now gone cold, though I don't really notice it.

In my father's eyes, I'm still an accessory—and an inadequate one at that. Yet every time he's tried to marry me off, it always falls through because he won't settle for anything less than an exorbitant price for my hand.

After all, he knows that by marrying me off, he's handing off his kingdom too. And his kingdom is in dire straits, so tangled with debt that it will take a hefty pair of shears to cut through it. Lucky for him, Tyndall apparently has solid gold ones.

The soft whispers of my ladies make my gaze snap to them, the hair on the back of my neck rising like a bristling cat's.

Get out. Go away. Stop your mindless, stupid chatter.

That's what I want to say. That's what I would do, if I were queen.

If this marriage contract actually goes through, I can have a husband who can come to love me. I can actually have some power here in my own kingdom, even though I have no magic to speak of.

I can have some control. I can be happy. I can have a child of my own and raise another Colier heir worthy of the throne, who will have enough magic to keep it.

Tyndall Midas feels like the answer to my unspoken hope. So I close my eyes, deciding I'm actually going to voice them.

Great Divine, hear my prayers...

I wake with a start.

My eyes are wide, my ears throbbing with the sound of my own whispered plea in my head, like an undying echo. Even my cheek seems to sear from Tyndall's long-ago touch, like it was just moments ago, rather than years.

Fool.

I was a naive, ignorant fool.

Sharp bitterness rises like shards of ice on my tongue that I try to swallow down. The dream was an exact replica, as if that memory was plucked from my consciousness and played out behind my tired eyes.

Why my mind would torment me with that now, I've no idea.

Probably because I'm stuck in the back of a wooden cart, using my coat for a blanket, with a curved hillside as the only form of shelter. Why is it that when you're physically vulnerable, your mind decides to become vulnerable too?

I sit up, my movements stiff with aggravation. The shelter from the snowy hilltop is paltry and laughable, but it keeps the wind at bay somewhat. What it doesn't keep at bay are the memories that keep jumping up in my mind like snapped springs, breaking through the mattress to cut right into me without warning.

Times with Tyndall repeat while I'm asleep. But when I'm awake, I see Jeo. I see my freckled saddle getting stabbed in the snow, his blood as red as his hair. I see the shadowed man distorting dark and light, eyeing me beneath a hood and pointing at me like death incarnate come to hunt me down.

My body involuntarily shivers, though it's not from the cold. The cold doesn't even seem to touch me.

"My queen?"

Shifting my body, I slam a barrier between those memories as I lean over the cart. I see Sir Pruinn sprawled on the ground with the horses, their saddle blankets spread beneath them as a feeble layer against the snow.

Despite our hard travel, he doesn't look rumpled. His tailored clothing is still unwrinkled, his boots holding their shine, and his jaw clean-shaven, though I don't know when he's had time to shave. His skin doesn't even seem to be chapped from the freezing cold air that always pelts at our faces.

"I wish to get moving for the day, Sir Pruinn."

He sits up from where he was resting against the animal, seeking its heat, head tilting up as if he needs to do that in order to confirm it's still dark out. "It's not yet dawn."

"It's not far off," I reply before I turn and grab my coat, pulling it on. The waterskin Pruinn gave me falls out from its folds, hitting the wooden planks of the cart with a thump. "The water has frozen."

I hear him sigh, but then he's up and on his feet, stretching slightly before he comes over to take it. As he does, he brushes against my fingers, and his dark and severely arched eyebrows lift. "My queen, you should really reconsider sleeping on the cart. The horses offer warmth—"

"And they'd offer their stench too," I say, cutting him off.

"Yes, but..."

"I'm fine on the cart, Sir Pruinn," I say primly. "What I'm not fine with is wasting time."

Without waiting for a reply, I step off the cart and trudge through the snow to do my morning ministrations. It's completely uncivilized being exposed and forced to squat like an animal, with the snowfall as a washbasin.

When I'm finished, I come back to where Pruinn has already hitched and fed the horses. Fortunately for us, the bottom of the cart was loaded with bales of hay and a couple bushels of food. Even with rationing, our supply has already dwindled to half.

We haven't discussed what will happen if the horses run

out of hay and can no longer carry us. Or what will occur once our own reserves run dry. I'm not sure I want to know.

I walk over as he's finishing up with the animals, the sky dim. A drab veil is cast over it, as if even the clouds feel subdued this morning. "How many more nights am I expected to be out in the elements of Sixth Kingdom like this?"

He rifles through his shoulder bag, pulling out a familiar pouch. After digging into it, he hands me an oat bar. That, plus jerky and dried fruit, makes up the entirety of what we've been living off of, along with melted snowfall for water. "Since we're getting such an early start, we should be out of it by tomorrow."

My hand drops, oat bar and thirst forgotten. "We'll be out of the elements tomorrow?" I say, hope burgeoning in my tone. There are no cities or villages out this way, of that I'm sure, but perhaps a traveling merchant such as himself knows of a lone homestead? Somewhere that we can sleep *inside* and be fed something more than travel packs?

But Sir Pruinn shakes his head, pulling the hood of his coat over his shorn blond hair, just as it begins to lightly snow. "Not the elements. We'll be out of Sixth Kingdom."

This stops me short. "Already?"

"Remember the map?" he says with a smile, his gray eyes almost twinkling. My hackles rise, because he's talking about the map that apparently shows me how to reach my heart's greatest desire. "It showed me a shortcut."

My back stiffens. "Of course it did."

"I thought that would make you happy, my queen."

Would it make you happy, Princess?

I grind my teeth loud enough to drown out the memory of Tyndall's words in my head, and then spin back toward the cart, settling myself into it for another long day of endless traveling. Toward what? I've no idea. Perhaps it's all a lie, and Sir Loth Pruinn, the strange albeit magnetic traveling merchant, is nothing but a fraud. Perhaps he's leading me to the ruined Seventh Kingdom, where he'll toss me off the edge of the world.

I would be happy.

Fool.

Naive, ignorant fool.

CHAPTER 23

AUREN

It's been a whole week. Seven days of training. I sleep until dusk, by which point Slade has already disappeared to wherever he goes, and then I get dressed and come here to train with Judd until I want to pass out. Then I wash myself as best I can without getting my bandages wet, and join everyone for dinner.

I don't cook it. I think we've all agreed that's for the best.

After dinner, I usually join in with the others playing cards while Hojat reads or mixes up some new tincture to try on Digby or myself. The storm still hasn't stopped. I can hear it blowing through the entrance of the cave at all hours, raging against the shelter of the Grotto.

And me, I stay up long after everyone else goes to bed, not falling asleep until dawn. I don't trust myself to be up with the sun. But...I haven't gilded anything. Not a single time. Not even while I've laid asleep in the bed. My borrowed clothes are the same brown and black color as before, the blankets and furs on the bed untouched by my power.

I don't know what that means, but I'm silently stewing in worry, avoiding the topic at all costs.

When I woke up in that cave and felt the power coursing through me, I just needed it to *stop*. To be shut away. Because my gold can't be trusted. Especially not that facet I've never even known that I was capable of before.

Now…now it seems like it's broken completely. As if whatever I did in Ranhold that night has changed my gold-touch irreparably. But I'm just going to focus on getting stronger physically for now. So I sleep the daylight away instead of obsessively worrying about why my gold-touch seems to have dried up.

"You're looking at your feet again."

Judd's voice makes my head wrench up. "Sorry."

"Can't have your eyes buried into the ground," he tells me. "Or the beam. Now take three steps forward. No looking."

I bite my lip, fighting every instinct to look down. The wooden beam beneath my feet must be at least ten feet long. When I came into the Teeth yesterday, it was waiting for me in the very middle of the room. I can't even imagine how heavy it must be. When I asked Judd, he said Slade and Ryatt had brought it in earlier for me. I'm a bit disappointed that I missed the sight of them carrying it.

For the past two days, I have been doing nothing but these beam exercises. It's forcing me to re-learn how to balance.

I've fallen off more times than I can count. My legs ache, the arches of my feet feel sprained, and even my toes are sore. But I don't quit.

"One," Judd counts as I place one foot in front of the other. "Two, three... Good."

He walks the length of the beam on the ground beside me, the blue light of the Teeth's jaw casting a long shadow behind him.

"Now I want you to turn around and walk three steps the other way."

I groan. "Do I have to?"

Judd laughs. "Come on, Gildy."

He's had me do this very move so many times, but I always lose my damn balance. My body still wants to rely on the ribbons that are no longer there. Still, I force myself to twist my back foot and spin around...only to go pitching right off the beam and landing ass-first in the needling hay on the ground.

They're pokey. It doesn't feel great.

I let out a growl of frustration, slapping my hand against the beam and then getting even more aggravated when tiny splinters break off into it. I yank off my glove and toss it to the floor.

"Again."

I cut Judd a look. "I hate you."

"Gotta walk before you can run, Gildy. Or in your case, gotta balance before you can stop falling on your ass."

"Thank you for bestowing that wisdom."

He dusts off the shoulder of his black coat. "Anytime."

I stand back up onto the beam, trying to ignore my throbbing feet and smarting ankles, my arms automatically lifting up to try and steady my balance. The muscles in my legs tighten to keep me steady.

"Walk all the way to the end."

I nod and go slowly, but my eyes flick down to double-check I'm not about to go walking right off the edge.

"I saw that. No peeking."

I swear this man has an uncanny ability to know where I'm looking. Yanking my eyes back up, I keep my line of sight at the other end of the cave.

"Don't overthink it. There you go... Now stop and turn."

I do it without thought, spinning on the ball of my foot... and I actually don't fall over. Instead, my other foot plants perfectly in front of the one I just swiveled, and then before I know it, I'm successfully facing the other way.

My eyes go wide, and a huge grin comes over my face. "I did it!"

"Very good," he says with a clap. "Now let's do that ten more times."

My smile melts right off my face. "Shouldn't we just end on this high note?"

"Nice try," he says, walking up to be parallel with me. "Now that we know you can do it, you're going to master it."

Judd isn't kidding about doing it ten times. I probably do it about forty more times in all, because he doesn't count it if I fall or flail or stumble.

The jerk.

By the time I manage to complete my tenth one, I collapse

on the ground, knees up in front of me, elbows leaning on them as I drop my head toward my lap and pant. I'm covered in sweat and splinters, and my feet are *killing* me.

"My ankles feel like they want to burst through my skin."

"You did well," Judd says, coming up to me and passing me some water.

I guzzle it down, not even caring that some of it drips from the sides of my lips and goes down my chin. When I hand it back to him, I say, "Thanks for pushing me, Judd."

"Anytime. Now, don't forget to get some snow and use it to ice your feet and legs. Because tomorrow, we'll be doing more beam work."

I groan, rubbing my spasming calf. "I hate icing them."

"But it helps."

"It does," I relent. Not only does Hojat help to ice my sore muscles, but he's also been placing snow packs on my back. As much as I hate it while it's on, it really has helped a lot.

"Ready to go?"

I nod, and when I take Judd's hand for him to help haul me to my feet, I don't even flinch. Already, I'm getting more used to touch. It's strange how much has changed in such a short amount of time.

Together, we leave the cracked entrance of the Teeth, spilling out into the main cave of the Grotto. As soon as we do, I see a figure striding for us, and even though my eyes don't adjust right away, my body knows exactly who it is.

When Slade's close enough that I can see the shadowed lines of his face, his intent attention spills my heartbeat into a scattered runoff.

"You're limping," he says by way of greeting, stopping in front of us.

"I'm okay, my feet are just sore."

"I told her to ice them," Judd tells him. "But she did good today. Her balance has already improved. She's ready to move on as soon as her back is a bit more healed up."

Slade nods, and I can see approval cast over his expression. "I'd like to take you somewhere, if you're willing."

My brows lift in surprise, and my pulse picks up in pace. It seems like he's been avoiding me. We share dinner together with the others, but he always goes off to do things while I fall asleep on my own, and then I wake up the same. The only indication that he's actually stayed in there with me is that the fire is always tended to, the pillow on his side always indented. I can't really blame him though. I'm the one sleeping away the day.

"It will be something relaxing, I promise," he tells me, obviously picking up on my hesitation.

"Okay," I say with a nod, though I feel guilty for making it seem like he has to convince me. He's still feeling really guilty about the whole rot thing. "I'd like that."

Relief flashes through his eyes just before Judd claps us both on the shoulders. "You two have relaxing fun. I'm off to go make Lu play cards with me. She got all my money again last night." He turns and walks off, his silhouette disappearing in the direction of the house.

I look up at Slade, very aware that we're alone. We haven't been alone, not really. Not since I woke up in that cave and practically jumped him.

Clearing my throat, I ask, "Where are we going?"

"You'll see."

Then he turns and kneels down in front of me. "Hop on."

I blink. "What?"

"I saw your grimace every time you took a step. I want to carry you, but I don't want to hurt your back. So hop on."

My feet shift in place, but even that sends a shock of pain down my arches. "Are you sure?"

He glances at me over his shoulder. "Am I sure that I want your body pressed against mine while I carry you so that you're not in pain? Yes."

I can't help but feel a little thrill at the way he looks at me.

"Alright," I say quietly.

Tentatively, I wrap my arms around his neck, and he instantly lifts me up, my legs going around his hips. It immediately makes me think of the *other* time my legs wrapped around him, only I was latched onto his front, grinding against him and desperate to be mindless, to not have to think, to be punished and pleasured as my world came crashing down around me.

Slade adjusts me on his back as he straightens up, his strong hands coming down to grip my thighs. The thick leggings do absolutely nothing to keep a barrier against his touch, because I can feel it searing into the skin of my legs, making me tingle.

"Are you sure this is okay?" I ask, since my hourglass figure means I'm no twig.

His fingers dig into my thighs, letting a dark chuckle

rumble against my chest. "More than okay, and I think I proved that fact the other day, don't you?"

I don't need a mirror to know that my cheeks are flaring with a gilded blush.

He starts to walk, heading in the opposite direction as Judd, away from the house. His steps are steady, his touch strong, but I can't help the nerves that are jumping around in my veins.

"Relax, Auren."

It's like my body was waiting for that command, because as soon as he says it, I'm able to release the vise grip around my nervousness. Slowly, I let my body ease, my breasts pressing against this muscular back, my cheek resting on his shoulder. I silently revel in it. This feeling is still very new.

I've never felt so *safe* as I do when he's holding me. When my body is against his. It's not safety with strings attached, it's not comfort with conditions. He holds me like he wants nothing else in return, and it's so foreign that I still find myself in awe at how this can be for *me*.

"Your thoughts are awfully loud back there," Slade says.

I glance up at the thinning lines of blue along the ceiling. "I'll try to keep it down."

"On the contrary, I want you to voice them."

"I was thinking...that this is still very new. That there's so much we don't know about each other."

He doesn't answer right away, instead letting his thoughts percolate in the air. "That's true," he finally replies. "I suppose the two of us have learned to be very good at keeping secrets."

I let out a little laugh. "That's an understatement."

"But I think that's what I'm looking forward to the most," he confesses, his voice sounding sensually low. "Peeling you back, layer by layer. Learning you inside and out." His hands squeeze my thighs, and even though he's not talking about anything sexual, my body still responds like he is, my mind imagining him peeling off the layers of my clothes and laying me bare in a completely different way. "I'm looking forward to every edge of you that you'll reveal to me."

I swallow thickly, trying and failing to keep the heat from gathering low in my belly. "I look forward to that with you too."

His head turns to the side so he can look at me over his shoulder. "Good."

The thought of baring myself to him—in more ways than one—always sends my pulse racing. It's invigorating and vulnerable, so scary and yet so thrilling.

I don't know if I've been avoiding him or he's been avoiding me since I woke up, or maybe it's a combination of both, but all of that just feels so complicated compared to this quiet moment in the dark.

"Where are we going?" I ask him again.

"Such impatience."

I roll my eyes. "Like you'd let me lead you somewhere without telling you where it was."

"Oh, Goldfinch, I'd follow you to the end of the world and tip right off the edge, all because of a crook of your finger."

My stomach does a flip. "Oh."

"Oh, indeed."

He continues down the cave and takes a sharp left. "Almost there."

Then I see what looks like a dead end but is actually an enclave blocked by a short rock wall. As soon as Slade slips around it, there's a...*smell*.

My nose wrinkles. "Did you just..."

"Did I just what?"

Great Divine. It's *strong*. I have to suppress the urge to plug my nose.

I clear my throat. "I just can't help but notice that it smells. Badly. All of a sudden."

A startled laugh barks out of him. "That smell isn't coming from me, I assure you. Though I'm a bit worried that you think I could produce something so...pungent."

"I was worried too, believe me." The smell is consuming the air, but then I realize that the air is also *wet*, and there's a steady bubbling sound getting louder and louder.

"Here's the culprit," Slade tells me, just as he rounds another turn, where the small cave opens up to a room full of steam. The humidity instantly sticks to my skin and clothes, and the soft sound of bubbling draws my eye to the pool of water just ahead. "I chose this cave to build the Grotto because it was big enough to have a house and a training area, but this private hot spring was a definite perk."

"Is this the only one?"

"In here, yes. But there are others. The villagers who live here have a couple past the pavilion, inside the mountain there. It's much larger and has a couple smaller ones split away for more privacy."

"Amazing," I say, because while the pool of water is probably only just as long as Slade's bed, everything about this enclave is cozy and intimate. I've gotten so used to · the constant cold air that I practically melt into this steamy warmth.

As soon as Slade sets me down, I look around the softly glowing space. "It's so pretty." The veins of fluorescence running around the slightly domed walls and ceiling are reflected back in the water beneath, the blue clinging to the foggy air.

I walk closer, the rock beneath my boots slick with puddled moisture. The hot spring sits in the middle of the room, and there's a short area of raised rock that makes a shelf around it. The water itself is in constant movement from the gentle bubbles rising at the center. Kneeling down, I dip a finger into it and practically purr at the heat.

At a noise behind me, I turn around, only to find Slade shrugging off his coat and laying it onto a rock that's jutting up from the ground.

When I see him whip off his shirt next, my eyes go wide. His body never fails to make me surge with heat. All those perfectly defined muscles, those roots weaving beneath his pale skin and curving around his pecs, spreading up his collarbone and down his shoulders. He's so incredibly, beautifully fae.

"I figured you deserved a reward for training so hard," he says, and I have to force my eyes back up to his smirking face.

I blink over at the hot spring, excitement bubbling up as much as the water's heat. "We're getting in?"

His grin flashes through the dim room. "I wouldn't bring

you all the way in here just to tease you. I know your back isn't bandaged anymore, but Hojat said it's not quite ready for a soak. But I figured we could soak our feet and legs together."

"Great Divine, *yes*." I think I might weep in joy on behalf of my poor, aching feet. "But…why'd you take off your shirt if we're soaking our feet?"

"Don't worry, you won't submerge in the water—not until your back is all the way healed. But even so, we'll need to strip, otherwise our clothes will get soaked near the hot spring. The steam is very thick."

My eyes cast over to the bubbling pool, and he's right, I can see with my own eyes how dense the steam is, but that doesn't make me stop from panicking.

"I promise, the steam will feel nice."

My heart knocks against the rails of my ribs. "I'm sore," I blurt out.

Slade's lip twitches. "I will be the perfect gentleman," he assures me. "I only want to take care of you, to help you relax. Nothing more. And I've seen you bare before. There isn't an inch of you I haven't touched."

Heat that has nothing to do with the hot springs comes bubbling up into my core. But it's tempered with an edge of distress.

I don't have bandages wrapped around me anymore. If I take off my shirt, he'll see. He'll see the ugly, leftover bruising. The crinkled, frayed stubs. He'll see the ruin of my back.

And I still can't bear that.

I don't know when he moves behind me, but I startle at his soft voice. "Let me."

His fingers skim against the back of my neck, right where the first button is, and I can feel the heat of his breath press against my skin far more than the steam in the air.

I freeze, my fingers gripping the front of my collar while my emotions go jumbled and confused, like puzzle pieces all shaken up.

"No," I tell him, taking a step away. "I'm just going to leave this on."

He moves back into my line of vision, but I don't meet his eyes. The silence between us is like silt, the murky waters convoluted and confusing. But even in that silence, I know he hears. I know that he's listening to what I'm not saying.

Don't look. I don't want you to see.

"Alright," Slade finally says, his tone quiet.

I hear him walk toward the hot spring, and then a rustle of clothing tells me the moment he drops his pants. I feel my already heated cheeks flood with a blush.

My eyes flick up to see his completely nude body, his back facing me. I've never gotten to appreciate him from this angle before. I watch as he walks his way into the hot spring, the steam almost completely enveloping him. Yet it doesn't obscure the way his ass flexes before he steps in deeper, until his lower half disappears beneath the surface of the water.

He sticks to the perimeter, avoiding the bubbling center, and then the rest of him disappears for a second too as he dunks his whole body under. When he comes back up, he pushes his dripping black hair away from his face, and the movement is so incredibly sexy that, despite the moisture in the air, my mouth goes dry. Slade is all hard, sculpted muscles, an endless plane of strength and masculine beauty.

Right now, I feel lacking. Sweaty from training, hair tangled, my skin probably in heated blotches, and my back...

More than anyone else, Slade adored my ribbons. And now they're gone, and I just feel so...incomplete. Inadequate. I don't know if I'll ever *not* feel that.

"Coming in?" he asks.

With a nod, I kick off my boots and then peel off my leggings and socks, leaving them on a protruding stone. The shirt hits my thighs, and I walk closer, wrapped up in the steam, eyeing the water and his pinkening skin. "How are you not boiling alive?"

"The bubbles are from the hot water constantly coming up to circulate, but the flow is quite slow. It's not too hot, I promise."

There must be some kind of rock shelf inside the spring, because he sits down, facing me. He spreads his arms out on either side of him, hands resting on the rim of the cave's floor. It puts his muscles on full display, his lines of power only just barely visible as they bunch around his shoulders.

"Come here," he tells me, patting the rock beneath his hand. "You can sit and let your legs soak."

Nodding, my bare feet pad over the slick, warmed rock floor. I stop just beside him and then carefully sit down on the lip of the hot spring. The steam envelops us both so thoroughly that it makes the rest of the cave seem almost non-existent, basking us in a milky blue glow.

I dip one foot into the water and then instantly groan at

the delicious heat. Without wasting any more time, I slip my other foot in, letting my legs rest all the way down until the hot water laps at my calves.

"Great Divine," I breathe out, relishing in the heat. "This feels nice."

"I thought you might like it."

I brace my hands behind me. "This makes up for the stench."

He chuckles, and the noise makes my toes curl in the water. I slowly start to relax, fingers gently tugging at the hem of my shirt that rests on my upper thighs. Already, the material is damp, the fabric sticking to my breasts as the thick steam clutches against my skin, leaving me feeling dewy and warm all over.

"You sure the steam is okay?" I ask nervously, my back itching ever so slightly.

Slade nods. "Hojat said it was fine for a bit."

Letting out a sigh, I enjoy the feel of the bubbling water beneath my sore feet, my eyes skimming over the visible parts of him. "Your lines—they're usually spread to more of your body."

He looks down at his chest as if to see what I'm seeing. "They're not as pronounced after I expel magic."

With his arms free and bare, the lines of his power are like black blades of grass shifting slightly in a breeze.

"Do you have to do that a lot?"

"I've learned how to hold it in for long periods of time."

I frown. "That must be painful."

"It can be," he admits. "But I learned control a long time

ago, and part of that has to do with knowing when to hold back…and when to let go."

His eyes bore into me, and I know he's trying to steer me into this conversation, to turn it around to me. But I don't want to go there.

Not yet.

"Slade."

"We need to talk about it," he says firmly.

Memories of that night in Ranhold start to surround me just as much as the cloying steam. The amount of power I felt was indescribable. It seemed to feed something dark in me, seemed to multiply and grow. Having your magic suddenly feel so uncontrollable and foreign can be terrifying in itself, but it wasn't just the magic. It was me. *I* lost control.

Just like I did in Carnith.

I swore to myself I'd keep my magic locked up tight, but I failed all over again. It feels like I'm fifteen years old, with brand new magic dripping from shaky fingers and no clue how to manage it.

"Is that what this is?" I ask, my voice gone sharp, eyes cutting into him. "You only brought me in here to force me to talk?"

Slade's shoulders go tense, and he slowly lowers his arms into the water. "I would never force you to do anything," he says, his voice darkened, like the crisped edges of a leaf, curling and blackening with the burn. "And you should know that."

"Well, that's not strictly true, is it?" I say, the words flying from my mouth before I can stop myself. "I don't remember asking you to rot me."

Something stretched and harsh radiates between us. My pulse raps against my temples. I have to suppress the urge to place a hand over my chest, as if I'm afraid the rot is going to stir to life because I brought it up.

Slade leans forward slightly, the steam curling between us like sinuous specters, and I wish I hadn't said it. I wish I could pull the words right back into my mouth and swallow them down. Because I don't blame him. I don't resent him. If anything, I'm thankful, so I don't even know why I said it other than the fact that I'm lashing out so I don't have to face my own whip.

"You're right," he says, and despite the heat of the room, a chill lopes down my back. "But I will tell you this now, Goldfinch, and you will hear it. When it comes to your *life*, when it comes to the option between you living and dying, I will always step in. I will *always* choose to do whatever needs to be done to ensure that you *fucking live.*"

My inhale gets snagged against the rungs of my ribs, banging against it with hollow uselessness.

"I hate that I had to use my power against you, but don't mistake my guilt for regret, because you will be sorely mistaken. I would do it again in a fucking heartbeat."

His gaze is too intense, his words too hard-hitting. My eyes lower, my own guilt bubbling up as much as the heated water.

"I'm sorry. I don't know why I said that," I confess. "I'm not mad at you for that at all. If I were in your position, I'd have done the same thing. I'm grateful you were able to stop me. I wouldn't be here right now if you hadn't intervened. I will always be in your debt."

He doesn't say anything at first, and I worry that I've really upset him, but then I suddenly feel his hand lift my leg. I startle, because I didn't hear or see him move, but now he's right in front of me, his deft, strong fingers massaging into the sore arch of my foot as he stands in the water in front of me.

Our eyes lock as he presses into every sore inch, thumbs circling, hands moving my foot up and down. "You are not indebted to anyone, Goldfinch, least of all me," he murmurs as he continues to release the tension and the pain, like the real magic is in his touch. "You are priceless. You are worth more than gold. And the world owes you so much more than what you've been given."

I think a tear might drip onto my lashes, but I pretend it's the plugged-up steam.

Slade and I stay quiet after that. He massages both of my feet until I can't suppress the groans, until my arches no longer feel stretched and sore. Then his masterful hands move up to my calves, his firm touch pressing into the knots, rubbing every tender part. Because that's what he always does for me. He finds every aching part and helps me work through it.

Even when I don't want to.

CHAPTER 24

SLADE

F inally, the storm has broken.

The sky is bruised, with clouds of black and blue clinging to the horizon as night starts to give way.

With it, the air has finally stopped blowing, and all that's left of the blizzard from the past several days is what it dumped on the ground. A good six feet now borders all of Drollard, though the villagers were diligent and made sure to constantly clear off the paths and the fronts of houses, while the mountainside shelves helped to keep some of the snowfall from piling up in the pavilion. With the snow left to collect everywhere else, Drollard feels extra sheltered from the outside world.

I stride through the village with my hands buried in my pockets, and the only reason I don't slip over the icy paths is because of the grains of salt and sand that have been scattered around like birdseed.

I pass the slant-roofed homes, though all is quiet and still since it's not yet dawn. Smoke puffs up from the chimneys and breathes against the ceiling of the mountain's overhang, dissipating into the sky.

The pavilion is empty, save for the parked carts that the villagers use to gather supplies whenever they get a shipment in. A few arthritic trees cling to the ground, their knobby limbs and bent branches holding up tufts of needles and snow.

Just beyond, the pavilion is covered beneath the lip of the mountain's overhang, and it's here, past piles of firewood, past the stone fire pit, where the door to the Cellar is located. I check there first, but aside from a large room stocked full of supplies and a single cold-weary guard, there's no one there. He gives me a nod as I pass, and I then disappear into a split in the mountain just beyond, where the walls have been smoothed and filed back just enough to let a person through.

The cracked path is long and jagged, and for a while, I'm walking completely blind, no light afforded anywhere in the miserly fissure. When I finally make it to the end and squeeze out, the mountain is slightly more generous. There are a few blue lines spread through the cave's anemic walls, casting off the palest of glows.

Despite being out of the elements, it's colder inside here. The kind of cold that's stagnant and inert, the kind that never leaves. Yet despite that, I find myself growing hot as I get closer to the iron door set into the shadowed rock. By the time my footsteps bring me to the barred window so that I can look in, the cold is only acknowledged by the clouds of exhale that leave my mouth.

"How long have you been back?" I don't turn as I ask the question—I don't need to. I sensed him in here as soon as I walked in.

Ryatt stretches out his legs from where he's sitting. His shadowed form is blocking the firelight from the heat lantern hanging beside him, its orange flame fed from the oil in our very own mines.

"Couple of hours," he says roughly, making me finally turn to him.

"There's only one." My tone is tilted with a question.

He scratches the back of his head, making his black hair stand on end in some places. He normally keeps his longer than mine, always grumbling when he has to stand-in as Rip and cut it shorter. "You said you needed one to question."

"I said I needed *at least* one to question," I correct.

He doesn't look the least bit contrite. "If you wanted them all alive, you should've sent Judd. You knew I wasn't going to let all of Midas's rats come back here. You got what you wanted," he tells me, tipping his head toward the cell. "I got what I wanted with the others. Especially since they made it so hard to fucking find them all."

"How many were there?"

"Four. The lucky bit was my timberwing spotted theirs. That's how I finally found them holed up against some hill not far from here. Once they heard you'd arrived, they took off, scampering like the rats they are, but the storm took them out and grounded them."

At least the storm was good for something. Ryatt and I

had been out searching for days, looking for them, and I was starting to worry we weren't going to find them.

"You took satisfaction in killing the other three, I take it?"

Ryatt's wicked grin flashes. "They made a much better adornment in the frozen wastelands dead than they did alive."

Nodding, I once more look through the barred door, where I see a pitiful heap of a man slumped against the floor, shivering inside his gold-trimmed coat. I wonder how many days Auren spent gilding shit like this. How much of her energy and time and strength was spent on feeding Midas's reputation and ego. Just thinking about that makes anger burn down my back.

"You're up early," Ryatt says, face pitched in my direction, half of it blue, the other half completely shadowed.

I say nothing, taking a seat on the barrel just across from him. The truth is, I'm still struggling to sleep. Auren won't sleep at night, and I get barely a few hours tossing and turning before I give up before dawn, just as she slips in.

My brother makes a noise deep in his throat. "She's still not getting up during the day?"

I cut a look over to him. "She's adjusting."

"Is she?"

"What the fuck is that supposed to mean?"

Ryatt shrugs a shoulder. "I see the look on her face anytime someone mentions the gold. She's terrified of it."

"She's not," I snap, anger making my teeth clench.

"If you say so."

"Why are you so fucking concerned?"

"Why aren't *you*?" Ryatt counters. "We all saw her that night.

She might look like a mountain on the surface, but she's a volcano ready to erupt. And when she does, it's not some small thing."

"She's fine."

Ryatt doesn't let it drop though. Not that I would expect him to. Half of his personality is arguing with me.

"She's scared of her own power—and rightfully so. But fear is a dangerous thing when it comes to magic. You should know that better than anyone."

We stare at each other across the narrow path, on opposite sides of the cracked corridor. Blue streaks spread out from behind him, smearing him in their light, while the flickering lamps counter their glow.

"It's going to take time."

"And how much time can you afford?"

I rake a hand through my hair, tugging at the ends. "As long as she fucking needs."

He shakes his head, disgruntled and contrary. "You might be a king, but even you can't sustain that. Besides, you hate it here."

"I don't hate it here."

Ryatt rolls his eyes. "Sure you don't. That's why you only visit when you absolutely have to."

My back teeth feel like they might crack from how hard I'm grinding them. "I have a kingdom to run."

He scoffs. "Right. But before you had that, you had this village to protect."

I snap forward, elbows dug into my knees. "I do protect this village. You don't know even *half* of what I do to protect it. Of what I've sacrificed."

Ryatt levels me with a stare that probably rivals my own. "Do you really want to talk of sacrifices, brother? Because I've given up my whole *identity* to serve yours."

Sometimes, the chasm between us feels insurmountable. Like now, when we're so at odds, the distance from his side to mine can't be crossed.

"Have you even gone to visit?" he demands.

My spine locks up tight. "Don't ask questions that you already know the answers to. The sound of your voice isn't that soothing."

He ignores my jab. "Should've known."

"I've been a little busy, Ryatt."

"Right." Disdain drips down as he heaves to his feet. "Well, perhaps try to fit it into your schedule, Your Majesty." He bends at the waist into a mocking bow before striding off.

With ugliness buried in my chest, I watch him walk away, back stiff, steps carrying the weight of his anger.

It's hard to correlate the sight of him like this when my eyes also hold another time—of when he was more than a foot shorter than me, a scrawny little thing with wild black hair and jam smeared on his lips.

There was no walking away then. He always followed behind me or tried to clutch onto my arm, tethering us together with a mischievous smile. There were no angry glares aimed my way. We sought games and adventure instead of avoiding each other as we do now.

My anger expels with my exhale, dissipating in the cold air.

I lean back against the cave wall, feeling the threat of my spikes pushing against the inside of my arms.

Like my memories are too close to the surface, an old condemning voice rings clear in my head. *"Control, Slade. Are you some common fae to lose it so easily? Or are you going to be worthy of the blood in your rotted veins? Pull those spikes back, or I'll pin them to the estate wall and let you hang there till you learn."*

Maybe it's muscle memory of the countless days I spent under commands like that, but my spikes sink back below, the skin on my arms no longer bulging with the threat of their presence.

Control.

It was the first thing drilled in my head since the moment I started to change. Most fae are around fifteen or sixteen when their magic comes in.

I wasn't afforded that much time.

I still remember the itch. The way I raked my nails over the backs of my forearms, or tried to reach along my spine. I felt like a bear in the woods needing to scratch against the bark of a tree. Every time my spikes stabbed out of me, they ripped my skin to shreds, blood gaping from the gashes they cut.

For a year, they would bleed every time they came out—until crimson soaked every sleeve, the back of every shirt dotted with a perfect row, while more drops of blood dripped down into my eyebrows.

Worse still was the look I got—and that cutting voice. I learned how to suppress my spikes, learned how to only draw them out when I wanted them to come. I even stopped flinching when they stabbed through my skin. And soon,

I even stopped bleeding. As if even my blood was afraid to show itself to my father.

"There you are."

I glance up at Lu as she flits inside, though she's not alone. There's a messenger hawk gripping her shoulder, and neither of them look very pleased about it.

"This asshole just showed up. Flew right to the front door and started beating on it like its beak was a knocker." She tips her head at it, but when it pecks at her head, she bats it away. "She won't let anyone get the message. Wouldn't even trade for it," Lu says, holding out her palm where a handful of dried jerky waits. The hawk makes a noise of scorn, the hoarse sound accompanying a sharp dig of its talons into Lu's shoulder.

She winces, giving it a glare. "See what I mean?"

I stand up and walk over, and the bird immediately jumps from her shoulder to land on my arm, and holds out its leg. "Good girl," I croon, drawing a finger down the side of her neck. She clicks her beak together, eyes blinking at me as I take hold of the silver vial attached to her leg and remove the rolled parchment within.

My eyes flick over the words, and I've only made it halfway through when my fingers start to tighten over the paper. By the time I get to the end, I'm crumpling it, my entire body gone taut.

"What's wrong?"

Instead of answering, I pass Lu the letter, and I watch as her expression goes through the same emotions as my own. "Son of a bitch."

Her hand drops, crinkled letter still clutched as she looks at me. "Queen Kaila certainly didn't waste any time."

"No. She didn't."

Lu regards me silently for a moment. "What should we do?"

It's not exactly a surprise, but I thought we'd have a little more time. Because that's what Auren needs. Time.

Time to stand on her feet. To acclimate to the loss of her ribbons. To gain confidence. To be ready to face the world *and* her magic. She just killed her manipulative captor, discovered a new facet of her power, almost died in the process, and left everything she knows. She needs a fucking breather.

"Nothing," I finally answer.

Lu's black brows jump up. "Nothing?"

I shake my head. "It's an intimidation tactic meant to bully us. It's not going to work."

"But what if they come to Fourth?"

"Queen Kaila has two empty kingdoms to contend with and a frozen Barrens between us."

"But the other monarchs..."

"Can suck my dick."

She rolls her eyes. "As much as I'm sure they'd enjoy the invitation, they're still an issue."

"And an ocean away," I point out. "We have time."

"If you say so."

My skin twinges, and it's not because of the hawk's talons still clutching my arm. "I have it under control."

I always do.

"Alright." She nods before glancing over my shoulder to the cell door. "I take it Ryatt finally found them?"

"He did." Holding my hand out, I take the jerky from Lu, feeding it to the hawk with another stroke. The bird tucks its head against my neck in thanks before she turns and takes flight, zooming out of the cave and letting off a distant screech as she takes to the air.

Lu shakes her head. "You have every damn bird and timberwing under your spell."

"What can I say? I'm just likable."

She snorts, both of our attention catching on the cough that sounds from the cell.

"Looks like he's awake," she says, and anticipation has already begun to wind its way around my limbs like silken ropes. "You want me to stay?"

I shake my head, removing my coat and rolling up my sleeves. "No. I'm going to have a nice little chat with Midas's spy."

Lu nods and then leaves me to it. As soon as she's gone, I step up to the door, peering inside where the pitiful heap is now a man sitting up, eyes wide with fear when he sees my face.

I let myself in using the key tucked into the iron lock, and the door slams shut behind me so loud that the man flinches.

And everything, the tiredness, the contention between Ryatt, the worry of Auren, the news from the letter, it all coalesces into something clotted and acidic, ready to bubble over and burn. Lucky for me, I have the perfect candidate to take it out on.

I flash the man a wicked grin, feeling the way my rot twists against my chest, reaching down my arms. He trembles all over, face slack, eyes wild.

"I don't believe we've been properly introduced. I'm King Rot, and you're in my territory."

The man pissing his pants isn't going to be the worst scent by the time I'm done with him.

I walk around closer, letting rot creep from my steps and crawl up the walls like strings threatening to knot him a noose. "Now, I want to know everything you reported to Midas, and everything he ordered from you."

The man gulps, Adam's apple bobbing in undulating fear. "And...and if I do, you'll l-let me go?"

I laugh. The noise makes him flinch, but then his mouth opens wide in shock as I lash my magic into him, rotting the bottom row of his teeth from his gums. Letting the enamel brown and crumble till they slip from their places and disintegrate to the ground.

"Oh, no. You won't be leaving this room alive. But it's up to you how I let my rot toy with you."

It's funny how quickly he sings. Or rather, lisps.

He doesn't tell me anything I hadn't already figured out, but doling out punishment helps my dark mood. Only a little. But it helps.

When I walk away a couple hours later, with the sun in the sky and the taste of sweet rot and cold ash in the back of my throat, I should be relieved that we were able to get all of Midas's spies and send them to a frozen grave.

But relief is the furthest thing I can feel, and Midas's people no longer matter.

It's the rest of Orea I have to worry about now.

CHAPTER 25

SLADE
Age 15

There's a festival today in the city—a celebration of the winter solstice. I know this because we passed it on our way to the hills. There was already dancing in the city streets, blue lights hovering in the air with magic. Tonight, after the sun goes down, they'll offer sacrifices to the cold stars and play music to the moon.

I passed by it all on the back of my horse, and that was the closest I've ever been to one of the city's festivals. My father has chanted his entire life the importance of staying separate from the rest, to hold ourselves above.

"Get your head out of the clouds," my father seethes, making my head snap back in his direction.

"It wasn't in the clouds," I reply. It was firmly on the ground...back at the city.

He raises a thick brown brow, his bald head so shiny

that it can be blinding when the sun hits it at certain angles. "You're slipping. Pull the rot back in where I told you."

I look down at the ground and grimace when I realize he's right—the rot has spread past the circle he's drawn in the ground around me.

When we first started doing this lesson, there was no circle. He would just bring me out here, and my rot would explode out, killing everything in view. It was uncontrollable. Destructive.

Slowly, I've learned how to pull it back. To only rot the ground, coaxing it back from a tree, avoiding a lake.

It's taken a lot of time and endless hours of practice, but now, I have a tiny circle drawn around me, the top line hitting the tip of my shoe. It takes a lot of willpower to keep the rot contained in such a small area.

Some fae have to work to expand their power. Not me. My power has always wanted to rip out of me. It is containment and control that have taken years of practice.

When it became clear what my magic truly did, it scared me. I was a danger to everyone and everything, was terrified of my power. When my father figured out I was scared, he dragged me out of the house. Took me right through the city teeming with fae. He told me I either had to control it or I'd have their deaths on my conscience. I threw up twice during that exercise and rotted an entire street, but I didn't kill anyone. Not that time.

He loves to force me to train with consequences. Says it's not real otherwise. So I had to learn very quickly, but it didn't happen without very real ramifications.

The people celebrating in the city wouldn't want me

there, even if I were allowed to go. That's what happens when you rot someone right in front of them. Even though I was able to pull it back, to make sure the fae lived, the city never forgot.

My father may be known as The Breaker, but I'm The Rot.

It doesn't help that I can never hide who I am. I might be able to hide away my spikes, but the rotted lines that run down my arms and up my neck are a constant reminder.

"Concentrate," my father snaps, arms held behind him as he walks just outside my circle.

"I am." I grit my teeth, while lines of rot squirm beneath my feet. The grass is dead, the ground gone dry and hard, like anything alive in the soil has shriveled up and died.

The rest of the landscape is gently changing for winter, but even so, the hills still have patches of grass, the trees holding on to the last of their leaves. If my rot were to spread, there would be nothing gentle about it. There would be no natural progression from life to death, or the circle of nature's rebirth.

There would just be a blight.

With his foot, my father draws another circle, concentric to the smaller one around my body. "Put the rot between the two."

With a nod, I concentrate and look down at my feet as I move the rot away from me. I push it out further to the other side of the line, sweat beading on my forehead as I struggle to make sure it stays contained.

My father nods in approval. At one point in my life, I would've been ecstatic at that. But I'm long past that now.

I loathe him.

Even though I've never seen him strike my mother since that day seven years ago, I remember.

I watch.

My beautiful, kind, strong mother, yanked from her world and looked down on by all fae, has to put up with a tyrant and yet still manages to love her sons. To find moments to smile for.

I learn this for her. Not for him.

I learn so that one day, I can be strong enough to take her away from him. So that I can bring her somewhere in Annwyn where no one's heard of The Breaker. Where no one hates Oreans. Where we can be happy and free. But to do that, I have to learn to be strong. And who better to teach me than the male I want to beat?

"Tighten it at the back, Slade."

I look over my shoulder to see where it's slipped, but he snaps his fingers. "Eyes forward. You don't need to see it to know where it is."

My teeth grind together. But instead of opening my mouth and saying something that will piss him off, I close my eyes and sense my power. Even though my magic is external, I learned that I can feel it internally. The rotten veins beneath my skin are the same as the rotted lines I force into the ground. But although I can feel it, it doesn't mean it always wants to listen to me.

My father draws another circle, and then another, and then another. He has me doing all sorts of new things I've never tried before, like making half the rot go in one section, the other half going somewhere else, spreading in opposite directions. It leaves the once lush grass dried and dead, with cracks of earth showing through. Despite the cool air, I start dripping sweat, my body shaking from the physical and mental exertion.

"You're getting sloppy," he says with a sigh. "Control, Slade. Are you some common fae to lose it so easily? Or are you going to be worthy of the blood in your rotted veins?"

"We've been going at this for hours," I reply, though I'm careful to keep my tone neutral. The sun is going down, and something about being out here without it makes everything seem harder. "I'm tired."

My father sneers at that word. Even though he's hundreds of years old, even older than my mother, the only lines he has in his face are from the frowns dug between his brows and bracketed around his downturned mouth.

"You're tired," he mocks, practically spitting.

My stomach drops, because I know what's coming next. In the next blink, he's snapping a finger in front of me, and the ground shakes, splits, breaks.

I stumble, almost crashing down when the shaking relents. The ground is breaking in perfect circles, right where he drew my lines. Gaps in the earth surround me, making it seem like they could break all the way through to the world's core, crumbling beneath my feet.

But he's not done with his display.

With another snap of his finger, he makes the full tree just behind us break in half, the huge trunk snapping like a twig and falling over with a crash.

The ground barely stops shaking when he lifts his hand again.

Snap.

The sound is so loud, but I don't register that it's not only coming from him, it's coming from me. Just like that, he's snapped the bone in my finger exactly like he did to that tree.

A scream flings out of me, and my knees hit the ground in a plume of dust as I cradle my hand now searing with pain. My father peers down at me without expression while I try not to throw up.

All the spikes have torn from my body, ripping through my shirt, though at least they don't make me bleed anymore. I look up at him from the ground, shaking in the shock of pain, but I say nothing. Nothing. Because I will not ask. I will not beg.

He lets me stay in that agonizing limbo for several long seconds. Then, he snaps his finger again, making me flinch. But as quick as the noise, the break in my bone is gone. So is the break in the tree. The ones on the ground.

My chest heaves as I look up at him, and he tilts his head, eyes flicking over my face with an indecipherable expression. His eyes drop down and then he grips my chin, his fingers even colder than the power running through my veins. He turns my head to the side roughly. Scrapes the side of my cheek. "Interesting," he mutters before letting me go. He looks at me with great satisfaction. I don't like it one bit.

"What?" I ask, bringing my own hand up to scratch the spot that feels oddly itchy. I don't do it with my tender finger, though. The bone may not be broken any longer, but my nerves are still screaming, letting out ripples of confused pain.

Instead of answering me, he says, "Control. My father taught me, and I will teach you, and you will not fail."

I swallow hard, but all the rot in my veins has petered out, all the lines in the ground shriveled to nothing.

"Now pull those spikes back in, or I'll pin them to the estate wall and let you hang there till you learn to control yourself."

I grit my teeth.

Fist my sore hand.

Feel a line of blood drip from my eyebrow.

I stare at The Breaker, and I hate.

One day, I think to myself. One day, I will break you instead.

But until then, I will learn control.

CHAPTER 26

AUREN

I'm being nudged.

Nudged in the arm while I'm trying to sleep. I don't *want* to be nudged while I'm trying to sleep. I say exactly that, but it comes out as a mashed-up grumble while my face is still stuffed against the pillow.

I hear a chuckle in reply, which makes my eyes squint open. Slade is standing beside the bed, his nudging hand nowhere to be found. Smart male.

"Is it night already?" I ask groggily as I stretch my legs out and start to sit up.

"No, it's about midday."

My eyes flick over to him just as I set my feet on the ground. "Oh good, I still have time then." I start to lower myself back down again.

A damn nudging hand at my arm stops me.

"Actually, I'd like you to get up now."

I stop and look up at him. "For what?"

"Training."

I frown. "I train with Judd at night."

His expression is unreadable. "You're not training with Judd."

My attention snares, our eyes tangling together. "I'm training with you." It's not a question, but his head tips down in a nod nonetheless, while mine shakes. "I can't yet."

He arches a brow. "Why not?"

Excuses clog up in the back of my throat like a newly formed dam until I'm running dry. I automatically resist, anxiety sloshing against my internal barrier. But then my determined words come leaking through the cracks to my ear.

The next time someone wants to try and use me, control me, I want to be ready.

That's what I said to Judd.

I want to master my own strength—physically and magically.

That's what I told Slade.

I can't do those things if I don't learn to control my magic. So I swallow hard, trying to dam up the flooding fear.

"Okay."

Pride flashes over his face. "Get ready, and then we'll go."

Every step I take from the Grotto is made with tightly strung nerves. They're braided around my bones, twined around my chest, woven so thoroughly throughout my body that every step is stiff with apprehension.

This is my first time being out of the Grotto. My eyes sting as we step out of the cave and into the veiled daylight, my hand a shield above my eyes as I take in the wintry landscape. The mouth of the cave has been shoveled, with the barest scrap of a stone pathway visible below a layer of sand and salt.

"This way."

I follow Slade out and to the right where we trudge up another shoveled path. Although the storm has broken, the sky is still cloaked with clouds, a slight wind chafing my cheeks. This strip of Deadwell has a shore of flat snowfall and a rising tide of mountains at my right. One of them bends over slightly like a comber wave, and there's a shelf protruding from its belly, keeping us in perpetual shade.

I tighten my arms around myself, hands buried in my pockets as we travel up a slight incline around the mountain's base.

"We're almost there," he tells me when he notices me starting to breathe harder. "It's far enough away from everything."

That gives me some peace of mind, but even so, I'm too nervous about the training to get any real comfort. We could walk to the very peak of this mountain and I'm not sure it would be far enough.

He nudges my arm. "It will be fine, Auren."

I appreciate the reassurance, but I don't have the same certainty.

"You saw me in the ballroom," I say, more harshly than I mean to.

"I did," he replies. "And it showed me how incredibly powerful and strong you are. Which means you can master it."

Pressing my lips together, I keep my eyes on my feet, while my anxiety twists and twines.

"Watch your step. The path will be a bit steeper from here."

The snow is piled higher here, and there is no discernible path, but it's not as stacked up as it is to the left of us. We only make it a few more paces when someone calls out behind us. "Your Majesty!"

We stop, both of us turning to see a man hurrying forward. He's wearing a thick coat with a deep fur collar stretching all the way up his throat, and on his arm is a large messenger hawk, its chest dotted with brown and white speckles. "Believe this is for you, Sire."

The man flicks his gaze to me, eyes widening as he takes me in. I try to give him a smile, but he quickly looks away.

As soon as Slade reaches him, the bird instantly lets out a shrill purr before holding out its leg to him. Slade strokes its neck and then takes the vial from its leg. He unrolls the scroll, eyes flicking back and forth over the paper. He's turned slightly away from me, but from his profile, I see a frown appear on his brow. I walk over, a sense of unease building in my gut.

"What's wrong?" I ask when I'm right behind him.

His shoulders tense up, but only for a moment. "Nothing," he says before he takes the scroll and shoves it into his pocket.

He looks back up at the man while giving the bird another pet. "Thanks, Selby."

"Of course, Your Majesty. What should I do with him?"

"Let him rest in the Perch. I've no need for him."

The man nods and then turns away with the bird in tow, disappearing down the incline.

"Everything okay?" I ask, looking to Slade.

"Of course," he replies easily. "Shall we?"

He already starts leading the way again before I can say anything more. I hesitate for a moment, and it's on the tip of my tongue to assuage my curiosity and outright ask what the letter said, but I stop myself when a thought occurs to me.

Do I even have a right to ask him something like that?

Surely he'd have offered up the information about it if he'd wanted me to know. My feelings shouldn't be hurt that he didn't.

He probably has a lot of letters that he receives and sends every day as part of being a king. I shouldn't feel so sensitive about it. Like we said, we still have a lot of work to do in peeling back each other's layers.

I follow after him, my eyes latched onto his back while I try to shrug off these swirling scruples. After all, he's a king, and that's something I keep forgetting. He's a king, and I'm...

I'm about to fail miserably at using my magic.

Therein lies the heart of my troubled thoughts. I haven't said anything to anyone, haven't even let myself really face it. But the fact of the matter is, my gold isn't working right. Not only that, but I murdered people with it left and right, without a single thought of hesitation.

What if I do that again?

When Slade finally leads me off the path and brings us into a cave, I'm in my own head so much that I don't even take in the space until I nearly walk right onto the gold-stained floor.

I suck in a breath, eyes sprinting from one end of the cave to the other. I recognize it immediately. It's where I first woke up. Where I blinked and I was already moving, power already coursing through my veins.

Too late, I realize I'm staring at the hardened gold that's splashed and splattered over the walls and floor, lost in its shallow depths while Slade watches me.

Blinking, I shake myself, pasting on an unaffected expression.

"We're training here?" I ask, and though I try to keep it steady, my voice sounds heavy with the weight of the implications.

Slade continues to study me for a moment before he dips his head. "We are," he tells me, his tone heeding something I can't quite catch.

Those anxious nerves, those curled and twisted strings I'm all tied up in, they pull taut, making even my throat too tight to swallow.

He walks a few feet away and kneels down, right where a wave of gold has frozen, and he drags a finger over the hardened crest.

I don't know why, but I shiver.

He cocks a brow. "Cold?"

"No."

He stands again and removes his coat, but just as I try to insist that I'm not cold, he places it on the ground. "Come sit."

I hesitate for a moment, but my feet lead me to him, and then I lower myself onto his coat, tucking my legs beneath me.

He sits down too, and even though we're two feet apart, the distance feels inconsequential. Slade's presence—his attention on me—it's always eaten up the space between us.

"It's daytime," he says, motioning toward the cave's opening where daylight still spills in. "Your power has always been uncontrollable during the day, right?"

"Right. Normally, as soon as something touches my skin during the day, my gold comes rushing out." My eyes fall to the black leggings and gloves on my body. "But ever since I woke up, it's different. Nothing is being gold-touched."

"What do you feel?"

Worry bombards me, and I lift my hand as if I can see what lurks inside while flashes of memory of that night in Ranhold ping against the backs of my eyes, shooting scene after scene through my vision.

I quickly bury my hand beneath my leg. "Nothing. I feel nothing."

"Try to gild the rock."

With wary weight, I slip off my glove and press my palm to the jutting stone just to my left. It should be instantaneous. Gold should immediately spill out of me.

But it doesn't.

Slade cocks his head. "Are you trying?"

My eyes slash up. "What's that supposed to mean? Yes, I'm trying."

315

"Are you sure? Because you say your gold-touch was always uncontrollable during the day, but you could control it, to an extent."

"What are you talking about? Of course I couldn't."

"But you did," he argues. "You could gild things so they were only plated in gold. Or you could make things completely solid gold. Remember the coat you wore? You managed to keep your magic only gilding the inner lining so it didn't spread. That was you controlling it."

I blink. "I've…I've never thought about it that way."

"You've always had control. You just need to learn how to wield it. I think you're scared. I think you're holding yourself back, and *that's* why your gold isn't coming—because you're blocking it."

Anger trips up through my veins, making my mind stumble. "I'm not."

"Auren…" I don't care how persistently calm he still is, that tone rattles me down to my bones. "I know you."

"Maybe you don't," I spit back with far more vitriol than I intended. I've gone as stiff and as cold as the frozen gold, caught in my own momentum. I steel myself, readying for the backlash, preparing for the fight.

But he doesn't give it to me.

Instead, Slade watches me with that unerring green gaze, face betraying nothing.

"Maybe you're wrong," I go on, wanting to break that shuttered expression, wanting to crack open the eggshell view that he has of me and show him the rottenness inside. Prove that he didn't put it there. "Snippets and unanswered questions—that's what we have. So don't sit there all superior and act like you know everything, because you *don't*."

I don't even know all of me.

And that's the splinter that's caught in my chest, unable to be plucked free.

My magic changed—so wholly that I'm terrified of it. My ribbons are gone. Like leaves stripped from a vine. And I...

"I am not the same person I was when I walked into Ranhold."

"That's true," he concedes. "But I still know you."

A balking, frustrated laugh tumbles out of me. "Are you out of—"

"Let's talk about that night."

My words lurch to a halt. My heart does too. I feel it snag against my throat. "We don't need to talk about that night. We were both there."

A look of frustrated sadness lines his face. "Talk to me, Auren."

"What do you want me to say?" I demand. I'm up and on my feet before I even realize I've moved. "This." I gesture around the room, at all the gold that doesn't feel like me. "This doesn't make any sense. That night at Ranhold doesn't make any sense. My gold isn't working right, and what I did that night...I never should've been able to do that."

"And what did you do?" he presses, and I curl my hands into fists because I—

"I *killed*."

That's the thing that nobody is saying. The thing that I haven't been able to face.

"How did I even *do* that? I felt my power leave me when the sun set," I say as I begin to pace around the cave, skirting the solidified splotches. "I shouldn't have been able to use any part of my power, but that..." I stop, looking down at the ground. "There was something inside of me that just snapped open."

"It needed to happen."

My head shakes, voice cracking, and my anger cracks with it.

Because I'm not angry at him. I'm angry at *me*. And it's easier to hold that anger than to feel anything else, because I don't know how to navigate these other emotional landscapes. They're dark and terrifying and rocky, and I feel lost as I try to cross them.

I hate my snappish tone. Hate how the first thing I do is try to push him away because of some internal feeling like I'm going to lose him anyway.

"I'm sorry," I tell him. Sincerity fills my tone, and I drop my guard, drop my snappishness that he doesn't deserve, and I tell him the truth.

"I became a beast. I killed a lot of people that night, and I could do it again. What if I go full fae here?" I ask. "What if I lose control and gild all of Deadwell, and you can't stop me? I remember what I did that night, just like I remember what happened leading up to it. How I was on that mezzanine. How confused and helpless. I felt angry and alone, and then I finally found you..."

Slade's eyes are an empty, starless night. "I want you to ask me, Auren."

My brows scrunch up in confusion. "Ask you what?"

318

"I want you to ask me those questions that have been on your mind since you woke up. I deserve to hear them. You deserve to voice them. One in particular. So *ask me*." His gaze is dark, his tone hard. But not with the fight that I was trying to pick. Not with anger at all. With *anguish*.

I suck in a breath. Because right away, I know what he's referring to.

There *is* one question that's burned into the back of my mind. I've carried the taste of its ash on my tongue, felt the char of its presence seeping down my throat.

Everything between us becomes so *heavy*. So stretched. A perilous point where there is no soft side to fall on. The longer I stay silent, the more misery saturates Slade's face. But the question continues to burn. Smoking up my head, raking flames down my spirit.

"Ask. Me."

One tear. One tear leaks out of me, so hot that I wouldn't be surprised if it steamed against my cheek.

But I ask.

Looking him in the eye, my own anguish now matching his, I ask the one question I haven't wanted to. "Where were you?"

When I was drugged.

When I was shoved into that room with Digby.

When my ribbons were slashed, right along with my soul.

When I was propped up on that mezzanine, confused and lost.

"I thought you were going to come. But you didn't." My voice is choked, shaken, and every word I say lands a flinch across his face. "So where were you?"

CHAPTER 27

SLADE

Where were you?

It's the way she says it. The smallest warble in her throat, so tiny that anyone else would miss it. But not me.

When it comes to Auren, I make it a point to notice everything.

So I hear it—the pain. And I know that by initiating her to ask this question, I'm leading her down the path of that night. A night I'm sure she doesn't want to think about, much less talk about. But we need to.

She looks at me steadily, golden eyes shining almost as much as the blue veins running through the cave. "I thought you were going to come," she tells me, and the confession bleeds like a wound from her tongue. "But you didn't."

I have been beaten. Stabbed. Head held beneath water until my lungs burned. I have been ripped apart by the fury of my power to the point where it felt like my skin was flayed from my body.

But none of that is as painful as hearing those words out of Auren's mouth.

It's a physical thing, this culpability. Guilt isn't a strong enough word for what I feel, for what I carry.

As if it wasn't enough that I fucking *rotted her*, I let her down. And somehow, that's far worse.

All her damn life, people have let her down. Over and over again, she has put her faith in them, and they have failed her. And then the night when she needed me, that's exactly what I did.

Failed her.

My mind flashes to that night. The night before it all went to shit. She left my tent, a secret smile curving her plush lips, and all I wanted to do was drag her back in and devour her all over again.

I wish I had.

If only I'd taken her hand and asked her to stay. If only I hadn't let her go back into that castle.

When Hojat tended to her, and I saw the state of her back...

A tightness punches me right in the sternum. Her ribbons. Her charming, unprecedented, beautiful ribbons. Gone. Hacked away. Left in a frayed and bloody ruin.

I don't think I'll ever get that sight out of my mind.

It's no wonder that she can't bear for me to look.

"So where were you?" she asks me, and even though I wanted her to ask, I still flinch.

"I fucked up. In every possible way."

322

Scenarios keep running through my head. If only I'd done *one* thing differently, maybe I could have stopped it.

"Lu told me that Queen Kaila had overheard you two when she walked you back from camp. She doubled back after the queen was gone, had to bypass countless guards. By the time she made it to your room, you were sleeping. She stayed waiting in the halls until dawn and then saw that you went down to gild for Midas. She waited to make sure it was all okay before she came back to camp and told me what happened. I ordered her to get some sleep first, because she was about to fall over. I knew she needed rest before she could search for Digby. So I sent Judd in her stead, but he turned up empty."

Auren listens intently, and it's as if I can see her mind merging her timeline with mine.

"I tried to warn Mist—the saddle who's carrying Midas's baby," she tells me. "Tried to warn her about Queen Kaila, but she didn't want to listen to me. And then I was going to try and sneak out and tell you what happened, but Midas came, wanting me to use my magic. So I made him a deal."

I guess it immediately. "Digby."

She nods. "I was a fool."

"No, Midas was just a fucking monster."

She glances down. "I used my magic all day. Thought he was going to actually let me have Digby back. I'd say that's the definition of a fool."

I hate the bitterness in her tone, because it's directed at *herself*.

"Auren—"

"Keep going," she tells me.

I swallow back my other words with a nod. If she wants me to keep going, then that's what I'll do. "The night you and I were supposed to meet at the library, I went through Ranhold's gate to get inside. Lu was with me, ready to search for Digby."

I force myself to dive straight in, without inflection, without pause. Because while I haven't spoken it aloud, in my head, I've gone over the events leading up to finding Auren too many times to count.

"Ryatt was supposed to be waiting there for us, but he never showed up. We didn't think too much of it, because him being late isn't out of character. We went inside, but instead of us going our separate ways, we were headed off by Midas at the entry."

"What did he want?"

My jaw jumps as I grind my teeth. "He pulled me into a fucking *meeting*. He was stalling me. I just didn't know it at the time. What I also didn't know was that there were problems with villagers coming too close to our army's camp, so Judd and Osrik were dealing with that. Meanwhile, Lu wasn't having any luck finding Digby, and then I found out Midas had detained Ryatt."

Her brows jump up in surprise. "He arrested him?"

"I didn't find out until later."

Understanding dawns in her eyes. "Ryatt was detained because of me. Because Midas thought that he and I..."

"He told Ryatt that he'd wrongfully touched what didn't belong to him," I tell her, my jaw gone tight. "By the time we got out of this pointless meeting about our fake fucking alliance and trade deals, it was very late, and with the ball happening the next day, the castle was busy. There were servants and guards everywhere. It took some time, and we had to go up to my room first, but then Lu finally left to start her search for Digby, while I went up to the library. I knew you wouldn't be there since it was much too late by then, but I looked for a note or any indication that you'd been there."

I hear her swallow.

"I didn't see any," I say, and then I wait, on edge. Because I have pieced together what happened as best I could with the others, but now I'm finally going to hear it from her own lips.

"I never made it to the library," she says quietly, and when she looks back up, her eyes are far away, all the way back in Ranhold.

"I tried to go up to your room, but there were too many guards. I didn't want to tip off Midas. I already knew things were precarious with Queen Kaila," I add.

"I wasn't there anyway," she tells me. "Or maybe I was back there by that point, I have no idea. If I'm piecing the timeline together correctly, Midas had already..." She chokes on emotion, has to clear her throat before she can get the rest out. "It had already happened. Maybe I was already stuffed back into my room by then, I don't know. I was pretty muddled."

My ribs feel like they've been chained together. Not a single link allowing any give to breathe.

"I didn't listen to my fucking instincts," I tell her, anger at myself practically spitting out of me. "I tried to go see you again. I could *feel* that something just wasn't right, but Midas kept me too distracted. Before I could get to your room, he called all of us into more damn meetings before the ball was set to start. I was so tied up that I didn't even realize the shit happening all around me. It was only when Lu showed up and signaled to me that I realized she'd found him."

"Digby?" Auren asks.

"No. Ryatt," I tell her. "Lu was looking for Digby, but she found my brother in a holding cell instead. Ryatt told her that he saw Digby being handed off to another set of guards. We had to wait for the ball to start before she could go back down to get Ryatt out, and then while she distracted the guards and led them back to the ball, Ryatt got Digby."

She processes it all with a slow nod of her head, tipping like a buoy in the sea.

"Will you tell me what happened?" I ask, though I fucking hate the pain that it causes her.

"He drugged me."

Her declaration makes my eyes flare. My entire fucking chest feels like it splits open, chains be damned. "*He fucking what?*"

She pauses at the seething horror in my tone, her gaze flicking down to where my spikes have all torn through my shirt, like the black fangs of a snarling beast.

"Like I said, I was a fool," she goes on, a single shoulder lifting. "I let him lead me downstairs, and he *did* bring me to Digby. That was the only honest thing he ever did." Tears start to fall down her cheeks, her brow pulled into pain. "He was beaten. I thought he was dead at first. And I was *furious*. I wanted to hurt Midas. Make him hurt as much as Digby was hurting. But then he had me held against the wall and he...he..."

My chest cleaves. "Auren—"

"They hacked at my ribbons. One by one. I felt *everything*." She's trying not to cry, but the sobs squeeze her throat and make my own close up so tightly I can't take a breath. "It hurt. It hurt so *badly.*"

Where were you?

I didn't just fail her. I allowed her to be fucking destroyed.

"I passed out after that—from the pain or the dew, or both. I woke up but only briefly, and then the next time I woke, I was given more dew. I don't remember everything after that. Just snippets."

My teeth ache with the sharpened canines that've shoved their way down, my cheeks itching with the scales that I know now adorn me. That whole day leading up to the ball, my stomach had felt like there were claws raking down it. But then, like a magnet drawing me in, I finally saw her that night. Up there on that balcony. And even though I didn't know any of this yet, even though we had hundreds of people between us, I could *feel* it. Could see it in her erratic, fitful aura.

I thought you were going to come. But you didn't.

I should've rotted the whole fucking ballroom right then and there.

The hate I feel for myself is so intense that my spikes throb down my spine, as if they want to stab me in half.

Auren sucks in a breath, and for a second, I think she's just catching her breath, but when I see her eyes have dropped down, I follow her gaze to my arm. My arm, where my spikes are pulsing, and rivulets of blood have seeped through my torn skin.

I guess that explains why my back feels like I'm being

chewed up, though it's *nothing* compared to the pain I feel scouring through my chest.

"I've never seen that happen."

I shake my head absently. "It hasn't. Not for a long, long time."

When I lift my head to look at her again, glittery lines from her tears are drying on her cheeks. Tears that never should've been there. Not if I'd done my fucking duty and protected her the way I promised.

Disgust consumes me, and I curl my hands into fists. "Where was I?" I say with a sigh, making her eyes slam back to mine. "*I wasn't fucking there.*"

I wasn't there.

While she drained her magic.

While she was *drugged*.

While she came face-to-face with a beaten and bloody Digby.

While she was held against the wall and mutilated.

And yet, she came down from that mezzanine, she fought her way through a crowd, and she stood in front of *me* to face Midas, claiming me in front of everyone, looking like she was ready to fight the world in order to protect me.

And I...

I wasn't fucking there.

CHAPTER 28

AUREN

I *sit here, a thick layer* of a coat beneath me, gloomy
daylight filtering in behind, and all I can do is stare at the
male in front of me.

If anguish was a person, it would be him.

He shoves a hand through his hair, grip tugging at the
black strands while his face is twisted in a pained expression.

I wasn't fucking there.

Just the way he said it, I could tell it had been beating
inside his skull with raised fists, reverberating in his mind
over and over again like a malicious echo.

I can't help but drop my gaze to where the spikes on his
arms have ripped through his skin, making him bleed. I've
never seen that happen any of the other times he transformed.
But I can also tell this wasn't just a normal transformation.
When he was listening to my account of what happened, his
spikes tore out of him in a violent burst. Whatever magic is

associated with his usually harmless metamorphosis couldn't keep up with his furious emotions.

But seeing this side of him—seeing Rip—it makes me let out a shuddering breath. Because even though he's still him no matter what form he's in, I somehow *missed* him. This is the version of him that I knew first. The version of him that I trusted and pined for.

Tortured black eyes lift to me, and I shiver at the sight of his aura pulsing around his body. It's moving like aggravated shadows, an overcast of dense torment. But it's not a falsehood. It's not a maneuver or a tactic. He's not doing it with purpose or to manipulate my emotions. In fact, he's trying very hard *not* to show emotion.

Seeing him like this makes me wonder how I ever looked at Midas and believed a damn word he said. If Midas ever showed any emotion other than anger, he did it as a scheme.

"An apology is an insulting, shallow word," Slade forces out. "I hate that all I have to offer you is a cheap word. *Sorry* is inadequate." He shakes his head, his shoulders tense, though I doubt it has anything to do with the spikes that tore from his back. "I failed you so utterly. You should loathe me for it. You should never be expected to forgive me for that. But I'm a selfish piece of shit, because I will try to earn your forgiveness anyway."

Earn it. Not ask for me to give it.

This is so incredibly foreign and bewildering.

"Rip—"

"If I had done *anything* differently, things could've been avoided. I should've known something was wrong when Midas headed me off. I should've gone straight to your room afterward to check on you. Should've never let you leave the camp in the first place. I should've found you in that holding cell and saved you before he could hurt you."

"But, Rip—"

"I should have rotted that entire Divine-damned ballroom right there on the spot, consequences be damned, because I let him fucking *hurt* you. I just stood there. I just stood there while he threatened to kill you. You should fucking hate me forever, blame me, because I failed—"

"Rip!" My voice lashes out like a whip, cutting off his tangent. He startles, black eyes snapping to me. When I'm sure I have his full attention, I say, "I don't want that."

He shakes his head, his jaw working. "I know you didn't want me to rot everyone. Even after everything you went through, you still came down to protect *me*." He scoffs in disgust with himself, as if he didn't deserve that.

"That's not what I mean. I'm *glad* you didn't intervene."

He rears back as if I've shocked him. "What?"

My nod is slow, but definitive. "I'm glad you didn't."

Confusion mottles his features. "How could you *not* have wanted me to intervene? I failed you—"

"No, you see? The problem was that I have been failing myself."

His lips press together, and a heavy silence drops between us. I let my finger drag across the cave floor.

"I won't lie and say I didn't wish for you to swoop in and rescue me in the moment," I admit. "But hindsight gives the best perspective, and I'm glad you didn't."

He sucks in a breath, as if that wasn't what he was expecting at all.

"You didn't fail me. That was on me. For so many years. Would it have been easier and more painless for me if you'd shown up? Yes. But the truth of the matter is, I needed that final straw. I don't regret it, because I needed to *snap*. I needed to find my edge."

I'd avoided it all my life, and it was jagged and painful and steep, but I found it.

"But I should've—"

"No," I say, cutting him off. "I needed to do that for myself. No one rescuing me. No one fighting my fight. It *had* to be me. Do you understand?"

Emotion wars on his face. I can tell he still thinks he's failed, still hates that he wasn't there. And I understand that. I do. But...

I meet his eyes so that he can see the truth in mine. "I had to be the one to save myself."

Something ruminative swirls in his gaze. "And you did. You *fucking did*," he says, pride lacing through every letter. "But I *hate* that you feel guilty. Midas got what he deserved. He was the real fucking monster. Not you. If you want to blame anyone for his death, you can blame me, because I should've been the one to kill the bastard before he hurt you. But I can't fucking stand that you regret—"

"Wait a minute," I interrupt, slashing my hand through the air.

He stops, eyes pinned to my face.

And suddenly, I realize this last piece he's been struggling with—what he's been thinking all this time. This is the narrative that's crooned in his ear. I've been fighting the memories that night, fighting the truth about my ribbons, about my wayward magic, while I lefst him to churn in this alone.

I look him straight in the eye. "I want you to listen to me very carefully."

He seems to brace himself, like a man without shelter locking his knees in a torrential storm.

"Fuck Midas."

He blinks in surprise. "*What?*"

"You heard me. Fuck. Midas."

Great Divine, that feels good to say.

He shakes his head like he's trying to clear it, like he can't believe what he's hearing.

"My guilt is about the innocents who got caught up in my rampage. My uncertainty is about my magic. But Midas? No. I'm glad I killed him," I say, my tone dogged and firm. "The only thing I regret is that I didn't do it sooner."

He continues to stand there watching me, like he's waiting to see a crack in the plastered lie. But he won't find one, because I mean every word. "You're truly glad?" he asks carefully.

I nod. "And relieved. I've never felt such relief before. It's just...gone."

"What is?"

"The cage."

He doesn't ask me to elaborate, because I can see by his expression that he knows exactly what I mean.

"I'm still processing."

"His death?" he asks.

I shake my head. "No. The depth of his control over my thoughts. My decisions. My life. Even now, I find myself cringing away from people, not just because of my power, but because he never wanted me to be touched. I saw things one way; he told me I was seeing it wrong. I felt something; he convinced me I was crazy or overreacting."

It all comes rushing up. So many little moments. Times I was too blind to see. Too cowered by silver-tongued words in a gold-plated castle.

"It's *everything*," I explain. "The little things. How submissive I'd become. How *trodden*. I was nothing but a road to him. A means to get to where he wanted to go, and I paved that path in gold. Even now, I worry I'll never really be rid of him. I worry that I'll still be walked all over. What if I never truly heal from his manipulations? What if the damage he's done to my person is never undone?"

There's a long thoughtful silence before he says, "The emotional trauma you've endured will take time, and you need to know when to be gracious with yourself and when to steel yourself. But if you're ever doubting, just stop and listen to the voice in your head. So long as the voice is *yours* and not his, then you know you're beating the bastard."

Beating the bastard.

I like the sound of that.

"To be honest, I was bracing myself for the guilt to hit me, for regret to shove its way in. Midas manipulated my emotions for so long that I fully expected the damage of that conditioning to rear its ugly head. But what he did to me…"

I clear my throat and look away, one hand feeding into my coat pocket. My fingers twist the piece of my ribbon around, the satin fabric looping around my hand, bolstering me.

"I don't feel regret or guilt," I admit. "I'm just fucking *angry*. Angry that I let it go on that long, that I let him take so much. I'm angry at everyone who ever wronged me or used me. And I'm angry that I didn't figure out how to save myself sooner. I don't know what I'm going to do with all this inside me, but I'm not afraid anymore. I'm not trodden with guilt or regret. All I feel is *anger*."

Rip's mouth curves. "Good. Use your rage to complete your courage."

I suck in a breath of air, the fae beast inside of me practically purring at his claim.

"Anger can do a lot of things," he goes on, thumbing over the sharp tips of his spikes. "It can drag you down, make you bitter. But if you wield it another way, it can be a stepping stone for your determination."

"You sound like you're speaking from experience."

"I am. I learned to use my own rage to my advantage."

The idea that this sharp anger that's carved into the recesses of my chest could actually be put to use intrigues me. "So you're not going to tell me to live and let live? To work through my anger and move past it?"

"Absolutely fucking not. I'm going to teach you to *use* it."

CHAPTER 29

AUREN

I don't want to become bogged down by my anger, dragged under it, to turn into some bitter, miserable person. But using my anger in a different way? In a way to bolster me up? Now that—that is something I can get behind.

I've always been more passive in life. I think passivity is often mistaken for weakness. Really, it's just a different way to cope. To survive. The safest way I learned to react to situations was to endure. To let things blow over. To please. To peace keep. To constantly regulate my own reactions and thoughts and emotions so that the tyrant could be appeased into a lesser form of abuse.

So from an early age, I learned that my anger wasn't safe. Then, I learned that it was irrational. Then, it was just plain wrong. I was always in the wrong.

Fuck that.

My Divine-damned *mind* was warped into the mold of someone else's purpose.

The abuse came in shades of gray. Some were darker and more noticeable than others. Some, I probably haven't even noticed yet. My healing from this isn't going to happen overnight.

But...I'm free now. Truly free. For the first time in twenty years, I have the chance to decide who I'm going to be, *how* I'm going to be. And I don't want to waste it on *him*. I want to sever his effects as meticulously and as thoroughly as he severed *me*.

So if I can learn to use my anger in a way that moves me forward rather than keeps me here, pinned to a painful past, then that's what I want to do.

When I look up at Slade, my resolve looks with me. "I do want you to teach me how to use my anger," I tell him. "But the truth remains that my gold isn't working right." Shrugging, I look down at my hands. "I could see myself using the gold as this beast—this fae side of me—but I can't call to it like that. I don't have control over it in that form. And now, it's not working at all."

My gold-touch has never been something I had to put much effort into using. In fact, it's always been the exact opposite. I had to be more careful, to work harder for it *not* to come out.

When I unleashed in that ballroom, it could've been cataclysmic. I'm lucky Slade stopped me when he did, because my rational mind had no control. I could've killed Slade or the Wrath or Digby. My gold could've seeped through the rest of the castle and down into the city, killing innocents.

"My gold can't be trusted. *I* can't be trusted." I finally say the words aloud, the same ones that have been churning in my gut, making me swallow them down again and again.

Slade frowns. "You unleashing like that, defending yourself while your magic unfurled with another layer you'd never been able to utilize before, it's not a bad thing, Auren."

I'm not sure how he can say that. Then again, he rots people. Probably not the best judge of good versus bad.

"Regardless, I haven't gilded anything," I say, picking at my leggings. "Not a single thing since I woke up. My gold-touch has always happened involuntarily. *Always*. If the sun's up, my gold would come whether I wanted it to or not. But since I woke up...nothing."

He looks contemplative for a moment, eyes skimming around me. "Your aura looks strong. But physical magic like ours can be finicky. It's why training is so important."

"I think my magic is broken," I confess on a thick tongue. "I think when I somehow called the gold to me that night, when I snapped and my fae nature came out, I did something with my magic that I'm not supposed to be able to do. I corrupted it in some way, and now it doesn't work right. At least, not without me going full-fae, and I can't keep letting myself snap like that. Because what I did..."

My voice plugs up. Tongue parched from the memories that torment me.

I see the flashes playing in my head in fragments. The rush of power I called. The things I destroyed.

The people I killed.

I can hear the screams, too.

Because of what I did. Because I lost control.

Look at what you did.

That sudden voice pops in my head like a shrill whistle flung from a combative hand, calloused fingers shoved between teeth, the blown blare tossed against my ears like a slap.

Look at what you did.

I jerk away from it, as though the person saying that is in front of me rather than in my head.

"Auren?" My eyes spring to Slade, to the concerned line between his brows. "What just happened? Where'd you go?"

"Nothing. Nowhere."

His eyes narrow. Watch. Observe me like he's not just looking at my eyes but looking right through them. Looking into my head where these memories swirl.

"I see."

My shoulders tense. "You see what?"

Rip leans forward. "You know what I think?" he says instead of answering me. "I think you already explained why your gold isn't working."

"What are you talking about?"

"You said that both you *and* your gold can't be trusted."

"It's true."

He raises a finger and points at me. "And that right there explains it. Because our emotions are tied to our power, Auren. That includes fear of our own magic."

My pulse spikes. Maybe I'm imagining it, but I swear his gaze drops down to the vein in my neck as if he's observing me *that* closely.

"You're afraid of what you did in Ranhold," he says, and my heart bangs against my ribs, my eyes forgetting to blink.

"Of course I am."

He leans closer to me, and I want to lean away, want to hold up a hand in front of my face so he can't read me so thoroughly.

Defensiveness rises up in me like a sudden tide. "I shouldn't have been able to control the gold like that, but I did, and because of that, I killed people. I lost control."

"You aren't just afraid of what you did that night. You're afraid of your gold, aren't you?"

The question hits me full in the chest. He doesn't even need me to answer.

"You can't be afraid of your power, Auren. I know you've had to try and hide away and suppress it your whole life, but—"

"I barely had any control before, and now I have to worry about going fae beast? I don't even have the reprieve of nighttime?" I let out a scoffing sigh. "I *have* to be afraid of it, Rip. Because when I lose control like I did at Ranhold and like I did at—"

I snap my mouth shut, eyes gone wide.

Slade's head cocks. "Like you did *where*?"

No.

I don't want to think about that.

I *never* let myself think about that.

"Did you lose control before, Auren?" he asks quietly.

My jaw grinds together. Unrestrained heat hits the back of my eyes.

"I don't want to talk about that," I say, jumping to my feet. "That has nothing to do with this."

He's on me before I can even go three steps. His hand gripping my arm, turning me back around. And I hate the frown of concern on his face, because it just makes me feel worse.

"My magic is just broken. That's all," I say obstinately.

Adrenaline pumps through my veins, my limbs tingling, breath quickening like my instinct to flee is urging me on. But Slade doesn't remove his hold on my arm. I'm stuck in this spot, unable to run away from this conversation.

"No. Your magic isn't broken, Auren. You have more ability with it than ever, and you're just blocking it."

I feel my shoulders go tense.

"Something happened to you, didn't it?" he asks softly. "You've lost control of your magic before and something bad happened. So Ranhold, all of this, it's bringing up something else from your past."

My chest rises and falls so fast, and yet it feels like I'm not getting in any air at all.

"Breathe, baby," Slade says softly, now using both hands to rub up and down my arms in soothing strokes. "Tell me what happened."

My head shakes, cheek torn by a line of moisture. "No."

It's not a stubborn answer. It's a plea for him to drop this. Sympathy crosses his expression, but he doesn't give in. The bastard *never* gives in. "Tell me."

I'm scrambling, still hearing those screams, still seeing me lose control. Then and now, here and there.

Look at what you did.

I squeeze my eyes shut. But that single word, the one

I've tried to bury so far down, it just falls out. Like a piece of cracked ceiling that finally caves, landing out in the open with an existential crack.

"Carnith."

The word lands with an echoing slap. Unbidden, tearing free without my consent. I wish I could shove it back up in the hidden recesses, take away the sound that's echoing between us. I shouldn't have let it drop. I should've taken what happened at Ranhold and crammed them both away.

"What happened in Carnith, Auren?"

I go still. Like singing strings of a harp suddenly pinched between fingers, choking off their sound.

"I don't want to talk about Carnith."

"I think we should," he says. "I think what happened in Ranhold has brought up whatever trauma you experienced in Carnith, and I think both of those things are what's repressing your magic now."

"My magic just can't be trusted."

"This was a new side to your power you hadn't used before. It takes practice. You'll master it."

"Or I'll kill everyone. Just like I almost did at Ranhold. Just like I did in…"

"Carnith," Slade finishes for me.

My heart is beating so hard that I'm surprised it's not bruising my veins.

"Tell me," he urges quietly, his eyes soft, accepting. Like no matter what I tell him, he couldn't possibly judge me for it.

He *should* judge me for it.

"I've never talked about it," I admit on a croaked whisper.

His thumbs brush over my cheeks. "I want your past, remember? Your memories, your thoughts. Tell me, Auren. I want to help."

How can I deny him? He's here. He's not walking away, no matter how hard I've pushed. No matter how little I deserve him. From the very beginning, he's always seen every part of me.

I think it's time I showed him one part that he hasn't.

CHAPTER 30

AUREN

I was lucky.

That's all I kept thinking, over and over again. I got away from Derfort Harbor. From Zakir. From Barden East. From being the painted girl, the harbor's most expensive saddle.

I got away, with a wayward leap into an unknown boat, captained by a no-nonsense woman. Captain Mara was true to her word. She took me aboard, and I earned that passage every day by scrubbing the salt-stained boards, and coiling rope, and emptying chamber pots, and peeling vegetables.

But I didn't mind it at all. Because it meant freedom. It meant escape.

I was lucky.

So although I slept in a swinging hammock with blistered hands and a capsized stomach, I was happier than I'd ever been during my entire time in Derfort Harbor. And after weeks of sailing, when the blisters had started to become calluses, and my stomach had learned to stop heaving for every chopped wave and blown-in storm, the ship arrived at Second Kingdom.

Captain Mara put me on a boat and paddled me right to the docks, and even gave me a coin to go with the others I had in a pouch sewn into my dress. She stood in front of me on that dock, where the call of gulls competed with the shouts of sailors, and she tucked the coin right into my shirt pocket that she'd given me and said, "You've got terrible sea legs. Best stay steady on solid ground, okay, gold girl?"

She left with a pipe in her mouth, already shouting to her crewmates over the bustle.

And I...I was in Second Kingdom, where the sand was white and the sun was baking, not a single cloud in sight to dump on the city in a flood of fishy rainwater. It was so unlike Derfort, but it was still a harbor, and I had no desire to stay anywhere near one of those.

So I found the first safe-looking passage I could with a family in a cart, and I was lucky, because they were happy to take me with them if it meant a little extra coin in their pocket. They had two young babies who I could help with on the trip, and I didn't have to worry when I closed my eyes at night.

When I left them, I found a trio of sisters to travel with next, and that's how it went, my luck staying with me from city to city, always finding women to travel with. I was gawked at, whispered about, some people came up and asked me why I'd painted my skin, but other than that, I was left alone, and I made sure to buy a cloak with a deep hood the first chance I got.

The landscape dried up the further I went into the desert, beaches and palm trees changing to sand serpents and cacti. But I kept going, trying to get as far away from the sea as I could. So long as I was near the ocean, it felt like I was still too close to Zakir West and Barden East.

My luck started to run out with my coin. The further I got from the harbor, the leerier people were of a strange golden girl traveling with them. I had to pay more for them to agree to let me hitch a ride, and that was if I could even get people to talk to me. The further I traveled, the more brutal the desert landscape and the heat became.

I thought it was hot before, but that was at least with the cold ocean air carried in from the beach. Out here, the sun was relentless, the wind hot. Despite the delicate appearance of the silky soft dunes, the sand felt as if it could burn through the soles of my shoes. Water was so expensive that a single bloom sliced off a prickly pear ate up my reserves for both water *and* food.

Despite all of that, I *liked* the sun. The way I could tip my head up and feel as if the warmth was soaking into my pores, cleansing each clogged up sodden year I'd spent drenched in Derfort.

But in the desert, though the sun blazed during the day, at night, temperatures plummeted. It didn't matter that I layered every piece of scant clothing I had. My clothes were no match for the chill that came every time the sun set.

In such desolate terrain, there was nothing there to hold the heat, nothing to block the stripping wind, and it seemed to be an entirely different place when the sun went down. I'd woken more than once with scorpions creeping over my skin or sand serpents slithering in my hair. I'd woken with coyotes yipping in a frenzy as they went in for a kill or with other travelers shouting in a way that made me want to steer clear.

And then, the problem was my back.

I thought it was some kind of sunburn at first, the powerful rays baking right through my shirt and burning the length of my spine. It itched, and my skin peeled layer after layer, leaving me feeling raw.

After the itchiness came the pain. It throbbed from just between my shoulder blades all the way down to the very bottom of my back. It was gradual at first, then it became constant. So bad that I couldn't even lie on my back to sleep or walk without wincing. And while it continued to peel and itch and hurt, I had to keep going. To try and ignore the pain as much as I could, even though I'd usually collapse into a wrung-out heap by the time I stopped traveling each day.

When the sun set, I got the relief from the burn. The night sky was so clear, its dark face freckled with stars. Those were the nights that I could forget about the pain and remember that I was free.

Free of Derfort Harbor. Free of Zakir. Of what went on at *The Solitude*.

But I had no idea what I was supposed to do. The only thing I'd ever focused on was getting away. I'd gone as far as I could go. I'd crossed a sea and left the shore to wade through dunes the color of ash, feeling my skin peel away beneath the brutal beating of the sun.

I knew I needed to find a place to stop, but every village

I came to, the people were wary and I wasn't welcome. So I kept going. The severity of my situation truly set in when I slept against the back of a shop, shivering all over, stomach grumbling, mouth parched, a layer of sand gritted over my skin and hair.

I knew no one, had nothing. I'd spent my last coin on filling up my waterskin and a sack filled with nuts and dates. I was tired. Scared. Alone—I had never felt so utterly alone.

And that's when I found Milly. Or really, when Milly found me.

She jabbed me awake with her walking stick. Stared down at me with one milky eye and told me to come with her.

I was going to bolt. I knew better than to just trust someone, especially when you had no money or items to barter your safety with. But even though she was blind in one eye, Milly must've seen that on my expression, because she said, "Run off if you want, but I got rabbit in the kitchen and water in the well. Don't have a building to sleep up against, but I'm sure the bed will do."

I sat there, stunned, taking in the silver gleam of her hair, the way her shoulders stooped so that her body was in the shape of a teapot—bent elbow leaning on her cane just like a handle.

"What?" I asked, wiping the tangled hair out of my face as I looked up at her, my knees bent, worn boots tucked beneath my dress.

"How old are you, girl?"

"Fifteen."

"Hmm." She leaned even more on her cane, the cheeks

of her lined face making little C shapes on either side. "You break some kind of law? Steal something?"

I shook my head while she glowered at me. "Well, alright then. Let's go."

I gaped at her, trying to think of all the ways she might be tricking me. Before I could figure it out, she turned around and started to hobble away, skirts swishing at her calves, silver hair tucked into a tight braid.

When I didn't move, she looked over her shoulder at me. "Well? You gonna sit there on the street all night and get pecked at by vultures? Or are you coming? Because I got a bad hip and worse patience."

I'd like to say I had some gut instinct telling me I could trust Milly and that's why I went with her, but the truth was, I just really wanted that rabbit and water.

Milly led me to a mule hitched to a cart on the dark street, and I sat beside her as she took the reins and plodded us away. When the street ended, when the cluster of village buildings was left behind, she still guided us on, tired hooves clomping through the sand, just a sliver of a crescent moon lighting up the way.

Thirty minutes later, when I was about ready to fall over in exhaustion, my whole back screaming in itchy pain, the first signs of Carnith came into view.

Most of the villages and cities I'd passed had oases or rivers, low as they may be, and Carnith was no different. It was a quaint village curled around a tiny oasis, date palms propagated around the water.

Milly's house was right in the middle of the cluster

of buildings. They were all nestled between sand dunes, a mountain far off in the shadowed landscape. Each home was curved and short, looking like it was molded from clay and left to bake in the sun. Hers was set a bit further back than the rest, a short clay fence surrounding it. The slightly angled tin roof shone silver as she led the mule through the gate and then to a small stable whose ground was littered with straw, while a trough and stall were visible through the archway.

Still leery, I waited at the front of the building, watching as she clumped down the cart's steps. "Well, don't just gawk, girl. Come over here. You're going to learn how to unhitch Sal and to feed and water and brush him. Tomorrow, when I go do my deliveries, you'll learn to hitch him back up." She eyed me, one brow raised higher than the other. "You'll learn to ride him too."

All I could do was stare wide-eyed at this strange woman until both she and the mule seemed to tsk at me.

So, I learned how to unhitch Sal. And how to brush him. Feed him. Water him.

When I was done, Milly gave me fresh, cool water from her well that tasted earthy and crisp. I could've drunk forever, except she knocked me with her cane again and told me that was enough because she didn't want me vomiting all over her front yard.

Then I helped her polish off the rabbit that had been drying over her fireplace, and my mouth watered the entire time I ate it. She squinted over at me from across the fire as I ate and said, "Huh. You're shiny."

And that was that. She didn't seem to mind that I was

gold, didn't even seem that surprised by it, as if she'd seen so much in her old age that nothing fazed her much anymore.

After I'd eaten my fill, she shoved aside a drape hanging from a doorway and showed me a room with a small straw bed with a small square window, and told me to get some rest.

I didn't sleep at all that night because I was too wary, too nervous. I was still wondering what she was going to do, because in my experience, people didn't help or give anything away for free.

But Milly did.

So I stayed that night, and the next, and the next, until I started to actually sleep, and my wariness turned into gratitude.

Despite her advanced age and being blind in one eye, I quickly realized that Milly was hard to keep up with. She worked from dawn until dusk, and sometimes even later when she had deliveries to make or markets to go to.

The back of her house was cultivated with desert wildflowers and pallets of wood flush with beehives. She taught me how to gather honeycombs from them. How to make jelly from prickly pears. How to sew my own clothing, lay snares for small game, build a fire, ride Sal.

Over time, my gratefulness merged into warmth. Milly was tough as nails and quick of tongue, but she was kind. She taught me to be self-sufficient, and she gave me a roof over my head and food and water in my stomach, and in return, I threw myself into helping her as much as I could.

For a time, everything was great. We lived together in this small clay bungalow, and I was content. Milly was the first person I loved in Orea. She was like the grandmother I never knew. Brisk and weathered and exacting when it came to how to do things and do them right.

Yet there was a softer side to her too. Like when, that first morning, she took one look at the dark circles under my eyes and said we were having a *down day*. How, with knobby knuckles and arthritic hands, she brushed out my wet and hopelessly tangled hair. How, when she was combing and noticed me flinch, she demanded to know what was wrong with my back.

She found me sleeping outside and took me home. She saw my gold skin and shrugged it off. And then, as she tended to my raw, peeling back, she discovered my ribbons sprouting out of it, and she didn't even bat an eye.

"Got ribbons growing out of you," she'd said. So matter-of-fact there wasn't even a note of inflection.

I was panicked.

She was pragmatic.

"Best not pluck them out. I think they're meant to be there."

Practical as always, she tended to the sore skin every night and told me to leave them be, told me not to fuss my head about it. Because people grow hair all over their bodies, so it wasn't that strange to grow this. Said she had chin hairs longer than what was growing from my back, though that wasn't true for very long.

It was her deadpan, unruffled attitude that kept me from having a breakdown. It was her quiet care as she tended to them every night that had me crying with the acceptance she showed me.

So I kept working alongside her in the garden or scrubbing the bricks in the well or taking care of Sal or helping to mend or wash or cook, and I was content, yes, but I was also *safe*. It felt like living out there with Milly, at the edge of a small village, in the middle of a desert, I was finally safe.

Until one night, everything changed.

I fell asleep the way I usually did. Curled on my side, watching the thin fabric of the curtained doorway as it ruffled from the breeze through the open window. Moonlight streamed in, the same soft, milky color as Milly's eye, and I listened to her rasping, dried-up tenor as she sang while she sewed.

Her singing reminded me of my mother.

It wasn't until hours later, when dawn had just barely crested, that I jerked awake. I think it must've been the sound of the front door shutting or maybe just a disturbance in the air. I sat up in bed with a start, heart already pounding before my mind could catch up with the danger my body was warning me of.

But then I heard it. Footsteps. Steps far too heavy and steady to be Milly's limping hitch. There was the sound of something landing on the floor, a loud sniff, a shuffle, a cough. And that's when I froze on the bed. Because that was a man. A man who must've broken in—a man who was going to hurt Milly, hurt me, steal what wasn't his and abuse us because he could.

Because that's what men did. They took and they hurt and no one ever stopped them.

My back itched. My fingertips ached. My heart continued to hammer.

I couldn't let anything happen to Milly. She was too old, too frail, and that wicked tongue of hers would only make things worse.

It had to be me. She protected me, so I had to protect her. This surging need to keep her safe was all-consuming. I looked around the sparse room for anything that I could use as a weapon, creeping off to grab my boot from the floor.

As I crouched against the wall, watching the flapping drapery on the doorway, my adrenaline surged. I wasn't going to let anyone hurt Milly. I wasn't going to let anyone hurt me.

But as the heavy footsteps started to make their way closer, my fingertips prickled. Pricked. As if little needles were suddenly pressing into them and threatening to splinter.

As soon as the curtain was moved aside with a callous shove, I leapt forward and slammed my boot across his face. He cried out with a curse, whirling on me, an enraged, weathered expression lit up by the moonlight. He shoved me so hard that my sore back hit the wall with a crack, stars bursting in front of my eyes, and this time it was me crying out, the sound magnified in the dim lighting.

"You want to try and attack me?" the man shouted, enraged, spittle landing on my cheek. His breath reeked of alcohol. "I'll show you what happens, girl."

He didn't even hit me with his hands. Instead, he yanked off the heavy sack from his back and swung it at me. Hard. I don't know what he had in there, but it felt like an anvil crashing right into my head. My shoulder. My ribs. Tucked against the wall, as if I could sink right through it, I tried to raise my arms to protect my head as the man snarled and swung.

Then I heard Milly.

She was slow at the best of times, but after she'd been lying down in bed for more than a few hours, her achy joints stiffened up and made it even worse. And yet, I heard her hurried shuffle, her walking cane scraping against the tile floor.

Panic surged through me. It was one thing for me to take these kinds of hits, but Milly couldn't sustain that. Her brittle bones might very well shatter. I heard her scratchy voice calling my name. Heard the fear in it.

Her fear added to my surging adrenaline. It made it swell. Made it *snap*. Made my fingertips ache and burn and then *bleed*.

I felt the liquid dripping down my palms, but I barely paid any mind to the red-hot blood seeping from my fingers. Because Milly was getting closer, and the man was swinging back his foot to kick me in a crushing blow, and I launched myself at him.

Like an animal, I snarled as I jumped at him. Clawed at him. Raked my bleeding fingers down his face. Not Milly. He wasn't going to hurt Milly. I wasn't going to let him come into her home, steal her hard-earned coin, and hurt us.

The man stumbled as I attacked him, tried to pry me off, but I slammed my hands against his head and *pushed*. And the blood on my palms smeared and gushed, and I was too frantic to even care.

And then, his snarls turned to gurgles. His prying fingers left my body to instead claw at his face.

The slick blood pouring from my hands made me lose

my hold, and I landed on the floor again, but then my feet were wet too, like I was suddenly standing in a puddle of my own blood, or maybe it was his? But that didn't make sense, because I'd only scratched and hit him, and he'd hit me, and why was there so much blood? Was it raining? Was the roof leaking? But why was it so warm? So thick?

My frenzied mind couldn't come up with a single explanation, but the air held the metallic clang of blood, and the liquid was warm. So warm.

Milly tore through the doorway. Eyes wide, hand spasming over her hold on her walking stick that she held like a weapon. She raised her cane, ready to hit, but then she jerked to a stop, good eye taking in the man.

"*Felton?*"

"You know him?" I asked, but my voice felt strange. *I* felt strange.

"He's my brother. Comes every few months. What—"

The man made a strangled noise, and then his knees hit the floor. There was a splash on impact. I flinched back when some of it splattered across my face.

"Felton!" Milly cried, and I knew. Knew I'd made a mistake. Knew it by the way she turned, uneven steps hurrying away and then coming back, this time, holding a lantern in her hand to help the dim dawn to light the room.

When the light hit the room, I couldn't make sense of it.

The amber hue that drenched everything. The shine reflected from the lantern. The man was on his knees, clawing at his throat, making the most disturbing noises. But he wasn't marked with streaks of red. The floor wasn't puddled with rain. My fingertips weren't bleeding. It wasn't the metallic warmth of blood I was smelling.

It was...*gold.*

Milly's hand flew to her mouth. The cane she was holding fell to the floor, splashing as it landed. Her expression was horrified. "Felton!"

The cry tore out of her as another burbled noise came from him, and my eyes went wide when she held the lantern closer to his face. His face where liquid gold had scored down his cheeks where I'd hit him, and wrapped around to his mouth. He was trying to cough as it drained down his throat, trying to get the viscid liquid away from his neck where it strangled and squeezed.

"What did you do?" Milly shouted at me, looking from me to him. *"Look at what you did!"*

He struggled for a moment longer, and then his kneeling form crashed to the floor with a splash.

Milly *wailed.*

She scrambled forward, but the slippery floor made her go crashing down. I lurched forward to catch her.

I shouldn't have.

I shouldn't have, because as soon as my hands caught her arms, the gold spread to *her*. Like a conscious, intentional thing, it moved and encased, staining her clothes, blotching her skin, pooling in her mouth.

She couldn't even scrabble and fight like the man did. And I was in shock. Utter, horrifying shock, as I watched this terrifying gold so viciously attack the one person I loved.

I tried to pull it away. Tried to claw at it where it poured in her mouth and dripped down her neck, but that only made it worse. More gold rained from my palms, surrounding her in a hostile downpour, making me snatch my hands back. I stared at them, watching more and more stream down, and I couldn't stop it.

What did you do?

Denial tried to beat through my chest, but as I knelt over her, saw her one wide, milky eye, saw the way the gold was squeezing her and her brother against the floor...

There was nothing but panic then.

I scrabbled up, slipping on the wet tile, and I ran. I screamed. For help, for someone to come, for anyone else in the village to fix her, for this to all be a nightmare, despite the hot sun peeking over the horizon.

But as I screamed, as I ran out of her house and into the yard, my gold came with me. It followed my feet, nipping at my heels like a feral dog.

The first person who ran out of their house at my cries took one look at me and stopped dead in his tracks. I stumbled at him, hands gripping his arms, begging him to help me as tears poured down my cheeks. Tears that were no longer clear but the same gold that wept from my hands.

I shouldn't have touched him. Shouldn't have grabbed him. Because the gold pounced on him too. He fell, just as they had. Landing at my feet with a violent, panicked pitch, dying right there in front of my wide eyes, all because of a touch.

Shouts rose up and down the village. More people came out. I was shivering, crying, screaming, and this curse just kept rolling out of me in waves, flooding from my feet, pouring from my hands, more and more and more.

"*She's cursed! She's come to curse us!*"

"*We need to burn her!*"

No no no no

I was already burning with this nonstop cascade, and Milly—

When a group of men came running at me with lit torches, I knew they were going to hurt me. I knew I deserved it. But I needed them to go see. Needed them to help Milly.

"Please, please."

They ran at me, eyes lit with fire, flames reflecting off the gold that gathered around me. With a spike of my fear, I tried to turn and run away.

But my gold didn't.

It streamed out of me, poured from Milly's doorway, gushing down the street like a flash flood, swallowing up the village in its wake.

It didn't even take long for the gold to inundate the cluster of houses. For it to stream into every doorway and window, and drop from the rooftops. For the screams to rend the air. And then choked gurgles and running feet to abruptly halt.

It should've taken longer to murder an entire village.

I was stuck in shock, bare knees on the molten road, eyes blinking around the destruction I'd wrought. There was just a puddle left at my feet, the entire village splotched and blotted and *dripping*.

The flame from the torches littered on the ground mocked me. The dawning sun shone in accusation.

What did you do?

The gold didn't dry up until my tears did.

And by then, everyone was dead. Men, women, children. Milly.

Not even poor old Sal was spared.

My palms were a mess of congealed, tacky gold I had to scrub off, and my feet were the same. I could feel the thickly dried tracks on my cheeks as I ran through the village. Splotches of gold were everywhere, smothered against faces, fisting around chests, staining doorways and window panes like splatters of blood.

I killed *everyone* in Carnith.

I'm not sure when I collapsed, but when I woke up, night had come. The shadows of the gilded dead surrounded me. Houses far too quiet, not a single fireplace lit. I ran back into Milly's house, sobbing, exhausted, walking over the streaks of gold on the floor that felt as sticky as the honey Milly harvested.

I knew I couldn't stay. Knew I had to get away. So I stripped off my syrupy clothes and washed up, dressing in a clean shirt and pants, along with my cloak. I found Milly's knapsack and filled it with as much food and water as I could carry, and then I fled.

I couldn't bear to stay in that house. In that village. So I ran to the next one over. That was as far as my exhausted feet could carry me. Stayed in a hidden alleyway, unable to sleep, because all I saw was that splash of gold glinting across Milly's mouth and cheek and good eye, the milky one untouched, staring ahead, unseeing in a completely different way.

The next night, that village was raided. With men who brought torches and threats. I thought they'd found Carnith and they'd known what I'd done. I thought they'd tracked me down to kill me, that they were going to punish this village for unwittingly harboring a cursed girl.

Of course, I didn't know then that it was *him*. Didn't know that he'd followed me across the ocean on a hunch and that he'd found Carnith, where his master plan morphed. He didn't need the clout or wealth from being Derfort Harbor's east-end crime boss. Not anymore. So he shed the false name and had his men burn Carnith to the ground and bury the gold, hiding the evidence entirely.

Then he tracked me down, had half his men attack the village to make it look like a raid, while the other half swooped in to save the day. He had his own men killed not long after that. No one was allowed to know who he was or where he came from.

No one was allowed to know about me.

And I followed him. With newly-formed magic and a miserable, terrified heart, I followed him, looking at him like he was my savior. My protector. With his prodding, I learned how to use my magic when he said we'd run out of money. For him, I had to learn how to use it, but more importantly, how to hide it.

When I first got to Second Kingdom, I thought I was lucky.

But it turned out the villagers were right.

I was cursed.

CHAPTER 31

QUEEN MALINA

Perhaps the cold should bother me more than it does, yet I think I have simply grown numb.

Numb when I had to flee my own castle.

Numb when I had to flee my own safe house.

Numb as I flee my own kingdom.

That could be the reason why I don't truly feel the blizzard as it boils around us like bubbles of frost, an agitated, bulbous cloud steaming out a mist of snow.

Or, it could be the shock.

I've lost track of the days since we crossed out of Sixth—since we entered the cursed land of what used to be Seventh Kingdom.

No one comes out here. For one, it's forbidden, and two, it's impossible to sustain life. There are no trees and no birds that fly overhead, like there's something corrupted here in both soil and air.

Or perhaps it's just too cold.

As a girl, I was taught history lessons about the monarchs who once ruled here. About the great strides they made in seeking the unknown. The kingdom itself was once intriguing as well. Like the great glacier lakes that used to draw so many people to sightsee. Icebergs jutting from the frozen water like the teeth of a giant sea serpent come to bite through the ice.

This used to be a formidable kingdom, and despite the harsher climates, it once had a thriving city too. The heart of the Orean and Annwyn union, the doorway between sister worlds where fae and Oreans alike could pass back and forth.

Now, this place is broken.

If it weren't for Sir Pruinn, I would've turned back the moment I noticed the split and ravaged landscape. I can now say with complete certainty that the lessons I had on the destruction of Seventh Kingdom were not exaggerated. The fae destroyed this place so thoroughly that not a single person survived. Not a single inch of the *land* survived either, and it still hasn't recovered. After three hundred years, nothing about this place shows any signs of repair. It's not just demolished, it's...*unnatural*. Sometimes, I think I can feel some of the pulsing, evil magic hovering in the gray mist that clings to the fissures.

All around, there are jagged strips of land like serrated knives, where some of the earth has simply crumbled away. As if some great quake shook the kingdom, shattering it into pieces. All that's left are broken-off strips on a flattened expanse, a gray and white void that lies bleak and empty.

I keep my face on the horizon as Pruinn drives the cart

onward. I made the mistake of looking down into those empty crevices of earth once, seeing them gorged with whorls of mist, and the sight made me dizzy. Because in those huge cracks, there's nothing—no darkness of shadow that tells me the core of the earth is below. Instead, there's just the gray emptiness that goes on forever and ever. As if you could fall over and never stop falling, because whatever happened here was born of magic and not of nature, and these cleaves through the ground are an anomaly of destructive power.

And it doesn't stop. That's how this entire landscape has been, no matter how long we've been traveling. Somehow, Pruinn has used the map to guide us, knowing when to turn past different rifts and when to brave the pinched strips of land. So far, we haven't ended up stranded, though I almost wish we would. I wish we had no option but to turn around.

But turn around to what?

That's the question that has been tormenting me. As much as I have absolutely zero faith in Pruinn's charlatan magic that this map can point me to my heart's desire, where else do I have to go?

My husband sent an assassin to kill me. My own people rebelled against me. There's nothing left for me in Sixth Kingdom anymore.

Perhaps that's why I'm numb.

Who am I if not Malina Colier, Queen of Sixth Kingdom?

So we travel on.

I'm not even certain how the horses are still alive. It's not as if we're in a place Pruinn can forage for food, and I can't believe he still has barrels of hay for them. This place isn't just desolate, as parts of Sixth are. It's sterile, empty. Creepy.

And yet, the further we go, the keener Pruinn seems to become.

"We're not going to find anything," I've told him again and again.

To which he always replies, "Trust the map."

Fool.

I doze off, buried beneath the hood of my coat, lulled from the sway of the cart. I've since stopped being worried about one of the horses' hooves slipping on one of the edges and sending us falling into the gray abyss. At this point, I can't seem to drudge up the energy to care.

Perhaps that's where my heart's desire is—an endless end.

I get tugged out of my sleep when the cart comes to a sudden stop, and I hear a scrap of Pruinn's voice over the wind. I turn to see why he's stopped before nightfall, but I freeze in place when I see the silhouette looming before us.

At first, I think it must be one of the old icebergs I read about, except much larger than I ever imagined. It's caught in a still sea of white snow, its jagged tips as sharp as canines sneering up toward the sky. It's asymmetrical, as if three quarters of it were broken off and sunk into the ground, leaving only this last bit remaining.

Yet, as I continue to squint at it past the gray mist, I recognize the shape isn't quite the deadened pronged berg I thought it was.

It's...a castle.

What's left of it anyway.

"Is that what I think it is?" I breathe, my eyes still locked on it.

Pruinn sits at the cart's seat, holding the reins loosely in his hands, his short blond hair looking muted in the dismal daylight. "It is."

I shake my head, disbelief rolling around beneath my skull. "How is this possible? I thought the castle was completely destroyed."

"I suppose not."

All this time, I was taught that the city and castle itself were swallowed up by the magical void, but as I stare at the decrepit form still standing, I realize that wasn't true. Seventh Kingdom was broken and destroyed, yet it's still *here*. Like a skeleton partially preserved.

Pruinn pulls us onward, toward the monolithic bones of what once was a pristine palace. When we're so close I can actually see the scrape of stonework, raw and chipping on the sides of its remains, I also see what lies beyond.

My eyes were playing tricks on me before, because it isn't just more flat, frozen ground stretching far beyond it.

I thought I saw giant fissures as we traveled here, but all of those combined are *nothing* compared to this. This isn't just a cracked crevice left mangled in the earth. No, the land just beyond where the castle sits is *gone*.

As if a huge chunk of the flattened earth has simply been torn like a piece of paper and tossed away. Roiling clouds of colorless mist drag against the craggy lip of the land, and beyond, there's nothing. Below, there's nothing.

The hair on the back of my neck lifts, and I have the

sudden and intense feeling I'm being watched. I glance all around us, but I don't see a single speck stretched along the white snow. Perhaps it's the magic that's stalking me, like it knows life has dared to breach the void.

With that eerie sensation I can't quite shrug off, Pruinn brings us right up to the very front of the ruins. The structure has been fossilized in the freeze, preserving the abraded stone. I can't make out where any windows or balconies may have once existed, but the general shape of a hacked off rooftop and reaching walls still remain.

Pruinn jumps off the driver's bench of the cart and comes around, holding a hand up to help me get out. "This is where your map ends, Your Majesty," he tells me, just as a grin widens over his face. "So let's go find your heart's desire."

Somehow, Pruinn managed to find an opening so we could actually go *inside* the remains of the castle. It's now nothing more than a shadowed cavern, collapsed in some places, the rubble frozen stiff.

It's awful—like walking inside the chest of some giant beast long-since perished. Mist swirls around in here too, so the only real difference from outside to inside is the way our steps echo ominously. As I walk around, that tingling sensation happens again—the one that feels as if I'm being observed. As if the castle itself is watching me, finding me lacking.

Well, I find it lacking too.

"I hate to disappoint you, Sir Pruinn, but this is definitely *not* my heart's desire."

We stop just inside the middle of what I'm guessing used to be a grand entry hall, the ceiling at least thirty feet up, now covered in ash-colored frost.

Turning around to look at him, I clasp my hands in front of me. I'm travel weary, filthier than I've ever been in my life, and now all I have to look forward to is...the journey back.

"I don't know what I was thinking, letting you bring me here," I say, my tone gone as brittle as the ice chips beneath my feet. "I hope you're happy. You've just proved how much of a fraud you truly are, and now we're at the end of the world for no reason."

My anger runs frigid and cold.

"This isn't my heart's desire," I say again, spinning around to gesture to the ruins. "Why did you bring me here? This is a shattered and severed land that has no hope of ever becoming what it once was."

Just as I have no hope of ever becoming what I once was.

A throat clears behind me, making me go rigid. "Actually, Your Majesty, that's where you're wrong."

I whirl around at the new voice, eyes flaring wide at the two men standing before me.

The first thing that stands out to me is how thoroughly ill-fitting they are in this forsaken detritus, because both of them are impeccably dressed. As if they aren't in the middle of ruins but ready to step into some sort of royal celebration.

The second thing I notice is the men are nearly identical. A thick curtain of hair down to their shoulders, the same height, even the same stance. The only difference I can pick out between them is they each have moles dead center in the middle of their cheeks, yet on opposite sides of their faces.

"Who are you?" I ask, taking a startled step back. That sensation of being watched comes back full force, making the mist in the air seem denser as it curls near my side.

"I am Friano, and this is my twin brother, Fassa," the man on the left says, the corresponding mole on his left cheek. "We are pleased to make your acquaintance, Queen Malina Colier."

I glance warily at Pruinn, but he's simply watching me with an encouraging look I wish I could slap right off his face.

"How do you know who I am, and what are you doing here?"

Friano grins, showing a row of perfectly even teeth. "You are the queen of Sixth Kingdom. Of course we know who you are. Tales of the beauty of the Cold Queen have stretched even here."

My brows lift in surprise. "Are you saying that you *live* here?"

They both nod in unison, and this time, Fassa answers. "We do, Your Majesty."

"How is that possible? No one can live here. This place is utterly desolate."

"Ah, yes," Fassa replies brightly. "Brother, if you could...?"

"Of course." With a nod, Friano lifts a finger in the air and spins it around, and like a wave rippling through our surroundings, the castle *transforms*.

Within moments, gone are the ruins, and in its place is

Seventh Kingdom's castle restored. Slick gray walls, dazzling blue windows, and black marble that's whole and polished beneath our feet. What was the stripped off bones of a cavern is now a revived and elegant entry hall.

It's like a timepiece turned backwards, reversing all the damage that had been done and returning this place to its rightful glory.

All I can do is gape as I try to take it all in, my mind not quite believing my eyes. "How...?"

"We have been waiting for you, Your Majesty."

I rear back, looking between the two of them before my gaze hooks into Pruinn. "Did you know they were here? That this would happen?"

"I knew that we would find *something*," he says before tapping on the pocket of his coat where I can see a hint of the rolled-up map. "I always trust my magic."

Bewildered, I look back at the twins. My hands automatically run down my wrinkled, stained dress. They're standing here looking fresh, while I'm begrimed and sloppy, my normally perfect hair a tangled twist at the back of my head. "Why were you waiting for me?"

They share a look, matching grins gathering on their faces. "Because we have prayed to the gods for a rightful heir of Orea to help us restore Seventh Kingdom to glory, and they brought us you."

My mind snags on his words, a jolt of hope burgeoning from my weary limbs. "What are you talking about?"

Fassa comes forward and gently takes hold of my palm, like a noble would just before kissing it for good graces. He doesn't raise my hand to his mouth though, and instead holds it, his own hands feeling far too warm.

Or perhaps I'm far too cold.

"You are the answer to our prayers, Your Majesty. You are the queen this land needs. You coming here proves it."

"Proves *what*?"

"Isn't it obvious?" he asks, his dark eyes sparkling with hope. "You're going to be the queen who saves Seventh Kingdom."

CHAPTER 32

AUREN

*I*t looks very good, my lady."

Hojat gives me a cursory tap on my shoulder, letting me know I can sit up, since he already buttoned up the borrowed shirt along my spine.

"How much longer do you think I need to have the salves put on me?" I ask as I sit up, feeling only slight discomfort pull at my back.

"Not much longer, I think. You are healing quite fast."

"On the outside, maybe," I mutter. "Thank you, Hojat."

He glances at me from the corner of his eye, and I can see him hesitating for a moment until he turns back around to face me, his leather satchel strung over his shoulder. "My lady, I have not known you very long, but I know you through your wounds, I think."

I don't know how to take that comment for a moment until he taps at his dragged down skin, the left side of his face like candle wax melted and then cooled, left there to droop. "People with scars, we know. We see. We understand." He taps his wilted eye next. "There is hurt past this, yes?"

My mouth goes dry. "Yes."

He nods, hand dropping down to hang at his side. "I can heal your body, my lady. But my tonics and salves won't heal your mind, I'm afraid. It's up to you to do that."

"And did *you* do that? Heal your mind?"

A sad smile twists his already crooked mouth. "I like to think so, and I like to think that you will, too." He holds out a dried lotus flower, its petals a vivid purple, surrounded by bright yellow middle strands that look like some sort of sea creature you'd find in the ocean. "To put beneath your pillow."

Taking it, I flick my gaze back up to him. He's been leaving peonies beneath my pillow, just like he did when he tended to me in the army. Back then, I remember him telling me that where he was from, it was good luck to put them beneath your pillow when you were ill.

And I remembered something similar.

Peonies for good health. A willow branch for luck. Cotton stems for prosperity. The fleshy leaf of a jade to bring harmony.

And a lotus for resilience.

I can't believe I didn't think more about this coincidence before. "Where did you say you learned this tradition?" I ask carefully.

"Ah," he says, and something indecipherable glitters in his eyes. "This was passed down to me. I learned my trade from a very good healer."

Healer. Not mender.

Mender is the Orean word for it. But *healer*...

"Are you... I mean, you can't be, but..." I falter, eyes skimming over him like I haven't seen him before. The way he's never balked at my ribbons, at my power, at anything to do with Slade... "Where exactly are you from?"

"My accent does not give it away?" he teases with a tap on his nose. "I was born in Southern Orea. Though, I lived here for a while. Trained here."

My brows lift. "Here? As in..."

"Drollard Village, yes. A bit colder than where I was raised," he says with a smile that crinkles his scars.

Slade has told me very little about this place so far. I only know that it exists without actually existing. The strip of desolate land is all that he acquired when he decided not to declare war.

But why?

Why this place?

What's so important here that he wanted to make it part of Fourth Kingdom when it was outside his territory?

Perhaps it's just because of the rot. I've heard of how his power has surpassed his own territory and leached into Fifth. But I can't help but feel like it's more than that. Why keep an entire village hidden?

My mind spins with questions, but before I can ask Hojat anything else, he's already leaving the room and shutting the door behind him. My eyes drop down to the lotus while barely-there memories try to stick to my mind. They're nothing more than pieces of lint clinging with nothing but static.

A willow branch hanging from a bedpost. Peonies tied with a ribbon and tucked beneath my pillow. Waking with the crushed remnants, fingers brushing against the dried shards, the scent of them tucked into the fabric of my pillow.

Gently, I place the offering on the bed, feeling a wave of nostalgia wash over me, knotted curiosity tying down my limbs.

After making myself get up, I use the washroom and wash my hands before I comb back my hair to rid it of tangles, and tie it off in a simple braid that will work for training. But then I realize that I don't have another clean pair of leggings in my closet. Slade was going to bring me more from his room, but he must've forgotten.

I hesitate for a moment, debating whether or not I should just head off to meet Judd for training, but I need to wear the thicker pants to help cushion against the splintered hay. So I push back my shoulders and leave the room, heading down the hallway until I get to the very last door at the end.

My fingers curl around the doorknob, but it takes several seconds before I gain the courage to actually turn it. When I do, I stop in the doorway, staring at the bed.

Gold covers the entire mattress, the whole of it spreading from headboard to foot, perhaps an inch thick where it's pooled in the center, the liquid now frozen and still. I walk slowly over to it, staring down at my gilded reflection within.

Since Slade brought me to the cave a few days ago and I confessed everything that happened in Carnith, he's backed off. Talking was good for both of us, but when it comes to my magic, I'm not ready. I want to concentrate on getting physically stronger first, and then I'll feel like I'll be able to tackle my gold.

Maybe he's right. Maybe I *am* blocking my power. But in a way, it's a relief. I've gone so many years with it dripping from me uncontrollably. If only I'd snapped sooner and grappled this kind of control, my life would have been so different. So maybe it's selfish, but I'm not ready for this intermission to end. I'm not ready to unblock it.

Even now, looking down at this frozen pond on the bed, I don't want to touch it, to connect with it. I want to be me without the gold-touch for just a little while longer.

I give myself one last long look at my reflection before I turn away, going into Slade's closet where, thankfully, I find a pair of leggings to slip on. I don't look at the bed again as I walk out. It's only once I've shut the door behind me that I let out a shuddering breath.

"There you are," Lu calls, walking up. "I was looking for you."

"What for?"

She stops in front of me, dressed in her usual army leathers, and for once, her slippers are nowhere in sight. "Since it's a nice night, I figured you might want to go out and walk around. You must be feeling cabin fever by now."

A laugh escapes me. "I lived in a cage for ten years."

"Oh. Right." Lu shrugs. "Well, anyway, what do you say I take you into the pavilion where you can meet the villagers?"

I hesitate. So far, my only venture out of the Grotto has been when Slade took me to the other cave where we spoke. Between the house and training with Judd, I haven't had any real reason to leave the cave, and I've felt protected here. Like the rest of the world can't touch me. So long as I stay in here, I don't have to face anything or anyone else yet.

"I can't. I'm supposed to meet Judd for some training."

"You've been working hard, you can skip tonight."

I paste a forced smile on my face. "No, I'd better not. I don't want to let Judd down."

"Well, you get extra points for being a dependable student," I hear Judd say right before he comes into view, rounding the corner from the living room with floppy mustard-colored hair and a grin. "I think it'll be good for you to get out and walk around with Lu. Emphasis on the *walk*. You could really use the practice with that because you're still a bit shit at it."

"Ha ha," I say dryly.

He gives me a playful wink.

"You want to come with us?" Lu asks as he comes nearer.

"Nope, you enjoy."

She gives him a skeptical look. "Don't even *think* about it."

"Think about what?" he asks, sounding far too innocent for it to be real.

"If you go into my room while I'm gone, I'll know."

"Will you?" he counters, eyes glittering.

"Dammit, Judd, I didn't steal the damned wine!"

"Mm-hmm," he says, seeming completely unconvinced.

He nudges her in the arm as he walks by to head for his bedroom. "Have fun with Gildy Locks tonight. Drink some wine for me since I can't because our barrel is *missing*."

Lu rolls her eyes, and Judd disappears into his room before I can try to convince him that I want to train instead.

"So…" I whisper, glancing at Lu. "Did you steal the wine?"

She snorts. "Of course I did. Ready?"

"Umm…"

She arches a dark brow. "You don't live in a cage anymore, Gildy. Gotta venture out sometime."

She's right. I know she is. I can't hide inside forever. But what if I snap again? What if the fae beast in me wrenches out and I flood the village with gold, killing more innocent people?

"My power…"

"You've got this. And if you don't, I'm sure I can distract you with my magic."

My head tilts. "Does your magic work that way?"

"No idea. Let's go."

I can't keep the hesitation out of my voice. "Okay."

She tilts her head, motioning me forward, and I follow her into the living room. "Grab your coat," she says, and I head for the peg, pulling the coat off and slipping it on. The heat of the fire is saturated through the fabric, enveloping me in its delicious warmth. "It's not late yet, so the pavilion still has people around."

I nod as I do up the last button and then slip on my boots.

Lu pulls up the hood over her shaved head. "Ready?"

"Is it too late to go train?"

She rolls her eyes and tugs me forward by the arm. "Come on, Gildy."

Together, we head out of the house and go through the Grotto's cave, and with every step, my heart pounds. All I keep thinking of is when Slade stepped in front of me, when I finally came back down from the rush of the power driving me and realized I'd killed people and flooded the room.

Outside, the night is bright, the moon full and shining against the snow, making everything seem to glow. Yet I find no comfort in it. The night used to give me reprieve. It used to be *safe*, marking the time where I didn't have to worry about my magic and every single touch of my skin. But I can't trust it now.

"You've got this," Lu says, and I follow as she heads to the left, our steps crunching over a snowy pathway.

Stuffing my hands into my pockets, I feel for the ribbon, twining it around like threading fingers through a friend's hand.

The air is stiff and icy, not a hint of a breeze, and every exhale I let out condenses into a cloud. I pull up my hood to try and keep the chill from clinging to my face and ears, but it seeps in anyway. Yet even though it's freezing, there's something therapeutic about breathing in fresh air. Only once you feed it into your lungs do you realize how stale you've been.

I take a moment to look around, head tilted up at the looming mountains. In the dark, they look crooked and notched, with cracks running through like some long-ago giant took an ax to them, blade chopping into the rock again and again.

We're at the base of the smallest mountain, its form hunched like the stooped spine of someone bracing against the cold. Above us, the natural shelf near the base of the mountain continues, keeping our path hidden and shadowed, while meager clumps of trees pepper the slope.

"Look at you," Lu says beside me. "You're not leaking gold out of your ass or setting a rabid molten bird after your enemies, so I think you're going to be okay."

"Thanks," I deadpan.

She gives me a grin and pats me on the shoulder. "Relax, Gildy. Look up at the sky and relax."

My eyes lift. "Clouds are covering most of it, and this mountain's shelf is doing the rest."

"You know what I mean."

"So...what now?" I ask.

"Now, I show you around," she says, turning to face the other way, toward the larger mountain. "Back that way is the Perch—the timberwings' roost. You see how that path winds a bit? You just follow that. You passed it when Rip took you to train the other day."

"Are there a lot of timberwings here?" I ask, avoiding the training topic. The creatures are pretty rare and don't live in the wild anymore. Monarchs are the only people in Orea that I've known to own them, using them for personal transport and war.

"We always have three here," Lu explains. "But right now, we have more since our own are roosting."

My brows lift. "You have your very own timberwing?"

"All the Wrath do. Why, you jealous?" she asks with a grin.

I suppress a shudder, remembering the way Queen Kaila's beast snapped at me, its drooling, sharp fangs grinning at me from a stretched maw and wet feathers. "Nope. Definitely not."

"Hey, they're not so bad. Lots of people are afraid of them, but if you train them right, they're big softies."

"I'll take your word for it."

She laughs and then points up further. "Past the Perch is the Mole. It's one of our hidden lookouts where the guards keep watch."

"Why is it called the Mole?"

"Because it looks like a growth on the side of the mountain. It's a damn pain to get up there, too. Takes about a hundred rickety, slippery stairs, and then you're stuck in a cramped post with only a tiny heat lantern and a lookout glass to keep you company."

"Sounds cozy."

Lu turns. "Come on. Down this way is where the villagers live. Their homes are all stacked together one after the other, beneath the mountain's awning. Everything was built beneath it so that timberwings couldn't spot anything from above," she explains.

Just then, the houses come into view, each one only slightly different from the one beside it. They all look like they were carved right into the mountain, rock roofs slanted over them and wooden doors lathered in frost. Each door is just a few feet away from the other, most of which are grappling with vines that have crawled up the stone, some heavy with hardy-looking berries.

"These houses seem small."

"It's deceiving."

We pass by the first few homes, tiny stone chimneys jutting up from the roofs and fanning out smoke. After a few more moments, the path that parallels the homes slopes down a bit, and I can see a large open space ahead where the base of the mountain is pushed in.

"That's the pavilion," Lu explains. "It's where everyone hangs about when they're sick of being in their houses, which right now, everyone is, since that blizzard lasted so long."

The pavilion is half exposed, while the other half is tucked into the mountain's belly. The rock overhang juts out quite a bit here, but there's an orange glow of a large fire burning half beneath it. I can smell the meat cooking before I see it, but my eyes are locked onto all the villagers gathered around. Some of them are standing by the fire, some joined at tables beneath the overhang in the cave, most of them with a cup in their hands or food in their mouths. It reminds me a little of seeing Fourth's army camp for the first time.

"It's not much, but that's basically the entirety of Drollard," Lu tells me as we come to a stop beneath a trio of trees just outside the circular stone ground that's laid out for the pavilion.

"Okay, let's go get some food."

I grimace. "Do I have to?"

"Yes. All you're going to do is go over there, grab some meat, drink some wine, and meet some people."

I shift on my feet, my stomach churning. "Meeting new people is rarely rewarding."

She snorts. "Spoken like a true Wrath. Except for maybe Judd. He's annoyingly friendly." The ruby gem piercing above her lip glints as she turns toward me, her eyes taking me in. She can probably see the fear on my face, because she says, "What did I say, Gildy?"

I let out a breath. "I got this."

"Damn right you do. Now let's go."

CHAPTER 33

AUREN

*I*t's been an hour.

An hour of rooting myself against the cave where I've grown into a wallflower, not moving from this spot. Several feet away, the fire still burns brightly, though the meat that was cooking has been all but picked clean, nothing left but bones and the remnants of dripping fat that make the flames hiss and spark.

My gloved hands are still clutched around the wine cup that Lu shoved at me, though I've only taken a few sips. I want to have a clear head to make sure my magic doesn't creep up and take me unawares. But I haven't felt a thing.

Slowly, I've been able to relax. Yet that's when I noticed that the people of Drollard are...odd.

It's not the staring. I'm used to that. Plus, I think with a village this small, *any* new face would be cause for staring, whether they were gold or not.

As soon as I walked up with Lu, attention snapped to me. The people at the tables, the ones milling around the fire pit, more beneath the mountain's overhang—they all turned to stare. There was even a terrible squeak from someone who was playing a small stringed instrument on his lap.

But with a few introductions from Lu, they seemed to relax, their overt stares changing to discreet flicks of their eyes. So it's not the staring and the uneasiness around a stranger. It's something else. Something I can't quite put my finger on.

Lu and I are sharing a seat on part of the cave wall that juts out as the perfect bench. I've been content to sit back and watch, while Lu's gone into more depth about pointing out little things about the village, probably just to fill the silence and make things less awkward.

"So, you feeling gold murdery yet?" she asks. "Have the urge to make gold start pissing down the walls?"

"Umm…no."

"See? You're doing great."

With a snort, I shift my weight, trying to get a bit more comfortable, but a jagged edge of the mountain scrapes against one of my severed ends. I flinch up with a hiss, pain shooting down my spine.

"You alright?"

A shaky exhale leaves my lips. "Fine," I grit out.

From my peripheral, I can see her dark brown eyes watching me, yet not with pity or concern. "It hurts?"

I give her an incredulous look, because *of course* it hurts. "Yes."

She points right at my face, the gesture catching me off

guard. "But that means you feel. That means you're *alive.*" This isn't the laid back, friendly Lu talking. This is Lu, the captain of Fourth's army, addressing a soldier.

A hard swallow jostles my throat. "Only part of me," I admit.

Twenty-four strips didn't make it.

"That's okay," she says without a hint of doubt, a hard glint caught in the edges of her eyes. "Just make that the strongest part."

My lips tip up, her words stabilizing my spine and making the pain dull slightly.

"That's the plan."

She knocks her cup against mine again. "Good fucking plan, Gildy. Best one you've ever had, I think."

I think so too.

"Thanks, Lu."

She doesn't ask me for what. She knows.

Lu kicks a foot up in front of her, arm dangling over her knee, while my eyes dart around to the villagers once again. "Can I ask you something?" I ask.

"Go for it."

Luckily, we're far enough apart from people that I don't think our voices will carry. "It's… Something seems…off."

She spares me a fleeting glance from the corner of her eye. "Was that a question?"

I blow out a frustrated breath. "I can't explain it, but something just feels strange about the people here."

I'm anticipating Lu rolling her eyes or making a joke or calling me out for my paranoid and very vague description, but she doesn't. Instead, an indiscernible look crosses her face as she turns away and lets her head rest against the wall behind us. "Hmm."

My brows crinkle together like paper. "Why do I get the impression that you're not telling me something?"

"Probably because I'm not telling you something."

Before I can demand some answers, she shakes her head. "It's not my place."

My lips press into a thin line. "Slade," I say, not even really needing to ask.

"There's a reason he needed to make sure Deadwell became part of his territory. There's a reason Fourth's outpost is right at the border, not far from here. There's a reason that people might seem...off to you."

Her reply only fills my head with more questions. Yet if there's one thing I know about Lu, it's that she's incredibly loyal to Slade. If she says it's not her story to tell, then I wouldn't be able to pry it from her no matter what I said.

"It seems Slade and I still have a list of things to talk about."

"Yeah, he likes to be dramatic about being the whole brooding, silent type. It's become his whole personality."

A laugh escapes me, and I shake my head, looking around again. A few of the villagers said hello to Lu when we first came over, another passing us food, but for the most part, they've been content to leave us be. I was glad about that at first, but now, I'm wondering why exactly that is.

"How often do you come here?"

She lifts a shoulder. "Not that often. Just when we need to

stop in and talk to Ryatt or help bring in some more supplies, or sometimes I come here with Rip so he can…do what he needs to do."

I don't miss that vague answer. "And how many people live here?" I ask. "I didn't see that many houses."

"There are thirty-two," she tells me. "Not counting the Grotto. And inside those houses lives fifty-seven people."

"*Fifty-seven*? I've been to saddle parties that had more participants."

She snorts.

"With an environment as harsh and closed-off as this place, I suppose it makes sense that it's not exactly a bustling population," I say. "But Hojat mentioned he came to live here. How did that happen?" I press. "How did any of these people end up in a place that doesn't exist?"

Lu gives me a long look, taking a sip of her drink instead of answering.

I sigh. "Yeah, yeah. It's not your place."

"You catch on quick."

"So pretty much everyone is here tonight," I muse, looking around again.

"Seems like it."

"I don't see any children," I note.

"There's one—he's probably almost two now. Most likely tucked up in his bed with his mother at this hour."

"Just one child out of all these people?" I ask curiously, eyes scanning. I wouldn't be surprised at that news if the villagers all seemed older, but the opposite seems to be true. All I see are men and women in their prime.

"There was another," Lu says, taking a long drink, a dabble of red wine blotting her bottom lip before her tongue sweeps it away. "You met him, actually."

"I did?"

"Yep. Twig."

I immediately remember the little boy who was in the army camp. He brought me my meal when I first met with Rip and Osrik.

"He was born in Drollard?"

Lu nods. "Every child who's been born here—though it hasn't been many—they've all gone into the army."

"Why?"

She sends me a sidelong glance.

I blow out a frustrated breath. The list of things I need to ask Slade is growing by the minute.

Just then, a pretty blonde-haired woman comes up to talk to Lu, greeting her with a warm smile. Again, I get that sense of strangeness. The woman is nothing but affable, there's nothing out of the ordinary with her expressions or overall appearance, and yet...

And yet.

My eyes skate over the pavilion, watching everyone as they mingle, their feet stepping over the rough stone, each brick spiraling toward the center. A couple of men toss some logs on the fire pit, shooting sparks up into the air, while another group mills around a wine barrel, filling up cups and smoking something from a pipe in a shape I've never seen before.

It's all very...pleasant.

So why then is the hair on the back of my neck standing up?

Just then, my ears prick with the sound of raised voices. At first, I think it's just more of the villagers having a good time, but after a second, it becomes clear that the tones aren't lively, they're *angry*.

I strain my ears, trying to pinpoint where it's coming from as my eyes scan my surroundings. Then I turn my head and find that it's coming from further inside the pavilion's cave.

I didn't really pay attention to anything past the tables where people were eating. But now, I see there are a couple of tunnels at the end. Well, one is a tunnel, and the other seems to be a crack in the mountain that's making a very narrow path. Their shadowed recesses are nearly impossible to see from here, even with the strung lanterns hanging near the entrances.

When the voices lift again, a few of the villagers at the tables turn to look. My skin prickles when the thick baritones cut through the air, though not clearly enough for me to make out any actual words.

But I don't need words, because I know that voice.

I'm up and on my feet in an instant, wine cup left behind on the bench as my steps take me deeper beneath the pavilion. I skirt around the tables, clinging to the opposite wall of the cave, trying not to draw attention to myself. The first tunnel I come to is wider, and there are crates sitting just inside, supplies overflowing.

I start to head inside of it when the voices lift again, and I realize they're coming from the fissure that's tucked into the corner and bathed in shadows.

"Another one? How many is this now?"

I recognize Ryatt's voice instantly, though it's hissed out between the clenched teeth of palpable anger.

"Six," I hear Slade answer.

"*Six*? Fucking hell. How long are you going to ignore this?"

My steps falter, eyes going wide.

"We still have time."

A bitter laugh comes from Ryatt. "Keep telling yourself that."

"What do you expect me to do?" Slade's voice suddenly snarls.

"I expect you to protect Drollard. I expect you to not bring in a threat. To go be a fucking king."

"Stop insinuating that I don't protect Drollard. I do everything I can to ensure its safety," Slade snaps back.

I suddenly feel very awkward, just standing here listening in on this conversation. I turn my head back to where Lu is, finding her still half turned toward the woman, though she keeps shooting me curious looks.

I'm about to turn back around when I hear Ryatt say, "If that were true, then you wouldn't have brought her here."

I freeze. He's talking about *me*?

"Auren is not a threat," Slade all but growls.

My heartbeat begins to drum heavily in my chest.

"We all saw her in that ballroom. If that's not a threat—"

"She won't do that here." Slade sounds so sure, but my entire body goes slick with anxious sweat.

"You don't know that," Ryatt counters. Slade starts to reply, but Ryatt cuts him off. "You *don't*. And I want her gone."

A sharp twist of pain jams in my stomach, and I look away, though instead of my gaze catching onto Lu again, this time I see the villagers. See all the people who I could hurt if I lose control.

Suddenly, fifty-seven doesn't seem like such a small number.

Shame crawls up my neck and grips me by the throat.

"It's not up to you, Ryatt," Slade says, his voice gone low with the kind of anger held beneath the lid of a simmering pot. "And she's making progress."

"Yeah?" Ryatt snips back. "If she's making so much progress here, then why haven't you told Auren the truth? Why haven't you told Auren about her? Are you ashamed?"

There's a long, heavy pause.

That heaviness falls through my stomach like a rock down a well, cracks echoing in my ears every time it slams against my nerves.

Why haven't you told Auren about her.

Told Auren about her.

About her.

The rock lands hard, shattering into the spoils of dread.

Her.

CHAPTER 34

AUREN

Ryatt's sentence is still reverberating in my head when a hand at my elbow makes me jump. I whirl around to find Lu standing at my side with a frown on her face. "What..."

"I will when she's strong enough. I can't overwhelm her with this," I hear Slade say.

Lu's black brows vault upward when she realizes I've been eavesdropping.

"She—"

Lu clears her throat. Loudly.

I'd glare at her, but to be honest, I don't want to hear anymore.

Why haven't you told Auren about her?

Are you ashamed?

There's a pause, then footsteps, and then I feel him right at my back.

I don't turn around. My shoulders are stiff, my emotions

like turbid waters beneath the falls, clouded with churning sediment, roiling with thoughts that fall out of my control.

"You guys do know that voices carry when you're in a Divine-damned tunnel, right?" Lu drawls.

Movement in the corner of my eye has my gaze catching onto Ryatt's face. The anger that he spewed seems to have emptied him out, because instead of hate on his face, there's remorse instead. He opens his mouth like he's going to say something to me, but then he shakes his head and turns, walking away.

Lu looks over my shoulder. "Who pissed in his porridge?"

Braving his expression, I turn, letting my eyes flick up. "You didn't tell me you were bringing Auren out tonight," he says to Lu.

"She needed to get out of the Grotto."

All three of our attention snags to the fire, where Ryatt is now surrounded by villagers. Looking at him, you would never know that he was practically spitting anger just a few moments ago. Right now, he looks relaxed. Happy. There's no indication whatsoever of the emotion that must still be churning in his head. Instead, he seems completely at ease in the camaraderie of the people around him as they laugh and talk.

Until his eyes snap to mine from across the space, making my stomach go sour as I turn away.

I want her gone.

We all saw her in that ballroom.

Fifty-seven people.

I open my mouth to say...*something*, but every turbulent

thought grinds to a halt when I spot something against Slade's cheek. "Is that blood?"

He lifts a hand to his face and tries to wipe it away, but all that does is spread it.

"Is that yours? Are you hurt?" Maybe he and Ryatt actually came to blows before I came over?

But Slade shakes his head. "It's not mine."

"Then whose?" Ryatt didn't look like he'd gotten hit, didn't have any visible blood.

Slade's eyes dart to the right. Back toward the tunnel, and a chill scatters down my spine.

"Whose blood is that?" I ask again.

His green eyes flick to Lu, and they exchange a loaded look.

"Gildy," she says, moving up beside me. "How about you and I go finish up our wine—"

I shove away before either of them can stop me, plunging into the fissure where Slade and Ryatt just were. I hear him calling my name, but I ignore him, just as I ignore the darkness I'm suddenly plunged into, even the way the claustrophobic walls seem to press in on me as I scramble through.

Something drives me forward, my pulse pounding in my ears, and then I'm through the crack and stumbling into a dimly lit cavern. The first thing I see is the thick iron door. A barrel and chair shoved against the jagged walls. Lanterns hanging from a hook. Somehow, the fluorescence in here looks more sinister, like the veins of the mountain have spoiled into a sickly green in some parts.

I hear footsteps behind me, so I push forward, my pulse

thumping loudly in my ears. I approach the door, peering through the slats at the top. At first, I can't even discern what exactly I'm looking at.

But the smell...

"Auren."

Slade's hand comes down to my arm, trying to gently pull me away, but I shrug him off. My eyes are adjusting to the dark, my mind telling me what I'm seeing, even as it simultaneously revolts against it. But there's no denying that person-sized lump.

The smell wafting from the room grows more intense the longer I stand here, and I pin my lips together, trying to hold my breath. Yet the putrid scent feels like it's sinking into my pores, clogging my skin with its foulness, making my stomach roil. And there's a sound, an incessant buzzing that seems to vibrate all the way through my bones.

I'm about to turn away, about to ask Slade who this is, when a pair of swollen eyes spring open, the shine of them catching in the low lantern light.

I gasp and stumble back a step.

How can he be *alive*?

This man—if he can even be considered a man anymore—is looking right at me where he's lying on his side in the middle of the dirt floor. Even with the low lighting, I can see that his body is swollen beneath shucked up pant legs and sleeves. His skin has browned and peeled back, his hair nothing but tufts of rotten strands clinging to a molded scalp. There's curdled blood on his lips, and his teeth...

"Great Divine..."

Slade's arm wraps around me and tugs, and this time, I let him pull me away, my steps unsteady as he leads me further down the tunnel. When I feel a breeze of air, I turn my head in that direction, taking in great gulping breaths.

"I didn't want you to see that," he says as I brace a hand against the wall of the cave.

I look up at him. "Who *is* that?"

"Didn't you recognize the clothing?"

"I was too busy noticing his fingers rotting off his hand."

Slade's lips press together, and he looks away, his sharp-jawed profile bathed in warring shadow.

Breathing out, I take a second to think past the shocking parts, to remember the rucked up clothing, and my eyes go wide. "His coat was gilded."

He turns back to look at me, his face grim as he gives me a nod. "Yes. He was a spy for Midas. Sent here to get information after we made the Deadwell deal," he explains. "They tried to flee when I arrived, but Ryatt tracked them all down."

I swallow hard. "They found Drollard."

"They did," he confirms. "Ryatt took care of the others, but he saved this one for questioning."

Everything he's saying makes sense. I know this is the real world, where people have to be ruthless to protect their own. But to see it...

"Did you get whatever information out of him that you needed?" I ask, though my voice doesn't quite sound like my own.

His head tips down. "I did."

"And the village is protected?"

"It is."

"So…it's finished."

Slade's brows pull together. "What do you mean?"

I gesture toward the cell door. "Your questioning. It's finished. So you can put the man out of his misery."

There's a pause. A pause that's far too long.

My hand snags out and I grip his arm. "*Slade*. You can't keep him like that."

"Why not?" he asks, shoulders stiffening. "He's a spy. He was going to report everything back to Midas. All of my carefully kept secrets would've been *destroyed*."

I see the anger in his face, the way the skin around his eyes tightens. "I know. But you and Ryatt stopped all of that. So you need to stop this too. He's obviously unable to talk anymore. What you're doing is cruel."

His eyes flicker. "I've done things far crueler."

Instantly, all the memories of putrid corpses and rotted land spring back to my mind, and nausea crawls up my throat. "I know that too."

"Do you?" he challenges, the fierce glint in his eye flashing. "Because I'm not sure you do."

My hand drops, like his words have weighed down my limbs. "I'd like to go back to the Grotto now."

His gaze sweeps over me, but my own keeps drifting back to that door, back to the buzzing noise I can still hear. The noise of tiny flies infesting the flesh of a rotting man.

"I'll walk you," Slade rumbles.

He places a hand on the small of my back, and we leave the

cracked mountain, my arms scratching against the fissure as we go. It feels like it takes even longer to get out than it did to get in.

Finally, sounds of the villagers begin to trickle in, and a moment later, we step back into the pavilion. All is as it was. Drinking and mingling, the man in the other corner still playing his instrument. It seems like I stepped out into a different world. I wonder what they'd think if they knew there was a person just inside this mountain whose tongue had begun to disintegrate right there in his mouth.

The walk back is quiet, and no matter how many breaths I take, I swear I can still smell the stench.

When we get to the cave, Slade stops me with a hand on my arm. "Tell me what you're thinking."

Too many thoughts at once.

Slade's plunged in blue light, though there's no missing the apprehension in his eyes. "I'm King Rot for a reason, Auren."

"I know," I tell him. And I do understand. I know he's gotten his reputation for a reason, just as I know that he does things to protect his people and his secrets.

But he's right—there is a difference when you see it firsthand. Just like when I crossed out of Sixth and saw the bodies trussed up like meat on a skewer. Just like I saw those guards in Ranhold, collapsing on the floor as their organs began to rot. It's different to see it, and it's different when I know a man has been left to suffer just to appease whatever it is inside of Slade that drives him to do it.

Because he's King Rot.

And I...

I have a piece of that rot inside of me.

CHAPTER 35

AUREN

When *Slade and I reach* the Grotto, I come to a grinding halt. Because I'm not doing this. I'm not going inside and stewing in questions. The old Auren would've done that, would've been too nervous to bring the subject up. But that's not me anymore, and Slade isn't Midas.

He stalls next to me. "What's wrong?"

"We're not going inside," I tell him, chin tilted up, steel in my chest.

"We're not?"

"No. Turn around and lead the way," I say, hand gesturing toward the outside.

"Lead the way...to where?"

"To *her*."

"Auren, what you heard..." His words shred into frustrated scraps.

"I know what I heard. And you and I...there are still a lot of secrets. So many things we don't know. But I'm not going to just go inside and fester, waiting around until you think I'm ready to hear what you have to say. So take me to her. You said past, present, and future, right?"

He sucks in a breath, but I look him in the eye without faltering. Because the only way to walk a new path is to stop yourself from using the same stumbling stride.

Even if his present is as shocking as a living corpse.

Even if his past might break my heart.

Even if his future isn't guaranteed.

Emotion drips thickly down my throat, clinging to the back of my tongue. "I won't ever again give myself to someone who doesn't give himself back to me. So if there's someone else here...I need to know about it."

I see his throat bob, his eyes flicker. This is a split in the path. He knows it, I know it. If this were Midas, he'd pick one way.

But Slade...

Slade picks another.

"Okay, Goldfinch. Let's go."

Instead of heading back toward all the villagers' homes that I passed by on my way to the pavilion earlier, Slade turns outside of the Grotto, veering right, toward the Perch and the gold-splattered training cave. I shoot him a wary look but stay at his side as he leads me up the snowy slope, the heart of the village disappearing behind us.

We go past the Perch that Lu mentioned, and then, when I practically run into it, I spot a set of short, rickety stairs made of white wood and shallow steps. I crane my head up, gaze following them to spot the Mole high above us, stuck to the side of the mountain like a bulbous lookout.

Its structure is camouflaged with snow and rock, some sort of tarp weighed down with snowfall that seems to cover the entire thing and hide the view of it from above. All I can see from here is the barest glow of firelight, which means someone is probably up there right now, keeping watch.

Turning back around, I continue to follow Slade, neither of us breaking the silence. I'm so nervous that my stomach is riled up tension with acidic nausea burning a path up my throat. Meanwhile, Slade seems like he's wound tight enough to break in half, his arms so stiff at his sides that his stride is wooden.

His unease only adds to mine.

The clouds have clogged the moonlight, so the landscape isn't as bright as it was earlier. Now, as we curve around the base of the mountain, shadows are like specters, while dingy light stretches against the snow. My legs grow tired the further we walk, and it feels like the temperature plummets in a matter of minutes. Even with my hands buried in my coat, the frigid thief sweeps through the air and snatches any sort of warmth I try to hold onto.

Then, the training cave appears ahead, but instead of going straight through, Slade takes a sharp turn, disappearing into a smaller opening almost completely obscured by the sharp rise of a slanted rock that blends into the rest of the mountain. I would never have noticed the gap there if I hadn't seen him disappear through it.

Hesitantly, I follow him, my body slipping behind the rock and then immediately turning left to disappear inside the mountain.

My mouth drops open at how big it is. Even larger than the Grotto, this cave system reaches so high I can't quite tell where the ceiling actually is.

"Why are we here?" I ask, but I wince as soon as I do. Because although I spoke quietly, my voice seems to echo in the hollow, grand space. "Why aren't we back at the village where the houses are?"

Slade turns to me, cloaked in sapphire light. "She doesn't live with the villagers."

A snag catches in my lungs, the cords of apprehension laced around my ribs, not letting me take in a full breath. "And...who is she?" The question spoken out loud sounds so quiet compared to the way it screams in my head.

His troubled gaze is turned away, eyes buried in the depths of the cave. The trepidation on his expression does nothing to ease me. "She..." His mouth shifts and wavers, and then his eyes bolt to mine. "I wish I could've prepared you more, but just...be calm, okay? It's important."

Be calm?

"How do you expect me to be calm when I don't even know what situation I'm walking into?"

"I know," he says with some sympathy. "But now that we're here, it's just best that I show you."

That doesn't make me feel better at all.

Still, Slade turns, and I go with him, deeper into the cavern that seems to never end.

Yet as we walk in further, I keep thinking of the things Ryatt was saying. Of that man back at the cell, the memory so fresh in my head that I can actually hear the buzzing flies all over again.

But then, the cavern veers off, and right there in the middle of the space is a house. It's a miniature version of the one back at the Grotto, except this is practically glowing. There are thick stretches of fluorescence that curve and curl, like waves in a sea. They sparkle against the lightless parts of the cave, a swirling galaxy in a moonless sky.

The house itself is a simple structure, a door right there in the middle, a slanted roof that has stains of calcium streaked through it, and a puddle on the ground that seems to have sagged the stone floor beneath the eave's edge. I'm not sure what color the stone bricks really are that make up the structure, but I wouldn't be surprised if they soaked in the glow and began sprouting their own light.

Slade gives me a moment to take it all in, and then we're moving again, heading straight for it. Except...

That buzzing sound is still in my ears.

Either my time outside that cell door traumatized me more than I realized, or...

No. It's not the buzzing sound of flies rooting for a putrid meal. It's an incessant, low *hum*, and it's very much real.

"What's that noise?" I ask, but my body has turned, feet still moving, heading around the house instead of toward it. The noise is coming from somewhere back there, somewhere past the curve of the cave where I can't see. It's louder now, a sound so low that I can feel it from the bones in my feet to the skull of my head.

Closer. I need to get closer. I need to get to—

A hand stops me, snapping me out of my daze. "Come this way, Auren."

Slade's voice makes the hum's pitch turn to near nothing.

I shake my head at myself, letting him bring me back toward the house. Yet the strange pull I feel makes me look over my shoulder, and when I do, the hum rises ever so slightly.

I wrench my head to face forward again, my pulse pounding. "What *is* that?" I ask, drawing my hands up to ward off a chill that's spread over my entire body.

"One thing at a time." Slade glances down at me just as we reach the door of the house. "Ready?"

"How can I be?" I ask frankly.

"Fair point," he concedes, but then he takes my hand in his. My stomach jolts at the gesture, and I look down at our entwined fingers, as if I'm making sure he really did it. If we were about to go to a lover's house or a secret wife or a favored saddle, he wouldn't hold my hand…

Right?

Before my stomach can churn itself right up my throat, Slade opens the door.

No knock. No calling out. Just turns a creaking knob and lets himself in. The heels of my shoes seem to stick with dread as I enter, and I try to prepare myself. Try to shove away my emotions and raise walls so that no matter what hits me, I'll stay standing.

The first thing I notice is the warmth and the comforting firelight. It permeates the entire open floor home, so I can see everything from one end to the other. Which isn't surprising, considering there's a huge fireplace that dominates the wall directly ahead of us, and the whole house comprises one large square space.

There's a bed in the far corner, with a carved partition placed in front of it so that only the foot is visible, a bright yellow knitted blanket flung over the mattress. Directly across from the bed are two cushioned chairs on a rug before the fire, and a small round table between them where a teacup sits on top.

To our left is an open kitchen with a narrow shelf countertop and an iron stove that's gone cold, with a washbasin directly beside it. Just past the small round dining table is a set of shelves no higher than my shoulders, every inch of them taken up with books.

For a moment, I'm so caught up in tracking every little detail in the house, that I don't even see the person sitting in one of the chairs in front of the fire until I catch movement. All I can see is the back of a head at first, and my fingers dig into Slade's hand.

Slade clears his throat, and the head tilts in a movement of acknowledgement, but not startled. "I'm sorry I haven't been to see you."

The person in the chair turns, and my fingers squeeze Slade's hand even harder when they get up and turn to face us.

My eyes go wide.

She's beautiful.

She's young, maybe around my age, yet petite, like every single bone is delicate. She has pale skin and big eyes, black hair tucked back into a loose ponytail that rests at her nape. She looks to Slade, and her face splits into a smile that drives a knife through my chest because of how heartbreakingly *joyful* it looks.

She crosses the room and throws her arms around him, me yanking my hand from his with only a split second to spare.

I watch as they embrace, feeling completely out of place, like I'm watching something too private.

She pulls away, beaming up at him, and while Slade takes hold of her fragile hand, he turns to me. "Auren," he begins, and my heart feels like it's going to either burst or break, I'm not sure which. "I'd like you to meet my mother."

CHAPTER 36

AUREN

All I know is that I can't have heard right.

So I keep waiting for my ears to correct my mind or for Slade to correct himself or for the woman to laugh and shake her head.

But none of that happens.

I'd like you to meet my mother.

When I realize that his words aren't being taken back, I look from her to Slade. "Your...mother."

He nods slowly.

I dart my eyes back to her because I don't want to be rude and talk about her as if she isn't standing right here. I study her again, closer this time. There are very faint lines next to her eyes, a dusting of silvery hairs right in front of her ears, but those are the only things that could possibly age her, and even still, it doesn't. She looks as young as me.

She's smiling at me so openly, and I'm struck with the

green of her eyes and the shape of her mouth. Now that I'm no longer worried about a lover, I can recognize that there's a big family resemblance. But she looks like his sister, not his mother.

Clearing my throat, I then give her a soft smile. "It's nice to meet you, Lady..."

"Her name is Elore," Slade says, pronouncing it *Eh-lore*.

"Lady Elore," I say. "I'm Auren."

The woman beams at me, green eyes flicking over my face with open study. After a second, she swivels her smiling face to Slade and taps him on the cheek, and then she reaches over and taps my cheek next.

I startle slightly at the gesture, but she doesn't seem to notice. She just continues to tap my cheek, like she has no qualms, no hesitations about me. As if she can tell with a look exactly who I am to her son.

When she drops her hand and looks to Slade again, they share something between them for a moment, and it seems so personal that I have to look away when I catch the shine in Elore's eyes.

Then she does the most motherly thing ever, reaching up to try and straighten a part of his hair that's sticking up, before she tsks and then fixes the corner of his collar. Just those gestures make Slade's declaration all the more believable.

My mind races, and I look down at my loose leggings and borrowed coat, hand running over my messily braided hair while I try not to panic that I'm meeting Slade's *mother* while looking so rough.

Before I can think of a polite conversation starter, Elore

walks away, heading for the kitchen. I watch as she starts to light the stove, a soft hum coming from her.

"How can she be your mother?" I murmur to Slade. "She looks the same age..."

He gives me a sad sort of smile. "Come, let's sit."

Together, we walk to the small dining table and slip onto the wooden chairs. Elore finishes lighting the stove and gets to work bringing a kettle to set over it and then bustles around, setting down plates from the hanging cabinets in front of her.

"Let me help you," I say as I get back up again, but she doesn't respond or even turn around. Instead, she continues to gather a few crackers and then slices up cheese, all while I stand awkwardly off to the side. She doesn't stop humming.

I swear, the tune sounds familiar.

When I shoot Slade a look, he says, "It's alright. Come here."

Hesitating for just a moment longer, I drag myself back to the table and take a seat. I continue to watch her, my brows carving deeper and deeper into a frown. Because just like back at the pavilion with the other villagers, I feel it.

That sense that something is *odd*. Off.

I turn back to Slade. "I don't understand."

"My mother doesn't speak anymore. Very rarely," he tells me.

It's on the tip of my tongue to ask why not, but I swallow it down, because I don't want to be insensitive in front of her just to satiate my instant curiosity.

Elore walks over to set down the plates, her profile leaning down directly in front of me, and I let out a gasp. Eyes

413

riveted to her, I notice something that I should've realized right from the start. Her ears are rounded.

"She's...not fae." I instantly remember Slade telling me that he's only half.

Yet when I speak the word *fae*, she suddenly stiffens. The humming abruptly cuts off, and a shudder seems to travel through her.

Slade is on his feet in an instant, coming around the table. He takes her shaking hands in his and lowers himself so she will meet his eyes. "It's alright," he soothes, his thumbs stroking over the back of her frail looking fingers. "You're alright."

She starts to nod, blowing out a shaken breath, but the kettle begins its shrill cry, making her flinch.

"It's just the tea," he murmurs. "Do you want me to get it?"

Elore gives a slow nod, and he sits her down at the empty chair like she's the most fragile thing in the world. I watch her shaking fingers, her face that's gone even paler. I feel stuck in inaction, not knowing what I could possibly do or say to help.

Yet Slade stays calm, his sure steps taking him over to the kettle that's begun to cry. He pulls cups from hooks on the wall, and when he starts to pour out the tea, he hums. The same gentle, soothing tone.

By the time he brings the cups over to us and then sits down again, Elore has calmed, her eyes no longer strained, mouth no longer turned down. She sends Slade a small, sad smile.

I nibble on the crackers, sip on my tea, and for the next half hour, I just watch them.

It's a bit fascinating. Slade talks quietly, telling her about what the snow looks like, about how hard the wind blew during the blizzard. He speaks of his timberwing, promising to bring her a feather next time. He tells her about the mulled wine he found at the Cellar and says that he'll bring her more of that too.

Be calm, Slade told me before we came. Just...*be calm*.

But he wasn't saying that because he was going to show me something upsetting; he was saying it because his mother obviously *needs* calm. It's not just that she doesn't speak. There's something else caught beneath the depths of her silence. I'm not sure where her mind is or what she could possibly be thinking, but seeing her reaction to the word *fae* was startling.

It's clear from the patient and assuring way Slade acts with her that he does everything he can, from the pitch of his tone to the mundane topics he speaks about, to keep everything as relaxed and simple as possible.

For the next half hour, that's how the time passes. He talks in a soothing rumble, while she watches him with a smile on her face. It doesn't matter that she doesn't talk, because the affection is as clear as the crystal cups we sip our tea from.

And while I'm burning with questions, I let them simmer in the background, because it feels like Slade has pulled back a veil, letting me see a part of him that not many people do. I'm experiencing a part of his past and present, something vulnerable and private and *precious*. Because I can see by the way he is with her, his mother is precious to him.

It makes my heart hurt for the loss of my own mother.

When the tea is gone and our plates have nothing left but crumbs, Elore cleans up with a smile on her face. I try to offer to help again, but Slade shakes his head and leads me to the chairs by the fire. "She likes her routines," he tells me. "It would upset her if you do any of that. She likes things a certain way."

I settle into the chair and try to collect all the questions that have been building up like a wall, laid brick by brick. Glancing over my shoulder, I make sure she's occupied with her task before turning back to Slade. He's leaning forward slightly, an elbow on the armrest and his chin in his hand, like he's waiting.

"I don't even know where to begin," I say, blowing out a breath.

"I know this was a lot."

I blow a sardonic laugh through my nose. "That's putting it mildly. To be honest, I was expecting to walk in here and have to come face-to-face with your lover."

Slade's brows immediately slam down. "You think I would show you such disrespect?"

I shift in my seat. "I have no idea what to think. We don't—"

"Know each other," he finishes for me, feeding my words back to me. When I nod, he runs a hand through his black hair, mussing it up again, frustration betraying in the way he yanks on the strands. "I will admit that I'm not used to being open, but I will. For you."

"Your Wrath know."

"My Wrath know everything because I have been with

them for years. Those layers peeled back after being together for more than a decade. With you...the timeline is different. I don't want to overwhelm you."

"Like with the...prisoner."

His nod is slow, eyes piercing.

"I'm on your side. It's just, seeing that..."

"My power is not easy to see."

The memory of my gold swallowing people whole like a bestial bird flashes in my mind. "You've seen the worst parts of my power and didn't blink twice."

"There's no shame in your reaction to my power," he replies.

I feel shame though, because the last thing I want to do is judge him for his magic. He certainly didn't judge me. "Why are you keeping him alive?"

"Because I *want to*," he replies, making something scrape down my gut. Slade watches me like he wants me to see every word he's saying, to envision his every intention. "I want you to understand something, Goldfinch. I am not good. I will rot every person in my way, will bring a blight to every corner of the world if I have to."

I shake my head. "No, you wouldn't. You're good. You're—"

"No, Goldfinch," he interrupts. "I'm good to *you*. But I am every bit the villain that I warned you I was."

His previous words ring in my ears.

I'll be the villain for you. Not to you.

I can see in his face that he means what he says, and based on the man he's keeping... But I can also see the bracing.

Like he's steeling himself, waiting for my impending disgust. Waiting for my rejection of it, for my argument against his nature.

Yet I went to Slade with my eyes wide open. I told him I wanted everything, and when you ask for *everything* from a person, you don't get to pick and choose. You take them as they are. Even King Rot.

Which is why I don't even hesitate to reach over and clasp his hand in mine. It's why I can hold his gaze, without fail. It's why I say, "If you're a villain...then I'll be a villain with you."

A slow, sexy grin rises from the grounds of his grim lips.

"But…" I go on. "I still want you to put that man out of his misery now. There has to be a limit to your villainy."

He laughs, stroking a finger over my hand. "Alright, Goldfinch."

A noise from behind abruptly cuts off the moment between us, and Slade and I swivel around. At the door, Ryatt walks in, entering the same way Slade did. No knocking, no calling, just letting himself in.

"Hey, I brought you some tarts from Jelma that she—" His words cut off at the same time that his eyes find us across the room. He hesitates for a moment before shutting the door behind him and turning back around.

Slade rises to his feet, and I follow suit, while Ryatt infuses the whole house with a pregnant pause.

We all saw her in that ballroom.

Are you ashamed?

I want her gone.

My eyes flick away. No wonder he didn't want me here. Their *mother* is here.

Ryatt clears his throat, and from my peripheral, I see him walk over to Elore. "Here," he says with a soft offering.

I look up as she takes the tart that's wrapped in a gingham cloth. A smile spreads over her face as she uncovers it, and then she goes up on her tiptoes to peck a kiss on his cheek. Ryatt blushes.

She grabs a spoon from the counter and then sits down with it, happily eating right from the tin. Ryatt watches her for a moment before he finally turns and approaches us.

Beside me, Slade goes rigid, and the blackened veins at his neck pulse and jolt just past his coat's collar, their sharp ends like the mouth of an irritated snake.

There's an awkward shift of Ryatt's feet as he stops in front of us. "So...you brought her."

"I did." Slade's voice is clipped, and I wonder what other words were exchanged back at the pavilion before I overheard the tail end of their argument. I'm incredibly curious about their dynamic. The line between love and hate seems to have blurred between them, and I'm not sure I understand it. I'm not even sure if *they* understand it.

While I'm busy trying to guess at their brotherly relationship, Ryatt's eyes fall to me. "I apologize for the things you heard back at the pavilion," he says, surprising me. "I didn't intend for you to overhear. It's clear you're in control enough not to destroy Drollard," he says as he motions around his mother's house.

"No apology necessary," I reply. "You were right to be worried."

Slade slams his eyes into me, and I know he's about to jump in to defend my honor, but I don't let him.

"No, Slade," I go on. "It's true. My magic pretty much exploded out of me uncontrollably, and now it's not working at all. You and I both know I don't have a handle on it, so I understand why Ryatt doesn't want me here."

To his credit, a look of contrition tugs at Ryatt's expression.

"I'm glad I overheard."

Both of them look at me like they don't quite believe me, but I mean every word.

"I won't hurt this village." My eyes move over his shoulder to where Elore sits at the table. "Especially when I know how important it is."

Even if I have to keep my magic blocked off forever.

Ryatt studies me for a moment and then gives me a single nod of acknowledgement before he looks at Slade. "How was Mother when you came in?"

"Fine. Happy," he replies, still a little gruff.

Ryatt looks over his shoulder. "She misses you when you're gone too long."

Slade doesn't reply, but his gaze is tracking his mother, a flicker of pain dug into the strained lines around his eyes. After a second, he notices me watching him, and just like that, the expression is gone.

"Why does your mother live separately from everyone else? And how is she…here?"

A condensed, heavy breath slips from his mouth and seems to burden his shoulders. "I suppose it's time to show you the rest now. Though I'm sorry I can't space out all of these revelations, but I don't want you to think I'm keeping anything from you."

Ryatt's eyes go comically wide. "You're going to show her...*that*? Right now?"

At his tone, I feel my body fill with uncertain tension. "What exactly are you going to show me?" I ask, wary of the resigned look on his face. I don't know how it's possible, but I'm even more nervous about this than I was about the existence of a possible lover.

He takes my hand, expression resigned. "I'm finally going to tell you why they really call me Rip."

I leave Slade's mother's house feeling like I'm walking straight through the silk strands of a spiderweb. This uneasy, viscid feeling clings to me all over, no escape from their unsettling fibers.

"Do you have to have so many damn secrets?" I grumble into the dark.

Slade chuckles. "Sorry. I'll do my best to tell you all of them."

"So, just to be clear, there is definitely no favored saddle you have locked in a cage somewhere or an ex-lover that you keep in this village?"

He shoots me an unamused look. "No."

"Good. Good."

I'm trying to fill in the silence with nervous chatter,

because I have no idea what to expect. Every single one of Slade's secrets has always been pretty groundbreaking, and I don't think this one will be any different.

Now that we're back out in the heart of the cave, the buzzing sound has returned. Even pitched at its low hum, it sets my teeth on edge. Slade leads me around Elore's house and then deeper into the cavern. The bright, cheerful blue glow soon dims, the huge rivers of fluorescence splitting off and becoming nothing but small rivulets in the stone. Without enough light from the mountain to counteract the size of the space, it feels as if the shadows close in on us, the massive space seeming smaller than it really is.

And still, there's a constant hum that I can feel vibrating through my skin.

"You can hear that too, right?"

"I can."

He doesn't seem concerned, nor does he elaborate, so I have to believe that whatever the reason is for this hum isn't dangerous. It also must have to do with whatever he wants to show me.

My nervous chatter returns. "In my head, I'd pretty much narrowed the reason for your nickname down to having ripped abs. Or making women want to rip their clothes off. Something like that."

He laughs beside me, the sound counteracting the awful hum and making my anxiety subside just a bit.

"Very good to know where your head has been. But to be *extra* clear, I have no desire for anyone to rip their clothes off except for you."

"Clarity is really good." I nod firmly. "We should keep doing it."

"We should keep doing it," he replies with a wicked grin. I have a feeling he's talking about something different.

Despite my attempt at some levity, my heart starts to pound in an anxious thrum. I try to squint ahead of us, but it's getting darker, and aside from rock formations and stalagmites, I can't see anything.

The hum is louder now. It pulls me forward, like a moth to a flame, the source of the sound sinking into my ears and calling to me. Goose bumps scatter down my arms because I know this reaction isn't right, but I'm too drawn to do anything about it.

"It sounds like we're getting closer..." I muse, voice dropping.

The cavern breaks off, and Slade leads me through the smaller tunnel, the walls dotted with condensation. There are milky beetles hanging from the stringy lines of blue glow overhead, and the further we go down this tunnel, the stronger the vibrations become. At first, it stays as low and steady as the hum, yet both of them seem to amplify a thousandfold within a matter of seconds until it's so consuming that I want to shove my hands over my ears.

What could possibly be making that noise?

But then, we're out of the narrow tunnel, and I stop dead in my tracks.

Light hits our faces as we stop in the massive cavern that puts all others to shame. It's like the entire mountain has been hollowed out, eaten from the inside.

And I can see why.

In the very middle, stretching vertically as high as ten people standing one on top of the other, is a...slash in the air.

I don't know how else to describe it, and my eyes are trying desperately to take everything in so that I can make sense of it. But I can't.

This isn't some crack in the cave floor or wall or ceiling. This isn't some jagged fissure illuminated with the natural fluorescence that runs through the rest of the mountain. No, this is something else entirely.

This cleave in the air shouldn't exist.

When I look at it too long, it hits me with a sense of vertigo, like when you're standing on a precipice so high that your eyes can't make sense of the ground's distance.

It looks as if a giant has sliced open the air with a dulled ax. Its edges are ragged and peeled, opening up into some bottomless chasm and hanging suspended. And the humming noise comes from inside of it, some unknown force trilling with power.

Inside of this air's split, there's a strange, mottled light peeking out. Except, the light is disrupted, like lying beneath a tree at high noon, when the wind blows through the leaves and keeps shifting the shade.

The hairs on the back of my neck are standing upright. The pulse in my veins has been completely drowned out. And for some strange reason, I want to go closer.

I don't even realize that I'm walking forward until Slade clasps my hand, tugging me back. I snap my eyes away from it.

"What...what *is* that?" I ask breathlessly.

There's an exhale hewn from the depths of his lungs. "This is where I tore a rip into the world."

CHAPTER 37

SLADE
Age 15

I'm startled awake in my bed, and I sit up, pointed ears cocked. I'm not sure if it was something I dreamt or if it was a real sound that woke me, until I hear someone shouting and footsteps running down the hall.

I fling the covers off and get out of bed, quickly tugging my shirt back on from where I left it in a heap on the floor. I shove my feet into the boots beside the door and hurry out, tightening the drawstring in my pants as I go down the hall and head for the stairs.

Shouts rise up, and when I hear something shatter, I start to run. My boots skid to a halt against the carpet when I see a group of our servants gathered at the bottom of the stairs, crowding the entry hall just ahead. They're all standing there frozen, not moving or talking, and the backs of my arms start to prickle.

I push my way forward, though I'm not even noticing

the faces I'm passing, because I'm focused ahead. There are more people that I have to get through to get into the entry hall, everyone dressed in either their nightclothes or rumpled ones from yesterday, as if everyone hastily dressed to see what the commotion is.

As soon as I push my way to the front, I freeze in place.

A gray, morbid light streaks in through the entry hall.

Since this room is in the center of the estate, there are several open doorways that lead to different parts of the house, and every single one is full of more servants. As if my father called them all here, like he does when he hosts public punishments.

The windows at the left are casting predawn streaks across the marble floor, making the red wallpaper look deeper, the same color as a bead of blood left on the tip of your finger.

Right there in front of those dreary streaks of light stands my father. He shouldn't even be home yet, not for a couple more days at least, because he was called to the king for business, but here he is. Red shirt crisp, black boots laced straight, and fury in his eyes, even at this early hour.

He's gripping my mother by the wrist, holding her arm up at an awkward angle. A group of servants stands just behind her. It's like the entire room is balancing on shards of glass and no one dares move, or else we'll get sliced open.

Because the look on my father's face...

It's not only anger spattered over his brow and darkening his eyes. It's not only a slight downturn of his mouth. This is something more. His whole face has gone red, blotches of it bursting against his neck that I can see from across the room in this poor light. The muscles in his arm are strained where he's holding my mother, his grip so tight that his fingers are leached of blood. And his eyes...they aren't just angry or irritated or disappointed.

No, they're enraged.

Like everyone else, my mother is in her nightdress, her hair hanging loosely down her back. I know something is wrong just by the state of her undress. She would never leave her room without at least her robe and slippers on.

"I want to know who knew of this!" my father shouts, his glare skimming around the entire entry.

The servants are all watching wide-eyed, faces tight, fear making some of them tremble. But not one of them speaks up.

"I want to know!" he roars.

When my mother winces, I finally snap into action and stride over, loose boots slapping against the tile floor. "What are you doing?"

My father jerks his head in my direction, and something cruel enters his eyes. My mother looks as pale as a ghost. "What am I doing?" my father repeats, the last word ending with a whip of laughter that has nothing to do with happiness. "Oh no, this is all about what your mother has done."

I flick my eyes to her just as a tear races down her collapsing cheek.

"Tell him."

She flinches at my father's order, but her lips stay shut, gaze staying on me.

"Tell him!" he screams, shaking her arm so hard that her whole body shakes with it.

I'm immediately transported back to being eight years old, when my body froze up and the scream only stayed in my head. Yet this time, the word tears from my throat. "Stop! You're hurting her."

He lets go, but I'm under no false pretenses that he's actually doing it to appease me. He shoves her at the servants behind her, but Jak catches her before she can stumble.

My father looks at me. "Since she won't tell you, I will," he spits, like venom streaming from a snake's fangs. In response, my own canines seem to throb in my gums. "What did your mother do when she thought I wasn't going to be home for the night? She invited another into her bed. Spread her legs like an Orean whore."

Shock makes my spine prickle and stiffen. It just takes a split second. Just the tiniest shift of my eyes as I look at her, and I already know. I can't believe I didn't put it together before. All the times he brought in fresh flowers for her or made sure to serve her first. The small smiles exchanged between them.

Jak's still holding her arms, keeping her locked against his chest as if he, a magicless Orean servant, can stand to protect her against my father. He's so opposite from my father in every way. Jak is quiet. Kind. A head full of hair and lines on his face from smiling rather than scowling.

My mother looks at me like she's afraid of my reaction.

"There, you see?" Father says, pointing at my face. "Slade didn't know. The truth is right there in the disgust on his face."

I hate the way Mother takes in a shuddering breath.

"You're right, I didn't know," I reply, taking a step

forward. *"But if there's disgust on my expression, it's not for her. It's for you."*

My father goes still. "What did you say?"

"Why wouldn't she seek affection from someone else?" I spit out. "You treat her like garbage."

The surprise that enters his eyes is nothing compared to the surprise at myself that I managed to say that to his face. Every word is true, and if he thinks I would ever take his side over hers, then he doesn't know me at all.

He whips around, eyes flaring on the gathered crowd. "I want to know which of you knew about this affair and failed to report it to me! I want to know how long it's been going on!"

None of them say a word.

He pounds a fist against his chest in a shaky rage, making some of his power slip out, a break appearing in the middle of the floor. The crack of the marble reverberates throughout the room, shaking up through my feet.

"Control, Father," I mock, throwing his constant command back in his face.

He snaps his finger so fast I don't even see it, I just feel my pointer finger break in half, right where he did it the last time. A grunt skids past my lips, the pain exploding down my entire hand.

"Stop it, Stanton!" my mother cries. "Slade has nothing to do with it."

My father doesn't turn away from me, doesn't acknowledge her right away. He just watches with sadistic retribution while I try not to vomit. After several long seconds, he snaps his fingers again, and my bones jolt back together with a sickening click.

I have to grit my teeth so hard that my jaw cracks, but I keep everything contained, keep it controlled. After all, that's what he taught me all these years. To be in control. To master my power.

"You're right, Elore," I hear him say while I blink away the rest of the pain. "This has to do with you...and him."

In my next breath, my father has shoved Mother away and gripped Jak by the throat. Jak tries to fight back, but it's no use. He's not a retired, wealthy warrior. He's an Orean servant, skin tanned from all his time outside, body lean instead of the bulk of muscle my father has from all his years in the army. Jak might be a strong Orean, but he's no match against the force of my father.

My father's voice drops dangerously low. "I brought you into my home, allowed you to live in Annwyn and sustain long life. Yet you deign to seek what does not belong to you?"

Jak's weathered hands scrabble, though he can't even get a single finger off his throat. His face starts to go unnaturally red, his lips gasping for air he can't take in.

"Stanton, stop it!" My mother tries to yank at my father's arm, but he shoves her away. She would've gone sprawling, but I catch her before she can fall.

"I want to know how long this has been going on," he says, releasing Jak's throat just enough for him to suck in a breath of air and squeeze out hoarse words. "Was this the first time?"

Jak's eyes flick to my mother, but that only enrages my father more. He shakes Jak like a rag doll. "Was this the first time?"

The entire room feels swollen. Like the air right before a torrent, inflated with a downpour ready to burst and flood us all.

The crack of thunder is Jak's hoarse answer. "No."

My father throws him so hard and so far, tossing Jak across the room, making him smash into one of the windows. The glass shatters, the first of the torrent raining down.

He falls into a heap, and my mother screams and tries to run to him, but my father holds her back. "How long, Elore?"

She tries and fails to rip from his grasp. His expression might be enraged, but hers is one I've never seen before either. Hers is pure, open hate. And that hate is like the wind that blows this storm around us, whipping it into a frenzy.

Her chin tips up, green eyes unfaltering. "For eleven years."

"Eleven years?" Utter shock consumes my father. A surprised gasp even falls out of me. How did she keep that secret for so long?

But then I realize not a single servant gasped, none of them looked shocked, and that's my answer.

They helped them.

My father's black eyes glitter with something ruthless. "You will regret that, Elore," he grounds out, like the rumble of an angry cloud.

I don't know whether I want to thank them for helping give my mother a sliver of happiness or tell them off for not making her be more careful.

Right now, my mother seems to be well past the point of caring about being careful.

"I have loved him for much longer. The only thing I regret is not allowing myself to have that love far sooner."

My father's temper explodes.

In the next instant, he's across the room, boots crunching over the broken glass. Jak has gotten to his feet, but before he can do anything, my father snaps his fingers, just as he snaps Jak's leg.

The crack makes me jolt, and then an agonizing scream tears from Jak's throat. My mother goes running over, but with another snap, my father breaks the entire room.

Everyone on either side stumbles from the shake, my own knees slamming down onto the marble tile as the house shifts.

The noise is deafening.

The whole estate breaks right down the middle. Everyone is screaming, falling, debris crashing down on our heads. When the walls split, the ceiling clefts, dirt spraying from the fissure in the floor. I have to scramble back when the crack spreads so wide I nearly fall into it.

When the shaking stops, I manage to stand up again and pull my mother up with me. The servants all get to their feet again too, everyone giving the broken floor a wide berth. Mother looks down at the massive crevice now between her and Jak, the gap too far to jump.

The two of them look across at each other, and the expression on their faces makes my whole chest hurt.

"Jak..." my mother says, voice cracking, eyes wet.

He swallows hard from his spot on the floor, face now covered in sweat and visible pain. "It's alright, Elore."

"Don't say her name!" my father screams, and then his

power breaks Jak's arm next, snapping it so hard that the bone pierces through his skin.

"No!" My mother's scream rends the air, and she tries to jump across, but I grab her at the last second. "You won't make it! You'll fall," I tell her over and over again as she tries to get away.

"This is what you get for choosing Orean trash," my father seethes. "I want you to remember this, Elore. Remember that this is what you get for betraying me."

She goes stiff in my arms. The whole room seems to suck in a breath of air. And then, my father lifts his hand and snaps.

And Jak's neck breaks.

There's no time for my mother to scream. No time for me to blink. Jak's neck cracks in an unnatural angle, and his wide, agonized eyes extinguish their light right before us.

When his upper body hits the floor, my mother's body does too.

I've read the word keening *before. I've heard of it plenty of times. But I have never actually heard someone let out a keening cry like my mother does.*

It wrenches from her body with so much force that it sends chills down my spine. It's so loud that I can't even hear my pounding heartbeat.

The sound she makes is terrifying. Unrecognizable.

I'm in so much shock that I'm just standing there uselessly, wondering how the hell all of this happened so fast.

My father moves his power effortlessly, unbreaking a single portion of the floor's fissure so he can walk across until he stands right in front of me. "This is why females cannot be trusted, Slade."

My hands curl into fists, and I feel the spikes above my brows pierce through my skin. A single drop of blood slips past my eye. He looks at me coolly, unimpressed. "Lack of control. Now we know where you get it from," he says with distaste.

Anger pours like a flood from my chest, and I feel the spikes in my back straining, ready to—

"Mother?"

I whip my head to the left and see the servants parting, and then my brother is standing there. He looks pale and scared, so young in his pajamas with a blanket clutched in one hand.

"Ryatt..." my mother cries.

He hesitates, eyes bouncing from the break down the middle of the house to my mother's crumpled face. But then, his eyes land on Jak's unmoving body.

"Father!" The word yanks out of his little voice, and he rushes forward, pushing past the servants that try to protect him. My heart leaps into my throat, but he skids to a stop in front of the crack when my mother manages to snag his shirt, stopping him before he can try to leap. He collapses into a fit of sobs against her shoulder.

And my father... I see his thoughts churn. See them clot and thicken.

"It cannot be."

If my mother was angry before, she looks terrified now. Especially when my father takes a threatening step forward. "No," she heaves out. "You will not touch him," she says, gripping onto Ryatt even harder.

And I stand there in shock, looking from Jak to my little brother, disbelief grappling me.

And yet...fae have a hard time conceiving. It's common knowledge. It's why our long life is so important for our species. But my father was able to have not only one heir but two, and fairly close in age. He always put it down to the fact that my mother is Orean, but that's not it.

Eleven years, my mother said. She's been having this affair for eleven years. My brother is ten.

Ryatt isn't my father's heir.

My mother looks wild. Her black hair is disheveled, scraps of ceiling caught in its dusty strands, an angry scratch dragged down her cheek. When he broke Jak's neck, he broke my mother's heart, but she's not going to let him hurt Ryatt too. I can see it in her red-rimmed eyes.

My father staggers, the back of his heel hitting the broken crack behind him as he realizes that Ryatt isn't his.

My heartbeat feels like it wants to rupture through my veins and explode out my ears. Ryatt is still crying, clutching our mother's nightdress, while she tries to drag him behind her.

"You dared to sire that bastard's whelp?" The dark tone in my father's voice seems to suck away the dawning light in the room.

My mother's bottom lip trembles as she tries to block Ryatt. The other servants look like they want to intervene, but they're too afraid to face my father, and they're right to have that fear.

"I should've known I couldn't trust an Orean."

With another snap of his finger, the ground shakes again and there's a violent snap, and I realize that my father has trapped us all in this room, a circle of cracks surrounding us, keeping us all in this entry.

By the time I steady my feet beneath me again, my father has walked up behind me, and I flinch when his hand slams down onto the back of my neck, squeezing slightly. "You gave me a powerful heir," he says to my mother, that voice of his still booming, still edged with impossible rage. "So I have no further need of you or the false spare."

Cold terror solidifies in my gut.

I know my father. I have been training with him for seven years. I have seen exactly how ruthless he can be. I have seen him break houses and streets. Mountains and trees. Tendons and bones.

But I will not let him break my mother and brother.

He may be as loud as thunder, but I'm as quick as lightning.

Faster than a blink, my spikes have burst from my skin and rot explodes from my veins.

I whirl on my feet and shove him back with all my strength. He cracks into the wall where some of the servants scramble, another group of them surrounding my mother and brother, trying to pull them away.

Good.

Because now that I've openly attacked my father, I've drawn a line in the sand. I either have to kill him...or watch everyone I love be killed.

I've let him lord over us for fifteen years. Let his cruelty dictate our lives. I have watched my mother sink further inside of herself, watched Ryatt's wary eyes lose their glint every time my father treated him just as badly as he treated me.

But I haven't put up with his training and his cruelty for nothing. I did it because I think I knew that one day, we would be here. On two sides of the line. I knew it was going to be him or us.

And I choose us.

So when my rot explodes out of me, it's seven years' worth of pent-up retribution.

The tile floor cracks, the earth between us crumbling with decay. Lines of poison leach from my skin and spread through the floor, slithering toward him like serpents ready to attack.

My father is straightening up, cruel eyes locked on me, acting as if that hit into the wall didn't faze him in the least. "You think you can fight me?" he hollers. "I made you!"

He shoves his hands forward and sends out a burst of power toward me. I feel it, like the moving air of a thrown punch. On pure instinct, I throw my own magic at it, and the very air seems to detonate in on itself.

My father and I both go flying back from the force, my head cracking against the broken tile as rot continues to seep from my pores. I hear crashes and screams, but that's all secondary. My sole focus is on him. I don't know how I was able to block his magic like that, or how exactly I wielded my own in that way, but now that I know I can, hopeful determination bolsters my bones.

"You are done breaking," I tell him, my chest heaving,

lines writhing up and down my skin. From the corner of my eye, I can see some of the servants cowering, not just from my father, but from me. And I know what I must look like—this fae packed with spikes and rot, and I feel like I am every inch a wicked fae, from scaled cheeks to flashing canines.

But I don't care. I will be a monster if it means I can destroy one.

He snaps his finger, but instead of trying to break me, my father breaks the floor right from under me. I hear my mother scream my name as I start to fall, but I jump up as the ground crumbles, barely managing to catch myself and roll. I don't even get fully on my feet before I send rot streaming toward him, rotting the ground in putrid corruption as it coils around his legs. I see him grit his teeth, and I know I'm molding his muscles, breaking down his blood, decaying his bones.

And I realize with startling clarity that I can kill him. Right here, right now, I can rot him on his feet. But for some stupid reason, one I hate myself for, I hesitate.

That hesitation is all he needs, making my rot falter and pull back. With ruthless speed, he snaps his fingers, and even though I ready myself to block, his magic doesn't come for me.

Behind me, I hear my mother scream.

I whirl around, seeing her nearly fainting backwards, arm broken in the same exact spot Jak's arm was. Ryatt is crying, the sound of the two of them pounding my ears.

I feel a prickle in the back of my neck, only barely managing to spin around before a fist is suddenly thrown into my face. I go sprawling, the skin of my palms slicing open when I land on the broken tile. I roll over, finding my father looming over me. *All over my arms, my spikes pulse erratically. I push myself to my feet, refusing to show fear, refusing to back down, no matter how much my mother calls my name.*

"You are such a disappointment, Slade," he tsks.

"Believe me," I pant. "The feeling's mutual."

Something flashes in his eyes, and I know. I know that this is it.

This is it.

I call up everything in me. Every scrap of magic I possess. I recall every moment where he pushed me, degraded me, hurt me. I think of every single time my mother's back went stiff, when her eyes filled, when Ryatt cowered. I let all that anger flood my mind and let it fuel me.

Power boils through my veins.

My father lifts his hand.

Time drops its speed.

The storm of the room roars. Or maybe that's the sound in my own throat—the sound in his throat too.

In an instant, my father sends magic hurtling at me with a force that makes my skin prickle. But I'm ready.

If I thought the air exploded before, it's nothing compared to this.

Our power collides.

And that raw, brutal, killing magic rips right through the air between us.

Magic isn't supposed to react this way. I've never heard of it happening before, but maybe because I carry my father's blood in my veins, it's allowing our power to react to each other.

The estate cracks, a fissure appearing between us. But this one isn't a physical break or palpable rot. This is something else.

A metaphysical rip in the air appears. It's broken with jagged darkness and rotten lines. It crackles like a lightning storm, thunders with a barrage of deafening blasts. Wind whips from it like a cyclone, tearing off pieces of wallpaper and spinning it around, sucking it through the gash like blood, making it disappear.

My father's eyes are wide, face leached of color, and the fact that he's showing any hint of panic should worry me, but I'm too focused. Too caught up.

I pour more and more of my power into it. I let it collide with his, ripping this break in the air even further, filling the whipping wind with the stench of decay and hate. My hands shake, my father sweats. We grit our teeth.

Pain lances down my bones, and for a second, I think maybe he's broken something, but no. My magic is draining me too fast, too strong. My spikes are going up and down in volatile bursts, and my heart feels like it's going to explode.

"Slade!" Distantly, I feel my mother's hand on me, trying to pull me away, feel Ryatt on my leg. But I don't stop.

I can't.

And right then, that's when my father sees it in my face. Sees that I'm not going to give up. The booming outcry that comes from his sneering lips makes a fierce scream come from my own.

Because I would rather die than let him win.

The wind tears at my clothes, tosses dirt into my eyes,

the smell of rot clogs my throat, his power pushing, pushing, pushing against mine so hard that my entire body shakes.

Control, Slade.

All those lessons. All the punishments and lectures and hours of exhaustion and pain. I put up with it because I knew I had to learn, had to push so that I could have just as much power and control as he does.

I learned control so that I could take his away.

I shove everything I have. Everything I am. I shove so much it feels like two parts of me rip right down the middle. And that's when that preternatural tear in the air finally erupts.

I feel it the second the magic explodes—feel it because it explodes through me.

The power finally comes to a head, breaking my father and me apart with an ear-piercing explosion.

For a second, I'm weightless. Numb. Caught in the air right alongside my mother and brother.

But then that slow, slackened time snaps back into place. The rip in the air is suddenly like a massive maw of a bodiless beast, and its dark, storming mouth opens wide. It suspends in the air, facing my half of the room, ready to devour us all.

I don't even have time to land back on the ground before those lightning teeth snap shut around our entire cracked half of the room. Then it devours us all in a storm of blackness, and all I know is agony and falling and echoing screams of dozens of people.

That ripped mouth swallows us down, down, down into the darkness of nothing, through time and magic and hallowed air.

And then we land in the belly of the beast, and my ripped apart body and poisoned power succumbs to unconsciousness.

I wouldn't know that I'd ripped a tear in the world until I woke up four days later. I wouldn't know that I'd ripped myself in half in the process or that I'd ripped the other people into Orea with me, who would now depend on me forever. I wouldn't know that everything was about to change.

Unconsciousness was my only reprieve, but I wouldn't know.

CHAPTER 38

AUREN

R*ip.*"

That's the first word out of my mouth when he finishes speaking. Because now, I know what it means. Now, I know how much it signifies. All this time, his greatest secrets have been carried by his most common nickname.

I'm not sure when I sat down, but I think my legs gave out somewhere around the time when Slade told me the story of how his power first manifested as a little boy, and I've stayed planted here all the way up to that fateful fight between him and his father. The fight that led him here.

I didn't speak even once. His words are dredged up like an excavation, something that's been buried for years, too painful to be unearthed. But he told *me*. He dragged up all of those moments from his past and laid it bare. Now I have answers to questions I hadn't even thought to ask.

When he finishes, silence fills in the hollowed out air. For several long seconds, my mind whirls, my thighs shifting over the rock beneath me. It's a lot to take in, so I don't think I even *can* right away. There are so many more layers that this tomb of memories has unearthed, and I think only time will truly help me to comprehend the magnitude of it.

I clear my throat, gaze shifting to the giant slash in the air before I glance back to him. "So that's how you got to Orea."

He nods slowly, staring at the stormy rip. "Yes."

"Do you think...do you think that's how I got here? Someone else made a rip in the world?" I ask.

Heavy eyes lift to mine. "I don't know. I've thought of that a lot, ever since you told me you were smuggled here. It makes me wonder if any other fae have been living in Orea all this time, hiding in plain sight."

"But do you think that I..." I trail off, head motioning toward the rip.

Slade shakes his head. "No. When I'm not here, this is always guarded, and not a single person has come through since that day. If anyone had, I would've felt it, because my power force is tied to it."

All of this information brings up thousands of more questions, like dust pluming in the air after something huge just dropped. But one look at Slade's face makes my questions settle back down. His face is drawn tight, eyes carrying more shadows than can be blamed on the cave.

He looks exhausted, more vulnerable than I have ever seen him, like the raw edges of a rock that's been chiseled, left with a bared surface he's not used to showing.

"I know what you went through was horrible, but for

what it's worth, I am glad that you're here in this world with me," I say quietly.

His eyes soften. "Oh, Goldfinch. I would've found you in whatever world you were in. In whatever life."

My lips tip up in a soft smile, because I believe him. "You would've found me in them all."

When he nods, I slowly get to my feet, taking careful steps over to him. Instead of saying anything, I place my hand over his curled fist. He immediately relaxes his fingers, allowing me to slip my palm against his, to thread our fingers together. A tremor of a breath quakes from his chest.

I gently tug on his hand, and there's only a moment's hesitation before he lets me lead him away. We make our way back through the dim cave, past his mother's house, through the little notch in the mountain and back into the snow.

Our fingers stay laced together as I lead him down the slope, all the way back to the comforting glow of the Grotto. But instead of going to the house, I keep leading him on. He gives me a confused look, but as soon as we pass the entrance of the Teeth, he knows exactly where I'm leading him.

It's not until the smell of sulfur clogs my nose and the cold air is replaced with steam and warmth that I finally let go of his hand.

Slade watches me with a frown snagging his brows together. "What are—"

His words cut off when I toe off my boots and shove off my leggings. I see the knot in his throat bob up and down as I shrug off my coat, placing my clothes on a rock beside us.

In only my borrowed shirt that skims my bare thighs,

I then walk around to his back and gently slip off his coat, placing it with mine. When I face him again, the confusion has been replaced with hooks of rapt attention that pierce straight into me.

My heart might be racing, but I shove aside my nervousness as I look up at him. "You bared yourself to me. It's time I do the same."

He sucks in a breath as I turn around and look at him expectantly over my shoulder. Only hesitating for a moment, he then steps against me until the heat of his body seems to permeate into mine.

I feel his hands at the top of my shirt, his fingers skimming over the collar. He pauses, as if he's giving me a chance to change my mind, but I won't.

When he undoes the first button, I shiver in both anticipation and worry.

One by one, he bares my back, until the last button is unclasped. He gently pushes the shirt down, slipping it off my arms and laying it on the rock with our coats. And now I'm exposed completely. The sight of my ruined back on full display, my own vulnerability and painful memory exposed to him.

My body trembles. My stomach is tight. And my eyes—my eyes burn with the memories of being held up against a wall while I was severed two dozen times.

But then, Slade's lips are there at the nape of my neck. A soft press of his mouth before he starts to pepper feather-light kisses down my back in painstaking inches. I realize, with tears springing to my eyes, that he's placing his lips between each pair of cut ribbons. There are still some ends hanging on, like hangnails I've refused to yank off. The bruising is all healed, and I know that when these last pieces fall off, my back will be smooth and empty, with no sign of what was there before.

In perfect increments, his kisses go down, down, down.

I tremble even harder, my eyes filling with so much emotion that the cave blurs in front of me. His hands come up next, the barest brush of his fingertips soothing the frayed pieces of me I can no longer feel.

His finger skims over the length of my spine, leaving trails of chills in their wake. And as he continues to place tender touches of adoration against my skin, all the shame melts off of me like snow in the sun.

Without saying a word, he's comforting me. *Healing* me. Until he's on his knees, placing the very last kiss against the ruined ribbons at the base of my back, his grip on my hips grounding me to his touch.

When he stands up and turns me around, he lifts his hands to swipe away the tears on my cheeks. "I see you, Goldfinch," he murmurs, his eyes so full of tenderness that I still can't believe I'm on the receiving end.

"I see you too, Rip," I whisper.

My hands drop to the ties of his pants, and unlike the time in the cave when I first woke up, my movements are gentle, slow. Because I want to relish in this moment. I want to take my time.

The outside world—anything outside of the Grotto's cave—it doesn't exist.

When the ties are loose enough, Slade toes off his boots and helps me shove down his pants, and then he's just as nude as I am, but both of us have revealed so much more than just our bodies.

I drag my eyes up his thick muscled thighs to his cock that's already begun to harden, hanging thick and heavy. With my eyes still locked on it, I slowly lower myself to my knees before him, just as he did for me.

He sucks in a harsh breath as I grip his length in my hand. I take him in my fist, fingertips skating over the softness of his skin even as he hardens beneath my touch. Then I lean in, licking a line up the crown of the head, and his entire body goes rigid.

"Auren—"

Whatever else he was going to say in that mangled tone is cut off as I take him in my mouth. His hands instantly go to my head, fingers threading into my hair. I keep my mouth exploratory for a few seconds, taking him in, licking around the size of him, savoring the way he tastes and the stretch of my lips.

"You're teasing me," he rumbles, and I try to smile around him, eyes flicking up. "Suck me, baby. I want to see those cheeks hollow out."

A flutter sets off in my stomach, and I immediately do exactly what he wants. I suck him, bobbing my head up and down, and the groan that he makes shoots heat right between my thighs.

"Fuck, Auren," he grits out. "That *mouth*."

The thrill I get from the way he comes apart makes me

bolder, and I start to suck him down until he reaches the back of my throat. I gag, but Slade's hands pull my head back slightly. I look up, and his eyes are burning into me with pure carnal hunger. Just like he did with the unbuttoning, he waits, watching me closely, checking on me, making sure I'm okay. The pure *trust* in that makes me even more eager to make him lose control.

With the right person, there is power when you kneel. There is adoration with submission. There is balance with control.

Which is why I look up at him and say, "Fuck my mouth, Slade."

His eyes flash with carnal hunger. "Put your hands on my thighs," he tells me. "Good. I want you to tap me if I get too rough or you need a break."

I nod, letting him know I understand, and he starts to direct my movements, sliding me back and forth over his cock. He lets me get used to him calling the shots for a few moments, and then he starts to move faster, harder, fucking my mouth as though he craves it fiercely, his movements bold and rough and deliciously erotic as he pumps his hips.

"*Yes*," he growls. "This dirty fucking mouth taking my cock so perfectly." He sweeps my hair up, fisting it in his hand, tugging just enough to keep my head firm, but not enough to hurt. "That's what you are, you know that? Fucking *perfect*."

His hard length bumps the back of my throat again and again, making me gag, making saliva spill from the corners of my lips.

"That's right, drool all over my cock, baby. Get it nice

and wet and sloppy, because I'm going to fuck you with it soon, and I want you *dripping*."

He may have called *my* mouth dirty, but his is positively *filthy*, and I can't get enough of it.

Slade pulls me off, and I gasp in lungfuls of air, my eyes watering slightly. "You are gorgeous, and I want nothing more than to watch my cum flood your mouth, but I want to sink myself inside your pussy even more."

With a smile, I wipe my chin and rise to my feet, and then I start to walk backwards toward the hot springs. He watches me without moving, the lines on his skin twisting and curling around his pecs, as if they want to reach for me.

When my heels hit the edge of the hot water and I start backing into it, legs embraced in the heat, I raise my hand and curl my finger toward him. "Then come on, King Ravinger. Because that's exactly what I want, and I'm healed enough for a nice, long *soak*."

He's on me before my lower half can disappear beneath the surface, his fingers digging into my ass as he lifts me up. He wades us further in, and the water feels *so good* the deeper we sink into it—the deeper we sink into *each other*.

Slade stops at the side of the pool and puts me down, and I notice the incline here is sharp, lifting me several inches higher than him.

"Turn around, baby," he tells me. "Brace your hands on the rim of the pool."

Swallowing hard, I turn, my fingers curling around the smoothed rock as I grip it. "Good girl," he purrs as his hands come around me, one curling possessively around my pussy, while the other goes to my breasts.

"Goddess..." I breathe as he circles my clit with two fingers, moving over me like a master musician plucking the perfect strings. My body sings for him in all the right notes.

When he sinks a finger into me, still keeping the other curled to caress my clit, we both groan. His mouth comes down to nibble at the side of my neck, while his other hand squeezes and caresses my breasts, twisting my nipples and making the peaks stiffen.

"Slade, I want you," I moan out, my head tipping back against his.

"And you'll have me," he replies, kissing the back of my neck. "There's a short shelf just in front of you—I want one knee propped up on it."

Out of my mind with thrumming need, I quickly raise my knee, finding the smooth rock exactly where he said it would be.

"Perfect," he tells me as his hand on my breasts falls away. Then, his finger leaves my pussy, the crown of his cock taking its place.

I'm instantly being stretched, my breath catching as he pushes in with agonizing slowness. Inch by inch he sinks into me, and somehow, him going slow just makes me feel *fuller*. The hot water surrounding us makes everything slicker.

When his pelvis hits my ass, he gives it a squeeze, while a groan travels through his chest. "So fucking good. So tight and ready."

I feel his lips on my back again, and I realize that this positioning he put me in was entirely purposeful. But then, everything Slade does is for a purpose, so I shouldn't be surprised. He doesn't keep us face-to-face, he has me like this with my back still bared to him, and when he places kisses there again, it's like he's replacing the violence and marking me with tenderness instead. Reminding me that I'm not ruined. That despite it all, we're here, together, and that sometimes, our worlds have to rip in order for us to end up where we're meant to be.

"Slade, I need you to move," I tell him, all while he strokes, caresses, makes my body melt and all my reservations thaw into draining rivulets.

His hand comes back to my clit with almost reprimanding quickness, and a garbled breath gets stuck in my throat as his fingers start to rub me in rapid, determined circles.

At the same time, he drags himself out and then thrusts back into me. Again. And again. And *again*. His pace is steady and hard, and when he uses his other hand to grip my thigh and tilt me up just a little bit more, a jolt of heat slams through me.

My back arches as an embarrassing mewling sound escapes me, though the bubbling sound of the water drowns some of it out.

"Yes, yes," I chant, feeling his touch on my clit like a thousand different lightning bolts coursing down my limbs, up my stomach, even heating the soles of my feet. Feeling him hit that spot inside of me that makes me want to crash into a crescendo.

"Faster, Slade. I want to come. I want to come with you."

"I'll give you what you want," he says, voice heated and hungry, dominant and protective. "Hold on."

I straighten my arms, bracing myself, and Slade starts fucking me hard and fast, making the water splash around us. The slapping water is somehow the perfect addition to the erotic noises that accompany his groans and my own.

"Your pussy is clamping down on my dick like it wants to milk me dry," he hisses in my ear, sharp teeth skating over the curve. "You're close, aren't you, baby?"

"Yes! Please!"

His fingers strum my clit, harder and faster and harder and—

I combust. In the heat of the water with the waves of it crashing against my arms and chest, I catch fire from my feet to my chest, tingling with release.

Slade lets out the sexiest sound against my ear as he jolts, his cock pulsing cum into my body, and I melt against him as my own waves slowly ebb.

Panting against each other, Slade gives me one last kiss against my back before he turns me around and sits me sideways on his lap. He holds me there with my head tucked against his chest, with the steam curling around us like a curtain meant to keep us hidden from everything else.

After a while, after the silence has become a comfort, the bubbling water nothing but a humming background noise, I look up at him, making him tilt his head down to look at me. "This is it, isn't it?" I ask quietly, feeling so soft and secure in his arms. "This is real love." That word. That huge, momentous, meaningful word just falls out of me, rippling the waters between us, but I know it's true.

Before, when I thought I had that, it was nothing like this. It was nothing like *him*. After tonight, I see with such clarity. I see what's right in front of me.

Slade's arms tighten around me, and then he places a kiss on my forehead. "Yes, Auren. This is love."

CHAPTER 39

AUREN

S lade and I spend the rest of the night in bed. He makes love to me two more times before I fall asleep, only to wake up with his mouth between my thighs while his tongue does wicked, wicked things.

I'm not sure what time it is when we both fall asleep again, but when I wake up the next time, I'm alone in bed. It's not anything unusual since I've been keeping opposite sleeping patterns in fear of suddenly gilding something. Still, I can't help the pang of disappointment at not having him here.

Looking at the clock sitting on top of the fireplace mantel, I see that I didn't sleep as long as I usually do. It's late afternoon, which means it's still daylight. Normally, I'd turn over and bury myself beneath the blankets, content to hide until night. But my stomach decides to growl hollowly right at that moment, because it's been a long time since the feast at the pavilion. Especially considering how...*active* Slade and I were last night.

It helped, to fall into each other instead of getting bogged down with all those revelations. But now that I'm alone and have time to process, all I can think about is this village. About all the long-lived Oreans inside of it.

Mostly, I think about his mother.

I can relate to her. She was taken away from her world, trapped with a cruel man. Coveted for her magic, kept away like a trinket to bear him fruit. I wonder what happened when she went through that rip, why she no longer speaks.

Perhaps her voice broke that day, right alongside her lover's neck.

It makes sense now, why I kept picking up something odd about the villagers and Elore. I must've been sensing their connection to Annwyn, as subtle as it may be.

But mostly, the thing that keeps cropping up in my head is wondering how I got here. If Slade and his father wielded their magic and tore the world...did someone else do the same? Was I smuggled through some rip that might still exist somewhere in Orea? The thought that another fae could've been sold to the flesh market, treated just as I was, makes my heart hurt. And yet, if there are other fae in Orea...where are they?

My thoughts roll in and out on a steady tide until my stomach really starts to complain, and I force myself out of bed. "It'll be fine," I murmur as I leave the warmth of the blankets and wander into the adjoining room. I'm not going to gild anything during the day.

I have to start taking baby steps, and getting up with the daylight is the first one. The last thing I want is to lose control and hurt this village. I would never forgive myself.

After using the washroom, I wander into the closet. Now that my back is mostly healed, I decide to ditch Osrik's shirts in lieu of one more my size. I pull on clean clothes and then head back into the bedroom, my gloved hand pausing on the handle of the door. With a deep breath, I open it and step out, walking down the long hallway to head for the kitchen.

When I'm nearly to the open doorway of the living room, my steps come to a halt at the sound of voices straining past the walls.

"Rip, we can't keep ignoring these."

That's Lu's voice, and her tone sounds...worried.

"I know," Slade replies, a heavy resignation weighing down his words.

There's a pause, and then I hear Digby say, "They're idiots if they really think this about her. If you ask me, it's just a bunch of caterwauling."

"Doesn't matter," Judd replies. "They feel threatened. They're too arrogant to think Midas was the liar. And anyway, it's political. If there's one thing you can always be sure of when it comes to rulers, it's that they will always try to spin a situation to their advantage."

My brows pull together in a frown.

The front door suddenly opens, and I jump, pressing my back against the shadowed wall as Ryatt comes stomping inside. If he was really looking, he'd spot me, but he stalks inside and rounds the doorway, his shadow spilling into the hall.

"Is it true?" he growls, making everyone else go quiet. "Is it?"

"Yes, it's true," I hear Slade say.

Ryatt makes a noise of frustration, and I see his shadow start to pace. "Fuck."

A simmering unease sloshes against my stomach, tainting the hunger I had and replacing it with nausea. I know there's something going on—something Slade hasn't told me yet. That much was clear when I overheard him and Ryatt at the pavilion, and I got the same feeling when Slade received that hawk and didn't offer an explanation. Sure, it could've been something minor, but I don't think so.

For a second, I consider turning back around. Going back to the bedroom and hiding from all of this. But I can't keep doing that. It's time I take another step. So even though my anxiety is spiking up, like water levels rising to my ears, I force myself to push away from the wall. To walk into the living room.

As soon as I do, I see everyone gathered around the kitchen table. Slade's eyes immediately flick up to me when I appear through the doorway, and I see the stress on his face a second before he wipes it away.

"Auren."

Everyone else at the table turns to look at me, as does Ryatt, who was standing in the kitchen doorway with his back to me.

None of them quite have the poker face that Slade does. But even if they did, I'd still be able to sense something was wrong from their stinted silence. Even Hojat, whose presence is always so calm, has strained lines of worry creasing his face.

My eyes fall to the scroll that's been rolled out on the table. It looks like it's been passed hand to hand, crinkles marring the scrawled words.

"What's going on?" I ask, my eyes dragging back up.

Lu and Judd look to Slade, and even Digby cocks a brow at him, like he's waiting for Slade to come clean.

When Slade hesitates, Judd cuts in with an easygoing grin. "Hey there, Gildy. Heard you found out why we really call him Rip. Bit of a show-off, making a whole-ass rip into the world, don't you think? Personally, I preferred all the rumors that *we* came up with to explain his nickname," he tells me. "It was fun spreading them."

Lu smirks. "Like he got the name for ripping people's heads off in battles."

Judd nods. "Or having ripped muscles—the women liked that one."

"Rest In Peace."

"Ripping people a new one."

"Being a rip-off."

"Ripping through lives."

Judd's eyes light up. "Or ripping some nasty ass far—"

"Enough," Slade says with a sigh. Judd snickers.

"Thanks for that," I tell them. "And yes, it was quite the surprise. But I really just want to know what's happening now." My eyes look around the room. "There's something that's been going on since we've been here, right?"

To my surprise, Ryatt is the one who answers. "Yes, there has been."

"Ryatt," Slade growls.

"What?" he snaps back. "She's up. She's healed. And now, she's *asking*. You're wasting time—time that's not only yours to waste. It's not *hers* to waste."

"What does that mean?" I ask, unease churning through my stomach. "Is this about...Midas?"

Hojat shifts in his seat. Judd's eyes move to Slade again. Lu flicks her wooden lip piercing with her tongue.

"What does the letter say?" I ask warily.

It's the look on Slade's face that makes my chest tighten, that makes cold dread flood my veins.

"What does it say, Slade?"

Instead of answering, he gets to his feet, digs a hand into his pocket, and pulls out a handful of scrolls. My eyes widen when they spill onto the table. "The monarchs have demanded that you answer for the death of Midas—that you stand trial at a royal Conflux. They claim..."

My heart crashes against my chest. "They claim what?"

He lets out a weary sigh. "They're claiming that you stole Midas's gold-touch. That you became jealous when he announced his betrothal to Queen Kaila, and you killed him in a fit of rage. And...that you've seduced me."

My mouth parts in shock, ribs cracking with the force of my heartbeat. "And that...that's what those letters are? A kind of summons?"

"Some of them."

I swallow hard. "And the others?"

He hesitates.

"*Slade.*"

"We were just informed that our shipment of supplies never arrived. It was supposed to get to the outpost, enough for the army passing through and also to replenish Drollard, but it didn't arrive. I looked into it, and it seems that the ships never came to port."

My frown deepens as I try to understand what this has to do with what happened in Ranhold.

"What ships?"

Ryatt cuts in before Slade can answer, turning his body toward me. "What my brother is trying to say but doing a shitty job of, is that the other kingdoms are now sabotaging us for harboring you."

My eyes go wide.

Slade shoots him a glare before he tries to explain. "Fourth Kingdom is mostly wetlands, swamps, and mining mountains. Outside of that...there's the rot," he says. "Partly used as a deterrent, partly because I have to expel the power. But that means that my kingdom doesn't make for very good farming land. Other than fish, we have to import most of our food from trade agreements between the other kingdoms."

He pauses.

"So the shipment..."

"It's not coming, Gildy," Judd tells me from his spot at the table. "The kingdoms are pissed off that Slade's ignored their guidance and hasn't shipped you off for the summons. This is their way of warning us."

My eyes fly to Slade. "But what about Drollard?"

"We have reserves."

"Yeah, but it's not infinite," Ryatt says.

"Not to mention the army," Judd adds, running a hand over his mustard yellow hair. "They've been on the move for months now. Their supplies will be dangerously low as they pass into Fourth. Not good for morale."

"Neither is an absent commander, and a king not in his kingdom," Ryatt says pointedly.

"You need to get back," I say aloud.

Slade looks at me stoically, as if he's not carrying the weight of a kingdom on his shoulders. "We'll go when you're ready."

He's not returning because of *me*. Because I've been dragging my feet, too tentative to get a hold of myself and face the changes of my power, face the repercussions of my actions at Ranhold.

"I'm holding you up, Slade," I tell him honestly. "You need to go back to Fourth Kingdom."

Anger flashes across the sharp planes of his face. "You think I'd leave you behind? Not a fucking chance."

"I don't want to be left behind, but the other monarchs know I'm with you. Maybe it's best if I do stay here."

"No."

I let out a sigh. "Slade—"

He presses a hand against the table. "It's not happening. We're not separating. Besides, I can better protect you back in my kingdom. It would also be best if I'm there, in case the other monarchs decide they want to retaliate with more than holding up an outpost shipment. But before we can go…"

I fill in his gaps. "I need to figure out my magic."

He nods.

"Right, so she can possibly kill everyone in Drollard," Ryatt mutters.

Slade opens his mouth to tear into him, but Digby beats him to it. "Don't speak about my lady in that tone," he grounds out.

Surprisingly, Ryatt actually looks a bit chastised before he covers it up with derision. "Shouldn't you be in bed healing?"

"Watch your mouth," Slade barks. "You will treat Auren's guard with respect."

Digby glares at him. "I don't need your defense, *boy*," he says to Slade before he turns back to Ryatt. "My leg and ribs are better," Digby retorts. "I'm healed enough to kick your ass."

Judd snickers.

"Something funny?" Ryatt demands. "Sorry we can't all laugh everything off and pretend it's fine like you do, but Drollard is in serious fucking danger of being starved out if your king doesn't get off his ass and fucking *do something*!"

My eyes flare wide, bouncing between them as they all seem to snarl and snap at each other like a bunch of hungry dogs.

Across the table, Lu gives me an eye roll. "You see what I put up with all the time?" she tells me before getting to her feet. Then she hops on top of the table and, quick as a whip, launches a dagger from...I don't even know where, and makes it slam point-first into the wood, pinning the letters down.

Everyone stops talking at the same time, looking up at her.

"Now that I have your Divine-damned attention..." She

places her fists on her waist, looking down at them like the captain she is. "I need you all to tuck your dicks in for a second and try to think rationally. Like a woman."

Despite the severity of the situation, I can't help but grin.

"It's clear what we need to do," she goes on, and she points at Ryatt. "You need to stop being a prick. Slade cares about Drollard and everyone in it—and you know this. Just like *we* also know that you're stressed as fuck about it because this place is your home. But like I said, stop being a prick."

Ryatt looks mulish, but he keeps his mouth shut.

Her finger moves to Judd. "Stop being an instigating asshole."

"And you," she says next, pointing at Slade. "You've been gone way too long from your kingdom, and you know it."

"You..." she says to Digby next, making him look up at her warily. "Keep up the good work. Same for you, Hojatty," she adds, and the mender gives her a shy smile.

"And Gildy." I stare cautiously at her finger, bracing myself for her words. "You need to yank up your big girl britches and figure out your magic. Because we all know Rip sure as hell isn't going to leave without you, and frankly, you need to do it before we let you near another ballroom. It's time."

I know she's right. I'm past the point of dragging my feet. I need to be stronger physically *and* magically. So even though it fills me with dread, I nod. "I know."

"I know you do," she replies. When she drops her hand to her side, everyone seems to relax a little. I'd find it funny if I weren't so anxious. "Now, we're not going to argue and waste time anymore. Os is already getting the last third of the army crossed back into our territory. Which means we are going to have thousands of tired troops we need to take care of, and letters to answer. We need to come up with a plan. Together."

Collectively, everyone nods.

Lu hops down from the table and then looks to Slade, and I see his own demeanor shift. He looks like he did in his Rip form—the devious commander of the world's most fearsome army.

He braces his hands against the wood, eyes skimming over the rolled scrolls beneath his fingers. "The other kingdoms think they can try to bully me into handing over Auren, but it's not going to work," he says, and I finally hear it—the rage that he's kept hidden, the need to act that he's been suppressing. After a moment, he lifts his head from the letters, and a wicked grin spreads over his face. "Maybe I need to remind them of why no one fucks with King Rot."

CHAPTER 40

AUREN

Yesterday, as everyone filled me in on all the political moves that've been happening since Ranhold, I realized just how *sheltered* I've been. How much they've tried to shield from me. But now that those shields are down, they included me in all the talks. Several times, one of them would look over to me and ask my thoughts on the matter. I startled the first couple times, caught myself frowning in confusion another.

I've been a silent witness to hundreds of political meetings over the years, but the key word is *silent*. I was never invited to voice an opinion, never allowed to ask questions. I was just the caged pet meant to be gawked at.

We all spoke for hours, and admittedly, I was out of my element. I'm not used to being asked for my judgment on things like this. But that's just another reason why Slade and his Wrath are different. They all work together. Even when they argue, Slade isn't pulling rank and meting out punishment. He opens every discussion, hears everyone's say in the matter, from his Wrath to his mender—to even my *guard*. He listens to everyone, taking it all into account.

Midas would never have done that.

And despite such difficult topics, Slade seemed *relieved* after. Like this was a weight he's been pulling behind him, secreted away from view as he silently shouldered the responsibility. But now that it's all out in the open, he seems more self-assured and ready.

But me? My mind has been turned to mush, like porridge that's had an overabundance of oats added. It's a sticky slop with too many grains of thought congealed together in my head.

My sleep is fitful that night. I'm not sure when we finally all go to bed, but by the time we do, I wake up in desultory pieces, as fragments of dreams cut through my consciousness. I'm overloaded with brand new information coming at me from all directions.

I dream of the rotted prisoner. Of Ryatt screaming in my face to leave his home. Of Elore, only I see her from Slade's account, of when he made that rip in the world, of her screaming until her voice no longer worked. I dream of Queen Kaila holding me hostage with ropes of collected whispers. I dream of my gold bursting out of me and encasing all of Drollard.

When my eyes drag open after that last dream, I decide not to close them again.

I'm done.

Not with sleep—but with me. With this heavy undertow, where I'm trying to move one way but I actually keep dragging myself back. And I'm not just holding myself back either, I'm also holding back a king who needs to protect his kingdom.

I know what I have to do.

So, I carefully get out of bed, even though we only just got into it a few hours ago. I quietly dress and then go to the door, checking on Slade's sleeping form before I slip out. From the hook beside the banked fire in the living room, I grab my coat and shrug it on before stepping into my boots. The house is quiet and still and *cold*, but I'm shrouded in a nervous warmth.

The normally creaky front door of the Grotto doesn't make a sound as I open it and slip out. Ahead, the cave yawns open with the barest hint of dawn cresting against the landscape. I walk toward the muted light, tucking my hands beneath my arms as I leave the protection of the cavern.

The air is placid and raw, the kind of cold that sticks to your breath and makes your lungs feel like ice. I turn my back on the silent village and aim up the slope, my steps sure, my mind determined.

Because I'm going to master my power.

If Slade could learn to do it when he was *eight*, then I can do it now. I have to.

So I drag my ass up the freezing hill, with my body encased in the shade of the mountain to my right. I go past the Perch, past the Mole, cursing under my breath as my boots sink into the snow and my legs burn. I forgot how long the walk was to get up here. But finally, I pull myself into the cave that's polluted with the splashes of gold I left behind.

My eyes adjust to the dim lighting, to the solidified gold that's pooled in the center of the rocky floor. When I move closer though, a shadow that I'd mistaken for one of the rock formations shifts. I jump back in surprise, a yelp popping out of my lips.

I stare wide-eyed at the timberwing that unfolds its wings, lifting its head to look at me.

"Great Divine, you scared me," I say shakily, hand covering my now racing heart.

The giant beast raises its nose, like it's scenting me.

I'm going to go out on a shaky limb and say that's not a good sign.

It watches me entirely too closely from its spot on the gilded ground, while I debate what the hell to do.

"The last time I was conscious around a timberwing, it wanted to eat my face off, so I need you to go."

A pair of glowing eyes blink.

The thing is bigger than a horse, with massive wings held against its dappled body, taloned feet tucked beneath it. If it was surprised by my appearance, it certainly doesn't show it, nor is it threatened by me. And why would it be? It's got a mouth full of razor-sharp teeth.

I take my hand away from my chest long enough to flick at it. "Go on. Shoo."

I honestly didn't really think that was going to work, so I'm not surprised when it just continues to sit there. A sigh comes out of me, and I cross my arms. "Look, I just had to walk a very long way to get here. Through the snow. Uphill. So I'm not leaving. I need this space to practice my magic because I can't be in a populated kingdom without getting a hold of my power until I'm sure I won't gild a whole castle. Again."

The beast yawns.

"Oh, you're bored?" I drawl, fisting my hands at my hips. "Fine, then. If you get gilded while I'm practicing, don't come crying to me about it. It'll be entirely your fault."

It licks its lips and tucks its head back beneath its wing, like it's bored of me and wants to return to its nap.

"Stubborn beast," I mutter under my breath.

It makes a noise deep in its chest, causing me to jump a little. Because yes, I'm still very scared of it, but I'm scared of a wasted trip uphill even more. At least, so long as this thing doesn't start coming at me with its teeth. Then I'll take the hill.

"Okay, I'm just going to start, then," I call as I walk to the other end of the cave.

It doesn't stir.

Letting out a breath, I warily keep it in my sights as I walk further away, careful to keep plenty of distance between us. I reach a spot on the floor where there's a puddle of solid gold, and just behind it, a wall with some more gold splattered onto it.

I think this is *the* wall. The wall where I basically launched myself at Slade. My cheeks heat as I remember the animalistic way we clashed.

Bright side, at least the timberwing wasn't there for *that*.

473

I carefully lower myself to the ground, crossing my legs beneath me. I stare at the frozen gold, its color dulled in the hazy dawn light, and I look at my slightly distorted reflection. With the way the gold solidified, it makes my face look sharper, eyes almost glowing as much as the timberwing's, and my expression looks more...*fae*.

For a second, I'm a little caught off guard, because it's as if I'm looking at that *other* side of myself. At the Auren who was more beast than person, at the fae who burst free for vengeance and blood.

Or maybe it's just a trick of the eye.

I stare at the reflection, palms on my knees, searching for a gleam in my eye, a malevolent spark, anything to recognize that part of me that unleashed.

"My magic isn't working right," I say aloud, looking right into my eyes. "It hasn't been ever since I woke up. And I'm pretty sure that's because of that night in Ranhold."

My reflection watches, and I'm probably just feeding into this, but I swear, I see myself smirk.

"But this is *my* power," I say, fortifying my words. "It's mine to control."

I think my reflection might be daring me to prove it's true.

I scrape off my glove, letting the leather fall to the ground beside me. Turning my hand in front of me, I look at my palm, at the shape of my fingers, the lines on my fingertips.

Behind me, the dawn is brightening ever so slightly, birthing a new day, and I hope it awakens my magic. Yet when I press my hand against the floor of the cave, nothing happens.

No gold drips from my fingertips, no slick liquid metal coats my palm.

"Come on," I murmur beneath my breath, keeping my skin pressed against the cold rock floor. It's funny how I would've given *anything* to have been able to touch during the day without gilding anything. But now, I need to do everything I can to get my gold-touch back.

It's time to stop blocking my power.

I press my palm hard against the rock, my fingertips digging into it like I want to claw my way through, but still, nothing happens. A breath of frustration tears past my lips with jagged edges that cut through the quiet. From the corner of my eye, I see the timberwing pick up its head, and I freeze in place.

When it doesn't leap up and decide to eat me, I give it a heedful once-over. It stares right back at me, unblinking, and as I stare back at it, a chill travels down my spine. My eyes drop back to my gilded reflection, then back to the timberwing, and a jolting recognition shoves its way in my head. It suddenly reminds me of the beast, the one that clawed its way through my barriers and burst free.

Slade said I'm not a monster. He said the beast is the fae side of me. Now, I don't know much about being a fae, and I know next to nothing about beasts, but there's one thing I do know.

Beasts can be tamed.

"That's it," I hear myself say, and the timberwing cocks its head at me. The fae in me has no problem whatsoever with controlling the magic, because it's inherent. My

problem is that I've always fought or hidden my magic—
and my fae nature.

I never embraced it. Never embraced *myself.*

Maybe I always had this ability to control gold, to call to
it even after the sun went down. Maybe I just never found my
voice to summon it before.

But I have a voice now.

Looking back down, I press my hand against the rock,
the cold biting through my skin. "This is *my* power," I say
beneath my breath. "It's not gone. It's not broken. It's just
changed. *I've* changed."

I close my eyes and let out a deep breath. I shove away
all other thoughts, focusing entirely on searching for that side
of myself that burned and scraped, the part that simmered and
inflamed. I delve deep, fully expecting for this not to work
right away, but it's as if this part of me was there all along.

Just *waiting.*

Like a savage predator poised in the shadows of my soul,
it lies eager and alert. Glowing eyes alight on me, wings of
burning gold tucked against its body like flames. It looks at
me, and I look at it, but it's a bit like going through a tunnel.
I'm not sure where its sight begins and mine ends, how long
the stretch lasts between the bright pupil, or if the two are
even separate at all.

I feel my lips curling, relief filling me. Because the
beast—the *fae*—in me isn't something to be feared. It's *me*. It
always has been. I feel that now.

And my power, it's not some uncontrollable force, nor
has it dried up. It's there, like an eternal fire of gilded flames

burning in the center of my soul. I feel my magic just as I feel the beat of my heart. It's in my veins, coursing through my limbs, simmering beneath my skin. All I need to do is reach out and take control of it.

When I open my eyes again, a sense of calm has washed over me, because this time, I know what to do. It's instinct.

I stoke the flames of the beast's wings, and the gold drips down through me. I don't try to pull or panic, I don't try to force it or inundate myself with doubts.

I simply call to it with my newfound voice, and it answers.

The smile widens on my face when I feel the familiar warmth beneath my skin. A second later, my palm goes slick. I let out a whoop when the gold streams out of my hand and starts to gild the floor, merging with the frozen puddle before me.

I look up at the timberwing with a triumphant smile. "I did it!"

The beast blinks at me, and I don't even mind that it doesn't look impressed, because I'm too excited that I finally managed to use my magic on command while fully conscious and in control.

I immediately celebrate by yanking off my other glove. I press my palms against my leggings, my shirt, my socks and boots, elated, ecstatic, feeling like for the first time ever, I can *celebrate* my own magic.

When I'm gilding my gloves, a clap sounds behind me, and I whirl around in surprise. Slade's there, leaning against the wall of the cave, looking offensively sexy. No person should be able to look that effortlessly good in the light of dawn.

But I'm sure glad he does.

He's wearing unlaced boots caught over low-slung pants and a wrinkled shirt with its sleeves shoved up his forearms. He's not even wearing a coat, like he rushed out before pulling one on.

He stops clapping, his hands slipping into his pockets, while the grin on his face and gleam in his eye make my stomach flip. "Well done, Goldfinch. I knew you could do it."

CHAPTER 41

AUREN

"Try and pull it back in," Slade tells me.

His back is resting against the cave wall—a wall that's now gilded in sweeping waves that mimic the veins of fluorescence surrounding us.

Argo, Slade's timberwing, is here too, just as he has been for the last four days. He never approaches or growls, but instead keeps a keen eye on me and my gold—or acts completely bored by my presence.

My brow furrows in concentration from where I sit in front of a rock formation at the back of the cave, my gold cascading over the dark stone like a slosh of paint dripping over the top. I try to pull it back into my hand that rests on the pointed tip, but no matter what I do, the gold keeps spreading down.

"I can't," I tell Slade with frustration, my fingers stretched and bent over the stone, glutinous gold dripping from me.

My hand is shaky, the rest of my body tired from the strain of control I've been practicing non-stop for several hours already. Since Slade first followed me and saw me finally have a breakthrough with my magic a few days ago, I've been dragging him up here from dawn until dusk to help me practice.

I've learned a lot in a short amount of time. Like the fact that I can't make *new* gold during the night. That power is still purely tied to the day. Yet I *can* control any gold around me during nighttime, just like I did back in Ranhold.

"Alright, take a break. Breathe."

"I don't want to take a break," I say stubbornly, my mouth pinched as I stare at my ornery gold. "I want to get this."

Slade drags a foot up to lean an arm over his knee, looking casually sexy from where he sits across from me. "I know you do. And you will. You've done amazing work already learning control. Take a breath, and then try again."

Nodding, I relax my strained fingers and shake them out a bit as I let out a centering breath. Every day, Slade has been helping me master the new facets of my magic. I quickly realized that my confidence boost of calling up my gold-touch again was just the first step. I have so much more to learn and experiment with, and a lifetime of old habits and thought processes to undo.

Instead of suppressing my power, I'm trying to *push* it. To figure out exactly what I'm capable of. But I'm decidedly *in*capable of bringing my dripping gold back up to me yet and undoing what I've gilded.

But I'm determined to learn.

Slade's been having me do things step by step. For the first couple of days, I practiced simply calling my magic to gold-touch certain things in a controlled way, and then to essentially turn it off like a spigot so I don't gild anything I don't want to.

It's not easy. I struggle with both aspects. But I suppose that's to be expected after so many years of uncontrollably gilding anything that my bare skin came into contact with. I'm still careful about keeping covered during the day, just in case.

But...a flicker of golden light lives in the back of my head with this unbelievable possibility—that one day, I can be in complete control.

It's what spurs me on.

That I can one day walk barefoot in the sunlit grass, without the risk of spreading metallic death beneath my heels. That one day, I can bare my arms and legs to the cast of the day, with no fear of what might brush up against me. That I can eat and drink from dawn till dusk and actually taste my food, without the bitter taste of metal sliding down my throat. The possibility that I can go without gloves, that I can touch and feel and hold whatever I want, without worry, no matter the time.

I want to get to that *one day* so desperately.

After letting out a calm exhale, I once again stretch my fingers over the gilded tip of the short stone before me. As soon as I touch it, I call the gold to seep from my fingertips, and it starts streaming down in slow, steady drips.

"Good."

Slade's murmured praise bolsters me.

I reach inside of myself, looking for that effortless control that came out of me in Ranhold. If I was able to grab hold of *all* the gold in the entire castle, I can control this one gilded rock.

This is my power. I control it. It answers to me and me alone.

The concept of recalling the gold back to me is completely unnatural, and something that I'm fighting to figure out. Yet because of Ranhold, I know I'm capable of a lot more than I realized, either because my magic evolved, hatching from the chains I'd been wrapped in, or because this was always something I could've done with training—I'll never know which. All I know is I'm going to figure this out, because I don't want to keep living in fear of my power. I want to live in *control* of it.

Like liquid pouring from a glass bottle, I envision shoving a stopper in, ceasing its flow. The visual helps me ground what I'm trying to do with my magic, and I feel my power respond, the gold trickling to a stop against the rock. My hand shakes from the effort, but I hold on, scrabbling to keep steady with my concentration. Now that I've successfully *stopped* gilding, I need to take it just one step further.

Continuing my trick of visualization, I picture someone opening the bottle and tipping it out, letting gold collect in my palm.

"Good, Auren."

I distantly hear Slade urging me on, but my concentration is almost replaced with giddiness when I feel the gold come back up, sliding into my hand. I shove down my excitement, continuing to call more back to me, and when I have a good amount pooling in my palm, I start to picture pouring it back into my unstoppered bottle, letting it drip into that narrow opening.

The weirdest sensation comes along with it. The gold that was pressing up against my palm just...sinks back into me. It's like dropping a piece of fabric in a puddle. Except the puddle is my moving gold and I'm the cloth.

It takes a long time, but slowly, I manage to soak it all up. When I sense the last drop disappear, I open my eyes to find that the rock is now bare of every single speck of gold.

With the biggest smile stretching over my face, I whip around to look at Slade, pointing triumphantly. "Did you see?"

His lips kick up, making the skin beside his eyes crinkle. "Well fucking done."

With a giddy laugh, I leap up and then bound into his lap, keeping my bare hands braced against the wall behind him, arms resting on his shoulders.

Our faces are just an inch apart, chests pressing against each other, and the surge of confidence inside feels like bubbles inflating me, making me buoyant.

"Do you know what this means?" I ask.

His hands grip my waist, fingers moving in a slow draw of mirrored strokes. "What?"

"This is going to change *everything*," I breathe. "If I can master this, then I can touch anything, any hour of the day. I can be casual and unrestricted. I won't have to live in the dark anymore."

In more ways than one.

"Because even if I gild something, I can *un*gild it."

A low hum comes from his throat, and he lifts a hand like he's going to touch my face, but I rear back, batting his hand away with my elbow. "What are you doing?"

"I'm going to grab your face and kiss you."

My stomach tightens, because that sounds like a *very* nice reward, but then my eyes snap to the outside of the cave. "It's still daylight."

"But you just proved that you can *un*gild something if need be."

He tries to move again, and I leap up out of his lap. "Let's not get hasty. That was only my first time."

Slade gets to his feet, and the look in his eye makes my body go hot all over.

"You know how to call your gold-touch, and you also know how to make it retreat now," he says as he begins to prowl toward me with a hungry look in his eye.

I lift my hands up in front of me to ward him off. "I only just learned how to do that three seconds ago!"

He doesn't reply, just keeps coming for me, and great Divine, the *look* on his face. His dark green eyes sweep down my figure like he's thinking very dirty thoughts.

"I could still slip up. Now's not the time to test this, and I definitely shouldn't test it on you."

"You haven't gilded anything involuntarily since you woke up," he points out, still prowling toward me.

I back up, shaking my head. "Let's just save the kissing for when the sun goes down. It'll be like old times. It's too soon to do this right now."

My back hits the cave wall, and he's *right there* pinning me in place without even touching me. "On the contrary. This moment has been a long time coming."

His broad chest blocks out the light of the cave, his head tilted down to look me in the eye, and I can't breathe. My mind screams with doubts and fears, even as my body whispers with desire, spine bending ever so slightly to get closer to him.

"Slade."

"Auren." He leans in close, the plume of his warm breath skating against the skin of my cheek. "You've touched me during the day already."

"But—"

"You're not going to suddenly gold-touch me."

Watching him from a few feet away is one thing. But when he's this close, when the exhales make our chests skim against each other, and when I can see every facet of his green-flecked eyes, it's hard to think. It's hard to doubt. It's hard to fear. He's so all-consuming that my mind just stutters to a stop.

"Kiss me," he says.

My breath hooks at the back of my throat. "We shouldn't."

"Oh, but we should." He shifts again, so close that I can feel the air move between our cheeks.

My mouth has gone dry, my whole body flaring with want I can't tamp down. I'm practically clasping the wall at my back as if it'll keep me from melting right into him, but I'm not sure how much resistance I can truly put up.

Behind me, molten gold slips from my palms, wetting the stone wall. "My power's slipping," I whisper shakily as he softly blows against the bend of my neck. Chills flare from his purposeful breath, my skin somehow feeling both cold and hot at the same time.

"Kiss me," he commands again.

I want to.

"You want to," he says, like the jerk is reading my mind.

I immediately shake my head. "No, I don't. I don't even like kissing you. It's the worst."

The corner of his mouth twitches. "Is that so?"

"Yes," I reply tartly. "You have bad form. I should've told you before."

A laugh escapes him just as he reaches down to trail a finger over my collarbone. Even though it's covered in my shirt and coat, that simple touch makes me think of skin-to-skin, which I'm sure is exactly the point. "Bad form? That sounds unfortunate."

"It—it is."

"Mm-hmm." Slade moves his finger lower until it grazes against my abdomen and then catches against the waist of my pants. "Have I told you how much I enjoy watching your ass in these pants?"

"The sentiment is mutual."

Another laugh escapes him, making my stomach tumble over itself.

He leans back to look at me, the heat of his body like a warm blanket I want to dive beneath. "Kiss me."

My fingers dig into the stone, and I hear the soft patter of gold starting to drip onto the floor. "My magic..."

"You have control of it," he says, his tone nothing but pure confidence.

"I could slip—"

"You won't."

"Your timberwing is watching us."

"He's sleeping."

"What if I—"

"Auren," he says, cutting me off. "Stop doubting yourself and *fucking kiss me*."

I slam my lips against his so quickly that he's still forming his last word when I fuse our mouths together. My lips slant and search, urgent and *desperate*.

Slade instantly has his hands on my hips, yanking me against the hard lines of his body. The move has me panting, and as his tongue delves into my mouth and commands desire, I moan right into him so he can swallow it down.

After a few moments, I pull away, gasping for air, my hands clinging to his corded arms. "I didn't gild you," I say breathlessly. "I kissed you—touched you, right here in the middle of the day, and I'm controlling my magic."

The pride shines through his eyes so bright that I can bask in it.

A hand comes up to tenderly tuck a piece of loose hair behind my ear. And then, as if the male has no fear whatsoever, has complete confidence in my new shaky hold of my magic, skims his bare finger along my swollen lips. "You're amazing, you know that?"

His words make a wave of bashfulness rise up.

"You have taken everything thrown at you in such a short amount of time. Look how far you've come, Auren."

"I want to get so much further."

I want to get as far as I can.

"You will," he tells me.

This time when I kiss him, I fall into him easily. I relish it. Revere it. I'm caught in the rapt earnestness of this moment, and I just *indulge*. Because here I am, in a place that doesn't exist, with a fae king who shouldn't be, kissing in the midst of daylight when I've always had to shut myself away from the light.

After so many years of being chained to the presence of the sun, I'm here, in the middle of the day, kissing. Touching. *Feeling*.

The overwhelming moment has a tear slipping down my cheek to mingle between our lips, until I've flavored our kiss with the brine of my emotions.

Slade pulls away, a frown dug in between his brows, and I answer his silent question. "I just...never thought I'd have this. Never thought I'd ever be able to really *live* during the day."

"You can," he tells me. "You will."

The idea is so incredible that it doesn't even feel real. Sniffing, I wipe at my eyes, and a smile spreads across my face.

"What does that smile mean?" he asks, taking in the glint in my eye.

"I'm just thinking about all the *other* things we can do now. At any hour of the day. Without any clothes covering my skin at all."

Slade reaches behind me to grip my ass. "*Excellent* point."

He moves to kiss me again, which will probably lead to some other *excellent* things, but a chuff beside us pulls us apart again. We both look over at Argo, whose glowing eyes are leveled on us with judgment.

"I told you he was watching."

Slade makes a noise under his breath. "That's enough practicing for today," he says, taking my hand as he starts tugging me toward the exit. He scoops up my gloves from the floor and puts them in his pocket.

Then he pulls me out of the cave and into the snowy day, walking fast enough to make me laugh. "The things I'm going to do to you..."

Elation surges up through my chest because I am positive I want to do every single idea he has in his head. I'm out of breath by the time we get all the way down the slope and back to the Grotto. When he shoves the door open and we burst inside the house, a laugh bursts with me.

Until Slade and my own steps come to a jarring halt at the sight in the living room.

Everyone is gathered with a serious look on their faces, and they're all *standing*. That doesn't bode well.

All the excitement drains out of me in an instant, my smile vanishing as we step into the room.

"What's wrong?" Slade asks, his gaze falling to his Wrath.

Ryatt passes Slade a rolled scroll.

"It seems Queen Kaila has grown tired of waiting for a written reply, so she's sent her advisor to Fourth Kingdom," Ryatt says, a grim look on his face. "Her brother Manu will arrive in two days' time."

CHAPTER 42

AUREN

We're out of time.

I know it, and everyone else in this room knows it too.

I've held us up. The only reason we've stayed here for so long is because they've been patient with me. Slade's been supporting me, letting me work through things at my own pace, even at the detriment of his own kingdom.

"If Manu arrives at Fourth and finds out you're not there, it will raise questions, and they could start searching, which risks someone finding Drollard," Ryatt states.

"We can stall him for a few days at most, but any longer and he'd grow suspicious about where you were," Lu puts in.

I feel everyone's attention shift to me, and I swivel my attention to Slade. "We need to go."

It's not a question, but he nods anyway. "Are you ready for that?"

This facet of control over my magic might be new, but I can do it. Ever since I faced the fae beast side of me, I'm not afraid. I'm not going to explode into a fit of gilded rage.

That is, not unless I want to.

All I have to do is continue to practice my control, and I'll be able to master my magic. I *will* master it. Because I just got my first real taste of touch during the day, and I'm not going to give that up.

So there's no answer other than the one that I say. "Yes. I'm ready."

There's a collective thrum of support that sounds in my ears, and then the group seems to launch into action.

"Right. Hojat, is Digby cleared for travel?"

"I stay with her," Digby says stubbornly, and my lips tilt up.

"His ribs are still on the mend..." Hojat begins carefully.

"I stay with her," Digby repeats on a gruff grunt. "Ribs are fine."

Hojat sighs and then gives a reluctant nod. "I'll need to bind you, and you'll have to be buckled in carefully. As soon as you get to Fourth, you need to rest."

Digby waves him off. "Fine."

Slade walks further into the room, and I perch myself on the armrest of the chair while he plans with the others. "If we ride hard and high, and only take a few breaks, we can get to Fourth in four days."

Judd shakes his head. "The timberwings are going to be frothing by that time."

"We'll push them, but not too hard. But if we take longer than four days..." Slade trails off.

Lu crosses her arms in front of her, her face thoughtful. "I'll write back—make sure they know we're on our way but that they'll need to stall Kaila's brother."

Slade nods. "We'll need food packs and to make sure all four timberwings have a quick hunt before we go. And we'll need to update Os so he knows we'll be at the castle when he arrives."

"Four timberwings?" Ryatt asks. "I thought you'd be doubling up?"

"We are. The fourth timberwing is for you," Slade replies.

Ryatt blanches. "I'm not going with you. I should stay here, make sure Drollard is safe, and help with the extra hunting to keep up our reserves."

"I need you with me."

Anger flushes over Ryatt's face, making his pale cheeks dapple with color. "I'm your fucking *stand-in*!" Ryatt growls back. "If anything, I should go back to the army. But we all know you're the real commander. I just have to take up the gauntlet when you're off playing king."

My eyes bounce between the brothers, watching as the tic in Slade's jaw pulses. I wonder if he's ever noticed that Ryatt does the very same thing?

"And I'll be *playing king* when we get back. Which means I'll need you by my side, and I'll need your presence among the soldiers when they return. I can do it when I'm able, but I'll have to be careful with Manu sniffing around. He might not have the magic his sister does, but we can't underestimate him."

Ryatt scoffs, rubs a hand down his bristled face. "Fine.

I'll leave Drollard. But I'm going back with the army, not to the kingdom, and I'm taking Hojat with me. Our soldiers have been without our best mender for too long *and* their stand-in commander. Plus, I can send a few of the soldiers here to guard the village."

A sigh escapes Slade. "Ryatt—"

"I'm not going to the kingdom with you," he snaps before he turns and starts stalking down the hall. "If I have to be away from here, then I'm going to be with the army, whose morale is probably real fucking low at the moment since two-thirds of its captains abandoned them, *and* their king and commander. I'm going to them, and I'll be ready to leave in an hour's time, and don't fight me on this. I'll come play your double at the castle when I get there with the rest of our soldiers."

Slade's jaw pulses. "Fine."

Ryatt gives him a terse nod over his shoulder. "And for fuck's sake, don't you dare leave without saying goodbye to her."

The door slams behind him as he storms out.

For a second, no one says anything.

Glancing around, I then clear my throat. "So...I take it he doesn't like being Fake Rip?"

"He's grown weary of it," Slade replies.

Lu snorts. "That's one way to put it." Her dark eyes flash to me. "It never used to bother him before. He used to like it in the beginning. It was good for him too. Taught him some good things."

"What changed?"

"He started to resent that he wasn't *himself*," Lu says with a shrug. "Can't really blame him either."

My eyes flick to Slade. "Why did you decide to be your own army commander? That ruse can't be easy to maintain."

"I became a soldier so I could better learn how to protect Drollard and to discover more about Orea. The signing bonus was a big incentive too," he says with a shrug. "We needed the money, and Fourth was recruiting, and they didn't care about age. But I soon realized I was *good* at being a soldier. Even more, I realized I *liked* it. I quickly worked my way up, faster than anyone else ever had, using only my physical strength. Fighting always triggered my spikes, so I let it be part of my soldier persona. It set me apart."

"I bet it did."

"I never used my rot magic. Never wanted to," Slade says. "But Fourth's king was a tyrant, and by the time I hit twenty, I realized how much dissent there was in the kingdom. The king was also doing things at the border that could've jeopardized Drollard's secrecy. So, I decided to take my other form and challenge him for his crown with my rot magic. I won, and Ravinger became king, while Rip became commander. I made sure to quell any pushback by using both forms and keeping my identities separate."

"And you still wanted to lead your army after that?"

"The army is unstoppable with Rip," Judd chimes in. "He's stronger, faster, and more alert. His fae instincts have helped us win more battles than I can count. And his spikes scared the shit out of people. He became notorious in his own right. The rumors of the two of them alone were enough to keep people in line."

"Commander *and* king. Seems like a lot of work."

Slade tips his head. "I had to win a lot of battles when I took position because of other kingdoms trying to test the new king's weaknesses. But it's not as if I could just rot the world, so I met them on a battlefield instead. Grew Commander Rip's reputation. Once that was established and our army's strength was realized, the challenges stopped."

I nod, taking this all in. "And so your brother fills in for you as Rip when you need him to?"

"Yes."

"But what does Ryatt want to do?"

All three of them look at me blankly.

I gape at them. "You've never *asked* him?"

They look a bit sheepish now.

"Alright. We'll just...table that for now. But maybe sometime, you could...retire Rip?" I offer. "And Ryatt can either lead your army for *real*, as himself, or do whatever it is he actually wants to do—which you'll find out, when you *ask* him," I say pointedly to Slade.

He flashes me a smirk. "Noted."

"Alright, I'll go to the Perch to get that message sent off, and I'll make sure the caregiver knows we need our timberwings ready as soon as they're finished hunting," Lu says as she starts to walk toward the front door. She pauses just at the doorway to the hall and looks over her shoulder. "Don't do too much this time, Rip."

Slade stiffens but doesn't reply. She sighs and then walks off, the door closing after her.

As soon as she's gone, Judd jumps up. "I'm going to go get the damn wine while she's out. I know she stashed it somewhere. Whistle if she comes back."

I can't help but smirk.

Judd looks at Slade just before he disappears down the corridor. "I'll get food and water packs ready and start closing up the house, too. You go do your thing, but like Lu said, don't do your thing *too* much."

When he walks off, I frown over at Slade. "What are they talking about?"

His steady eyes settle on me. "Well...there's more that I haven't explained about the rip."

Slade and I enter the cave, the dim blue shade surrounding us in its subterranean midnight. I let my head tip back, let my gaze run across the shadowed dips and curves of the ceiling. The fingers of the stalactites reach down, pausing in their grasp, while the little clouded beetles cluster together against the fluorescence, making their whole bodies glow.

I may not have been in Drollard for long, but I'll miss these caves. I'll miss the way they've given me shelter from the world for these past few weeks. Like a cocoon for a caterpillar, I've been encased in their hollows, enveloped in their protective shells. But now, I'm ready to leave their protection—to face the world outside.

I'm still no winged butterfly, but I do feel as if I've been reborn. My metamorphosis has been twenty years in the making, but I'm ready to be what I'm supposed to be.

My old life had to end, had to be cut away, burned down to nothing but gilded ashes. And I can either remain stagnant in these ashes or I can root down into them and sprout up anew.

I can *thrive*.

But these cocooned caves—I will miss them.

"It's peaceful here," I murmur.

Slade nods, but I can tell that he doesn't hold the same quiet esteem I have for it.

"You don't like it here, do you?"

A little chuff escapes him. "I was responsible for yanking all of these people with me from Annwyn. The raw magic of the rip killed some of them and badly injured others, my mother included. We were stuck in these caves for *weeks*. We had nothing. No food, no homes, nothing but the clothes on our backs. One of the Oreans tried to jump back *into* the rip, but it nearly killed them."

I try to picture that, picture him going from this horrific fight for his life—a fight for his mother's and brother's lives— and then suddenly being yanked through a rip in the world and shoved here, in the middle of nowhere.

"Did you know you were in Orea when you fell here?"

"Not at first. But I figured out pretty quickly that we weren't in Annwyn anymore. I could feel it."

An old memory trickles into my mind, like the gentlest first drop before the rain. "Yes. I remember that—remember how strange Orea felt in comparison. I don't really remember Annwyn all that much, but I do remember that when I came here, something just felt...lacking."

Slade nods, and I know he knows exactly what I mean.

Elore's house comes into view, its rooftop practically

gleaming. "How did you all survive?" I ask. "This isn't exactly the best place to suddenly be thrust into."

"It was good in the sense that no one was here to see us arrive, no one here to see the rip. But it also meant that we were stuck in this frozen wasteland with nowhere to go. And I was responsible for it."

"You didn't know it would happen. The rip was partly your father's fault too. And who knows what he would've done to everyone if you hadn't gotten them all away."

"Not everyone fell through the rip, but for those of us who did...those first few days still haunt me."

My heart aches at the stark rawness of his voice, at the way his tone drags like grit against an open wound.

"Every single Orean was ill when we first fell here. No one could do much more than roll over and vomit. It was up to me to take care of everyone, to make sure no one else died, including going off to find food." My heart twists painfully in my chest. "We stayed in this cave, close to the rip, but the adjustment was agonizing for them. Their bodies weren't used to Orea anymore or to losing the fae-blessed connection to Annwyn. For a while, I wasn't sure if they would survive."

"Great Divine," I say, swallowing thickly. "What did you do?"

"Luckily, the illness wore off for most, and then I discovered the timberwing nest here, right where the Perch is now. The flock was completely wild, and I nearly lost a hand a time or two, but I finally won one of them over. I think it might've been the last wild timberwings in Orea."

My brows lift in surprise. "Argo?"

Slade shakes his head. "Argo's mother. Without her, I wouldn't have been able to hunt large game for us to eat. Wouldn't have been able to get to the coast where I was able to steal supplies. We survived off bare bones for the first couple of months, but slowly, we made a life here. A few of the villagers had magic too, which helped. One of them could form rock, and he helped build the houses and hide Drollard's existence."

"I can't believe you were able to do all of that," I say with awe. "Especially in a completely new world you'd never even been to before, all while you were essentially ripped in two."

"I made a lot of mistakes in the beginning. I wish I would've figured things out sooner. We might not have lost some of the others. But in the end, traveling through the rip was too taxing on them, and the conditions here were terrible. A lot of them blamed me for it."

"You were *fifteen*," I point out.

"And very fae," he counters. "With a mother who could no longer talk or interact and a brother who was ten years old and scared out of his mind. The Oreans didn't resent me right away, but it came. With time. Especially when they realized I could leave and they could not."

I pause. "What do you mean?"

He stops to turn toward me. "Lu told me what you said at the pavilion, that you could sense something was...off about them."

"Yes..." I say.

"You were picking up on their life force being connected to Annwyn."

My eyes go wide. "What?"

"Everyone here in Drollard—they'd been taken from Orea by my father hundreds of years ago, when the Bridge of Lemuria still stood. Living in Annwyn fae-blessed them with long life. But when we came here... The rip is their last connection to Annwyn. If they stray too far from it, they will die instantly."

My hand flies to my mouth. "So none of them can *ever* leave here."

"Only Ryatt and myself and the very few children who have been born."

"Like Twig."

He nods. "Like Twig. We worry that leaving a child here too long will make them dependent on the rip as well, so I bring them to Fourth Kingdom with me when they're old enough to be away from their family."

"But what about Ryatt?" I ask. "He's technically not fae like you, so why is he able to leave?"

"The only theory I've come up with is our mother must have a very strong fae bloodline—far stronger than Orean—which would make sense with how powerful her magic used to be. So I suppose that's what made it so his life force isn't dependent on the rip, either."

I drag a hand through my hair, eyes straying off to the crevices of the cave, though I'm not really seeing them.

"I know this is a lot to take in."

Blowing out a breath, I nod. "Yes, but I'm glad you're telling me."

This time, it's Slade who squeezes my hand. "As I

said before, I will tell you everything. I just don't want to overwhelm you."

I give him a soft smile. "For what it's worth, I'm proud of you. For saving everyone. For protecting them. For figuring out everything when you were only fifteen years old, when you could've easily given up."

Slade reaches up and trails a light finger over my cheek. "Giving up isn't in my nature."

"You are very stubborn when you set your sights on something."

"My sights rarely steer me wrong," he replies as we start walking forward again.

As we near Elore's house, I ask, "Why doesn't your mother live with the other villagers?"

"Falling into the rip affected her more than anyone," he says quietly. From his profile, I can see the heaviness in his eyes, the weight seeming to settle on his shoulders. "Her magic, her words, her *light*, it was like it was all just extinguished. She's only spoken a handful of words since we passed through. Sometimes, I'm not even sure she recognizes me."

"I don't think that's true," I say, my heart squeezing. "I saw the way she looks at you. She adores you."

"I wish she spoke," he confesses thickly.

My throat constricts. "It must've been really hard on you and Ryatt when you first got here."

"There was a healer who came through with us—she was half fae. She tried to help my mother, but whatever happened couldn't be reversed. So it's hard to be here and to see her like this. To know I'm responsible for everyone here. I know that's selfish..."

"It's not," I tell him firmly. "I understand."

"Ryatt sure doesn't," he says with an edge of bitterness.

I hum thoughtfully. "Ryatt loves your mother, and you can tell he deeply cares for the people here. He doesn't hold the same guilt you do, so he doesn't understand why you avoid it. Perhaps to him, you're abandoning it."

"I would never abandon this place," Slade says as he comes to a stop in front of his mother's house. "Or her."

"I know. I'm sure Ryatt knows that too, deep down."

Slade glances over at the dark door, like his gaze is sanding over its ridges.

Something pulls hard in my chest. "You're going to miss her," I say quietly, noting the subtle tells of grief caught in the somber mesh of his eyes.

"That's the thing," he replies. "I miss her even more when I'm *here*. Because my mother got ripped from me when I ripped the world, and she's never been the same since."

My heart soaks up the sorrow of his words until I'm full with it, like a cloud soaking up the vapor and condensing into itself.

Slade clears his throat, shaking his head at himself. "Here I am, complaining that I miss someone who's just a door away, while you were stolen from your parents at such a young age. I'm sorry."

"Why are you sorry?" I reply. "One person's pain doesn't negate another's. Our heartaches are not competition, but the bridge to empathy. So that we can look at one another and know that on some level, we understand. That's one beautiful thing about grief, I think. That sometimes, we can find someone in the world to look at from the other side of the bridge of our torments and know that we are not alone."

The way Slade looks at me is so foreign, I can't even place it. And then he leans down and places a kiss against my brow, the gesture so tender my heart almost hurts from it. "You are remarkable."

My skin tingles where his lips touched. "I think the same of you."

He shakes his head again like he can't quite believe it, and then he opens the door. The two of us stride in, and Elore picks up her head from where she's sitting in the chair by the fireplace, sewing a piece of clothing. As soon as her eyes land on Slade, her face lights up, just like she did the first time.

Hurrying to her feet, she places the clothes on her seat and then comes over, meeting us halfway. She looks him over from head to toe, and even though he gives her a smile, worry creases her brow, as if she can sense that he's troubled, despite his attempt to cover it up.

She places her hand on his cheek and looks him in the eye, so I decide to give them a moment alone. As Slade murmurs words of assurance to her, I wander to the bookshelf, my fingertips running over the spines. Without the barrier of my glove, my fingertips graze against the texture of the books, and I relish in the simple feel of it. Of the way my gold doesn't come spilling out involuntarily.

As I linger, I glance over the titles absently, wondering about Elore, about what happened to her when she went through the rip. It's certainly evident to me that she knows who Slade and Ryatt are, but maybe that's not always the case. Maybe when she went through the rip, the chaotic magic affected her too much, and since her diviner power is tied to speech, it overwhelmed both her magic and her ability to speak.

I hear them behind me, and I turn to see her fussing over Slade, practically pushing him down into a seat at the table. "Alright, alright," he says with a smile.

Elore turns to me and then points to the seat right beside him. Getting the hint, I quickly come over and sit down. She pats me on the head, and then I watch as she bustles over to the cupboards and starts grabbing things from them, placing everything on a square of checkered fabric.

"What is she doing?"

"Packing me food," Slade says with a smile. "Knowing her, she'll probably be packing enough for you as well."

"Oh, she doesn't have to do that," I say, worrying my lip. "With the shipment not coming in..."

"She has plenty of food stores, I promise," Slade tells me quietly. "And she insists on doing this every time I leave, no matter how much I try to convince her otherwise."

I look over at her as she hums softly while she bundles the fabric and ties the ends, holding everything inside. "She's your mother. She wants to take care of you."

Elore comes over and places the food in front of me, giving me a warm smile.

"And take care of you, it seems," Slade says fondly.

"Thank you," I tell her.

I reach for the bundle, but her hand comes out and grabs

hold of mine, and she sits in the seat to my right. Her gaze hooks into mine, and the two of us just look at each other. I feel shy at first with the way she's studying me so openly, but after a moment, I find myself calming. There are so many similarities I recognize between her face and Slade's. Her grass-green gaze flicks over me, and I wonder what she sees. I wonder what she *thinks*.

She doesn't say anything of course, but as she looks at me, I can almost hear a hundred words from her effusive eyes. It makes me wonder what these eyes looked like when she used her diviner power; what those secret scrawls held.

When her hand comes up to cup my cheek, I go still. Elore gives me the softest, kindest smile that I have ever seen. And despite her youthful face, it's so *motherly*. Maternal. Like she somehow sees the little girl inside of me and she's come to comfort her. It makes my eyes want to well up right here in her kitchen.

Her soft palm gently rubs my cheek, and then she drops her touch away and looks past me to her son. She nods at him, and he nods back to her like they're communicating in their own silent language. Then he murmurs, "I know."

I glance between them, and this time, my eyes do start to well up, because I think I just got approval from Slade's mother. I didn't even realize just how much I needed that until this moment.

When we leave, I walk out first so that Slade and Elore can say their goodbyes in private. After he comes out a few moments later, I reach down and grip his hand, and he grips mine right back.

Then, hand in hand, we walk to the rip in the world.

CHAPTER 43

AUREN

The rip seems to draw me forward just like before.

Light and dark congeals at the center, and a mimicry of stars glitter within its clouded depths. We stand before it, and even despite the cold of the cave, there is the faintest stream of warmth hinting from an unfelt breeze.

I walk closer to it, only stopping when Slade's hand comes down to my arm. "It has a very strong draw," I say.

"It's Annwyn. The two of us will always feel that call to home. But no one has come through since we arrived here— which I think must mean that this is the only side that has an entry point anymore or that the magic is too unstable. It's dangerous. Which is why I had to dissuade some of the people not to try to go back through it."

"You said it nearly killed one person who tried to go back."

He nods. "The rip was even more unstable then, but it

could also have to do with them being Orean. I dissuaded anyone else from trying."

"Why would they even *want* to go back?" I ask curiously. "I thought they hated it there?"

"They did, to a point. But they'd been in Annwyn for hundreds of years. It had become familiar to them. Adjusting to Orea was not easy, especially since knowing they could never leave this remote, difficult place. Knowing that all their loved ones would've long since passed. For some of them, loved ones were left behind with my father."

With the guilt I hear in his voice, sadness gnaws at me like the brittle teeth on an infected creature, chewing a hole right in my chest.

"Why are we here?"

Instead of answering directly, he instead says, "We'd been here in Orea for several weeks when the rip started to fail."

My eyes snap to him.

"The noise...it was like a thunderstorm churning up an angry sea, and the wind was right there with it. It woke everybody up. I could tell right away that the magic was collapsing."

I immediately think of all the villagers, of the implications of what would happen if the rip *did* fail.

"What did you do?"

"Shoved so much magic at it that I passed out," he says with a dry chuckle.

"Great Divine."

He runs a hand over the back of his neck. "Yeah. At first,

nothing was happening. I was just rotting everything out. Thousands of beetles dropped from the ceiling, their husks raining down on us. The blue fluorescence blinked out—I think we were even in danger of the whole damn mountain caving in on us. And still, nothing was helping. But then I figured out it wasn't rot power it needed. It was that raw, indefinite power that my father and I had somehow made together when we clashed. I was able to channel that same force and feed it into the rip. It nearly drained me to death, but it worked, and it stabilized the rip. It's something I've had to do ever since."

My mind whirs. "You're saying you've had to feed raw power into this rip all this time so that it doesn't close?"

Slade nods, and I just stand there completely dumbfounded. "I didn't even know fae could do that."

"Neither did I," he says with a humorless laugh. "And I can't use that power for anything else. I have enough rot power to take out all of Orea, and I *need* to expel it. It would be nice if that's what the rip needed, but it's not. My rot magic has no effect whatsoever. Too bad, because expelling rot can be invigorating, while expelling raw power is always exhausting."

"So...you have to come out here to Deadwell to expel your rot power, but then you also have to feed *raw* magic into the rip?"

He tilts his head. "Yes."

"How often do you have to do this?"

"Depending on how much power I can feed into it, the longest I can leave it is about eight weeks."

I stare at him with awe. Not only is this male unparalleled

with his rot power and his overall extent of control, but he has to drain himself every two months to sustain a rip between *worlds*. "Wow. You are...really, *really* powerful."

This time when he laughs, the sound is genuine, and he turns to look at me, unleashing that charming smile he seems to save just for me. "Have I dazzled you, my lady?"

I drag my boot against the floor. "I mean, maybe a little."

"Wait until I show you my kingdom."

Excitement bubbles up in me, because the fact that I'm actually going to Fourth Kingdom hasn't really sunk in.

"Alright," he says, rubbing his hands together. "I want you to back up and stay over there by that rock where it's safer," he says, head tilting to the right.

Nodding, I turn and walk several paces away until I sit down on the rock he indicated. My hands gather in my lap, my knee bouncing up and down in nervous anticipation.

Slade turns back toward the rip, walking so close to it that his black hair gets windswept, the panels of his coat blowing back.

His feet are planted, hands outstretched, and although I can't see his face, I sense the moment his power rises up, because every hair on my arms and the back of my neck rises with it. His body goes taut, and when the force of his raw magic comes barreling out of him, my back slams against the rock behind me.

Despite the fact that my back has mostly healed, the force makes me hiss out a breath of pain. But it's immediately forgotten when I see the ripple of air that's now streaming from Slade's hands. Adrenaline courses through my body, like all my senses are on high alert from the presence of such power.

Wind blows out of the rip, the cracked air shoving and elbowing its way through the torn air. Everything in it seems to shudder. The dark and light that churn inside start to shake. The pricked stars begin to spin, so fast that it's like watching a million fireflies get caught in the whirl of a tornado.

Slade pours out more and more power, so much that I feel pinned in place, unable to move from my spot. Spikes tear out from his back, the first one appearing at the top just between his shoulder blades, before the other five appear, one after the other until the shortest one just above his hips. They break through his arms too, which is when I notice that his hands have started to shake.

But still, he shoves more power out of him.

My eyes jump between him and the rip, my heart beating, speeding like it's going to pass me by and leave me here breathless.

His ears go pointed, aura bursting off his silhouette like thick black steam. It's not a calm, clinging shadow, but an erratic and unsettled swell like capsizing waves. When his entire body starts to shake with the effort of the magic pouring through him, my mouth goes dry, worry slamming through me.

"Slade..."

I know he can't hear me, but his name slips past my lips anyway, eyes unblinking as I watch him. The magnitude of the magic he projects presses against my skin in some invisible force, like static clinging to my arms and charging up through my teeth.

His aura continues to churn erratically until its usual inky depths start to turn shallow and pale.

I jump to my feet, pushing against the brunt that wants to push me back. With gritted teeth, I walk over, every step a challenge to get closer to him. Wind tears through my hair, making my clothes plaster against my body, all while the rip seems to try to shove me away.

"Slade, stop," I call out when I'm just a few feet behind him. He either doesn't hear me or he's too focused on his magic, because he doesn't react to my voice. But his aura has gone slow, like water bogging up, weighed down as he continues to expend.

Pushing forward, I don't stop until I'm right at his side. "Slade, you need to stop," I say, just as I reach out and grip his wrist.

He jerks in surprise at my touch, and one of the spikes on his arm slices into the skin of mine. I release him with a surprised hiss of pain, looking down at the gold blood that trickles from the cut.

Slade's face snaps to me, black eyes blinking away the faraway look of concentration. In an instant, his gaze drops to where I'm bleeding, realization scouring over his face like the raking of nails to drag him down.

"*Fuck.*"

With great effort that makes his whole body shake, teeth clenched and muscles bunching, Slade manages to fist his hands, and the power cuts off in a blink.

The sudden loss of its magnetism makes him stagger, and his body pitches to the right. He almost falls over, but I shove my shoulder against his side and keep him upright, my arm stretching around his waist, careful to not touch the spikes on his back. "I've got you," I say, though I struggle to keep my feet planted beneath me with his weight bearing down. He pants like he just ran across the Barrens without stopping. I can feel his exhaustion as he sinks into me.

"Do you want to sit?"

Slade shakes his head. "Just...gimme...a...second."

I help him stagger over to the cave wall, and he braces himself against it, still pulling in lungfuls of air. His pallor has gone gray, his aura sticking around him like the drip of sap on a tree.

Worry indents into me, leaving me feeling raw and pitted. I stay at his side just in case, and my pulse only starts to calm down when he finally catches his breath and looks over at me.

"Are you okay?" I ask, the distress lifting my tone.

He ignores my question and instead grabs my arm, pushing up my sleeve to reveal the cut. "Fuck," he hisses out. "I'm so fucking sorry."

I glance down at the slice against my skin. "It's fine. It's not even very deep, and it's my fault for grabbing you."

With a creased brow, he reaches into his pocket and pulls out a clean handkerchief to gently wipe away the blood before tying it around my arm. His fingers caress my skin just below the fabric, and when he looks back up at me, tormented black eyes fade back into green. "I hurt you."

"You didn't. It's barely a scratch," I say as I pull my sleeve back down. "But you were worrying me."

He lets out another deep breath and then straightens up

from the wall. "I know, I'm sorry." He runs a hand through his messy hair. "I wanted to expel enough power into it just in case I can't come back for a couple of months. It's always a difficult push, and I let it get away from me. The rip doesn't like for me to cut off my power."

My eyes look over to the tear, which is now back to its calm swirl, sparkling stars blinking, and the faintest lightning boiling within churning clouds.

Slade takes my hand, bringing my attention back to him. "Are you truly ready?" he asks, eyes watching me steadily. "To leave Drollard, to go to Fourth Kingdom?"

To leave the cocoon.

Slade delves into my thoughts with the look in his eye, like he's always been able to root right down inside me. "Because fuck the rest of the world, Auren. If you need to stay here, we'll stay here."

My lips tip up, even as emotion drags down my chest. "I'm ready."

CHAPTER 44

QUEEN MALINA

T*ime seems to move differently* at the edge of the world in Seventh Kingdom.

The days have bled together, and somehow, Cauval Castle has been the respite I didn't know I needed, a balm to soothe the wrongs that have nicked into my soul and tried to bleed out my purpose.

I thought this place was in ruins, but Fassa and Friano have shown me the truth. They were called here, just as I was, to preserve the castle and wait for a rightful queen to take its throne.

They were waiting for me.

Even though the twins are the only ones here other than Pruinn and myself, they've somehow made everything seem so *full*. The gray and white marble walls gleam, the floor tiles are as blue as glaciers, and a soft light always seems to cling to the lanterns and leave off a lush glow.

There must be excellent castle staff, too, though I've never seen a single one. Yet the dining table is always laid out with hot and perfectly spiced food for each mealtime, my bed is made each time I return to my room, and my bath is filled whenever I want to soak and wash.

There's always music playing as well, a song I can hear even when I sleep in the feather bed at the top of the turret. Soft and lyrical, as if it's carried in by the mist that clings to the windows. The air smells nice too—permeating from the frosted flowers that drip with crystalline petals, their bouquets set in vases all around the castle.

I get out of bed with a stretch, poising my hands over my head, curling my toes beneath my feet before I walk into the bathroom to clean up, and then I enter the closet. Everything is just my size, each gown the perfect combination of the white Colier color along with the glacier blue of Seventh Kingdom. I choose a dress with a long flowing train that sounds like the faintest chimes when I walk, the hollow beaded crystals at the hem dragging along the tiles and adding to the soft hum in the air.

Coiling my white hair up into two full braids that make a crown on my head, I pin it in place in front of the mirror, and then, hands dropping, I study myself. My cheeks and nose are no longer chapped from the frozen wind of our travels, my lips no longer peeling. My ghostly pale skin is so smooth I nearly look ethereal, and whatever soaps I've been using have made my hair seem lusher and shinier.

Yet for a split second, as I look into my own icy blue

eyes, I see a flash of darker blue, and instead of my own face, I see a smattering of freckles dusted like cinnamon, hair as red as blood, a grin pulling at lips.

Jeo.

I hold my breath, but I don't need to brace myself for any emotion. Instead of feeling much of anything about him or how he died, I feel a sense of contentment. He died in sacrifice so that I could be here.

Now, even when I think of Highbell, I know that it was *good* that my people betrayed me, because it led me on this path. Tyndall's treachery doesn't matter to me anymore. The frigid fear, the hate, the bitterness, it's simply...gone. Melted away within these remedying walls.

That's how I know being here is *right*. For the first time in a long, long time, I am at ease.

When I'm ready, I glide down the stairs and enter the breakfast room. The three men are already there, the food steaming in wait for me, just as it has been each morning.

"Good morning, Your Majesty." The twins speak and move in unison so often that I've grown used to it.

"Good morning."

They sit back down once I take my place at the head of the blue-painted table, a pillared centerpiece of crystal bulbs holding soft candlelight that prisms inside of it. I hum as I eat, soothed by the pretty music, enjoying the sunshine that streams in through the blue-tinted windows.

I should've come here long ago.

"My queen, how are you feeling today?" Friano asks, mole dimpling into his left cheek.

"I'm feeling very well. My stay here has been just what I needed."

"No less than you deserve."

Fassa nods and tugs at the shiny gray sleeve of his shirt. His brother wears the same thing, and both of their hair hangs like black drapes that frame their faces. "It's true," Fassa says. "We are so lucky that the fates have divined you to come. We wanted nothing more than to give comfort to you after such a treacherous journey."

"*And* after all your betrayals," Friano adds with a tsk. "From your husband and your own people, no less."

"But no matter," Fassa picks up. "Here is where you are, and here is where you belong."

"Exactly," Pruinn agrees, and his magnetic eyes draw me in, the smile on his face letting me know I should've trusted him all along. "You are going to attain your heart's desire, Your Majesty."

"Yes, and we think you're ready," Fassa and Friano say in unison.

I straighten up eagerly, feeling my heartbeat quicken. Since the first day I arrived, the twins haven't spoken more about my role in Seventh Kingdom. They told me that all I needed to focus on for the time being was recovering after all my hardships. To be catered to like the queen I am.

"I am ready," I say with confidence.

The twins grin. "Come, let us walk."

They take me into an atrium.

For a moment, all I can do is stare around the space as a flood of memories come back to me. "This...this reminds me of the atrium back in Highbell. Back before it was all gold-touched."

I'm not choked up with emotion—I feel far too content for that—but walking in this space brings me both awe and pleasure. These are the plants that I can thank for the bouquets set all throughout the castle. The room's walls are painted a soft blue, before doming into a ceiling of glass that makes the blossoms sparkle, the silvery stems on which they grow matching the mist that clings to the windows.

As my eyes skim around, I notice that a cloud of mist has seeped *inside* the atrium as well. It swirls near one of the window panes, congested in a dense, large collection as if there's a crack in the glass, letting it stream inside. My skin prickles ever so slightly just before I turn away.

"We thought you might like it, Your Majesty."

With a nod, I walk down the aisle, the low heel of my shoe clicking across the blue-tiled floor as I gently skim a fingertip over the budding petals beside me. The soft floral scent seems to sink into my lungs and brush through my pores.

"It's beautiful," I say as I turn away from the flowers to face the twins, while Pruinn stands just off to the side, his gray eyes roving over the rows of plants as if he wants to clip a few blooms and stuff them in the merchant's bag that's always slung across his shoulder.

"Come, sit," Fassa offers, and the twins part to reveal a dainty bench of gray stone set right in a semi-circle of blooms.

My heart turns automatically, nose pulling in the smell in

this close proximity. I could bathe in this fragrance—have my bed brought up right here to slumber in its sweet perfume. It's just so *calming*. I take a seat, while the twins also sit down on an identical bench that I somehow missed.

"Your Majesty," Friano says, pulling my attention back to him. Both twins are leaning forward slightly, their elbows balanced on their knees and hands clasped in front of them, brown eyes boring into me as their sleek hair brushes against their shoulders. "Seventh Kingdom went from power to ruin. Much like you."

"But together, we can fix both of those things," Fassa says, dark eyes glinting. "We can restore this kingdom and you to your rightful places. We can help make you the most *powerful* queen in Orea."

Eagerness travels up my spine. From my peripheral, I see Pruinn grin.

Because that—that is my heart's greatest desire. I've been an unwanted heir, an unwanted wife, an unwanted queen. Yet if I was powerful, nothing like that would ever happen to me again. I'd make sure of it.

"Yes," I breathe. "That is what I want."

Friano smiles. "Then we will achieve it," he says simply.

"How?"

They exchange a look, and my yearning sharpens. "My brother and I have very unique magic, my queen. They work only in tandem. I can instill something new."

"And I can restore something old," Friano finishes.

My brows lift. "Restore...like this castle?"

"Quite."

"But our magic always has a price," he explains. "Not only do they have to perform at the same time, it also requires a sacrifice."

"Yes," Fassa goes on. "We won't lie, this magic will be the largest we have ever performed, but we believe in this purpose— believe that this is why the gods have given us our power."

His brother cuts in. "So, in order to restore a kingdom and bestow a gift to a queen, we need two things. The first is we must wait for the new moon, when the gods bless new beginnings and our powers are at their peak."

"And second, that the blood of a pure Orean royal is willingly offered to restore this Orean kingdom," Fassa finishes.

"Me."

They both nod. "You."

I swallow hard. "Exactly how much blood...?"

"Never fear, Majesty," Friano says affably. "Just a few drops will do. And by doing so, by offering this to us, I believe my brother's magic will instill magic into *you*, giving you exactly what you need to rule."

My gaze bounces between them as I take this all in. The scent of the flowers is nearly intoxicating as my breathing quickens.

I'm suddenly reminded of a memory. My seventeenth birthday, when my father called me to his office and told me just how ashamed he was of me. Just how disappointed.

Most Oreans who inherited magic showed some sign of it by the time they were fifteen. I'd been waiting for two extra years, and there wasn't a single morning I didn't wake up and pray for something—anything—to come out. I just needed the tiniest scrap of magic, and my father wouldn't hate me so much, my people wouldn't gossip about me, the servants wouldn't pity me.

I waited and waited and *waited*. Yet nothing ever came. I still remember that look on my father's face, the sneering hate. Without magic, I was useless to him, to Highbell. A wasted heir who couldn't hold the throne on her own. A disappointment in the Colier line.

All my life, that's been my worth—my own lacking.

So this...this fantastical sliver of a chance that they're telling me has my breath quickening, my gaze sharpening. The heart in my chest tenses at the possibility.

Having power is all I've ever wanted.

"My magic works in mysterious ways, my queen," Fassa goes on. "I believe the gods will see all those who have wronged you, all of your betrayals and hardships, and they will allow my magic to bestow something glorious in you. Something...*powerful*."

"Magic," I breathe. "You think you can give me magic of my own."

"Is that not your heart's desire, Majesty?" Pruinn cuts in quietly where he's leaning against a gray pillar. "My magic is never wrong. It led you here for this reason."

My mind whirls as much as the mist that covers the atrium's glass roof. A small laugh escapes me. "It sounds too good to be true."

"You deserve it," he says with a soft smile.

"Exactly," Fassa cuts in. "The gods knew that you were the queen this land needs—that the Colier line is pure and right. The moment you arrived, we could feel that you were perfect. You are the queen that will raise Seventh Kingdom to glory. *You*. No one else."

Me.

My blood seems to sing, rightness flooding into my veins.

"What do you need me to do?"

The twins grin, and both of them stand to walk over to me in synchronized steps. They each hold out a hand for me to take. "All you need to do is say you agree."

I've never been more ready to do anything in my life.

I take their hands, letting them lift me to my feet. "I agree."

Behind them, Pruinn murmurs, "And so the bargain is struck."

I feel as if I'm gliding on clouds when I walk out of the atrium. The others stay behind as I leave, and I head down the hallway with the lovely fragrance of the blossoms still in my nose. I'm absentminded as I walk, yet just as I pass by a window, I jerk to a stop and turn around.

The mist.

It's leaked in here too, churning with both the light from the window and the shadows of the corridor. It's so thick I can't see through it, and that prickling feeling on the back of my neck returns.

It's silly that I start to back up, but I find my feet doing it anyway, even though I try to tell myself it's only mist.

I twist my ankle when I take another blind step backwards, and just as I suck in a breath at the pain, the mist tosses and seethes in front of me, making my eyes go wide as the light around it bends.

Then, I'm frozen in place as a hooded man steps out of the shadowed, swirling air.

"*You.*"

A deluge of fear dumps all over me, like a downpour of rain, though it doesn't quite flood away my repose.

I know who he is, even though I only saw him once for those brief seconds. I've memorized that shadowed face hidden beneath his cloak.

"You killed Jeo. You tried to kill me."

The man lifts his gloved hand, pulling back his hood and revealing his face to me, and I suck in a breath. Just as he manipulated the light and shadow around him, his brown skin is marbled, pale patches around his nose, mouth, and chin, and another at his neck. His eyes are deep ebony, no differentiation between his iris and pupil.

"You followed me all this way to kill me?"

At the back of my head, I recognize I should feel a sharper stab of fear, yet I don't. I can't.

The man tips his head down, while the mist billows at his sides.

"Yes," he says, and the sudden sound of his voice sends a shockwave down my spine. It sounds rough. Labored. As if he hasn't spoken in a very long time. His expression too is flat, no pulling of his cheeks, no creases in his lips. Perhaps he always looks stony and blank. "That is what I was bid to do."

My back stiffens. "And you think you're going to do that now?"

I'm a second away from calling out to the others when he shakes his head. "That doesn't matter now. I have been watching, Queen Malina, and I don't like what I've been seeing."

I feel my brows pull into a frown of offense. "I beg your pardon?"

"Do you not feel it? The magic in the air?"

"If you're not going to kill me, then you can turn right back around and leave this place," I snap. "I should have you drawn and quartered for what you did to my saddle and guards."

"You could try," he says. "But you wouldn't succeed."

Anger curls down my back. "You're ruining my day, and I was having a rather good one."

"That's just it," he says, taking a step forward, and it's far too close to be appropriate. So close, in fact, that I can feel the heat from his body as the misty shadows around him follow his movements, nearly stroking over my skin and making me shiver, making my pulse jump. "You've been having a good day every day since you've gotten here. You haven't questioned anything at all."

"What would I question?" I reply with scorn. "I'm a queen, this is a castle. They're treating me as they should, especially after the ordeals I suffered."

The man makes a noise that I think is supposed to be a laugh, though it sounds like gravel being scraped against glass. "I thought you were supposed to be at least a little bit intelligent with all of that cold bitch cunning."

"How *dare*—"

"Look around you," he says, cutting me off. "*See. Observe*. You can't trust the people here."

I scoff. "Coming from the assassin who's here to kill me."

His dark eyes go flat. "Maybe I should finish you right here and now, since you're so unwilling to listen."

I open my mouth as if I'm going to reply, but instead, I shout out as loudly as I can for help.

The man doesn't move. He doesn't so much as twitch. The assassin simply watches me with dark eyes that I think might be made entirely of shadow. My heart slams against my chest when I hear footsteps running my way, but I can't look away from him.

"Wake up, and don't smell the flowers, Cold Queen, before it's too late. You have to find a way to break whatever bargain you've made, because at this point, I don't think your death is going to cut it."

He pulls up his hood and disappears in a swirl of fathomless smoke, and by the time the three men reach me, there's nothing here but gray-tinged light coming in from the window.

"What is it? What's wrong?" the twins ask, faces synchronized with concern.

I have no idea why I lie.

"Nothing," I answer, shaking my head, putting on an unadorned smile. I already feel so much better with them here. "I twisted my ankle and thought I would need help to walk back to my turret, but I'm alright."

They look at me with worry. "Are you sure, my queen?"

"Yes. Could you have luncheon brought up to my rooms later? I think I'll stay up for the rest of the day."

They both bow at the waist, cutting a bend into their crisp shirts. "Of course, Your Majesty."

I nod in thanks and start to turn, but not before I see Pruinn watching me with a frown. I turn and walk away, limping slightly as I go, warily eyeing the mist outside each window.

Yet by the time I get back to my rooms, when I'm basking in the bath soon after, the shock of seeing the assassin has faded. As I breathe in the perfumed steam, I sigh in contentment, all my worries bubbling away with the suds of the soap.

He was trying to scare me, trying to deter me from gaining power, because I'll bet he can't kill me while I'm in this castle. Fassa and Friano are too powerful. I'll bet the assassin simply hoped to lure me away so he can finish the job. Trick me so that I don't end up more powerful than Tyndall.

He said he's been watching? Fine. Come the new moon, he can watch me rise up to glory and be rewarded with power.

Then he truly won't like what he sees.

CHAPTER 45

AUREN

Three timberwings soar through the sky, cutting lines into the clouds and leaving trails of vapor behind.

We've been flying hard, day and night, only stopping for a handful of hours so we can all sleep and the timberwings can have some much needed rest and time to hunt. Being around Argo while I practiced my gold-touch helped me not be quite so scared of him, but it's still a bit terrifying to be strapped to his back hundreds of feet up in the sky.

Although, I have it easy. Slade keeps me tucked against his chest, layered in coats and blankets, his strong body the perfect pillar for me to sleep and rest against while he holds the reins.

He's been exhausted for the whole trip, ever since he expelled so much of his power into the rip. And even though he never complains, I can see the weariness clinging to him every time we dismount. I offer to take the reins so he can rest instead, but he always declines.

Stubborn male.

The other timberwings always ride close enough to see. Digby sits behind Judd, and just past him, on a timberwing with more snowy feathers than the rest, is Lu. I think they might be keeping an extra eye on Slade, just in case.

When we packed up our meager camp this morning out on a mountaintop of rock and snow, Slade told me if we made good time, we'd be arriving at Fourth Kingdom tonight.

I felt it several hours ago—the permanent change in the air. Steadily but surely over the past few days, the air has become less stark, the whipping wind not as frigid. Now, as dusk descends, the temperature is almost...*warm*. I keep trying to steal looks below, desperate to see the landscape of Fourth Kingdom, but we're above the clouds, the coverage too thick to see through.

And then, night falls.

That's exactly what it looks like, too. A brooding darkness seems to tumble over the sky, crashing against the lingering dusk and shattering it into obscurity. But this night is different. It's not shoveled out to the bare bones of sparse cold. It's not sharpened with pricks of frigid ice or whipped through with the bluster of frozen wind to beat against our backs.

Instead, there's a warmth beneath night's cloak, one that I haven't experienced in a very long time. Ten years of living and breathing the numbing cold that never ends. Of footsteps crunching over snow, of eyes that never saw the unhindered sun. Of skin always covered against the arctic elements.

In my part of the world, in Highbell and even in Fifth Kingdom, the sun never could break through those frozen clouds. Never could compete with its blizzards and sleet. So as we fly through the night, I bask in the warming air, feeling like a layer of perpetual frost is slowly melting away from me.

When I'm nearly lulled to sleep by its balmy comfort, I feel Slade lean down against my left cheek. "We're here."

My breath catches in my throat, and I turn around to ask him how he knows, when Argo suddenly lets out a loud call that knocks me back. Slade's arm tightens around my middle, hand splaying over my stomach. "Hold on."

I might've gotten a bit used to flying on Argo's back, but his landing dives are another thing entirely.

My hands grip the saddle strap in front of me, thighs locking around the beast just as it points its nose at the ground and starts to drop. A scream threatens to spew from my mouth, but I manage to grapple it in my throat.

The dive sends my braid whipping backwards and air streaming against my face, making it almost impossible to keep my eyes open. Slade holds me firmly against him as we start to plummet past the clouds.

My stomach lurches, feeling like the rest of my body is dropping without it, while Argo's body streams down, down, down, a coat of condensation streaming off his feathers like backwards rain.

And then, just when I think I might actually vomit from the speed of this nosedive, Argo tips up his body and lets out his massive wings. A rush of air sucks into my lungs as our descent goes from breakneck to surprisingly gentle.

Regaining my equilibrium, I take another shaky breath, just as Slade's lips are once again at my ear. "Look, Auren."

My eyes peel open to the dark.

And I see...

The ground is dark. Not glowing white from the moon and the snow. No snow. There's not so much as a flake of it anywhere in sight. And just that, just *that*, is enough to make my eyes go wide. But then, my gaze truly takes in what I'm seeing.

There are rivers *everywhere*. As far as I can see, their streams are glittering below like roots stretching out from an ancient tree. They arc and bend, sparkling surfaces reflecting the lights that seem to be sewn into their twisting hems.

In the night, I can only see the shadowed contours of buildings and walls, but lights are peppered throughout the city, giving off this effervescent feel amidst the shimmering water.

The other timberwings drop down to fly at our sides, and Slade lifts a finger, pointing ahead. I lift my gaze from the ground to follow the direction he's indicating, and my mouth drops open.

There's a massive mountain just ahead, so large that I can't truly take in its scope until the light of day. But right at the base of it sits Fourth Kingdom's castle.

It's dark, even despite the way its windows glow with light from within, and more lights litter the pinnacles and parapets. There are pointed turrets at the top, and notches of vertical grooves in its high, smooth walls. Yet instead of ramparts or outer defensive walls around it, there's a massive moat that surrounds it. With the moat at its sides and front, plus the mountain at its back, it looks more like a fortress than a castle.

One of the other timberwings lets off a call into the air, making the others answer, as if they're celebrating our arrival. I almost want to let out a call right along with them, and I hear Judd do just that.

But even though I'm more than ready to be done flying, Fourth Kingdom really is beautiful from up here. With dewy air and radiant rivers, friendly lights dappling the dark landscape, it's a sight to behold, and as Argo and the other timberwings fly straight for it, my anticipation bubbles up like foam on a lake.

Behind me, Slade's mouth skims against the shell of my ear. "Welcome to Brackhill."

Hidden behind the rising spires at the very back of Brackhill Castle, there's a flat-top roof open to the stars.

One after another, the timberwings circle overhead in a kind of synchronized dance. Argo is the first to touch down as he lands in the center, his talons clicking against the ashen stone floor. The roof is amazing, with the view of the mountain behind us and the protected yet open sight of the sky. It makes me forget how travel weary I am.

"This is beautiful."

Slade's voice comes against my ear. "It's our private entrance when we get back to the castle on our timberwings."

"I love it."

The others land beside us, and Slade reaches around to unbuckle us from the saddle's straps. He swings up and off, stomping his feet for a second before he grips me by the waist and lifts me off. As soon as my feet hit the floor, my legs tingle, and I groan at how sore I am from riding nonstop.

"You did very well for your first long trip," Slade tells me. "I'm sorry we couldn't take more breaks."

"Getting here faster was better anyway."

Judd jumps down and stretches his back, rolling his shoulders. "Fuck. It's good to be home and out of that Divine-damned snow."

Lu grins from where she's petting her timberwing and feeding it a scrap from the pouch around her waist. "If you're thinking it was just shrinkage from the cold, you're going to be really disappointed."

Slade laughs under his breath, and Judd chucks a glove at her face. She catches it, of course.

"Your Majesty, welcome back."

I nearly jump as a guard peels away from the smooth wall to tuck into a bow. He's dressed all in black leathers, very similar to the Fourth army soldiers, except he has the sigil of the twisted tree sewn in brown thread onto the left flap of his vest, and boots that are far less travel-worn. My eyes dart around the rest of the wall, which I thought was empty, but I quickly notice that there are three other guards hidden in the shadows.

"Marcoul, you're a sight for sore eyes," Slade greets the gray-haired man with a clap on his back and a smile. "Has the royal envoy arrived?"

"Yes, Sire," the guard replies. "They were given approval, and they're staying on the third floor."

Slade nods, sharing a look with Lu as she comes striding over. "Good. Anything else we should know about?"

"Nothing for me to report."

"Thanks, Marcoul."

The man bows and slips back into his post, body nearly disappearing against the shadows. I notice that the lanterns along the top of the wall that surrounds this open roof have very precise placement. Just enough to light the way for timberwings to land, but plenty of shadow to keep the guards hidden, especially with the twin turrets behind us.

Turning around, I look for Digby, immediately noticing the way he's gone pale, the hunch of his body and the sweat beaded against his brow.

I hurry over. "Are you alright?"

"Fine," he says gruffly. "Can someone show me my room?"

"And send for a mender," I add, ignoring his glower.

Judd appears at his side. "Come on, old man," he says cheerfully. "You get the best room of the house—the one right next to mine."

Digby huffs, but he starts to hobble away with Judd, going through the domed archway in the center of the wall, leading to a set of stairs that feeds down into the belly of the castle. As soon as they're a few paces away, I join Lu and Slade. "Don't worry," Slade tells me. "Judd will make sure our castle mender sees to him right away."

I blow out a breath of relief. "Thank you."

"You need anything?" Lu asks, turning to Slade.

"I'm good. Go get some sleep."

She nods but then lets out a sigh, looking down at her feet. "I already miss my slippers."

"Why don't you just get a pair out here?" I ask.

"They wouldn't be the same," she says forlornly, just as she turns and goes the same way Judd and Digby did.

Slade walks over to Argo and scratches him on the neck. "Go get yourself some food and settle back into your favorite perch." The beast trills like he understands completely, nudging his arm. Then he leaps into the air, the others following him, disappearing toward the mountain right behind us.

At my curious look, Slade says, "Their perch is built into the mountain just below."

"They're smart creatures."

"Very," he replies, coming to stand beside me. "It's late, but I can still give you a tour now if you want to stretch your legs?"

It's on the cusp of my lips to say yes, but then I notice the fatigued lines cutting through his face, tucked into the corners of his strained eyes.

"No, let's just go rest. You can give me a tour tomorrow."

With a nod, he places his hand on the small of my back and leads me toward the archway. Three steps past it, and we're descending a set of spiraling stairs rimmed in iron. My gloved hands skim down the curved banister, the steps slightly dizzying. When we reach the bottom, there's a corridor with worn gray rock and a long stretch of green carpet in the very center, while sconces held in iron casings flicker against the bare walls.

The ceiling is dropped here, the path narrow and feeling slightly claustrophobic, but then, Slade takes me down another set of stairs, this one wide and straight down. When we get to the bottom, the whole castle seems to open up around us. I clasp the open banister, looking down three more flights of stairs to see the grand hall below.

Dark wood and smooth white walls dominate the space. The open upper level corridors are somewhat like the ones in Ranhold, since I'm able to see clear across to the other side, every staircase and hallway visible within the squared center.

Except here, there are elaborate wood carvings that stretch from the pillars that secure the staircases, going all the way up to the ceiling. The thickly pitched wood reminds me of the inside of a musical instrument, complete with curved hollows and the daintiest of copper strings pulled from the points in the middle of the ceiling, leading down like draped tapestry to the arched windows.

"This is amazing," I say, hands curling around the smooth wood beneath my fingers.

Across from us and down a level, I can see the others, just as they split off from a lower staircase. Lu continues down one direction, while Judd and Digby turn right and go down the hall across the castle from us, and Judd leads a limping Digby inside.

"He's more hurt than he's letting on," I murmur with concern.

Slade slides up beside me. "His injuries were pretty extensive, but Hojat is the best mender there is, and if he truly didn't think he should've made the trip, he would've put his foot down. Digby is tough, and I have another good mender here too. He'll be looked after."

"He was my guard for a long time. The only one I could ever trust. I always kind of looked at him like a sort of father figure. He didn't just guard me. He *protected* me. Sometimes, even from other guards."

I see Slade's head turn to look at me.

"Midas was always very strict about me being guarded in Highbell, but he wasn't as good about his threats as he thought he was," I explain. "It was a common occurrence for some of the guards to behave...less than gentlemanly."

I see his fingers tighten against the railing, and then with a perfectly serious tone, he says, "If you give me names, I'll rot their brains from their skulls."

A startled laugh escapes me as I turn toward him. "I think a lot of them didn't really have impressively thriving brains to begin with, so we'll just let them rot in their own time."

"Fine," he says, sounding slightly disappointed.

I laugh again, but a yawn takes over the tail end of it, making my jaw nearly crack from how wide it is.

Slade reaches down and takes my hand in his. "Come on, let's get some real sleep, on a real bed with real pillows and blankets."

"You really know how to sweet talk."

Chuckling, he leads me down a set of stairs, but instead of going to the opposite end where the others are staying, we keep on this opposite end. We pass a guard on our way, who tips her head down in greeting, shooting me a curious look as we go.

The hallway walls on this level are studded with strips of the same carved and curving wood, making the ceilings appear taller. Every few feet, there's a window tucked into the wall's notches, the bubbled glass plaited with strips of iron. It's too dark to see anything outside, so our reflections are all the windows reveal for now.

At the end of the corridor, Slade opens the door and then slips to the side, holding out a hand for me. As soon as I enter, there's an immediate sense of familiarity, because the room just *feels* like Slade. There's a masculine fireplace molded with an intricately carved black corbel. Set on the floor in front of it, there's a trio of dark sofas and a table at the center.

On the opposite end is a doorway, and Slade leads me through there where I find a bed set on a raised platform, four stone pillars at each corner made of the same stone as the floor. It makes the big bed look even bigger, and the black and dark green bedding looks so plush that I can't wait to drop right inside of it.

"Do you need anything to eat?" Slade asks behind me as he gently removes my coat.

"I think I'm too tired for food right now."

He takes my coat and disappears into another door where I can see clothes and weapons hanging inside. I hear the telltale sound of boots being dropped, and then he comes out again, his own coat gone as well. In his hands is a shirt that he hands to me. "We'll get you some proper clothing tomorrow, but for tonight, you can wear my shirt."

"That seems a little intimate," I tease as I pluck the clothing from his fingers.

Slade chuckles. "If you consider *that* intimate, then I'm in great need of making some things up to you." He reaches one arm behind him and strips the shirt from his body in one smooth motion that makes my mouth water, gaze pivoting to his abs.

"Eyes up here."

They snap up on command, and heat catches in my cheeks. "I wasn't checking you out," I say.

"No, I seem to remember it was my ass you liked to do that with."

I narrow my eyes on him, and even though he's right, I will never admit it. "I don't know what you're talking about."

"Mm-hmm. Come to bed, Goldfinch."

I point a finger at him. "No ravishing, Ravinger. We're both tired and you're still recuperating from a power drain. We need to sleep."

His eyes skate up my body as if it's something to relish, when really, I probably look like a wind troll with tangled hair and three-day-old clothing. "Fine. But I'll be ravaging you tomorrow. I'll wear tight pants to set the scene."

I roll my eyes, though my lips can't help but tip up into a smile. "Good luck with that," I tell him. "Can I use the bathroom to wash up?"

"Of course," he says as he walks over to the bed. "And you don't have to ask. Everything in this entire castle is yours. You may go wherever you like and do whatever you please."

He pulls back the covers while I just stare at him for a moment.

When he notices me still standing there, his brows crinkle. "What?"

I snap out of it. "Nothing."

Turning around, I quickly go through the only other door in here and close it behind me.

Go wherever you like and do whatever you please. He said it so casually. As if it's normal. As if I've ever heard it before in my life, when in fact, I have not.

A smile pulls at my cheeks, and it stays there the entire time I'm in the bathroom. My bladder feels like it's about ready to burst, so I quickly take off my gloves and use the toilet, and then wash my face and hands. I strip out of my old clothes, pulling on Slade's shirt before I find a comb and try to brush through my tangles as best I can. I head for the door on another yawn, but I hesitate whether or not I should put my leggings and socks back on, but no. I don't gild anything unless I want to.

As if to prove it to myself, I press my fingers against the comb again, calling up my magic, smiling when gold drips down the length of it. As soon as it's gilded, I drain the magic up, pressing my fingers against the marble countertop to make sure not a single drop comes out.

It's amazing how much easier it's already become.

When I walk out with a smile on my face, I'm ready to tell Slade that I'm actually going to sleep in *only* his shirt, but I stop when I see he's already fast asleep. His breaths are feeding in and out, his face relaxed, body slumped onto the plush bed. He looks so unburdened in his sleep that I just watch him for a moment, wishing he could have that same weightlessness when he's awake.

On bare feet, I pad over to the other side of the bed and slip beneath the covers as quietly and gently as I can so I don't disturb him. I try to leave some space between us out of habit, yet as soon as I'm in the bed with him, he seems to sense me.

His arm comes out, gripping me by the waist, and he tugs me over as if I weigh nothing, sliding me right up against his body. I hold my breath in surprise, going still, but he doesn't wake. He simply lets out a long exhale, as if he can relax even more now that I'm tucked against his side.

I fall asleep just as quickly as he did, with a sigh and a smile drifting from my lips.

CHAPTER 46

SLADE

I *wake up with a jerk*, eyes focusing on the crack of light cut from the edges of the heavy black curtains. Then my gaze falls to the bed beside me—the *empty* bed.

I sit up, running a hand down my face, realizing I didn't even wait for Auren to come out of the bathroom last night before I passed out. I didn't want to worry her, but the power drain was worse than usual. I got carried away, exhausted myself more than I should've, especially knowing I had Auren to protect on the journey home.

I suppose there's something to be said for returning to your own bed after months of being away. Last night was the best sleep I've had in months. The only thing I'm missing now is waking up with Auren beside me.

I wonder if she's still worried about staying in bed past morning. I can understand that she's had over a decade of conditioning herself to being up before the dawn, to not eat, drink, or touch anything once the sun comes up. But she doesn't have to do any of that anymore. She has more control than she knows, though some habits may be hard to break.

Getting up out of bed, I head for the bathroom where I wash up and then go into the closet to dress. Once I'm ready, I leave the bedroom, expecting to find her in the sitting room, but it's empty. I head for the door, and as soon as I step into the hall, one of my guards is doing his rounds, walking in the opposite direction.

When he looks over his shoulder and sees me, he stops, turning his back against the wall to give me a nod. "Your Majesty."

"Morning, Vaen. Have you seen Lady Auren?"

He shakes his head. "No, Sire, but we just did a shift change. I can go ask the previous guards?"

I shake my head. "That's alright, I'll find her."

Taking the stairs, I go down a level and head for the private breakfast room near Judd's rooms. We always eat our casual meals in there, hardly ever using the formal dining except when we have to. I pass another guard on the way, and then let myself in.

Lu looks up from the table just as she knocks Judd's propped feet off the top. "Well, look what the rot dragged in," she singsongs. "You overslept."

My brow arches as I walk forward. "Does being a king have no perks?"

"No," she and Judd both answer.

My gaze sweeps around. "Where's Auren? Did she already eat?"

"We thought she was with you," Lu tells me.

"Yeah, we haven't seen her yet this morning."

Dread fills me. "Neither of you have seen her?" I look around again, noticing Digby isn't here either. "Have you checked on Digby this morning?"

"No, but it's early."

I nod and head for the door. "She's probably with him."

"Or she might've gone to walk around the main floor?" Judd offers.

I should've given Auren a tour last night so she knew where everything was, or at least where to go for breakfast. "You put Digby in the silver room?"

"Yep."

When I get back out into the hallway, my stride takes me right to where Digby's staying, and I knock on the door. There's no answer right away, but I wait a moment, and then knock again, louder.

Worry crawls over my spine, making me roll my shoulders back, and I see Judd and Lu coming over from the corner of my eye. Just as I'm about to pound on the door with my fist, I hear him call out to wait. There's a shuffling noise, and then the door is yanked open by a bleary-eyed Digby, who clearly just rolled out of bed, his gray hair sticking up. He looks at me, gaze casting to the others behind me. "Yeah?"

"I take it Auren isn't with you."

His brows draw together. "No."

I spin around, my worry now coalescing into something tangible that presses right on my ribs, restricting each breath.

"I'll check the kitchens and the dining room," Lu says, spinning on her heel.

"The library too," I call after her, and she nods over her shoulder. Then, a thought occurs to me that makes my blood run cold.

"What room was Manu given?"

Judd's brows shoot up, like he hadn't thought of that either. "The blue room on the third floor. Do you think..."

"I don't know." I'm already striding away, my ribs continuing to constrict. "But if he did *anything* to fucking hurt her—"

Judd catches up with me, his face drawn tight.

"Alert the guards," I order. "Have a full scale search, have them—"

"Oy!"

Judd and I stop in our tracks, jerking around to look behind us. Even Lu, where she's already on the east stairwell, looks up and stops.

Digby leans against the door jam, glowering at me. "You don't know where Auren is."

Impatience prickles my neck, but I answer his non-question anyway. "No."

He limps over to me, and even though my mind is screaming at me to hurry up and go find her, I impatiently wait for him.

He looks up at me from beneath bushy eyebrows, lips pinched together with clear disapproval as he stops in front of me and gives me a once-over like I'm about to get lectured. "I thought you were smart."

I blink down at him. "*What?*"

He shakes his head and lets out a sigh. "My lady isn't in the kitchens or the dining room or the library."

Judd and I share a look while Lu comes walking over. "Okay...so you *did* see her this morning?"

"No," he says. "But I don't need to have seen her to know where she is. Just like *you* would know if you'd pull your head out of your ass for a second."

My jaw grinds so hard I'm surprised my teeth don't crack. "Explain."

"My lady lived in the north of the world for *ten years*. That's a decade of nothing but snow, seen through cages and windows and caves and *restrictions*." His arms cross in front of him. "If you know her at all, you'll know right where to find her. So where do you *think* she is right now, boy?"

He pins me with a pointed look, and realization dawns on me.

Digby nods tersely. "Good to see you're not completely hopeless." He then turns around and limps away, shutting his bedroom door while I'm left staring after him.

Judd gives a low whistle. "I think you just got told off, Rip."

"I never know if I should be insulted or impressed," I admit out loud.

"Let's just go with the second one," Lu tells me. "So...do you want us to help you look?"

I shake my head and start to walk away. "Digby was right. I think I know where to find her."

I take the stairs two at a time, back through the narrow corridor, and then up the spiral steps all the way to the roof.

I considered going out to the ground floor and checking the gardens, but Auren didn't have any proper clothes, so I think she would've preferred to go somewhere more secluded.

Just as I reach the top, I notice all three watch guards hanging around the archway, each of them looking in the same direction. I have a feeling I know what they're looking at and why they're in here, trying to give a semblance of privacy, rather than being at their normal stations on the roof.

When they notice me, they bow. "Sire."

I stop in my tracks when I see her. She didn't just come up to the roof. No, she also climbed up onto one of the turrets as well. She's there, lying against the steepled shingles, her golden skin glowing against the black stone that surrounds her.

For a moment, all I can do is watch. She looks like a sunlit goddess, gleaming in the light that's been sheltered from her, soaking up the rays as if the sun is blessed to shine on her.

"How long has she been up there?" I ask the guards quietly.

"Since dawn."

Nodding, I let my feet carry me toward her. "Go take a break."

I don't turn to look, but I hear their retreating footsteps as they wind down the spiral staircase, leaving us alone. I walk to the other end of the roof, my eyes zeroed in on the gilded figure.

The thought of her scaling the tower wall, even though it's only about ten feet tall, makes my nerves twist. I stop at the base of the turret, and then, using the nails driven into the side, climb up. Instead of entering through the walled opening where the guards keep watch in the tower, I keep going, my leg swinging up to the turret's steep roof.

I straighten and walk over to her, finding her elbows propped up beneath her, bare legs stretched out and crossed at the ankles. Hair flowing down her back, face tipped up toward the sky.

She's *basking* in the sun, and it looks as if that's all the daylight was ever created for. She's so breathtaking up here in only my shirt, that I have half a mind to drag the guards back and demand they pluck out their own eyes for seeing what's mine.

Yet my possessive thoughts are driven away when I notice the streaks down her cheeks.

Alarm has me dropping to a kneel beside her. "Goldfinch," I murmur quietly so that I don't scare her. But I must not have been as stealthy as I thought, because she doesn't so much as flinch. "What's wrong? Why are you crying?"

Her eyes flutter open, lashes clumped together with gilded tears. But she looks at me, and my heart stops. "Can you hear it?" she whispers.

I pause, ears straining, but all I hear are faint sounds from the city below and the constant draw of the waterfall at the base of the mountain.

"Hear what?"

And she smiles, through the tears dried on her cheeks,

through the glassiness of her eyes. The sight is so damn beautiful that it's hard to breathe.

"The sun," Auren answers quietly, tone filled with a tentative, innocent joy. One that you're afraid of saying too loud in case it breaks. "She's singing to me."

Emotion clogs in my throat as I watch her tip her head back again. Watch her eyes close. I draw a knuckle down her soft cheek. "And what does she sing, Goldfinch?" I murmur.

Her smile breaks through like the sunlight above us. "The song of home," she says. "The sun is singing the song of home."

My chest swells, and when she reaches a hand up and tugs at my arm, I lie back with her, situating until we're arm to arm, leg to leg.

"Listen," she whispers.

So I do. I thread my fingers through her own, and I listen.

But my song of home doesn't come from the sun. Mine comes from her.

CHAPTER 47

AUREN

I have no idea how long Slade stays up on that rooftop with me, but by the time we climb down, I'm buzzing with bolts of energy. It doesn't matter that I woke up before the dawn, I feel invigorated. Restored. *Alive.*

"I want to be outside today," I tell Slade as we walk toward the archway where the guards are standing.

"Eyes up, gentleman," Slade says, and I don't understand for a minute until I look down and realize I'm still only in his shirt...and nothing else.

Their heads tip up comically fast, eyes going so far up that it's a wonder they don't see clear to the back of their skulls.

"I probably need some clothes, huh?" I say.

"It would be preferable so I don't feel like stabbing daggers into my loyal guards' eyes."

One of the said guards lets out a choked cough.

"I'm going to frown upon eye stabbing, for the record."

"I'll make a note of it."

I pause just before we go through the archway, looking over my shoulder at the open, clear sky. At the unobstructed *sun*. I haven't seen it in so long.

I'd forgotten the way it felt.

The way I could just let my eyes drift close. Let my head tip up. How the light shone red through my lids and the way warmth seemed to lay against my skin, from forehead to feet. The way it sunk into my pores and soothed every memory of cold away.

It called to me.

Even before it rose in the sky, I heard it. I slipped out of bed and wandered back upstairs, letting its soundless voice draw me here where I could stand on a roof beside a mountain and just...*feel*.

Ten years. It's been *ten years* since I felt sunshine like that on my face. Without any clouds to block it, without any storm to sully it.

Not once, while I was up there on that roof, did my magic try to come out unbidden. Instead, I let it pool in my palm, growing warm in the morning sunlight, letting it bask for a moment just as I was. Then, when I called for it to sink back into my skin, it did. Easily. So easily that it was almost effortless.

I think my gold missed the sunlight, too.

"Auren?"

I turn away from the sun's caress to look at Slade, who's watching me with something on his expression that I can't quite read.

I give him a small smile. "I was lying back and enjoying the sunlight so much that I didn't even think to get a proper look at your kingdom."

He continues to study me, and I wonder for a second if I've said something wrong. But then he tells me, "How would you like it if I showed you around today?"

My heart skips a beat. "You mean...leave the castle?"

"Would you like that? To see the city?"

"Would I *like* that?" I repeat breathlessly. "I..." My words trail off, like I'm too overwhelmed to speak them. Aside from the trip from Highbell to Ranhold, I've never been allowed to leave the safety of the castles I've been kept in. "Walk out into the city, just like that?" I ask.

He nods.

"But..." I look around at the guards. "But I'm *gold*," I point out.

Slade's lip quirks. "So you are."

I take a quick step toward him and lower my voice. "People will recognize me as Midas's gold-touched *pet*," I say, spitting out that word with disdain.

"They might, yes," he replies with a nod. "This is *your* life, Auren. If you wish to stay away from prying eyes, then that's what we'll do. But you don't have to hide here. You are nobody's pet to be kept. Your life is your own, and the choice is yours."

The choice is mine.

So unprecedented. Choices have never been mine, so I don't want to waste a single one.

"I don't want to stay inside anymore." The confession

rushes out of me, like the words are afraid that if they don't speak quickly enough, the opportunity will be taken away.

He grins, instantly making my own lips tug up. "It's your first day out of the snow and the cold. I think that's cause to celebrate."

I smile so wide that my cheeks hurt, but then it falters. "But what about Manu? Don't you have things you need to handle now that we're back?"

"Manu and the kingdom can wait for one more day. You're more important."

My heart feels like it swells and does a flip all at once. "Are you sure?"

He places his hand at my back—very *low* on my back— the tips of his fingers grazing the curve of my ass as his voice tilts down close to my ear. "Come on, Goldfinch. Let's go exploring."

Exploring.

I can't deny the thrill that goes through me at that word. With a grin, I race ahead for the stairs, and I feel a rush of air when my shirt rides up just a little too far. I clamp my hands down on the hem at my butt, looking over my shoulder. "Whoops."

Slade's eyes are zeroed in on my ass. "Eyes are still up?" he calls over his shoulder.

"Yes, Sire!" three voices shout back. *Quickly.*

With a face that's half exasperation and half amusement, he makes his way to me until I can feel the warmth of his body at my back. "Come, Lady Auren," he practically purrs. "Let's go get you some clothes before I forget all about

554

exploring and decide to clear the castle so I can explore *you* instead."

My breath stutters.

"Honestly, that's a good second option..."

He chuckles darkly behind me, making me tingle all over, just as he gives my ass a little tap. "Get moving."

I practically float all the way down the stairs.

I end up wearing simple brown leggings and a black tunic, both of which are soft and comfortable and so much thinner than I'm used to compared to the thickly woven fabrics in Sixth and Fifth. Slade gives me a cloak as well, and because of habit and precaution, my gloves are securely over my hands.

The others opt to go to the city with us, but when I try to talk Digby into staying, he just glowers at me and then walks off to get ready.

When Slade takes me down to the large open entry hall, everyone's already there waiting. Lu is wearing her usual army leathers, while Judd is wearing a bright orange tunic that rivals the mustard of his hair, making him look a bit like a poppy flower.

Digby is wearing borrowed clothes just like me, still scowling, as if he's ready to ward off more lectures about how he should stay here and rest.

"I'm surprised you both wanted to come," I say as we reach Lu and Judd by the main doors.

"Of course we do. We haven't done anything fun in

ages," Judd says. "King Rot is always dragging us around the world and making us destroy his enemies."

Slade rolls his eyes. "Last I checked, *you* haven't destroyed anyone this trip."

"That's true," Judd replies, as if he's disappointed about this. "No wonder I'm so bored."

"Which is exactly why we need a trip to the city," Lu puts in.

"Yep. Pub drinks," Judd says with a wag of his brows. "You haven't lived until you've been to the Burnt Cat Tavern."

I scrunch up my nose. "They don't *serve* that, right?"

"Only on Tuesdays," Lu quips. "Ready?"

Am I ready?

I'm not sure, because I haven't been out in an unprotected public like this in a very long time.

"It's your choice, Auren," Slade murmurs beside me, and I know that if I changed my mind right now, he'd turn us back around and let me stay in his rooms, no questions asked.

"I'm ready."

Digby is at my side in a second to escort me out of the castle, just like he did all those months ago when I left Highbell for the first time. That was the catalyst, the tipping point for all the chopped trees to start falling down. The moment that changed the course of my life.

When Brackhill's carved black doors open wide, I see a flash of Highbell's gilded ones in my head. But instead of stepping out into a frozen night, I walk over the threshold and am greeted by the warmth of day.

The front is paved with dark cobblestones smoothed

from tread. The stones ring around an impressive obelisk statue that's straight ahead, the onyx stone pillar reaching up toward the sky and creating the perfect walls for the climbing vines to wrap around.

I turn to look at the castle, and my eyes go up and up and up. With grooved black walls, arched windows, and pointed rooftops, Brackhill looks intimidating, stately, and beautiful all wrapped up into one. The way it's set against the mountain makes it look bigger than it is, and the moat of sparkling water on either side wraps around it like a crystalline cloak, with a small dark bridge curved right in the middle.

Slade points at the gathered horses ahead, where there's a dark carriage at the back with a driver seated and ready. "We can take the carriage down, if you like. It's a bit of a slope from here, but once we get past the falls, it'll only be a few minutes into town."

I glance at the carriage and then at the loose horses that the others are walking toward. Lu swings her leg up and over a reddish-brown one, while Judd shows Digby to a smaller dappled mare.

"Actually," I begin, tearing my eyes away. "I'd rather like to ride."

"Would you?" Slade asks, looking pleasantly surprised.

"Yes. I still remember riding horses when I was little," I say. "But after, I rode quite a lot with Midas. Until we reached Highbell, and then..."

And then I never rode again for a decade.

"I don't think I want to be stuck inside the walls of a carriage on such a nice day. At least for right now?"

He nods like he completely understands that. "Then we'll ride."

"I'm not sure if Digby should be on a horse…"

My guard hears me, tossing back a brusque, "I'm fine."

When I look to Slade, he just shrugs. "You know he's too stubborn to stay behind."

I let out a sigh. "Yeah."

In no time at all, Slade's staff has brought out two more saddled horses. Slade's monster of a stallion looks both statuesque and a bit mean, with a shiny black coat and probably a good eighteen hands high.

Meanwhile, I get a pretty buckskin horse with golden skin and a black mane, who looks far more agreeable. I walk over to get a better look at her. "A bit of a mix of our colors, don't you think?" I ask Slade.

He smirks as he comes over to help me mount. "Her name's Honey. She's a sweetheart, though she's been known to have a temper."

I stroke a hand down her neck. "Then we'll get along just fine." I continue to pet her for a second, running my hands over her dark mane, but when my smile slips, Slade notices.

"What's wrong?"

"There was a horse that I rode out of Highbell. Crisp. I don't know what happened to him after the Red Raids, but he was a good horse."

Of course, when I think of Crisp, I think of Sail, and when I think of him…

"I don't know if I've ever really processed what happened that night. I thought you were the bigger monster," I admit with a humorless laugh. "I was a fool. If only I'd learned to use my magic after dark back then. I'd never have let the captain…"

"Let the captain *what*?"

My eyes spring to Slade's face. "Nothing."

His gaze goes dark, and he takes a step forward, giving us more privacy from the staff and the others mounting their horses. "Did he hurt you that night?"

There's a threat of dark promise in his tone. "Not me. Rissa. I helped her too late. By the time the sun came up…" I trail off, shaking my head. "He's a golden statue somewhere in the middle of the Barrens, hopefully piled over with mountains of snow by now."

The muscle in Slade's jaw jumps, his posture gone stiff.

"I'm sorry for bringing that up," I say with a shake of my head. "I don't know why I did. Let's just…move on? I want to enjoy the day and not think about *that*."

He seems to gather himself, burying the anger in his eyes. "Alright. But I want a list, Auren."

"A list?"

"Of everyone who's ever hurt you."

My eyebrows jump up. "Why?"

"I think you know," he tells me, his sharp gaze cutting right through me. "And we are going to talk about all of this very soon." I swallow hard, but I can't deny the thrill that shoots down my back, because I've never had this before him—this fierce protector.

I've had a false one. If only I'd known what a true one looked like, I probably never would've been fooled in the first place.

Clearing my throat, I try to wave him off, try to lighten the mood again. "Well. We have a lot of things to still talk about. Like why everyone here wears such tight pants," I say as I look around at all the guards. "Not that I'm complaining."

Slade cocks a brow, but the last of the anger seems to edge out from his eyes. "The only ass I want you checking out is *mine*."

I give off a lazy shrug. "I can't make any promises," I say breezily before I nock my foot into the stirrup and start to mount the horse. As I swing my other leg over, there's a sharp pinch on my butt. I sit down in surprise, jolting the horse a little as I shoot Slade an incredulous look over my shoulder. "Ow!"

He gives me a shrug as he walks to his stallion. "We'll discuss *that* more later as well."

I smirk as I gather the reins.

As soon as we're all situated, the five of us plus a few guards at our back begin to make our way across the bridge ahead.

Digby stays faithfully at my right and slightly behind me, while Slade rides just beside me at my left. Judd and Lu lead the way, while guards trail behind us. Even with this many of us, our party is small compared to what a normal royal enclave would be. I don't think Midas ever traveled without a host of guards, though perhaps that's because everything he owned was gilded, and he had no real power of his own to protect his stolen wealth.

Slade is a force all on his own.

We travel over the bridge, passing the long stretch of

moat, and then we breach the top of the grassy hill, where the city opens up beneath us like a perfect picture. Rivers are everywhere, winding through the city, spilling into lakes both big and small.

There are boats everywhere too, and I can see several areas of river docks and bridges. The houses seem to be built so close to the water that people have docks for gardens and boats instead of horses. Some of the buildings are even built up on posts, right on the water. And all along, the ground is green and the air is warm and wet, and it's like nothing I've ever experienced before.

As we begin to make our way down, grass hugs the winding line of the road, and trees are speckled along the hills, spread out enough to breathe. To our right, far enough that I can't quite hear the rushing water, are waterfalls that pour from the side of the mountaintop at least a hundred feet up. Water pitches down in a plunge of white froth, creating fractured rainbows within the clinging gray mist.

I can't see the bottom of the falls since it's blocked with trees, but the water carries itself to me, the river stretching out to greet the road. Just a stone's throw away, it winds alongside the path before splitting itself in several different directions. At the base of the hill, I can see where it branches off throughout the city, feeding all of the massive waterways cut into the land.

"I don't think I've ever seen so much green or so much water in my life." I turn around to look at Digby over my shoulder. "Are you looking, Dig?"

"I'm looking, my lady."

Beaming, I turn to Slade, finding that he's already watching me. "Such a pretty view."

"I'm glad you like it," he says.

Being out here is sublime, with the sun on my scalp and the fresh air in my lungs.

When we make it to the bottom of the slope where the land levels out, the road and the river both swerve toward the largest lake. "It's called Compass Lake," Slade tells me. "See how it's circular save for that point there?"

My eyes track the line from the lake that seems to stretch out like a prong, pointing back toward the castle.

"Compass always points us the way home," Lu calls back.

I glance at Slade curiously. "Is it home to you? Brackhill?"

His face grows contemplative for a moment. "I don't think anywhere in Orea will ever truly feel like home."

I nod in complete understanding, because I've always felt the same. But this place, I think it could feel like *almost* home. I think it could feel like enough.

Though nothing will ever really compare to Annwyn. I may have been taken away as a child, I may have forgotten most everything about it, but I still remember the *feel* of it. But maybe that's just what home is. A feeling.

The closer we get to the river, the more people we see. At first, there are just a few carts and horses that pass us by, but soon, we're right in the hub of activity, where the city is bustling.

Fishermen pull in their nets from stretched out piers. Shop buildings are lined up one after another along the street, their backs facing the lake, and their fronts made of smoothed stone the color of dolloped cream, with roofs pitching back straight to the water. Almost all of them have their doors flung wide open, probably to feed the fresh breeze in. Without the soft wind drifting off from the water, the humid, warm air would feel much more stifling. As it is now, there's a perfect balance of warm and cool.

The moment people realize that their king is in their midst, there's a concentric effect that surrounds the city. Like a ripple, people start to call out or bow or cheer or line up. It's not just King Ravinger they call for either. Both Judd and Lu are apparently well known too, because the people seem to respect and recognize them just as much.

But I see it. The moment their excitement at seeing the army captains and their king shifts to something else. The moment when they spot me. There's a definitive stiffening that treads over the crowd, a rigidness to their stares and tight mouths moving, and I hear snatches of those tense words the further we go down the city's road.

That's her—the golden saddle.

She killed King Midas.

She stole his magic.

What if she steals our king's magic too?

I jolt on my horse so hard that I pull against Honey's reins too tightly, making her jerk to a stop. Two of the guards instantly come up on either side of Slade and me, as if to form a barrier between us and the crowd as their proclamations continue to be voiced. I loosen the reins, and Slade comes closer, while I yank up the hood of my cloak.

"What do they mean?" I ask, eyes spinning all around me. Even with Judd and Lu in front and the guards at our sides and back, I still feel exposed to this shock of impliable judgment. "Why are they saying I stole magic?"

I can see Slade's hold tighten on the reins, see his hesitation in the tic of his jaw muscle. "That's the story that's spread from Fifth Kingdom," he admits. "The story that Queen Kaila has helped spread."

"And you didn't think to tell me?" I practically hiss between my teeth.

"I didn't think this rumor was so widely accepted."

I look around at the leery faces as they strain to see me as our horses pass. "I'd say it's pretty damn accepted, Slade."

He can't argue otherwise.

"Do you want to go back?" he asks.

I start to nod, but then, I stop myself.

I've always had to shy away from crowds, always had to fit into Midas's narrative. And now, even though he's dead, he's still steering my public reputation.

For ten years, he took my power and pretended it was his own and now...

He's still taking. And yet, they're calling *me* the thief.

My power has never been my own, and for the first time, when I'm finally proud of it, when I'm finally mastering it, he's tainted this too. Made it seem like I took it from him?

The thought makes my blood boil so hot that the backs of my eyes sear with moisture.

"No," I say definitively, expression hardening. "I'm not a thief, and I'm not going to hide."

I'm not going to let Midas use my gold-touch to his death's advantage.

Pride flickers over Slade's face as I shove back my hood, letting it drop behind me. "I'm not going to run away like I'm guilty," I declare, sitting up straighter. "Let them look."

CHAPTER 48

AUREN

"You were right," I say across the long table. "The Burnt Cat really is the *best*."

Judd beams at me, lifting his tankard up in a toast. "Told you so. Best wine in Orea."

Nodding, I help myself to another drink, only to realize it's empty. I frown at the bottom of my wood cup, as if the sweating grooves inside will somehow produce more deliciousness. I'm vastly disappointed when it doesn't.

"I ran out."

"Would you like to have more?" Slade asks, though how I hear him inside such a noisy tavern, I'm not sure.

"Yes, please."

Judd led the way straight here, and the tavern owner quickly brought us into this private seating area in the back. The lighting is low, a fresh breeze coming in from the window behind me, and our round table is blocked by stacks of wine barrels that smell amazing.

I have to admit, the wine has helped my mood.

Slade lifts his hand, and the tavern owner comes bustling over. He's a short and stout man named Barut, with thinning hair and even thinner lips. Barut wipes his hands on his muddied apron. "What can I do for you, Sire?"

"Can you bring another pitcher of wine for the table? And we'll have more bread and cheese as well, Barut."

"Of course!" he says with a clap, beaming over at me with a crooked smile, his two front teeth tilted over each other like crossed arms. "How is everything else?"

"Perfect as always," Judd calls over.

The man's cheeks go ruddy with a bashful blush. "So glad to hear it, Sir Judd."

When he leaves and it's just the five of us again, I glower into my cup. I kept my chin up while we were outside on the street, but this widespread rumor of me stealing Midas's magic is both ironic and infuriating. Needless to say, my mood has plunged. Everyone else is trying to keep the atmosphere positive still, but I can tell that the rumors are bothering them too. Digby, however, is not amused in the slightest. Every time he heard someone say something about me outside, I thought he was going to leap off his horse. I think only his sore ribs held him back.

"Are you alright?" Slade asks, his arm braced on the back of my chair.

I nod. "I'm fine." When I realize how surly that sounded, I lift my gaze to him. "Thank you for taking me to the clothing shop—you didn't have to buy me all of that, by the way."

"You need clothes," he says with a shrug. "Plus, it's purely selfish."

"How so?"

He leans in close. "I get to rip every single piece off you. It's like getting to decide on the wrapping paper for my own gift."

A blush rises to my cheeks, and I check around the table, but Judd and Lu are talking, and Digby is busy glowering into his cup. "You sure that's a good idea?" I challenge? "I might steal your magic."

Slade gives me a pointed look. "You need to ignore them."

"That's pretty hard to do when I wasn't prepared."

He drags a hand down his face. "You're right, I'm sorry. I should've told you what some of the rumors were saying. I just wanted you to have a good day here."

"I know," I say, blowing out a breath. "I just hate that he's somehow made it so that my magic still isn't mine."

Slade's mouth tightens. "If people truly want to think that, then they're fools."

Just then, Barut comes back over, setting a tray of everything down in front of us. "There you are, Majesty. Enjoy."

Slade gives Barut a nod of thanks and then pours me more wine. I hum at my first sip.

Bright side, wine can't gossip.

I take a bite of the creamy cheese too, chewing on my

thoughts as much as the food before I ask, "Doesn't it bother you? That people think I'm seducing you for your magic?"

"I don't give a fuck what other people think."

"That's such a man thing to say," I reply with a slight roll of my eyes as I take another bite. "Women in this world have to be more careful. Perceived reputations can be life or death."

"That's true," he concedes, watching as I take another drink. "Reputations can also mean power."

"Says the king."

He leans in close, lips almost brushing my ear. "Says the king to the fae female who's conquered him completely."

I lick my wine-stained lips. "I've conquered no one."

"Goldfinch, you could conquer the entire world with a single look, if only you'd open your eyes."

"That's dangerous advice, considering what happened in Ranhold."

"That's all part of the fun, don't you think?"

I level him with a look. "I think I'm starting to learn that you're just as unhinged as some of the Orean rumors have claimed."

His devilish smirk only grows. "Oh, love, I'm worse."

The racing organ in my chest does a flip when he calls me *love*. "You're better than you give yourself credit for. You're good. To me, to your Wrath, to your people."

"If you knew what I was thinking right now, the last thing you'd call me is *good*."

I bury my blush in my cup as I take another long gulp. The heat of his words and the look in his eye have buoyed my mood significantly. He's at least tied with the wine.

"So, Gildy, where do you want to go next?"

My head jerks forward at Lu's question. "Oh, umm..." Everyone looks at me expectantly. "I'm not sure."

"We could take her past the watermill," Judd supplies. "Or maybe the perfume shop. Lots of ladies like to go there. Or the hattery."

Lu rolls her eyes. "Does she look like she wants a frilly hat?"

"We could go to the market at the docks," Judd offers instead. "But there will be lots of people down there."

I cast a questioning glance at Slade as I finish off the last of my cheese and a bite of bread. "Too many people?"

"We're all with you," he tells me. "Besides, like you said, you're not a thief, so you aren't going to hide like one. Let them see that these rumors are wrong."

With a nod, I look to Digby. "You up for it, Dig?"

"I go with you," he says simply as he drains his cup.

"Alright then. Let's do it."

Slade stands up and offers his hand to me, which I take after one last sip of wine.

As we make our way out of the tavern through a back door, I thank him for lunch. "The food here is much better than in Ranhold."

Lu makes a noise of disgust behind me. "They ought to be ashamed of themselves, drenching everything in syrup. Salt is far better than sugar."

"Ah, so *that's* why you're not sweet. Even your tastebuds reject it," Judd says as we all spill out onto the path. Lu tries to trip him, but he's nimble enough to leap right over her foot.

571

I take a deep breath of the outside air. The lake is just feet away, separated by the wooden dock and railings. There's an array of small boats tied up along the docking lines, each of them bobbing slightly in the water.

Slade walks over to the guards waiting around by the carriage, handing them the parcels of food he had Barut make up for them. The men give him nods of thanks, and I'm struck by how different things are here.

Midas would have *never* given his guards food. It wouldn't have even crossed his mind. It didn't matter if they'd been stuck outside in the horrible snow or waiting around for hours inside. And yet, he got the reputation of the *Golden King*, while Slade is nothing but rot and ruin.

After Slade helps me up onto Honey, we all make our way down to the market, leading our horses around the tavern and down to the busy road once again. Luckily, it's wide enough for our group plus the unmoving horses and carriages parked up and down the path. Just like up at Brackhill Castle, the roads are cobbled, the black stones scuffed, and the rest of the street lined with brick sidewalks where people walk in and out of the storefronts.

Just like before, I keep my head straight and my chin up, and I don't pull up the hood of my cloak. Out here in the sun, my hair and skin gleams, so it's very apparent that I'm not hiding, as everyone's gaze draws toward me.

The air is thicker now, the warm humidity causing my palms to sweat even without wearing gloves. But Judd leads us right to the market on the docks, and the fresh breeze rolls right in, a constant cool exhale blown in from its sparkling surface.

The guards dismount first, one of them coming over to guide my horse to a hitching post. As soon as we're all on our own two feet, the people in the market have all stopped to turn and see.

More gasps and shouts ring out as they greet their king and army captains, nearly every stall owner calling out to them. The shoppers have all stopped and turned too, parting as we start to walk down the path. The market consists of rolling carts set up along the street, while others sell their wares right from their bobbing boats.

Judd and Lu go look at a stall of weapons, while Digby hangs back with me. Slade gets a bit inundated with the public, but they keep a respectful distance while the guards watch over everything.

My eyes spring from one spot to another as I take in everything that's being sold. Shawls and blankets, boots and buckles, jewelry and cloaks. So many of the shops cater to the fishermen as well, with fancy carved oars, perfected fishing nets, and poles that are as tall as the buildings. It's a conglomerate of merchandise, too many things to track, too many voices to hear at once.

But I do hear one. One that seems to cut through the crowd, like a vocal arrow that's nocked and aimed right for me, hitting its target with deadly accuracy.

"Do you see who that is? The gold one? You've heard of her! She's the gilded pet—King Midas's favored saddle. The one who stole his gold-touch and killed him because she was jealous."

My gaze sweeps left, where I see the group of men

huddled together against the wall of a stall selling battered fish tails. Brown eyes collide with mine, a middle-aged face peering at me beneath the floppy brown brim of his hat.

"Gilded Lady!"

I tear my eyes away from the men, finding a woman waving at me, gesturing to her cart where she's selling bracelets. "I have perfect bracelets for you, Gilded Lady!"

With a smile, I wander over to her stall, but the men's voices seem to follow me.

"Thought her being gold was just rumors," a different man says, while I hear the telltale puff of a pipe.

"Nah, my cousin went to Highbell once. Said he saw her through a window at one of the public executions. That's her, alright."

"Whaddya think she's doin' here?"

The smiling stall owner pulls out bracelet after bracelet for me, but I don't see any of them, too preoccupied with what the men are saying.

"Midas died, didn't he?" the man counters. "Looks to me she's got herself a new king already. Latched on from one to the other mighty fast."

"Fucking women," the other one says with a sardonic huff. "Always diggin' their claws into the next best thing, ain't that right? Hopping from one man to another. That's all they do."

"Yeah, I heard she slit his throat and then stole his magic. His gold-touch went rampant after that, gilded all of Ranhold, killed a hundred people inside, but she escaped."

"That's why I don't trust saddles," another one says, his

raspy voice sounding one syllable away from a coughing fit. "If they're paid to fuck, they won't give a fuck."

Several hocking laughs sound out.

I nearly jump when Slade's hand comes to the small of my back. "Did you want something?"

Blinking, I focus on the bracelets set out in front of me, suddenly feeling guilty that the lady has probably been showing me things and talking to me, and I haven't paid attention at all. "No," I say, shaking my head. "They're beautiful, but I don't need any jewelry."

"No one truly *needs* jewelry, my lady," the woman says. "But it's nice to have something pretty." She holds out a simple band that has a black jewel in the center of it.

My fingers trail over the soft silver metal. "It is very pretty."

"We'll take it," Slade says, passing the woman money. Her whole face brightens up.

"See that?" I hear the man say. "Got her claws into our king, didn't she?"

"She must fuck like a goddess and squirt out gold cum."

More jeering laughter. The raspy man finally ending it with a whooping cough.

My fingers fist at my sides, and gold starts to lather against my palms.

Behind me, Digby goes ramrod straight a split second before he lurches forward. I whirl around and catch his arm just in time, feeling the gold in my palm glob up and soak into his sleeve. "Don't," I tell him with a shake of my head.

"My lady—" he grits out.

"It's fine."

His face goes red, but at least the rest of his bruises have faded away. "It's *not*."

"What's wrong?" Slade asks, coming up beside me with the wrapped up bracelet, his gaze bouncing between Digby and me.

I drop my hand, tuck it into my pocket. Though Slade's eyes don't miss the faint handprint on Digby's shirt.

"Nothing's wrong," I say with a smile, though I think it's shaky, because his gaze turns more intent, and he looks around us, as if searching for whatever might have upset me.

But one look over my shoulder, and I see that the men have scattered like rats from a sewer. The gold in my palm hardens like an angry stare.

"Actually," I say, turning back around. "I think I'd like to head back to the castle now."

"Really?" Slade asks.

I nod, and he watches me for another moment before he goes to speak to the others. I look back at Digby, noting his expression is pulled tight, brows shut in together with a crease. Brown eyes casting off disappointment like a drawn out shadow.

"Should've let me say something to them."

His grumbled words almost unearth some of the soiled weight that's been dumped on my chest.

"You can say something until you're blue in the face, and it won't do any good. People rarely change their opinions when they're argued with. They only tend to listen to the voices of those they already agree with."

"It isn't right. What they're saying about you."

576

I look around, catching the eyes of more people, their willful stares making me itch like the searching scratch of wayward fingers.

"Or maybe it's exactly right," I say beneath my breath.

Digby's eyes sharpen on me, but Slade comes back up before he can say anything else. "I think I'd like to sit in the carriage on the way back, if that's alright," I say.

Slade stops short, gaze diving into my own like he wants to swim past the surface and find what lurks beneath my deepest depths. "What's wrong?"

"Nothing," I say again, trying to perch that false smile on my face.

He looks over his shoulder at the others as they mount their horses. "You all go on ahead. We'll catch up."

Surprise flits through me, but I say nothing. Digby gives me a look before he follows Judd and Lu to the horses, while Slade leads me toward the carriage. I see the guards untether Honey, as well as Slade's horse, attaching their reins to their own mounts.

All while more stares follow me, more voices chipping in.

"That's the gilded pet. She killed Midas, you know. Caught him with another lover and stabbed him in a fit of jealousy."

"You think that's paint on her skin, or you think it's really gold?"

"What do you reckon a lock of her hair is worth? Must be nice to walk around with wealth growing out of your scalp."

"She's nothin' special. Take away the gold and what do you got? A jilted saddle who forgot her place."

"What's she doing here? Wasn't one king enough for her? She's gotta go and try and trap the eyes of ours too?"

"Hopefully, he'll see through her gilded charms and rot her where she stands."

"D'you think a golden girl can rot?"

I shut my eyes against the words, hoping that it'll shut my ears as well. But still, they batter against me, like hail on a window, threatening to crack.

The driver of the carriage opens the door for us, and I settle inside first, sitting down on the plush green velvet seat. It's bigger than the carriage I had to ride in while I was nothing more than a would-be captive in Fourth's army, and it's more elaborate too. Similar wood carvings are etched into the walls, geometric shapes drawing the eye to concentric diamonds and circles that overlap throughout the ceiling and walls.

When Slade gets inside after me, the door snaps shut behind him, and most of the light and even some of the noise is sealed out. The whole carriage jostles as the driver gets into his seat, and I hear the sharp click of his call as the horses begin to pull us forward.

Slade sits in the seat directly across from me, his wide legs opened on either side of mine. Some of the daylight feeds in through the curtained window right beside us, though it's filtered through sheer green fabric.

Despite the sounds of the market, the excited voices when people see the royal emblem on the carriage as we ride by, and the clopping of the horses' hooves, Slade's quiet voice is the loudest thing in my ears. "Now, I want you to tell me what's really wrong, and no lying, Goldfinch. I'll know if you do."

CHAPTER 49

AUREN

His gaze is the piercing sort that I've never learned how to dodge. It cleaves into me, perforating my walls and reaching past the smile I've still got pinned up against my cheeks.

The cracks form in my cheeks first, whittling my lips back down, no longer able to hold up the lie.

"Better," Slade says, the moment my smile drops. "Now, tell me what's wrong."

"It's not important."

"Don't be dismissive. We do not lie to one another."

I let out a snort. "I'm pretty sure our entire foundation was stacked with lies."

"Maybe in the beginning before we knew we could trust each other, but we've moved past that now."

He reaches forward, snagging my hand, tipping my palm up before I even realize I should try to hide it. I feel the skate of his gaze as he takes in the blotted smears of gold.

"Your gold comes out with your anger." His thumb brushes against the clammy metal drying on my skin, rubbing it over every line and groove.

"They were talking about me—some men in the market. But I think they might've been right."

His thumb pauses, smears against the pad just beneath my index finger. "What did they say?"

My eyes lift up so that I can look at his face as I speak. So that I can gauge his reaction. "They said that I jumped from one king to another."

The stern line of his brow lifts ever so slightly as he flicks his eyes up to me. Waiting. Watching.

"Isn't that what I've done?" I challenge, pulling my hand away from his touch. "I've gone from Zakir, to Midas, to you. Letting men take care of me." I shake my head at myself, reeling from the outside perspectives. "I thought I was making changes, making strides to be independent, but what if I'm not? What if I'm making the same mistakes all over again?"

He jerks back, spine gone stiff against the carved wall. "You think you and I are a mistake?"

I toss up my hands with exasperation, because the more I talk, the more frustrated I am. "No. But what if I am hopping from one king to another? I just got away from a one-sided relationship riddled with abuse. I'm finally free of all that, free to *live*, and I've *never* had that before. Ever. Maybe trying to show my face today was a mistake."

My chest rises and falls with the waves of my

acknowledgement, while his stays still and quiet like a breezeless air.

"For twenty years, I've been caught beneath the will of another. What if I want to just...leave? To escape all the bullshit and stay in a little cabin in the middle of the woods where no one can find me? Or what if I want to travel all of Orea, never setting down roots, never staying anywhere long enough to outstay my welcome? I could...learn something new. Climb a mountain. Practice music. I could get a job somewhere. Build something. Get a pet. I could go flirt in a pub. Swim naked in the sea. Go dancing. Make a friend. Kiss a stranger. Maybe *that's* what I want."

My eyes flash up at that last bit, and I catch myself bracing for his reaction.

For a long while, he's quiet.

I sway with the movement of the carriage, or maybe it's the movement in *myself*—jerking me side to side with wavering emotions, while I wait for him to respond.

How he can be so still, I have no idea. Not when I'm a motley of riotous shifting. Not when words are bouncing around in my skull hard enough to give me whiplash.

"Well?" I demand. "Aren't you going to say something?" Gold slips along my wrist, spilling from the crease of my hand. "I just told you I want to kiss someone who isn't you. I'm freaking out about the fact that this whole newfound independence might not even be *real*, all while realizing the public is calling me a seducing, king-hopping thief, and you're just sitting there!"

My face is hot, my chest tight.

He sits forward, bent elbows flanking his knees, threaded hands coming up in front of his chin.

"Do you want me to yell at you? To get pissed off?"

"No—I don't know," I say, feeling more and more insecure about what the hell I'm even saying. What I'm feeling.

Catching me completely by surprise, he suddenly plucks me up from my seat and sets me on his lap. I jolt in surprise, but his steady hold keeps me in place.

"What are you doing?" I demand, floundering as I glance to the carriage window. Although the curtain is covering the glass, it's still slightly sheer.

"Your aura is quite erratic right now," he says, his tone conversational. As if it's completely natural for me to be on his lap. As if the dozens of people we can hear just outside don't even exist. "Usually, it's calm, like the glow around a morning sun right as it drifts above the horizon." He shifts his hips, and my breath snags in my throat when I feel him hardening beneath me. "But when you're angry or overwhelmed, it starts to jump and swirl like its own gleaming tempest ready to bait and blind."

"So?"

His lips curve up with the force of my snapped retort, his fingers digging into my waist. All of a sudden, I'm reminded of just how thin this clothing is. Just how few layers are between my skin and his.

"You want to be independent? You want to live your life however you see fit?"

I tilt my chin up. "Yes. Is that a problem?"

His eyes darken, like shadows filtered through a forest floor. "I must've made myself unclear." He lifts a hand to wrap it around my throat, not to hurt or strain, but to hold. To bend.

My head is tilted to the left, my neck curved in invitation for his lips to descend. "You want to travel the world?" he murmurs against my skin, making it pebble, making it rise up to meet his touch. "Then I'll be your escort." His lips press against me, closed at first, just the tiniest feel of pinched breath between the seams. "You want to hide away? I'll build us whatever cabin in whatever remote wood you want."

His mouth opens, a rush of warm breath drifting out to coat my neck. But I feel that warmth drift down, lower and lower, until it's a swirl of ardor kindling in my stomach.

I reach up, sifting my fingers through his thick hair, twining the black strands in my grip. I tug hard, jerking his own head, making *his* neck bend too. And he meets me with a flash of a grin that makes that kindled fire start to spark.

"Who said you're invited?" I challenge with demure provocation.

He chuckles.

That low, sensual laugh that will always ruin me. It travels from his chest, making my own arch up to meet it, just so I can feel it. So his laughter can travel from him into me, and I can feel like I'm basking in something entirely different from sunlight. For my insides to revel in this sensual heat.

"Oh, Goldfinch."

Oh, Goldfinch.

My toes curl. My head turns as much as his hold on my throat will allow.

"You haven't been paying attention. Not at all."

I suck in a breath at both his words and the way his teeth come down to clamp on the skin beneath my ear. The nibble of his teeth, the slip of his hot tongue, it makes my eyes flutter closed, makes my breath flutter, too.

He bites down harder than I expect him to—not enough to break the skin, but enough for my eyes to spring back open, for my breath to suck in a gasp. Outside, the carriage wheels bump over the choppy road, our weight shifting with a slight turn. People's voices are just a backdrop cacophony.

His fingers tighten, thumb lifting my jaw as he leans back to look at me, and then he shifts his hold so his hand is wrapped around the back of my neck instead. "This isn't going to be some casual dalliance. This isn't going to be temporary," he purrs, reciting his previous words back to me. "I get your soul."

A kiss pressed to my cheek.

"Your mind."

Another pressed to my forehead.

"Your body."

His hold tilts my body back, making me arch, making my head fall against his hand as he presses a third kiss to my chest. His lips close around the button just below my collarbone.

I don't know how he does it, but his mouth slips the button out of its gap, makes the fabric flare out an inch. The smallest amount of skin is bared, and yet my entire body tingles as if he's just stripped me nude.

"I get your past."

Another button.

"Your present."

Another inch.

I'm panting now, three buttons undone. Only the thinnest bandeau trimmed with dainty black lace covers my breasts.

"Your future."

The hand from my neck glides down my back. Pinning my spine. Arching me up even more. The solid line of him digging into my ass.

"That's what you promised me, isn't it, Goldfinch?"

My entire upper body is balanced on his hand, my knees bent, thighs on either side of his waist. A scorch of his breath presses right over the curve of my breasts, the hook of his teeth dragging down the front fabric. The friction makes me want to catch fire.

When I don't answer, too caught up in what he's doing, reveling in this lust of heat, he nips me right there on my breast, making me jump. His grip on my waist keeps me locked down on his lap—on the stiffness of his cock. "Isn't it?" he demands.

"*Yes.*"

He soothes the spot with a kiss, leaning back up. "That's right," he tells me. "Now reach up."

"What?"

His chin jerks upward. "See that wooden loop there? It's meant as a knocker for the driver, but I want you to grab hold of it."

I follow his gaze to the ceiling, to the hinged circlet just above my head. "Slade—"

"Do it."

His instruction tightens my stomach with arousal, and I swallow hard. "Bossy."

"King," he drawls.

Reaching up, I feel the loop of wood and pull it down, let my fingers curl around it. With my arms up, I somehow feel more exposed, more vulnerable.

More *excited*.

"Happy?" I counter, grip shifting, tone brazen.

He doesn't reply. Instead, his fingers come down to the last remaining buttons on my shirt. Scooping them through the slits, letting each one come undone.

"What are you doing?"

Outside, people say too much to grasp. In here, he says nothing at all.

Somehow, that's louder.

Both hands come up, calloused and warm, slipping the center of my shirt apart like peeling open the pages of a book. He lets the fabric rest at my sides, stomach exposed, breasts heaving inside my bandeau.

My skin crackles, every nerve ending sitting up in wait for what he's going to do next. But I don't expect him to slip down to the ties at my pants. To pull the string and let them loose.

One of my hands snaps down, finger and thumb circling his wayward wrist. "What are you doing?"

He pauses, black brow crooking up. "Did I tell you that you could let go of that handle?"

My heart skips a beat. "Slade..."

I receive a pat against my ass from his other hand, so swift and sharp that it makes me flinch. "Hey!"

"I want your hands up and gripping it."

I don't know what it says about me, but when Slade looks at me with this hunger in his eyes, when his rumbling voice slips out words of sensual command, I buckle. Boil. *Burn.*

My hand comes up to take hold of the loop, my chest automatically arching back up. Bending toward him.

He nods in satisfaction. "Now, where were we..."

His hand slips down to the waist of my pants, fingertips grazing inside and making the skin of my stomach jump.

"You want to climb a mountain—I'll be right there to make sure you don't fall," he goes on, just as the first inch of his fingertips grazes over my panties.

"You want to build something? I'll be handing you the tools."

My head whirls and my nerves whip, and when his hand molds against me, when I know that he's just found the wetness gathered there, I quake.

"Mmm, you're wet for me, Goldfinch."

I can't help my wobbling breath. "Yes." I shift my hips, an urge for him to move, to touch where I've begun to throb.

He answers my silent beckon. His fingers come up to my clit, rubbing and circling, making a moan drift past my lips. My hold on the loop tightens, grounding me, even as it helps me lift my hips, seeking his touch.

"You want to flirt in a pub?" Slade asks, mouth coming down against my breasts, over the thin band right at my hardened nipple. His lips close around it, tongue wetting the fabric, just as his finger moves past the edge of my panties and slips inside of me.

The gasp that tears from my throat is a corrugated rip that seems to echo inside this confined space.

"You can flirt and play all you like," he purrs, tongue lapping, moving to my other nipple, making it match in wet heat. "You can make men and women desire you, *crave* you, and I will crave right along with them."

My heart is flexing in my chest, wrinkling my ribs, making it hard to catch my breath. His finger begins to pump. Curl. Thumb lapping at my clit and making it surge. Making me *need*.

"Slade..."

His other hand comes up to cup my face, demanding my mouth that I willingly give. A harsh nip, a soothing lick, his plush lips pressing against mine.

The perfect dance.

"You want a friend? I'll be *very* friendly to you for the rest of our lives."

He looks at me, thumb brushing over my bottom lip while his other thumb presses even harder against my clit, building the pressure, making me squirm.

"Great Divine..."

Slade takes my jaw, turns my cheek.

"And you want to kiss a stranger?" he adds, the caress of his breath a dark smolder. "Go right ahead." His touch at my core is pressed harder, a second finger fed in. His thumb moves faster. Deliciously so.

I can't think, and yet, all I can do is hear him. *Feel* him. It's his words and his touch and everything inside of me wanting to burn and to burst.

"If you need to kiss and fuck and play in order to feel free, then that's what you'll do."

I arch up even more, body begging, seeking...all while my mind spins with his words. His mouth is against my ear, hand supporting my waist, the other using friction to make me ignite.

"But remember, Auren. Your body—your pleasure— you gave it to *me*. So I will be there, wherever you decide you need to be. At a pub. In a sea. On a bed. I'll be there with you. Watching you. Joining you. You are mine, and I am yours, and whatever pleasure you seek, I will be there to watch you get it, and I will feed it to you tenfold afterward because you are *mine*, and I will see that you get what you need."

His words. His filthy, delicious words.

They're a balm against the turbulent doubts, coating me with provocative assent.

"Slade—"

"Come for me, Goldfinch."

And I do. A strike, so hot it feels cold, charges through my body, making me arc. I cry out from the bolt, from the pleasure at his touch, at what he's said.

It charges through me with pure electricity, until I'm struck and thundering, my whole body flashing from blinding pleasure that makes me tremble head to toe.

It takes several seconds for me to see clearly again, for my eyes to blink past the bliss still dotting my vision. My entire body feels raw, like the charred ground where lightning just hit, and I practically slump in his arms.

But he chuckles.

And I know that chuckle.

"Don't get too comfortable. We're just getting started."

CHAPTER 50

AUREN

T*he residue of my relish* slowly fades away, so it takes
me a second to process what he's said. There's an
impish glint flashing in Slade's eye that makes my
stomach tumble.

Hands dropping from the loop, I shift on his lap. "What?"

"We're having a very serious conversation, and we're
not quite done yet."

"Really? Because I'm sure I just finished," I say with a
smirk.

A grin stretches across his handsome face, his dark lines
swaying against the skin of his neck.

"And besides, maybe I want to go and try to kiss one of
those strangers we were talking about," I tease.

Shocking the hell out of me, he reaches over and flicks
back a corner of the curtain. "Pick one."

I instantly slam my body against his chest, eyes wide as

I look out the corner of the revealed window, at the people we pass on the street. "*Slade*," I hiss.

"Don't worry, they can't see you. Not unless you want them to."

There must be something wicked about me, because my blood heats.

His hand tucks the bottom corner of the curtain into the notch in the window frame, keeping it folded back that sliver of an inch. "I'm going to fuck you in this carriage, Goldfinch."

A full-body shiver takes over, my hands pinned to the slope of his shoulders. "There are people outside," I say breathlessly, even now, turning to look through the curtain. "I shouldn't have even let you do what you already did. What if someone sees? Hears?"

"Yes, what *if?*"

I didn't think he could be any more scandalous than he already was, but Slade does nothing by halves. And when it comes to the heat between us? He always magnifies it, always catches me off guard with the way he can make my mind swim with lust and my body bend to hunger.

"We're in the busiest part of the city. These streets are packed with people. Yet here you were, on my lap, writhing when I fingered your wet pussy."

My hands tighten around the hard tones of his muscles. "Slade."

He grinds up into me, his rigid length hitting my sensitive spot and making me jolt. Simply the thought of him sinking into me makes my pulse race. The thought of him doing *that* while just a thin carriage wall separates us from everyone else.

Even now, I can hear an ensemble of unintelligible shouts and speech, of hooves and creaks, doors slamming open, dozens of feet shuffling against the paths.

It makes my heart gallop.

As if he can read my mind, one side of his mouth tips up. "You want to experience things, so let's experience them. We'll start with seeing if your pussy gets wetter with a hint of exhibitionism."

He grinds up again, shakes an exhale from the recesses of my chest.

"And if you want to *experience* someone else? Then you say the word, and I'll take you to the nearest brothel and you can take your pick."

His fingers knot into my waist, sliding me back and forth over his cock. Again. And again. And *again*. It doesn't matter that I just had an orgasm, because with the way he plucks at my body and strums me into a cadence of lust, I'm once again growing hot, growing wet.

My entire face feels like I'm hovering over a steaming bowl, leaving me with a flushed sheen. "How can you just say things like that?" I ask, my voice jagged with the pulls of my hips.

"There's no shame between us. Especially not sexually."

To prove his point, he somehow spins me around until the curve of my ass is caught deep against his groin. He clips his thighs beneath mine and spreads them wide, spreading *me* wide. The waist of my undone pants gapes, too big and too loose to do anything but sag around my hips like the envelope of an invitation already ripped open.

"Fae are carnal. Sensual." His hands come down, easily

slipping right back where they'd left. All four fingers glide up and down over my mound, pressing down hard, a firm drag of slow burn friction. "Your desires are not to be staunched or controlled. I am not intimidated by your curiosities, because they're natural—and because you have been restrained for far too long. I'm never going to clip your wings, Goldfinch."

His dark words wrap around me, and I tip back against his chest, let my spine move with his breath. Though my eyes still dart to that wedge of window, at the bodies moving just outside. Everyone out there makes everything he's doing in here that much more tantalizing.

Slade uses a hand to turn my cheek, to lock our gazes together. "When I say you're mine, it's not cheap ownership. I don't see you as a figure to lock to my arm like a toy to keep away from all others."

That was the only *mine* I knew.

"So what are you saying exactly?" I ask with a faltered breath.

"I mean you're mine to please. To *pleasure*." The motive in his eyes matches with the drag of his hand, the curl of his palm as he presses against my throbbing clit and makes me see sparks of light behind my eyes. "You're mine to protect. To adore. To hear. To see. To experience. To *love*."

A pitted lump burns in my throat.

"You're mine, Auren. As wholly as I am yours. If there's something you crave, if there's some freedom you want to try the taste of, then you will do it, and I will be right there with you. Watching you devour your wants. And then I will devour *you*."

I turn to face him more, to take in the sharp lines of his jaw, the sincerity in his eye. "You'd really go anywhere with me, do anything? Even stand back if I wanted to kiss someone other than you?"

"Make no mistake. I will watch you with hunger and feast on the scene of your thrill. But after you've had your fill, I'll be there, driving my cock into your sweet cunt, purging all others from your skin as I take you. Over and over again. Until you remember that *I'm* the one you crave the most. The one who will always give you what you need. Until you remember that you're mine all over again."

Great Divine.

"So what will it be, Goldfinch?" he purrs into my ear. "What will it be?"

Innocent words. Wicked meaning.

My chest slings with gasps, my body a million prickles all over. My thoughts spinning.

What will it be?

I slowly lift up from his lap, turn. And with the shaft of light feeding in from that peeking window, I kneel. Right there on the cramped floorboards between the stretch of his open thighs.

And I look at him, eye to eye, truth to truth, and say, "I choose *you*."

His eyes flare. Hands tighten into fists at his sides as if it's the only way to keep from snatching me up. Because he knows what I'm saying. And from the intensity surging through his expression, he also knows that I mean it.

It's always going to be him.

Poised between his legs, I undo the ties at his pants, slipping the cords out of their loops. I look up at him, and with his gaze searing into me, I tug. His hips lift just enough for me to draw them down, just enough for me to see an inch of dark hair.

When I peek up at him, he nods. "Go on, Goldfinch. Slip your fingers down to my cock and claim what's yours."

A rush goes through me as I reach up and tug at the front of his pants. I delve beneath the gap and grip his length, pulling it free.

He groans. Kicks his hips up slightly in the sexiest position shift I've ever seen.

Still watching him, I fist his cock and squeeze, pumping him slowly. Once. Twice. Three times.

"The fact that you're not threatened by any of those things I told you, the fact that you'd support any of my decisions and wants...I have to admit, it's a huge turn-on," I tell him.

"Yeah?" Slade asks, as he reaches down and grips my chin. "Show me."

A new current charges through me in a rush, igniting me all the way to my core. When he's like this, when he shows me this dominant lust, it spreads through me like a wildfire, and all I want to do is burn.

And I want him to burn with me.

I lower my head, flick my tongue out at the beaded drop collected just at his tip. My tastebuds curl around the taste of his musk, my tongue a tease as I swirl around the head. Lapping at it. Wetting it. Provoking it until it jumps in my hand.

"Mmm, you want to play?"

In answer, and maybe just to catch him off guard, I suddenly part my lips and suck in the head of his cock. An inhale grits through clenched teeth as I dip my head, trying to go lower, trying to take him as deep as I can go.

But he's thick. Long. And so incredibly hard. My jaw acclimates, loosening as I move up and down over him, trying to go a little bit deeper every time.

"What a perfectly indecent mouth you have," he says, just as his hands come down to thread through my hair, delving into my braid, fingers jabbing through.

"Let me see," he tells me. "Mouth open. Tongue out."

I ease off him, lips parting to fulfill his request. My tongue lies flat, stuck out as far as it can go. His hand comes down over mine at the base of his cock.

"Yes. Look at that," he says as he taps his crown against my outstretched tongue. "Naughty tongue. Profanely plush lips. And you here, willing to kneel between my legs with your eyes on my dick. Such a perfectly wicked girl you are."

These thrills at his words are collecting in my stomach, a bounty of lust for me to consume.

He releases his hold, letting my hand grip him on my own again. "I want you to tap my thigh if it's too much, okay?"

"It won't be too much," I quickly say.

He smirks. "Don't tempt me. It's best not to push your limits while we're in a moving carriage."

I swallow hard as I wonder what exactly these *limits* are that he's referring to.

Before I can ask him, his fingers thread deeper into my

hair and he leads my head down. I go easily, lips parting around him as I take him in again. But this time, his hand is at my head, guiding me.

He goes slow at first.

Lets me get used to his thickness, content to let me lick and swirl around the underside of him as I bob up and down, while my hand still clenches his base.

But when I come up, pausing too long at the crown, he pushes me back down. "Deeper this time, Auren."

I relax my jaw. Take him down. And he pushes me further and further until I begin to gag. He keeps me there for a moment, and maybe it's a test, but I don't tap his thigh. I want to do this for him. I may be the one kneeling, but there is power here on my knees, with him in my mouth, with him beneath my grip. Such power here.

He pulls my head back, lets me gulp in some air before feeding his cock right back into my mouth. "Relax your throat, baby," he murmurs huskily. "Let me feel you swallow me."

I push past my body's inclination to gag or to gasp, throat working to try and gulp like someone dying of thirst.

And then the carriage lurches, jostling me up, bringing me back down hard and fast and rough, his cock hitting the back of my throat.

"Fuck," he hisses. His free hand comes to my throat, thumb pressing gently, reverently. "I can feel me inside you, right fucking here."

I swallow again, tears rimming my lids and slipping down my cheeks, my cut-off breath straining my chest.

When he guides me back up, and I gasp in my inhales,

breathing leveling out, I don't wait for him to guide me slowly this time. Instead, I go down on him with a fervor, sucking and bobbing so fast that it tears a vicious growl from his throat, and his fingers tighten against my scalp with a sting.

And that's when I strike.

With the fist curled around his base, I let my gold drip.

It comes out in solvent heat, hedonic liquid metal that I have wrapped around his length, sliding around him, glazing him in slippery luster that makes Slade lurch on the bench. "*Fuck...*"

The gold seeps out and coats him like oil, until he practically rips me up from the floor. I lean over him, taking in the wild, fierce look on his face, his eyes merging from green to black. "That was a *very* wicked way to use your gold-touch," he says as he tears down my pants until they hang around my ankles. He reaches up and grabs my hand still wet with gold, and he presses it firmly on my mound, making me gasp.

With my gathered wetness already there, the pooling liquid in my palm makes me so slippery, so slick that I nearly fall back into the bench.

"That's it," he croons. "Now sink down on my cock. I want you facing out. I want your eyes on the window. I want you to see all those people right outside while I fuck you. Claim you."

A whimper comes from my lips as I turn around. He grips my shaky frame and leads me down. Achingly slow. The crown of his cock breaches me, stretches me, and he gives it to me inch by inch. Sinking me down, lower and lower, so slow that I can feel every bit of him.

He moves my knees apart, spreading me wide, and then right before I reach the hilt, he slams me down that last inch, making my lips fall open with a noise of surprise that bounces off the confined walls.

"Goddess..."

His mouth comes up against my neck, pressing, breathing, licking. One hand comes up to grip my breast, to delve beneath the fabric and twist my nipple, to knead my heated, heavy flesh.

"Fuck me, Auren. Bounce on my cock."

I brace my hands on his knees as I lift myself up and down, shakily at first, movements slightly awkward. But then he uses his hands to hold my waist steady, to help guide me up and down, and I get a rhythm. Tilt my hips so that he hits that spot inside of me.

The first moan slips out.

My eyes dart to the window. To that sliver of light poking through, to the bodies moving. Heads, feet, shops, windows.

They could see something. Hear something. Could see me fucking their king, could hear him groaning my name as I claim him behind these paper-thin walls. All the rumors, all the accusations of me seducing him for his magic, right now, it seems almost laughable.

Because he has so thoroughly seduced me.

"Are you looking, baby?" he murmurs. "Are you looking at all those people just outside while you fuck me? While we do this *very* filthy thing right here where everyone could see?" He jams up into me from beneath, and I swear, it's like a lightning bolt of pleasure striking.

I moan. Too loud. "*Slade...*"

"Shh, Goldfinch," he says, a hand coming up to cover my mouth. I arch my back, biting his finger between my strained jaw.

I need. I need so intensely that my body is climbing up, my eyes watching. My legs moving faster up and down him, slamming harder, chasing the peak that keeps rising and rising.

"Don't make a noise," he purrs, though it sounds like a challenge. Like he wants me to *scream.*

And he must, because his other hand comes down to my achy clit and starts thrumming over it to match the pace of our fucking.

We're loud.

Too loud.

His head knocks against the wall behind him. My moans start coming in earnest. The skin of my ass slapping against his thighs, and I don't care.

I don't care if they see—if they hear.

In fact, I *like* it. The thrill. The what-if. The vulgarity of this wild fucking. Like it's a wicked secret bound to come out.

"I can feel your pussy quivering," he whispers. "You want to come, baby?"

My answer is mumbled against his clamped palm. "*Yes...*"

It's an answer.

It's a plea.

"I want your slick to coat my cock. I want your pussy to clamp down around me so hard that it demands me to come with you. I want to burst inside of you until my cum and your gold comes dripping from this hot"—*thrust*—"tight"—*thrust*—"cunt." *Thrust.*

I explode.

With his hips thrust up so deep inside of me I can feel him in my stomach, I burst into flames and bliss. My orgasm is tremulous and quaking, a full-body shiver that makes me scream against his hand.

I feel his choppy thrust up into me, and then I hear the most erotic groan as he spills inside of me, delivering on his wet promise.

Perfection.

Pure perfection in his wicked seduction.

When my orgasm fades, I slump against his chest, and he holds me there in his lap, the bounce of our rushed breaths pairing together.

And I realize right then, that those men back at the market? They weren't wrong.

I did jump from one king to another—from one male to another.

But the difference?

This time, I actually chose right.

CHAPTER 51

AUREN

fter we get back to Brackhill, we find the others have already returned, since apparently, Slade had the driver take us the long way.

Not the first time he's done that with me. He definitely took me the long way on our journey to Fifth Kingdom.

Bright side, I didn't have to explain my current state of disarray. No amount of finger-combing or trying to act natural was going to fix my mussed hair or the burnished blush on my cheeks.

I washed up, taking the longest, warmest bath I could, and came out smelling like jasmine and honeycombs. After, Slade sat me in front of the seat by the window and brushed my hair in soft, languorous motions.

It made me want to curl up and purr.

Now, with a simple braid down my back and a few tendrils loose around my face, I choose one of the dresses we bought while we were out in the city. It might not be tailored directly to my size, but it fits, and the color reminds me of thunderclouds.

I slip it on over my head, the square neck showing just a hint of cleavage, the shirred ruffle material stretched around my breasts. Just below, the skirt gathers in ashen layers dragged down past my ankles, the sleeves just a sparse bit of sheer folds hanging from the tops of my shoulders. It's simple but pretty, and it's a hell of a lot more comfortable than any of the dresses I had to wear in Fifth Kingdom.

Slade comes striding out of the closet, fingers doing up the button at his wrist. His long-sleeved shirt is black as usual, but with thick brown strands threaded at the shoulder seams, and bicone brass buttons trimmed down the front. The shirt is tucked into black pants that hug his groin and thighs *very* nicely. With boots and the formal jacket he pulls on, he looks intimidating and sexy, his hair still slightly damp from his own wash-up.

His gaze casts down my figure and back up again, and he comes over to slip an arm around my waist and pull me close. His lips press against the top of my head. "You look beautiful."

"So do you," I say as he pulls away.

Digging into his pocket, he pulls out the dainty bracelet he bought from the market and slips it onto my wrist. "You should gild this as soon as you can," he tells me.

"Why?" I ask curiously, finger running over the dark gemstone.

"You can't create new gold in the night, but you can still

call to it. I always want you to have some on you so you can protect yourself."

I smile. "Smart."

He curls a strand of my hair around his finger and then tugs it gently, gaze searching my face. "Are you ready for this dinner?"

My fingers twist together. Not really, but Slade and I discussed at length how we're going to handle Manu when certain topics arise. Still, it's nerve-wracking, especially knowing what they want.

Instead of voicing those concerns, I say, "I've been a fixture in the backgrounds of many political talks."

"But you won't be a fixture, and you won't be in the background. You'll be at my side."

That fact both intimidates me and encourages me.

"What do you think Manu will say?"

Slade shrugs. "He's advisor to his sister. Everything he says tonight will be his political strives to strengthen Kaila's position. It'll be interesting to see what angle they choose to play."

"They're summoning me to a Conflux. I'd say their angle is that they hate me."

"Hate has nothing to do with it," Slade replies. "When it comes to the games the monarchs in this world play—me included—it's about strategy. There are no feelings involved, it's just about power. How to get it, how to keep it, how to attain more of it. And most of all, how to make sure others don't have more power than them."

"Like the rumor of me stealing Midas's magic," I muse.

"Indeed."

"These political schemes are exhausting."

"They can be," he says. "But being a king was the only way I could ensure protection of Deadwell, and taking over Fifth Kingdom wasn't viable at the time. Plus, I hate the cold."

I snort.

"Shall we?" he asks, holding out his arm.

I grab the new elbow-length gloves from the foot of the bed and pull them on before I slip my hand into the crook of his arm.

Together, we leave his rooms, my free hand skimming the curved railing as we begin our descent to the bottom floor. The flat soles of my shoes pad silently across the tile as we go across the entryway and head for the back of the castle, the space tightening into a corridor. Dark wood wainscoting stretches halfway up the walls, each one carved into a perfectly symmetrical square and clasped with leafy wallpaper above it.

Slade leads me past the iron wall piece at my left, the metal formed into a twisted tree, its roots stretched down as if disappearing into the paneled wood.

"Sire." The guard standing watch at a doorway nods at Slade as we approach.

"Has the ambassador from Third come down yet?"

The guard shakes his head. "Not yet, Your Majesty. He's still in his rooms."

"Good."

The door is swiftly opened for us, and the dining room holds the same wainscoting, though the wallpaper in here is deep green, spliced by tall, pointed windows. My eyes immediately lift to the wooden chandelier hanging in the center of the room. It stretches at least ten feet across, looking like the crown of a tree was cut off and flipped upside-down. A polished stump is suspended from the ceiling, its branches perched out like the perfect canopy. Every inch of the wood has been smoothed, long since stripped of its leaves and bark, leaving the raw wood beneath with its rings and knots. Hanging from the branches are little lanterns no bigger than my hand, at least four dozen of them hanging at different lengths, casting warm light on the table below.

Seated at the dining table are three people whose voices dim at our arrival, but then when their heads lift and they see who's come in, chairs are pushed out, smiles spreading over their faces.

"You're back," a deep baritone voice greets.

Slade grins as a man stands up to meet us. He has dark brown skin and rich sepia eyes that are crinkled at the sides with his smile. There's a dusting of silver strands in his shortly shorn hair, and he's wearing a similar outfit to Slade.

"Good to see you, Warken."

The man claps Slade on the shoulder. "You too. We'd started to think you finally decided to duck out and hang up your crown for good."

"Don't tempt me," Slade replies with a grin. "You know you'd all do a far better job than me."

"For politics, yes, but your threat of rot is effective," a feminine voice says.

The woman who was sitting next to Warken strides over, the warm undertones of her dark complexion glowing beautifully in the lantern light, her ruby red dress cinched over her full-figured body and swishing at her feet. The tresses of her hair are coils of curls that brush against her shoulders, silver and black blended together.

"We heard you already decided to sneak off into the city before you'd even come to say hello," she says with affectionate reprimand, just before she gives Slade a hug.

"Wanted to drag it out a little bit longer," he replies.

The third person from the table comes over too, but this woman is much younger, her face the spitting image of the older woman, though perfectly smoothed with youth, the apples of her cheeks filled with a vibrant bronzed glow. She's curvaceous and beautiful, with the same kind of warmth about her as the other woman.

"It's about time," she teases as she comes up, just as her umber eyes flick to me with curiosity.

Slade turns back to face me. "Everyone, this is Auren, as I told you in my letters. Auren, this is Warken and Isalee Streah, and their daughter, Barley. Warken and Isalee are my Premiers. They're always in charge of the kingdom while I'm away. They act as the sole guardians of Fourth and ensure everything is taken care of in my absence...and in my presence," he adds with a smirk. "They're far better rulers than I am. I may sit on the throne, but they do all the leg work."

"Only because he hates it," Warken says with a chuckle. "Doesn't have the knack for politics and proper procedures. That's where we come in."

Slade shrugs, not denying it in the least.

"It's very nice to meet you all," I tell them with a smile.

"Great Divine, you're even more beautiful than he described," Isalee, the older woman, says as she comes forward. Her delicate hands grip mine as she beams at me.

"Described?" I ask, flicking my eyes over at him.

"He said gold was his new favorite color," she says with a grin. "I can see why."

My cheeks heat.

"It's a nice shift from rot brown and mold green," Barley quips.

A snort escapes me, and then Isalee moves over for Warken to take my hand. "If you get sick of this one, we have two sons," he tells me with a mischievous sparkle in his eye.

"Father," Barley says with a roll of her eyes. "You can't keep trying to marry my brothers off every time you meet someone new."

Warken sighs. "I'm going to be dead in a grave before any of you have babies."

"You're only fifty. You're fine," she retorts. "Besides, Dis prefers men most of the time, and he's always busy at the brewery."

My eyes widen. "Wait a minute..." I look between them, thoughts clicking into place as I remember something.

My family owns a brewery back in Fourth. But I got off easy. My older brother is named Distill. Unlucky, that. But we're both a bit jealous of our sister, Barley. She's got the best name of the lot.

"You're related to Keg!" I blurt out with excitement. Now that it's clicked, I can see the family resemblance, though he takes more after his father—I can see it in their eyes.

"You know our son?" Isalee asks, affection clear in her tone.

"When I asked about his name, he said you owned a brewery." My eyes dart to Keg's sister. "He said you got the best name out of the three of you."

They all laugh, Barley smiling with a hint of satisfaction. "That's because I did."

"Their father named them," Isalee says, rolling her eyes but sending a fond smile to her husband.

Warken just rolls back on his heels, completely pleased with himself. "My family has owned the brewery for generations. Thought it would be fitting."

"You also own the most land in Fourth. And run the most successful spice trade. Plus the bathhouses. And the water mills. Could've named us after any of those," Barley says. "Not that I'm complaining, because I *did* get the best name."

He waves her off. "The brewery is my favorite." Leaning in closer to me, he says, "It's *very* lucrative."

"Wark," his wife cuts in. "It's not polite to talk about money."

My lips tip up. "I'm gold. It's really fine."

Warken laughs. "Ah, I like you," he says, wagging a finger at me. "So, tell me, how is our Keg doing? Did you know he was supposed to come into politics with the rest of the family?"

"Yes, and he didn't. He was the smart one of the bunch," Barley says dryly.

Warken cuts a thumb over to Slade. "He joined *this*

man's army instead, deciding that instead of making power plays and writing up delegations, he'd rather cook."

"Well...his slop was very good," I joke. "Best cook in the army, if you ask me."

"So you two met properly?" Isalee asks.

I nod. "Yes. He was very nice to me, right from the start. And he fed me, so he was an instant favorite."

"Well, let's get you fed with us too," she replies warmly. "We have some things to tide us over before the dinner formally starts." Her dark eyes shift to Slade. "And we should speak before Third's advisor arrives."

All of us go to the table, where Slade pulls out a chair for me right beside him. Warken, Isalee, and Barley all sit across from us, leaving the seat at the head of the table open.

"Shouldn't you be sitting there?" I say to Slade as he takes a seat beside me.

"I'd much rather sit next to you," he says with a wink.

"He also likes to play mind games," Warken chuckles. "Placing Manu there is a good way to do something unexpected and put him on the spot a bit more."

The table is a thick slab of wood, so dark it's nearly black, the edges left raw, showing off the grains and irregular trim. There are already small plates laid out, along with polished silverware and wooden goblets, and Slade quickly serves me some fresh bread and wine before serving himself.

Once we're situated and I've already taken my first bite, Slade looks across to them. "Alright. Lay it all out."

Isalee sets her own cup down with a nod. "Since you left with the army to travel to Fifth, we've made sure the outpost at Cliffhelm was repaired and the soldiers there relieved. Of course, when the supply shipment didn't arrive, we made sure to send over a backup cargo that should be getting there within the week. Then as you know, we had new recruits for the army that are in the training camp in Farncroft."

"Good," Slade says. "And the mines?"

It's Warken who answers. "They've hit another very productive pocket three weeks ago. We've been making sure to work it, refreshing the laborers there too, keeping morale up with pay increases as they work the fissures to extract the oil."

"And the north mountains?"

"Ahead of schedule on the mineral deposits—that vein has been incredibly easy to extract. We've been having it worked quickly in order to prepare for possible conflicts with the other kingdoms," Warken explains, his hand rubbing over his chin thoughtfully. "So our reserves are up. We have plenty of funds to do what needs to be done with weapons and new armory and food stores."

"But therein lies the problem," Barley adds, cutting her eyes up to Slade. "We just got word from another one of our ports. Our imports have slowed."

"From where?"

"Third Kingdom."

Beside me, Slade's body stiffens. "How many shipments have arrived?"

Barley shares a look with her mother before replying. "Three."

He physically jerks back. "*Three?*" His eyes skate across

the table. "How can that be? I know you sent word that the supply shipment for Cliffhelm seemed to have some foul play when it went missing, but this..."

"Best we can tell," Warken begins, his face grim, "is that this is no longer an isolated incident. It's no longer shipment sabotage. Third Kingdom seems to have slowed our imports drastically."

Slade's fist closes around his butter knife like he's envisioning stabbing someone in the eye with it. "So that's their play. We can mine all the rock and gems in the world to pay for the imports our kingdom needs, but it does nothing if the trade agreements in place aren't going to be honored."

My stomach sinks. "The three ships that *did* arrive—why didn't they block those?" I ask.

"All three had been on extended journeys," Isalee tells me. "One ship was nearly sunk in a storm, holed up at the edge of our territory awhile for repairs. The other two had been gone for weeks, dropping off and picking up along their trade route. We believe the only reason all three of them actually docked at our port was because they hadn't been able to be reached to cut us off."

"What was on the ships?" Slade asks.

"One had grain, another was salted meat, and another had fabrics."

The table is quiet for a moment as Slade takes all of this in, and the uneasy feeling in the pit of my stomach grows and festers.

"So they're cutting Fourth off," I say quietly.

Warken nods solemnly.

The lines of power flail beneath the skin at Slade's neck, tucking into the beard of his jaw. "Fucking bastards."

"They're playing the game," Isalee says. "Queen Kaila is cunning, and she moves quickly. We knew her traveling to Fifth was a power play. She's had to adjust. Now with what happened with King Midas and Prince Niven, she's pushing the narrative that Fourth is harboring a traitor."

I swallow hard. "Me."

She tips her head.

"Just so you know, I didn't steal Midas's magic, and I'm not here to steal Slade's."

"Oh, you don't have to worry," Warken tells me. "Slade doesn't trust very many people, so when he does, we know that they're trustworthy. That includes you."

The compliment warms my chest, makes some of the anxiety melt from my shoulders.

"The other kingdoms are going to do their best to spread this version of you to the public, so we need to supply a different one," Isalee tells me. "Which is why I think it was good for you to go into the city and be seen."

"Exactly," Barley adds. "Go out and show them that you're not some devious woman. *You're* the victim of King Midas, not the other way around. We need to push back on their other story, give the people the truth and a reason to band behind you."

"You think that will work?" I ask cautiously.

"We've already started circulating it. If anything, it will give people cause to stop and think rather than just accept whatever is spoon-fed to them," Isalee says.

I glance at Slade, giving a nod.

"In the meantime," Isalee goes on, looking to Slade, "Queen Kaila is putting major pressure on Fourth to... *encourage* Lady Auren to attend the Conflux."

"Strong move, considering we share a border," Slade muses. "I have to say, I didn't expect her to cut off imports. Third is usually too attached to the wealth our mines provide them. I assume you've already cut off our exports to them?"

"Of course," Isalee says with a nod.

"But our reserves—they're full?"

Barley finishes taking a drink from her cup. "Our stores are very healthy. We were preparing for a war with Fifth or Sixth Kingdom. With some adjustments, we can handle Third and the lack of their shipments."

"Alright," Slade replies. "The army should be arriving back in the capital soon, and when they do, we can offer a payout for those who volunteer to increase our own food production." His eyes look between them. "You own the biggest portion of farmable land. Can you sell the kingdom your crops?"

"Already done," Warken replies. "And if you send more laborers, we can get this year's harvest sooner than usual."

"Good. We will have the volunteers go to every border of Fourth. We may not have very much viable land for crops, but we can sure as hell fish—both here in the rivers and in the oceans."

The three of them nod.

"It's nearly time for the advisor to arrive for dinner," Isalee points out. "And I for one am very interested to see how Third Kingdom plans to sway you."

Slade's expression hardens. "They can go to hell. I'm not sending Auren to a fucking Conflux."

His snarled reply has the back of my neck prickling.

"Of course not," she replies easily. "Let's speak with him. I'm convinced there's a way to politic and negotiate our way out of this that doesn't lead to famine or war. We just need to find it."

"Let's hope so," Slade says darkly, the roots spreading down to the backs of his hands like webs forming to ensnare. "For *their* sakes."

CHAPTER 52

AUREN

When the thick door is pushed open, I look up as Manu Ioana walks inside the room. He takes one look around before he turns to a man who must be his guard, dismissing him. Once the door closes behind him, Manu begins to make his way over, and we all get to our feet.

His long black hair is collected at the nape of his neck, the deep blue sleeves of his shirt swishing as he walks. The fabric is lustrous, and when the light hits it, it makes it look like the first weak rays of daylight hitting the surface of water.

The thump of his boots matches that of my heart, because as much as I liked Manu when I met him back at Ranhold, now his sister thinks I'm stealing magic and wants me to face some sort of formal trial.

"King Ravinger," Manu says when he stops in front of us.

Slade says nothing and only tips his head.

His keen brown eyes sweep to the others. "Ah, you must

be the Streahs," he says in greeting. "It's nice to put faces to the names signed on the correspondence."

"Likewise," Warken supplies.

Slade motions his hand toward the head of the table. "Please, sit."

Manu hesitates when he realizes we mean for him to sit at the head of the table, but when he catches me watching his inward dilemma, he shoots me a wink before easing down into the chair.

I think the castle workers must have been peeking through the cracks in the door at the back of the room, because as soon as we're all seated again, servers come out, laying down full plates of food. Steaming meat speckled with herbs, some sort of mash with a buttery gravy, and root vegetables are laid out in perfect precision on the plates that are set in front of us.

"Thank you," I say to the woman who serves me.

Then, we start to eat, and the first ten minutes of the dinner is a lie.

It's packed with pleasantries and trivial topics, while I skate the food around my plate with the fork and listen to Warken and Isalee open up the discourse with Manu with easygoing repartee.

Slade, however, is quiet. Watchful. It makes his presence that much more intimidating, but I have a feeling that's his intention.

I'm about to take another tiny bite of the meat when Manu's attention shifts to me. "Lady Auren. I have to admit, seeing you now compared to that first dinner meeting is quite a change. For the better, I believe."

I'm not exactly sure how to answer, so all I say is, "Yes."

"Not that I didn't enjoy your harp playing," he adds with a grin.

"I've gone off that instrument, truth be told."

His keen eyes gleam. "I'm sure you have, Doll, and I don't blame you in the least."

My heart skips a beat, and I steal a sideways look at Slade, but he's still watching Manu, his attention unwavering, his expression closed off.

"The dinner is delicious," he says, sopping some of the gravy up with his bread. "Much better than that sugary glue that Fifth Kingdom seems to be so fond of."

"Yes," Slade says, speaking up for the first time. "And yet, your queen sister has decided to break our trading agreement and slow our imports. This does not please me."

Silence screeches in with the tine of Manu's fork scraping against his plate.

One second passes. Two, three, four.

The pause is gluttonous, eating up the space between us all, making the air bloated and uncomfortable.

Manu sets down his utensils. Then his friendly disposition. In the span of a second, he's gone from an amicable dinner guest to royal advisor. He's so very different from that first dinner when I met him. The easygoing jokes, the almost contagious camaraderie. Queen Kaila is a force, someone you always have to watch your words around. But I wonder if everyone, including me, has underestimated her brother—and if that's exactly what he wants.

"Alright, King Ravinger, I see we've made it to the

serious part of our discussion. Though, I do appreciate you letting me finish most of my dinner first."

"Perhaps I shouldn't have, considering your kingdom isn't giving my people the same courtesy."

Shit.

My eyes snap to Slade, nearly freezing in the coldness of his tone. Manu doesn't appear fazed in the least. Though, I suppose being a queen's advisor means that he'd have to have many difficult conversations and train himself not to react. I wish I had that same perfected ability to keep my emotions and thoughts locked away from my expression.

Manu doesn't rise to the bait. He steeples his fingers in front of him, looking back at Slade calmly. "You haven't answered the queen's correspondence. She's trying to get your attention."

"And which correspondence would that be?" Slade replies smoothly. "Would it be the demands or the threats? Because I can tell you now, I do not tolerate either."

It's a challenge.

A catechism.

A pointed statement to pierce Third Kingdom through.

Manu's brow lowers. "The fact of the matter is, Your Majesty, you are harboring a traitor and a murderer." He doesn't look at me as he says it.

"Your claims are that Lady Auren killed King Midas," Slade replies. "And yet, you weren't in the room when his death claimed him."

Manu's gaze shifts from Slade to me and back again. "We have witnesses that state she stole his magic. It was clear to everyone in that room that the gold wasn't in his control."

My pulse thumps loudly in my ears.

"Again, did you *see* Lady Auren kill him?" Slade presses.

"Whether I did or did not is irrelevant, because it's the entire point of the Conflux. She's being called to Second Kingdom to stand trial, where all of the evidence and witnessed accounts will be taken into consideration," Manu explains.

"And yet," Isalee cuts in, "there wasn't just one very public, very violent death of a royal—there were *two* that night. So what is being done about the death of Prince Niven?"

Manu turns to look at her. "The Lady Auren will also be investigated for his death."

My eyes go wide.

A growl forges from Slade's chest. "You know as well as I do she didn't have anything to do with Niven. In fact, the person who truly should be questioned about the prince's death met his own grave shortly after."

"So you're implying King Midas killed the prince?" Manu asks.

"Of course I am. Just as I'm implying he had a hand in King Fulke's death as well. Yet he was never suspected for either."

"Yes, it is quite suspicious," Warken says.

"Which is exactly why you should bring her to the Conflux," Manu replies. "You will be there to sit on the council and answer any insight, and we can properly question her."

Warken arches a brow. "Surely, you don't mean to force

King Ravinger to attend the Conflux in the ruse of questioning *him* as well?"

"No ruse. But the public believes that Lady Auren seduced King Ravinger into rotting the prince." Manu shifts his gaze to Slade. "Your detailed explanation can go on record so the public can be set straight."

Barley lets out a scoff. "That *public* believes such things because Queen Kaila has backed that narrative."

"My sister has done what she must in order to keep Fifth stable after such a horrific event."

"Yes, there's no doubt you have all been hard at work at crowning the new king of Fifth," Isalee says.

Her statement cuts with an underlying edge.

Manu gives her a bland smile. "The fact of the matter is, we have two dead monarchs, and the people are demanding answers. We *have* to call for a Conflux." His gaze tracks to Slade. "Which is why I'm here to formally call both you and Lady Auren to attend."

Slade leans forward, his power coiling beneath his skin. "*We decline.*"

The first show of emotion appears in the frustration that pinches Manu's lips together. "I'm sure you'd like to, King Ravinger, but a king is dead because of what happened that night in Ranhold. You know as well as I do that the situation demands it."

"And yet, as my Premier has pointed out, there was no trial when King Fulke was killed."

Manu's expression tells me this is the last thing he wanted Slade to bring up. He covers it well, though, with a sardonic twist of his lips. "King Fulke's death, although still tragic, was completely different. He was betrayed by his own people. The man who killed him was already put to death for his crimes."

"Claimed the king who had everything to gain with Fulke's death."

Manu laughs. "Come now, Ravinger. King Midas was a long-standing ally to King Fulke."

Slade looks back at him, completely unimpressed. "Allies turn on each other all the time. Do they not?"

Another barbed question.

Manu's expression holds a smile that somehow manages to be leached of anything pleasant.

"I can see we are not going to come to any sort of healthy discourse tonight, Your Majesty, so let me tell it to you bluntly." He reaches into his pocket and pulls out a scroll, handing it to him. When Slade doesn't open it, Manu says, "It's all laid out for you there. First and Second are in agreement with us. Lady Auren must stand trial."

"And I've already said, we decline."

"I would think long and hard about that, King Ravinger," he replies, motioning toward the scroll. "Because depending on your answer, First Kingdom and Second Kingdom are ready to put a block on their trade coming into your kingdom as well. We both know your own kingdom—spread with wetlands and rot—cannot sustain the food your people need. Your kingdom can't survive without us. So unless you agree to send her, all trade agreements will officially be halted."

I thought the room's silence was gluttonous before, but this one is downright *insatiable*. It gorges itself on us, devouring every word, every movement, until we're halted by its consuming mouthfuls.

Warken is the first to break through it. "I see. And are your kingdoms prepared to live without Fourth's exports? Last I checked, Third in particular was *very* keen on buying up more rights to our oil supplies—without a lot of wood to burn in their area, they rely on our oil for eighty percent of their lantern oil."

"The monarchs have decided that justice is far more important."

Slade slowly rises to his feet. Manu's bobbing throat is the only tell of apprehension that shows through as Slade's hands brace against the table. "Tell your sister she's not the only one who can starve a kingdom," he practically growls. "I will rot her land from march to beach, leaving nothing in its wake. Or maybe I'll just rot *you*, right here and right now, and really send a message."

I flinch at the threat, watching his lines pulse beneath the skin at his neck.

Manu shoves his own chair back, its shrill scrape making my ears cringe. "I can see we're done here for the night," he says coolly. "I will stay for one week, King Ravinger, and then on the seventh day, I must have your final answer." His gaze strays to the others. "I suggest you advise your king carefully, especially on the threats of rotting entire kingdoms. We all know your army is the strongest in Orea, but right now, we also know that your army is fatigued from traveling to Fifth and back. Can a tired army—even under the direction of your twisted Commander Rip—defeat *four* other kingdoms?"

He hums beneath his breath as he looks back at Slade, running his hands down to straighten his shirt, pulling the luminescent blue to swell and settle like lapping waves. "All we're asking for is a fair trial, as is the right of our joined alliances. Do not be so quick to declare war on the rest of Orea, King Ravinger, to be responsible for hundreds of thousands of deaths. And remember, you and your rot cannot be everywhere at once."

Manu's eyes find me for a split second before he turns and drifts away, the door shutting behind him like the slap of a tidal wave that threatens to swallow us whole.

When Slade relays everything to Lu, Judd, and Digby, it's met with a commotion of blunt anger and cursed threats. Except for Dig—who's reaction isn't one of noise, but of the burrowing of his scowl.

"Fucking Queen Kaila," Lu says with a shake of her head, the shape of the dagger shorn into her hair looking sharper with the warm light cast off from the fireplace.

We're in a new room I haven't been to before, this one on the top floor, just a few doors down from Slade's personal rooms. There isn't much in here apart from a large table at the center and a small bar top to the left with bottles and goblets just waiting to be poured and filled. A scattering of glasses is set around the table, clutched in hands or left abandoned.

"How long?" Judd asks.

Slade takes a long drink before he answers. "Warken and

Barley ran the numbers. If we implement rationing immediately across the entire kingdom, we can keep our people fed solely on reserves for...roughly four weeks without any imports."

Only a month?

My eyes shift to Slade, his elbow bent on the table, hand running over his jaw in thought. I'm stranded in the sticky unease, wondering how monarchs can justify making innocent people starve. The stickiness glues up my memory, tacking to the time when I went through Highbell's city—into the denied parts of the shanties. The hardship carved out into every rundown building, the weightless rags hanging on people's thin forms. I only had that single glance at the people's hardship, at how they'd gone without.

"Four weeks?" Judd whistles. "Well, that's not ideal."

"I thought they'd be too stuck on our oil and gems to do something that bold," Lu adds.

Slade drains the last dregs of his drink. "Morale will drop with the rationing. Which means unrest and spikes in crime. We'll need more patrols. Not an easy ask of the returning army when they're coming off of weeks of travel through the frozen fucking Barrens." He shakes his head. "We can sustain a siege from another kingdom. Our army can win against any other that meets them in battle. But we can't win against *all* of them at once. Not with our food supplies cut off. Not with our army already tired."

"They're hitting when we're most vulnerable," Lu goes on. "And cutting off our food... It's a pretty steep punishment for not agreeing to bring Auren for this stupid trial."

"They're scared of her," Digby says. When everyone turns

to him, he shrugs. "If they're believing these rumors, then they'll be thinking she can steal their powers too. They don't want that."

"What they truly don't want is to make an enemy of me," Slade practically snarls. "Starvation takes a hell of a lot longer than rot."

Cold sweat curdles in frigid droplets against my skin, the dark threat of his words like a heavy fog I can't see through, can't breathe through. Beside me, I feel Slade's tension as if it's a string tied from his chest to mine. The taut line thrums with strain, knotting me with stretched pressure.

An entire kingdom. All of Fourth can only go one month living on reserves, or they're in danger of starving. And that's just Slade's people. If he retaliates against the other kingdoms, it won't just be Fourth that suffers, but everyone.

"Slade…"

"Don't," he snaps out. "Don't even suggest it."

"But maybe I should go. I don't want your people to suffer. Or any innocent person."

Green eyes brined with anger flick to me. "You are *not* going."

My gaze drops down with the weight of the guilt on my shoulders.

Lu reaches over and taps me on the back of my hand. "Slade's right, Gildy. That's the worst plan. We can't give in to threats and blackmail. Fourth is strong, and so is Rip. They're too afraid of him to do anything for long. In the meantime, we'll figure this out, and he'll retaliate just enough to make them back off."

That's what I'm worried about.

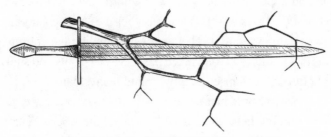

CHAPTER 53

OSRIK

The army is fucking tired.

I've been pushing them hard, trying to get the hell out of Fifth. The goal was to get to Cliffhelm. Since the outpost is right at our border, I was planning on letting the army stock up on supplies, have a few days to rest, and then travel the rest of the way through Fourth Kingdom at a slower pace.

But that all went to shit.

The shipment never showed up to Cliffhelm, so instead of being able to recoup, I was forced to send the soldiers off quicker than I anticipated, because we were seriously lacking in supplies.

Luckily, the terrain changes a lot more as we get further into Fourth. The last bit of snow is on the balding heads of the mining mountains. Dust rises around their bases in a halo, evidence of our own people working the veins and getting up gems and oil.

Before we could get into the better part of Fourth where the landscape finally has trees and wildlife and shit, we had to get past the layer of rot. Doesn't bother me so much anymore, I'm so damn used to it. There's rot surrounding the entirety of Fourth's border, so I've walked past decayed plants and sunken right through collapsed, sickly ground many, many times.

This rot isn't just an eyesore, either. Because we get a lot of rain out here, the cracked, wasted land *stinks*. With the warmer weather and the perpetual rot feeding on the wet soil, the air is the scent of rancid meat and molded fruit.

Smells like home.

It makes for a shitty day of travel though, and everyone tied a thick piece of cloth around their faces. But this rot is a damn good deterrent for enemies. No one wants to cross this shit, not even our own army.

As soon as we passed the last of the squishy, mildewed ground, I let the army stop to rest. Luckily, the breeze is on our side, keeping the stench downwind. But no one has much of an appetite tonight, much to Keg's annoyance. Good for our dwindling supplies though.

The camp is quieter than normal. The lieutenants have been trying to keep everyone's mood up, so the talk about hunting fresh meat tomorrow night is the damned slapped-on bandage on the gaping morale that we need.

We're done with the snow, done with the rot, and back in our own kingdom. Now we just have to get to the Brack—Brackhill Castle and capital—and they can finally fucking take a break and go home to their families after being gone for these long months. Definitely a morale boost.

I'm sitting around one of the large campfires with a bunch of the soldiers, listening to the right and left flanks talking shit to each other, not even suppressing my smirk.

"Judd and Lu would be proud," Ryatt says next to me. "Their rivalry is going strong."

"Good way to pass the time."

Ryatt nods, head turning to the group playing music just to the left of us, Keg right there in the center of them. Behind us, the horses are grazing, a skimpy clump of trees offering shelter at our backs.

As I take a swig of some shitty wine that Himinn brought me, my mind strays to Rissa.

Been doing that a lot lately.

She fucking kissed me. It was weeks ago now, but ever since, I've been feeling like a damned animal in a rut. I've caught her scent, tasted her mouth, and every time I'm around her—or even when I'm not—I'm thinking about grabbing her lush ass, pinning her up against the nearest tree, and fucking that temper right out of her.

But her head's not in it yet, so I've been giving her space.

Her body sure as shit is. There's no denying the way her eyes dilate or the way her cheeks go all fucking cute and pink when she's around me. But body responses don't equal consent. I want her fierce temper to unfold into a wanton hellion as she comes around my cock, clawing at my back with demands because she *wants* it.

The fact that she ran away like her ass was on fire after she kissed me, and the fact that she didn't leave her tent for the following two days, told me she wasn't really ready.

I meant what I said—I'd never take advantage of a woman. We've got a pull, no doubt about it, but my instincts tell me she's trying to fight against it. I'm not going to lie, a fancy woman like herself is definitely not used to a gruff soldier like me. I'm way too fucking rough around the edges for someone like her, but I want her anyway.

It's a huge turn-on when she goes toe-to-toe with me. All of the women I've had in the past were submissive, and I liked that. But the fire in Rissa heats my blood like never before, makes me picture all the ways she would take what I gave her and deal it back tenfold. Arguing would be our foreplay.

But when she didn't come out of her tent, I had my answer, so I've been avoiding her ever since. Not letting myself ride next to her carriage during the day, trying not to look for her every time I walk around camp, keeping my distance.

I still make sure the front of her tent is shoveled and her food is delivered, but I'm just not the one to do it, even though it fucking bothers me. How this woman got under my skin so quickly, I'll never know.

"Alright, I'm turning in," Ryatt says as he gets to his feet. "Sick of wearing this fucking helmet."

"I prefer it. Means I don't have to look at your ugly mug."

Even though I can't see it, I can feel him roll his eyes. "Yeah, fuck off."

"Just admit that you missed me," I tell him. "I know that's why you came back. Using Hojat as an excuse."

I chuckle when Ryatt flips me off and then walks away in the direction of his tent. The soldiers around him nod deferentially and clear out of the way. Him coming back has been a big morale boost too. Definitely helped to have him here while we crossed over the last of the rot.

I know I should turn in soon too, but I take another drink of wine, listening to Keg and the others strum and blow into their instruments. But when I'm wiping the drink off my beard, I suddenly catch the faint scent of flowers.

Think of the vixen, and she will appear.

I look up as a shadowed silhouette blocks the flames in front of me. The little she-demon stands there in borrowed clothes that swim on her, all but hiding her form beneath my oversized shirt and coat. I could've given her someone else's spare set, like Himinn who's much closer to her size, but the thought of her wearing any other man's clothes other than my own sets my teeth on edge.

"Evening, Yellow Bell," I drawl.

She glares at me, hands on her hips, and then glances around at all the soldiers. I shoot them a look, making them instantly scatter. With a small pocket of privacy now, Rissa sits down on the vacated log the others were sitting on, tucking her legs beneath her.

The brazen woman reaches over and plucks the cup right out of my hand and takes a sip of my wine. A grimace pulls at her face that's Divine-damned adorable, but I'm more focused on the way her pink tongue slips out and drags across her lips. "You've been avoiding me," she says.

My brows lift. "Thought you *wanted* me to avoid you."

She opens and closes her mouth like she's not sure how to answer. It's only because of how watchful I am of her that I've discovered her tiny tells. She's got a very good poker

633

face usually. Most people probably wouldn't notice the way she curls her pointer finger, scraping it against her thigh when she's anxious. But I do.

"You kissed me, then you left. Figured that meant you didn't want to repeat the mistake after all," I say with a smirk as I take the cup back from her, making sure to drink from the same exact spot she just did. The way her eyes darken lets me know that she's fully aware of it, too.

"Well, it *was* a mistake," she finally replies.

"Yeah? Well, it all depends on whether or not you *want* to make those mistakes, Bell."

She faces me fully, the fire making one side glow a soft orange and her coiled hair look like a sun-ripened peach. "Why would I want to?"

"Didn't you ever have your rebellious years when you were young?" I ask. "Sneaking out to get drunk when you knew you shouldn't? Picking fights even though you knew you weren't going to win four against one, but instigating it anyway because you wanted to punch something? Fucking someone you knew you were gonna regret, but doing it anyhow because you had an itch to scratch? Some mistakes are just too damned gratifying."

Rissa snorts and shakes her head, but she doesn't deny it. "Why does it not surprise me that you'd pick a fight with four men?"

"I didn't become captain because I shied *away* from fights. Or killing."

"What did you do before you became a captain?"

"I was a mercenary in First Kingdom."

Her eyes widen.

"Don't ask questions unless you're ready to hear what the answers might be," I tell her. "I killed for coin, and I was good at it. Liked it, even. Does that bother you?"

I watch as she processes what I've said, watch as thoughts practically stream across her blue eyes. "Well, some people claim that saddles fucking is just as big a sin as people killing, so I suppose I have no room to judge."

"The world can judge us all it wants, doesn't mean we have to give a shit."

"Eloquent," she says dryly, though her lips tilt up into an almost smile, and the sight is like a punch to the gut. What would she look like if she *really* smiled?

I shouldn't be thinking questions like that. Which is exactly why I need to keep avoiding her.

"Never said I was a poet."

Getting to my feet, I leave the cup on the log before straightening up. "Enjoy the fire." I start walking away to head for my tent, but light footsteps rush after me.

"Why are you leaving?" she asks as soon as she reaches my side.

"It's getting late. Gotta get up before dawn to start breaking all this shit down again, just like I do every morning."

I can practically feel how loudly she's thinking, but it's not until I reach my tent and stop to turn to her that she drudges up the determination to speak. "I've been thinking. I know we're going to reach Fourth's capital soon, and...well. You know my plans on leaving, but I thought..."

I've never seen her so unsure before, stumbling over her words and looking around nervously.

"You thought..." I prompt.

"Maybe you were right. About making good mistakes."

I arch a brow but say nothing.

Irritation blooms over her face. "Do I have to spell it out? I want to fuck."

Her blunt words make me rear back in surprise, and I instantly go hard, my dick pressing against my leather pants.

I cross my arms in front of me. "You don't know what you really want."

Her irritation morphs into full-blown anger. "Excuse me? Don't presume to speak as if you know what I'm thinking. I'm here, aren't I? *I* approached *you*."

"Yeah, but *you* also kissed *me*, and that didn't stop you from regretting it after. I'm all for actively enjoying some fucking great mistakes, but I'm not interested in regret. That's something else entirely, and we both know that's exactly what you'd condemn it as."

She can't even deny it. I see it right there on her face, and it fucking guts me. Her stunned silence says it all.

"Thought so," I tell her as I let out a sigh. "Go back to your tent, Yellow Bell."

Embarrassed hurt flashes across her features, which feels like a knife digging into my stomach, but I hold my ground.

"You think you know what you want, but you don't. Not yet. So come and find me when you figure that out."

Red blotches dot her cheeks, and a bitter laugh escapes her. "You know what? Fine. I just thought we could do it to pass the time, get whatever this is between us out of our systems. But you're out of your mind if you think I'd *ever* come back to you now. I know my worth."

I level her with a look. "So do I."

Her eyes widen fractionally, and her delicate throat bobs. Guilt wracks me because I know I've embarrassed her, know I probably just put the last nail in the coffin to this thing before it could even open in the first place, but I also know if I let her instigate this now, it won't be right. And I *need* it to be right— for both of us. Because I think there could be something here, and I don't want it to be ruined by letting her try to *get me out of her system*. Fuck that.

"You are the worst bad mistake I'm glad I never made," she hisses.

"And you're still the best mistake I can't wait to make," I retort with a smirk. "When you're ready to admit it."

Letting out a growl, she turns and stomps away, and as soon as she disappears from view, the amusement wipes off my face.

Fuck.

I hope I made the right decision. Because if I'm wrong, I just pushed her away for good, and that means *I'm* going to be the one with regret.

CHAPTER 54

SLADE

I t takes ten minutes on the back of Argo to make it to the city's army base.

At the bottom of Banded Mountain, you can spot the corners of a few of the buildings if you're standing on the west tower of the castle. It's a checkered collection of squares tucked in with the forest trees, walled up and meant to house a few thousand soldiers.

Right now, it's about to house far more than that.

As I fly toward it, I see streams of soldiers marching in, this bird's eye view making them look like a flowing river of black leather. Their progression is rife with curves and turns as thousands of men and women tread across the landscape, passing over the largest bridges and cutting past the castle, their sights set on the looming mountain.

This is the last of them to arrive, so Osrik and Ryatt will be here too. It's taken three days for them to all filter in, and when the final troops pour past the entrance of the wall, the base is going to be crammed full. Normally, when I've called most of my army here, they're only at the base for a short period of time. But with the situation as it is now, I cannot quickly discharge them to return to their homes.

That fact won't be well received.

They've been gone for months, and they've been traveling *hard*. However, their arrival will be stained like the spill of bitter juice when they find out that war is looming and they can't return home yet.

With the river of the army flowing in, I direct Argo to drop lower when we make it to the base's wall. Shouts rise up from below, cheers from the soldiers who recognize Argo from the sky.

I don't deserve their cheering.

Argo's wings slice through the air, tucking between the limbs of the trees as he gets even lower. With a tug on his reins, he shifts to the right, heading for the building pitched with beams on all four sides, its roof a pinnacle of pine tar, the dark grain of the wood walls blending in with the trees around it.

As Argo begins to circle in his telltale sign of landing, the soldiers below move out of the way, just as the beast touches down, his talons sinking into the grass.

All around me, soldiers bow their heads as I unbuckle from the saddle and jump down. After giving Argo a pat on his hindquarters to let him know he can go off to hunt, I turn around, nodding at the crowd before I head for the building.

My boots tramp up the three sparse steps leading to the door, and as soon as I get inside, four heads swivel in my direction. Judd and Lu are sitting at the left of the table, Ryatt and Osrik at the right. Osrik's long beard is even more unruly than usual, the hair on his head in much the same condition.

"You look like shit, Os," I say in greeting.

He grunts, thick arms crossing in front of him. "Sorry I didn't primp. Been busy dragging *your* army across the continent through the freezing ass snow."

I smirk as I take a seat next to him. "I appreciate it. Did you have any trouble?"

"Aside from the expected grumbles every now and then, and a few fights breaking out? No."

"Good." My eyes shift to Ryatt. His helmet is on the tabletop, though other than that, he's still in full armor. "And you and Hojat got back fine?"

"Of course. Good thing too, because the frostbite running through the camps wasn't pretty. We've lost too many fingers and toes," he says, his tone dripping with displeasure.

"Hojat was worried about that."

Ryatt levels me with a look. "What's going on, Slade?" he asks. "Why haven't we started dismissing everyone who isn't in the standing army? Why are you keeping everyone here?"

I look between him and Osrik, and then I catch them both up on everything that's happened, including the dinner we had with Manu three nights ago. Os spools out a string of curses several times during my explanation, but Ryatt grows quiet. I know my brother. The quieter he becomes, the more furious he is.

"Well, fuck," Os says when I finish. He rubs the back of his head. "This isn't good."

"Understatement of the year," Judd mumbles as he picks at the dry edge of the wood table.

"We knew they'd do something to try and force my hand, but I didn't expect this. Queen Kaila and the others are going hard."

Judd yanks a splinter off the edge, using it to pick at the grains on the tabletop. "What I don't get is why they're risking pissing off King Rot."

"Someone has to take the fall for two dead monarchs in one night," Lu replies. "They're choosing Auren as their target."

"They're scared of her," Osrik says. "These fucking rumors. No wonder the other rulers have their knickers in a shit twist. They're worried she's gonna steal more magic."

"The rumors and propaganda have spread more than I realized," I admit. "The public's opinion is focused on bringing Auren to trial. All while Kaila is quietly trying to sink her claws into Sixth."

Osrik's eyes sharpen. "*What*?"

I nod. "Last report I had was that she took a trip to Highbell. Made some announcement about how she and Midas were betrothed right before he got killed. Had a bullshit ceremony to fucking honor Midas's life. She's trying to dredge up support there."

Judd shakes his head. "Trying to take over more territory with the public's fucking blessing."

"They like her," Lu cuts in. "She's perfected her public charm."

"All while they try to starve us out," Os says. "A fucking month of reserves, and we'll be completely wiped out."

I look between all of them, even Ryatt, whose eyes are stuck on the table. "I need to pull volunteers from the army. I need massive efforts thrown into bringing in our own food."

"We all know Fourth is made up of mostly swamps and marshes. Not exactly the best farmlands, that's why we've always relied on the other kingdoms. And can crops even be harvested that quickly?" Judd asks.

"Some," Osrik pipes in. "Radishes, spring onions, spinach, turnips—those we can harvest in about a month."

Everyone stares at him.

He shrugs his shoulders when he notices. "What? You shits know I was from First Kingdom."

"Yeah, as a mercenary," Judd replies, his brows lifted up. "How the hell do you know about farming?"

Osrik shifts in his chair, the bulk of his body making the wood creak in protest. "Hired to kill a farmer who didn't pay his taxes once. Ended up staying there to help him so he could pay instead of murdering the poor fuck."

Lu grins at him. "Aww, Os. You're such a soft-heart."

"Fuck off," he grumbles. "My heart's rock-hard."

Judd's eyes practically light up. "No, that's not your heart, that's your—"

"Let's not," I cut in.

Judd just laughs.

"Alright, so we send soldiers to fucking plant seeds and shit, but we'll need some actual farmhands who know what they're doing to supervise, *and* we need a place to do it," Os says.

"Yes. I'll talk to Barley," I reply. "She knows Fourth's

land like the back of her hand. If there's any other viable land we're not tapping into already, she'll find it. And I've already had her and Warken put together a plan to increase our fishing and hunting."

"But will it be enough?" Lu asks.

I meet her worried eyes, because the same worry is in mine. This is what my Premiers and I have been working on night and day. "I don't know. Isalee is running the numbers. But for now, we've come up with a plan to make a backdoor deal with First Kingdom. They want more lantern oil, so we'll give it to them in exchange for supplies."

"Will the king go for that?"

"We will need to charm him enough so he can't help but take the deal." My attention moves pointedly onto Judd.

He ruffles a hand over his hair. "Ah, shit. You need me to go to First Kingdom and schmooze King Thold, don't you?"

"My Premiers are too busy to leave, and out of all of us, you're the most charming."

"That's not saying much. But fine, I'll go try to schmooze him to give up some food in exchange for oil and gems."

"Thank you."

"But what if he refuses?" Judd asks.

I scrub a hand down my face. I really fucking hate being a king sometimes. "Then we'll try to find another way to ensure people don't starve."

From the corner of my eye, I see Ryatt lift his head. There's a slow roll of his shoulders as his neck straightens, his eyes meeting mine before he finally breaks his silence. "*Are you fucking kidding me?*"

The only reason I don't rear back in surprise is because I've been bracing myself for his reaction since I walked in.

When I say nothing, he looks around at the others, head shaking. "Are all of you honestly just going to sit here and not even say it?"

"Say what?" Lu asks.

Ryatt tosses his arms out in frustration. "Oh come on! It's obvious! How can everyone be fine with the fact that there's a damn good chance the entire kingdom is going to *starve*?" His fierce gaze snaps back to me. "Auren needs to go to the Conflux."

Fury gropes beneath my skin. It pokes and pries, trying to wrest me open and ooze out onto the floor. I glare at my brother, feeling that fury charge the air of the room.

"How can you say that?" Lu demands. "We all know the trial is a joke."

"Yeah," Judd agrees. "If she shows up, it won't be good."

Ryatt shakes his head. "No, they just want a show. They need to put on a spectacle, slap Auren's wrist, and send her on her way. They know they can't push too hard and risk angering Slade, because he'll rot their entire kingdoms to the core. All she has to do is show up, let them run their little power trip, and come back. Then there's no risk of war, no risk of starvation—"

"Listen to me very fucking closely," I snarl out, my voice low and deadly. "I'm not bringing Auren anywhere near them, and if you suggest that again, you and I are going to have a *very* big problem."

The look he gives me is so piercing I can almost feel it stab through my skin. "I think you should at least consider it.

With you there, they can't do shit to her. You're supposed to put the kingdom first. You're supposed to protect your people."

I see red.

"What do you think we're talking about?" I demand. "That's what I'm trying—"

"No," he cuts me off. "You're trying to protect *Auren*. You're willing to let your people *starve* at her expense."

"No one is going to starve," I growl.

He lets out a scoff. "You don't know that. Everyone in Fourth is going to be impacted. And the army doesn't deserve this. They just marched on a frozen fucking kingdom *for no reason*. You dragged them across the Barrens twice, and now that they're just getting back, you're going to make them stay here at the overcrowded base or go off to become farmhands? It's ridiculous, Slade, and you fucking know it."

Lu looks between us. "Hey, I think we should all just relax—"

"Fuck that," Ryatt says, erupting from his chair like spitting lava, his outburst making the others spring to their feet, their bodies tense as if they're just waiting for a fight to break out between us.

Ryatt barbs a finger in my direction, ignoring them completely. "Your priorities have already changed. Your loyalties are in the wrong place. Be a fucking king and take care of your damned people like you promised you would!"

"I am." My tone is smooth on the surface, but the sharp and jagged angles are below, steeping in barbed and boiling anger. "Which is why you will put your helmet on. You will gather the army. And you will carry out the orders as I've commanded you to."

"Fuck you!" he bursts out, foot swinging back to smack into the chair, sending it flying across the room and crashing into the wall.

I don't even flinch. The others watch on anxiously.

I get to my feet slowly.

Unfurled from my spot so I can brace my hands against the table top. So we're leaning head to head, eye to furious eye.

"It must be so easy for you, brother," I say quietly, fury an undercurrent dragging my enraged tone forward. "To throw your tantrums. To pass your judgments. So *easy*. You know why?"

His cheeks are snagged with red ire, mouth silent.

"Because you have *never* had to make hard decisions," I tell him. "I have always been the one to do that. You just get to sit by with your outbursts and your righteous anger, and tell me what a shit job I'm doing at everything, while you haven't *ever* had to carry the load that I carry. And *that's* what you don't get. You'll never get it."

His eyes flash, but his impatient anger will never win out against my enduring rage.

"I am not going to be blackmailed. I am not going to send Auren to be put on a stage for the world to rip her apart for their own political gain. I am not a dog to be called to heel, and if you *ever* question my motives for my kingdom again, then I won't hesitate to put you in your place."

His chest heaves. Eyes flared, fists curling at his sides like he's going to leap across the table and throw the first punch.

I fucking hope he does.

"So you can stand there and spew whatever bullshit you want as my brother. But at the end of the day, I am also your fucking *king*, and you will do as I command."

The silence between us is a sword.

Double ended, pointing in both directions between us. It hovers in the air, stabs against my skin, keeping us held beneath sharp tips and readying to pierce us both through. We're both held motionless, waiting to see which of us is going to fall on it first, which of us is going to bleed.

My relationship with my brother has always been complicated. Since he went from an innocent boy to a man layered thick beneath mantles of resentment.

And I always take it.

I always fucking take his anger, his arguments. Because for the most part, I deserve it. I destroyed our mother's mind. I've imprisoned her in a cave she can never leave. I've made him non-existent, stuck beneath a helmet to play a part as my double.

And my father killed his.

But when it comes to this, when it comes to *her*, I'm not going to fucking take it.

Because he's right. My priorities *have* changed. And I will let the world corrode and crumble in order to protect her. But that doesn't mean I won't do everything I can to protect my people too.

For several moments, nobody in the room moves. I don't think Lu is even breathing. We're all waiting to see if he's going to explode, to finally throw that fist he's making and aim for my face.

But he doesn't.

I'm not sure who's more surprised.

Instead, he turns and stomps out of the room, letting the door slam shut behind him. The moment it's closed, my tense shoulders immediately slacken, hands dropping away from the table.

"Well," Judd says, breaking the awkward silence. "That didn't go so well."

Lu sighs. "You know how he is. He's protective of the army."

"We all are," Os replies. "And the rest of the kingdom. Doesn't mean he has to act like a little shit about it."

She glances at the door. "He'll come around."

Os grunts.

"So...is anyone else feeling a little Wrathy?" Judd prompts as he rolls back on his heels with a grin. I appreciate the gesture—appreciate him trying to lighten the mood. "When you give Manu your answer, they're probably going to have some retaliation planned," he says to me. "Does that mean we get to go fuck shit up for the other kingdoms?"

"Absolutely."

His grin widens. "I was hoping you'd say that."

"While you go off to First Kingdom to make this deal, I need someone to be my eyes and ears in Sixth. I want to see what Queen Kaila is doing."

"I can go," Lu volunteers.

I give her a nod of thanks before my eyes track to Osrik. "Can you pull some of our best soldiers to watch the borders?"

"Of course."

"The first sign of anyone approaching, I want to know about it," I say.

"You gonna go all King Rot on their asses?" Judd asks, rubbing his hands together like the idea thrills him.

I give a slow nod. "If they push me, then that's exactly what I'll do."

CHAPTER 55

AUREN

I've been practicing my magic.

This morning I was in the bedroom, plating the pillars, practicing making the gold reach up in swirling patterns and then sinking back into my skin. I'm getting better and better at it, and there's some pride in that, which is something I've never been able to have when it came to my magic. It's a quiet thing, soaking through my spirit and reinforcing the changes I'm trying to make, the confidence I'm trying to build.

After a couple hours, I decided to go outdoors to get some fresh air. I spotted the gardens from the roof, and now that I'm here, I think it might be my new favorite place. It's protected by a high ashen wall on the east side of the castle, so it feels private, especially with the mountain standing watch just beyond.

There seems to be only one guard that passes by on his

rounds about every thirty minutes. Even so, I'm careful, which is why I like this little spot, where I'm mostly obscured by the shrubs. Since the rumors about me stealing Midas's gold are so fresh and rampant, the last thing I want to do is make a spectacle of myself or give anyone cause to fear me.

Plus, I like working out in the sunlight.

There are divots of glass stonework in the grass, like flat blue marbles bigger than my foot and spread a step apart. They trail from the doorway, past the first row of flowers, curve with the twisting turns around the bushes, and lead past the walls of shrubs all the way to the very center of the garden where there's a fountain and a wrought iron bench.

Though the ironwork is pretty, the bench isn't the most comfortable, so I sit on the grass instead. With my back against the base of the onyx fountain, I work with my gold, experimenting with different textures. I ball it up like dough, roll it around in my hand, and then liquefy the pliable sphere.

Slade's been busy with his Premiers, with his Wrath, and with his army, so I've been trying to use all my spare time to work on my magic. Meanwhile, Digby has taken on helping me with the physical training part of it, since Judd has been busy and is set to leave on a mission for Slade. Digby doesn't do anything physical since he's still healing, but he instructs me on my stances, helps me run through strengthening drills, and has taught me a few blocks.

I haven't even had Slade alone for more than a few minutes at a time since our ride in the carriage. I can't truly comprehend even a sliver of the amount of responsibilities he has as a king, but I can tell that he handles things much differently than Midas.

The biggest difference for me personally though, is that he tells me all about what he's doing. He keeps me involved. Answers my questions. Encourages them, even. It's strange to get used to.

But tomorrow, he's supposed to give Manu his final answer. Already, the mandatory rationing has been put into effect. Even here in the castle, where Digby and I have been sharing meals alone together, there's smaller portions, simple ingredients. But even with these segmented servings, my stomach still churns with guilt, and I try to leave more behind to be saved.

Every night this past week, I've woken up in a cold sweat, my nightmares returned. Sometimes, the dreams are about the shanties, of the frozen poverty kept in the crooked cracks of Highbell.

Other times, it's my ribbons.

The sound of the sword swinging down. The slice of agony as it tore through me, silken limb by silken limb. I dream about falling, without any ribbons to catch me.

But last night, my nightmare changed. It wasn't Highbell I was seeing, but Brackhill. The same streets I rode down with Slade, except the people were crying. Bone-thin. Rabid with starvation. And Queen Kaila stood at the other end of the street, my voice caught around her like a babbling breeze that only she could control.

That dream stayed with me all throughout breakfast, turning my stomach sour. It stayed with me during training with Digby until he crossed his arms and told me we were done for the day because I was too distracted.

Now, it's still clutching at me, tugging at my shoulders like an incessant beggar.

I feel like I need to do something, but Slade won't hear of it. The few scraps of moments I've gotten with him are spent with his insistence that everything is going to be fine. That his plans will work and the rationing and extra food production will be effective.

But what if it's not?

I press my fingers over the bracelet he gave me. It now shines solid gold, though I kept the black gemstone in the center and braided a chain of gilded pattern around it.

I lean my back against the fountain, listening to the soft trickle of the water. It's calming comfort, as is the feel of the cool grass beneath my bare feet and the warmth on my scalp. If I could, I'd strip down naked, just so every inch of my skin could feel the kiss of the sun.

But that would probably be frowned upon.

I pluck a small flower from the grass and spin it between my fingers. It's a purple blossom, the yellow center reminding me of the color of Judd's hair. I draw up a tiny bit of gold, making it coat the greenery, delicately sinking into the veins of the leaves.

Dropping it, I lean back, letting my bare feet sink further into the grass. I feel my magic press against my arches and toes, wanting to come out. I let it slowly pool, the warmth of the gold competing with the coolness of the grass.

When I drag my feet back to spread the gold, I blink

down between my feet, pausing. I lean closer to get a better look, brows falling together.

At first, I think I'm seeing a reflection or a speck of dirt, but I see that's not the case. It reminds me of when a piece of bread has been left too long over a fire, its crust singed from the flames. There's just one splotchy edge around my gold that's darker than the rest, making it look charred.

Frowning, I dip my fingertip in it, watching the dark blot dip down, but then it just mixes with the rest, going away completely.

Strange.

Shifting over, I tuck my legs beneath me, hovering my palm over the spot of the gilt grass, calling the gold back to me. I rub my hands together and tilt my head up to the sun with a content sigh.

"Lady Auren?"

My eyes flash open and see Manu approaching. He's dressed in a teal vest with a softer blue shirt beneath and a matching cravat, his long black hair loose around his shoulders. "It is good to see you in such an...informal setting," he says as he looks down at my bare feet with a smile that lights up his whole face and reminds me of the Manu I met back in Ranhold.

I quickly snatch up my shoes, slipping them back onto my feet as I stand. "I didn't expect to see you out here," I say.

He looks around, his expression easy and open. "I found this garden the first day I arrived. It's my favorite place here. I spend hours out here day and night," he confesses. "The warmth has been a nice break from Fifth Kingdom. Though, not quite as warm as it is back home in Third. I have to say, I do miss the beach."

That makes one of us.

Manu might be easygoing right now, but I'm on edge.

He must see it in the way I'm holding myself, because he lets out a small sigh. "Look, Doll, this business with the Conflux, it's nothing personal. I like you. But monarchs have their own laws to follow, and when two die in one night..."

"You know I had nothing to do with Prince Niven," I say. "That was Midas. He wanted to take over Fifth. He told me so himself."

Manu's face grows contemplative as he picks off a leaf from one of the taller shrubs and twirls it between his finger and thumb. "Then that's exactly what you'll say at the Conflux, if you choose to go."

"Slade—King Ravinger," I quickly correct myself, "won't ever agree to that."

He cocks his head. "Do you know what a Conflux is?"

I falter for a moment, because Slade hasn't told me much about it. "I know that it's some sort of trial that the royals call during special occasions."

"Yes, but if you look throughout history, it's not really a *trial*. It's a spectacle."

I blink in confusion. "I'm sorry?"

"A Conflux is what royals call for either another monarch, family members of a royal, or a person of high status. Instead of following the normal laws of Orea, those called to a Conflux are exceptions. Brought forward because the subjects of Orea *need* to see that even people involved within the monarchy are handled and held to some type of law. In this case, a gold-touched pet who's rumored to have stolen her king's power and helped assassinate a prince," he says pointedly.

My face grows hot. "Why are you telling me this?"

He tosses the leaf aside, letting it flutter to the ground. "Because, like I said, I like you. I think King Ravinger might be rotting your head, because all of Orea is not your enemy. *I'm* not your enemy. Let Second Kingdom do what they do, which is to call you in for questioning, you'll explain your innocence, and they can give you a slap on the wrist."

I roll my eyes. "Yeah, right."

"It's true," he says with a shrug. "The history of the Conflux proves it. I think the most severe punishment was a fine for a hundred thousand gold coins in the last hundred years."

"Whether that's true or not, it doesn't apply to me."

"Think about it—nobody truly wants to go against Ravinger. We know how powerful he is. But if we let King Midas's death stand without questioning? The people will be incensed. They'll get dangerous ideas. Whether it's to kill another royal without consequence or to take it upon themselves to mete out judgment, both of which we don't want. That certainly wouldn't be safe for you."

I feel the underlying threat of his words like a papercut slicing over my skin.

Manu comes closer, dark eyes imploring. "Piece of advice, Doll, never let the people come up with their own narrative, because you'll rarely like what they say. But if you take control of this now, if you give testament, then all the monarchs will be able to put on the show that everyone needs to see. We can move past this, and all this talk of war can be put behind us."

My moiling thoughts twist in an eddy. I have no idea what to say or what to think.

Luckily, I'm saved a response when a guard comes striding forward. "My lady?" The man stops short when he notices Manu and then looks uncertainly between us.

I paste on a forced smile. "Yes?"

"There's someone here to see you."

I hesitate, surprise filling me. "Alright."

"I'll leave you to it, Lady Auren," Manu says as he begins to walk away. "Just...think about what I've said."

The guard and I both watch as he departs, and I let out a strained breath before I turn back. "Is there really someone here to see me?" I ask. "Or did you make that up?"

"I've been told there's someone here requesting to see you."

My brows draw together. "Who?"

"I'm not sure, my lady. I was only sent to fetch you." He looks around nervously. "I'm sorry that you were out here alone with the Third Kingdom's advisor. I will alert the other guards and make sure that doesn't happen again."

"It wasn't anyone's fault," I say, because the last thing I want is for Slade to get angry at his guards. "Lead the way."

He nods and I follow behind him to return inside the castle, and I wipe my hands over my brown dress, hoping there's no grass stuck to me anywhere.

To my surprise, he doesn't lead me anywhere upstairs, but toward the front door of the castle.

"They didn't allow whoever it is to come inside?" I ask.

"No, my lady. Not without your permission."

That takes me aback. What must they think? That I have any kind of authority here? It's strange, even to me.

When we reach the entrance hall, there are three guards waiting by the open door, and at first, I can't see who's behind them. Yet when the sound of our footsteps echoes in the large, open space, the guards turn, and my eyes widen at the two figures standing there.

Rissa and Polly.

I stop in my tracks, mouth slightly open in surprise.

"Well, are you just going to stand there?" Rissa asks, delicate blonde brow arched up. "Or are you going to invite us in?"

I wasn't sure where to bring them, so I settled for the drawing room on the second floor. I haven't been in here before, but it has plenty of seats and a nice view of the river through the window.

Polly is glaring daggers at me from her spot on the chaise where she sits next to Rissa. Her black dress is covered in mud at the hem, as if she walked through the rivers, straight up to Brackhill's door. It seems like it's hanging off of her too, her curves far less noticeable than they were before. Her blonde hair is lackluster and tangled in a braid, but it's the circles under her bloodshot eyes that are the most shocking. That, and the state of her peeled lips and cuticles. As if she's been picking at the skin there, shucking them off strip by strip. Polly has always been beautiful, but right now, she's rundown and almost sickly looking.

"What are you looking at?" she snaps, and I jerk my eyes away from her.

I turn to Rissa, and although she too appears as if she's lost some weight and looks travel-worn, she doesn't look worse for wear.

"I didn't expect to see you," I tell her.

Rissa looks around the room, eyes lingering on the green striped wallpaper. "Yes, well, when we left Ranhold, I had every intention of taking a cart and getting out of the city, but Polly was in a bad way."

Polly's eyes tighten, her head swiveling. "I was *fine*."

Rissa presses her lips together. "You were *not* fine."

"Well, I didn't *want* to go!" she snarls. "You had no right—"

"I took you out of that place before you could kill yourself on dew. As your friend, I had every right."

Polly turns away, cheeks lifted with color as she stews in her anger.

I watch this exchange in anxious fascination. For years, these two were thick as thieves, always laughing and talking, always so drop-dead gorgeous and put together. It's almost like they're two completely different people.

Yet I can somewhat relate. The aftermath of leaving Midas's grip hasn't been easy for any of us.

I have snippets of that night with them, of Rissa coming

to collect Polly, and my stomach twists. "I forgot," I admit. "I forgot to tell you to go to the army. How did you know?"

"Some woman with daggers shaved into her hair," Rissa tells me. "She helped us get out of the castle, too."

Relief surges through me. I need to remember to thank Lu the next time I see her.

"So you stayed with Fourth's army?" I ask. "They didn't give you any trouble?"

Rissa tightens her hands into balls in her lap. "Nothing I couldn't handle. The hairy giant brute came in and grunted some words every so often, but aside from him, it was fine."

"Hairy gi—Wait, are you talking about *Osrik*?"

Rissa sniffs. "Yes."

An unruly laugh escapes me. "Please tell me that's not what you called him to his face."

She blinks her crystal-blue eyes at me. "Of course I did. He wants to behave like a lumbering boor, then I'll call him as such."

I cover my mouth with my hand, trying to suppress more amusement. "I can only imagine how well you two got along."

For some reason, her own cheeks turn pink, and she looks away. "Yes, well. We've just arrived, and it was a *long*, long journey."

"Of course," I say soberly. "Did you want to...rest here?"

Rissa says yes at the same time as Polly turns and snaps out a no.

I look between them.

A trundled, weary sigh escapes Rissa. "Polly—"

"No," she says, lurching to her feet. "I'm done. *Done*, Rissa. You just dragged me out of Fifth Kingdom, across the Barrens, past disgusting, rotted swamplands, all the way to this stupid kingdom, and I'm done!"

Her chest heaves, her voice shrill.

"I was trying to *help* you—"

"Well," Polly seethes, eyes alight. "I didn't *want* your help."

Rissa looks stricken.

"That's right," Polly pounces, peeled finger pointed at her face. "That's what you're not getting, what you haven't understood through this entire Divine-forsaken trip. You didn't rescue me. I was happy there."

"You were high!"

"So? I liked it. I liked the way it made me feel. And it was my choice."

Anger flashes through Rissa's eyes. "I wasn't just going to leave you there to drug yourself to death!"

"I wasn't going to," Polly snaps. "Not that you'd believe me. But you know the difference between you and me? All those times you talked about buying out your contract? You never once noticed I didn't want that. You thought that everyone—me included—wanted out as much as you did, but you were wrong."

"What are you talking about?"

"I *like* being a saddle, Rissa. You were the only one that started to hate it. But guess what. We might look alike, but we don't think alike. Because I'm a damn good saddle, and I want to keep doing it. I like being desired. I like the power sex gives me. Being a royal saddle was the best position I could hope for, and you dragged me out of there without my consent. So I am *done*."

The jolted tangle of silence that quakes between them has my eyes darting left and right. I feel entirely out of place hearing this, so I do my best not to make any noise at all.

After a moment, Rissa seems to deflate, as if Polly's words stuck a needle in her spine, letting the air out of her stiffened back. "I'm sorry, Polly," she whispers, emotion thick in her voice. "I didn't understand. I didn't listen."

"You're right. You didn't," she snaps. "You always think I'm just being stupid Polly. Immature Polly. High, irresponsible, bitchy Polly. And maybe I am those things, but I am also a damn good saddle, and there's no shame in that."

"*Of course* there's not," Rissa says imploringly. "I was a saddle by choice in the beginning. I never thought that."

"Good. Because you were a damn good one too, and I liked that we were a team. But we can't be one anymore. Our king is dead and now we're here, and we both want different things."

A sheen of moisture glazes over Rissa's eyes, and she dips her head slightly. I've never seen Rissa so cowed. "You're right. I'm sorry."

Polly gives a sharp nod, and then her back seems to loosen some of its stiffness as well. She drags her gaze to the window, arms crossed in front of her as she lets out a sigh. "Well. At least this place isn't so damn cold," she muses.

Rissa seems to take that as some sort of consolation and sends her a soft smile. "Yes. No more cold."

The two women share a look, some of the hostility seeping away.

Of course, then Polly turns and levels her eyes on me. "Now, I need a bath to wash off weeks of traveling from my body, and a new dress so I can look my best. And then I want some coin and a carriage ride to the best and most expensive brothel in the city, because they're about to employ their best saddle. Unless of course King Rot wants a new royal saddle," she says with an arrogant twist of her lips.

I ignore that part, my eyes flicking to Rissa. "Some coin?"

She shrugs. "I told Polly that since you're here with King Rot, you'd give us some help. Saddle to saddle."

"She tried to drug me," I say dryly.

"On Midas's orders," Polly retorts. "And what was I supposed to do? I couldn't disobey him. Women have to do what they have to do."

I let out a sigh, but sympathy rises up in me even though I don't want it to. After everything, I don't want to keep giving myself to people like Polly and Mist. But she's right. Women have to do what they have to do. I just think our idea of that happens to be two very different things. "I'll have something for you before you leave."

I think surprise flashes over her eyes for a moment, but she shutters it before I can tell for sure. "So," she begins, looking around the room, finger dragging over one of the high back cushioned chairs. "You changed kings quickly."

I look at her coolly. "On the contrary. I changed far too slowly."

She says nothing at that.

I get to my feet, closing the distance between us. "For

what it's worth, Polly, I hope you can be happy here in Fourth Kingdom."

Her eyes narrow, like she doesn't believe me. "Of course I'll be happy," she says defensively, as if she's out to prove herself right, no matter the cost.

"What about you?" I ask Rissa. "Are you wanting to leave the kingdom? Because I have to warn you, I'm not sure where in Orea is the best place to be right now."

"Actually, I was thinking of…staying here."

My brows jump up. "Staying?" I didn't expect that. All Rissa's been talking about is leaving. Traveling. Getting far away from everything that reminds her of her life as a royal saddle. Maybe she wants to stay to watch over Polly, but for some reason, I think it's more than that.

"Yes," she replies tartly, ending the discussion in that succinct single-word answer as she gets to her feet. "Now, I'll need a bath and a dress too, and also a room where I can sleep. I can't even tell you how utterly *sick* I am of sleeping in a tent and being caught in the shadow of that hairy oaf every night."

That's the second time she's mentioned him.

"Did something…happen between you and Osrik?" I ask carefully.

The flare of irritation in her eyes is withering enough to make my brows lift. "Me with that lout? Of course not," she replies hotly.

So hot that there's another blush burned on her cheeks.

Interesting.

"Right," I say slowly. "Let's…go get you those baths."

"Honestly," Rissa grumbles behind my back as she and Polly follow me out of the room. "Me and him. The very idea."

The very idea indeed.

CHAPTER 56

AUREN

It feels like all of my nerves have condensed right into the pit of my stomach.

Tonight, Slade has to give Manu his official answer. Night has already dripped from the sky and sunk into the land, slowly blotting out the last remaining hours.

I'm on the roof, my hair loose down my back, some of the strands tickling my cheeks. The sky is speckled with clouds that carry the scent of warm rain, but for now, it seems content to only bring a cool breeze.

My fingers are curled over the top of the wall as I look toward the army camp. I can't see very much of it from here, since the mountain and the trees block most of it, and the castle itself hides the rest. But I can hear it.

I can hear the sound of thousands of soldiers down there, the same noises that I heard when I traveled right alongside them. I can see a few sparse fires through the trees lit up like little orange suns burning in pinpricks along the ground.

The army base is so full that roughshod buildings have been erected to house more of them, while the rest of the overflow has either been given lodging in the city inns or right here in the castle itself. To say it's full is an understatement.

The Wrath have been sleeping down at the base every night, too. I think it helps the soldiers to see them down there, to know that their captains and commander aren't just coming up to their plush rooms in the castle. I could tell Slade was torn, but he's been staying here with me instead.

A noise above has me picking my gaze up and shooting toward the sky. I jump in surprise when a huge shadowy figure circles above, yelping when Argo lands right next to me.

I send him a glower. "You jerk. You scared me."

He licks his chops, his long tongue grazing over his dagger-like teeth. Some of them seem to look darker than the others, maybe blood from an animal he hunted. When he licks his maw again, this time chewing something after, I wrinkle my nose. "Gross. Can you rinse before you come up here and slop your chops at me?"

He cocks his head, iridescent eyes flashing. The sheer size of him alone still makes me a little nervous in his presence, although I have to admit, he has grown on me.

But I still flinch when he suddenly walks up to me and nudges my arm.

I go ramrod straight, my heart skipping a step. "Did you want something?" I ask nervously.

I hear footsteps approach and turn around to see one of

the guards walking up. "Pardon, my lady, but we've spoiled His Majesty's beast. He comes up here for this." The man digs into his pocket and holds out a piece of food.

Taking it, I look down at my hand, seeing the food isn't jerky like I expected, but a large cookie of some sort. "Are you telling me that timberwings have a sweet tooth?"

The guard shrugs with a sheepish smile. "Don't know about all timberwings, but this one certainly does."

Laughing, I turn around, only to find Argo looming over me, staring at the cookie in my hand intently. "So, this is what you want?"

He makes a chuffing sound deep in his throat and blinks at me innocently.

I scoff. "Mm-hmm, nice try with the puppy dog eyes," I tell him before I make my tone sterner. "If you bite my hand off, I'm going to be *really* mad."

Holding my hand out, I present the cookie on my flattened palm, and no sooner have I reached out a single inch than Argo is coming up to snap up the treat. I flinch, eyes shut tight, but rather than feeling his razor-sharp teeth mauling me, he's surprisingly gentle. All I feel is the smoothest nuzzle of horse-like lips before both his mouth and treat are gone.

When I open my eyes again, he's happily swallowing it down, looking quite pleased with himself. This time when he licks his teeth, he's gathering crumbs.

"Nothing like washing down a bloody hunt with a cookie, right?" I ask him.

He makes a noise like a hoarse chwirk, and I reach out to pet him.

Beside me, I hear the guard suck in a breath. "Lady Auren, I wouldn't—"

Before his warning finishes, my fingers come down to the bark-colored feathers at Argo's neck. I brace myself for the beast to snap at me, but to my surprise, he curls his head the other way, as if he's directing me where to scratch. Tentatively, I scratch at his neck, finding that the plume is much softer than I anticipated.

The guard lets out a sigh of relief. "Wow. He never lets anyone pet him other than His Majesty."

A surge of gratification fills me as I run my hand over him again. "Good boy," I croon. "Thank you for not mauling me to death."

I pet him for a few more seconds, and as soon as I drop my hand, he clicks at me. That's the only warning I get before he's lurching down and then leaping up, a burst of air tossed back our way as his wings take him higher.

I shove away the hair that got blown in my face, smiling to myself as I watch his shadowy figure disappear. Turning to the guard, I say, "Thank you for the cookie."

He bows his head. "Any time, my lady."

As I make my way back downstairs, all the content feelings from the roof slowly dwindle away, step by step. When I'm back on the floor of Slade's rooms, my anxiety has compressed right back into my stomach again, solidified and heavy.

I take a breath before I go inside and shut the door. When I get into the bedroom, I see that the window is opened, letting in the cool night air, ruffling the green curtains in slow swells.

"There you are," Slade says. He gets up from the chair beside the unlit fireplace, a stack of papers in his hands. He tosses them down onto the seat as he straightens up. My eyes roam over his figure, black pants tucked into his boots, a leather jerkin belted at the waist. He's shaved too, the black beard that had been getting thicker now back to just a scruff of a shadow along his jaw, and his hair is combed back.

"You look beautiful," he says as I walk over.

I pinch the skirt of my dress, lifting the ruby red fabric. "You picked this one out."

Dark eyes follow the dip of the top, the scooped neckline gathering in a cinch just below my breasts. "The color suits you."

"It's nice not to wear gold all the time. It's nice not to *see* it everywhere too," I admit, glancing around the room, taking in the dark floorboards, the rich green bedding. Even something as simple as being able to see the true color of grains of wood or thread in a sheet is still somewhat anomalous. After so long of being constantly surrounded by it, of every single thing in Highbell being gilded by my hand, it's a breath of fresh air to be out of that singular outlook.

A life lived in shades of gold casts its own sort of shadow.

His fingertips graze across the golden bracelet on my wrist. "But gold will always be my favorite color."

I smile at him, but that happiness drifts away with my troubled thoughts, while my stomach tries to churn and churn my leaden nerves. My hand delves into the hidden pocket of my dress, and I scoop out my ribbon, twirling it around my thumb for a moment before I set it on the bedside table.

I turn back around to face him. "Can we talk?"

"Of course."

I move toward the bed, sitting down on it, bracing my hands on either side of me so I don't fidget other than slightly swinging my feet. "I don't know if saying no tonight to Manu is the best thing."

A flash of disappointment passes over his features. "It is," he says decisively. "They're trying to intimidate us—to corner us."

"But the army is tired. And the food shortage..."

"You sound like Ryatt."

I pause. "So he agrees?"

A lackadaisical laugh tempers up from his chest. "When it comes to my decisions, Ryatt usually always believes I should be doing the opposite."

My teeth trap my bottom lip. "I'm just worried."

Slade's face softens, and then he walks over to me, stopping just in front of my knees. His hand comes up to slide beneath my jaw, to tip my head up as he leans down. "I don't want you to be worried. Fourth Kingdom is strong. *I'm* strong."

"I know you are, but your people—"

He suddenly bends his knee and places it right between my legs on the mattress, trapping the fabric of my skirt as his weight pins my legs down.

"What are you doing?" I ask, my voice coming out in a breathy surge.

He leans in, and I lean back, making him smirk. "I don't want you to worry. We are going to be just fine."

672

"But—"

With his hold still on my jaw, he swoops down and skims his lips over mine, making my words die on my tongue and trickle out with my shaken breath.

It's not even a full kiss, not really, but just that barest of touch makes my body react, makes me melt against him.

He pulls away, verdant gaze burgeoning with flickers of heat in their deep green depths. "You have a good heart, Auren," he tells me, thumb brushing over the edge of my jaw. "I just want you to trust me in this. Trust that I can keep you *and* my kingdom safe."

"I do trust you," I reply honestly. "But you said so yourself, if they do this, if they push you, you're going to retaliate."

Instead of trying to deny it, he places his other knee onto the bed too, this one on the outside of my right thigh. I thought my skirt was pulled taut before, but now, it's even more restricted, binding my legs in place. His hands brace on the mattress on either side of my hips, and even though I lean back slightly, he leans with me.

"I will retaliate," he says, speaking just inches away from my face. "I do not shy away from using my magic. I do not feel remorse for revenge. I will do whatever I need to do, because no one is allowed to threaten my kingdom or try to hurt you."

I swallow hard, and I shouldn't be turned on right now. Not when we're talking about something so serious, not when he's telling me that he feels no guilt for spreading his rot at the cost of lives and land.

But I am.

There's always this pulsing pull between us, one that reverberates through the air that only we can feel.

"I don't want you to have to kill for me."

The side of his mouth ticks up, and he grazes his cheek against mine, the scratchy texture of his shaven face making my own cheek prickle with heat. "It's far too late for that," he purrs darkly. "The fae instincts in me will not rest until the threats on you are eliminated, and the king in me will not sit by while others threaten my people. I will not be able to tolerate it. No one is allowed to threaten what's mine, because I will not *lie down and take it*."

He leans forward more, pushing me with the move, and now it's *me* lying down. It's my body on pinpricks, hearing the word *take it* in a completely different context. The heat in his eyes tells me that's exactly what he intended.

His arm muscles bulge as he holds himself over me, his eyes dipping down my chest, making liquid heat pool at my core.

"But...that's bad," I say lamely, even as my hips try to lift up. Try, and fail, because he still has my skirt pinned. It sends a thrill down my spine, being completely at his mercy, being held beneath his body.

Lie down and take it.

"Me and you," he says, leaning forward, making that pull more potent, the pulsating draw more magnetic. "There is no shame in what we are."

What a dangerous thought.

He nibbles at my bottom lip, licking at the seam. When I don't open, he pinches down harder, drawing the tiniest, sharpest point of pain that somehow makes my body fill with anticipation. I let my tongue slip out, finding the bead of blood there, but he presses his lips to mine again, stealing the taste.

"We are powerful," he tells me, one hand coming down to drag from collarbone to the cusp of my cleavage, a trail to ignite, to spread this kindling desire.

I shouldn't be wanting the burn. I should be pushing him away, talking about this decision without the distraction of his seduction. But I can't. I can't, because every time he touches me, he incites an uncontrollable craving.

So I arch up, a silent plea for him to dip his hand beneath the fabric, to grab my breasts, to touch me all over. I arch, and he bends, and that's all there is.

"Say it." His lips come down to my hardened nipple, sucking it in right through the dress. I whine at the contact, head tipping back. He moves from one to the other, licking, tugging, *teasing*.

"Touch me," I demand instead.

His teeth clamp over me, biting down hard just like my lip. My nipple sparks with a delicious jolt of pain, making me cry out. "*Say it*."

My hips once more try to lift up. Fail. Try again. I'm pushing against the constricting fabric, making my body feel stuck and tight all over. Making me feel utterly constrained— and all the more intensely aroused because of it.

I want to grind against him, for him to press against my beating core, for him to keep me here, caught beneath him, while he doles out my pleasure.

"We're powerful," I repeat, giving in to his request, my breath embarrassingly fast as I do.

"That's right," he tells me, eyes locked onto mine, holding me in place with his gaze just as much as he's holding the rest of me. "With gold and rot, we will protect what is ours. We will be our worst when we need to and be our best together. And at the end of the day, we will fucking destroy our enemies." His hips punch down, finally—*finally*—giving me that friction I need, and I moan, shuddering all over.

"Because why, Auren?" he asks, a seductive croon bade from his lips.

His hard length grinds down into me, hitting my clit, making me flare.

"Because..." I pant, eyes locking on him as I reach toward the ties of his pants, pulling them loose.

Instead of being afraid of the whole damn world, I could make the whole damn world afraid of me.

I sink my hand in and grab his cock at the same time that I say, "Because. We will be the villains for each other."

He grins. Slow, emphatic, *licentious*. "That's exactly right."

CHAPTER 57

AUREN

There's something *freeing and exciting* about this wicked confession to each other. Maybe it's the fae in me. Maybe it's the rot that's rooted in my soul. But whatever it is, it speaks to that beast that lives within the confines of my chest.

I squeeze Slade's cock hard, tearing a groan from his wicked lips. "Make me come, Slade."

His eyes flash. His mouth tsks. "You are my equal. My female. My partner. But when it comes to your pussy, I'm in charge."

I arch an imperious brow, even as my stomach skips over itself. "What if I want to be in charge of your cock?"

A dark, low chuckle comes out of him. "Do you, Goldfinch?"

I nod slowly, finger trailing over the throbbing vein running down the length of him. Right when I'm about to touch the crown, I retract my hand, and with my gaze boldly holding his, I lick the length of my palm, lapping at it until it's nice and wet. His eyes slam shut as I grip him again, stroking up. My touch roving until I grip his balls to knead and roll.

"*Fucking. Hell.*"

I don't even try to suppress my smile, but then I feel precum leak from his tip and drop onto my belly. Again and again, more of it dribbles out, and I don't know why, but seeing his cock actually *leaking* because he's so turned on by me makes me feel even *more* powerful, and in an entirely different way than he meant. The crude liquid continues to seep, soaking into my dress, making the fabric stick to my skin.

This time, I'm the one who tsks. "Look at the mess you've made, King Rot," I say, just as I take my finger and swipe some of the beaded drops still collecting at his tip. His eyes flare as I bring my digit to my mouth and *suck*. His salty flavor bursts on my tongue, and I hollow my cheeks until I pull my finger out with a pop.

He lets out another curse. "Are you trying to kill me?"

My smile returns, as does my grip on his dick. "Kill you? Considering what I want, that wouldn't be very handy."

He grits out a chuckle. "*You're* being very handy."

I let out a laugh, but it's cut off when he reaches down and presses *right* against me with the heel of his palm.

"I can give as much as I get. Just remember that, Goldfinch."

I shudder, concentration interrupted, the smooth continuation of my strokes on his cock turning sporadic. His palm, however, continues its circling and pressing against me without missing a beat.

I'm not sure what it is about the tight pull of my skirt constricting me, but it makes his persistent grind even more intense. It's like I'm more aware of every little feeling. The ruby fabric pinning me. The heat from his palm. The wet spots he's left at both my belly and the cooling marks over my nipples from his mouth.

All of it settles over me, wet and warm, like the slow buildup of condensation. It coats me, from blushing cheeks to straining thighs to my hand still massaging his cock, another bead of precum gathering like a drop of dew.

I wish I could lean forward enough to lick it up.

"Don't tease me," I say, hips trying to jolt upward again, trying to make him press down harder. "I want to come."

"Is that right?" he says, as unhurried as ever.

"Yes," I try to snap out, though it sounds more like a whine. How he can make me feel so desperate so quickly is like a spell he's able to cast. I've never been so deliriously lost in lust as I am when I'm with him. And then, like pure magic, his hand moves faster, harder, making me moan, making me arch, making me *build and build and build and*—

"No!"

His hand is suddenly gone, and so is my orgasm.

I glare up at him, chest rising and falling like I've just run up five flights of stairs. "Why'd you stop? I was about to come."

The infuriating male gets up from the mattress, his weight gone, dress no longer fastened down. My legs tingle from the relief, and I sit up on an elbow and then instantly slip my hand down my front. I shuck up my skirt, drive my fingers right down, ready to circle over my aching clit—

My wrist is manacled by a resolute grip, caught beneath my dress, stopping me *right before* I could reach my needy spot. "Let go."

Ignoring me, he shoves his pants down with his other hand and then instead, brings my hand back to his dick.

Instead of stroking it, I *squeeze*. Hard. Not in a firm, sensual way. Not like I usually do for him, but callous and pissed, full of warning. But the asshole doesn't even flinch. Nope, he just *groans*. As if me squeezing him like I want to juice a lemon is pleasurable.

"Mmm, so aggressive," he says darkly, shoving his hips forward as if asking for more. "Trying to punish me?"

"Yes." This time, I try to reach for his balls. Let's see if he likes *that* part of him handled so hard.

But he must be attuned with my movements, because he snatches my wrist again, and then as quick as a blink, I'm flat on my back and both of my wrists are pinned above my head.

"You lost the privilege of your hands, my lady."

Excitement bursts through me, scattering across the bottom of my stomach. Maybe our fae nature makes us more similar than I know, because I seem to like it when he's aggressive too.

But I scowl at him anyway.

"If you're not going to make me come, I'll do it myself."

"No," he says with a shake of his head. "You won't. So

long as I'm in the room, I'm the one who will bestow pleasure upon you. I'm the one who decides when you come."

I lift my head slightly. "Then do it," I challenge.

If my body could speak for me, it would've come out as a plea.

He gives me a dark look, eyes roving over my disheveled appearance. "Keep your hands above your head. Don't move them."

I swallow hard with a nod, and as soon as I do, he releases my wrists.

He stands over me, finger dragging down with his gaze. "Look at this," he murmurs, his other hand grazing around the wet spot on my stomach. "You've made my cock a dripping mess. It's practically salivating to feast on your pussy."

My hips lift in invitation.

He fists his dick, giving himself a couple lazy strokes, and the move is so sexy that it makes me red-hot from the waist down.

"Mmm. Maybe I should just make you watch. I could spill the rest of my cum all over your pretty dress. Watch you writhe and whine as I hold back this cock that you want so badly."

My breath snags. "*No*," I say, shaking my head.

Even with the sconces burning along their spot on the walls, it's still dim in here, and with him standing over me, stroking himself, it makes me feel even more carnal, as if the dark is the safe keeper of all things lustful and wicked.

He continues to move his hand forwards and back. "You don't even know what you've unlocked, letting my cock drip all over your pretty dress," he says, movements slow. Even. As if he's not torturing me with this erotic tease. "It makes me want to sink my teeth into your neck and leave a mark in your skin. Makes me want to strip you down, your mouth open, tongue out, and cum all over your chest, your pussy, your face. Makes me want to smear it over your tits, rub it against your pouting lips, watch you swallow it down as I smooth the cream right over your throbbing pussy."

My eyes have gone wide, my pulse jumping with titillation. "Great Divine..."

"You'd be so covered in me that I'd be able to smell it," he growls, as if he's already feeling possessive of the idea, already wanting to bring it to fruition.

I almost want to let him.

Then, without warning, Slade reaches down and wrenches up my skirt, exposing me. He rips down my sopping panties in the next blink, and then he's on his knees, his face buried in my pussy.

My whole body jolts as he licks up my slit, his tongue flat and insistent, licking me like I'm his favorite taste. "Mmm, all this wet cream just for me."

His voice rumbles against me, sending vibrations that feed my core like I'm some hungry beast, desperate to be satisfied.

He spears his tongue, fucking it into me, and I whimper and writhe, trying to grind my hips up to make him pay attention to my throbbing nerves, but he pins me down with my bunched up skirts again.

"Slade," I wail out. "Lick my clit."

He pulls away his lapping tongue to look up at me from his spot between my legs, my juices coating his chin. "My dirty fucking girl wants her clit licked?"

"Yes! Make me come!" I'm practically sobbing with need, squirming and twitching wildly from side to side, trying to break free of his hold while simultaneously loving the restricted control.

"Mmm, I love it when you're needy and writhing."

His face comes down, and a bolt of pure electricity comes with him when his mouth latches on to my swollen clit and sucks and nips, his tongue flicking out to lick me with a fervor.

My hands dive down to his head, fingers feeding through his thick hair. I yank and pull, forcing his head to stay *right there*, for his tongue to keep eating me out like he's feasting on my clit, because I'm going to—

His hands wrench my wrists away just as his mouth does.

This time, the most embarrassing wail comes out of me. "No, I was so close, you bastard!"

His hands pin mine down against the bed. "I told you not to move your hands," he says with wicked chastening. "It's very naughty not to follow instructions."

It feels like my entire body is throbbing now, everything concentrated down to that one bundle of needy nerves that still isn't getting what I want. He keeps bringing me to the peak and then leaving me hanging. I feel like one single flick of his tongue, and I could go barreling over.

"You have to finish what you started," I plead. Because I'm too wound up. Too needy. He made me this way, and now it feels like if I don't get the release that he's built, I'll be left bereft and devoid.

Which is why I act like a crazed animal when he releases my hands to stand up, smirking down at me as he says, "No."

I surprise even myself with how quickly I move.

One second, I'm lying on the bed, and the next, I'm up and shoving him so hard he staggers back. I don't know if it's because I've actually used enough force or if it's because I caught him by surprise, but either way, his feet shuffle backwards several steps.

Before he can solidify his footing, I'm on him, an animalistic noise that tears from my throat. "*Fuck. Me. Now.*" My snarl is demanding, my hand on his cock. "If you don't give me what I want, I'm going to knee you in the balls so hard all that cum you want to paint on my body will be choked up for a week."

Most men would probably gape and recoil at that threat.

But Slade?

He goes fucking *wild.*

My ass is in his hands, my dress is rucked up at my front, and then my back is pushed up against the nearest wall. But I don't even feel when my head cracks against it, because I'm laughing, laughing that I've pushed him like this, made him lose control.

"I was going to tease you some more. Keep playing with that pussy until you scream. But now you've pushed me too far. You're about to be fucked hard right against this wall, Lady Auren."

I shove my lips against his, biting down hard, making

him hiss when I draw blood before I pull back and smirk. "*Good.*"

He thrusts into me full hilt, so hard I think the world must split open.

Or maybe that's just me.

I cry out his name, nails digging into the leather of his shirt, feeling so full, so invaded, stuffed full of his cock and loving every inch of it.

"Is this what you needed, Goldfinch?" he growls against my ear.

"*Goddess, yes.*" Because I do. I need to not think. To not worry. I need for all of my awareness to be reduced down to nothing but something carnal and fierce and utterly satisfying.

Slade only gives me one slow drag out, and then he starts to fuck me right here, every thrust forceful and fast, making the wall creak and shake as he slams into me again and again.

And then he reaches one hand up, fingers demanding entry to my mouth, two thick digits pressing past my lips. "Suck."

Just that, and I moan. I moan, and I slather my tongue all over his fingers, sucking them deep into my mouth.

Those wet fingers go to my clit, rubbing, circling, pinching, and I'm going to combust, I'm going to—

He pulls it away. Just as my pussy was about to contract, just as I was about to explode.

A furious sob rips out of me. "*No...*"

"Yes," he purrs in response, his dick pulsing in me, feeling like it's growing even harder, even thicker.

"I need it," I beg.

"You were very naughty, weren't you? Shoving at me like that, making demands." His dark voice somehow makes my heated skin erupt with a chill of shivers. "I should bring you to the edge again and again. I should keep battering at this pussy, keep teasing this clit, make you mindless in your need. Bring you up again and again, never letting you slip off that peak."

I already feel mindless, and if he keeps teasing me, I might die. "No. *Please.*"

Maybe it's the throatiness of my plea, but Slade captures my mouth and starts kissing the absolute hell out of me.

There is no slow stroke of a tongue. No light nip of teeth. This is messy and dominating and fucking *sexy*. He owns my mouth as he owns the rest of my body—thoroughly and possessively and yet with a level of trust between us that allows me to completely let go in the thrill of such wild passion and give it back tenfold.

He only pulls away when I turn my head to gasp for breath, and then he rips me away from the wall, expertly slamming me up and down over his cock as if the weight of me makes no difference to the capacity of his strength. If he wasn't already deep before, he's even deeper now.

Every inch of me is impaled, stuck on the relentless cock that's shoving in and out as he lifts me up and down. It's *bliss*. It's agony. It's both wrapped up together, making my vision spin with crackling stars.

Because I need.

I need I need I need

My back hits the bed with a jump, and he folds my knees up to my chest, fucking into me like a male possessed.

"I'm going to let you come this time," he tells me, and I nearly cry in relief and in need, my breasts bouncing obscenely with the intensity of his rough thrusts. "And when you do, you're going to gush all over my dick and scream my name, and then you'll thank me for edging you because you're going to come harder than you ever have before."

I think this is probably an exaggeration.

It's not.

His hand comes down to my clit, but instead of rubbing it, he smacks it. A quick slap right over the throbbing nerves, and that sting of pain immerses me like being tossed in a tub full of water, stunning my senses and enveloping me in the shock. And then he rubs, shoving that twinge straight over into pleasure just as he growls out one commanded word.

"Come."

The orgasm ruptures through me, tearing me into pieces.

I come, and come and *come*, and he keeps rubbing and rubbing and *fucking*.

When the rupture peaks and ebbs, he somehow just rolls me right into another one, like he's gone right from tossing me into a bath to then dumping me into a river, its dangerously quick current sweeping me away before I can grasp anything around me.

And when I come again, still rippling with the aftereffects, *he keeps going.*

He keeps going, and I'm not sure if I'm going to die or pass out or just drown in pleasure.

But what a way to be swept away.

"Good girl," he says, and my pleasure lifts and twists on just that word. "You feel exquisitely *filthy*."

I'm shaking all over. I think I might be crying. I'm so wound up, so overly sensitive, so magnified that I toss my head back and forth, begging, begging.

But somehow, I'm begging for more while also begging for him to end this euphoric agony.

"You like that, don't you, baby?"

I can't even speak in anything but moaned-out mumblings.

His lips come down to scrape against my throat, tongue licking along the line of my jaw before his mouth captures mine. "You're so fucking gorgeous. Gushing as I fuck you." And I am. I can hear how crudely wet I am by the sound of our skin slapping together, the way his dick is coated in me. "I want your sweet pussy to cinch around me, Auren," he purrs. "Choke my cock and make me come with you."

My babbling beg is indecipherable, but surely, I can't do it *again*.

"One more. You can give me one more, because you're my perfect fucking female who loves when I fuck into you so hard that you see stars. You love it when you tease me, squeezing my balls, making my dick so wet it weeps. Isn't that right, Goldfinch?" I'm out of my mind with crazed need, with blissful exhaustion, with a peak that seems to never end. "So give me. One. More."

My body willingly bends to his demand. I feel my back arch up, feel my whole body shake. And then I give him one damn more.

The rapturous torment cleaves through me, and I'm not

sure how I have enough breath to scream his name, but I do. My pussy clamps around him, and he buries himself so deeply inside of me, hot jets of cum gorging into me.

And my body just dissipates. Mind completely blissed-out. I sink against the mattress with a shaken sigh, in such a state of spent, contented bliss that my eyes go dark, lids fluttering shut.

Because that one more ruined me in the best possible way.

The last thing I remember is a warm cloth wiping away the stickiness between my thighs, the gentle tucking of my hair off my face. The effortless shift of my body as I'm moved on the bed, pillow below my head and covers over the rest of me, and a tender kiss against my forehead.

Then, I'm gone to the world.

CHAPTER 58

AUREN

I wake up, prying my eyes open like they've been glued shut. My whole body is heavy, as if I've just had the best nap *ever*.

And then I remember why.

Orgasms.

Orgasms, and how thoroughly King Ravinger just *ravaged me*.

I came in here to talk to him about Manu, to ask him about the severity of the threat to his kingdom. About the Conflux, and if it really is a slap on the wrist or if Manu was blowing smoke to block the fire.

But instead of talking, he seduced me.

The prick.

Glaring at the empty room, I slam my hands down on the bedding and leap out of bed, stalking toward the closet. I think I only fell asleep for a few minutes, so I need to get down to the dinner with Manu, but I certainly can't wear this dress. Not with its certain...noticeable spots that are now dried and stiffened on the front.

I yank off the pretty ruby fabric, thankful that Slade doesn't have maids come in his room, because there is absolutely *no way* I could ever let someone else scrub this. I will be doing that myself in the bathroom later.

I shimmy my hips into a pair of black leggings and then pull on a shirt this time. Should've been wearing pants earlier. Then maybe I wouldn't have let myself get seduced and become so easily distracted.

Stupid.

It's just...*that male*.

He does the smirk and the chuckle and the lines of power with his scruffy jaw and his dirty words, and I just melt. Every time.

It's also his cock. He has a really good one.

Glaring around at his closet, I call to the gold that I wrapped around the pillars in his bedroom, and it immediately floods toward me from the other room. As soon as it's near, I direct it with my movements, slapping a hand against his favorite leather jerkin. My gold immediately engulfs it, making the fabric go all shiny and gaudy.

The sight makes me feel instantly better.

So I do his favorite pants next. Not *my* favorite pants— the ones that hug his glutes just right and make his butt look *really* good—but the other ones. Then I gild his extra boots. His coat. Even the daggers he has hanging on the walls. All of these things that he will not be able to wear anymore, because someone will definitely see.

When I've used up all the gold from the pillars, I dust my hands off, looking around in satisfaction.

It's the little things.

Personally, I think he deserves it. He basically sexed me into unconsciousness so he could go off to give Manu his final answer at dinner without me being able to discuss it at length beforehand. There are a lot of lives at stake here, not just mine, and despite his certainty on the matter, it's worth talking about.

Just as I'm about to leave the closet, my eyes catch on the feathered coat. The one I wore after I left the Red Raids. The one that Slade had in his closet back in Ranhold. But that's not all he's somehow been able to retrieve. From its pocket, I catch a peek of the fae book I'd brought to him back in Fifth. The book I never got to ask him about, because, once again, he'd distracted me with sex.

This seems to be a theme.

I add it to the list of things I need to talk to him about and then go into the bathroom. After I wash up and comb out my tangled hair, I throw it into a braid and then leave Slade's rooms. Walking out into the hall, I hurry to make it to the dining room in time.

Except, when I get there, the room is empty. The table cleared off. I stop in the middle of the doorway, staring at it, my heart starting to beat quicker and quicker.

When I see a servant come in at the back of the room, I call out. "Excuse me?" The young man pauses, eyes going wide. "I'm sorry, but when did the dinner end? The one with the advisor from Third Kingdom?"

"About an hour ago, Lady Auren."

Shit. I missed it.

I missed it, and Slade didn't even try to wake me up.

My lips press together in a hard line. "Do you happen to know where King Ravinger and the Third advisor went?"

"His Majesty went to the army base. Sir Ioana, I believe, was set to depart soon." Frustration brews in my gut.

"Thank you."

He nods and hurries away, disappearing like he's worried I might ask him something else. Or maybe he's afraid I'm the magic-stealer that's going to throw gold at him.

I stare at the dark room, unsure what to do for a moment. Slade left me in post-edged orgasmic bliss, probably snoring in his bed, and then came down here *alone* to once again say *I decline* to the Conflux. He didn't even wake me up to tell me before he ran off into the moonlight to visit the army base.

I should've gilded more of his things.

I'm pissed. I'm worried. I'm so scared about how this is all going to play out, and now that the answer has been given, consequences will pile up quickly. It's all happened so fast, slipping right through my fingers before I could get a real grip on it.

Spinning around, I start walking away, wondering if I can catch Manu before he leaves. I start heading in the direction of his room, the silent soles of my shoes padding down the hall. If I can talk to him again, maybe I can convince him to tell his sister not to cut off Fourth's imports and spur on Slade's need to retaliate.

Yet when I find another servant and ask them where Manu's rooms are, she tells me that he's already left. That he and his guards were seen just a few minutes ago walking out of the room.

My heart sinks.

For a moment, I consider going down to the army base to talk to Slade, but I'm too jumbled up to do that right now. I find myself walking toward the gardens instead. The guard just inside opens the door for me. "Getting some fresh air, Lady Auren?"

"Yes, thank you."

Despite my troubled thoughts, the outside air does help. As soon as I step outside, I breathe it in, the cool air calming me slightly. And I need some calm, because my stomach is a churning mess, my emotions agitated. Manu is probably on his way right now to his sister.

Fourth Kingdom might starve because of me.

It doesn't matter what kind of positive impression we're trying to push out to the public about me—once they realize I'm the reason for them going hungry, they'll turn on me more than they already want to.

The guard follows me out, trailing quietly behind me while I'm deep in thought. Yet I only make it a few feet when I notice someone on the bench near the row of roses. "Rissa?"

Her blonde head lifts up, white dress practically glowing in the moonlight. I walk over to her as she gets to her feet.

"I haven't seen you very much since you arrived," I say as I come up to stand in front of her.

"That's because I've been loath to get out of the bed," she says, tucking back a loose strand of her hair. "After traveling in a tent for so long, I needed to get reacquainted with a feather mattress and not feeling like my toes were going to freeze right off my feet."

"I'm sorry you had such a long, rough journey."

"Yes, well. We can't all infatuate kings and ride timberwings across the Barrens, now can we?"

I snort out a quiet laugh as I look out at the garden. Other than a few lanterns lit along the outer stone wall, it's dark yet peaceful out here, the moonlight casting off just as much shadow as it does light.

"Want to walk?" I ask her.

She tips her head in a nod, and we start walking toward the hedges, our steps slow as the guard trails a respectable few feet behind us to give us privacy.

"How's Polly doing? I hope she got the coins I sent down to her."

"She did. And she left straight for the brothel after."

I can tell just by the tone of her voice that it bothers her.

"I know you don't want that for her, but she seemed like that's what she wanted for herself," I say gently, breathing in the scent of jasmine as we pass by its vine trailing up intricate latticework.

"I know she does," Rissa says, quickly glancing at me from the corner of her eye. "I know that now," she amends. "I just...I'm going to miss her."

I'm surprised at the rare moment of vulnerability she's showing, and that's when I realize how sad she looks. Rissa is always hard-as-steel. Seductive. Smart. Blunt. But sad? Never.

I look back at the guard, motioning for him to hold back while Rissa and I stop just inside the first row of hedges. "I know Polly expressed some...anger at you for getting her out of Ranhold," I begin carefully. "But I think deep down, she knows you saved her life. Whether she wants to admit it right now or not, she was probably going to die on dew."

"And she better not ever try anything like that again," Rissa snaps as she glares at the leaves of the shrub like they're personally offending her. "Because she *will* get herself killed next time, and I'm not going to swoop in and save her. I'm not going to watch her go through *weeks* of withdrawals."

I wince, just imagining how that must've been. I have no idea what a body would experience after being cut off from dew, but based on Polly's haggard appearance and the fact she had to go through that while traveling with the army through a frozen wasteland, the experience probably wasn't good. I can imagine what Rissa had to endure to get her through it all.

Better her than me.

"Polly will come around," I say gently, reaching down to take Rissa's hand. She startles for a second, and I fully expect her to pull away. Yet to my astonishment, she actually squeezes my hand.

She lets go almost immediately, but still.

When she sees the smile creep up my face, she scowls at me. "No."

"No, what?" I ask, still grinning.

"I know you're thinking we're great friends now. It was a squeeze of comfort, nothing more."

"I don't know," I say with a breezy shrug. "It felt like a friendship squeeze."

She huffs and starts walking away. "Shouldn't you be off with your king, doing something romantic?"

"I'm not feeling very romantic at the moment," I confess. "Besides, he's back down at the army base again."

"They do like to spend all their time there, don't they?" she replies, looking put out. "Captain Oaf is always down there."

I quirk an eyebrow just as we reach the fountain and bench where I was practicing my gold the other day. "And that...bothers you? That Osrik is at the base a lot?" I try to ask as nonchalantly as possible, but I think I fail miserably, because she stiffens up.

"Why would it bother me?" she asks defensively, arms crossed in front of her as she stands before the fountain. "He's a lout and a ruffian. An army base is the perfect place for him."

"Mm-hmm."

She swings her head in my direction, narrowing her eyes and opening her mouth to deliver some retort.

Yet whatever she was about to say gets cut off suddenly when we both hear a noise behind us. I turn just in time to see my guard suddenly fall to his knees. I rush over, thinking he's choking or passed out, but then I see the second figure behind him. The one holding the knife.

Eyes wide, I watch the guard fall flat on his face with

a gurgling noise that twists my stomach. Fear pounds in my veins, and then I hear, "Auren, watch—"

I whirl around at Rissa's warning call, and I freeze in place. There's a man I don't recognize holding one hand over Rissa's mouth and the other pointing a dagger right at her heart. Her blue eyes are wide and terrified, the color drained from her face.

Just as I lurch toward her, something smacks into my temple. Not enough to make me pass out, but enough to send a shock of pain and dizziness through me, throwing me off as I stumble back.

I call upon my gold, but since it's night, all I have at my disposal is my bracelet. It melts against my wrist, dripping down my hand to collect in my palm. It's a tiny amount, *too* tiny, but it's all I have. If I can get it to the man who just hit me, to sharpen it like a needle and stab him through the eye, then I could—

A putrid smelling cloth is suddenly slammed over my nose and mouth. I sputter and cough, inhaling something sharp and bitter and consuming. It coats my tongue, sticks to my throat, burns my eyes, flares in my chest.

No, no, no!

Panic is a scream in my head, blaring through my ears, pounding through my veins. But with the blow to the head and this dizzying drug trapped against my face, I immediately slump, unable to hold my weight, unable to do anything.

I can't move my legs. Can't control my arms. My fisted hand tries and fails to get the gold to help. It slows and clogs against my palm like mud in a bog, too thick and gluey to move.

Someone catches me before I collapse, and it's all I can do to hold up my head. It's all I can do to keep my eyes open. It's like looking through a vortex, everything moving, everything violent and blurred. The cloth is just thin enough to let me breathe in and out, but it's forced and suffocating, making my heart race.

My mind, however, seems to be slowing down. So are my blinks. I'm trying to stay awake, trying to make sense of what's happening. The gold is dripping off my hand like drying paint, just as drugged and paralyzed as I am, and it falls from my fingers in a useless drizzle onto the lush grass.

Rissa is struggling, muffled screams against the cloth, her terrified eyes locked on mine. And I have nothing. No other gold around to help us, my magic too tainted from this poison to use it even if there were and my body weren't incapacitated.

And then two people walk forward. One of them is an unfamiliar man wearing a long white robe. A robe—and a large necklace hanging down with the emblem of Second Kingdom. My heart splits in fear, but then, my eyes fly to the second person moving out of the shadows.

Manu.

"It's nothing personal, Doll," he says quietly, dressed in blue so dark it's nearly black, his arms bare, hair tied back tight. "But I am loyal to my sister."

"And to the law of the Divine," the robed man says.

Manu nods stiffly. "Let's go. We can't afford to be anywhere near here when Ravinger gets back."

I try to scream against the cloth, but all that comes out is a blustering breath.

"What about this one?" someone asks—the man holding Rissa. "She's just a saddle."

It's getting so hard to keep my eyes open. So hard to hold up my head. Rissa doesn't look away from me, though. So I don't look away from her either.

"Just knock her out and leave her," Manu says.

Relief trickles through me, though the drug has even affected that, making it murky in its echoing gurgle.

But then the robed man shakes his head, and my entire body tightens. "No. We can't afford loose ends. Kill her."

My stomach roils. My lungs feel like they're melting in my chest, continuing to pull in polluted air, but my bitter-stained tongue is too leaden to let out a cry of protest anyway.

When I see the man holding her start to plunge the dagger through her chest, time speeds up. Like it's trying to get this over with, like my body and mind are far too slowed down for what's happening.

I try to scream, but all I get out is the faintest of whimpers, and my vision starts to go black, my head pounding.

I watch as Rissa's eyes flinch with pain and shock as she's stabbed through.

Fast. Too fast I can't stop it. Too fast that I can't do *anything*.

The blade goes in, stuck through her body as easily as someone skewers a piece of meat. Her mouth parts in shock, gaze still locked on me, and then that shock turns to something else.

Something finite and fatal.

She slumps, and I slump with her.

Her body is tossed onto the garden grass with carelessness. There's a bloodstain blooming amidst the flowers right there on her white dress, the blade still sticking up from her chest.

And it feels like a blade sticks right through my own heart, while a silent scream rends through my head.

Then, everything goes dark.

CHAPTER 59

SLADE

In just a week, the whole base has been saturated with the smell of shit and leather. The underground pipework has gotten clogged from overuse, so new latrines had to be dug. The rationing has been a nightmare to regulate too. There are still some soldiers sleeping in tents, even with the base putting up new buildings as quickly as we can make them, and there are nearly two hundred soldiers that Hojat and the other army menders are treating for travel wounds and sicknesses.

Morale hasn't been the greatest. Not with the reduced food. Not with the tight living quarters and the fact that no one's going to be dismissed to return home any time soon.

Queen Kaila and the other monarchs want to be difficult. Want to spread this narrative of Auren being a villain. Of me harboring a traitor. Of making Midas into some kind of martyr.

It's all fucking noise.

But they can spread their sounds as much as they want.

The queen may be a master of words, but I'm an expert at ignoring the clamor. I'm not the type of male to be swayed by sensationalized commotion meant to sway a populace.

Rot is silent.

So they can be as vociferous as they want, but at the end of the day, I will lay them to silent waste if I need to.

Across from me, Ryatt finishes up his reports. Things have been strained between us, but for all his bluster, he's been carrying out every order. He looks wrecked though, eyes red from lack of sleep, his frown more pronounced than usual. His hair is still sweaty from wearing his helmet outside while he got updates from the list of volunteers who'd agreed to leave Brackhill to go and source more food.

So he might not agree with my decision, but he's doing what needs to be done. When push comes to shove, he always does.

Aside from him, Osrik is the only other one sitting in this meeting. Judd and Lu left a week ago. Lu flew to Sixth Kingdom to get me a better handle on what's happening there, and Judd has gone to First Kingdom.

"...And we've got forty more going up to the plot of land Barley suggested," Ryatt finishes.

"How soon are they estimated to arrive?"

"I signed them off on a timberwing rotation. They're taking them ten at a time—half of our Perch, not counting our own beasts. Once they return, we'll switch them out, sending the next ten, and so on, giving the timbers plenty of time to rest before the next batch."

"Good."

"But it's not enough," Ryatt warns.

I nod my head, because that's true. Or it would be, except... "First Kingdom took the deal."

His eyes go wide. "They did?"

"Just got the reply from Judd," I explain, patting the letter in my pocket. "The King of First agreed to reroute his ships going to port at Second and instead head for ours. Once there, we'll get our supplies of food, and he'll get a fuck ton of oil at a *very* good price."

Ryatt lets out a weighted exhale. "Well, finally some good fucking news."

Nodding, I say, "We needed it."

"It certainly helps our food supply, but we still have problems," he cautions. "The army is grumbling more than normal. We're lucky we've always trained them to stand up to harsh conditions, but even they're taking a morale hit with all of this shit."

"I know."

Ryatt shoots a look at Osrik across from him before returning back to me. "They deserve better than this," he says, leaning forward so that his metal chest plate clinks against the table. "They got dragged across the fucking continent for show, dragged back, and now they have to prepare for yet *another* war that you might instigate."

"I'm not instigating it."

"You know what I mean," he says, waving me off. "They're loyal. You know they are. And they're the strongest, most fierce, and feared army in Orea. But they're losing faith in their leadership."

"I know that too," I say before Os and I share a look. "Which is why I'm going to officially name *you* as the new army commander of Fourth."

My brother lurches back, shock crossing his face. "*What?*"

I nod. "It's already done. I filled out the paperwork, and Os turned it into the lieutenants. You might want to prepare a speech."

Ryatt looks bewildered. "You can't be fucking serious."

"You're ready," I say. "And honestly, you've been ready for a while. It's time I pass the reins officially."

"You're really going to give it up? Going to trust me to lead them? We argue all the fucking time."

"I trust you."

He looks at me warily, as if he doesn't quite believe me. "I'm sure there are going to be things I disagree with from time to time, but I'm also sure that you have this army's best interest at heart, as well as all of Fourth Kingdom," I tell him.

He doesn't take the bait of the compliment, but he does look a little bolstered. "I thought you liked being commander way more than you liked being a king."

"I do. But this army doesn't need me anymore."

"What about Rip? Half the army's fear factor is because of the notorious rumors about you."

I give an easy shrug. "I'll make sure I bring Rip around plenty to show a united front to the soldiers, and I'll fight when I need to, but for all intents and purposes, Commander Rip is retiring so we can bring in new blood for the coming days. As far as being notorious...I'm sure you'll make a name for yourself."

He snorts and shakes his head but doesn't voice any other doubts. "What about Drollard?"

"How often you visit is up to you. But as the true commander, you will have more responsibilities, and that means you won't be able to go there as often."

"That's fine," he says quickly—eagerly. And that right there is all I need to know to confirm that I made the right decision, that he *is* ready for this. He gestures over at Os. "How come Os or one of the other fuckers isn't getting this position instead of me?"

"You think any of us want it? Fuck no." Os rumbles out a laugh. "We're much better off continuing to be your captains and telling you when you're shitting the bed."

"Thanks," he says dryly.

"So you accept? Officially?" I check.

He stands up, and I stand with him, and to my surprise, he holds out his hand and we shake. Much different from the last time we stood across this table.

"Thank you."

I give a nod as he drops his hand, and I pat him on the shoulder. "Don't screw up."

Ryatt rolls his eyes, but it doesn't have any of his normal acrimony in it. "I'm going to be on your ass about any decisions you make that affect the army, you know," he warns me.

"Oh, I'm aware," I say with a smirk.

Another reason why I know I'm making the right choice. Ryatt needs this—needs his own identity, his own purpose, and Auren showed me that. It's something I should've given him a long time ago.

Just then, there's a knock on the door, and Os thumps over to open it. I see one of the runners pass off a sealed vial, saluting Os as he's dismissed.

"What is it?" Ryatt asks.

Os twists open the lid and dumps out the scroll inside before passing it to me.

Taking it, I quickly unroll it, eyes scanning over the contents, and then my stomach drops. "Fuck."

"What?" Osrik asks, snapping out the word in a graveled voice.

"One of the mines. It fucking *collapsed*."

Both he and Ryatt tense. "Which one?"

I look up from the paper, barely able to stop myself from crushing it in my fist. "Oil."

Os lets out a curse. "Well, that's fucking convenient."

"Way too convenient to be a coincidence," Ryatt seethes, looking over at me. "What's going to happen with the First Kingdom deal?"

"It'll fall through if there's no oil at the port to meet his ships," I say through a growl.

"Can we prove it was sabotage?" Os asks.

"The foreman is looking into it."

"This is bad," Ryatt says, scrubbing a hand over his face. "What the fuck is with her? Queen Kaila has never pushed you like this before."

My rot pricks and writhes beneath my skin, the roots jabbing beneath my jaw and threatening to dig deeper down my arms.

"This is her chance to weaken us, and she's taking it."

I shove the letter into my pocket and stride for the door. Ryatt pulls his helmet back on as he and Osrik follow behind me. As soon as we're outside, the noise of the base is amplified, the smell of smoke from the fire pits clogging my nose.

Instead of fresh meat that should be cooking over the flames, I know they're probably eating some kind of travel gruel. I'm lucky that the soldiers are so loyal to me and their captains, or I might have more fighting and grumbling on my hands. The way they proceed from here on out will be a true test of their fealty.

The soldiers walking around give us a wide berth, but there are more respectful nods than guarded looks of irritability. Probably because I gave everyone a pay raise. Yet if the mines on the other side have been caved in too...

One problem at a time.

Just as we reach the run-in shed where some of the horses are kept, another horse comes galloping toward us, dirt kicking up beneath its hooves. The rider yanks it to a stop, practically leaping off its back when he sees us. I'm instantly on alert, stopping with Os and Ryatt at my sides as the man hurries over. I can see right away by his uniform that he's one of the castle's guards.

"Sire," he says, running up, face flushed. "There's a problem."

Tension thickens the stance of my shoulders. "What is it?"

"There was a woman attacked in the gardens."

Everything in me becomes chaotic. A jolt of noise in my ears, a jump in my chest, even my vision seems to flare.

"Lady Auren?" A million things run through my mind, but the guard shakes his head.

709

"No, Sire. The Lady Rissa."

Osrik's head reels back. "*What?*" he snarls. "What the fuck do you mean she was *attacked*?"

Most people would be a bit intimidated when being faced with all of Osrik's fury bearing down on them, but this man holds steady. "She was stabbed, sir. The guards patrolling found her and another guard out there with fatal wounds."

Osrik shoves past the guard and leaps onto his horse before I can even finish processing what the man said.

Ryatt and I sprint to our own mounts, trying to catch up as we race back to the castle. The three of us get back in record time, the horses pulled to a stop at the front courtyard. When we toss the reins to the handlers, Os is already through the side door, running the shortest path toward the gardens.

As soon as we're inside, there's an obvious turmoil in the energy of the castle. Servants are whispering in groups, quickly skittering away when they see us coming.

When we get outside, the garden is lit up more than usual, extra torches stuck into the ground, and dozens of guards are filling the area.

"Where is she?" Osrik snarls at the first guard he comes to.

"Over here, Os!" His head snaps to Warken's voice, and the three of us make our way past the rows of bushes and shrubs, following the stomped over flowers and grass until we get to the center of the garden where the fountain churns.

Warken, Isalee, and Barley are here, and even Keg is with them, standing beside the fountain, their faces grim. We have to pass by a gathered group as they stand over the body of a fellow guard.

I kneel down at his side. One of the castle menders is hovering over him, inspecting the slash across the young man's throat. The mender checking the wound has blood on his hands, and there's more of it stained against the grass. I hear Ryatt curse beneath his breath.

"Where's—" Osrik's question cuts off when some of the people shift, and his eyes latch onto a figure on the ground just behind the fountain.

All I can see are the edges of a white skirt and one bare foot, a shoe kicked off lying uselessly a foot away.

Os rushes over to her, falling to his knees on the ground. "*Fuck!*"

After rounding the fountain, I can see Hojat leaning over Rissa's body. There's a stain of blood seeped through her chest, a silver dagger still embedded there.

I've seen Osrik lose his shit many times.

I've seen him snarl and yell, punish and kill. I've seen him slaughter without remorse, insult without batting an eye, make threats with indifference.

But I have *never* seen him like this.

It's like his eyes are trying to adjust seeing the blade sticking out of her, like he can't quite correlate the blood soaked through her dress.

His eyes snap to her colorless face and closed eyes, and he reaches out to grab her shoulders. "Rissa." His voice is strained. Chapped. As if her name was torn from his throat and whipped raw in the wind.

Unmoving, he shakes her gently. "Rissa!"

"Sir Osrik," Hojat gently chides, reaching out to tug away

his hand. I see Osrik's hands tighten for a split second before he lets Hojat pull him away.

"No. *Fucking no!*" Os snarls right in her face, denial and fury battling it out. "You will wake up, you stubborn woman. You can't be fucking dead. Hear me, Yellow Bell? You can't be fucking dead because we have mistakes to make."

He chokes off, and I stand in shock as he suddenly folds his huge body over her slight frame, tipping his forehead down to hers, squeezing shut agonized eyes.

Ryatt and I are both frozen at his display, while Isalee's eyes glitter with moisture, and a thread of a tear stitches its way down Barley's cheek.

How am I going to tell Auren?

"Sir Osrik?" Hojat says gently. "Lady Rissa is not dead."

Shock plummets through me, and Osrik's head whips up so fast he almost headbutts our mender. Disbelief crosses his expression as he looks back down to her.

"The dagger just missed her heart, and because it was left inside her, she didn't bleed out," Hojat explains. "But I will need to get her into the castle's infirmary to perform surgery immediately. I'm just waiting on a carrying board." Just then, a couple of mender's aids with their red bands around their biceps come rushing through the garden, carrying the board.

"I'll carry her," Osrik grunts out as he gets to his feet.

Hojat winces. "I'm not sure if—"

"I said, *I'll carry her.*"

"Os..." I step forward, but Hojat waves me away.

"It's alright, Your Majesty," he says before looking back at Osrik. "Carry her *very* carefully. Slow movements, support her neck, and try not to jostle her chest. She's alive, but just barely. I'm not sure if she'll make it once I remove the dagger. You need to prepare yourself, just in case."

Giving a stiff nod and grinding his teeth so hard he nearly cracks his jaw, Osrik leans down and collects her in his arms. It's the gentlest thing I've ever seen him do. As if he's picking up the thinnest pane of glass, and one wrong move will make it shatter.

With Hojat leading the way, he carries Rissa out of the garden and into the castle, disappearing from view.

"What the fuck happened?" I ask as soon as he's gone. There's a blood spot and the impression of Rissa's body still left on the grass. My eye catches on a glint of something else further in the distance, but a worker walks over it before setting a bucket down beside the blood and starts to wash it away. When I squint in the dark, whatever I'd seen before is gone.

Warken watches as the menders lift the dead guard's body and carry it inside before he answers. "The patrol that came through the garden alerted me. When we came out, we found the guard and the woman. I sent for you immediately."

"The working theory is that the guard followed her out here. Perhaps he was jealous or possessive of her, and so he killed her before slitting his own throat," Isalee says.

"It wouldn't be the first time something like this happened to a woman. Especially a beautiful one," Barley says.

"Yeah, but *here*?" Keg says with a shake of his head. I know he's been spending time with his family since he returned with the rest of the soldiers, and I bet he didn't expect to see violence like this *outside* of the army.

"Do you know the guard personally?" I ask my Premiers.

Isalee shakes her head. "Just the basics. We'll look through his file, but as you know, no one is allowed to serve who's had a history of violent attacks or aggressive behavior."

"The lady hasn't been here that long," Ryatt points out. "How could the guard get infatuated with her so quickly?"

"It happens," Keg says. "My brother and I have had to beat off more than a few men who couldn't take no for an answer from Barley."

A nearby guard pushes his way forward. "Holman wouldn't have done that!" he says, face blotchy with emotion. He's young, probably only twenty or so, and the way he sniffs and rubs his nose on his sleeve tells me that he knew the guard personally.

"How did you know Holman?" Isalee asks.

"He was my best friend," he says with another sniff. "I'm tellin' you, I know how this looks, but it wasn't him. He wouldn't have done that. He fancied a few of the women here, sure, but he never said anything about the lady. He would've told me."

I nod, and my eyes drift behind him to where Marcoul, my head guard, comes walking over and tugs the man away.

"What do you think?" I ask Isalee and Warken with a lowered voice. "Do you want help looking into it?"

"No, we'll handle it," Isalee replies.

With a nod, I say, "I need to go tell Auren. I left her sleeping earlier. She'll want to be in the mender's wing while Hojat works on Rissa."

Ryatt comes with me back inside the castle, my brow

furrowed as we head upstairs. "You don't think the guard did it, do you?" he asks quietly so that none of the staff hears.

"No, I don't."

I'm not sure why, but I have a bad feeling in my gut.

"I don't either. Something just isn't sitting right." We're quiet until we reach Ryatt's floor. "I'm going to dip in my room so I can change out of Fake Rip," he says as we split off. "I'll meet you down in the mender's wing."

With a nod, I turn and go up another flight of stairs, and then cut down the hall to my rooms where I let myself in. Yet when I make it into the bedroom, I find the bed empty. With a churning feeling of unease, I scoop up her cut ribbon from the bedside table and put it in my pocket. In the closet, I see the rumpled remains of the ruby dress she was wearing earlier. I see my black and brown clothes now shiny gold.

And I know.

Right then. That churning feeling in my gut pushes at me, nauseates me. The glint of my clothes makes me immediately think of that glint I thought I saw on the grass outside in the gardens. A thought I dismissed too quickly.

My heart fucking bulges like it's going to explode, surging with fear and fury.

I check the bathroom. The front sitting room. The private room where we take our meals. The library. The kitchens. The roof. And when I'm up there, with the wind whipping at my face, I'm panting and pounding and fucking *panicked*. Because she's not here. She's *not fucking here*.

"Sire?"

I spin around to find Marcoul behind me along with several other guards, Ryatt included.

"What's going on?" my brother asks as he pushes his way forward.

"She's gone."

The friction of those two words abrades my mouth, sparking such searing panic that it burns my throat with acid.

What happened in the garden had nothing to do with the guard. He wasn't a murderer, he was a victim, same as Rissa.

My eyes churn, skin rippling, spikes trying to shove up through my arms and down my back, my gums aching as my fangs drop down.

I whip around, and the look on my face makes my brother's eyes go wide.

"They took Auren. They fucking *took her*!"

I stuff two fingers in my mouth, letting out a shrill whistle so loud that it makes the guards flinch. But Argo is hunting this time of night. He could be miles away, too far to hear me. Lady Rissa and the guard Holman weren't found for at least a half hour, and it took even longer for the guard to fetch me, for me to come up here...

"What do you want us to do?" Ryatt asks, coming up beside me.

"I think you got your wish," I snarl bitterly. "I think that fucking prick kidnapped Auren to take her to the Conflux."

Ryatt pales.

Whirling, I start sprinting away, because I need a timberwing. I'll take Ryatt's if I have to, his is the second fastest, and if I have to yank the beast from the roost, then I—

716

A deathly loud call shrieks through the air, and a second later, I hear the landing with the screech of sharp talons against the tiled roof. Argo snaps at the guards, making them jump back, before his iridescent eyes blink at me.

I waste no time. I'm up on his back in a blink, and he's tearing off into the night sky in the next.

"Wait!" Ryatt's voice is snagged away by the wind as I hold onto the reins, leaning into the climb.

I don't fucking care.

I will *not* wait.

Because they took her.

But I won't fucking stand for it. I don't care how long it takes me to catch up to them. I will ride day and night until I get to Second Kingdom if I have to.

And when I get there, they will *all* wish they'd never taken her away.

CHAPTER 60

AUREN

I peel my eyes open like peeling off a layer of skin. My lids snag, not wanting to separate until I rip with a little more force, leaving them stinging.

As soon as I look around, I wish I'd left my eyes closed.

Immediately, I know that I'm not at Brackhill anymore. Not just because of this room that I'm in, either, but because I can feel the difference in the air. Fourth Kingdom is warm and muggy, as if the warmth dances with the moisture of the rivers. Yet the air here lacks any signs of moisture altogether. It feels thinned out. Stretched by an empty, arid heat that would bake any sort of precipitation right out of itself.

I remember snatches of consciousness, of being held against someone as we flew through the air. I remember that foul cloth pressed against my mouth and nose, over and over again, between brief moments where broth and water were poured down my throat.

But now I'm here, finally climbed out of the chasm of unconsciousness, and I know where I am without even looking out the barred window. This room is the color of sand, the texture of the walls swiped with whatever tool the carpenter scraped the plaster on. I sit up from the single-person bed I'm lying on, my slippered feet hitting the rust-colored tile floor.

There's one small table in the corner of the room, with a strangely shaped waterskin and some food. How long those have been sitting here, I don't know. But my mouth tastes awful, so I risk taking a drink. I take the first sip tentatively, but when the water doesn't seem to be laced with anything I can pick up on, I down the whole skin, realizing how parched I am as soon as the drops hit my tongue.

I try to call up some gold, but despite the fact I can see daylight streaming in from the window, my body feels depleted. Like a tree barely able to glug out a single bead of sap. I still feel the aftereffects of the drug coursing through my body, making me feel sick and disconnected.

So even though I'm leery of the food, and my stomach isn't interested, I force myself to choke down the flatbread and fruit. I'm hoping that something in my stomach will help soak up whatever drug is still in my system. My head aches, my stomach feels like someone reached in and flipped it around, and I'm covered in a layer of grit.

Makes sense, since I was kidnapped and dragged to the desert of Second Kingdom.

My certainty of where I am and what's happened surrounds me, like a crowd suddenly jamming in at me on all sides. The memories push in, while my fear and fury push back.

Manu and someone from Second Kingdom did this. Had me drugged, kidnapped me and dumped me in this place and—

My hand slaps over my mouth.

Rissa.

"Great Divine..." A dry sob tears out of me like a husk torn from desiccated corn. They killed her. They killed her right in front of me, as if she were nothing but a nuisance, a life not meant to bother with.

My eyes well up, and it *hurts*. Like the dagger was pierced through *my* chest. They could've used the same drug to knock her out. Could've spared her. Instead, they stabbed her through and left her to crumple to the ground.

Rissa and I have a complicated relationship, stemming from years of resentment. But...I understood her. She used her wits, honed her seductions, learned to get ahead in a world of men, and then she wanted to forge a new path, doing whatever she needed to do to protect herself and get what she wanted.

I respected that. And when it comes to saddles, respect is the last thing society ever gives them.

Saddles fill the wants of men and women, work to satisfy sensual cravings. They perform and please, actualizing desires, earning both a sense of power and their own wealth by doing so.

And what happens? People hate it. They call it a sin, a vice. They beat it down. Claim that saddles are deplorable and dirty, the bottom dregs of society, unimportant and low-ranking. Except, behind closed doors, those very same people expect to have their urges satisfied. Expect to be pleased and pleasured, brought bliss and assuaged of their basest of needs.

And yet, a saddle isn't even worth a life.

She's just a saddle.

As if that made her less. As if she was so beneath them her death didn't matter.

But it matters. It matters to me. *She* mattered.

I wish I could've told her that. I wish, back at that garden, when she squeezed my hand in a rare show of warmth, that I'd have squeezed harder. Because she was strong and smart, and she deserved that new life that she wanted. The one she worked *so* hard for, and now, she'll never have it. All because of me. All because I asked her to take a walk.

Tears stream down my cheeks in chunks, as if my sorrow is heavy. It feels heavy, like a weight pressed down on my heart, and I don't know how long I cry for her, but I hope I'm not the only one. Because Rissa wasn't *just a saddle*. She was a saddle and she was also many other things too, and none of those things meant she didn't deserve to live.

When my tears stop, I feel dried out. I don't know if it's just the grief or if there are still some aftereffects of whatever drug they used on me, but my whole body drags. They must've kept me unconscious for days to get to Second Kingdom. The thought that I was left vulnerable to them like that makes me shiver.

I might not have been in this place in over a decade, but I remember this heat. I remember the grit that seems to be all over me too, of traveling through the dunes, of being caked in its grainy wind and baked through by the sun.

Funny how, when I first came here, my ribbons had only just started to sprout from my back.

So painful coming in.

So painful taken out.

I hated them then, but now, I'd give anything to have them back.

Absently, my fingers go to my back, to the empty spots where only smooth skin now remains.

Every single one of them, gone.

My ribbons and I have had so many parallels that I never appreciated before. As if my whole journey has been exhibited through their presence.

Like the fact that my new beginning here in Second Kingdom also marked the new beginning of them growing from my back. After that, I kept them hidden, just like I kept myself. Resented them, like I resented myself. Then, when I was finally coming out of my shell, so did they. Just thinking of the way they caught me, flirted with Slade, wrapped around his ankle...

I'll never have that again.

Just as I was coming into my own, so were they.

But then, I was cut down to the core, and with every strike, so were they.

That night marked an end for me *and* for my ribbons. Yet it was an ending I badly needed. I needed to be forced to stand on my own two feet, without anything to catch me. I only wish they could have been spared that same journey. But I needed to be cut down to finally rise up on my own like a phoenix from the ashes.

I wish my ribbons would do the same.

But there is no phoenix, and the only thing resembling

ashes are in the Ash Dunes that reside somewhere in this Divine-damned kingdom.

A noise jerks me out of my thoughts, and I drop my hand and turn around just in time for the door to swing open as a woman steps in. She has a white wimple draped over her head, the fabric thick, stiff, and perfectly creased on either side. It completely covers her hair, and all that's visible is a square opening for her face that sets at the edges of her cheeks and the middle of her forehead.

Her figureless robe is much the same, with similar creased draping in the starch-white cloth, covering her from jaw to feet. A slight train is gathered behind her, and her sleeves are long and wide at the ends, swallowing her hands so that not even that part of her is showing.

She has a sharp, pointed chin and her eyebrows are gone, as if she's shaved them away, while her eyelashes are so thin and fair that they're barely visible. Her eyes snag my attention though. Both of her brown irises are cracked on the outer sides, split with light green. It's a mirrored image from her right eye to the left, the green making her gaze look eerie.

"Welcome to Wallmont Castle," she says, voice serene and tilted with a slight accent, her lips twisted into a pleasant smile. "The Conflux is about to begin. I've come to prepare you."

"I'll pass, thanks," I say as I lean against the wall.

Her pleasant smile doesn't falter, but she does turn her head to look over her shoulder, and that's when two large men come through the doorway. They wear their own sort of wimples, only theirs are gray, the fabric shorter and thinner, in the same shape as chainmail hoods on soldiers. Their tunics are a cream color, not quite the stark white that the woman is wearing, and their gray pants are loose, the ends rumpled where they're tucked into knee-high boots.

They're both young, one with brown skin and one white and covered in freckles, and they both look at me without emotion as they stride forward. I press myself against the wall, anger curling in my stomach. I have a split second to decide if it's more important for me to hide my magic or to get out of here.

I opt to get the fuck out.

Curling my fingers into fists, I call to the gold. When I feel it pool in my palms more this time, my heart leaps. I let it gather until it starts to drip between the cracks of my fingers. It's slow, but it's something.

The first drop that falls to the floor makes the freckle-faced man's eyes go wide. With a push, I shove my hands out in front of me, fingers spread, letting the rest of it splash down. In a blink, I use the gold to slither toward them and wrap around their feet like thin snakes, the clinging liquid twining up their legs, stretching and hardening around their limbs. I yank more gold from my palms, a small stream pouring out, reaching for the woman next—

And I'm suddenly hit with pain.

It's unlike anything I've ever felt before. It doesn't strike like lightning, doesn't burn like fire. It doesn't pierce through me or feel like a limb slicing off.

This feels like being *pinched*. As if invisible hands have delved through my belly button and grabbed onto my organs.

As if phantom fingers have dug around to my veins, taking the tubes and compressing them so hard it makes my blood stop.

My heart, my stomach, my lungs, my muscles, my throat—these pinching fingers grip my insides and make everything freeze up. This horrible, pressing pain lances through me, and I fall to my hands and knees, making the gold cut off, squelching between my fingers, soaking through my pants.

I can't breathe, can't move, as these horrible contractions squeeze every part of me harder and harder and—

It suddenly stops. As if every single pinching point was released at the same exact time. I'm shaking, covered in sweat, choking in rasping coughs.

Through blurred eyes, I look up to see the woman gliding forward, stopping just before the liquid gold can stain her pure robes.

"There, none of that now," she says, her placid tone so out of context in this situation.

I look up at her with fury and try to call my gold again, though the echoing bruises inside my body make it so much harder. I barely manage to get a new trickle forming from my palms when I see her lift her hands, the sleeves falling back just enough to show her pressing her forefinger against her thumb and *pinch*.

Just like before, that pinching pain erupts inside of me.

This time, I collapse on the ground instantly, choking through a clamped throat, while everything inside of me cinches in agony, compressing like it's going to make my organs burst and bleed.

"Stop..." I croak out, writhing on the floor.

"No more trying to use that magic, Lady Cheat," she says. "This will happen every time you attempt to use what isn't yours."

The pinching ceases, and I twitch on the floor, feeling like I'm covered in a million internal bruises. It takes me a moment to recover before I even realize what she said.

"What did you call me?" I pant.

"Lady Cheat," she says in her same serene voice. "The gilded saddle who cheated her way into the Golden King's heart *and* his power, before she stole both and then his life. You're a cheat and a fallen woman, and this is the best place for you."

All I can do is gape at her.

She watches me as if she expects me to reply. When I don't, she prompts, "Well? Did you or did you not trick and steal and kill, Lady Cheat?"

"I guess that's the reason I was drugged and kidnapped, right?" I retort. "For me to go on trial and be asked that very question?"

Her fractured eyes glitter. "Indeed."

I drag myself up to a crouch, my trembling muscles nearly giving out as I force my body to stand. Splatters of gold stain the room, the shallow puddles already starting to dry. It's left splotches all over the men's pants and boots, none of the gold responding, just as limp and wrung out as I feel as it lies on the floor in useless strips.

"Come with me now, unless you'd like to try to use your stolen magic again?" she asks amicably, her pale lips reminding me of the white sands of this kingdom's shore. "Oreans who

727

relinquish themselves to the Conflux are forbidden from using power."

Wincing, I sit up straighter. "Well, I didn't relinquish myself, so you can fuck off with that rule, and I won't be going anywhere."

This time when she pinches her fingers together, it feels like my skull is being flattened. I scream, falling over with my hands against my head, my eyes feeling like they're about to burst like grapes. Agony ripples through me until I'm sure my skull is going to crack and my brain turn to mush.

It's only once I feel blood leaking from my nose that the pain ends.

Slumped against the wall, I glare at this woman with so much hatred through my blurred eyes I'm surprised she doesn't catch flame. My body feels destroyed, like I've been shoved in a shrinking room while the walls closed in on me, crushing me in its claustrophobic hold.

But I bleed gold. Cry gold. So I use my tears and my blood and try to move it, try to shrink them to pins so I can stab her through her horrible fingers and needle through her throat, but she presses again, cutting me off before I can do a single thing with that either.

"I can do this all day, Lady Cheat."

I snap my eyes up at her, tears of pain bunching up my lashes. "Then do it," I challenge. "Because I do not relinquish myself to the Conflux. So you can suck my gold and go to hell."

For the first time since she came in here, the woman's spurious smile falters. The men behind her shift their feet. When she brings her hands in front of her chest, I flinch, thinking she's about to use her awful magic on me again, but instead, she laces her fingers together and bows her head. "Great Divine gods, I beseech you to purge these blasphemous words from our ears and redeem our spirits' light."

In unison, the guards behind her murmur, "Purge the world of darkness."

"And illuminate our purest selves," she finishes.

A chill goes down my spine.

"So you can torture someone with pain power, but you think it's a sin to say the world *hell*?" I spit out mockingly.

She drops her arms and looks at me, a hard glint in her fragmented eye. "The afterlife is not for you to speak of. I have visible proof now you indeed stole the Golden King's magic."

"I *never* stole it," I snarl. "This magic was always mine. He used me. *He* was the thief, and I'm glad he's dead."

There's a small intake of breath through her lips. "We can add liar to your name as well. Thieves and cheats do not have the right to reference a spirit's hereafter, and certainly not liars and murderers."

"But you have the right to torture and hold me captive?" I retort.

She straightens her shoulders, looks down the thin bridge of her nose at me. "I am Isolte Merewen, Queen of Second Kingdom and First Matron of the Gathering of Temperance. The gods bestowed this power of pain on me so I may exact punishment on immoral souls. It is no sin, my lady. It is my duty as a patron of sanctity."

My lips press into a thin line. Everyone in Orea knows that Second Kingdom holds very strict factions of religions. The more famous offshoot, however, are the Deify. They live in the Mirrored Sahara with their silence, tongues cut from mouths like tumors off a limb and discarded, as if their speech was an abscessed infection sacrificed to the gods. The Temperance I've heard of too, but barely. I certainly didn't know this plain woman was the queen, leading the whole kingdom *and* this sect of puritanical doctrine.

"You will come now for Cleansing."

I lift my chin. "I will not."

I brace myself for the pain to hit, but this time, she simply nods at the men. I kick out as they come for me, but my movements are slow, ineffective. Like a kitten swiping uselessly in the air. With one on either side of me, they haul me up between them and start towing me from the room, gold smearing beneath my dragging slippers as the queen leads the way, as if she's so unthreatened by me that she's unafraid to show me her back.

I try to make gold flow from my palms, but it's listless and heavy, dense jelly that's caked against my skin, unable to drip. Unable to move.

Queen Isolte looks over her shoulder at me and says, "Pain is a pyramid, my lady. It stacks up, builds its layers. You think you can endure, think you can continue to climb its height, but you're wrong. I can guarantee that you will not want that pain to pile up so much that you reach the pinnacle, because you will not survive that sharp peak. Of that I can promise you."

Inside, I seethe. Amidst bruised bones and crushed organs, my anger broils.

I get dragged out of the small room and into a narrow

corridor. Instead of windows, there are skylights gracing the sandy ceiling, casting pillars of light every few feet.

The men haul me up a short stack of wide steps, and then we're in a wide domed room filled with archways, all of them open to the outside. I can see palm trees surrounding us, their thick fronds swaying with a shaded breeze that blows through. A layer of sand covers the white-tiled floor, but a bright yellow sun is painted in the center, its rays pristine and surrounded by a cerulean sky, just like the sails from the ship I rode when I fled Derfort Harbor.

We pass by it, heading to an archway to the left. I'm taken across sunbaked stones, the front of my ankles screaming from being bent back as they continue to drag me. The dense collection of palms are joined by cactus and olive trees, and the air erupts with the scent of oranges as we pass by citrus trees weighed down with heavy fruit ripe for picking.

Down the short outdoor path, the men bring me into another part of this sprawling building. After traveling down one more narrow corridor, I'm finally dumped into a dark room, my legs buckling as soon as I'm dropped.

Bracing my shaky hands beneath me, I push myself up into a sitting position, my eyes sharpening to adjust to the dim lighting. The room is shaped like a circle and completely without windows, the only light feeding in from the archway and a fire burning in a pot at the back of the room. The tile is the color of rust, the walls and ceiling matching it, and despite the stuffy heat, a chill goes down my spine, because this room has a wooden table with iron shackles chained to it. Part of the wall is covered in hanging whips too, and there are more sinister things that I can't quite see because there's a wall of women blocking my sight.

They're all gathered together like some morbid choir about to break out into song. They're dressed the same as the queen, except where her robes are pure white, theirs have strips of gray sewn into them. Some have a lot, the strips going all the way down to the hems, while others only have a single one around their waists. Just like Queen Isolte, their hair is covered in white wimples too, their hands swallowed by funneled sleeves.

"You can go," the queen tells the men, and I watch as they walk away. I have a feeling that I'd rather stay with them.

When I look back at Queen Isolte, the expression on her face tells me that I'm probably right. Turning to the women, she says, "Ladies of the Gathering of Temperance, it's time to perform a Cleansing."

CHAPTER 61

AUREN

I've learned that the strips on their robes represent the amount of sins the Temperance Matrons still have left to expel from their souls.

For a pious bunch, they're talkative, jabbering at me about their righteous order, about how so many of them sinned until they were brought in and shown the light. They tell me how blessed I am to be here and how it's a calling from the Divine, that my mortal soul is in danger and only they can help me.

They think very highly of themselves.

"We are joyful to have you here," one of them says. "To perform the Cleansing is a favor of the gods, and they deem us to be worthy of the task. It is a gift that helps our own internal purification too."

When they start closing in on me, I scramble back on my heels and hands until my back hits the wall. "Don't touch me."

The one nearest me widens her blue eyes. "Oh, my lady, we are not allowed to sully our skin in such a way," she says, a pitying look of misguided tenderness over her face. "The sleeves of our robes will keep us pure. Our skin will not touch."

I blink at her, and that split-second distraction is all they need to grab hold and drag me to the other end of the room. Although they're manhandling me, the woman was right— their bare hands don't touch me.

I don't know if I should feel insulted or not.

My body still feels like I've been crushed from the inside out, but I try to fight them anyway, try to kick out of their grasps. But it's like a baby bird trying to deter a hawk, and I accomplish nothing but making myself dizzy with echoes of pain.

They shove me into a narrow tub that's so thin that I can't rest both my legs down. Instead, I have to prop one leg over the other, and because it's not long enough either, my knees are forced to bend. The back of the tub is narrow too, so I'm cocked to the side, only one shoulder able to rest against the grains of the rough wood.

No matter how much I splutter and struggle, they have plenty of hands to hold me down. The water is tepid, and the lack of a temperature gives me the creeps, makes me cringe as I'm held in its depths.

My clothes soak through immediately, the end of my ragged braid plastered against my chest. As if it weren't bad enough to be restrained in the most uncomfortable tub ever made, the Matrons start to pour pitchers of lukewarm water over my head. A trio of them do so one after the other, while the others start to grab my clothed limbs and scrub me with painfully firm bristled brushes.

I cry out, trying to wrench myself away, trying to appeal to their righteous attitudes with the facts of my capture, but it's no use. I'm surrounded by white veils and devout insanity.

Bright side? At least they're so against touching that they're using these awful scrub brushes *over* my clothes. I think my skin would be peeling off in raw strips otherwise.

The soap they use smells sharply astringent, burning my scalp and cutting into my pores. And all while I'm being roughly handled, they preach to me about their gods. The ones who reward purity of the flesh and obedience of the mind. The ones who demand self-restraint and sacrifice.

They say nothing of the goddesses. Of matronly love or female fortitude.

When they haul me out of the tub, I get dumped beside the huge bowl of burning flame, clothes dripping all over until I'm given a scratchy blanket to soak up some of the water.

Someone combs my hair, doing it so gently that it makes the rough scrubbing of my skin seem even more of a shock. I try to shove her away anyway, but one of the other Matrons snaps a paddle against the back of my hand, making me hiss in pain. "Sit, my lady, and be still. Take this time to prepare for prayer."

"I'll take this time to prepare to flood this room with power, soaking *you* all through and then scrubbing at your skin until it's raw," I snarl back.

If they want to make me a villain, then I'll fucking be one.

She sucks in a breath, and I feel a small sense of victory at having shocked her. After being drugged and kidnapped, tortured and dragged here, my sense of control is slipping and making me feel like a cornered animal. I want nothing more than to tap into my fae nature, to wrench out the beast inside of me and melt down the world beneath a vat of gold, but Queen Isolte's magic is absolutely crippling.

But that doesn't stop me from wanting to try. I just need a little bit longer to recover. Just need to bide my time and pretend I'm powerless. I don't need much gold. All I'd need to do is take out this bitch of a queen. Maybe I'll make my gold squeeze *her* between a metallic vise. I bet she wouldn't be so smug then.

Speaking of...

"Lady Cheat will do nothing of the sort," Queen Isolte announces as she comes into my line of vision. She stands with her back against a mural of a priest in all white presiding over a dozen Matrons kneeling at his feet. The gray strips of sins on their robes match the number of lashes against a supposed "sinner's" back as he slumps against a pole. There's light shining on the priest, glinting off the whip as if he's the gods' gift to the world and his meted out punishment is something to be revered.

My stomach churns.

"She will submit to the rest of her Cleansing with grace," the queen goes on. "These threats hold no merit in this room, for they are spoken by the wickedness inside of her that we must help rid her of."

The other Matrons murmur their agreement.

My eyes narrow on her. "And tell me, how do you rid yourself of *your* wickedness, Queen Isolte?"

I feel more than see the others go still. The Matron at my back pauses in her brushing.

"My sins have been absconded already," the queen replies brusquely. "We too go through the ritual of a Cleansing. Though we endure many of them, as well as perform our services to the Divine, and to our priests. It is why no strips mar my robes, why I have risen up past my soul's deficiencies. I have been chosen to lead the Guardians of Temperance."

"But you don't *really* lead it, do you?" I ask, notching my chin up toward the mural. "Women can't be priests, isn't that right?" I ask, going out on a limb.

Her jaw clenches, and I get a little thrill at pissing her off. I don't care that she's queen. I don't care that she has the magic to pinch my body to death. She's a cruel fanatic who thrives on lording over others and calling her acts of cruelty *holy*.

"The Matrons serve a fundamental part in the Temperance," she replies, and it's so rehearsed I know she's heard and spoken that saintly slogan hundreds of times before.

I smirk. "Sure they do."

She turns to the others. "Witness, sisters. Her acerbic attitude is only the wickedness revolting against the Cleansing."

"Nope," I retort, wiping water off my face. "My attitude solely comes from the way you seem to think you can treat me. The golden whore? Isn't that what you called me?" I don't give her a chance to respond. "You don't need to be following some made-up ritual and worrying about gods who don't give a shit about you. What you *should* be worrying about is *me*. Because this golden whore can purify you far quicker than any Cleansing can. And trust me, you'll come out golden and shining."

She levels me with a look, and the faintest of pressure appears at my stomach, pinching me down, making me want to vomit. But I don't wince. I refuse to.

Her jaw cricks as she bites out, "You know what would truly be golden? *Your silence.*" Despite the pain, a snort escapes me. She releases her hold on me a second later. "This is all normal, Lady Cheat. You are not the first woman to come into this room with corruption engrained in her spirit. Evil never wants to be cast out. It's up to us to compel it."

I nod toward the wall of whips. "Is that what those are for? Is that how you and your Matrons abscond themselves and compel others? By being beaten? Being whipped or Cleansed or tortured or made to live uncomfortable lives without touch in awful tubs and uncomfortable blankets? Is that what your lives have been reduced to? I feel sorry for all of you," I say, gaze sweeping around the room. Because I might not be able to bring out my magic, but I can bring out words that can fester doubt in their minds.

Her hairless eyebrow arches up. "We keep ourselves pure. Pain makes us focus on our inner wrongs, and bleeding is a way for those wrongs to be released. We do not expect such a worldly woman to understand. Your touch is besmirched, your soul wicked. We will do what we can to Cleanse you before you face your superiors and your gods, but if you do not capitulate, then perhaps the teachings of the Temperance will heal you."

"Temperance save you," the other Matrons mumble.

I lean forward, not caring that my hair tugs painfully against the other woman's hold. "I don't want the Temperance to save me."

She cocks her head, that stupid, serene smile back on her face. "Then what, pray tell, do you think will?"

I smile. More teeth, more bite to add to my answer. "I'll save myself," I tell her before my eyes move across the wide-eyed faces of the others. "And even if I don't, King Rot will."

Despite her colorless face, she somehow pales even more, and a telling hush falls over the room.

"Did you forget about him?" I ask with a smirk. "Because when he gets here, not even your gods will be able to save you."

My outburst led me to another pinch of pain that made me pass out for a few minutes. I came to while oil was being dumped onto my feet to *"expunge the vessels on which I touch holy ground."* Then, clothing is tossed at me. I debate fighting them on changing, but the queen's obviously looking for any reason to use her power on me. I have no hope of recovering unless I can play nice.

So, I groggily strip out of my sopping wet clothes to pull them on, and as soon as my old clothing lands on the floor with a plop, one of the Matrons hurries over to gather them up and then tosses them into the fire, making it hiss and steam.

There's gauze-like material to bind my breasts, but I ignore that. There's also not one, but *three* layers of different kinds of underwear. I go with one, much to their chagrin. Then I pull on a dark gray cowled dress that covers me from neck to ankle, the sleeves cinched unpleasantly at the wrists, the color apparently signifying the taint of my spirit.

Lovely.

I should probably be more afraid, but I'm more angry than anything else. I'm really tired of monarchs using me for their own narratives, when all I've ever wanted was to be left the fuck alone.

Now that I'm dressed, the Matrons surround me and start herding me out of the room. The residual soreness throughout my body makes me shuffle forward, hunched and wavering. I won't deny the fact that the queen did a number on me. The well of my magic feels like it's been stretched and squeezed, gummed up in a too-narrow tube. Yet I have to do something. Have to hope I can recover enough that my gold-touch will work. I probably shouldn't have talked back so thoroughly, but I couldn't help myself.

I tell myself not to open my mouth again. To bide my time so I can recover. Yet as soon as I pass through the archway to the outdoors, the queen's magic crushes back into me.

As if she somehow knew what I was planning, she suddenly attacks. Her power cinches me like a too-tight corset, cutting off my ability to breathe, making my heart feel like it's being fisted in someone's cruel hand.

I gasp, falling over into the Matrons to my right, their robed bodies staying straight and firm, a knock of elbows and shoulder bones smacking me back in my tiny circle between them. It's a wonder I stay on my feet, taking gasping, short breaths that make me feel like I'm going to hyperventilate. It's just enough pinching pain to make my body panic, to make it difficult to focus, yet it's also subtle enough to not knock me down into unconsciousness.

Pain is a pyramid, she said. And she's stacking more on top of me, brick by brick, like she sees my suffering as some shrine to her own power.

The oppressive heat doesn't help. It presses down on my wet hair and prickled body, my bare feet burning against the tile as we walk along the outdoor path. I don't pay attention to where I'm being led. I simply follow the white and gray striped sheep, trying to focus through the pain.

Although the heat is almost oppressive, the sunlight seems to *invigorate* me. Like it's tapping into something deeper, sinking into my skin and shining on that beast inside of me.

Because for me, the sun has always equaled power.

And in this world, if you don't have power, you don't survive.

I was shut away from it for ten years. Blocked away, kept apart in a snow-doomed kingdom where the sky was always covered with oppressive clouds. Before that, I lived at a harbor that dumped out rainwater and flooded the streets. Yet here... this is where my magic came out. Here is where my gold first came and my ribbons first sprouted. This is where it all began.

So even though my time in Second Kingdom was traumatic then, maybe there was a reason why my fae power ignited while I was baking beneath its sun.

Despite the queen's leash of pain, I channel into the sunlight instead. Think only of *that*, of it soaking into me and giving strength. Then I try to muster up enough gold, try to tap into it and ignore everything else.

To my elation, a few droplets gather against my fingertips, and I roll the thick beads between my thumb and fingers, finding comfort in its presence, no matter how little the amount, no matter how thick and gunky it seems.

All of my concentration is on my gold, gathering painfully slow drops. I'm hoping the Matrons are taking me back to my room or to continue their gods-awful rituals somewhere else, something to give me more time to gather myself and my power.

But instead, we veer further outside, down the tiled path that's patched with intermittent shadows cast off from the plants, while an unbroken cacophony of cicadas buzzes through the air. Sweat starts gathering at the back of my neck as I'm herded, my frizzy strands of wet hair sticking to my skin, my cinched sleeves dampened at my wrists.

My feet are on fire. The only saving grace is that the stickiness of the oil has made the fine sand stick to them, giving the only protective layer I have. I try to focus my magic to my soles next, urging the gold to coat the undersides. Yet I can't get a thick enough layer to do much, though I hope I'm leaving stained footprints behind me to taint their way.

The queen apparently gets bored with my suffering

in silence, because she releases the pinch on my heart and changes it until it feels like something has latched onto my spine and dug in its nails, tipped ends pressing sharply into me.

This time, I have no choice but to whimper, back arched slightly, feet faltering. I'm pushed from behind, urged incessantly forward, while every step makes my spine bite and needle.

I know the queen is behind me, watching my every move, probably getting some sick satisfaction from the noise I made. I transfer the small ball of gold from my left hand and add it to the collection in my right, and while it's only the size of a blueberry, it's *something*.

But with all my concentration focused on enduring the pain and keeping my small clump safe in my hand, I realize belatedly that I'm not walking on sandy tiles anymore. I'm walking on clay stairs, and the noise I'm hearing isn't just cicadas anymore.

It's people.

A lot of people.

I look behind me, seeing the single-level castle draped across the feather-soft sand dunes and blended with a bounty of vegetation hugged around the sparkling water of an oasis.

But before me, down this steep outdoor staircase, is a sprawling metropolis. Far off in the horizon, I can see just a sliver of the sea. It streaks across the edge, separating the land and sky. All the way from here to there, there are blocks of flat-roofed buildings spread out in such a vast collection that I can't even fathom how many people must live here.

The buildings are the same color as the sand they're surrounded by, yet with pops of bright yellow and blue paint. The streets look like copper rivers woven through, and there are flags with their yellow sun emblem, as well as the official sigil of Second Kingdom—two concentric circles, one inside another, representing the great Divine overlapping all of life.

But the building nearest us, the one this path leads to, is surrounded by a sea of people collected beneath giant canvases stretched between pillars. Just in front is a circular building, and from my vantage point up here, I can see a short wall that circles around it all, its joined architecture clearly reminiscent of the kingdom's sigil.

I can't go a single step now without grimacing and hissing out breath. The oil and sand is no match for the brutal heat of the sunbaked tiles. I can't even rush, because the Matrons are setting the pace, and they either don't care about my feet or it's all part of my burning walk of shame.

By the time I make it to the bottom steps, I don't even care about the people who are staring and shouting incomprehensible words. It feels as if layers of skin have scalded right off my feet, leaving them raw and agonizing, as if I've been walking over a mile of fiery coals.

And the queen's pain continues. Steady. Punishing. So constant that I can't take in a full breath, my heart feeling like it can't complete a full beat.

I'm sweating buckets. Everything inside of me shakes and reverberates with echoing agony that's sapped all my strength as I'm led down a narrow path. The bodies of the Matrons close in on me as we get closer to the building. I can see a sea of people gathered, shouting, hands in the air as if this is some kind of frenzied event.

Then I'm led up the charring steps of the domed building. When I get to the top, the women part like waves, and I see I'm on some kind of outdoor stage. The building is at my back and the canvas-covered city square in front, so full of people that I can't even see the ends of the crowd. They're not wasting any time. There will be no waiting in my room, no other ritualistic Cleansing.

This is it.

I'm shoved inside a circle of thin pillars on the stage, and as soon as I am, the queen's magic is suddenly removed. In their haste to shove me inside, my shoulder and arm smack against the poles, and the gold ball drops from my hand. I don't dare draw attention to it though.

I can't enjoy the release of the queen's pinched pain, because I'm trapped. Trapped and on display, reeling from pain and forcing myself not to pass out.

I try to shake the poles that surround me, but they don't move a bit, and I'm far too weakened anyway. They stretch up at least ten feet, and they're no thicker than my wrist, leaving the same measure of gap between them. The space inside the enclosure is a small circle, the same pillared door slammed shut at my back. The only relief I have is the fact that I'm in the shade now from the building's overhang, so the tile floor of the stage is blessedly cool against my scorched feet.

But then I look up and see the seven chairs set just beyond me, facing both the crowd and my enclosure, all filled with the monarchs of Orea.

They must be in order, from First to Sixth Kingdom.

The chair for Fourth is noticeably empty.

At the end, in First Kingdom's chair, sits King Euden Thold, a man with dark skin and a serpent crown on his head that glitters with gems of green and black. The moment I see him, I remember his power, because it's wrapped all over him, tame under his control. There's a viper draped around his shoulders. A cobra coiling the length of his arm. Another snake with a rattle at his ankle, and a bright green snake looped in his lap.

As if she's not bothered in the slightest by their serpentine presence, Queen Isolte sits poised beside him, while another man who must be her mustached and blotchy-faced husband sits at her other side. King Neale Merewen.

And to the right of *him* sits Queen Kaila.

My stomach twists like I've grabbed it with two fists and wrung it out like a rag. Beside her is the empty chair meant for Slade, which makes my stomach twist in an entirely different way.

Where is he?

Next to that, in Fifth Kingdom's spot, sits a man I've never seen before. He looks far too young and nervous to be in charge of an entire kingdom. But I suppose that's the point. This is the newly crowned King Hagan Fulke.

One of King Thold's snakes is on the new king's armrest. Hagan tries and fails to hold in his grimace, clearly uncomfortable with the serpent's presence, though too nervous to do anything about it.

He should have though, because in a blink, the snake

suddenly sinks its teeth into his hand in a lightning-quick move, making him jerk back. King Thold chuckles and calls the snake back, but while King Hagan should have a bleeding, punctured hand, instead, there's nothing there at all. He may be a timid sort of person, but apparently, his skin is impervious to fangs.

Beside King Hagan, the chair is empty, the last one in the lineup, meant for Sixth Kingdom. Meant for Midas. Yet he's not here, and at least I can get some satisfaction from that.

But the scraps of that meager satisfaction disintegrate when King Neale Merewen stands, voice booming across the square, reverberating off the circular wall behind to amplify his speech. "The monarchs of Orea join here together to assess the accused and uphold the integrity of Orean Law." He turns to me, eyes disapproving, flat hair tucked back in thinning strands. "As King of Second Kingdom and upholder of the royal decree, I now declare that the royal Conflux has commenced."

CHAPTER 62

SLADE

I've been flying for days. So many that they've bled together with every darkened dusk stitched in the sky.

Argo is fast, but he has to take breaks to sleep and to hunt, and this amount of distance would normally be broken up with either a fresh timberwing at the coast or with plenty of rest between.

I had no such advantage.

We've had to deal with storms that dumped water on us, beating wind, and an improvised route. Yet crossing over Weywick Sea was the worst. I made sure to cross the shortest amount of distance over the water, having us stop right at Third Kingdom's outermost island, but even so, we nearly didn't make it across.

When Argo landed on the shore of Second Kingdom, he collapsed. I stayed with him at the tiny canal that fed into the sea, and I was damn lucky that he woke up and had the energy to hunt for fish.

But every moment we couldn't travel was a pressure physically felt. Every second I didn't move meant I wasn't catching up to Auren. I knew that Manu probably had changed timberwings at least twice, while I was pushing Argo further than I had any right to.

But I had no choice.

I rushed to leave, which meant I had no supplies other than the clothes on my back, the ribbon in my pocket, and the sword and dagger at my belt. I sold that dagger to a fisherman in exchange for new clothing and some travel rations. It was only once he saw the lines of power creeping down my hands that he paled and ran away, though he was wise enough to keep the dagger.

The oppressive desert heat of Second Kingdom has already made me sweat through my leathers, and Argo takes an entire day and night to recover. He's fast though. Faster than any timberwing I've ever seen. If it weren't for the break he had to take, I have no doubt that we would've caught up to them.

We should've caught up to them the night Auren was taken, but the bastards evaded me. They must've had more of a head start than I realized. Even though I was trying to have Argo track them, the path he was traveling kept changing, as if they were purposely eluding us and taking weird as fuck routes, which they probably were.

Argo doesn't have much left in him. His wings are tired. His speed is next to nothing. It's even worse than that night we raced toward Deadwell, because the punishing heat is sapping what's left of his strength.

As for me, with the sun beating against me like furious fists, minimal food and water, and only blips of rest here and there, I'm running on pure fucking rage.

Rage, and the unmistakable guilt-laden fear.

Because they took her. They took her, and I wasn't there. I know she told me she was glad of how things happened in Ranhold, of how she *needed* to save herself. I know she's strong. That she can take care of herself, rescue herself.

But I should've fucking been there then, and I damn well should be now.

So I *will* fucking get to her.

Her ribbon practically scorches inside my pocket, a reprimanding reminder for the hurt that already happened to her when I wasn't there.

I need to be there this time.

I'm getting closer. I should reach Wallmont within the day. Everything hinges on them taking her there. Because if they've taken her somewhere else...evaded me once more...

No. I won't think of that.

We're maybe just a few hours away from the capital now, and a new surge of hope claims me.

Almost there, Auren.

Kick their asses until I get there, but when I arrive, those fuckers are mine.

At this distance as we race over the dunes, my power writhes and builds, the roots snapping at my skin, ready to sink into this arid land and rot it through. When we pass a smaller city just off the coast, I know we're getting closer, and it buoys my enthusiasm even more.

That's when it happens.

Just on the outskirts, when Argo dips below the clouds. If he weren't so overtaxed, if I'd been more focused, maybe we could've dodged it.

But the bolt came from nowhere, just a whistle I hear a split second before it pierces through his wing.

He lets out the most ear-piercing screech I've ever heard. His blood blows out in the wind, splattering me with blots of red. Argo pitches sideways, still shrieking, still trying to flap, to *fly*, but his stubbornness and skill is no match for the iron bolt stuck through the muscles and bones of his wing.

We fall.

I hold onto the straps of the saddle, leaning forward, draping myself over him and giving him all motion to move the way he needs to. There's no steering his direction, no trying to urge him on. All I can do is brace myself against his back as he plummets. Even through his pain and our violent descent, he still tries to slow our fall, still tries to search out the best possible place to crash-land.

I can say with absolute certainty that the sand dunes look far softer than they really are.

Argo takes the brunt of the fall, tucking in his legs and his one good wing at the last moment, and lurches to the side just as we hit.

Powdery sand explodes around us, and Argo lets out another shrill cry that rolls in my skull, clashing into me just as much as the impact.

I unbuckle myself as fast as I can and slide off his good side, boots sinking into the sand as I hurry around him to get to his injured wing. The bolt is big and heavy—probably set off as soon as we were spotted crossing outside of the city. We've fallen far enough away that there's probably a good mile between us and the city wall, but that's worse, because all I want to do right now is rot the fucker who did this.

I take in the damage to Argo's wing, grim realization settling over me as I take it in from all angles without touching. The iron arrow is stuck in the center of his right wing, matting his brindled feathers with blood. The end is far too thick for me to pull out without causing more damage and pain.

The one silver lining is that metal corrodes.

Argo cries, this time a noise more like a whimper, and it fucking *guts* me to hear him sound like that. The beast is one resilient and tough creature, and to see him broken down into this...

"I got you," I murmur to him, and his huge brown eye pins to me, as if there's a blink of understanding at what I'm about to do.

Touching it with as little contact as I can, I slowly spread rot down the metal. It looks like the iron does nothing at first, but then, it slowly begins to weaken. The color turns grimy with rust, pitting appearing along its length. When it begins to flake off in corroded strips and the metal appears ancient, I reach up and snap off the end.

Argo jerks, biting his teeth at me, but I move quickly and yank the rod out, tossing it behind me. He instantly curls his wing toward him and starts licking at the blood, which I take as a good sign that he can move it at all.

He's panting hard, froth gathered at his maw, and when

I move around him to check his legs, he gives me a warning snap again.

"Easy, beast," I say, though if I'd just been shot with a bolt and took the brunt of a violent crash to the ground, I'd be lashing out at everyone too.

When I press up on his chest and lean down to check the condition of his legs, my stomach drops. His left one is held at an odd angle where it's tucked beneath his tilted form, and I can tell without even touching it that it's broken.

"Shit."

Broken leg and a wounded wing that I don't know the full extent of. He's completely debilitated; there's no possible way that he can move, let alone fly.

I get back to my feet, looking around the barren land, but there's no shelter from the sun, nowhere for me to keep him hidden or protect him from the elements.

We're both sitting ducks in a boiling pond.

When Argo lays his puffing face down against the scorching ground, sand blows from around his nostrils and blooms in front of his mouth. He makes a dejected, beaten noise again, and it twists the blade of guilt lodged in my throat.

I tear off the waterskin hanging from my waist and start to drip the liquid against his maw. He instantly opens his mouth, and I pour water in until it's nearly empty. He licks his lips, looking at me with a steady blink before he slops his abrasive tongue against my hand as if in thanks and then closes his eyes.

Sucking down the last of the water, I sit against Argo's

good side, knees up, eyes pointing toward the direction of Wallmont.

The miles that still stretch between us from here to the capital seemed small just minutes ago. Now, they seem insurmountable.

So close.

Too far.

Argo can't fly. Can't walk. He's going to die out here because of me. I'll have to walk to the city that shot him down and steal a horse and race across the desert to get to Auren, and it's going to be too late. I've taken too long, and now, without being able to fly...

The moment I leave to head for the city behind me, I'm giving Argo a death sentence. My teeth clench together, my fists too. The choice I have before me is to either leave him here alone to slowly succumb to his injuries and the elements or to rot him where he lies, by the very touch he's learned to trust. A touch that, right now, lashes with incensed lines that have traveled down the lengths of my hands with volatile twists as it lengthens past my knuckles. The rotting depths of my anger seep into the ground and spread like ferreting veins that stretch out in a hunt to scour the land in punishment before I pull it back.

I wouldn't be surprised if the reach of my fury crossed all the way to Wallmont. I'm tempted to let it try. Let it swallow the city behind us too, cause every last person to spoil and molder.

Argo's been my faithful beast for years, and this is the thanks I give him. A desert grave where he's hurt and hot and vulnerable. My hand comes up to stroke the soft feathers of his neck, and when he lets out a near-silent purr, emotion thickens in my chest.

"I'm sorry," I murmur.

To him. To her.

So fucking sorry.

CHAPTER 63

AUREN

*I*nstead *of applause at the* king's announcement, the square grows quiet and anticipatory. As if everyone's waiting to hear what's going to be said next. Just in front of the stage, sitting on a slightly raised platform, sits a few dozen people. They're all dressed finely, clothing of nobles, but my eyes immediately find one face in particular in the crowd, sitting with his husband.

Manu.

He gives me the quickest glance before he looks away, and maybe I'm wrong, but I swear, I see the slimmest slice of guilt flash over his expression. He tried to tell me that the Conflux was going to be nothing more than a slap on the wrist, but this certainly doesn't feel like a slap on the damn wrist.

It's nothing personal, Doll.

Except, it was.

It *is*.

I start to turn away, but my attention then snags onto a young boy sitting just in front of me. He's wearing nearly the same white robe that Isolte wears, except his head is bare, showing off dark blond hair. He's young, maybe around ten years old, and based on the guards standing at his back, my guess is he's Second Kingdom's heir.

I wonder how many Confluxes he's witnessed.

"Let us state the claims against the accused."

My eyes snap to King Merewen.

Standing in front of his chair, he looks around the gathered crowd. The hairs in his long gray mustache curl slightly, the ends looking like they've been dipped in egg yolk, yellowed with age.

"The accused is here because witnesses have stated they saw the Lady Auren kill King Midas."

The crowd doesn't murmur, doesn't make a sound; instead, they get even quieter. It's almost eerie as I feel their silent attention drift to me, hundreds of eyes flocking around my body.

Taking deep breaths, I gulp down enough air until I'm able to think past the last echoes of pain that Isolte held me in. I don't believe in killing without thought. But her? I would gladly fucking gild her ass, just for her abuse of power alone. Because if she's done this to me, who knows how many other people she's done it to?

It is my duty as a patron of sanctity.

What a load of horse shit. I glare at her through the bars of the ca—

No. My mind slams down protective walls. I won't call

758

it that. I'm not in a cage. I'm just in a pillared enclosure. This is where everyone in a Conflux goes. It's just stone. My gold could tear it down in a blink.

The tiny ball of gold I'd dropped has rolled, but luckily, one of the stone rods has blocked it from going out of reach. Without trying to be obvious, I reach my foot out until I'm touching it with the tip of my pinky toe. One good thing about this robe is that it hides the ball from view. I'd step on it if I could, but the bottoms of my feet are in far too much pain. I don't know if I'm too weakened by Isolte's abuse to make any new gold, so maybe if I can just control the ball, get it to move up my leg and get it back to my hand...

Yet the moment I start to even *think* of channeling my power, gold abruptly gathers at my fingertips. I'm caught off guard for a moment at the immediate liquid that starts to collect, and I clasp the poles in front of me, letting it soak into the stone, keeping the liquid metal hidden beneath my grip. It's gathering quicker than it was before, even with the toll on my body, like I'm not even having to try. And something about that feels...*off*.

But I have to work quickly. Before Queen Isolte can use her power on me again. Before she can cut my proverbial knees right from under me, crippling my magic. So I let it gather, trying not to be obvious, and at first, the more I gather, the more bolstered I feel.

Until I realize that I can't stop it.

It's like I've been turned into a leaky faucet, uncontrollable drips spilling from my skin, gathering more and more. I try to curl my fingers and palms, try to hide as drips start to slip out and dribble down my arms so I don't alert Isolte, but it won't stop.

Not only can I not stop it, but I also can't *direct* it either. I have no control whatsoever. Like a raincloud suddenly deciding to sprinkle, it's become an irrepressible force.

Something is wrong.

I keep my hands fisted tight, not daring to move them. Luckily, what's dripping down from my hands to my arms is hidden beneath the sleeves of my dress. But some of it catches against the fabric and stains in blotches. Then, more of it spills out from the edge of my palm. When the first bead drops to the floor, my eyes follow its descent. And that's when my gaze notices the symbol etched into the tile beneath my burnt feet.

What is that?

I'm so distracted by the strange circular patterns engraved into the floor, that I don't notice that King Merewen has walked over until the nearness of his voice jolts my head back up. With wrinkles set into his olive-toned skin and the flat patches of gray hair on his head, he must be at least a couple of decades older than his wife. I rack my brain, trying to remember what his power is, and then recall his ability has to do with finding sources of water. For a desert kingdom, it's quite a handy trick.

"The accused is here because witnesses have stated the Lady Auren is a thief of power," he declares, gesturing toward me.

All the other monarchs are staring, gazes needling into the side of my face like they want to pierce their glares right through me.

"How do you answer to this accusation?"

I swallow hard, sweat gathering at the trim of my hair, pooling beneath my breasts and itching down my temples. "My answer is that there is no one here that witnessed how he died." More drops of gold from my palms fall to the ground. But I can't *do* anything with it. Can't guide it. Can't make it gather together or solidify or move out of this enclosure.

What the hell is happening?

I tighten my grip, attempt to gild the pole, but I can't even do that. Because of my movement, the king's eyes drop to my slicked palms, and his lips part in surprise. Isolte is watching me too, and from beneath her long sleeves, I wonder if she's about to press me down and wring me out.

I need my gold. It's here, it's continuing to drip, and I start shaking in concentration and panic, trying to get it to move, to use the only advantage I have, but I *can't*.

King Merewen's gaze flicks from my strained fingers to my tight face, and he *grins*. "Ah, I see. Allow me to give you a little history, girl," he says beneath his breath. "My great-grandfather had the power of runes. And the one you're standing on? It drains a person's magic out of them, like squeezing out a tube, but you won't be able to use it so long as you're in there. It just reveals."

My eyes go wide.

With a satisfied look, he turns back toward the other monarchs and says, "So, the accused has alluded that there were no witnesses. Queen Kaila, as the only living monarch present who was in Ranhold that night, what is your response to this?"

I watch as she gets to her feet, sleeveless dress pooling at the ground like a ripple of water, her crown set atop her thick, wavy hair. "My response is to present the actual words spoken that night to the Conflux with the use of my magic," she says, and my blood goes cold as she turns and defers to the king. "With approval from the gathered monarchs, of course."

All hands from the royals lift slightly, apparently giving their permission.

King Merewen nods. "Proceed, Queen Kaila."

Even though I brace myself for hearing it, it's no less shocking when my words, my *voice* is suddenly streamed from her lips like a rivulet of vapor. Magic bristles in the air as I'm wrenched back to that night, my bodiless words echoing across the square, filling the spaces and ears of everyone gathered.

"Don't touch him."

My voice shouts out with fury, making several people in the crowd flinch back and look around as if they're trying to see who spoke.

"What are you doing, Auren? Get away from him right now and come to me."

Hearing Midas's voice makes *me* flinch. Makes my grip on the poles tighten.

He's dead, I tell myself. *He's gone.* But hearing him again, so *real*, his whole voice bottled up and poured right out for me to hear, makes me want to pitch forward and vomit.

"Come to me," his voice commands.

Then my reply. Enraged and biting. *"Never."*

The crowd was silent and still before, but this disembodied display of impassioned voices has charged the air.

"Lower your swords away from my favored!" Midas's voice shouts out. It makes him sound protective. Like he's safeguarding me.

"I'm not your favored." My reply sounds heated. Crushed out between gnashing teeth.

"Clear the room!" Midas's shout rings out.

She purposely left out what I'd said before he gave that order. When I told everyone that *he* was the one who killed Prince Niven, not Slade.

Kaila puffs out more magic. Streams out more words.

But this time, it's my voice, Lu's voice, from an entirely different night.

"Thanks for sneaking me in and out. It was nice to spend time with Ravinger."

I'd said Rip that night. Not Ravinger. Which means Queen Kaila's power can not only store words, but manipulate them. Cut them off and paste others on to her liking. My stomach twists and curdles, saliva flooding my mouth.

"I'm sure. Better company than the golden prick, huh?" Lu's voice echoes out.

"Much better."

Now, the crowd can't keep quiet. There's a shuffle of noise through the masses, gathering, collecting, passing their judgments.

"It was him?" Midas's accusation now makes it seem like the perfect scorned lover.

"We're leaving."

People stare daggers at me, faces twisted into sneers.

Another exhale, and this time, it's Queen Kaila's voice herself from that night. *"It's clear that her loyalty lies with Fourth Kingdom. Let her lose her favor. It's what she deserves."*

Then Midas's voice sounding pleading. *"Auren, come here right now."*

"Never."

Another word out of context, used to her narrative's benefit.

"You want to leave? To be the whore of King Rot?" Midas's voice spits.

"Better the whore to the man at my back than the favored to you," comes my reply. *"We're leaving. You'd be wise to do the same."*

The way she's reenacting this makes it very clear that I meant it as a threat.

"You want to leave, Auren? Then go. Let Ravinger's pollution leave this kingdom."

The poor, rejected king, giving up his favored.

Kaila doesn't make it known what really happened next, doesn't make it clear that we *did* try to leave. No. Instead, she makes it sound like Midas was this spurned, betrayed king who was letting me walk away.

Which of course, isn't true at all.

Queen Kaila pauses, looks out at the crowd. "Lady Auren refused to leave. She attacked Midas right in front of me, and when he tried to use his gold to protect himself, he couldn't." Her head shakes and she makes a somber sniff, gathering more and more sympathy from the watchful faces. "Lady Auren was jealous he had announced his engagement to me. In her rage to get back at him, she seduced King Ravinger, and then she attacked."

My teeth grind together. Heart pounding against my skull. I don't know what's more prevalent, my anger, fear, or exhaustion.

"This next part is violent," she goes on. "I caution anyone with young children or sensitive dispositions to cover their ears."

Then she blows out another breath.

This time, there aren't voices that she feeds out, but *screams*. They rend out across the square, clacking against the walls, making the people balk and cringe and look at me with horror. The noises ring in my ears, my memories lining up with each one. I can see the guards swallowed by gold, melted through, sliced and slashed and smothered.

I did that.

Just like I was responsible for the carnage at Carnith.

Then there's Midas's voice. Tinged with the timbre of his plea. *"Auren."*

I can feel it—how the crowd turns on me. The pity they feel for King Midas. I'm already the villain in their eyes. But if there's one thing I've learned, it's that being the villain isn't always a bad thing.

"Thank you, Queen Kaila," the king announces. "But one must ask, *were* you in the room while King Midas was killed? Did you witness it firsthand?"

Kaila pauses before answering, "No, King Merewen. I had to flee."

"Flee? Why is that?"

"Because Lady Auren didn't just trick and kill the king," Kaila states. "She also holds a dark power that none of us knew."

"What power?"

Her sharp eyes look straight ahead, like a performer delivering her perfected lines to the audience. "I witnessed Lady Auren stealing Midas's gold-touch. And she killed him with it, just as she tried to kill me."

The crowd erupts into gasps and whispers.

King Merewen looks at me. "How does the accused respond?"

"I didn't steal anything," I grit out.

I don't trust these monarchs. What if they want to keep me in here and force me to gild things just like Midas? They have a goal in mind for this Conflux, otherwise they wouldn't have gone to such lengths to kidnap me. If I defend myself, will they only use it against me?

"No?"

"No," I reply through gritted teeth. "I didn't steal Midas's magic."

In the worst timing imaginable, all the gold that's been gathering beneath my grip starts to dribble down the poles in thick streams.

The gathered throng erupts with exclamations, fingers pointed, eyes widened.

"*It's true!*"

"*She's got King Midas's power!*"

I glare at the crowd, trying to scream back. "It's not his

power! It never was!" My voice is inconsequential. Drowned out by a sea come to wash me away.

"*She's a thief, a cheat!*"

"*Guilty! Guilty!*"

I yank my hands away from the thin pillars, but all that does is ensure that gravity is not on my side. Now, gold no longer drips slowly from my hands. It floods out of my skin, streaming from my fingers to puddle on the floor. It soaks the bottoms of my burnt feet, staining the hem of my dress, gathering higher, but being contained by some invisible barrier that doesn't allow it to pass the poles.

"*Guilty!*"

It's like being cut open at the wrists and watching myself bleed. I can't stop the flow, but I can feel its deluge draining out of me, weakening me even more.

That's when I notice threads of black appear inside the gold.

At first, it's just a single line of it that drips down in a heavy, dense drop and splashes at my feet. Then there's more, until it's streaking through every single rivulet, like someone has dumped black ink and swirled it around.

What is that?

The gold is *pouring* out of me now, and I know the monarchs are speaking, know the throng is shouting, but my ears are ringing, heart pounding, because these dark lines... they look like—

"Great Divine."

My head jerks up at Queen Kaila's voice, at the way she's pointing at me, the shock on her face so apparent that

I'd bet nearly everyone in the crowd can see. "She stole King Rot's power too!"

She screams it.

And the crowd screams with her.

But I'm in too much of a shock to say anything at all, because she's right. Those *are* the same seeking strands that Slade spreads through the ground, the same veins that writhe beneath his skin.

In some sick twist of fate, these lines of rot are spreading, digging, tunneling through my gold like roots twisting through to grow a plethora of festering weeds, right here for everyone to see. Rot sprouting from that single speck that Slade left inside of me, the seed that we thought was dormant.

"*She stole gold-touch! Now she stole rot! She can steal more!*"

"*Guilty! Guilty! Guilty!*"

My world tips. I stumble back against the poles, feet splashing in the pooled up metal. I need this pull on my magic to stop, need to cut it off, yank it out, but I can't.

I was drugged for days, I'm dehydrated. Hot. Exhausted. My feet are charred. Every place where Queen Isolte tortured me feels like one crushing wound. My magic is gushing out of me with a deadly and unstoppable force, and I'm trapped.

I'm trapped.

My whole body starts to tremble, eyes flaring around wildly, heart feeling like it's too big for my chest, too thundering for my pulse.

"Monarchs, give your vote!"

Every single one of them joins the voices of the crowd.

Guilty, guilty, guilty.

King Merewen turns to his people. "The royal Conflux rules that she is guilty!"

The voices of the crowd spread into a thousand cracks.

"The verdict is immediate execution."

And everything around me *shatters.*

Guilty guilty guilty.

CHAPTER 64

AUREN

There's a recoil that happens in your brain when something shocking occurs. Something so violently harrowing that your thoughts blanch and withdraw. As if your mind becomes a protective mother, shielding its child's eyes and muffling the frightening noises while the massacre occurs and she knows they're next. Subduing the receptors, mentally numbing the fallout—it's the last thing it can do to offer protection.

The last thing it can do to soften the impending blow.

So I hear the crowd continue their chant.

Guilty.

I see the shouting faces, the movement of the monarchs, the spill of my stained gold.

Yet all of it is dulled. Soft. Monotone. Slow like I'm in a dream. As if this is only a nightmare, and my mind is reminding me to keep me calm.

Except I know this isn't a dream. The worst things that have happened in my life have always been while I was awake. This is no different.

Where were you?

I asked Slade that question back in Deadwell, back in the sheltered protection of the cave. It seems so long ago. What I told him then will always hold true for me. That I was glad I saved myself.

But this time, I thought he was going to be here.

I thought he was going to come.

Where are you?

I'm strong. I've come a long way with my magic and my control. With my emotions and thoughts. Even my physical body has gotten stronger with the intermittent training. Yet none of that is going to help me break out of this enclosure.

I need help this time.

And I don't have it.

I don't know where he is or why he hasn't come, but whatever it is must be something terrible, because I know without a doubt, he'd do anything in his power to be here. To track me down and save me. Yet he isn't here, so I can only think the worst.

Something happened to him.

Did Queen Kaila have a hand in this? Did they do something to Slade? They had to have, or he would've come already. He wouldn't have let them even take me out of Fourth Kingdom in the first place.

This realization sinks in like a boulder crashing into an

ocean. It bottoms out, leaving the ground beneath my feet to shake, silt lifted up to muddy my vision.

"The Conflux execution must be carried out at once."

My eyes rock to the king.

"You have been judged culpable for your crimes in killing King Midas and stealing not one power but two."

"I didn't steal anything!" I scream out. "Gold-touch is *mine*."

No one believes me. No one even hears me. I search the other monarchs, but they look at me as if I'm a leech they need to burn, like they don't want me anywhere near them in case I steal their magic, too. The spectators in the square don't hold any sympathy for me either, their expressions pure hate.

To them, I'm nothing but a lying, murdering, thieving saddle who deserves this judgment.

"Please!"

My hands grip the poles again, wet with a gold that won't harden. The puddle at my feet is so much deeper now, reaching the middle of my shins. Black, liquid roots slink in its depths, the tipped ends stretching toward all sides of the enclosure as if they're trying to dig their way out but can't.

I can't get out.

Can't control my magic.

My back is barren.

And he's not coming.

My soundless sob is what breaks through the haze of my mind, snapping me back into full awareness. Without the buffer of my mental shield, I'm clutched in the chaos of my own condemnation.

The monarchs are all standing now, and there are guards surrounding my enclosure. Guards I didn't even notice approach. They wear no armor, but their uniforms are starch-white with belts of gray to hold the sins of their blades.

"Arm!" King Merewen orders.

Every single guard pulls out his sword. There are six of them in total—three in front of me, three in back, surrounding my small circle.

It seems like some sort of cruel irony for there to be six.

"Please!" I scream again, but no one cares to hear my plea.

My heart pounds like it's trying to break a hole through my chest and escape, but no part of me is leaving this enclosure.

Is this truly it? After everything. After fucking *everything*, is this my end? Condemned to death because of *Midas*?

Another cruel irony, that I should be executed because they think I stole gold-touch from *him*.

"Raise!"

The guards lift their swords. All six blades notched between the poles, their sharp tips pointed at me with lethal intent.

This enclosure is so small that the moment they stick these blades in, I'll be stabbed through on all sides. There is no escaping this.

There is no way out.

Tears stream down my face, futile drips that barely reveal the panicked terror I'm flooded with.

I spin around, trying to jostle the barred door, but it doesn't budge at all.

"*Please!*"

After all I did to be free, I'm going to die trapped behind bars anyway, locked in a cage I can't escape. *That's* how cruel life is.

It's almost as if I can feel Midas laughing over my shoulder.

I surge inside of myself, trying to pull out my fae beast, trying to break past the runes at my feet, to shove apart the poles that surround me.

Nothing works.

My beast is curled up, feathers withering with exhaustion. My gold can do nothing but drain out of my skin. The structure that surrounds me feels like it's closing in.

I'm trapped.

King Merewen meets my eyes from over the guards' heads. "Lady Auren, I now sentence you to die."

The blades close in.

And so do my eyes.

I feel the first piercings of the swords like a fingertip getting pricked by a wayward sewing needle. Sharp. Small. Just the very tip biting through my skin.

So I breathe. A single phrase caught in the exhale, joined with the sorrow of my heart.

Find me in another life.

Find me in them all.

And then there is no room for words. None for coherent

thought, because the first of those swords sinks in deeper, and pain erases everything else.

My body braces. My mind empties.

But then…the world *erupts*.

I don't understand for a moment. When the ground shakes. When the screams sound. I can't grasp that the blades pressed into my body are no longer firm or sharp. My numbed mind only registers something is off when they fall away from me.

My eyes snap open to see dust as thick as fog crowding in the air. Looking down, I see that the swords are no longer gleaming and silver, but mottled with rust the color of amber stones and tangerines, and then they suddenly disintegrate completely. I can feel them burst into powder where they've sunk into my body.

And the guards…

I watch the man in front of me as his body morphs. Terrified eyes go opaque, sinking down into their sockets. His jaw hangs open like his muscles can no longer hold it. His lips peel, exposing a row of browning teeth. His veins fester and burst, lesions peeling back up and down his neck. He tries to grab hold of the pole, but his hands shrivel down to the bone.

When he falls, his body swells and twitches, bloating up unfathomably large, before everything then seems to suck inward, shrinking and shriveling until he's just a husk of bones and dust.

I spin around at the thump and clang that surrounds me, seeing that all of the guards have met the same fate.

My head snaps up, my eyes searching, heart leaping…

And then I see him.

I'm not sure I've ever felt true elation until right in this moment. It's visceral, draping around me like the warmth of his body, my heart surging at the sight of him and making a sob wrest from my deepest depths.

He came.

He came for me.

A timberwing lands right in the middle of the square with a fierce roar, and the crowd screams as they flee, though they don't go fast enough.

The moment Slade jumps off the beast, the very *second* his booted feet hit the stones, rot slams out in every direction. It consumes the crowd of onlookers, tainted roots growing and spreading, infesting everything in its path. The people fall, one after the other, bodies left to languish and decay, the guards surrounding the crowd succumbing to the same fate.

I cling to the pole in front of me, trying to keep upright, as cries crack the back of my throat and leak past my lips. Our gazes lock together, my heart locked with it.

I can feel the fury pouring out of him in endless waves, and the amount of power pulses in the air, but it doesn't make my stomach roil, doesn't make nausea churn.

He walks toward me with a savage stride, making the ground crumble, making the square squelch into silence as he rots everyone in his path and lets his boots crush their decayed bodies into dust. Until there are no more screams. No more running. Only quiet death lies in his wake.

I'll be the villain for you.

He is the epitome of death and revenge. The personification of rage.

He destroys everything and everyone in his vicinity without glance or thought, and through the chaos, through the massacre, I *revel* in it.

Maybe it's the rot inside me. Maybe it's being fae.

But maybe, it's simply the fact that the person I love is willing to destroy the world to protect me. And *that* is its own kind of power that not even this enclosure can drain away.

So long as we're together, everything is okay. Because I will fight for him, and he will kill for me, and if we need to be the villains, then so be it.

Slade strides straight ahead with murder in his eyes, while the roots of his power writhe and coil along his forearms and neck, mirroring the rot that worms through the ground. When he's just ten feet away from the stage, his gaze splits to the monarchs and some of the nobles and guards.

They're huddled together on the stage, and I wonder for a moment if Queen Isolte is trying to squelch Slade's power with hers. If so, she's failing miserably.

She's no match for him.

No one is.

Which is why I'm surprised none of them have used these last several seconds to try and flee. Instead, they're shouting at King Merewen, telling him to hurry. I don't understand, but then I see the little boy—the one who must be the prince of Second Kingdom—his father holding his shoulders and positioning him in front of them.

Outrage slams into me like a fist. Are they hoping, by blocking themselves with an innocent kid, that Slade won't destroy them?

The thought is despicable, but they should know that when it comes to Slade's magic, he is precise. He could rot them all and not let a single bit of it touch the boy, just like he destroyed the guards that surrounded me.

But then King Merewen snaps something to his son. The boy nods and reaches into the pocket of his robe, and he pulls out a spool of thread. In a blink, he's yanked the thread between his fingers, and then he closes his eyes in concentration, pulling the unspooled thread into a taut line. Magic sparks to life in the air like someone just poured oil over a flame.

Slade is just three feet from the stage, already sprinting up the steps, when the boy's magic slams into place.

If I weren't holding onto the poles, I would've fallen down. The collected gold sloshes wildly at my legs. Yet my eyes are riveted ahead to where the entire stage is now covered in what looks like a veil of fabric the same color as the boy's thread. I'm also contained in a second layer that separates me from them, the veil slightly thicker where it surrounds my enclosure.

The whole thing swells and undulates like laundry hanging from a clothesline and blowing in a breeze. Stretching over us like a dome, it's not quite solid, the fabric turning translucent as it moves, glistening in the sunlight.

Slade slams into it, and the fabric bends around him before pulling tight and shoving him back.

"You cannot get through," King Merewen calls out with arrogant victory, still gripping the shoulders of his son. The boy continues to squeeze his eyes shut, his small fingers holding onto his thread.

Slade raises both hands and shoves them against the barrier. Feet braced, muscles bunching, rot pours out of his touch with livid fortitude, and I watch as veins stretch up around the domed fabric to spread its infection.

Instead of the rot making the billowing shield deteriorate, the corroded capillaries seem to do nothing at all. Slade growls out, pushing even more power, so thickly that it seems to tingle against my skin.

But it does nothing to the shield of blowing fabric.

The power suddenly cuts off, my riveted gaze blurring as Slade starts to pant, sweat dripping from his hair, anger grinding through his jaw.

"King Ravinger, as I said before, you cannot get through. My son's veil is impenetrable. But let us speak," King Merewen says, holding out his arms like he's some benevolent, enlightened man. "We are not your enemies."

Slade bares his teeth at him, giving a look that even chills my blood. "Anyone who hurts Auren is my enemy."

"But that's just it, King Ravinger. *She* is the enemy," Queen Isolte says.

Queen Kaila nods and steps past her brother. "Exactly. We've just proven it here at the Conflux, which is why it was so imperative we got her away from you. She's dangerous. Tricking kings and taking their power. We didn't want to stand by and let it happen to you too."

Fury makes the gold still pouring from my hands go molten. It lands in steaming drops that hiss as they fall.

"Her claws needed to be ripped from your mind. See for yourself," King Merewen says, gesturing toward me. "She has stolen gold-touch, but now, she has *also* stolen your rot. You should've turned her in sooner."

Slade's eyes jump to me, falling down to the gold now lapping at my thighs, at the rooting lines that swim in their depths. All while gold pours from my hands with an unnatural pull. My eyes feel heavy. My heart lagging.

"She stole *nothing*," he says on a growl. "Release her. Now."

"I'm afraid we can't do that," Merewen says. "You know the law. Once the accused has been found culpable, the judgment must be carried out."

The force of his furor makes Slade practically shake. "If you *touch* her, I will rot every single one of you right here, right now."

King Thold shifts on his feet, his snakes hissing with agitation. "Merewen, perhaps we should discuss this..."

"No," he snaps, the blotches on his cheeks growing redder. "The judgment has been made. Do you want her to steal *your* power too?" he demands before his eyes whip toward the new Fifth King. "What about you? Would you like her to seduce you and then steal yours?"

Both men say nothing to that.

"She killed a king. We can't stand by and do nothing," Queen Isolte puts in. "She's a tainted woman who needs to face her fate."

Slade looks at them, body so still that it's eerie. As if he even so much as blinks, he's going to tear them apart. "Drop this barrier and let her out. *Now*. Or what I did today in this square will be *nothing* compared to what I do next."

He grounds out the threat between bitten words so quiet that I have to strain to hear him.

"You can hide behind this shield for as long as your son can hold it, but I assure you, I will wait longer. The moment it drops, I will curdle your skin and wither your bones. I will decay you slowly, from the inside out, until you're nothing but an agonized corpse left to fester in the sun. Then, I will destroy every last person in your kingdoms, and I will not rest until all of Orea crumbles out of existence."

The other monarchs blanch.

Queen Isolte shakes her head in disbelief. "King Ravinger, we're trying to *help*—"

"Drop the shield *now*. I'm not going to ask again."

"But—"

"Drop it," King Merewen says, cutting off his wife.

She looks shocked. "The ruling of the Conflux is *holy*."

"Shut your mouth, woman," he seethes before he turns to his son. "Drop the barrier, boy."

But the boy doesn't open his eyes. Doesn't make a noise.

His father rounds on him with irritation. "Did you hear me? I said drop it!" The king goes to shake him, but as soon as his hand touches his shoulder, the boy crumples to the ground and starts to convulse.

"Hamus!" Queen Isolte scrambles to her son, falling to her knees beside him. She holds his cheeks, trying to stop his violent shaking, but it doesn't help. She rounds on her husband. "This is your fault for pushing him to use so much magic!"

I sway.

Even though it's nothing compared to the amounts of gold I've expelled before, this drain on my power is too continuous, too forced.

"Auren?"

It takes me several blinks before Slade can come back into focus. "I..."

Whatever he sees on my expression or hears in my choked off words makes the blood drain from his face. He whips his head back toward the others. "Get her the fuck out of there!"

"Merewen, get the barrier to drop, or he's going to fucking kill us," King Thold hisses as much as his snakes.

Queen Kaila looks torn between wanting to see me die and wanting to ensure she saves her own neck.

But the prince isn't waking, his body keeps thrashing, the thread tangled between his hands. His father curses and rushes over, tries to snatch the thread away, making Isolte scream. But even that does nothing.

And I...I fall back.

My shoulders hit the poles, and I look down at the gold that's now splashing around my chest, some of it reaching the puncture marks from the swords. Seeing them springs up the pain that surrounds me from all sides, my blood mixing with the rest.

"Slade..." My voice doesn't come out as more than a whisper, but he hears me.

He always hears me, even when I don't say a thing.

Expression full of animalistic fury, Slade rips out the sword from his belt, raises it up, and *slams* it down across the fabric. Even though it looks like it shouldn't hold any hope against Slade's sword, the threads absorb the blow, the sharp blade completely impotent, the barrier immune to the slash.

But he slashes at it again and again and again.

He throws his brute strength at it, trying to slam his body through it, trying to hack at it, trying to pour so much rot over the barrier that the noxious veins encompass so thoroughly that it nearly blocks my sight of him completely.

"Hold on, Auren! Hold on!"

But my knees shake, legs giving out. I don't sink down in the gold though, because the black, liquid roots seem to catch me, keeping me afloat.

Panic comes over his face, and that's when I know there's no hope.

He can't get to me.

There's pure torture in his eyes, and my entire soul just *cracks*.

My bottom lip wobbles. My love for him drains from me as much as my power, collecting around me, wishing it could reach him.

But it can't.

I can't.

He came for me, but he can't get to me.

Hot tears score lines down my shaking cheeks. But I try to pull them up. Try to give him a smile. "Find me in another life."

"*No!*" The anguish thrown from his throat feels like it tumbles right at my feet.

I blink, head cradled against the bars, and I watch as he

suddenly brings up both hands. And then I feel the hair rise on the back of my neck.

In the next instant, magic comes slamming out so forcefully that it steals the breath from my chest and holds it in its fist.

Raw magic blasts from his body and pours into the barrier.

As soon as it makes contact, the entire dome starts to vibrate. Several of the monarchs clutch their heads, cringing back, while the prince passes out, body going still.

Slade's power dominates the air.

He directs it all to the double-layered shield in front of me, pouring all of his energy into the spot around my enclosure. My skin is covered in chills, my ears ringing, even the rotted gold around me acts erratically. Unnatural wind gusts from the spot where he's trying to breach through the barrier, and I'm stuck in the storm of its charged ferocity.

His body quakes, veins shrinking and expanding in an eerie pulse. I can see his jaw muscles working, see the fierce determination in his eyes as spikes burst from his arms, even as I grow weaker and weaker.

"Just hold on!"

I'm trying, I want to say, but I can't get the words out.

"Hold—"

His words get ripped from his throat at the same time that a rip suddenly rends through the air.

I watch as the fabric right in front of me tears open, like someone grabbed it and ripped it in two. A rush of sweet-smelling wind blows back my hair as I blink at the twelve foot rip. It's torn through the poles, split right down to the ground, making some of my gold start to drain into it.

The gaping slash is clotted with roiling clouds of black and white that churn in its starry, electrified depths. It looks bottomless, ethereal, and as soon as I smell the air, the beast inside of me *sings*.

Because it carries the breeze of home.

It feels like I release a breath that's been locked in my chest for twenty years. With that long breath, my skin warms, my gold *glows*.

I was my parents' little sun. And with the world torn open, with the fragment of *home* just inside that rip, I actually *feel* like one. Like if I could just fall into that cracked-open sky, I could shine forever.

And yet, when I look away from the rip right in front of me, past its mirrored and mottled air, I see the look on Slade's exhausted face.

I see horrified realization in his dark eyes.

The shine, the warmth, the glow, it all dulls. It all chokes out like a fist at my throat.

"Auren..."

The moment he says my name, I understand.

He swallows hard, head shaking. "I was trying to rip through the barrier to get to you, but..."

But he tore a rip into Annwyn instead.

"Auren. You need to go into it."

My eyes go wide, liquid gold churning in waves around my shoulders. If the runes forcing me to drain out my energy don't kill me, I'll drown in my gold instead.

"Auren."

I glance from the rip to him, and I'm so terrified, but I know it's the only way, because he's tried everything else, and it's *home*. Annwyn is home, and—

But then I realize.

Then I truly see.

"The rip...you can't get to the rip."

His lips are pressed into a thin line, his eyes full of speechless agony.

"You have to come with me," I say, panicked, terrified, despairing.

He shakes his head, and my foundation shakes with it. "I can't. You have to go into it, baby. *You have to*. I can't get to you, and you can't stay there. You're fading."

My head shakes, tears pooling from my eyes. "I can't. I can't. Not without you," I beg. Fight. *Wail*.

"Look at me," he demands, even as his chest heaves. "You have to go in. You're strong. So keep your rage to fuel your courage and save yourself again."

Sobs wrench from my soul, anguish suffocating me. "But—"

"I *will* find you. I will find you in that life. I fucking promise you that. But you *have* to go." Two wet tears split down his cheek, and the sight makes anguish split through my soul. "*Please, baby*." His beg bleeds through the cracks of his voice. Stabs straight through my heart.

"*Slade*..."

He gives me a nod. Tries to give me his strength. His dark eyes and darker aura bore into me, surround me.

"I'll find you, Goldfinch. I swear to you. Now *fly*."

So with a sob suffocating my throat, I close my eyes. Lift my arms. Suck in a breath I wish was filled with his scent. Then, I tip down into that fathomless, familiar unknown.

Through the rip in the world, with a rip torn through my heart, I plunge out of Orea, into the storming depths of Annwyn.

Alone.

CHAPTER 65

SLADE

I watch her drop.

Watch her pitch into the churning, storming sky, ripped straight into Annwyn. Watch her disappear through the slash I tore open.

I need to keep my grip on the ragged, frayed ends for as long as I can. Give her as much time as I'm able. My fists are squeezing so hard I can't feel my fingers, power bleeding out of me too fast to sustain. But still I wait, shaking, draining, spikes punching through my spine while fangs pierce through the insides of my cheeks.

Not yet.

I feel my knuckles pop, feel my braced legs waver. Yet still, I hold the rip open, counting every second, because I don't know if the tear needs to stay open for her to be safe, for her to reach Annwyn. But if it does, then I need to hold on.

So I do.

When my knees hit the cracked, decayed ground, I do.

When my head bows, hands quaking, I do.

When my breaths come out in painful bursts, when my jaw pops, when my back arcs, when my heart feels like it's going to explode through my own festering veins, I do.

I hold it far longer than my body wants to, expel more power than I have. I hold on until my body can't give any more of this raw, exposed power. Power that I shouldn't even be capable of using, and certainly not to rip holes into the world.

When I've given my very last piece of power, the rip shatters shut.

The noise is nearly deafening as the air snaps back in place.

My power cracks with its collapse, like a piece of mountain crumbling off. Its jagged, plummeting form crashes into a sea that swallows it whole, leaving no trace of it behind. It's as if the rip was never even there.

I collapse onto the ground.

The world spins, my chest feels hollow, and I don't think I could muster a single scrap of power, rot or raw, even if my life depended on it. I feel like death, like I could roll over straight into a grave.

But I made her a promise.

So instead of allowing myself to succumb to the darkness my consciousness wants to pull me into, I roll over. Push myself up.

Fall to my knees again. Sway like a damn tree in the wind, slumping against the fabric barrier that's still standing. Silently yelling at myself, I try to threaten my legs to hold me, though they're not fucking listening.

Just when I worry that I really am going to collapse in unconsciousness, two hands appear, a hard grip wrenching me to my feet. I whirl, nearly stumbling right back down, but the hold steadies me, keeps me upright.

"Relax! It's me."

I blearily blink at Ryatt as he comes into focus.

"Fuck. You look..." Ryatt trails off, apparently unable to vocalize just how bad I appear. "Did you just do what I think you did?"

"Rip another tear in the world to save Auren? Yes."

"Fuck," Ryatt says. "I never should have said what I did before—that Auren should come here. I was so fucking wrong."

If I didn't feel like death, I might reel back from shock. "I don't think I've ever heard you admit you were wrong."

"Come on, I gotta get you out of here," he says with a grim expression. "You're in no position to defend yourself like this. When that barrier comes down, those fuckers might try to come for you."

I look over my shoulder at the monarchs and nobles, at the handful of guards.

They're fucking *lucky* I'm too weak to use any more power, that the shield was up and didn't let me rot them to dust. Because if things were different, if I weren't so wrecked right now, they'd be dead. Based on their faces, they know it.

Queen Kaila looks nervous. King Merewen is downright terrified. I think the new Fifth King might've shit his pants.

It only gives me the smallest twinge of satisfaction.

I glare at them all, and they fucking know. The next time I see them, I'll kill them.

The kid is still lying on the floor, but as I watch, he gasps and coughs, the first signs of him waking, and as soon as he does, his barrier begins to ripple, like a blanket being shaken out in the wind.

"Time to go," Ryatt urges. Turning away, he tosses my arm over his shoulders and all but drags me toward a timberwing. "Can you ride on your own? We'll go faster if you can ride in your own seat."

"I can ride."

"You sure?" he asks dubiously.

"I said I can ride," I grit out.

"Okay, okay, asshole. Let's go."

"How are you here?" I ask as I stumble to the beast. I hate to admit that I wouldn't have been able to walk this short distance if it weren't for Ryatt holding me up. "Whose timberwing is this? Where's Argo?"

"Our soldiers caught up to me—just like I told you they would when I found you in that desert. Argo's on his way back to Fourth as we speak," he tells me. "Probably already on a ship. He's in good hands, I promise. One of them is an animal mender."

Relief fills my chest.

In a forceful move, Ryatt shoves me up onto the saddle of the squatting timberwing and starts to quickly buckle me in. "We can catch up to the others, ride the same ship. I doubt any of these fuckers will try a damn thing once we're behind our borders."

But I shake my head, my hand snapping out to grip his wrist. "I'm not going to Fourth."

Ryatt pauses, jerking to look behind us at the shield as it starts to snap and fray. "What the fuck are you talking about?"

"I'm going to Deadwell."

He frowns, opens his mouth to say something, but then realization dawns. "You're going to the rip."

I nod. "I have to find her, and I'm not going to have the strength to use any more raw power. I can't open another rip right now."

Ryatt shakes his head. "Deadwell is a long ways from here. We'll have to change out the timberwings."

"You're coming with me?" I ask, surprised.

"I'm your brother. Of course I'm fucking coming with you."

I study his face, see the determination and fierce loyalty radiating through him. And I nod. Because at the end of the day, no matter how hard things are between us, no matter how many arguments we get into, we're brothers. He has my back, and I have his, and that's all there is to it.

"Now don't fall," he orders before he runs and jumps on his own timberwing—his own beast that he lent to me so I could fly here.

If he and his group hadn't found me in the desert, if I hadn't shown up here when I did, Auren would be dead. Just thinking about how close she was makes my blood feel like ice.

With a slight tap of our heels, the beasts jump into the air in tandem, just as the barrier falls away like a shirt yanked from a clothespin, caught in the wind and disappearing from view. The other monarchs are watching my ascent and scattering like ants, afraid I'm going to fly back down and catch them.

They should be scared. I hope they jump at every shadow. Twitch at every dark line that creeps into their peripheral vision. I hope they keep looking over their shoulders, watching, waiting for me to be there, hunting them.

The timberwing I'm riding lets out a roar, and the monarchs flinch, making a cruel smile twist my lips. Then we're up in the clouds, and they're out of view.

And we start our race toward Deadwell.

The journey is long, and I feel every moment keenly, just like I did when I raced from Fourth to reach Auren. Luckily, I was able to stay on the saddle, though I certainly wasn't conscious for most of the ride that first day and night. I was too weak to do much of anything, so Ryatt led the way and made the plans and kept us moving.

I slept when it was time to land, I ate when he shoved food in my hand, and held onto the reins with a strained grip, while my sapped strength slowly returned.

But something was different.

I was able to use my normal magic again on the third day, making the grass wilt and rot beneath my feet. However, two days after that, when my rot was back to normal, I tried to see if I could use raw power, tried to test if I could possibly open another rip without having to use the one in Deadwell.

I couldn't.

It wasn't as if I could dredge it up but only a splutter of it came out. No, I couldn't call on my raw magic *at all*. There's a pit deep in my center where the well of raw power used to be, and it's just *empty*.

As if I truly did dry it up, with nothing left but parched earth and untamed decay.

I didn't tell Ryatt. Didn't acknowledge it at all. Instead, I told myself I just needed more time. Shut up my fear by fueling determination in my thoughts instead. Quell my doubts by stuffing my hand in my pocket and feeling her ribbon. Auren needs me, and I'm going to get to her, simple as that.

So what if my raw power is barren right now? It will come back. It has to, because I don't want to think of what will happen to the villagers, to my mother, if it doesn't.

I got Auren out, and that's what matters. I just need to get to Deadwell so I can follow her.

All while we travel, I'm eaten away by unknowns. I don't know if she was hurt when she fell through the rip. I don't know where she is or if she's safe. Until I can see her with my own eyes and feel her beneath my own hands, I'm not going to be able to rest.

So when we finally reach Deadwell and the heart of Drollard Village, I feel like I'm ready to snap. Too many days have passed.

I need to find her. Need to be on the right side of the stars and in the same world where she exists.

My boots slam through the snow as I race past the quiet village. I'm so focused on getting to the rip, on getting to her, that I don't even notice just *how* quiet things are. Don't notice that there's no one out, even in the middle of the day.

Ryatt shouts my name as I sprint for the cave, but I don't slow as I continue up the stooped hill, boots slipping on the snow as I go. I reach the cave, pass my mother's house, steps echoing through the blue-lit hollows.

Almost there.

Just when I round the corner, just when I reach the opened up cavern and I should feel relief, I skid to a stop.

I blink. Again and again. Look around, left and right. Because surely, surely my vision is wrong. Or I took a wrong turn. Or—but no. No, because I know this cave, know this exact spot, and—

"Slade," Ryatt pants as he catches up, nearly knocks into me, both of us blurting words at the same time.

"Everyone is—" he begins, and, "The rip is—" I start.

"*Gone.*"

Our words join together with an echoing blow I feel punch through my gut.

The rip is gone.

The people are gone.

Auren is gone.

And my fucking power to get to her is...

Gone.

EPILOGUE

QUEEN MALINA

"I t's time."

I slowly turn my head from the window I was watching to see the twins standing there. I'm not sure how long I've sat here, blinking out at the swirling mist. Sometimes, I think I nearly get a peek at what's beyond, but it's far too thick to see through it. Yet now, it's pitch-black, so I know night has fallen long ago.

With a smile, I rise to my feet, glancing down at the white and blue dress draped over my body. I don't remember putting this one on, but it's thick and heavy, probably in preparation for tonight's ritual.

I follow behind the brothers, and it seems like in no time at all, we're already outside. Like in a dream, when you go from one place to the next in an instant, without any time or effort.

The night is so dark I'd be blind out here if it weren't

for the row of torches stuck into the icy ground. It makes the snow look like it's on fire, and I shy away from the flames, a bead of sweat collecting just at the nape of my neck.

Fassa and Friano lead me behind the castle and right to the end of the world.

With my feet poised at the edge, I look down into the brink. Just darkness and gray mist forever. Land and then nothing.

"This way, Majesty."

I turn and follow their voices until I find Pruinn standing beside some sort of pillar right at the rim of the land.

No, not a pillar, it almost looks like—

"Are you ready, my queen?" Pruinn asks, expression full of joy, his silver eyes pulling me in.

I breathe in the fresh, cold air.

"I am."

The soft music that I've had stuck in my head since I got here seems to grow louder. I hear it in my ears, feel it reverberating in my bones. The light of the torches seems to intensify too, though I don't like the heat. I wish I could sit in the snow and let it soak through my dress to cool me.

I can't sit though, because Fassa and Friano are both taking my hands, and then Pruinn has a small blade that he pulls from his pocket. The music is so loud, the firelight so hot...

The dagger is pulled across my palms in a single line that spreads from one hand to the other, cutting through the lines and marking it with the red of my blood.

"Repeat after me, Your Majesty."

So I do.

"*I am Queen Malina Colier of the Colier royal bloodline, and I willingly give my blood to restore what was lost and to gain what is new.*"

I'm not sure what magic feels like.

I never felt anything with Midas, and aside from feeling watched, I didn't sense the assassin.

Yet I feel magic now.

Fassa and Friano slam their palms against mine, threading their fingers in, turning my hands so that my blood coats their skin and then drips into the snow.

And magic *roars*.

Like we've awoken a slumbering beast from the belly of the earth, and it's come to claw its way out. Every drop of blood that seems to paint the ground pulls something from the center of my gut.

The world spins.

The magic bays like a wolf at the moonless sky.

Then comes the wind and the quakes.

The earth begins to shake so hard that I get my prior wish and go crashing down to the ground. My knees smack painfully into the ice, the splatters of blood blotched into the snow where it's dripped.

Everything shakes so violently, the wolf now sounding like it's grinding its teeth against the bones of its prey, gnashing and smashing.

I have no idea where the twins or Pruinn are. There's too much noise to call for them, and the world is rocking like a ship on turbulent waves, so my eyes cannot search for them either.

I clutch the ground like a safety net, the snowy mesh dissolving between my fingers. I get tossed aside, rolling until my back crashes into the pillar that I noticed before, the single stone post pitted but still standing.

Pain shoots down my back and shoulder, but then there's a new ache. Something not from the hit but in my veins. As if the pain is traveling through my very blood, from ankle to temple, freezing it in place.

My heart goes gluey, my pulse sluggish.

And the heat from the torches no longer bothers me, because I am blessedly, thoroughly *cold*. As if ice now pumps from my heart and frosts down my veins.

I'm not sure when the ground stops shaking. When this pain ebbs. But I pull myself up, hands gripping the pillar for support, and when I stumble to a stand, I turn around to look at the land.

But...Seventh Kingdom hasn't been restored.

The snowy land hasn't been pulled back together, healing the rifts or filling the cleaves. From what I can see lit up by the hundreds of torches, it looks exactly the same as before.

"It worked."

I spin around at the twins' voice to see both of them and Pruinn standing just beside me. Yet instead of looking at the land, they're looking at the endless chasm behind.

I realize right then that what I'm holding isn't some broken pillar. It's a *banister*. And it now has another identical one, both caught between a strip of gray, endless land stretching like a bridge. I stare down its length as far as my vision takes me, to where the mist now clings to the roped railing along the drooping path that stretches across the eternal abyss.

Clarity, sharp and cold, pierces through my mind.

Like I was asleep and then, suddenly dropped into the middle of an icy lake, I wake up.

Wake up, and don't smell the flowers, Cold Queen. Before it's too late.

The kingdom isn't restored to its former glory. The light of the torches shows me it's just as crumbling and ruined as I thought when I first got here. And there is no scent of flowers in my nose or music in my ears.

There's blood and something that seems to drum from the bridge.

Like the pulse of a beast.

As my hands clutch the banister, ice frosts beneath my fingertips, spreading down the restored stone pillar. I snatch my hands up, staring at the shards of ice stuck to my palm.

And that sound keeps pulsating from the ground.

I look up at the twins, fear freezing my heart. "What did you do?" I whisper.

The twins turn to me, and they seem more frightening somehow. The angles of their faces more severe, their eyes holding no kindness. Even Pruinn, whose gaze has always drawn me in, seems to somehow deter me now, especially when he accompanies it with a flash of a grin revealing sharp canines caught in his gums.

"You mean what did *we* do?" They and their mingled voices sound like a razor dragged across glass. But it's their ears. Their *ears*—

"With your blood and our magic, we restored what was broken."

My eyes cast down the bridge. To that drumming that travels down its length in a steady beat. Because I know the tale of this bridge. Every single Orean knows about it.

This is the Bridge of Lemuria.

My mouth goes dry. Gaze drags back to their sharpened faces, to the points of their ears.

"You're fae."

Terror wracks through me, and I stumble away, but they just watch me with detachment. Like I'm a snow bunny that's been caught in their trap, and they distracted me so much that I didn't even realize it.

"I told you she had pure royal blood," Pruinn tells them. "I could sense it."

"Well done," the twins praise.

"What did you do?" I say again, my voice as shaky as the ground was. "This isn't what I agreed to."

"But it is. You made the bargain, Majesty. We needed the blood of a pure Orean royal to accept the restoration of the bridge, and you gave it."

That drumming down the bridge gets louder, but I realize all too late that it's *not* drums. It sounds like...*footsteps*. Like a thousand marching feet thudding down the strip. My whole body trembles with the ominous pulse.

"What is that? Who's coming?"

I don't like the way their grins grow cruel. But it's their unified answer that makes terror bolt through my heart. "The fae are returning. And this time, Orea will be ours."

THREE QUEENS

PART ONE

There once were three queens,
though very different they were.
One was a lure, another so pure, the last was a cure.

There was a queen who was born, and a queen who was made.
And a golden gold vine who grew up through the shade.

One was night, and the second was dusk.
Two very different, two dipped with mistrust.
The third was another mismatch (this one was dawn).
But one thing they had in common? All three of them—*gone*.

Dusk disappeared down a bridge,
Night was meant to be killed.
And through a split in the air,
Dawn had to be spilled.

So tumbled down Fate,
while goddesses loomed.
From hatching shelled stars,
their destiny bloomed.

But fortunes can change and outcomes can snap.
And each kind of queen must learn how to tap
—into their power (for not all power is magic),
or their futures would only end up as tragic.

There once were three queens,
though very different they were.
(They needed to learn how to be sure.)

One was quite cold, the second was brave.
Of course, the third one, she always gave.
All of them—every one—caused others to crave.

And craving is danger
in a world of great greed.
So it was not yet certain
what planting would seed.

But plant they all did,
each queen, their own root.
Into the worlds,
their blood-watered fruit.

For each crossed a bridge of their own making,
each had the world, wanted for taking.

But blood, heart, and gold, must be unshaken,
for only they could determine what Fate would awaken.

TO BE CONTINUED...

READ ON FOR A SNEAK PEEK
OF THE NEXT BOOK IN
THE PLATED PRISONERS SERIES

FORTUNE FAVORS THE GOLD

GOLD

THE PLATED PRISONER SERIES

RAVEN KENNEDY
INTERNATIONAL BESTSELLING AUTHOR

CHAPTER 1

AUREN

I go loudly.

Loudly, loudly into the void.

The blaring rattle of a solitary fall.

I don't close my eyes against the strange dark. My grief wails like thunder, clapping past a broken chest, while echoed teardrops stream down my cheeks like rain.

The world ripped, and I was ripped from *him*.

It feels wrong. So wrong to be rent apart. Like fingers curled around my ribs, yanking me open. Hollowing me out.

Thick wind peels at my skin. Rushing air plugs my nose and condenses on my tongue. A howling clatter drowns my ears. The flash of lightning and stars surrounds me in the yawning dark.

Through it all, I can see the rip.

I can see the jagged edges of the torn sky above me, a betraying Orean air gaping like a wound in the dark. Liquid gold bleeds through, falling like gelatinous droplets, glinting as they drip down into the nothing. But that rip gets further and further away from me, my body plunging deeper into the starry unknown with unstoppable force.

I'm alone. Alone in this dark, endless void, torn away from Slade.

I keep falling and falling, further and further away from that rip. Further away from him. And as if that weren't terrifying enough, my senses are suddenly stripped away.

My sight. Sound. Feeling. Taste. Scent. All of it—*gone*.

The scream tearing from my throat is no more either. Or if it is, I can't feel it. Can't hear it pierce my ears.

Without my senses, without any way to experience what's happening, my grief and fear condenses. Time stretches and snaps.

I don't know what will happen to me in this void. I don't know if this is what it feels like to die. Though I do know one thing.

This

     is

        what

           it

            feels

             like

              to